I0592129

18th cent Junius, John Wade

Junius

Including Letters by the Same Writer Under Other Signatures, (Volume 1)

18th cent Junius, John Wade

Junius
Including Letters by the Same Writer Under Other Signatures, (Volume 1)

ISBN/EAN: 9783744717250

Printed in Europe, USA, Canada, Australia, Japan

Cover: Foto ©Andreas Hilbeck / pixelio.de

More available books at **www.hansebooks.com**

JUNIUS:

INCLUDING

LETTERS BY THE SAME WRITER UNDER OTHER SIGNATURES;

TO WHICH ARE ADDED

HIS CONFIDENTIAL CORRESPONDENCE WITH MR. WILKES, AND HIS PRIVATE LETTERS TO MR. H. S. WOODFALL;

A New and Enlarged Edition

WITH NEW EVIDENCE AS TO THE AUTHORSHIP, AND AN ANALYSIS BY THE LATE SIR HARRIS NICOLAS. G.C.M.G

BY

JOHN WADE,

AUTHOR OF " A COMPENDIUM OF BRITISH HISTORY." "THE CABINET LAWYER," ETC.

VOL. I.

CONTAINING THE ENTIRE WORK AS ORIGINALLY PUBLISHED, WITH ILLUSTRATIVE NOTES.

———

LONDON: GEORGE BELL AND SONS, YORK STREET, COVENT GARDEN.

1881.

ADVERTISEMENT.

NEARLY three generations have elapsed since the "Letters of Junius" were first published; and it may be safely affirmed that, during this long ordeal, no contemporary work has maintained a higher estimation—has received more marked and uniform approval from competent literary judges—or has called into existence so many commentators, editors, and investigators.

As there is little in the subject matter of these famous epistles that could confer upon them such enduring celebrity, they must be mainly indebted for it to the writer's extraordinary powers, the varied resources of which have enabled him, with the peculiar characteristic of genius, to dignify and immortalize that which, in its own nature, is secondary and perishable. In this respect Junius stands alone—he is the Napoleon of public writers; and, like the author of the first and noblest epic, though he has had a host of imitators, he is still without an equal.

The STANDARD LIBRARY would have been imperfect had it not included among its elect the most celebrated of political gladiators. The very complete edition now submitted to the public comprises all that was given in the three volumes published in 1812, and again in 1814, by the late Mr. George Woodfall—indeed all that was authentically known of Junius and his writings.

To specify more distinctly the merits of Woodfall's edition, now reprinted entire, it may be proper to enumerate its contents, which are:—1. The public letters of Junius as revised and annotated by himself, and published collectively, under his direction, subsequent to their appearance in the *Public Advertiser*. 2. A collection of Miscellaneous Letters, ascribed to Junius. 3. His private notes and confidential communications with Mr. Woodfall (published only after they had been preserved in honourable privacy for forty years). 4. Illustrative notes; and a copious Preliminary Essay, comprising a critical analysis of the Letters, and an examination of the various claims to their authorship.

In an edition already so complete little scope was left for useful enlargement. Nevertheless, even in this respect, something has been contributed. Besides a more careful discrimination of the authentic writings of Junius, the Editor, by the courtesy of the present proprietor of the Junius Manuscripts, and the abundant materials placed at his disposal by the publisher, has been enabled to present further illustrations. He has examined the formidable array of "inquiries" with considerable diligence, and the reader will have the benefit of the little that is to be gleaned from them.

But his most critical task is reserved for the second and concluding volume. Junius remains at least unavowed. The editor's own impression as to the authorship is strong, based, he thinks, upon adequate testimony; but his hero and his arguments must be deferred until the due season of publication. The solemn enunciation, that "I am the sole depositary of my own secret, and it shall perish with me," has to the present time been kept inviolate.

Since the present volume was put to press, the publisher has become possessed of some manuscripts relative to Junius by the late Sir Harris Nicolas, destined, it is believed, towards a new edition. This acute scholar had devoted his mind to the subject for years, and has drawn up an ingenious analysis, which will be presented to the reader in the next volume.

1854.

CONTENTS.

CONTENTS.

x

APPENDIX.

PRELIMINARY ESSAY*.

It was not from personal vanity, but a fair estimate of his own merit, and the importance of the subject on which he wrote, that the author of the ensuing letters predicted their immortality. Their matter and their manner, the times they describe, and the talents they disclose, the popularity which attended them at their outset, the impression they produced on the public mind, and the triumph of most of the doctrines they inculcate, all equally concur in stamping for them a passport to the most distant posterity.

In their range these letters comprise a period of about five years: from the middle of 1767 to the middle of 1772: and never has the history of this country, from its origin to the present hour, exhibited a period of equal extent that more peremptorily demanded the severe, decisive, and overpowering pen of such a writer as JUNIUS. The storms and tem-

* This able and comprehensive Essay on Junius and his Writings was affixed to Woodfall's edition published in 1812, and is ascribed to John Mason Good, a physician and miscellaneous writer of eminence, who died Jan. 2, 1827. Of its purport and the views of the writer some observations by the present editor will be found at the end. The commencement of the second paragraph requires passing explanation. The *Letters of Junius* as acknowledged by him, and published under his own revision in a collective edition in 1772, by Henry Sampson Woodfall, proprietor of the *Public Advertiser*, appeared in that journal between Jan. 21, 1769, and Jan. 21, 1772, concluding with a brief impressive letter addressed to Lord Camden, and a paper by Junius, explanatory of his views on long parliaments and rotten boroughs. Dr. Good includes in the term of *five* years the Miscellaneous Letters given in the second volume of the present edition, some of which Junius acknowledges to have written, at an earlier or later period, under different signatures; and other letters collected by Mason Good, of which the authorship is not equally well authenticated.

The omission of a quotation or two, of no present interest, and the correction of a few inaccuracies of language, are the only alterations that have been made in the Preliminary Essay.—EDITOR.

pests that, within the last twenty years, have shaken the
political world to its centre, have been wider and more tre-
mendous in their operation; but they have, for the most
part, discharged their fury at a distance.   The constitutions
of other countries have been swept away by the whirlwind;
but that of England still towers, like the pyramids of Egypt,
a wonderful fabric, overshadowing the desert that surrounds
it, and defying the violence of its hurricanes.   In the period
however in question, this admirable structure of government
was itself attacked, and trembled to its foundation; a series
of unsuccessful ministries, often profligate and corrupt, and
not unfrequently cunning, rather than capable; a succession
of weak and obsequious parliaments, and an arbitrary, though
able chief justice, addicted to the impolitic measures of the
cabinet, fatally concurred to confound the relative powers of
the state, and equally to unhinge the happiness of the crown
and of the people; to frustrate all the proud and boasted
triumphs of a glorious war, concluded but a few years before
by an inglorious peace*; to excite universal contempt abroad,
and universal discord at home.   Hence France, humiliated as
she was by her losses and defeats, did not hesitate to invade
Corsica in open defiance of the remonstrances of the British
minister, and succeeded in obtaining possession of it; whilst
Spain dishonourably refused to make good the ransom she
had agreed to, for the restoration of the capital of the Philippine Isles, which had been exempted from pillage upon this
express stipulation.   They saw the weakness and distraction
of the English Cabinet, and had no reason to dread the chastisement of a new war.

The discontents in the American colonies, which a little
address might at first have stifled, were blown into a flame
of open rebellion, through the impolitic violence of the very
minister who was appointed, by the creation of a new office
at this very time and for this express purpose, to examine
into the causes of dissatisfaction, and to redress the grievances complained of; while, at home, the whole of the ways
and means of the ministry, instead of being directed against
the arrogance of the common enemy, were exhausted against an
individual, who, perhaps, would never have been so greatly dis-

* In 1763, through the negotiation of the Duke of Bedford.

tinguished, had not the ill-judged and contumacious opposition of the cabinet, and their flagrant violation of the most sacred and important principles of the constitution in order to punish him, raised him to a height of popularity seldom attained even by the most successful candidate for public applause, and embroiled themselves on his account in a dispute with the nation at large, almost amounting to a civil war, and which at length only terminated in their own utter confusion and defeat*.

It was at this period, and under these circumstances, that the ensuing letters successively made their appearance in the Public Advertiser, the most current newspaper of the day†. The classic purity of their language, the exquisite force and perspicuity of their argument, the keen severity of their reproach, the extensive information they evince, their fearless and decisive tone, and, above all, their stern and steady attachment to the purest principles of the constitution, acquired for them, with an almost electric speed, a popularity which no series of letters have since possessed, nor, perhaps, ever will; and what is of far greater consequence, diffused among the body of the people a clearer knowledge of their constitutional rights than they had ever before attained, and animated them with a more determined spirit to maintain them inviolate. Enveloped in the cloud of a fictitious name, the writer of these philippics, unseen himself, beheld with secret satisfaction the vast influence of his labours, and enjoyed, though, as we shall afterwards observe, not always without apprehension, the universal hunt that was made to detect him in his disguise. He beheld the people extolling him, the court execrating him, and ministers and more than ministers trembling beneath the lash of his invisible hand.

That the same general impression was produced by the appearance of these letters *in* parliament, which is so well known to have been produced *out* of it, is evident from almost all the speeches of the day, as the ensuing extracts from speeches delivered by Mr. Burke and Lord North will attest.

* In the language of Lord Chatham, delivered May 1, 1771, in the House of Lords, "they rendered the very name of parliament ridiculous, by carrying on a constant war against Mr. Wilkes."

† They were generally copied from the Public Advertiser into all the daily and evening papers.

" Where then shall we look for the origin of this relaxation of the laws and all government? How comes this Junius to have broke through the cobwebs of the law, and to range uncontrolled, unpunished, through the land? The myrmidons of the court have been long, and are still, pursuing him in vain. They will not spend their time upon me, or you, or you. No: they disdain such vermin, when the mighty boar of the forest, that has broke through all their toils, is before them. But what will all their efforts avail? No sooner has he wounded one than he lays down another dead at his feet. For my part, when I saw his attack upon the king, I own my blood ran cold. I thought he had ventured too far, and there was an end of his triumphs, not that he had not asserted many truths. Yes, Sir, there are in that composition many bold truths, by which a wise prince might profit. It was the rancour and venom with which I was struck. In these respects the North Briton is as much inferior to him, as in strength, wit, and judgment. But while I expected in this daring flight his final ruin and fall, behold him rising still higher, and coming down souse upon both Houses of Parliament. Yes, he did make you his quarry, and you still bleed from the wounds of his talons. You crouched, and still crouch, beneath his rage. Nor has he dreaded the terrors of your brow, Sir; he has attacked even you—he has—and I believe you have no reason to triumph in the encounter. In short, after carrying away our Royal Eagle in his pounces, and dashing him against a rock, he has laid you prostrate. King, lords, and commons are but the sport of his fury. Were he a member of this house, what might not be expected from his knowledge, his firmness, and integrity? He would be easily known by his contempt of all danger, by his penetration, by his vigour. Nothing would escape his vigilance and activity. Bad ministers could conceal nothing from his sagacity ; nor could promises nor threats induce him to conceal anything from the public."

The following is part of a speech delivered by Lord North :—

" When factions and discontented men have brought things to this pass, why should we be surprised at the difficulty of bringing libellers to justice? Why should we wonder that the great boar of the wood, this mighty Junius, has broke through the toils and foiled the hunters? Though there may be at present no spear that will reach him, yet he may be some time or other caught. At any rate he will be exhausted with fruitless efforts ; those tusks which he has been whetting to wound and gnaw the constitution will be worn out. Truth will at last prevail. The public will see and feel that he has either advanced false facts, or reasoned falsely from true principles ; and that he has owed his escape to the spirit of the times, not to the justice of his cause. The North Briton, the most flagitious libel of its day, would have been equally secure, had it been as powerfully supported. But the press had not then overflowed the land with its black gall, and poisoned the minds of the people. Political writers had some shame left ; they had some reverence for the crown, some respect for the name of Majesty. Nor were there any members of parliament hardy enough to harangue in defence of libels. Lawyers could hardly be brought to plead for them. But the scene is now entirely changed. Without doors, within doors, the same abusive strains prevail. Libels find patrons in both Houses of Parliament as well as in Westminster Hall. Nay, they pronounce libels on the very judges. They pervert tho privilege of this house to the purposes of faction. They catch and swallow the breath of the inconstant multitude, because, I suppose, they take their voice, which is now that of libels, to be the voice of God."

It is not the intention of the editor of the present volumes to vindicate the whole of the method pursued by Junius towards the accomplishment of the patriotic objects on which his heart appears to have been most ardently engaged. Much of his individual sarcasm might perhaps have been spared with advantage—and especially the whole of his personal assaults upon the character and motives of the king. Aware as the editor is of the arguments in favour of occasionally attacking the character of the chief magistrate, as urged by Junius himself in his Preface, he still thinks that no possible circumstances could justify so gross a disrespect and indecency; that no principle of the constitution supports it, and that every advantage it was calculated to produce, might have been obtained in an equal degree, and to an equal extent, by animadverting upon the conduct of the king's ministers, instead of censuring that of the king in person. In the volumes before us the editor is ready to acknowledge that these kinds of paragraphs seem at times not altogether free from—what ought never to enter the pages of a writer on national subjects—individual spleen and enmity. But well may we forgive such trivial aberrations of the heart, in the midst of the momentous matter these volumes are well known to contain, the important principles they inculcate; and especially under the recollection that, but for the letters of Junius, the Commons of England might still have been without a knowledge of the transactions of the House of Commons, consisting of their parliamentary representatives—have been exposed to arbitrary violations of individual liberty, under undefined pretexts of parliamentary privileges against which there were no appeal —defrauded of their estates upon capricious and interested claims of the crown—and deprived of the constitutional right of a jury to consider the question of law as well as of fact. To the steady patriotism of the late Mr. Fox is the nation solely indebted for a direct legislative decision upon this last important point;—but the ground was previously cleared by the letters before us; it is not often that a judge has dared openly to controvert this right since the manly and unanswerable argument of Junius upon this subject, in opposition to

the arbitrary and illegal doctrine of Lord Mansfield, as urged
in the case of the King *v.* Woodfall:—an argument which
seems to have silenced every objection, to have convinced
every party, and without which perhaps even the zeal and
talents of Mr. Fox himself might have been exercised in vain.

But, after all, who or what was Junius? this *shadow of a
name*, who thus shot his unerring arrows from an impenetrable concealment, and punished without being perceived?
The question is natural; and it has been repeated almost
without intermission, from the appearance of his first letter.
It is not unnatural, moreover, from the pertinacity with which
he has at all times eluded discovery, that the vanity of many
political writers of inferior talents should have induced them
to lay an indirect claim to his Letters, and especially after
the danger of responsibility had considerably ceased. Yet
while the Editor of the present impression does not undertake, and, in fact, has it not in his power, to communicate
the real name of Junius, he pledges himself to prove, from
incontrovertible evidence, afforded by the private letters of
Junius himself during the period in question, in connection
with other documents, that not one of these pretenders has
ever had the smallest right to the distinction which some of
them have ardently coveted.

These private and confidential letters, addressed to the late
Mr. Woodfall, are now for the first time made public by his
son, who is in possession of the author's autographs * ; and

---

* There must have been some misunderstanding either of the *extent* of the
question, or the *nature* of the answer in that part of a conversation which
Mr. Campbell, in his Life of Hugh Boyd, states to have occurred between
Mr. H. S. Woodfall (editor and one of the proprietors of the Public Advertiser) and himself in relation to the preservation of these autographs.   " I
proceeded," says Mr. Campbell, " to ask him if he had preserved any of the
manuscripts of Junius? He said *he did not.*" p. 164. The veracity of Mr.
H. S. Woodfall is well known to have been unimpeachable ; and it is by no
means the intention of the editor to suspect that of Mr. Campbell. It is
probable that Mr. Woodfall understood the question to be whether he had
regularly preserved the manuscripts of Junius, or had preserved any of the
manuscripts of Junius which had publicly appeared *under that signature?*
No man, not even Mr. Campbell himself, could have suspected Mr. Woodfall
to have been guilty of a wilful falsehood ; nor can any advantage be assigned,
or even conceived, that could possibly have resulted from such a falsehood,
had it taken place.

It is equally extraordinary that Mr. Campbell, in this same conversation,

from the various facts and anecdotes they disclose, not only in relation to this extraordinary character, but to other characters as well, they cannot fail of being highly interesting to the political world. To have published these letters at an earlier period would have been a gross breach of trust and decorum: the term of trust, however, seems at length to have expired; most of the parties have paid the debt of nature, and should any be yet living, the length of time which has since elapsed has so completely blunted the asperity of the strictures they contain, that they could scarcely object to so remote a publication of them. Junius, in the career of his activity, was the man of the people; and when the former can receive no injury from the disclosure, the latter have certainly a claim to every information that can be communicated concerning him.

It was on the 28th of April, in the year 1767, that the late Mr. H. S. Woodfall received, among other letters from a great number of correspondents, for the use of the Public Advertiser, of which he was a proprietor, the first public address of this celebrated writer*. He had not then assumed the name, or rather written under the signature, of Junius; nor

should represent Mr. Woodfall as saying that "as to the story about Hamilton quoting Junius to the late Duke of Richmond, *he knew* it to be a misconception." In regard to the story itself, Woodfall knew it to be founded in fact from Hamilton's own relation—and has repeatedly mentioned it as such; but he may have meant that the story *as told by Mr. Campbell* was a misconception.

In effect the late Duke of Richmond himself distinctly informed the son of the late Mr. Woodfall, that such a communication with Hamilton had taken place, while his Grace was riding with Sir James Peachey, afterwards Lord Selsey, in the park at Goodwood, though he could not at that distance of time recollect the particular letter to which it referred. The clue to the mystery is that Mr. Hamilton was acquainted with the late Mr. H. S. Woodfall, and used occasionally to call at his office; whence it is highly probable that Mr. Woodfall had shown him or detailed to him a letter from Junius then just received, and intended for publication on a certain day. Hamilton alluded to the general purport of this letter, on the day on which it was to have been published, as though he had just read it; when, to the astonishment of his Grace and Sir James Peachey, to whom he thus mentioned it, no such letter appeared, though it did appear the next day or the day after.

* Dr. Good is a forcible, but careless writer; the letter referred to, the first of the Miscellaneous Letters, was published, not received on the day mentioned, and preceded by twenty months the appearance of the first letter of Junius. It was signed *Poplicola*, and, as it contained a severe attack on Lord Chatham, there is the strongest reason for doubting its assigned origin.—ED

did he always indeed assume a signature of any kind. When
he did so, however, his signatures were diversified, and the
chief of them were Mnemon, Atticus, Lucius, Junius, and
Brutus. Under the first he sarcastically opposed the ministry
upon the subject of the *Nullum Tempus* Bill, which involved
the celebrated dispute concerning the transfer on the part of
the crown of the Duke of Portland's estate of the forest of
Inglewood, and the manor and castle of Carlisle, to Sir James
Lowther, son-in-law of lord Bute, upon the plea that these
lands, which formerly belonged to the crown, had not been
duly specified in King William's grant of them to the Portland family; and that hence, although they had been in the
Portland family for nearly seventy years, they of right belonged to the crown still. The letters signed Atticus and
Brutus relate chiefly to the growing disputes with the American colonies: and those subscribed Lucius exclusively to the
outrageous dismission of Sir Jeffery Amherst from his post of
governor of Virginia.

The name of Mnemon was, perhaps, taken up at hazard.
That of Atticus was unquestionably assumed from the author's
own opinion of the purity of his style, an opinion in which the
public universally concurred; and the three remaining signatures of Lucius, Junius, and Brutus were obviously deduced
from a veneration for the memory of the celebrated Roman
patriot, who united these three names in his own.

Various other names were also occasionally assumed by this
fertile political writer, to answer particular purposes, or more
completely to conceal himself and carry forward his extensive
design.   That of Philo-Junius, he has avowed to the public,
in the authorized edition of the Letters of Junius: but beside
this, he is yet to be recognised under the mask of Poplicola,
Domitian, Vindex, and several others, as the subjoined pages
will sufficiently testify.

The most popular of our author's letters anterior to those
published with the signature of Junius in 1769, were those
subscribed Atticus and Lucius; to the former of which the
few letters signed Brutus seem to have been little more than
auxiliary, and are consequently not polished with an equal
degree of attention. These letters, in point of time, preceded
those with the signature of Junius by a few weeks: they are
certainly written with admirable spirit and perspicuity, and

are entitled to all the popularity they acquired :—yet they are not perhaps possessed of more merit than our author's letters signed Mnemon. They nevertheless deserve a more minute attention from their superior celebrity. The proofs of their having been composed by the writer denominated Junius are incontestible: the manner, the phraseology, the sarcastic, exprobratory style, independently of any other evidence, suffi ciently identify them. These, therefore, together with such others as are equally and indisputably genuine, are now added to the acknowledged letters of Junius, to render his productions complete.

It is no objection to their genuineness that they were omitted by Junius in his own edition published by Mr. Woodfall :—there is a material difference between printing a complete edition of the letters of Junius, and a complete edition of the letters that appeared under this name. The first was the main object of Junius himself, and it was not necessary, therefore, that he should have extended it to letters composed by him under any other signature, excepting, indeed, those of Philo-Junius, which it was expedient for him to avow; the second is the direct design of the edition before us; —and it would be inconsistent with it to suppress any of his letters, under what signature soever they may have appeared, that possess sufficient interest to excite the attention of the public *.

The first of the letters (signed Atticus) was written in the beginning of August, 1768. It takes a general, and by no means an uncandid, survey of the state of the nation at that period, and particularly in regard to its funded property, the alarming depression of which, from the still hostile appearance of France, the prospect of a rupture with the American colonies, the wretchedness of the public finances, and the imbecility of the existing administration, struck the writer so forcibly as to induce him, as he tells us, to transfer his property from the funds to, what he conceived, the more solid security of landed estate. The conclusion of this letter

---

* Mason Good's unhesitating affiliation of those unavowed letters on Junius will form a subject of after inquiry; that those signed *Poplicola,* *Brutus,* and others were not written by him, strong proof will be adduced; and thereby the impression entertained by some against the undeviating consistency of this famous writer be removed.—ED.

exhibits so much of the essential style and manner of Junius,
that it has every claim to be copied in this place as affording
an internal proof of identity of pen.

" We are arrived at that point when new taxes either produce nothing, or
defeat the old ones, and when new duties only operate as a prohibition : yet
these are the times when every ignorant boy thinks himself fit to be a
minister. Instead of attendance to objects of national importance, our
worthy governors are contented to divide their time between private pleasures
and ministerial intrigues. Their activity is just equal to the persecution of
a prisoner in the King's Bench, and to the honourable struggle of providing
for their dependants. If there be a good man in the king's service they dismiss him of course; and when bad news arrives, instead of uniting to consider
of a remedy, their time is spent in accusing and reviling one another. Thus
the debate concludes in some half misbegotten measure, which is left to
execute itself. *Away they go : one retires to his country house ; another is
engaged at a horse race ; a third has an appointment with a prostitute ;—
and as to their country, they leave her, like a cast-off mistress, to perish under
the diseases they have given her.*"

It was just at this period that the very extraordinary step
occurred of the dismissal of Sir Jeffery Amherst from his
government of Virginia, for the sole purpose, as it should
seem, of creating a post for the Earl of Hillsborough's intimate friend Lord Boutetort, who had completely ruined
himself by gambling and extravagance. This post had been
expressly given to Sir Jeffery for life, as a reward for his past
services in America, and it was punctiliously stipulated that a
personal residence would be dispensed with. It was an
atrocity well worthy of public attack and condemnation ; and
the keen vigilance of Junius, which seems first to have
traced it out, hastened to expose it to the public in all its
indecency and outrage, and with the warmth of a personal
friendship for the veteran hero. The subject being of a
different description from that he had engaged in under the
signature of Atticus, he assumed a new name, and for the
first time sallied forth under that of Lucius, subscribed to a
letter addressed to the Earl of Hillsborough, minister for the
American department, and published in the Public Advertiser
Aug. 10, 1768. A vindication, or rather an apology, was
entered into, by three or four correspondents under different
signatures, but almost every one of whom was regarded by
Junius, and indeed by the public at large, as the Earl of
Hillsborough himself, or some individual writer under his
immediate control; thus assuming a mere diversity of mask

the better to accomplish the purpose of a defence. Lucius Junius followed up the contest without sparing,—the minister became ashamed of his conduct, and Sir Jeffery, within a few weeks after his dismissal and the resignation of two regiments which he had commanded, was restored to the command of one of them, and appointed to that of another; and in May, 1776, was created a peer of the realm, which the Duke of Grafton had refused him, under the strange and impolitic assertion that he had not fortune enough to maintain such a dignity with the splendour it required. The sarcastic remark of Lucius upon this observation of his Grace, is entitled to attention, as identifying him with Junius in his peculiar severity of reproach.

" The Duke of Grafton's idea of the proper object of a British peerage differs very materially from mine. His Grace, in the true spirit of business, looks for nothing but an opulent fortune; meaning, I presume, the fortune which can purchase, as well as maintain a title. We understand his Grace, and know who dictated that article. He has declared the terms on which Jews, gamesters, pedlars, and contractors (if they have sense enough to take the hint) may rise without difficulty into British Peers. There was a time indeed, though not within his Grace's memory, when titles were the reward of public virtue, and when the crown did not think its revenue ill employed in contributing to support the honours it had bestowed. It is true his Grace's family derive *their* wealth and greatness from a different origin, from a system which he, it seems, is determined to revive. His confession is frank, and well becomes the candour of a young man, at least. I dare say, that if either his Grace or your Lordship had had the command of a seven years' war in America, you would have taken care that poverty, however honourable, should not have been an objection to your advancement;—you would not have stood in the predicament of Sir Jeffery Amherst, who is refused a title of honour, because he did not create a fortune equal to it, at the expense of the public."

He is not less severe upon Lord Hillsborough in a succeeding letter; and the editor extracts the following passage for the same purpose he has introduced the preceding.

" That you are a civil, polite person is true. Few men understand the little morals better or observe the great ones less than your Lordship. You can bow and smile in an honest man's face, while you pick his pocket. These are the virtues of a court, in which your education has not been neglected. In any other school you might have learned that simplicity and integrity are worth them all. Sir Jeffery Amherst was fighting the battles of his country, while you, my Lord, the darling child of prudence and urbanity, were practising the generous arts of a courtier, and securing an honourable interest in the antichamber of a favourite."

Having thus signally triumphed in the affair of Sir Jeffery
Amherst, our invisible state-satirist now returned to the
subject he had commenced under the signature of Atticus,
and pursued it in three additional letters, with the same
signature, from the beginning of October till the close of
November, in the same year; offering a few general remarks
upon collateral topics in two or three letters signed Brutus.
The characteristics of Junius are often as conspicuous here as
in any letters he ever wrote: it will be sufficient to confine
ourselves to two passages, since two competent witnesses are
as good as a thousand. The following is his description of
the prime minister of the day.

" When the Duke of Grafton first entered into office, it was the fashion of
the times to suppose that young men might have wisdom without experience.
They thought so themselves, and the most important affairs of this country
were committed to the first trial of their abilities. His Grace had honourably fleshed his maiden sword in the field of opposition, and had gone
through all the discipline of the minority with credit. He dined at Wildman's,
railed at favourites, looked up to Lord Chatham with astonishment, and was
the declared advocate of Mr. Wilkes. It afterwards pleased his Grace to
enter into administration with his friend Lord Rockingham, and in a very
little time it pleased his Grace to abandon him. He then accepted of the
treasury upon terms which Lord Temple had disdained. For a short time
his submission to Lord Chatham was unlimited. He could not answer a
private letter without Lord Chatham's permission. I presume he was then
learning his trade, for he soon set up for himself. Until he declared himself
the minister, his character had been but little understood. From that moment
a system of conduct, directed by passion and caprice, not only reminds us
that he is a young man, but a young man without solidity of judgment. One
day he desponds and threatens to resign, the next he finds his blood heated,
and swears to his friends he is determined to go on. In his public measures
we have seen no proof either of ability or consistency. The stamp-act had
been repealed (no matter how unwisely) under the preceding administration.
The colonies had reason to triumph, and were returning to their good humour.
The point was decided, when this young man thought proper to revive it
without either plan or necessity; he adopts the spirit of Mr. Grenville's
measures, and renews the question of taxation in a form more odious and less
effectual than that of the law which had been repealed."

The following is his character of the members of the cabinet
generally. "The school they were bred in taught them how
to abandon their friends, without deserting their principles.
There is a littleness even in their ambition; for money is
their first object. Their professed opinions upon some great
points are so different from those of the party with which they
are now united, that the council chamber is become a scene of

open hostilities. While the fate of Great Britain is at stake, these worthy counsellors dispute without decency, advise without sincerity, resolve without decision, and leave the measure to be executed by the man who voted against it. This, I conceive, is the last disorder of the state. The consultation meets but to disagree, opposite medicines are prescribed, and the last fixed on is changed by the hand that gives it."

The attention paid to these philippics, and the celebrity they had so considerably acquired, stimulated the author to new and additional exertions: and having in the beginning of the ensuing year completed another with more than usual elaboration and polish, which he seems to have intended as a kind of introductory address to the nation at large, he sent it forth under the name of Junius, (a name he had hitherto assumed but once,) to the office of the Public Advertiser, in which journal it appeared on Saturday, January 21, 1769. The popularity expected by the author from this performance was more than accomplished; and what in some measure added to his fame, was a reply (for the Public Advertiser was equally open to all parties) from a real character of no small celebrity both as a scholar and as a man of rank, Sir William Draper; principally because the attack upon his majesty's ministers had extended itself to Lord Granby, at that time commander in chief, for whom Sir William professed the most cordial esteem and friendship.

Sir William Draper appears to have been a worthy, and, on the whole, an independent man; and Lord Granby was, perhaps, the most honest and immaculate of his majesty's ministers. Junius did not begin the dispute with the former, and seems, from a regard for his character, to have continued it unwillingly: " My answer," says he to him in his last letter, upon a second assault, and altogether without reason, " shall be short; for I write to you *with reluctance,* and I hope we shall now conclude our correspondence for ever!" At the latter he had only glanced incidentally, (for upon the whole he approved his conduct,) and seems rather to have done so on account of the company he consorted with, than from any gross misdeeds of his own. Nothing could, therefore, have been more improvident or impolitic than this attack of Sir William Draper: if volunteered in favour of the ministry, it is impossible for a defence to have been worse planned;—for, by confining the vindication to the individual that was least accused, it tacitly admits that the charges advanced against all the rest were well founded; while, if volunteered in favour of Lord Granby alone, it might easily have been anticipated by the writer that his visionary opponent would be hereby challenged to bring forward pecadillos which would otherwise never be heard of, and that he would not fail, at the same time, to scrutinize the character of Sir William himself, and to ascribe this act of precipitate zeal to an interested desire of additional promotion in the army. It was too much for Sir William to expect that Junius would be hurried into an intemperate disclosure of his real name by a swaggering offer to measure swords with him; while the following rebuke was but a just retaliation for his challenge.

" Had you been originally and without provocation attacked by an anonymous writer, you would have some right to demand his name. But in this cause you are a volunteer. You engaged in it with the unpremeditated gallantry of a soldier. You were content to set your name in opposition to a man who would probably continue in concealment. You understood the terms upon which we were to correspond, and gave at least a tacit assent to them. After voluntarily attacking me under the character of Junius, what possible right have you to know me under any other? Will you forgive me if I insinuate to you, that you foresaw some honour in the apparent spirit of coming forward in person, and that you were not quite indifferent to the display of your literary qualifications?"

In reality Junius, though a severe satirist, was not in his general temper a malevolent writer, nor an ungenerous man. No one has ever been more ready to admit the brilliant talents of Sir William Blackstone than himself, or to apply to his Commentaries for legal information, while reprobating his conduct in the unconstitutional expulsion of Mr. Wilkes from the House of Commons. " If I were personally your enemy," says he in his letter to him upon this subject, "I should dwell with a malignant pleasure upon *those great and useful qualifications which you certainly possess,* and by which you once acquired, though they could not preserve to you, the respect and esteem of your country. I should enumerate the honours you have lost, and the virtues you have disgraced : but having no private resentments to gratify, I think it sufficient to have given my opinion of your public conduct, leaving the punishment it deserves to your closet and self."

The rescue of General Gansel, by means of a party of guards, from the hands of the sheriff's officers after they had arrested him for debt, was an outrage upon the law which well demanded castigation; and the attempt to quash this transaction on the part of the minister, instead of delivering the culprits over to the punishment they had merited, was an outrage of at least equal atrocity, and demanded equal reprobation. The severity with which the minister was repeatedly attacked by Junius on this subject is still well known to many: but the reason is not yet known to any one, perhaps, why the latter suddenly dropped this subject, after having positively declared in his letter of November 15, 1769, "if the gentlemen, whose conduct is in question, are not brought to a trial, the Duke of Grafton shall hear from me again." From his Private Letters to Mr. Woodfall, we shall now learn that he was solely actuated in his forbearance by motives of humanity: "The only thing," says he in a note alluding to this transaction, "that hinders my pushing the subject of my last letter, is really the fear of ruining that poor devil Gansel, and those other blockheads."*

In like manner having been betrayed by the first rumours of the day into what he afterwards found to have been too severe an opinion, and expressed himself with too indignant a warmth upon the conduct of Mr. Vaughan in his well known attempt to purchase of the Duke of Grafton the reversion of a patent place in Jamaica, he hastened to make him both publicly and privately all the reparation in his power. "I think myself obliged," says he in a letter to the Duke of Grafton, "to do this justice to an injured man, because I was deceived by the appearances thrown out by your Grace, and have frequently spoken of his conduct with indignation. If he really be, what I think him, honest, though mistaken, he will be happy in recovering his reputation, though at the expense of his understanding." Vaughan himself had so high an opinion of our author's integrity, though a total stranger to him, that he intrusted him with his private papers upon the subject in question, which Junius, in return, took care to employ to Vaughan's advantage †.

* Private Letter, No. 11.
† Compare his private letter to Woodfall, Dec. 12, 1739, No. 15, with his public letter to the Duke of Grafton, February 14, 1770, after he had

From the extraordinary effect produced by his first letter under the signature of Junius, he resolved to adhere to this signature exclusively, in all his subsequent letters, in which he took more than ordinary pains, and which alone he was desirous of having attributed to himself; while to other letters, composed with less care, and merely explanatory of passages in his more finished addresses, or introduced for some other collateral purpose, he subscribed some random name which occurred to him at the moment. The letters of Philo-Junius are alone an exception to this remark. These he always intended to acknowledge; and in truth they are for the most part composed with so much of the peculiar style and finished accuracy of the letters of Junius, properly so called, that it would have required but little discernment to have regarded the two correspondents as the same person under different characters,—*idem et alter*—if Junius himself had not at length admitted them to be his own productions, which he expressly did, in an authorized note from the printer, inserted in the Public Advertiser, Oct. 19, 1771. "The auxiliary part of Philo-Junius," says he in his Preface, " was indispensably necessary to defend or explain particular passages in Junius, in answer to plausible objections; but the subordinate character is never guilty of the indecorum of praising his principal. The fraud was innocent, and I always intended to explain it." Yet whatever were the signatures he assumed, or the loose paragraphs he occasionally addressed to the public, without a signature of any kind, we have his own assertion, that from the time of his corresponding, as Junius, with the editor of the Public Advertiser, he never wrote in any other newspaper. " I believe," says he, " I need not assure you that I have never written in any other paper since I began with yours; " Private Letter, No. 7. So also in another Private Letter, No. 13, " I sometimes change my signature, but could have no reason to *change the paper*, especially for one that does not circulate half so much as yours."

That he was not only a man of highly cultivated general talents and education, but who had critically and successfully studied the language, the law, the constitution and history of

examined these papers, and especially the passage, " You laboured then, by every species of false suggestion, and even by publishing counterfeit letters," &c.

his native country, is indubitable. Yet this is not all; the proofs are just as clear that he was also a man of independent fortune, that he moved in the immediate circle of the court, and was intimately acquainted, from its first conception, with almost every public measure, every ministerial intrigue, and every domestic incident.

That he was a man of easy, if not of affluent circumstances, is unquestionable from the fact that he never could be induced in any way or shape to receive any acknowledgment from the proprietor of the Public Advertiser, for the great benefit and popularity he conferred on this paper by his writings, and to which he was fairly entitled *. When the first genuine edition of his letter, was on the point of publication, Mr. Woodfall again urged him either to accept half its profits, or to point out some public charity or other institution to which an equal sum might be presented. His reply to this request is contained in a paragraph of one of his Private Letters, No. 59, and confers credit on both the parties. "What you say about the profits is very handsome. I like to deal with such men. As for myself, be assured that *I am far above all pecuniary views*, and no other person I think has any claim to share with you. Make the most of it, therefore, and let all your views in life be directed to a solid, however moderate independence: without it no man can be happy, nor even honest." In this last sentence he reasoned from the sphere of life in which he was accustomed to move; and, confining it to this sphere, the transactions of every day show us that he reasoned correctly. It is an additional proof, as well of his affluence as of his generosity, that not long after the commencement of his correspondence with the printer of the Public Advertiser, he wrote to him as follows: " For the matter of assistance, be assured that, if a question should arise upon any writings of mine, you shall not want it;—in point of money be assured you shall never suffer." In perfect and honourable consonance with which, when the printer was at length involved in a prosecution in consequence of Junius's letter to the king, he wrote to him as follows : " If your affair should come to a trial, and you should be found guilty, you will then let me know what expense falls particularly on yourself: for I un

* Letter, No. 6, dated Aug. 6, 1769.

derstand you are engaged with other proprietors. Some way or other *you* shall be reimbursed," Private Letter, No. 59 *.

"As you have told us," says Sir W. Draper, in his last letter to Junius, "of your importance; and that you are a person of *rank* and *fortune*, and above a *common* bribe, you may, in all probability, be not unknown to his Lordship (Earl of Shelburne), who can satisfy you of the truth of what I say." Sir William alludes, in this passage, to a short public note of Junius to the printer of the Public Advertiser, addressed in consequence of some verses which had just ap-

* Had Dr. Good been as industrious in his researches as a recent writer in the *Athenæum*, he might have ascertained, from an undoubted source, the direct effect of the pen of Junius on the pecuniary interests of Woodfall, in promoting the sale of the *Public Advertiser*. As the question is of some moment, by elucidating the influence of powerful writing on the popularity of a journal, we shall avail ourselves of the inquiries of our contemporary. By reference to the "Day-book," of the *Public Advertiser*, the *Athenæum* found that neither the first letter of Junius, nor many subsequent ones, had any immediate effect on the sale of the paper. But on the 19th of December, 1769, appeared his celebrated letter to the king, the effect of which was immediate and electrifying; to meet the increased demand from this formidable appeal, not 500 copies, as Mason Good states, were required, but 1750 additional copies. "To meet the demand expected, or which followed, for Junius's next letter (to the Duke of Grafton) published 14th February, 1770, 700 additional copies were printed; for the following on the 19th of March, the additional supply was 350; for the letter in April, 350—but not an additional copy was printed of the letter of the 28th May. There were 100 only on the 22nd August for the letter to Lord North. The letter to Lord Mansfield again awakened public attention, and 600 additional copies were printed. We have no detailed account of the sale in January: but 500 additional copies were printed of the *Public Advertiser* which contained the letter in April, 1771—100 of the June letter to the Duke of Grafton—25C for the first in July to the same—not one for the second letter to Horne Tooke of the 24th of July—200 for the August letter to the same—250 for the letter to the Duke of Grafton in September. With the letter to the Livery of London in September the sale *fell* 250—with the letter of the 5th of October there was neither rise nor fall—with the letter of the 2nd Nov. to Mansfield it may have risen 50, but we doubt it—and on the 28th with that to the Duke of Grafton it rose 350."—*Athenæum*, July 29, 1848. The *Public Advertiser* had long been a successful and rising paper, whose average sale, with the exception of two, was little inferior to that of our existing London daily papers. But the sale of a periodical, however important to the proprietors, is only a vulgar test of the influence of a writer; that of Junius was unquestionably immense; but it was at the court of George III., in his cabinet, among his ministers, judges and *employés*, and among the higher class of statesmen and politicians, that the tusk of Burke's " great boar of the forest" was most keenly felt.—ED.

peared in that paper, entitled " The tears of Sedition on the
death of Junius ; " in which he observes : " It is true I have
refused offers which a more prudent or a more interested man
would have accepted. Whether it be simplicity or virtue in
me, I can only affirm that *I am in earnest*, because I am con
vinced, as far as my understanding is capable of judging, that
the present ministry are driving this country to destruction ;
and *you*, I think, Sir, may be satisfied that my rank and fortune place me above a common bribe."* Sir William sneers
at the appeal, and treats it as the mere unfounded boast of a
man of arrogance and invisibility ; but the reader now sees
sufficiently that it had a solid foundation to rest upon.

That Junius moved in the immediate circle of the court,
and was intimately and confidentially connected, either directly
or indirectly, with all the public offices of government, is, if
possible, still clearer than that he was a man of independent
property ; for the feature that peculiarly characterized him,
at the time of his writing, and that cannot even now be con-
templated without surprise, was the facility with which he
became acquainted with every ministerial manœuvre, whether
public or private, from almost the very instant of its conception. At the first moment the partisans of the prime minister
were extolling his official integrity and virtue, in not only
resisting the terms offered by Mr. Vaughan for the purchase
of the reversion of a patent place in Jamaica, but in com-
mencing a prosecution against Vaughan for thus attempting
to corrupt him, Junius, in his letter of Nov. 29, 1769, exposed
this affectation of coyness, as he calls it, by proving that the
minister was not only privy to, but a party concerned in, the
sale of another patent place, though the former had often been
disposed of before in a manner somewhat if not altogether
similar. The particulars of this transaction are given in his
letter to the Duke of Grafton, Dec. 12, 1769, and in his
private note to Mr. Woodfall of the same date, No. 15. The
rapidity with which the affair of General Gansell reached him
has been already noticed. In his letter to the Duke of Bedford he narrates facts which could scarcely be known but to
persons immediately acquainted with the family. And when
the printer was threatened with a prosecution in consequence

* See Miscellaneous Letters, No. 54.

of this letter, he says to him in a private note, "it is clearly
my opinion that you have nothing to fear from the Duke of
Bedford. I reserve some things expressly to awe him in case
he should think of bringing you before the House of Lords.
I am sure I can threaten him *privately* with such a storm, as
would make him tremble even in his grave."* He was equally
acquainted with the domestic concerns of Lord Hertford's
family†. Of a Mr. Swinney, a correspondent of the printer's,
he observes in another confidential letter, "*That* Swinney is
a wretched but a dangerous fool : he had the impudence to go
to Lord G. Sackville, whom he had never spoken to, and to
ask him whether or no he was the author of Junius—take care
of him."‡ This anecdote is not a little curious : the fact was
true, and occurred but a short period before the letter was
written : but how Junius, unless he had been Lord Sackville
himself, should have heen so soon acquainted with it, baffles
all conjecture. In reality several persons to whom this transaction has been related, connecting it with other circumstances
of a similar tendency, have ventured, but too precipitately, to
attribute the letters of Junius to his lordship §.

His secret intelligence respecting public transactions is as
extraordinary. The accuracy with which he first dragged to
general notice the dismission of Sir Jeffery Amherst from his
governorship of Virginia has been already glanced at. "You
may assure the public," says he, in a private letter, Jan. 16,

* Private Letter, No. 10.

† The following are two of the paragraphs alluded to in Private Letter,
No. 42. "The Earl of Hertford is most honourably employed as terrier to
find out the clergyman that married the Duke of Cumberland, an errand well
fitted to the man. He might, however, be much better employed in marrying
his daughters at the public expense. Witness the promise of an Irish peerage to Mr. S——t, &c., &c." "Nobody is so vociferous as the Earl of
Hertford on the subject of the late unprecedented marriage ! "

‡ Private Letter, No. 5.

§ In the Miscellaneous Letters, No. 7, is the following passage, pretty
conclusively showing the little ground there ever has been for any such
opinion. "I believe the best thing I can do will be to consult with my
Lord G. Sackville. His character is known and respected in Ireland as much
as it is here ; and I know he loves to be stationed in the *rear* as well as myself." The letter from which the above is an extract, independently of its
containing the style and sentiments of Junius, is thus additionally brought
home to him by the printer's customary acknowledgment in the P. A. being
followed by the subjoined observation : "Our friend and correspondent C.
will always find the utmost attention paid to his favours."

1771, "that a squadron of four ships of the line is ordered to be got ready with *all possible expedition* for the East In dies. It is to be commanded by Commodore Spry. Without regarding the language of ignorant or interested people, depend upon the assurance *I* give you, that every man in administration looks upon war as inevitable."*

But it would be endless to detail every instance of early and accurate information upon political subjects with which his public and private letters abound. In many cases he was able to indicate even to the printer of the Public Advertiser himself the real names of those who corresponded with him under fictitious signatures. "Your Veridicus," says he in one letter, "is Mr. Whitworth†. I assure you I have not confided in him."‡ "Your Lycurgus," he observes in another letter§, "is a Mr. Kent, a young man of good parts upon town."

Thus widely informed, and applying the information he was possessed of, with an unsparing hand, to purposes of general exposure in every instance of political delinquency, it cannot but be supposed that Junius must have excited a host of enemies in every direction, and that his safety, perhaps his existence, depended alone upon his concealment. Of this he was sufficiently sensible. In his last letter to Sir W. Draper, who had endeavoured by every means to stimulate him to a disclosure of himself, he observes, "As to me, it is by no means necessary that I should be exposed to the resentment of the worst and the most powerful men in this country, though I may be indifferent about yours. Though you would *fight*, there are others who would *assassinate*." To the same effect is the following passage in a confidential letter to Mr. Woodfall: "I must be more cautious than ever: I am sure I should not survive a discovery three days; or if I did they would attaint me by bill."|| On many occasions,

---

* Private Letter, No. 28. The knowledge of this preparation was communicated four days before the meeting of parliament: the war, however, did not take place; but the preparation is now known to have been a fact, the ministry being themselves fearful that the temper of parliament would have forced them into hostilities, from which in truth they very narrowly escaped. See note to the Private Letter, No. 28.

† Richard Whitworth, Esq., M.P. for Stafford.

‡ Private Letter, No. 6.   § Id. No. 5. || Id. No. 41.

therefore, notwithstanding all the calmness and intrepidity he affected in his public letters, it is not to be wondered at that he should betray some feelings of apprehension in his confidential intercourse. In one of his private letters, indeed, he observes, " As to me, be assured that it is not in the nature of things that they (the Cavendish family) or you, or anybody else should ever know me, unless I make myself known: all arts, or enquiries, or rewards, would be equally ineffectual."* But in other letters he seems not a little afraid of detection or surmise. "Tell me candidly," he says, at an early period of his correspondence with Mr. Woodfall under the signature of Junius, "whether you know or suspect who I am."† "You must not write to me again," he observes in another letter, "but be assured I will never desert you."‡ "Upon no account, nor for any reason whatsoever, are you to write to me until I give you notice."§ "Change to the Somerset Coffee House, and let no mortal know the alteration. I am persuaded you are too honest a man to contribute in any way to my destruction. Act honourably by me, and at a proper time you shall know me."||

The Somerset Coffee House formed only one of a great variety of places, at which answers and other parcels from the printer of the Public Advertiser were ordered to be left. No plan indeed could be better devised for secrecy than that by which this correspondence was maintained. A common name, such as was by no means likely to excite any peculiar attention, was first chosen by Junius, and a common place of deposit indicated :—the parcels from Junius himself were sent direct to the printing office, and whenever a parcel or letter in return was waiting for him, the Public Advertiser announced it in the notices to its correspondents by such signals as " N. E. C."—"a letter," " Vindex shall be considered," " C. in the usual place," "an old correspondent shall be attended to," the introductory C. being a little varied from that commonly used; or by a line of Latin poetry. " Don't always use," says our author, "the same signal: any absurd Latin verse will answer the purpose."¶ And when the an-

---

* Private Letter, No. 10.   † Id. No. 3.   ‡ Id. No. 18.
§ Id. No. 47. || Id. No. 41.
¶ Private Letter, No. 43.—As instances of these signals of different kinds

swer implied a mere negative or affirmative, it was communicated in the newspaper by a simple *yes* or *no*. The names
of address more commonly assumed were Mr. William Middleton, and Mr. John Fretly; and the more common places
of address were the bar of the Somerset Coffee House as stated
above, that of the New Exchange, and Munday's in Maiden
Lane, the waiters of which were occasionally feed * for their
punctuality. But even these names and places of abode were
varied for others as circumstances might dictate.

By what conveyance Junius obtained his letters and parcels from the places at which they were left for him, is not
very clearly ascertained. From the passage quoted from his
private letter, No. 10, as also from the express declaration in
the dedication to his own edition of his letters, that he was at
that time " the sole depositary of his own secret," it should
seem that he had also been uniformly his own messenger; yet
in his private letter of January 18th, 1772, he observes,
" the gentleman who transacts the conveyancing part of our
correspondence tells me there was much difficulty last night."†
In truth the difficulty and danger of his constantly performing his own errand must have been extreme; and it is more
reasonable therefore to suppose that he employed some per

the reader may accept the following, taken from the Public Advertiser according to their dates.

August 12, 1771. A Correspondent may rest assured that his directions ever
have been, and ever will be, strictly attended to.

September 13.   C.
          17.   C.
          21.   C.
          27.   C.
October   19.   C.
November   5.   C.
           8.   C.
          12.   Vindex shall be considered.
          21.   Dic quibus in terris, et mihi eris magnus Apollo.
          26.   Quid rides? de TE fabula narratur.
          28.   Received.
          30.   ——— dicere verum
                   Quid vetat?
December   5.   Jam NOVA progenies cœlo dimittitur alto.
           6.   Received.
                   Quis te MAGNE CATO tacitum?
          17.   Infandum, REGINA! jubes renovare dolorem.

* Private Letter, No. 39.   † Private Letter, No. 51.

son on whom he could place an implicit reliance; while to
avoid the apparent contradiction between such a fact and that
of his affirming that he was the sole depositary of his own
secret, it is only necessary to conceive at the same time that
the person thus confidentially employed was not entrusted
with the full scope and object of his agency *. He sometimes, as we learn from his own testimony, employed a common chairman as his messenger†, and perhaps this, after all,
was the method most usually resorted to.

That a variety of schemes were invented and actually in
motion to detect him there can be no doubt; but the extreme
vigilance he at all times evinced, and the honourable forbearance of Mr. Woodfall, enabled him to baffle every effort, and
to persevere in his concealment to the last. "Your letter,"
says he in one of his private notes, "was twice refused last
night, and the waiter has often attempted to see the person
who sent for it."‡

On another occasion his alarm was excited in consequence
of various letters addressed to him at the printing office, with
a view, as he suspected, of leading to a disclosure either of
his person or abode. "I return you," says he in reply, "the
letters you sent me yesterday. A man who can neither write
common English, nor spell, is hardly worth attending to. It
is probably a trap for me: I should be glad, however, to know
what the fool means. If he writes again open his letter, and
if it contain anything worth my knowing, send it: otherwise
not. Instead of 'C. in the usual place' say only 'a letter'
when you have occasion to write to me again. I shall understand you."§

Some apprehension he seems to have suffered, as already
observed, from the impertinent curiosity of Swinney; but his

---

* Mr. Jackson, the present respectable proprietor of the Ipswich Journal,
who was at this time residing with the late Mr. Woodfall, for the purpose of
instruction in the London mode of conducting business, observed to the editor
in a conversation on this subject, that he once saw a tall gentleman dressed
in a light coat, with bag and sword, throw into the office door opening in
Ivy Lane a letter from Junius, which he picked up and immediately followed
the bearer of it into St. Paul's Church Yard, where he got into a hackney
coach and drove off. But whether this was "the gentleman who transacted
the conveyancing part" or Junius himself, it is impossible to ascertain.

† See Private Letters, Nos. 58, and 65, note.   ‡ Id. No. 58.
§ Id. No. 12.

resentment was chiefly roused by that of David Garrick, who appears from his own account, and from intelligence on which he fully relied, to have been pertinacious in his attempts to discover him. For three weeks or a month, he could scarcely ever write to Mr. Woodfall without cautioning him to be specially on his guard against Garrick: and under this impression alone he once changed his address*. He wrote to Garrick a private note of severe castigation, through the medium of the printer, which the latter, from an idea that it was unnecessarily acrimonious, resubmitted to his consideration with a view of dissuading him from sending it†, upon which our author desired him to tell Garrick personally to desist, or he would be amply revenged upon him. "As it is important," says he, "to deter him from meddling, I desire you will tell him I am aware of his practices, and will certainly be revenged if he does not desist. An appeal to the public from Junius would destroy him."‡

It is not impossible to form a plausible guess at the age of Junius, from a passage in one of his private letters; an inquiry, which, though otherwise of little or no consequence, is rendered in some measure important, as a test to determine the validity of the claims that have been laid to his writings by different candidates or their friends. The passage referred to occurs in his letter to Woodfall, dated Nov. 27, 1771; "after *long experience of the world*," says he, " I affirm before God, I never knew a rogue who was not unhappy."§ Now when this declaration is coupled with the two facts, that he made it under the repeated promise and intention of speedily disclosing himself to his correspondent‖, and that the correspondent thus schooled, by a moral axiom gleaned from his own "*long* experience of the world," was at this very time something more than thirty years of age; it seems absurd to suppose that Junius could be much less than fifty, or that he affected an age he had not actually attained.

There is another point in the history of his life, during his appearance as a public writer, which for the same reason must not be suffered to pass by without observation, although other-

---

* Private Letter, No. 41.
† Compare Private Letter, No. 41, with No. 43. The letter to Garrick will be found in the former of these.
‡ Private Letter, No. 43. § Id. No. 44. ‖ Id. No. 41.

wise it might be scarcely entitled to notice; and that is, that during a great part of this time, from January, 1769, to January, 1772, he uniformly resided in London, or its immediate vicinity, and that he never quitted his usual habitation for a longer period than a few weeks. This too, we may collect from his private correspondence, compared with his public labours. No man but he, who with a thorough knowledge of our author's style, undertakes to examine all the numbers of the Public Advertiser for the three years in question, can have any idea of the immense fatigue and trouble he submitted to in composing other letters, under other signatures, in order to support the pre-eminent pretensions and character of Junius, attacked as it was by a multiplicity of writers in favour of administration, to whom, as Junius, he did not choose to make any reply whatever. Surely Junius himself, when he first undertook the office of a public political censor, could by no means foresee the labour with which he was about to encumber himself. And instead of wondering that he should have disappeared at the distance of about five years*, we ought much rather to be surprised that he should have persevered through half this period, with a spirit at once so indefatigable and invincible. Junius had no time for remote excursions, nor often for relaxation, even in the vicinity of the metropolis itself.

Yet from his Private Letters we could almost collect a journal of his absences, if not an itinerary of his little tours for he does not appear to have left London at any time without some notice to the printer, either of his intention, or of the fact itself upon his return home; independently of which the frequency and regularity of his correspondence seldom allowed of distant travel. " I have been out of town," says he, in his letter of Nov. 8, 1769, " *for three weeks;* and though I got your last, could not conveniently answer it."†— On another occasion, " I have been *some days* in the country, and could not conveniently send for your letter until this night:"‡ and again, " I must see proof-sheets of the Dedication and Preface ; and these, if at all, I must see before the end of next week "§ In like manner, " I want rest most

---

* Junius, as already remarked (note, p. 1), is only known authentically to have been before the public about three years.—ED.

† Private Letter, No. 11.   ‡ Id. No. 7.   § Id. No. 45.

severely, and am going to find it in the country *for a few days*."*

The last political letter that ever issued under the signature of Junius was addressed to Lord Camden. It appeared in the Public Advertiser for Jan. 21, 1772, and followed the publication of his long and elaborate address to Lord Mansfield upon the illegal bailing of Eyre; and was designed to stimulate the noble earl to a renewal of the contest which he had commenced with the chief justice towards the close of the preceding session of parliament. It possesses the peculiarity of being the only encomiastic letter that ever fell from his pen under the signature of Junius. Yet the panegyric bestowed was not for the mere purpose of instigating Lord Camden to the attack in question. There is sufficient evidence in his Private Letters that Junius had a very high as well as a very just opinion of the integrity of this nobleman; and an ardent desire that the estimate he had formed of his integrity should be known to the world at large. In the whole course of his political creed there seems to have been but one point upon which they differed, and that was the doctrine assented to by his lordship, that the crown possesses a power, in case of very urgent necessity, of suspending the operation of an act of the legislature. It is a mere speculative doctrine, and Junius only incidentally alluded to it in a letter upon a very different subject†. The disagreement upon this point seems eagerly to have been caught at, however, by another correspondent in the Public Advertiser, who chose the signature of Scævola, apparently for the express purpose of involving the political satirist in a dispute with his lordship. " Scævola," observes he in a private letter, " I see is determined to make me an enemy to Lord Camden. If it be not wilful malice, I beg you will signify to him, that when I originally mentioned Lord Camden's declaration about the corn bill, it was without any view of discussing that doctrine, and only as an instance of a singular opinion maintained by a man of great learning and *integrity*. Such an instance was necessary to the plan of my letter."‡ And again, shortly afterwards, finding that the communication had not been received as it ought to have been, " I should not trouble you or

* Private Letter, No. 43.   † Letter 59.   ‡ Private Letter, No. 45.

PRELIMINARY ESSAY ON

myself about that blockhead Scævola, but that his absurd fiction of *my* being Lord Camden's enemy has done harm Every fool can do mischief, therefore signify to him what I said."* Not satisfied, however, with this hint to the printer. he chose, at the same time, under the subordinate character of Philo-Junius, to settle the point, and preclude all possibility of altercation, by an address to the public, that should dextrously mark out this single difference in a mere speculative opinion; and, while it amply defended the view he had taken of the subject, should evince such an evident approbation of his lordship's general conduct, as could not fail of being gratifying to him. This letter appeared in the Public Advertiser, Oct. 15, 1771†.

Lord Camden, however, was not induced by this earnest attempt and last letter of Junius to renew his attack upon Lord Mansfield; yet this was not the reason, or at least not the sole or primary reason, for Junius's discontinuing to write. It has already been observed, that so early as July, 1769, he began to entertain thoughts of dropping a character and signature which must have cost him a heavy series of labour, and frequently perhaps exposed him to no small peril. " I really doubt, says he, " whether I shall write any more *under this signature.* I am weary of attacking a set of brutes, whose writings are too dull to furnish me even with the materials of contention, and whose measures are too gross and direct to be the subject of argument, or to require illustration."‡

In perfect consonance with this declaration, in his reply to the printer, who had offered him half the profits of the letters at that time published under his own correction, or an equal sum for the use of any public institution he should choose to name, he makes the following remark, of which a part has been already quoted on another occasion: " As for myself, be assured that I am *far above* all pecuniary views, and no other person, I think, has any claim to share with you. Make the most of it therefore, and let all your views in life be directed to a solid, however moderate, independence: without it no man can be happy, nor even honest. If I saw any prospect of uniting the city once more, I would readily continue to labour in the vineyard. Whenever Mr. Wilkes can tell me

---

* Private Letter, No. 46.   † Letter 60.   ‡ Private Letter, No. 5.

that such an union is in prospect, he shall hear of me. *Quod si quis existimat me aut voluntate esse mutatâ, aut debilitatâ virtute, aut animo fracto, vehementer errat."* *

Even so long afterwards as January 19, 1773, in the very last letter we have any certain knowledge he ever addressed to Mr. Woodfall, he urges precisely the same motives for his continuing to desist. " I have seen the signals thrown out for your old friend and correspondent. Be assured that I have had good reason for not complying with them. In the present state of things, if I were to write again, I must be as silly as any of the horned cattle that run mad through the city, or as any of your wise aldermen. *I meant the cause and the public:* BOTH ARE GIVEN UP. I feel for the honour of this country, when I see that there are not ten men in it, who will unite and stand together upon any one question. But it is all alike vile and contemptible. *You* have never flinched that I know of; and I shall always rejoice to hear of your prosperity. If you have anything to communicate (of moment to yourself,) you may use the last address, and give a hint."†

* Private Letter, No. 59. " But if any one believes me to be changed in will, weakened in integrity, or broken in courage, he errs grossly."

† Private Letter, No. 63. The signals here referred to were thrown out on the very morning of the day on which this letter was written, and consisted of the following Latin quotation, inserted in the Public Advertiser for January 19, 1773, among the other answers to correspondents:—*Iterumque, iterumque monebo.* The printer, within a few weeks afterwards, availed himself of the liberty of making a communication to Junius by *the last address,* and, in the Public Advertiser of March 8, gave the following hint: "The letter from AN OLD FRIEND AND CORRESPONDENT, dated January 19, came safe to hand, and his directions are *strictly followed, Quod si quis existimat aut, &c."* The quotation is peculiarly happy: for it is not only a copy of what Junius had cited himself in his last private letter but one, and was hence sure to attract his attention, but is a smart replication to the passage in the letter it immediately refers to, " *You* have never flinched that I know of." The subject of some part of the communication at this time made by the printer to Junius, the editor has been able to discover, by having accidentally found among Mr. Woodfall's papers, and in his own hand-writing, a rough draft of one of the three letters of which it appears to have consisted. This letter the reader will meet with in the private correspondence, arranged according to its date, which is March 7, 1773, the day antecedent to the public notice given in the Public Advertiser as above. Among the answers to correspondents, March 20, we find another signal of the very same kind in the following terms, " *Aut voluntate esse mutatâ ;"* and in the same place March 29, a third ensign under the following form, "*Aut debilitatâ virtute;*' both of which it wi'l be observed, upon a comparison, are verbal cou

In effect, from the dissolution of the consolidated Whig party upon the death of George Grenville, the absurd divisions in the Bill of Rights Society, and the political separations in the city, our author had much reason to despair of the cause in which he had so manfully engaged.

To the moral character of Junius this letter is of more value than all the popular addresses he ever composed in his life. It is impossible to suppose it to flow from the affectation of an honesty which did not exist in his heart. The circumstances under which it was sent altogether prohibit such an idea: unknown as he was, and unknown as he had now determined to continue, to his correspondent, there was no adequate motive for his assuming the semblance of an integrity which he felt not, and which did not fairly belong to him. It was, it must have been, a pure, disinterested testimonial of private esteem and public patriotism, consentaneous with the uniform tenour both of his open and his confidential history, and conscientiously developing the real cause of his secession.

In truth it must have been, as he himself states it, insanity, to have persisted any longer in anything like a regular at-

tinuations of Junius's own quotation, and hence identify with double force the person to whom they relate. In the Public Advertiser of April 7, we find the following signal of a similar description, and it is the last we have been able to discover, "*Die quibus in terris.*" It is probable that these all related to matters of a personal concern, upon which, by the above private letter, the printer had still leave to address his correspondent: at least there is no reason for believing that Junius ever broke through the silence upon which he so inflexibly determined on January 19, or consented to reappear before the public in any character whatever. There were some very excellent letters signed Atticus that appeared in the Public Advertiser between the dates of June 26, 1772, and October 14, 1773, and exhibit much of our author's style, spirit and sentiments; and which, hence, by some tolerable judges, have been actually ascribed to him: but, for various reasons, independently of that afforded by the above private letter, the editor is convinced they are not the production of Junius. The talents they afford proof of, though considerable, are inferior; they contain attacks upon some statesmen who were never attacked by Junius; and it is well known from the following notice inserted among the addresses to correspondents in the Public Advertiser for June 19, 1773, as well as from other facts, that there was at this period, and had been for some time past, another writer in this journal who assumed the name of Atticus. "Some circumstances render it necessary that the printer should communicate a line to ATTICUS, *not his* OLD *Correspondent'*

tack; Lord Camden had declined to act upon his suggestion; the great phalanx of the Whig party was broken up by the death of Mr. George Grenville; the vanity and extreme jealousy of Oliver and Horne had introduced the most acrimonious divisions into the Society for supporting the Bill of Rights; and the leading *patriots* of the city had so intermixed their own private interests, and their own private squabbles, with the public cause, as to render this cause itself contemptible in the eye of the people at large. He had already tried, but in vain, to awaken the different contending parties to a sense of better and more honourable motives; to induce them to forego their selfish and individual disputes, and to make a common sacrifice of them upon the altar of the constitution *. Yet, at the same time, so small were his expectations of .success, so mean his opinion of the pretensions of most of the leading demagogues of the day to a real love of their country, and so grossly had he himself been occasionally misrepresented by them, that in his confidential intercourse he bade his correspondent beware of entrusting himself to them. " Nothing," says he, " can be more express than my declaration against long parliaments: try Mr. Wilkes once more, (*who was in private possession of his sentiments upon this subject*†;) speak for me in a most friendly but *firm* tone, that I *will not* submit to be any longer aspersed. Between ourselves, let me recommend it to you to be much upon your guard with *patriots*."‡

With his public address to the people, therefore, in Letter 59, he seems in the first instance to have resolved upon closing his labours, at least under the character of Junius, provided no beneficial effect were likely to result from it, and as the printer had expressed to him an earnest desire of publishing a genuine edition of his letters, in a collective form, in consequence of a variety of incorrect and spurious editions at that time circulating through the nation, he seems to have thought that a consent to such a plan would afford him a good ostensible motive for putting a finish to his public career; and on this account he not only acceded to the proposal, but undertook to superintend it as far as his invisibility might

---

* See Junius, Letter 59, and Private Letter, No. 65.
† See Private Letter, No. 66.   ‡ Private Letter. No. 45.

allow him; and also to add a few notes, as well as a dedication and preface.

Nothing can be more absurd than the idea entertained by some writers, that Junius himself was the previous editor of one or two of these irregular editions, and especially of an edition published but a short time anterior to his own, audaciously enough entitled " The Genuine Letters of Junius, to which are prefixed, *Anecdotes of the Author;*"* a pamphlet in which the anonymous anecdotist takes it for granted, from his very outset, that Junius and Edmund Burke were the same person, and then proceeds to reason concerning the former, from the known or acknowledged works of the latter.

It was not till the appearance of Newberry's edition, with which it is not pretended that our author had any concern, that even Woodfall himself had conceived an idea of the propriety of collecting these letters, and publishing them in an edition strictly genuine, in consequence of the numerous blunders by which the common editions were deformed; of these Newberry's was, perhaps, the freest from mistakes : yet Newberry's had so many, that our author, upon receiving a copy of it, addressed a note to Woodfall, begging him to hint to Newberry, that as he had thought proper to reprint his letters, he ought at least to have taken care to have corrected the errata : adding at the same time, " I did not expect more than the life of a newspaper; but if this man will keep me alive, let me live without being offensive."†

His answer upon Woodfall's application to him for leave to reprint his letters collectively, and subject to his own revisal, was as follows :—" I can have no manner of objection to your reprinting my letters, if you think it will answer, which I believe it might before Newberry appeared. If you determine to do it, give me a hint, and I will send you more errata (indeed they are innumerable) and perhaps a preface."‡ It was on this occasion he added, as conceiving it might afford him a proper opportunity for a general close of the character, though so early in his correspondence under the name of Junius, as July 1769, " I really doubt whether I shall write any more under this signature; I am weary of attacking a set

---

* See Mr. Chalmers's Appendix to the Supplemental Apology, &c., p. 24
† Private Letter, No. 4.   ‡ Id. No. 5.

of brutes, &c."*   In answer to Woodfall's next letter upon the same subject he observes, " Do with my letters exactly as you please.   I should think that, to make a better figure than Newberry, *some others of my letters may be added, and so throw out a hint that you have reason to suspect they are by the same author.   If you adopt this plan, I shall point out those, which I would recommend; for you know, I do not nor indeed have I time to give equal care to them all."†*

The plan for publication, however, though it commenced thus early, was not matured till October, 1771: when it was determined that the work should comprise all the letters which had passed under the signatures of Junius and Philo-Junius to this period inclusively, and be occasionally enriched by a selection of other letters under a variety of other signatures, such as will be found in the Miscellaneous Letters of the present edition; which, independently · ʃ that of Philo-Junius, our author, as has been observed already, not un-frequently employed to explain what required explanation, or defend what demanded vindication, and which he himself thought sufficiently correct to associate with his more laboured productions.   In the prosecution of this intention, however, he still made the two following alterations.   Instead of closing the regular series of letters possessing the signature of Junius with that dated October 5, 1771‡, upon the subject of " the un-happy differences," as he there calls them, " which *had* arisen among the friends of the people, and divided them from each other "—he added five others which the events of the day had impelled him to write during the reprinting of the letters, notwithstanding the intention he had expressed of offering nothing further under this signature.   And instead of intro-ducing the explanatory letters written under other signatures, he confined himself, in order that the work might be published before the ensuing session of parliament, to three justificatory papers alone : the first, under the title of "A Friend of Junius," containing an answer to " A Barrister at Law ; " the second an anonymous declaration upon certain points on which his opinion had been mistaken or misrepresented ; and the third an extract from a letter to Mr. Wilkes, drawn up for the purpose of being laid before the Bill of Rights Society, with a view of vindi-cating himself from the charge of having written in favour of

* Private Letter, No. 6.   † Id. No. 7.   · ‡ Letter 59.

long parliaments and rotten boroughs. This last, however, was furnished, not by Mr. Wilkes, but from his own notes, "you shall have the *extract*," says he, " to go into the second volume: it will be a short one."*

Of the five letters added after he meant to have closed, and had actually begun to reprint his series, four of them are either expressly addressed to Lord Mansfield, or incidentally relate to him, in consequence of his having *illegally* (as it was contended) admitted a felon of the name of John Eyre to bail, who, although possessing a fortune of nearly thirty thousand pounds sterling, had stolen a quantity of paper in quires out of one of the public offices at Guildhall, and was caught in the very theft. The other letter is addressed to the object of his steady and inveterate hatred, the Duke of Grafton, upon the defeat of his attempt to transfer the Duke of Portland's estate in Cumberland, consisting of what had formerly been crown lands, to Sir James Lowther, in order to assist the latter in securing his election for this county.

Such, however, was his anxiety to get this work completed and published before the winter session of parliament, that he was ready to sacrifice the appearance of the whole of these additional letters, even that containing his elaborate accusation of Lord Mansfield, and which he acknowledged to have cost him enormous pains, rather than that it should be delayed beyond this period. " I am truly concerned," says he in a private letter dated January 20, 1772, "to see that

---

* Private Letter, No. 45. The reader will readily pardon, and perhaps thank us, for pointing out to his particular attention the following exquisite paragraph with which the above letter closes, but which formed no part of it as originally addressed to Mr. Wilkes. It refers to an able argument that an excision of the rotten boroughs from the representative system might produce more mischief than benefit to the constitution. "The man who fairly and completely answers this argument shall have my thanks and my applause. My heart is already with him.—I am ready to be converted.—I admire his morality, and would gladly subscribe to the articles of his faith.—Grateful, as I am, to the GOOD BEING, whose bounty has imparted to me this reasoning intellect, whatever it is, I hold myself proportionably indebted to him, from whose enlightened understanding another ray of knowledge communicates to mine. But neither should I think the most exalted faculties of the human mind a gift worthy of the Divinity, nor any assistance in the improvement of them a subject of gratitude to my fellow-creature, if I were not satisfied, that really to inform the understanding corrects and enlarges the heart."

the publication of the book is so long delayed. It ought to have appeared before the meeting of parliament. By no means would I have you insert this long letter, if it make more than the difference of two days in the publication. Believe me, the delay is a real injury to the cause."*

The difficulties, however, of sending proofs and revises forward and backward were so considerable, that the anxiety of the author was not allayed: parliament met, but the book was not published. Junius became extremely impatient; yet still, in the most earnest terms pressed its publication before Alderman Sawbridge's motion *in favour of triennial parliaments*, which was to be brought forward in the beginning of March. "Surely," says he, in his private letter of February 17†, "you have misjudged it very much about the book. I could not have conceived it possible that you could protract the publication so long. At this time, particularly before Mr Sawbridge's motion, it would have been of singular use. You have trifled too long with the public expectation: at a certain point of time the appetite palls: I fear you have already lost the season. The book, I am sure, will lose the greatest part of the effect I expected from it—But I have done."

He was soon however consoled by intelligence from his friend Woodfall that, unduly as the book had been postponed, it was not for want of any exertions of his own ; and that, late as the season was, it would still precede the expected motion of Alderman Sawbridge‡. He, in consequence, replied as follows : "I do you the justice to believe that the delay has been unavoidable. The expedient you propose, of printing the Dedication and Preface in the Public Advertiser, is unadvisable. The attention of the public would then be quite lost to the book itself. I think your rivals will be disappointed : nobody will apply to them, when they can be supplied at the fountain head.—All I can now say is, make haste with the book."§

The Dedication, Preface, and the materials for his notes were all finished about the beginning of the preceding November (1771). The letters at large, excepting the first two sheets

* Private Letter, No. 51.   † Id. No. 55.
‡ The letters were actually published March 3, and Alderman Sawbridge's motion discussed the ensuing day—which motion, however, was lost by a majority of 251 against 83.   § Private Letter, No. 56.

which were revised by the author himself, were from the difficulty of conveyance entrusted to the correction of Mr Woodfall, with incidental amendments obtained, as they could be, by an interchange of letters. The Dedication and Preface were confided to the correction of Mr. Wilkes *, with whose attention the author expresses himself well pleased. "When you see Mr. Wilkes," says he in a note of February 29, 1772, "pray return him my thanks for the trouble he has taken. I wish he had taken more:" intimating hereby that there were still errors of which he was aware, and which he would have corrected if possible.

Yet though he thus continued to adhere rigidly to his determination never again to appear before the public in his full dress, or under the signature of Junius, as he expresses it in his Private Letter of November 8, 1771, he did not object occasionally to introduce his observations and continue his severe strictures in a looser and less elaborate form, and under some appellative or other, that might not interfere with the claims of Junius as a whole, as in the case of his series of letters to Lord Barrington, Nos. 105, 107, &c. These, however, it was not easy, in spite of the characteristic style that still, to an acute eye, pervaded them, for the world at large to bring completely home to the real writer, though many of them were frequently charged to the account of Junius by the political critics of the day, in different addresses to the printer upon this subject.

To judge of the moral and political character of Junius from his writings, as well private as public, he appears to have been a man of a bold and ardent spirit, tenaciously honourable in his personal connections, but vehement and inveterate in his enmities, and quick and irritable in conceiving them. In his political principles he was strictly constitutional, excepting, perhaps, upon the single point of denying the impeccability of the crown; in those of religion he, at least, *ostensibly* professed an attachment to the established church.

Of his personal and private honour, we can only judge from his connection with Mr. Woodfall. Yet this connection is perhaps sufficient; for throughout the whole of it he appears in a light truly ingenuous and liberal. "If undesignedly,"

* Private Letter, No. 40.   † Id. No. 57.

says he in one of his letters, "I should send you anything
you may think dangerous, judge for yourself, or take any
opinion you think proper. You cannot offend or afflict me,
but by hazarding your own safety."*   To the same effect in
another letter, "For my own part I can very truly assure you
that nothing would afflict me more than to have drawn you
into a *personal* danger, because it admits of no recompense.
A little expense is not to be regarded, and I hope these papers
have reimbursed you. I never will send you anything that *I*
think dangerous; but the risk is yours, and you must determine for yourself."†

Upon another occasion, being sensible that he had written
with an asperity that might alarm his correspondent, he again
begged him not to print if he apprehended any danger;
adding that, for himself, he should not be offended at his
desisting; and merely requesting that if he did not choose to
take the risk he would transmit the paper as sent to him, to a
printer who was well known to be less cautious than himself.
"The inclosed," says he in one of his notes, "is of such
importance, so very material, that it *must* be given to the
public immediately. *I will not advise*, though I *think* you
perfectly safe. All I say is that I rely upon your care to have
it printed either to-morrow in your own paper, or to-night in
the Pacquet."‡—To the same effect is the following upon
another occasion: "I hope you will approve of announcing
the inclosed Junius to-morrow, and publishing it on Monday.
If, for any reasons that do not occur to me, you should think
it unadvisable to print it, as it stands, I must entreat the
favour of you to transmit it to Bingley, and satisfy him that
it is a real Junius, worth a North Briton extraordinary. It
will be impossible for me to have an opportunity of altering
any part of it."§

Upon the printer being menaced with a prosecution on
the part of the Duke of Grafton, in consequence of the
publication of Junius's letter to him of the date of December
12, 1769, accusing this nobleman of having, in the most
corrupt and sinister manner, either sold or connived at the
sale of a patent place in the collection of the customs at
Exeter, he writes as follows: "As to yourself, I am con-

* Private Letter, No. 43.   † Id. No. 33.
‡ Id No. 38.   § Id. No. 34.

vinced the ministry will not venture to attack you; they dare not submit to such an inquiry. If they do, show no fear, but tell them plainly you will justify, and subpœna Mr. Hine, Burgoyne, and Bradshaw of the Treasury: that will silence them at once."*   The printer, however, was still fearful, and could not avoid expressing himself so to his invisible friend; who thus replied to his proposal of volunteering an apology: "Judge for yourself. I enter sincerely into the anxiety of your situation; at the same time I am strongly inclined to think that you will not be called upon. They cannot do it without subjecting Hine's affair to an inquiry, which would be worse than death to the minister. As it is, they are more seriously stabbed with this last stroke, than all the rest. At any rate, stand firm: (I mean with all the humble appearances of contrition:) if you trim or faulter, you will lose friends without gaining others."†   The friendly advice thus shrewdly given was punctiliously followed; and the predictions of Junius were more than accomplished: for the minister not only did not dare to enforce his menaces, but at the same time thought it expedient to drop abruptly the prosecution of Mr. Vaughan, which this attack upon him was expressly designed to fight off; and to drop it, too, after the rule against Vaughan had been made absolute.

Upon the publication of Junius's letter to the king, Woodfall was not quite so fortunate—but his invisible friend still followed him with assistance; he offered him, as has already been observed, a reimbursement of whatever might be his pecuniary expenses, and aided him in a still higher degree with the soundest prudential and legal advice. Upon a subsequent occasion also, he makes the following observation: "As to yourself, I really think you in no danger. You are not the object, and punishing you would be no gratification to the king."‡—But upon this subject, the following is one of the most important notes, as, although he expressly denies all *professional* knowledge of the law, it sufficiently proves that he was better acquainted with it than many who are actual practitioners. "I have carefully perused the *Information*: it is so loose and ill-drawn that I am persuaded Mr. De Grey §

---

* Private Letter, No. 15.   † Id. No. 17.   ‡ Id. No. 43.
§ At that time Attorney General.

could not have had a hand in it. Their inserting the whole, proves they had no strong passages to fix on. I still think it will not be tried. If it should, it is not possible for a jury to find you guilty."*

In his first opinion he was mistaken; in his second he was correct. The cause was tried at Nisi Prius—but no one has yet forgotten that the verdict returned was "guilty of printing and publishing *only*;" which in fact implied not *guilty* at all.

It is to this cause, as has been already glanced at, we are chiefly indebted for an acknowledged and unequivocal right in the jury to return a general verdict—that is, a verdict that shall embrace matter of law as well as matter of fact. From the ambiguity of the verdict, however, in the case before us, a motion was made by the defendant's counsel in arrest of judgment; at the same time that an opposite motion was advanced by the counsel for the crown, for a rule upon the defendant to show cause why the verdict should not be entered up according to the *legal* import of the words. On both sides a rule to show cause was granted, and the matter being argued before the Court of King's Bench, notwithstanding the bench appears to have been strongly and unanimously in favour of the verdict being entered up, the result was the grant of a new trial; which, however, was not proceeded in, for want of proof of the publication of the paper in question.

That Junius was quick and irritable in conceiving disgust, and vehement, and even at times malignant, in his enmities, we may equally ascertain from his private and his public communications. In the violence of his hatreds almost every one whom he attacks is guilty in the extreme; there are no degrees of comparison either in their criminality or his own detestation: the whole is equally superlative. If the Duke of Grafton be the object of his address, " every villain in the kingdom," says he, " is your friend †—the very sunshine you live in is a prelude to your dissolution." If Lord Mansfield fall beneath his lash, " I do not scruple to affirm, with the most solemn appeal to God for my sincerity, that, in *my* judgment, he is the very worst and most dangerous man in the kingdom."‡ An opinion corroborated by him in his

---

* Private Letter, No. 20.　　† Letter, No. 37.
‡ Letter, No. 69.

private correspondence: "We have got the rascal down,"
says he, "let us strangle him if it be possible."* In like
manner addressing himself to Lord Barrington, "You are so
detested and despised by all parties (because all parties know
you) that England, Scotland, and Ireland, have but one wish
concerning you;"† while his note to the printer, accompanying
this address, closes thus: "The proceedings of this wretch
are unaccountable. There must be some mystery in it, which
I hope will soon be discovered to his confusion. Next to the
Duke of Grafton, I verily believe that the blackest heart in
the kingdom belongs to Lord Barrington."‡ Even Scævola,
an anonymous writer, whom he knew not, is "a blockhead"
and "a fool,"§ for opposing him: Swinney, for his impertinent inquiry of Lord G. Sackville, "a wretched but a danger-
ous fool,"|| and Garrick, on the same account, "a rascal, and a
vagabond."¶

Yet it is not difficult to account for the more violent of his
political abhorrences; and which seem, indeed, to have been
almost exclusively directed against the three ministerial
characters just enumerated in conjunction with the Earl of
Bute: for his attacks upon the Duke of Bedford and Sir
William Blackstone are but light and casual when compared
with his incessant and unmitigated tirades against these
noblemen.

Firmly rooted in the best Whig principles of the day, he
had an invincible hatred of Lord Bute as the grand prop and
foundation-stone of Toryism in its worst and most arbitrary
tendencies: as introduced into Carlton House against the consent of his present Majesty's royal grandfather, through the
overweening favouritism of the Princess Dowager of Wales;
as having obtained an entire ascendancy over this princess,
and through this princess over the king, whose non-age had
been entirely entrusted to him, and through the king over
the cabinet and the parliament itself. The introduction of
Lord Bute into the post of chief preceptor to his Majesty was
in our author's opinion an inexpiable evil. "That," says he,
"was the salient point from which all the mischiefs and dis

---

* Private Letter, No. 24.   † Miscellaneous Letters, No. 111.
‡ Private Letter, No. 61.   § Id. Nos. 46 and 47.
|| Id. No. 5.   ¶ Id. Nos. 41 and 43.

graces of the present reign took life and motion."* Thus despising the tutor, he could have no great reverence for the pupil: and hence the personal dislike he too frequently betrays, and occasionally in language altogether intemperate and unjustifiable, for the sovereign. Hence, too, his unconquerable prejudice against Scotchmen of every rank.

The same cause excited his antipathy against Lord Mansfield, even before his lordship's arbitrary line of conduct had proved that our author's suspicions concerning him were well founded. Lord Mansfield was a Scotchman · but this was not the whole. Under the patronage of Lord Stormont, he had been educated with the highest veneration for the whole Stuart family, and especially for the Pretender; whose health, when a young man, had been his favourite toast, and to whom his brother was attached as a confidential and private agent. It was for these sentiments, and for the politics which intruded themselves in his judicial proceedings, where the crown was concerned, that our author expressed himself in such bitter terms against the chief justice. " Our language," says he, in Letter 41, " has no term of reproach, the mind has no idea of detestation, which has not already been happily applied to you and exhausted.—Ample justice has been done, by abler pens than mine, to the separate merits of your life and character. Let it be *my* humble office to collect the scattered sweets, till their united virtue tortures the sense."

His detestation of the Duke of Grafton proceeded from his Grace's having abandoned his patron Lord Chatham, and the Whig principles into which he had been initiated under him, to gratify his own ambition on the first offer that occurred: from his having afterwards united sometimes with the Bedford party, sometimes with Lord Bute, and sometimes with other connections, of whatever principles or professions, whenever the union appeared favourable to his personal views; and from his having hereby prevented that general coalition of the different divisions of Whig statesmen, which must in all probability have proved permanently triumphant over the power of the king himself. "My abhorrence of the duke," says Junius, "arises from an intimate knowledge of his character, and from a thorough conviction that his baseness has been the

* Letter to the King, No. 35, Note by Junius.—Ed

cause of greater mischief to England than even the unfortunate ambition of Lord Bute."*

It was not necessary for Lord Barrington to be a Scotchman in order to excite the antipathy of Junius. He might
justly despise and even hate him (if it be allowable to indulge
a private hatred against a public character of any kind) for
his political versatilities and want of all principle; for atro-
cities, indeed, which no man can yet have forgotten, and which
never can be buried in forgetfulness but with the total oblivion of his name.   Barrington, independently of these
general considerations, however, was the man who moved for
Wilkes's expulsion from Parliament, in which he was seconded
by Mr. Rigby.

These were the prime objects of our author's abhorrence ;
and in proportion as other politicians were connected with
them by principles or want of principles, confederacy, nation,
or even family, he abhorred them also.

His reasons for believing that the constitution allows him
to regard the reigning prince as occasionally culpable in his
own person, are given at large in his Preface.   To few people perhaps, in the present day, will they carry conviction.
But, bating this single opinion, his view of the principles and
powers of the constitution appears to be equally correct and
perspicuous.   Upon the question of general warrants ; of the
right of juries to return general verdicts, or in other words, to
determine upon the law as well as upon the fact; of the unlimited power of Lords Chief Justices to admit to bail ; of the
illegality of suspending Acts of Parliament by proclamation,
we owe him much ; he was a warm and rigid supporter of the
co-extent, as well as co-existence of the three estates of the
Government, and it was from this principle alone that he argued against the system of indefinite privilege as appertaining
to either house individually; and as allowing it a power of
arbitrary punishment, for what may occasionally be regarded
as a contempt of such house, or a breach of such privilege.

Personally and outrageously inimical, however, as he was
to the reigning prince, and earnestly devoted as he seems to
have been to the cause of the people, neither his enmity nor
his patriotism hurried him into any of those political extrava-

* Letter, No. 54.

gancies which have peculiarly marked the character of the present age : a limited monarchy, like our own, he openly preferred to a republic ; he contended for the constitutional right of impressing, in case of emergency, sea-faring men for the common service of the country ; strenuously opposed the supporters of the Bill of Rights, in their endeavours to restore annual Parliaments, and their fanciful but, as it appeared to him, unconstitutional plan of purifying the legislature by dis-franchising a number of boroughs which they had chosen to regard as totally corrupt and rotten ; and, anterior to the American contest, was as thoroughly convinced as Mr. George Grenville himself of the supremacy of the legislature of this country over the American colonies *.

Upon the first point he observes : " I can more readily ad-mire the liberal spirit and integrity, than the sound judgment of any man, who prefers a republican form of government, *in this or any other empire of equal extent*, to a monarchy so qualified and limited as ours. I am convinced, that neither is it in theory the wisest system of government, nor practica-ble in this country."† Upon the second point he appears to have been chiefly influenced by Judge Foster's argument on the legality of pressing seamen, and his comment on that ar-gument may be seen in his observations, Letters Nos. 59, 62, and 64. Upon the third and fourth points he thus ingenuously expresses himself : " Whenever the question shall be seriously agitated, I will endeavour (and if I live, will assuredly attempt it) to convince the English nation, by arguments to *my* un-derstanding unanswerable, that they ought to insist upon a *triennial*, and banish the idea of an *annual* Parliament.——— As to cutting away the rotten boroughs, I am as much offended as any man at seeing so many of them under the direct influence of the crown, or at the disposal of private persons ; yet, I own, I have both doubts and apprehensions, in regard to the remedy you propose. I shall be charged, perhaps, with an unusual want of political intrepidity, when I honestly confess to you, that I am startled at the idea of so extensive an amputation. In the first place, I question the power, *de jure*, of the legislature to disfranchise a number of

* Miscellaneous Letters, No. 10, as well as various others in the yeai 1768.
† Letter, No. 69.

boroughs, upon the general ground of improving the constitu
tion.—When you propose to cut away the *rotten* parts, can
you tell us what parts are perfectly *sound !* Are there any
certain limits, in fact or theory, to inform you at what point
you must stop—at what point the mortification ends ? "*

Junius has been repeatedly accused of having been a party-
man, but perhaps no political satirist was ever less so. To
Mr. Wilkes and Mr. Horne he was equally indifferent, except in regard to their public principles and public characters
In his estimation the cause alone was everything, and they
were only of value as the temporary and accidental supporters
of it. " Let us employ these men," says he, " in whatever
departments their various abilities are best suited to, and as
much to the advantage of the common cause, as their different
inclinations will permit. If individuals have no virtues, their
vices may be of use to us. I care not with what principle
the new-born patriot is animated, if the measures he supports
are beneficial to the community. The nation is interested in
his conduct. His motives are his own. The properties of a
patriot are perishable in the individual, but there is a quick
succession of subjects, and the breed is worth preserving." †
It was in this view of the politics of the day, that he privately
cautioned his friend Woodfall, as has been already noticed,
" to be much upon his guard against *patriots;*" ‡ and in the
consciousness of possessing a truly independent spirit, that he
boasted of being " disowned, as a dangerous auxiliary, by
every *party* in the kingdom," § his creed not expressly com-
porting with any single party creed whatever.

Yet there were statesmen whom he believed to be truly
honest and upright, and for whom he felt a personal as well
as a political reverence : and it is no small proof of the keen-
ness of his penetration that the characters, whom he thus
singled out from the common mass of pretenders to genuine
patriotism, have been ever since growing in the public estimation, and are now justly looked back to as the pillars and
bulwarks of the English constitution. His high opinion of
the general purity and virtue of Lord Camden we have
already noticed. " Lord Bute," says he, in describing several

---

* Vide the paper subsequent to Letter 69.   † Letter, No. 59.
‡ Private Letter, No. 44.   § Letter, No. 44.

others of whom he equally approved, " found no resource of dependence or security in the proud, imposing superiority of Lord Chatham's abilities, the shrewd, inflexible judgment of Mr. Grenville *, nor in the mild but determined integrity of Lord Rockingham."† He also seems disposed to have enter· tained a good opinion of Lord Holland ; and this is the rather entitled to attention, as the opinion was communicated con· fidentially. " I wish," says he, " Lord Holland may acquit him self with honour : if his cause be good, he should at once have published that account to which he refers in his letter to the mayor."‡ With respect to Mr. Sawbridge, and his worthy colleague, he observes, " My memory fails me if I have mentioned their names with disrespect ; unless it be reproachful to acknowledge a sincere respect for the character of Mr. Sawbridge, and not to have questioned the innocence of Mr. Oliver's intentions."§ And again, adverting to the former, " It were much to be desired, that we had many such men as Mr. Sawbridge to represent us in Parliament —I speak from common report and opinion only, when I impute to him a speculative predilection in favour of a republic.—In the personal conduct and manners of the man, I cannot be mistaken. He has shown himself possessed of that republican firmness, which the times require, and by which an English gentleman may be as usefully and as honourably distinguished, as any citizen of ancient Rome, of Athens, or Lacedæmon."

Yet the times were too corrupt, and the instances of defection too numerous, to allow so wary a statesman as Junius to regard even these exalted characters without occasional suspicion and jealousy. Much as he approved of the Marquis of Rockingham personally, he regarded him publicly as forming a feeble administration that dissolved in its own weakness ‖. He had more than once some doubts of the motives both of Lord Camden and Lord Chatham : their opposition at the commencement of the American contest he was jealous of ;

---

* Of all the political characters of the day, Mr. Grenville appears to have been our author's favourite ; no man was more open to censure in many parts of his conduct, but he is never censured ; while, on the contrary, he is extolled wherever an opportunity offers ; yet Junius positively asserted that he had no personal knowledge of Mr. Grenville. Compare Miscellaneous Letters, No. 29, with Junius's Letter, No. 18. † Letter, No. 15.

‡ Private Letter, No. 5. § Letter, No. 54. ‖ Id No. 23.

and ascribed it rather to political pique than to liberal patriotism *.   To his friend he writes thus confidentially: "The
Duke of Grafton has been long labouring to detach Camden ;"† and in unison with this idea he tells his lordship
himself publicly, " If you decline this honourable office, I fear
it will be said that, for some months past, you have kept too
much company with the Duke of Grafton."‡   And even as
late as August, 1771, when Lord Chatham had been progressively growing on his good opinion, he thus cautiously praises
him.   " *If* his ambition be upon a level with his understanding ;—*if* he judges of what is truly honourable for himself,
with the same superior genius which animates and directs
him to eloquence in debate, to wisdom in decision, even the
pen of Junius shall contribute to reward him.   Recorded
honours shall gather round his monument, and thicken over
him.   It is a solid fabric, and will support the laurels that
adorn it.—I am not conversant in the language of panegyric.
—These praises are extorted from me ; but they will wear
well, for they have been dearly earned." §
    In his religious opinions Junius has been accused of deism
and atheism ; but on what account it seems impossible to
ascertain : he has by others been conceived to have been a
dissenter || ; yet with as little reason.   To judge from the few
passages in his own writings that have any bearing upon the
question, and which occur chiefly in his letter, under the signature of Philo-Junius, of Aug. 26, 1771, he appears to have
been a Christian upon the most sincere conviction ; one of
whose chief objects was to defend the religion established by
law, and who was resolved to renounce and give up to public

---

* Letter, No. 23.   † Private Letter, No. 47.
‡ Letter, No. 69, to Lord Camden.   § Letter, No. 54.
|| Heron's edition of the Letters of Junius, vol. i. p. 69. [There is nothing
in Heron at the page referred to that has the least allusion to the religion of
Junius. What Heron, who was a more correct and careful writer than Good,
remarks on that topic, is at p. 46, from which we extract the concluding
sentence. " His (Junius's) allusions to religion, so far as they are contemptuous, relate chiefly to the absurdities of the Roman Catholic religion ;
a fact from which we may fairly infer, either that the course of his education
or the incidents of his life, led him into a particular acquaintance with these,
and an indignant disgust against them [Heron was a trained minister of the
Scottish Presbyterian Kirk], or else that he, in this instance, merely echoed
the voices of Pascal and Chillingworth."—ED.]

contempt and indignation every man who should be capable
of uttering a disrespectful word against it. To the religion of
the court, it must be confessed that he was no friend ; and to
speak the truth it constituted, at the period in question, an
anomaly not a little difficult of solution. To behold a sanctuary self-surrounded by a moat of pollution ; a prince strictly
and exemplarily pious, selecting for his confidential advisers
men of the most abandoned debauchery and profligacy of life,
demanded, in order to penetrate the mystery, a knowledge
never completely acquired till the present day, which has sufficiently demonstrated how impossible it is for a king of England to exercise at all times a real option in the appointment
of his ministers. The severity with which our author uniformly satirized every violation of public decorum, at least
entitles him to public gratitude, and does credit to the purity
of his heart : and if his morality may be judged of by various
occasional observations and advices scattered throughout his
private intercourse with Mr. Woodfall, some instances of
which have already been selected, it is impossible to do otherwise than approve both his principles and his conduct.

Whether the writer of these letters had any other and less
worthy object in view than that he uniformly avowed, namely,
a desire to subserve the best political interests of his country,
it is impossible to ascertain with precision, It is unquestionably no common occurrence in history, to behold a man thus
steadily, and almost incessantly, for five years, volunteering
his services in the cause of the people, amidst abuse and
slander from every party, exposed to universal resentment,
unknown, and not daring to be known, without having any
personal object to acquire, any sinister motive of individual
aggrandisement or reward. Yet nothing either in his public
or private letters affords us any tangible proof that he was
thus actuated *. Throughout the whole, from first to last, in
the midst of all his warmth and rancour, his argument and
declamation, his appeal to the public, and his notes to his
confidential friend, he seems to have been influenced by the
stimulus of sound and genuine patriotism alone. With this
he commenced his career, and with this he retired from the

* The only hints which can be gathered that he had any prospect at any
time of engaging in public life are in Private Letters, No. 17, and No. 65
but even these are of questionable meaning.

field of action, retaining, until the latest period at which we
are able to catch a glimpse of him, the same political sentiments he had professed on his first appearance before the
world, and still ready to renew his efforts the very moment
he could perceive they had a chance of being attended with
benefit.   Under these circumstances, therefore, however difficult it may be to acquit him altogether of personal considerations, it is still more difficult, and must be altogether
unjust, ungenerous, and illogical to suspect his integrity.

It has often been said, from the general knowledge he has
evinced of English jurisprudence, that he must have studied
the law professionally ; and in one of his private letters
already quoted, he gives his personal opinion upon the
mode in which the information of the King *v.* Woodfall was
drawn up, in a manner that may serve to countenance such
an opinion.   Yet on other occasions he speaks obviously not
from his own professional knowledge, but from a consultation
with legal practitioners.   " The information," says he, " will
only be for a misdemeanor, and I *am advised* that no jury,
especially in these times, will find it."*   In like † manner,
although he affirms in his elaborate letter to Lord Mansfield,
" I well knew the *practice* of the Court, and by what legal
rules it ought to be directed ;" yet he is for ever contemning
the intricacies and littlenesses of special pleading, and in his
Preface declares unequivocally, " I am no lawyer by profession, nor do I pretend to be more deeply read than every
English gentleman should be in the laws of his country.   If,
therefore, the principles I maintain are truly constitutional,
I shall not think myself answered, though I should be convicted of a mistake in terms, or of misapplying the language
of the law."‡

That he was of some rank and consequence, seems gene-

* Private Letter, No. 18.

† He speaks in like manner of legal consultation, and the difficulties he
laboured under of obtaining legal advice, from the peculiarity of his situation,
in Private Letter 70.   And in the same letter, he makes the following
pointed confession : " though I use the terms of art, do not injure me so
much as to suspect I am a lawyer.   I had as lief be a Scotchman."

‡ The late Lord Eldon, a competent judge, and who, to all intents, was a
lawyer, once remarked in the House of Lords, " that the author of the *Letters
of Junius,* if not himself a lawyer, must certainly have written in concert
with the ablest and the best of lawyers "—ED.

rally to have been admitted by his opponents, and must indeed necessarily follow, as has been already casually hinted at, from the facility with which he acquired political information, and a knowledge of ministerial intrigues.   In one place he expressly affirms that his " rank and fortune place *him* above a common bribe ;"* in another, " I should have hoped that even *my* name might carry some authority with it."   On one occasion he intimates an intention of composing a regular history of the Duke of Grafton's administration.   " These observations," says he, " general as they are, might easily be extended into a faithful history of your Grace's administration, and perhaps may be the employment of a future hour ;" and on another, that of Lord Townshend's, " the history of this ridiculous administration shall not be lost to the public." And on two occasions, and on two occasions only, he appears to hint at some prospect, though a slender one, of taking a part in the government of the country.   They occur in his private letters to Woodfall and Wilkes : to the former he says, "*if things take the turn I expect*, you shall know me *by my works*."† To the latter, " *though I do not disclaim the idea of some personal views to future honour and advantage,* (you would not believe me if I did) *yet I can truly affirm, that neither are they little in themselves, nor can they, by any possible conjecture, be collected from my writings*."‡

Of those who have critically analyzed the style of his compositions, some have pretended to prove that he must necessarily have been of Irish descent or Irish education, from the peculiarity of his idioms ; while, to show how little dependence is to be placed upon any such observations, others have equally pretended to prove, from a similar investigation, that he could not have been a native either of Scotland or Ireland, nor have studied in any university of either of those countries.   The fact is, that there are a few phraseologies in his letters peculiar to himself ; such as occur in the compositions of all original writers of great force and genius, but which are neither indicative of any particular race, nor referable to any provincial dialect.

The distinguishing features of his style are ardour, spirit,

---

* Miscellaneous Letters, No. 54.   † Private Letter, No. 17.
     ‡ Correspondence with Wilkes, *post*, No. 65.

perspicuity, classical correctness, sententious, epigrammatic compression : his characteristic ornaments keen, indignant invective, audacious interrogation, shrewd, severe, antithetic retort, proud, presumptuous disdain of the powers of his adversary, pointed and appropriate allusions that can never be mistaken, but are often overcharged, and at times perhaps totally unfounded, though derived from popular rumour, similies introduced, not for the purpose of decoration, but of illustration and energy, brilliant, burning, admirably selected, and irresistible in their application *.   In his similies, however, he is once or twice too recondite, and in his grammatical construction still more frequently incorrect.   Yet the latter should in most instances perhaps, if not the whole, be rather attributed to the difficulty of revising the press, and the peculiar circumstances under which his work was printed and published, than to any inaccuracy or classical misconception of his own. As to the surreptitious copies of his letters, he frequently complains of their numerous errors; "indeed," says he, " they are innumerable ;"† and though the genuine edition labours under very considerably fewer, and on several occasions received his approbation on the score of accuracy, yet it would be too much to assert that it is altogether free from errors. In

* The following character of his style and talents is the production of a pen contemporaneous but hostile to him.   It occurs in a letter in the Public Advertiser subscribed Alciphron, and dated August 22, 1771.   The writer had well studied him.

" The admiration that is so lavishly bestowed upon this writer affords one of the clearest proofs, perhaps, that can be found, how much more easily men are swayed by the imagination, than by the judgment; and that a fertile invention, glittering language, and sounding periods, act with far greater force upon the mind, than the simple deductions of sober reasoning, or the calm evidence of facts.   For the talents of Junius never appeared in demonstration.

" Rapid, violent, and impetuous, he affirms without reason, and decides without proof; as if he feared that the slow methods of induction and argument would interrupt him in his progress, and throw obstacles in the way of his career.   But though he advances with the largest strides, his steps are measured.   His expressions are selected with the most anxious care, and his periods terminated in harmonious cadence.   Thus he captivates by his confidence, by the turn of his sentences, and by the force of his words.   His readers are persuaded because they are agitated, and convinced because they are pleased.   Their assent, therefore, is never withheld; though they scarcely know why, or even to what it is yielded."

† Private Letter, No. 5.

truth this was not to be expected, for it is not known that a single proof sheet (excepting those containing the first two letters) was ever sent to him. "You must correct the press yourself," says he, in one of his letters to Woodfall; "but *I should be glad to see* corrected proofs of the two first sheets."[*] The dedication and preface he certainly did not revise.

Yet if the grammatical construction be occasionally imperfect, (sometimes hurried over by the author, and sometimes mistaken by the printer,) the general plan and outline, the train of argument, the bold and fiery images, the spirited invective that pervade the whole, appear to have been always selected with the utmost care and attention. Such finished forms of composition bear in themselves the most evident marks of elaborate forecast and revisal, and the author rather boasted of the pains he had bestowed upon them than attempted to conceal his labour. In recommending to Woodfall to introduce into his purposed edition various letters of his own writing under other signatures, he adds, "If you adopt this plan, I shall point out those which I would recommend; for you know, I do not, nor indeed have I time to give equal care to them all. As to Junius, I must wait for fresh matter, as *this* is a character which must be kept up with credit."[†] The private note accompanying his first letter to Lord Mansfield commences thus: "The inclosed, though begun within these few days, *has been greatly laboured.* It is very correctly copied, and I beg that you will take care that it be literally printed as it stands."[‡] The note accompanying his last and most celebrated letter observes as follows: "At last I have concluded *my great work*, and I assure you with no small labour."[§] On sending the additional papers for the genuine edition he asserts, "I have no view but to serve you, and consequently have only to desire that the dedication and preface may be correct. Look to it; if you take it upon yourself, I will not forgive your suffering it to

---

[*] Private Letter, No. 40. The truth is that the genuine edition was reprinted from Wheble's: the author correcting a few, and Woodfall a few more of the blunders which had crept into Wheble's text; though many of them still remained untouched. The letters in this and the former edition have been carefully collated with the Public Advertisers, and a numerous list of other errors have been consequently expunged.

[†] Private Letter No. 7.   [‡] Id. No. 24.   [§] Id. No. 40.

be spoiled. *I weigh every word; and every alteration, in my eyes at least, is a blemish.*"* In like manner, in his letter to Mr Horne, he interrogates him, "What public question have I declined, what villain have I spared? *Is there no labour in the composition of these letters†?* In effect no excellence of any kind is to be attained without labour: and the degree of excellence that characterizes the style of these addresses, intrinsically demonstrates the exercise of a labour unsparing and unremitted. Mr. Horne, in his reply, attempts to ridicule this acknowledgment: "I compassionate," says he, "your labour in the composition of your letters, and will communicate to you the secret of my fluency. Truth needs no ornament; and, in my opinion, what she borrows of the pencil is deformity." Yet no man ever bestowed more pains upon his compositions than Mr. Horne has done; nor needed he to have been more ashamed of the confession than his adversary. To have made it openly would have been honest to himself, useful to the young, and salutary to the conceited.

His most elaborate letters are that to the King, and that to Lord Mansfield upon the law of bail: one of his most sarcastic is that to the Duke of Grafton, of the date of May 30, 1769; and one of his best and most truly valuable that to the printer of the *Public Advertiser*, dated Oct. 5, 1771, upon the best means of uniting the jarring sectaries of the popular party into one common cause.

His metaphors are peculiarly brilliant, and so numerous, though seldom unnecessarily introduced, as to render it difficult to know where to fix in selecting a few examples. The following are ably managed, and require no explanation. "The ministry, it seems, are labouring to draw a line of distinction between the honour of the crown and the rights of the people. This new idea has yet been only started in discourse, for, in effect, both objects have been equally sacrificed. I neither understand the distinction, nor what use the ministry propose to make of it. The King's honour is that of his people. Their *real* honour and *real* interest are the same. I am not contending for a vain punctilio. Private credit is wealth; public honour is security. The feather that adorns the royal bird, supports its flight. Strip him of

---

* Private Letter, No. 46.   † Letter, No. 54.

his plumage and you fix him to the earth."* Again, "above all things, let me guard my countrymen against the meanness and folly of accepting a trifling or moderate compensation for extraordinary and essential injuries. Concessions, such as these, are of little moment to the sum of things; unless it be to prove, that the worst of men are sensible of the injuries they have done us, and perhaps to demonstrate to us the imminent danger of our situation. In the shipwreck of the state, trifles float and are preserved; while everything solid and valuable sinks to the bottom, and is lost for ever."† Once more : "The very sunshine you live in, is a prelude to your dissolution. When you are ripe, you shall be plucked."‡ The commencement of his letter to Lord Camden shall furnish another instance : "I turn with pleasure, from that barren waste, in which no salutary plant takes root, no verdure quickens, to a character fertile, as I willingly believe, in every great and good qualification." §

In a few instances his metaphors are rather too far-fetched or recondite. "Yet for the benefit of the succeeding age, I could wish that your retreat might be deferred, until your morals shall be happily ripened to that maturity of corruption, at which the worst examples cease to be contagious." The change which is perpetually taking place in the matter of infection gives it progressively a point of utmost activity ; —after which period, by the operation of the same continued change, it becomes progressively less active, till at length it ceases to possess any effect whatever. The parallel is correctly drawn, but it cannot be followed by every one. In the same letter we have another example: "His views and situation require a creature void of all these properties ; and he was forced to go through every division, resolution, composition, and refinement of political chemistry, before ho happily arrived at the *caput mortuum* of vitriol in your Grace. Flat and insipid in your retired state, but brought into action, you become vitriol again." This figure is too scientific, and not quite correct: *vitriol* cannot, properly speaking, be said to be, in any instance, a *caput mortuum*. He seems, however, to have been unjustly charged with an incongruity of meta-

* Last sentence in Letter, No. 42.   † Letter, No. 59.
‡ Conclusion of Letter to Duke of Grafton, No. 67.   § Letter, No. 69.

phor in his repartee upon the following observation of Sir W. Draper : " You, indeed, are a tyrant of another sort, and upon your political bed of torture can excruciate any subject, from a first minister down to such a grub or butterfly as myself."*   To this remark his reply was as follows : " If Sir W. Draper's bed be a bed of torture, he has made it for himself. I shall never interrupt *his repose*."†   We need not ramble so far as to vindicate the present use of this last word by referring to its Latin origin : he himself has justly noticed, under the signature of Philo-Junius, that those who pretend to espy any absurdity either in the idea or expression, " cannot distinguish between a sarcasm and a contradiction."‡

To pursue this critique further would be to disparage the judgment of the reader.   Upon the whole, these letters, whether considered as classical and correct compositions, or as addresses of popular and impressive eloquence, are well entitled to the distinction they have acquired ; and quoted, as they have been, with admiration in the senate, by such nice judges and accomplished scholars as Mr. Burke and Lord Eldon, eulogized by Dr. Johnson, and admitted by the author of the " Pursuits of Literature," to the same rank among English classics as Livy or Tacitus among Roman, there can be no doubt that they will live commensurately with the language in which they are composed.

These few desultory and imperfect hints are the whole that the writer of this essay has been able to collect concerning the author of the Letters of Junius.   Yet desultory and imperfect as they are, he still hopes that they may not be utterly destitute both of interest and utility.   Although they do not undertake positively to ascertain who the author was ; they offer a fair test to point out negatively who he was not ; and to enable us to reject the pretensions of a host of persons, whose friends have claimed for them so distinguished an honour.

From the observations contained in this essay it should seem to follow unquestionably that the author of the Letters of Junius was an Englishman of highly cultivated education, deeply versed in the language, the laws, the constitution and history of his native country : that he was a man of easy, if

* Letter, No. 26.   † Letter, No. 27.   ‡ Letter, No. 29.

not of affluent circumstances, of unsullied honour and gene-rosity, who had it equally in his heart and in his power to contribute to the necessities of other persons, and especially of those who were exposed to troubles of any kind on his own account: that he was in habits of confidential intercourse, if not with different members of the cabinet, with politicians who were most intimately familiar with the court, and en-trusted with all its secrets: that he had attained an age which would allow him, without vanity, to boast of an ample knowledge and experience of the world: that during the years 1767, 1768, 1769, 1770, 1771, and part of 1772, he resided almost constantly in London or its vicinity, devoting a very large portion of his time to political concerns, and publishing his political lucubrations, under different signa-tures, in the Public Advertiser: that in his natural temper, he was quick, irritable, and impetuous; subject to political prejudices and strong personal animosities, but possessed of a high independent spirit; honestly attached to the princi-ples of the constitution, and fearless and indefatigable in maintaining them: that he was strict in his moral conduct, and in his attention to public decorum; an avowed member of the established church, and, though acquainted with Eng-lish judicature, not a lawyer by profession.

What other characteristics he may have possessed, we know not; but these are sufficient; and the claimant who cannot produce them conjointly, is in vain brought forward as the author of the Letters of Junius.

The persons to whom this honour has at different times, and on different grounds, been attributed, are the following: Charles Lloyd, a clerk of the Treasury, and afterwards a deputy teller of the Exchequer; John Roberts, also a clerk in the Treasury at the commencement of his political life, but afterwards private secretary to Mr. Pelham, when suc-cessively chancellor of the exchequer, member of parlia-ment for Harwich, and commissioner of the board of trade *; Samuel Dyer, a man of considerable learning, and a friend of Mr. Burke and of Dr. Johnson; William Gerard Hamil-ton, another friend and patron of Mr. Burke; Edmund

* Anonymously accused of having written these letters in the Public Advertiser, March 21, 1772, et passim.

Burke himself; Dr. Butler, late Bishop of Hereford; the Rev. Philip Rosenhagen; Major-General Charles Lee, well known for his activity during the American war; John Wilkes; Hugh Macauley. Boyd; John Dunning, Lord Ashburton; Henry Flood; and Lord George Sackville *.

Of the first three of these reported authors of the Letters of Junius, it will be sufficient to observe, without entering into any other fact whatever, that Lloyd was on his death-bed at the date of the last of Junius's private letters; an essay, which has sufficient proof of having been written in the possession of full health and spirits; and which, together with the rest of our author's private letters to the printer of the Public Advertiser, is in the possession of the proprietor of this edition, and bears date January 19, 1773. While as to Roberts and Dyer, they had both been dead for many months anterior to this period: Lloyd died, after a lingering illness, January 22, 1773: Roberts, July 13, and Dyer on September 15, both in the preceding year.

Of the two next reputed authors, Hamilton had neither energy nor personal courage enough for such an undertaking†, and Burke could not have written in the style of Junius, which was precisely the reverse of his own, nor could he have consented to disparage his own talents in the manner in which Junius had disparaged them in his letter to the printer of the Public Advertiser, dated October 5, 1771; independently of which, both of them solemnly denied that they were the authors of these letters, Hamilton to Mr. Courtney in his last illness, as that gentleman has personally informed the editor;

* According to Mr. Britton (*Authorship of the Letters of Junius*) and who himself brings forward three at once—Barre, Shelburne, and Dunning—no fewer than thirty claimants or candidates have appeared as the veritable Junius; but the topic is reserved to the concluding volume.—ED.

† Hamilton, from his having *once* made a brilliant speech in the House of Commons, and ever afterwards remaining silent, was called *Single-speech* Hamilton. In allusion to this fact, and that he was the real Junius, there is a letter in the Public Advertiser of November 30, 1771, addressed to WILLIAM JUNIUS SINGLE-SPEECH, Esq. The air of Dublin, however, should seem, according to Mr. Malone's account of him, to have been more favourable to his rhetorical powers than that of Westminster: for this writer tells us that Mr. Hamilton made not less than five speeches in the Irish parliament in the single Session of 1761-2. *Parliamentary Logic, Preface* p. xxii. Lord Orford, indeed, contrary to general rumour, intimates that he was twice a speaker in the British parliament.—ED.

and Burke expressly and satisfactorily to Sir William Draper, who purposely interrogated him upon the subject; the truth of which denial is moreover corroborated by the testimony of the late Mr. Woodfall, who repeatedly declared that neither of them was the writer of these compositions. Why Burke was so early and generally suspected of having written them, it is not easy to say; but that he was so suspected is obvious, not only from the opinion at first entertained by Sir William Draper, but from various public accusations conveyed in different newspapers and pamphlets of the day; the Public Advertiser in the month of October containing one letter under the signature of Zeno, addressed " to Junius, alias Edmund, the Jesuit of St. Omers;"* another under the signature of Pliny Junior, a third under that of Querist, a fourth under that of Oxoniensis, and a fifth under that of Scævola, together with many others to the same effect: and, as has already been hinted at, an anonymous collector of many of the letters of Junius, prefixing to his own edition certain anecdotes of Mr. Burke, which he confidently denominated "Anecdotes of Junius," thus purposely, but fallaciously, iden tifying the two characters†.

* Note to Letter 61.

† In addition to the above proofs that Burke and Junius were not the same person, the editor might refer to the prosecution which Mr. Burke instituted against Mr. Woodfall, the printer of the Public Advertiser, and conducted with the utmost acrimony, for a paper deemed libellous that appeared in this journal in 1783. Considerable interest was made with Mr. Burke to induce him to drop this prosecution in different stages of its progress, but he was inexorable. The cause was tried at Guildhall, July 15, 1784, and a verdict of a hundred pounds damages was obtained against the printer; the whole of which was paid to the prosecutor. It is morally impossible that Junius could have acted in this manner: every anecdote in the preceding sketch of his public life forbids the belief.

Neither is it to be conceived, without greatly disparaging Mr. Burke's memory, that he could have written the letter to Garrick (No. 41); or have spoken in the terms in which Junius has spoken of Chamier, while he professed a warm and unreserved friendship for both. We may also further remark that the well known pamphlet, entitled " The Present State of the Nation," published in 1769 by George Grenville, was immediately answered by Mr. Burke in a tract entitled " Observations on a late publication, entituled, The Present State of the Nation,"—in which the political opinions of Mr. Grenville, and consequently of Junius, who, as we have already observed, was the general advocate of Mr. George Grenville, are censured with a vehemence peculiar to Mr. Burke, and altogether sufficient,

If, however, there should be readers so inflexible as still to
believe that Mr. Burke was the real writer of the Letters of
Junius, and that his denial of the fact to Sir William Draper
was only wrung from him under the influence of fear, it will
be sufficient to satisfy even such readers by showing that the
system of politics of the one was in direct opposition to that
of the other upon a variety of the most important points.
Burke was a decided partisan of Lord Rockingham, and continued so during the whole of that nobleman's life; Junius,
on the contrary, was as decided a friend to Mr. George Grenville.   Each was an antagonist to the other upon the great
subject of the American Stamp Act.   Junius was a warm and
powerful advocate for triennial parliaments; Burke an inveterate enemy to them.   To which the editor may be allowed
to add, that while Mr. Burke in correcting his manuscripts
for the press, and revising them in their passage through it,
is notorious for the numerous alterations he was perpetually
making, the revised copy with which the late Mr. Woodfall
was furnished by Junius for such part of the genuine edition
of his Letters as he re-examined, contained very few amendments of any kind*.

were there no other proof, to demonstrate that Burke and Junius could not
be the same person.   The reader may take the following extracts as specimens :—" *This piece is called, ' The present State of the Nation.' It may be
considered as a sort of digest of the avowed maxims of a certain political
school, the effects of whose doctrines and practices this country will feel long
and severely.*" * * * * " *A diversity of opinion upon almost every
principle of politics had indeed drawn a strong line of separation between
them and some others.*" [The marquess of Rockingham. * * * * "The
purpose of this pamphlet, and at which it aims directly or obliquely in every
page, is to persuade the public of three or four of the most difficult points in
the world—that all the advantages of the late war were on the part of the
Bourbon alliance; that the peace of Paris perfectly consulted the dignity and
interest of this country; *and that the American stamp act was a master-
piece of policy and finance;* that the only good minister this nation has
enjoyed since his Majesty's accession is the Earl of Bute; and the only good
managers of revenue we have seen are Lord Despenser *and Mr. George
Grenville; and under the description of men of virtue and ability, he holds
them out to us as the only persons fit to put our affairs in order.*"—
Burke's Works, vol. ii., 8vo edit., pages 11, 12, and 15.
    * Dr. Good here inserts the well-known speech of Mr. Burke on American
taxation, but, as the controversial questions that gave it its chief interest have
been settled, and it is readily accessible in the works of that eminent statesman, we have deemed its omission excusable.—ED.

Mr. Malone, in his preface to Mr. Hamilton's *Parliament-ary Logic*, offers a variety of remarks in disproof that this gentleman was the writer of the letters, several of which are possessed of sufficient force, though few persons will perhaps agree with him in believing that if Hamilton had written them, he would have written them better. The following are his chief arguments :—

" Now (not to insist on his own solemn asseveration near the time of his death, that he was not the author of Junius *) Mr. Hamilton was so far from being an ardent party man, that during the long period above mentioned [from Jan. 1769 to Jan. 1772] he never closely connected himself with any party. * * * * Notwithstanding his extreme love of political discussion, he never, it is believed, was heard to speak of any administration or any opposition with vehemence either of censure or of praise; a character so opposite to the fervent and sometimes coarse acrimony of Junius, that this consideration alone is sufficient to settle the point, as far as relates to our author, for ever. * * * * On the question—who *was* the author ?—he was as free to talk as any other person, and often did express his opinion concerning it to the writer of this short memoir ; an opinion nearly coinciding with that of those persons who appear to have had the best means of information on the subject. In a conversation on this much agitated point, he once said to an intimate friend, in a tone between seriousness and pleasantry,—'You know, H * * * * * * * *n, I could have written better papers than those of Junius:' and so the gentleman whom he addressed, who was himself distinguished for his rhetorical powers, and a very competent judge, as well as many other persons, thought.

" It may be added, that his style of composition was entirely different from that of this writer. * * * * That he had none of that minute *commissarial* knowledge of petty military matters, which is displayed in some of the earlier papers of Junius.

" And, finally it may be observed, that the figures and allusions of Junius are often of so different a race from those which our author [Hamilton] would have used, that he never spoke of some of them without the strongest disapprobation ; and particularly when a friend, for the purpose of drawing him out, affected to think him the writer of these papers; and bantering him on the subject, taxed him with that passage in which a nobleman, then in a high office, is said to have 'travelled through every sign in the political zodiac, from the SCORPION, in which he *stung* Lord Chatham, to the hopes of a VIRGIN,' &c., as if this imagery were much in his style,—Mr. Hamilton with great vehemence exclaimed, 'had I written such a sentence as that, I should have thought I had forfeited all pretensions to good taste in composition for ever !'"

Mr. Malone further observes, that Hamilton filled the office of Chancellor of the Exchequer in Ireland, from September, 1763, to April, 1784, during the very period in which all the

* " It has been said that he at the same time declared that he *knew* who was the author; but unquestionably he never made any such declaration."— MALONE.

ietters of Junius appeared before the public; and it will not very readily be credited by any one that this is likely to have been the exact quarter from which the writer of the letters in question fulminated his severe criminations against Government. The subject, moreover, of parliamentary reform, for which Junius was so zealous an advocate, Mr. Malone expressly tells us was considered by Hamilton to be "of so dangerous a tendency, that he once said to a friend now living, that he would sooner suffer his right hand to be cut off, than vote for it."

The only reason indeed that appears for these letters having ever been attributed to Hamilton is, that on a certain morning he told the Duke of Richmond, as has been already hinted at *, the *substance* of a letter of Junius which he pretended to have just read in the *Public Advertiser;* but which, on consulting the *Public Advertiser*, was not found to appear there, an apology instead of it being offered for its postponement till the next day, when the letter thus previously adverted to by Hamilton did actually make its appearance. That Hamilton, therefore, had a knowledge of the existence and purport of this letter is unquestionable; but, without conceiving him the author of it, it is easy to account for the fact, by supposing him (as we have supposed already) to have had it read to him by his friend Woodfall, antecedently to its being printed.

Another character that has been started as a claimant to the letters of Junius is the late Dr. Butler, Bishop of Hereford, formerly secretary to the Right Hon. Bilson Legge, Chancellor of the Exchequer, and father to the present Lord Stawell. Dr. Butler was a man of some talents, and was occasionally a political writer, and felt no small disgust and mortification upon his patron's dismissal from office. But he never discovered those talents that could in any respect put him upon an equality with Junius. He was, moreover, a man of mild disposition, and in no respect celebrated for political courage. To which general remarks, in contravention of this gentleman's claim, the editor begs leave to subjoin the following extract of a letter upon the subject, addressed by a friend of Dr. Butler's, and who himself took an active part in the politics of the times, to a high official

* Ante, p. 7, note.

character of the present day, and which he has been allowed the liberty of copying:—

" Mr. Wilkes shewed me the letters he received *privately* from Junius : *parts* of one of these were printed in the public papers at the request of the Bill of Rights. The autograph was remarkable—it was firm and precise, and did not appear to me at all disguised. Mr. Wilkes had been intimate with Bishop Butler when quartered as colonel of the militia at Winchester ; and, from some very curious concurrent circumstances, he had strong reasons for considering that the bishop was the author, and I had some reasons for conjecturing the same. Yet I must confess, that if these suspicions were stronger and more confirmed, yet I think I should require more substantial proofs; and my reasons are, that from all I was ever able to learn of the bishop's *personal character*, he was incapable of discovering, or feeling those rancorous sentiments, so unbecoming his character as a Christian, and his station as a prelate, expressed towards the Duke of Grafton, Lord North, Sir William Draper, and others—more especially the king. Nor do I think that his being the sole depositary of his own secret, which, as Junius says, would be, and I fancy *was*, buried in everlasting oblivion, when he was entombed ; would have encouraged him to have used such opprobrious language."

The pretensions of the Rev. Philip Rosenhagen, though adverted to in a preceding edition of these letters, are hardly worth noticing. He was at one time chaplain to the 8th regiment of Foot; and is said to have endeavoured to impose upon Lord North with a story of his having been the author of the letters in order to induce his lordship to settle a pension upon him. It is sufficient to observe, that Mr. Rosenhagen, who was a school-fellow of Mr. H. S. Woodfall, continued on terms of acquaintance with him in subsequent life ; and occasionally wrote for the *Public Advertiser:* but was repeatedly declared by Mr. Woodfall, who must have been a competent evidence as to the fact, not to be the author of Junius's Letters. A private letter of Rosenhagen's to Mr. Woodfall is still in the possession of his son*, and nothing can be more different from each other than this autograph and that of Junius.

It has been said in an American periodical work entitled " The Wilmington Mirror," that General Lee in confidence communicated to a friend the important secret that he was the author of these celebrated letters; but, whether Lee ever made such a communication or not, nothing is more palpable than that he did not write them—since it is a notorious fact, that during the whole, or nearly the whole of the period in

---

* And has descended to his grandson, the present Mr. Woodfall.—ED.

which they successively appeared, this officer was on the
continent of Europe, travelling from place to place, and
occupying the whole of his time in very different pursuits.

The friend to whom this communication is said to have
been made, is a Mr. T. Rodney, who declares as follows in
communication inserted in the above-mentioned American
periodical work.

" In the fall of 1773, not long after General Lee had arrived in America,
I had the pleasure of spending an afternoon in his company, when there was
no other person present. Our conversation chiefly turned on politics, and was
mutually free and open. Among other things, the Letters of Junius were
mentioned, and General Lee asked me, who was conjectured to be the author
of these letters. I replied, our conjectures here generally followed those
started in England; but for myself, I concluded, from the spirit, style,
patriotism. and political information which they displayed, that Lord Chatham
was the author; and yet there were some sentiments there that indicated his
not being the author. General Lee immediately replied, with considerable
animation, affirming that, to his certain knowledge, Lord Chatham was not
the author; neither did he know who the author was. any more than I did ;
that there was not a man in the world, no, not even Woodfall, the publisher,
that knew who the author was; that the secret rested solely with himself,
and for ever would remain with him.

" Feeling, in some degree, surprised at this unexpected declaration, after
pausing a little, I replied : ' No, General Lee, if you certainly know what
you have affirmed, it can no longer remain solely with him; for, certainly, no
one could know what you have affirmed but the author himself?'

" Recollecting himself, he replied : ' I have unguardedly committed myself,
and it would be but folly to deny to you that I am the author; but I must
request that you will not reveal it during my life; for it never was, nor never
will be revealed by me to any other.' He then proceeded to mention several
circumstances to verify his being the author; and, among them, that of his
going over to the Continent, and absenting himself from England most of the
time in which these Letters were first published in London, &c., &c. This
he thought necessary, lest, by some accident, the author should become
known, or at least suspected, which might have been his ruin, had he been
known to the Court of London," &c.

The account from which we have made this extract was
reprinted in the *St. James's Chronicle* for April 16, 1803.
which the editor prefaces by observing, " Of Mr. Rodney, or
of the degree of credit that may reasonably be attached to his
declaration, we know nothing ; but the subject is so curious.
that we think our readers will not be averse from having their
attention once more drawn to it."

The public do not in any degree appear to have been
influenced either by General Lee's pretended assertion or
Mr. Rodney's positive declaration : and this claim had totally

died away like the rest, when in 1807 it was revived by Dr. Girdlestone of Yarmouth, Norfolk, who endeavoured to establish General Lee's pretensions by a comparison of Rodney's statement with Mr. Langworthy's Memoirs of the General's life, in a pamphlet published anonymously, under the title of "Reasons for rejecting the presumptive evidence of Mr. Almon, that Mr. Hugh Boyd was the writer of Junius, with passages selected to prove the real author of the Letters of Junius." And in consequence of this revival of Mr. Lee's claim, the editor feels himself called upon to examine its foundation somewhat more in detail.

The passages selected are in no respect convincing to his mind, and do not appear to have been so to that of the public. But, without entering upon so disputable a question as that of a superiority of literary taste, it will be sufficient to remark that the great distance of General Lee from England during the period in which the Letters of Junius were published, together with the different line of politics which he pursued, render it impossible that Lee could have been the author of these letters.

The correspondence of General Lee previous to his quitting England for America, in August, 1773, as published by Mr. Langworthy in the memoirs of his life, and adverted to in Dr. Girdlestone's pamphlet, extend through a period of about thirteen months, from Dec. 1, 1766, to Jan. 19, 1768, and give us the following dates :—

1766, Dec. 1.	To the King of Poland, from London.
25.	The Prince of Poland, the same.
1767, May 1.	Mr. Coleman, from Warsaw.
2.	Mrs. Macauley *, the same.
4.	Louisa C., the same.
4.	Lord Thanet, the same.
Aug. 16.	King of Poland, Kamineck.
1768, Jan. 19.	Sir C. Davers, Dijon.

The dates of the letters written by Junius under his occasional signatures are as follows :—

1767, April 28.	Poplicola.
May 28.	The same in answer to a letter of Sir William Draper's of May 21.
June 24.	Anti-Sejanus, Jun.

---

* The letter was not addressed to Mrs. Macauley, but to Lady Blake.

1767, Aug. 25.	A faithful Monitor, on the subject of Lord Townshend's appointment to be Lord Lieutenant of Ireland, which took place the preceding August 12.
Sept. 16.	Correggio.
Oct. 12.	Moderator in answer to a letter of October 0.
22.	Grand Council.
31.	No signature, in answer to a letter of October 27.
Dec. 5.	Y. Z. on the King's speech, on opening the parliament November 24, 1767: the receipt of which will be found acknowledged by the printer in his usual method among the "answers to correspondents," November 30.
19.	No signature, on the subject of American politics.
22.	Downright.

It is only necessary for the reader to compare these two lists of dates, and places; as for example, London, and Warsaw, or Kamineck, during the two months of May and August, and to observe the rapidity with which the Letters of Junius were furnished, in answer to the different subjects discussed, to obtain a full proof that the latter list of letters could not have been written by the author of the former.

These remarks, however, relate only to the year 1767. Let us see how the account stands for 1769, being the year in which the author first appeared before the public under his favourite signature (with the single exception of Miscellaneous Letter, No. 52). It is difficult to ascertain exactly at what places General Lee was residing during this period. Langworthy's Memoirs abound with erroneous dates, which are not material, however, to the present question. The only serviceable hint that can be collected from them is, that he was rambling somewhere or other abroad, and "could never stay long in one place:" to which the editor adds, "that we can collect nothing material relative to the adventures of his travels, as his memorandum-books only mention the names of the towns and cities through which he passed. That he was a most rapid and very active traveller is certain," p. 8. The account furnished by Rodney confirms this statement, by telling us, "He then proceeded to mention several circumstances to verify his being the author; and, among them, that of his going over to the Continent, and absenting himself from England most of the time in which these letters were first published in London, &c., &c. This he thought necessary lest, by some accident, the author should become known, or at least, suspected, which might have been his ruin, had he been known to the Court of London," &c.

It is clear, therefore, that during the whole or the greater part of 1769, General Lee was rambling over the Continent; and of course had no possibility of keeping up a very close correspondence with any person at home. Yet the following table of the Letters of Junius, written either under his favourite or occasional signatures, or privately to Mr. Woodfall, will show that in the course of this very year, the author maintained not less than fifty-four communications with Mr. Woodfall: that not a single month passed without one or more acts of intercourse: that some of them had not less than seven, and many of them not less than six, at times directed to events that had occurred only a few days antecedently: that the two most distant communications were not more than three weeks apart, that several of them were daily, and the greater number of them not more than a week from each other.

1769, January	21.	July	8.	October	5.
February	7.		15.		13.
	21.		17.		17.
March	3.		19.		19.
	18.		21.		20.
April	7.		29.	November	8.
	10.	August	1.		12.
	12.		6.		14.
	20.		8.		15.
	21.		14.		16.
	24.		16.		25.
	27.		22.		25.
May	6.	September	4.		29.
	30.		7.	December	2.
June	6.		8.		12.
	10.		10.		19.
	12.		19.		19.
	22.		25.		26.

There is but one conclusion that can be drawn from a perusal of this table: which is, that the writer of the letters of which it forms a diary, could not have been travelling over the continent during the year 1769 to which it is limited, and consequently that General Lee, who was travelling over the continent, and who appears to have been chiefly in remote northern parts of it, could not be Junius.

The editor has observed that it is equally obvious General Lee could not have been Junius, from the different line of politics professed by the two characters: and not merely professed but fought for to his own outlawry by the former. Junius, it has been already remarked, was a warm and determined friend to Mr. George Grenville: a zealous advocate for the stamp act, Mr. Grenville's most celebrated measure; and a decided upholder of the power of the British Parliament to legislate for America, in the same manner as for any county in England. And it was because Mr. Lee was an inveterate oppugner of these doctrines, and was determined to fight against them, and even against his native country, if she insisted upon them, that he fled to the United States, took a lead in their armies, and powerfully contributed to their independence. The ensuing extracts taken from his letters contained in Mr. Langworthy's Memoirs, give his own opinions in his own words; and they may be compared with those of Junius that follow the preceding extracts from Mr. Burke.

" You tell me the Americans are the most merciful people on the face of the earth : I think so too ; and the strongest instance of it is, that they did not long ago hang up you, and *every advocate for the stamp act.*" *

" As to the rest who form what is called the opposition, they are so odious or contemptible that the favourite himself is preferable to them; such as Grenville, Bedford, Newcastle, and their associates. Temple is one of the most ridiculous order of coxcombs."†

" A formidable opposition is expected ; but the heads are too odious to the nation in general, in my opinion, to carry their point. Such as Bedford, Sandwich, G. Grenville, and, with submission, your friend Mansfield."‡

" We have had twenty different accounts of your arrival at Boston, which have been regularly contradicted the next morning; but as I now find it certain that you are arrived, I shall not delay a single instant addressing myself to you. It is a duty I owe to the friendship I have long and sincerely professed for you; a friendship to which you have the strongest claims from the first moment of our acquaintance; there is no man from whom I have received so many testimonies of esteem and affection; there is no man whose esteem and affection could in my opinion have done me greater honour. * * * * * * * * I shall not trouble you with my opinion of the right of taxing America without her own consent, as I am afraid, from what I have seen of your speeches, that you have already formed your creed on this article; but I will boldly affirm, had this right been established by a thousand statutes, had America admitted it from time immemorial, it

---

* Memoirs, p. 54, in a letter to W. H. Drayton, a member of congress.
† Id. p. 294.   ‡ Id. p. 297.

wonld be the duty of every good Englishman to exert his utmost to divest parliament of this right, as it must inevitably work the subversion of the whole empire. * * * * * * * On these principles, I say, Sir, every good Englishman, abstracted of all regard for America, must oppose her being taxed by the British parliament; for my own part, I am convinced that no argument (not totally abhorrent from the spirit of liberty, and the British constitution) can be produced in support of this right. * * * * * * * I have now, Sir, only to entreat, that whatever measure you pursue, whether those which your real friends (myself among the rest) would wish, or unfortunately those which our accursed misrulers shall dictate, you will still believe me to be personally, with the greatest sincerity and affection, yours, &c., C. Lee."*

It would be waste of time to pursue the claim of General Lee any further: though a multitude of similar proofs to the same effect might be offered if necessary.

Another character to whom these letters have been ascribed, is Mr. Wilkes; but that he is not the author of them must be clear to every one who will merely give a glance at either the public or the private letters. Wilkes could not have abused himself in the manner he is occasionally abused in the former; nor would he have said in the latter (since there was no necessity for his so saying) "I have been out of town for three weeks"† at a time when he was closely confined in the King's Bench.

Of all the pretenders, however, to the honour of having written the Letters of Junius, Hugh Macaulay Boyd has been brought forward with the most confidence: yet of all of them there is not one whose claims are more easily and completely refuted. It is nevertheless necessary, from the assurance with which they have been urged, to examine them with some degree of detail.

Hugh Macaulay Boyd was an Irishman of a respectable family, who was educated for the bar, which he deserted, at an early age, for politics, and an unsettled life, that perpetually involved him in pecuniary distresses; and who is known as the author of "The Freeholder," which he wrote at Belfast, in the beginning of 1776; "The Whig," consisting of a series

* Letter to persuade General Burgoyne to join the Americans. Memoirs, p. 323–330. See Junius's opinion of General Burgoyne, Letter 34.
† Private Letters, No. 2. This letter is dated Nov. 8, 1769. Wilkes entered the King's Bench Prison April 27, 1768, and was liberated April 18, 1770.—See, further, the private correspondence between Junius and Mr. Wilkes.

of revolutionary papers which he published in the *London Courant*, between November, 1779, and March, 1780, and the " Indian Observer," a miscellany of periodical essays published at Madras in 1793 *. In his public conversation he was an enthusiastic admirer of the style and principles of Junius; and in his political effusions he perpetually strove to imitate his manner; and, in many instances, copied his sentences verbally. On this last account the three advocates for his fame, Mr. Almon who has introduced him into his Biographical Anecdotes, Mr. Campbell who has published a life of him, and prefixed it to a new edition of "Boyd's Works," and Mr. George Chalmers, who has entered largely into the subject, in his "Appendix to the Supplemental Apology," have strenuously contended that Boyd and Junius were the same person; an opinion which, they think, is rendered decisive from the following anecdote, as given in the words of Mr. Chalmers himself.

" Boyd was in the habit of frequenting the shop of Almon, who detected him, as the writer of Junius, as early as the autumn of 1769. At a meeting of the booksellers and printers, H. S. Woodfall read a letter of Junius, which he had just received, because it contained a passage, that related to the business of the meeting. Almon had thereby an opportunity of seeing the hand-writing of the manuscript, without disclosing his thoughts of the discovery. The next time that Boyd called on him in Piccadilly, Almon said to him, ' I have seen a part of one of Junius's Letters, in manuscript, which I believe is your hand-writing.' *Boyd instantly changed colour;* and after a short pause, he said, ' the similitude of hand-writing is not a conclusive fact' [proof]. Now, Almon does not deliver these intimations as mere opinions; but he speaks like a witness to facts, which he knows to be true. It is a fact, then, that Almon taxed Boyd with being the writer of Junius's Letters; that *Boyd thereupon changed colour;* and that he only turned off the imputation, by the obvious remark, that comparison of hand-writing is not decisive evidence to prove the writer. Add to this testimony that Boyd was, by nature, *confident,* and, by habit, *a man of the town,* a sort of character who is not apt to blush. From the epoch of this detection, it was the practice of Almon, when he was asked who was the writer of Junius, to say, that he suspected Junius was a broken gentleman, without a guinea in his pocket."

Mr. Almon's own words in relating this anecdote are as follow: " The moment I saw the hand-writing I had *a strong suspicion* that it was Mr. Boyd's, whose hand-writing I knew,

* He is also said by his friends to have written various letters in the *Public Advertiser,* in the years 1769, 1770, 1771, and afterwards in 1779; the former under a questionable signature, the latter under that of Democrates or Democraticus.

having *received several letters from him concerning books.*"
And he afterwards adds in reference to Boyd's reply to him,
" though these words do not acknowledge the truth of the *suspicion*, they do not, however, positively deny it." *

This reply, " that the similitude of hand-writing is not a conclusive proof," is called by Mr. Chalmers an " *obvious remark ;*"
he might have added that the remark is just as *general* as it
is *obvious*, and consequently that it admits of no *particular*
deduction. It neither denies nor affirms, but leaves the question, or rather the *suspicion*, precisely where it was at first.

· But, say these gentlemen, it was preceded by *a change of
colour;* yet whether this change were to a flush or a paleness,
or any other hue, does not appear. Let it be taken for granted,
however, that they mean Macaulay Boyd *blushed*, and consequently that he exhibited, on the spur of the moment, a secret
sense of shame ; yet what had that man to be ashamed of,
upon a detection of this kind, who openly gloried in the principles of Junius, who had carried his own avowed sentiments
immeasurably farther, who was for ever publicly imitating his
style and copying his phrases?—this man, who was " by
nature *confident*, and by habit *a man of the town*, a sort of
character who is not apt to blush," nothing surely could
have given him a higher delight than to have been suspected
to have been Junius himself: nothing could more agreeably
have flattered his vanity. His cheeks *glowed* with a *flush* of
rapture upon the supposed detection, and he could not even
consent to dissipate the fond illusion by telling the whole
truth. *Shame* he could not feel ; and as to the passion of
fear, it must not be mentioned for a moment : *fear* would have
made him *turn pale*, but not have *blushed*.

Yet these gentlemen, in the ardour of their pursuit, prove
too much for their own cause; since we at length find that,
after all, there was NO SIMILITUDE of hand-writing whatever,
or at least none that could answer their purpose. The
letter shown by Woodfall, Almon asserted to be in the
common hand-writing of Boyd, the hand-writing employed by
him in his common and avowed transactions, and that he
knew it to be Boyd's on this very account. Now it so happened that Mr. Woodfall was also well acquainted, in conse-

* Letter from J. Almon to L. D. Campbell, Esq., Dec. 10, 1798.

quence of a similar corresponder.ce, with the hand-writing of
Mr. Boyd ; and Woodfall, whose veracity could not be ques
tioned, and who had far better opportunities of comparing the
autographs together, denied that the letters of Junius were
written in the hand-writing of Boyd ; adding, that Almon,
from the casual glance he had obtained, had conjectured erroneously.   The difficulty was felt and acknowledged ; and the
following ingenious expedient was devised to get rid of it.   It
was contended that Boyd had, about the period of Junius's
first appearance, accustomed himself to what he used to call,
and his commentators and biographers call after him, a *disguised* hand ; and that he uniformly employed this *disguised*
hand in writing these letters, in order to prevent detection.
And this ingenious discovery was afterwards brought forward
as an evidence of Boyd's good sense and discretion, and an
additional demonstration that he was the actual writer of
these letters.   " It would require strong proof indeed," says
Mr. Chalmers, " to satisfy a reasonable mind that the writer
of Junius's Letters would send them to the printer in his real
hand-writing.   It is impossible to conceive that such a man as
Boyd would take such successful pains to disguise his hand-
writing, if he had not had some design to deceive the world."
    But this is to involve the argument in even more self-con-
tradiction than ever.   Junius, whoever he was, wrote his
letters, we are told, in a *disguised hand-writing*, in order to
avoid detection : the letter which Almon saw was not a *dis
guised hand-writing*, but in the open and *avowed hand-writing*
of Boyd, with which Almon was well acquainted, and which
was made use of by Boyd *in his common transactions and
correspondence.*   Upon their own reasoning, therefore, Boyd
could *not* have been the author of the letters of Junius.
    But we are told, in reply to this second difficulty, that the
disguised hand-writing of Boyd, though different from his
common hand-writing, was nevertheless not so different, but
that those who were familiar with the latter could easily trace
its origin, and identify it with the former : " I have already
proved," says Mr. Campvell, " that those who are acquainted with
the *one*, would, upon inspection of the *other*, discover a strong
resemblance between them " *   The result of course is, that

* Life of Boyd, p. 157.

Almon penetrated the deception, although from *t* momentary glance, while Woodfall was incapable of doing so, notwithstanding his superior opportunities. Yet surely never was such a *disguise* either attempted or conceived before. The author wishes, we are told, to dissemble his hand-writing, in order to avoid detection; and he devises a *disguised* hand-writing that can only be traced home and identified by those who are acquainted with his common hand-writing; as if his common hand-writing could be identified by strangers as a matter of course.

A *disguised* hand-writing that should conceal him from all who were ignorant of his *real* hand-writing, and expose him to all who were acquainted with it, was a truly brilliant invention, and altogether worthy of Mr. Boyd's country and pretensions. Yet, after all, we must not forget, that the hand-writing supposed to have been seen by Almon, if Boyd's at all, was not the mystical, esoteric autography, the ἱερα γραμματα of the initiated, the disguised character that could be detected by nobody but those who were acquainted with his common writing, but the common and undisguised character itself, his general and avowed hand-writing employed on purposes of ordinary business, and which, says Mr. Almon, " I knew, in consequence of having received several letters from him CONCERNING BOOKS."

But this is not the only disguise which Mr. Boyd must have had recourse to, and which he is admitted to have had recourse to, if he were the real author of these celebrated epistles. He must have disguised his *usual style* even more than his *usual hand-writing*, and that by the very extraordinary assumption of an excellence which does not elsewhere appear to have belonged to him; for it is not pretended by any of his advocates that the *general merit* of any one of his *acknowledged* productions is equal to the *general merit* of the Letters of Junius; but merely asserted that there is in his works a *general imitation* of the manner of the latter, together with an occasional copy of his very phrases and images, and that he has *at times* produced passages not inferior to some of the best that Junius ever wrote. " Of all the characters," says Mr. Chalmers himself, " who knew Boyd personally, I have only met with *one* gentleman who is of opinion that he was able to write Junius's letters." And Mr. Campbell has hence conceived it necessary to offer two reasons for this palpable inferiority of style. The one is, that all the *acknowledged* productions of Boyd were written in a hurry—*stans pede in uno*,—while the letters of Junius, contrary indeed to his otherwise uniform method, were possibly composed with con siderable pains, and corrected by numerous revisions. The other consists of a long extract from the Rambler, in denial of the position that "because a man has once written well, he can never under any circumstances write ill."*

Now the whole of this reasoning, if *reasoning* it may be called, is founded on gratuitous assumptions alone, and may be just as fairly applied to any one else of the supposed writers of the Letters of Junius as to Mr. Boyd. It is admitted that he occasionally wrote passages of considerable merit; and it is admitted also, that he was an imitator of Junius's style, and a frequent copyist of his very words and images. But this last fact is against Boyd, instead of being in his favour, for the style of Junius is original and strictly his own; he is now here a copyist, and much less a copyist of himself. Boyd might characteristically write, as he has done in his Freeholder, "long enough have our eyes ached over this *barren prospect, where no verdure of virtue quickens,*" because Junius before him had written, "I turn with pleasure from that *barren waste in which* no salutary plant takes root, *no verdure quickens;*" but Junius could not write so, because his genius was far too fertile for him to be driven to the dire necessity of copying from his own metaphors, and even had he done it in the present instance, he was too manly a writer to have introduced into the simile the affected and con· temptible alliteration of "verdure of virtue."

If Boyd, therefore, wrote Junius, he must have been pos sessed of powers of which he has never otherwise given any evidence whatever, and must not only have *disguised his hand*, but. as well observed on a former occasion by the late Mr. W. Woodfall, have *disguised his style* at the same time; and this too "in that most extraordinary way of writing above his own reach of literary talent," judging of his abilities from every existing and *acknowledged* document. To conceive that a man of versatile genius might disguise his accustomed style of writing by adopting some other style *on a level with his own*, is not difficult; but to conceive, under the circumstances

* Campbell's Life of Boyd, p. 31

of his *authenticated* talents, that Boyd could disguise his avowed style by assuming that of Junius, is to conceive, though the difference between them was not altogether so extreme, that a sign-post painter might disguise himself under the style of Sir Joshua Reynolds, or a street fiddler under that of Cramer

In effect Boyd appears to have been an enthusiastic admirer of the writings of Junius, ambitious enough to try to imitate them, and vain enough to wish to be thought the author of them. By the deep interest he displayed in their behalf, he *once or twice* * induced his wife to challenge him with having written them;—when accidentally taxed by Almon with the same fact, he could not restrain his feelings, and his cheeks flushed with rapture beneath the suspicion; and when, upon a visit to Ireland in the year 1776, he wrote his address to the electors of Antrim, under the title of " The Freeholder," he so far succeeded by eulogizing Junius, by quoting his letters, and imitating his manner, as to induce a few other persons to entertain the same idea, and, what was of no small gratification to him, to acquire the honour of being generally denominated Junius the Second. Yet, say his advocates, he never dared to avow that he was Junius, because Junius had declared in his Dedication, " I am the sole depositary of my own secret, and it shall perish with me."

Upon the whole, however, these visits to Ireland are by no means favourable to Mr. Boyd's claims; for the letters of Junius published in August, 1768, under the signatures of Atticus and Lucius, were written during one of them; and from the rapidity with which they seized hold of the events of the moment, and replied to the numerous vindications and apologies of the government-party, *must have been written* (not at Belfast) but *in London, or its immediate vicinity*†. While

---

* Campbell's Life of Boyd, p. 136.

† Campbell in his Life of Boyd, p. 22, relates the following anecdote of that gentleman, which occurred during the before-mentioned visit to Ireland in the summer of 1768. " One evening while Mr. Flood sat at his own table, after dinner, entertaining a large company, of which Mr. Boyd was one, he received an anonymous note, inclosing a letter on the state of parties, signed *Sindercombe.* The note contained a request that Mr. Flood would peruse the inclosed letter, and that if it met his approbation he would get it published, which he accordingly did in a paper of the following morning, and the letter produced a very strong sensation on the public mind." Mr. Campbell proceeds to state that " every endeavour was made, without effect, to discover the author: that Mrs. Boyd always thought that Sindercombe was

his visit to the same country in 1772 was chiefly in consequence of extreme pecuniary distress, which had oppressed
him for the preceding eighteen months or two years, and had
driven him from the world, through a fear of being arrested;
such were the opposite circumstances of Junius, that the latter
was refusing, at this very moment, the moiety of the profits
resulting from the sale of his own edition of his letters, repeatedly pressed upon him, and to which he was fairly
entitled; and offering, from a competent purse, a pecuniary
indemnification to Woodfall on account of his prosecution by
the crown.

There is, however, a note inserted in Junius's own edition
of these letters *, in relation to Lord Irnham, and his baseness to a young and confidential friend, that has been conceived by these same gentlemen as almost decisive in favour
of Mr. Boyd's pretensions; the young man here alluded to
having been, as it should seem, one of Mrs. Boyd's guardians; the two families to which the fact relates, from the
peculiar motives they possessed for keeping it a secret, not
being supposed to have divulged it to any one, and Mrs.
Boyd herself having only communicated it in strict confidence to her husband. Yet the reader of the ensuing Private

her husband's production, and that many years afterwards she was satisfied
that her conjecture was founded in fact." If Mrs. Boyd were correct in her
conjecture, as to her husband being the author of the letter under this signature, it would of itself all but indisputably prove that he was not the writer
of the Letters of Junius; as on Dec. 26, 1772, nearly twelve months after
Junius had ceased to publish under this signature, and many months after he
had declined to write under any other, Sindercombe addresses the following
card to him:—

"*For the Public Advertiser.*

A CARD.   Dec. 26, 1772.
"SINDERCOMBE laments that Junius is silent at a season that demands his
utmost eloquence. Sindercombe has long waited with impatience for the
completion of that promise, in which every friend to liberty is so deeply
interested. Junius has long since pledged himself that the corrupt administration of Lord Townshend in Ireland 'shall not be lost to the public.' He
now calls upon Junius to fulfil that promise."
That is Boyd, the writer of Junius as Campbell contends, calls upon himself to fulfil a promise which he had not the smallest intention to perform, as
may be seen by reference to Private Letter, No. 63. Sindercombe is a signature of some peculiarity, and never appeared in the Public Advertiser during
the period in which the writer of the letters of Junius was a correspondent
in that paper, which the reader will perceive was from April 28, 1767, to
May 12, 1772.

* Letter, No. 67.

Letters, after witnessing the rapidity with which Junius became informed of Mr. Garrick's intimation to the king, and Swinney's visit to Lord G. Sackville, will have no difficulty in conceiving that Junius, though totally unacquainted with Mr. Boyd or his family, might have easily acquired a knowledge of secrets far more securely locked up than the present. In reality, from Mr. Campbell's own relation of this anecdote, it seems rather a matter of wonder that it should have been a secret to any one, than that it should have been known to Junius at the time of his narrating it; for it appears that at least six persons were privy to the transaction almost from its first existence: the debauchee and the prostitute, the injured bridegroom and his two brothers, and Mrs. Boyd as a part of the bridegroom's family *.—Yet, from these three slender facts,—Boyd's imitation of the style of Junius, Almon's suspicion concerning his hand-writing, and the anecdote of Lord Irnham, in conjunction with a few others of a nature merely collateral, and which, when separated from them, prove nothing whatever, these gentlemen undertake to "regard it as a moral certainty that Macaulay Boyd did write the letters of Junius."†

The late Mr. Woodfall‡, indeed, made no scruple of denying the assertion peremptorily, admitting, at the same time, that he was not absolutely certain who did write them. But this testimony, it seems, though from the printer of the letters themselves, and who, moreover, through the whole period of their publication, was in habits of confidential correspondence with the author, is of no consequence. Let us see by what curious process of logic this testimony is attempted to be invalidated: the reader will meet with it in Mr. Chalmers's pamphlet, who thus observes and reasons:—

"A few weeks after the publication of 'Almon's Anecdotes,' in 1797, Mr. H. S. Woodfall, meeting the anecdote writer at Longman's shop, complimented him on his entertaining book;

---

* Letter, No. 67, with a note by Junius.—ED.

† See Chalmers's Supplement, p. 94.   Campbell's Life, 173, 277.

‡ It may be fit to explain that there are in connnection with Junius three Woodfall's—the father, Mr. Henry Sampson Woodfall; the son, Mr. George Woodfall; and the grandson; the first, the original publisher of the Letters of Junius; the second, the publisher of the editions of 1812 and 1814; and the third, the present Mr. Henry Woodfall, who prints this uew edition in Bohn's Standard Library.—ED.

but said that he was 'mistaken in supposing Mr. Boyd to have been the author of Junius's Letters;' and then added, with an *emphasis*, that ' Mr. Boyd was not the author of them.' To these emphatical observations Mr. Almon replied that 'he had no doubt of Mr. Boyd's being the author of those letters; that as you, Mr. H. S. Woodfall, never knew who was the author, you cannot undertake to say who was *not* the author of those letters.' Mr. Woodfall departed without making any reply. What reply could he make? It is absurd in any man, who does not know the author of Junius's letters, to say that Macaulay Boyd was *not* the writer of them in opposition to affirmative proofs. Yet Mr. H. S. Woodfall afterwards told Mr. L. D. Campbell that 'Mr. Boyd was *not* the writer of Junius's letters,' without pretending, however, that he knew the true author."

Now every one who knew Mr. H. S. Woodfall, knew him also to be a man of strict unimpeachable veracity; a man who would not have ventured to speak decisively upon this or any other point, if he had not had very sufficient grounds. We are asked what reply he could have made? and are told that his negative assertion was *absurd* against the *affirmative proofs* offered. These *affirmative proofs* have been already sufficiently noticed; our next business then is to state what reply Mr. Woodfall could have made if he had chosen, and perhaps would have made if he had been differently addressed, of the *absurdity* of which the reader shall determine when he has perused it: it shall be founded upon *negative arguments* alone. Woodfall well knew the hand-writings of both Junius and Boyd, and was in possession of many copies of both; and knowing them he well knew they were different. He well knew that Junius was a man directly implicated in the circle of the court, and immediately privy to its most secret intrigues; and that Boyd was very differently situated, and that whatever information he collected was by circuitous channels alone. Junius he knew to be a man of affluence, considerably superior to his own wants, refusing remunerations to which he was entitled, and offering reimbursements to those who suffered on his account;—Boyd to be labouring under great pecuniary difficulties, and ready to accept whatever was offered him; or, in the language of Mr. Almon, "a broken gentleman without a guinea in his pocket." Junius he knew to be a man of considerably more than his own age, who, from a long and matured experience of the world, was entitled to read him lessons of moral and prudential philosophy; Boyd to be at the same time a very young man*, who had not even reached his majority, totally without plan, and almost without experience of any kind, who in the prospect of divulging himself to Woodfall, could not possibly have written to him "after LONG *experience of the world*, I affirm before God I never knew a rogue who was not unhappy†." Boyd he knew to be an imitator and copyist of Junius; Junius to be no imitator or copyist of any man, and least of all of himself. Junius he knew to be a decided mixed-monarchist, who opposed the ministry upon constitutional principles; Boyd to be a wild random republican, who opposed them upon revolutionary views: Junius to be a writer who could not have adopted the signature of Democrates or Democraticus; Boyd a writer who could, and who, we are told, did do so in perfect uniformity with his political creed. Woodfall, it is true. did not pretend to know Junius personally, but from his hand-writing, his style of composition, age, politics, rank in life, and pecuniary affluence, he was perfectly assured that Junius could not be Boyd.

It was possible, therefore, for Mr. H. S. Woodfall to have made *some reply* if he had chosen; and it was possible also for him to have said, *without absurdity*, and in opposition to the *affirmative proofs* of his biographers, that Macaulay Boyd was *not* the writer of Junius's Letters.

A thousand other proofs, equally cogent and insurmountable, might be advanced, if necessary, against the pretensions of Mr. Boyd. Among these let the reader compare the letter of Junius, subscribed "Vindex," March 6, 1771, Miscellaneous Letters, No. 91, in which he publicly ridicules Mr. Laughlin Maclean, upon his defence of the ministry, in regard to the Falkland Islands‡. Mr. Laughlin Maclean is

---

* Boyd was born in October, 1746, and Junius's first letter, under the signature of Poplicola, appeared in the Public Advertiser, April 28, 1767, when Boyd had not, as yet, attained his 21st year.

† Private Letter, No. 44.

‡ This Mr. Laughlin Maclean is the person whom a writer in 1849 in the *North British Review* (Sir David Brewster, it is said) has started as a new candidate for the honours of Junius. But the references in the text appear sufficient to dispose of the new claimant; that is, supposing Junius was *Vin-*

well known to have been the best and steadiest friend that Boyd ever possessed; and a friend who adhered to him uninterruptedly from 1764 to 1778*, iu which year Maclean commenced a voyage to India, upon official business relating to the Nabob of Arcot.   It was Maclean who, according to his biographer, furnished Boyd with the greater part of the secret transactions of our own government, and the intelligence he made use of in relation to the oriental concerns of the Nabob Mahomed Ali Khan; who largely and liberally assisted him with pecuniary aid while at home, and "faithfully promised him he would, on his return from India, assist in clearing him from all his pecuniary difficulties."   The proofs are unquestionable, that the above letter was written by Junius; and that he wrote it also in contempt and ridicule of Laughlin Maclean, who, instead of being, as Mr. Campbell affirms, an opponent of the ministry at this time, was an avowed defendant of them.   Will Mr. Boyd's biographers and advocates, after this anecdote, so far vilify his memory as to contend that it was written by himself?

dex, and wrote the commentary on Maclean referred to, and which will be found in our second volume.   Setting aside the great mistake committed in the article alluded to, as to the personal history of Maclean, there is nothing known of him to warrant the conclusion that he was competent to draw the bow of Junius; moreover, in the years 1769 and 1770, when Junius was in hot war, and unceasingly directing his keenest shafts against the ministry, Mr. Maclean was absorbed in his own pecuniary difficulties, consequent on gambling in India stock; and in 1772 he was collector at Philadelphia, while Junius is known to have been writing in London.—ED.

* See Mr. Campbell's Life of Boyd, pp. 117, 125, 209, 210. In p. 141, he gives us the following account of Mr. Boyd, in support of his assertion that he was the writer of these letters.   "From this time [Nov. 27, 1771] till the 20th of January following, Mr. Boyd's whole time was occupied in examining the law books and state trials above mentioned, and in writing with his usual secrecy for the Public Advertiser: Junius's elaborate letter to Lord Mansfield, in which he strove hard to make good his charge against him, is dated the 21st of January, 1772: about three weeks after the publication of this letter, Mr. Boyd went to Ireland; and Junius ceased to write under that signature for the Public Advertiser."   The reader will perceive by a reference to Private Letters, Nos. 40 and 48, that the letter to Lord Mansfield was finished some considerable time before it made its appearance in the Public Advertise.; and by comparing the dates of the Private Letters, subsequent to that publication, up to March 5, 1772, of which there are no less than seven, he will be satisfied that it was totally impossible for the writer of the Letters of Junius to have been in Ireland at the period described by Mr. Campbell.

Of all the reputed authors of these celebrated addresses, Dunning, Lord Ashburton, offers the largest aggregate of claim in his favour; and, but for a few facts which seem decisive against him, might fairly be admitted to have been the real Junius. His age and rank in life, his talents and learning, (though perhaps not *classical* learning,) his brilliant wit, and sarcastic habit, his common residence, during the period in question, his political principles, attachments and antipathies, conspire in marking him as the man: but, unfortunately for such a conclusion, Dunning was Solicitor-General at the time these letters first appeared, and for more than a twelvemonth afterwards: and Junius himself has openly and solemnly affirmed, " I am *no lawyer by profession ;* nor do I pretend to be more deeply read than every English gentleman should be in the laws of his country."* Dunning was a man of high unblemished honour, as well as of high independent principles; it cannot, therefore, be supposed that he would have vilified the King, while one of the King's confidential servants and councillors: nor would he, as a barrister, have written to Woodfall in the course of a confidential correspondence, " *I am advised* that no jury will find" a bill †.

Another person who has had a claim advanced in his favour upon the same subject is the late celebrated Henry Flood, M.P. of Ireland. Now, without wandering at large for proofs that Mr. Flood could not have been the writer of the Letters of Junius, it is only sufficient to call the reader's attention to the two following facts, which are decisive of the subject in question.

First, Mr. Flood was in Ireland throughout a great part of the summer of 1768, and at a time when Junius, whoever he may have been, was perpetually corresponding with the printer of the *Public Advertiser*, and with a rapidity which could not have been maintained, not only in Ireland, but even at a hundred, and occasionally at less than fifty miles' distance from the British metropolis. This fact may be collected, among other authorities, from the following passage in Mr. Campbell's Life of Boyd, and is just as adverse to the pretensions of the one as of the other.

* Preface to Junius.　　　† Private Letter, No. 18.

"In the summer of 1768 Boyd went to Ireland for a few months, on some private business. During his stay in Dublin he was constantly in the company of Mr. Flood."

Next, by turning to the private letter of Junius, No. 44, of the date of Nov. 27, 1771, the reader will find the following paragraph: "I *fear* your friend Jerry · Dyson *will* lose his Irish pension. Say "received."" The mark "*received*" occurs, accordingly, in the *Public Advertiser* of the day ensuing. Now by turning to the Irish debates of this period, we shall find that the question concerning this pension was actually determined by the Irish Parliament just two days before the date of the above mentioned private letter, and that Mr. Flood was one of the principal opponents of the grant, a circumstance which precludes the possibility of believing him to have written the letter in question. We shall extract the article from whence this information is derived, from the *Public Advertiser* of Dec. 18, 1771.

"Authentic copy of the conclusion of the speech which Mr. Flood made in the Irish House of Commons, on Monday the 25th of November last, when the debate on the pension of Jeremiah Dyson, Esq., came on before the committee of supplies:

"—— But of all the burthens which it has pleased government to lay upon our devoted shoulders, that which is the subject of the present debate is the most grievous and intolerable.—Who does not know Jeremiah Dyson, Esq. ?—We know little of him indeed, otherwise than by his name in our pension list; but there are others who know him by his actions. This is he who is endued with those happy talents, that he has served every administration, and served every one with equal success—a civil, pliable, good-natured gentleman, who will do what you will, and say what you please—for payment.

"Here Mr. Flood was interrupted, and called to order by Mr. M——, who urged that more respect ought to be paid to Mr. Dyson as one of his Majesty's officers, and, as such, one whom his Majesty was graciously pleased to repose confidence in. However Mr. Flood went on.

"As to the royal confidence reposed in Mr. Dyson, his gracious Majesty (whom God long preserve) has been graciously lavish of it, not only to Mr. Dyson, but to the friends of Mr. Dyson; and I think the choice was good : the royal secrets will, I dare say, be very secure in their breasts, not only for the love they bear to his gracious Majesty, but for the love they bear themselves. In the present case, however, we do not want to be informed of that part of Mr. Dyson's character ; we know enough of him—everybody knows enough of him—ask the British treasury—the British council—ask any Englishman who he is, what he is—they can all tell you, for the gentleman is well known.—But what have we to do with him? He never served Ireland, nor the friends of Ireland. And if this distressed kingdom was never benefited by his counsel, interest, or service, I see no good cause why this kingdom should reward him. Let the honourable members of this house consider this, and give their voices accordingly.—For God's sake let every man consult his conscience : if Jeremiah Dyson, Esq., shall be found to deserve this pension, let it be continued; if not, let it be lopped off our revenue as burthensome and unnecessary."

Let us proceed to the pretensions that have been offered on the part of Lord George Sackville as the real Junius. The evidence is somewhat indecisive even to the present hour. Sir William Draper divided his suspicions between this nobleman and Mr. Burke, and upon the personal and unequivocal denial of the latter, he transferred them entirely to the former : and that Sir William was not the only person who suspected his lordship even from the first, is evident from the private letter of Junius, which asserts that Swinney had actually called upon Lord Sackville and taxed him with being Junius, to his face*. This letter is, in fact, one of the most curious of the whole collection : if written by Lord George Sackville it settles the point at once; and, if not written by him, presupposes an acquaintance with his lordship's family, his sentiments and his connections, so intimate as to excite no small degree of astonishment. Junius was informed of Swinney's having called upon Lord George Sackville, very shortly after his call, and he knew that *before this time* he had never spoken to him in his life. It is certain, then, that Lord George Sackville was early and generally suspected : that Junius knew him to be suspected without asserting, as in the case of the author of " The Whig,"† &c., that he was suspected wrongfully; and that this nobleman, if not Junius himself, must have been in habits of close and intimate friendship with him. The talents of Lord George Sackville were well known and admitted, and his political principles led him to the same side of the question that was so warmly espoused by Junius. It is said, however, that on one occasion his lordship privately observed to a friend of his, " I should be proud to be capable of writing as Junius has done; but there are many passages in his letters I should be very sorry to have written."‡ Such a declaration, however,

* Private Letter, No. 5. † Id. No. 23.
‡ See Chalmers's Appendix to the Supplemental Apology, p. 7.

is too general to be in any way conclusive: even Junius himself might, in a subsequent period, have regretted that he
had written some of the passages that occur in his letters.
In the case of his letter to Junia, we know he did, from his
own avowal. It is nevertheless peculiarly hostile to the opinion in favour of Lord George Sackville, that Junius should
roundly have accused him of want of courage, as he has done
in Miscellaneous Letters, No. 7. And if we examine into
his lordship's style, and even into his own opinion of his own
style, we shall meet with facts not much less hostile. Of his
own composition he thus speaks in a letter published shortly
after his return from Germany, drawn up in justification of
his conduct at the battle of Minden:—" I had rather upon
this occasion submit myself to all the inconveniences that
may arise from *the want of style* than borrow assistance *from
the pen of others*, as I can have no hopes of establishing my
character, but from the force of truth."

And that his lordship has not in this passage spoken with
an undue degree of self-modesty, will, we think, be evident
from the following copy of a letter addressed by himself, upon
the preceding subject, to his friend Colonel Fitzroy.

COPY OF LORD G. SACKVILLE'S LETTER TO COLONEL FITZROY.

DEAR SIR, *Minden, August 2, 1759.*
The orders of yesterday, you may believe, affect me very sensibly. His
Serene Highness has been pleased to judge, condemn, and censure me, without hearing me, in the most cruel and unprecedented manner; as he never
asked me a single question in explanation of anything he might disapprove:
and as he must have formed his opinion upon the report of others, it was
still harder he would not give me an opportunity of first speaking to him
upon the subject: but you know, even in more trifling matters, that hard
blows are sometimes unexpectedly given. If anybody has a right to say that
I hesitated in obeying orders, it is you. I will relate what I know of that,
and then appeal to you for the truth of it.
When you brought me orders to advance with the British cavalry, I was
near the village of Halen, I think it is called, I mean that place which the
Saxons burnt. I was there advanced by M. Malhorte's order, and no further,
when you came to me. Ligonier followed almost instantly; he said, the
whole cavalry was to advance. I was puzzled what to do, and begged the
favour of you to carry me to the Duke, that I might ask an explanation of his orders:—but that no time might be lost, I sent Smith with
orders to bring on the British cavalry, as they had a wood before they could
advance, as you directed; and I reckoned, by the time I had seen his Serene

Highness, I should find them forming beyond the wood. This proceeding of mine might possibly be wrong; but I am sure the service could not suffer, as no delay was occasioned by it. The duke then ordered me to leave some squadrons upon the right, which I did, and to advance the rest to support the infantry. This I declare I did, as fast as I imagined it was right in cavalry to march in line. I once halted by Lord Granby to complete my forming the whole. Upon his advancing the left before the right I again sent to him to stop :—he said, as the prince had ordered us to advance, he thought we should move forward. I then let him proceed at the rate he liked, and kept my right up with him as regularly as I could, 'till we got to the rear of the infantry and our batteries. We both halted together, and afterwards received no order, 'till that which was brought by Colonel Web and the Duke of Richmond, to extend in one line to the morass. It was accordingly executed; and then, instead of finding the enemy's cavalry to charge, as I expected, the battle was declared to be gained, and we were told to dismount our men.

This, I protest, is all I know of the matter, and I was never so surprised, as when I heard the prince was dissatisfied that the cavalry did not move sooner up to the infantry. It is not my business to ask, what the disposition originally was, or to find fault with anything. All I insist upon is, that I obeyed the orders I received, as punctually as I was able; and if it was to do over again, I do not think I would have executed them ten minutes sooner than I did, now I know the ground, and what was expected; but, indeed, we were above an hour too late, if it was the duke's intention to have made the cavalry pass before our infantry and artillery, and charge the enemy's line. I cannot think that was his meaning, as all the orders ran to sustain our infantry :—and it appears, that both Lord Granby and I understood we were at our posts, by our halting, when we got to the rear of our foot.

I hope I have stated impartially the part of this transaction that comes within your knowledge. If I have, I must beg you would declare it, so as I may make use of it in your absence: for it is impossible to sit silent under such reproach, when I am conscious of having done the best that was in my power.—For God's sake, let me see you, before you go to England.

I am, my dear Sir,

Your faithful humble Servant,

GEORGE SACKVILLE.

Upon the claim, then, of Lord George Sackville to the honour of having written the Letters of Junius, the above are the chief facts which the editor is able to lay before his readers: he has laid them accordingly, and shall conclude with leaving them to the exercise of their own judgment.

END OF DR. GOOD'S PRELIMINARY ESSAY.

Dr. Good, in the above elaborate dissertation, appears to have fairly cleared the stage of all pretenders to Junius's honours up to the period of his editorship in 1812. Sixteen years later he seems to have considered the mystery as inscrutable as ever, though he admits that at the time he wrote the claims of Sir Philip Francis had not been publicly advanced. But with a full knowledge of Mr. Taylor's book—"*Junius Identified with a Distinguished Living Character,*"—he still continued sceptical; and in a letter addressed to Mr Barker, concludes despairingly, with the expression, "that the great political enigma of the eighteenth century was likely to lie beyond the fathoming of any line and plummet that will be applied to it in our days." We insert the entire letter from the late Mr. Barker's pleasant volume of literary *mélange* on the Junius question.

"DEAR SIR,   "*Guildford Street, Oct.* 13, 1826.

"Accept my thanks for your obliging copy of your first letter on the subject of Junius and Sir Philip Francis. Many years ago, as you perhaps may be aware, *I entered at full speed into this research, and beat the bush in every direction.* At that time, however, the claims of Sir Philip Francis had not been advanced, at least not before the public. But had they been brought forward, the arguments by which it is obvious they may be met, and many of which you have yourself ably handled, would, I think, have succeeded in putting him as completely out of the list as all the other competitors appear to be put whose friends have undertaken to bring them forward. The question is, nevertheless, one of great interest, as well on the score of national history, as of literary curiosity. Yet, like many other *desiderata*, I am afraid it is likely to lie beyond the fathoming of any line and plummet that will be applied to it in our days. I shall always be happy to hear of your success, and am, dear Sir, faithfully yours,

"To E. H. BARKER, Esq."   J. M. GOOD."

It will be observed, in the above, that Dr. Good indirectly acknowledges the authorship of the *Preliminary Essay;* and, on such authentication, his letter may be here properly appended.—ED.

JUNIUS,

CAREFULLY COLLATED WITH THE AUTHOR'S CORRECTED EDITION.

DEDICATION TO THE ENGLISH NATION.

REMARKS ON THE DEDICATION.

[THE Author of these Letters had the prudence or the good fortune to discontinue them, at a time when the name of Junius still retained all its first popularity. He was proudly conscious of their excellence, and believed them to be destined to literary immortality. In the course of their first publication, some of them had been, without his permission, collected and republished. At the close of the whole, he prepared them to be reprinted in that form in which he seems to have wished them ever after to appear. This Dedication was then prefixed, to express the Author's gratitude for the enthusiastic applause with which his Letters had been honoured, to recall upon them the popular curiosity, to suggest forcibly to the minds of careless readers the principal topics of which the Letters treated, and to explain that his Book was not to be regarded so much in the light of a collection of fugitive personal satires, as in that of a system of fundamental principles of British Liberty and Political Law, unfolded in a practical application of them, which was well adapted to confirm their truth, and to evince their importance.

. He bespeaks the continued partiality of the nation to his work, by representing it as the nursling of their favour. He boasts, that it cannot but survive the interest of those temporary and personal matters to which it owes a part of its present celebrity. He describes the principles which it inculcates, as worthy to make the people value it as a κτῆμα εἰς ἀεί, and transmit it to their posterity with the same care with which they would perpetuate the Constitution which it vindicates and explains. For the boastfulness of these assumptions, he apologizes, by observing, that the concealment of his person and real name, takes away from his vanity whatever might appear particularly weak, or might prove the most offensive. He maintains that the necessity for hindering the creation of precedents fatal to Liberty, makes it the duty of the People to watch against even the slightest encroachments of the Executive Power, as if these were innovations establishing, at once, the Reign of Despotism. Alluding to the great question of parliamentary privilege which at the moment engrossed public attention, namely, whether the power of the House of Commons to incapacitate any of its members, by a

simple vote of expulsion, from being re-elected to serve in the parliament out
of which he has been expelled; Junius boldly asserts that the sovereignty is
in the whole nation, not merely in its legislative representatives; urges, that
this is, both directly, and by frequent implication, the genuine doctrine of the
fundamental laws and the forms of the constitution; and earnestly warns the
people to make such conditions, as should leave this principle no longer in
doubt or contest with those whom they might choose to be their representatives at the next general election.   The liberty of the press, and the right of
juries to return in all cases a general verdict, he with equal earnestness describes as of infinite consequence to the support of British Freedom; the dis-
cussions in which Junius had engaged, and the judicial trials which his and
other similar publications had produced, having brought these two great safe-
guards of public writers into eager controversy, he, in a truly patriotic spirit,
is anxious rightly to impress the community with their vital importance and
constitutional bearings.   An alarm which had not yet subsided, had been
excited in regard to them, and Junius was anxious to keep alive the alarm
till the wishes of the people had prevailed and claimed respect for the exertions
which he had himself made on account of these objects.   The general
election that approached was the sole occasion on which he supposed that
the people might command the redress of every grievance.   Junius makes it
therefore, in this Dedication, his leading theme to rouse all the patriotism of the
people to an eager and resolute expectation of that event.   He concludes with
one of those flashes of haughty, indignant sentiment, in which one of his best
powers as a writer consists.   Such is the purport of this preliminary essay;
evidently intended to sum up the Author's merits, to state what was his primary design, to make a last impression that should hinder those from being
effaced which he had so successfully made before.   It does not appear to have
been laboured with Junius's happiest skill, nor with the most ardent and
trained exertion of his mind.   He seems to have sitten down to
write it, while its particular design was but obscurely conceived, while his
imagination was still in a sort of tumultuous ferment with the ideas which it
contains.   It was probably finished at one sitting, with labour of thought
rather exerted successively upon each particular part, than expanded, in the
progress of the composition, to a close consideration of the entire scope that
should give unity and effect to the whole.   .

It is, however, a genuine composition of Junius. The general cast of thought;
the structure and the colours of the style, rather expressing the native character
of the Author's genius, than bearing the marks of cold, artificial imitation;
the combination of reasoning, with the gorgeous ornaments of fancy, and
with those incessantly bursting fires of lofty and ardent sentiment, which are
kindled only in great minds, infallibly bespeak in this Dedication the spirit
of Junius; and would enable us easily to distinguish it as his, even if it did
not appear in connection with his Letters.   When it is noticed as not the
most powerfully written or the most correctly and elaborately finished of all
his pieces, it is not meant to deny that it is well adapted to the use for which
it was intended, and worthy of the admirable letters to which it is prefixed.]

I DEDICATE to you a collection of letters, written by one of
yourselves for the common benefit of us all   They would

never have grown to this size, without your continued encouragement and applause. To me they originally owe nothing, but a healthy, sanguine constitution. Under *your* care they have thriven. To *you* they are indebted for whatever strength or beauty they possess. When kings and ministers are forgotten, when the force and direction of personal satire is no longer understood, and when measures are only felt in their remotest consequences, this book will, I believe, be found to contain principles worthy to be transmitted to posterity. When you leave the unimpaired, hereditary freehold to your children, you do but half your duty. Both liberty and property are precarious, unless the possessors have sense and spirit enough to defend them. This is not the language of vanity. If I am a vain man, my gratification lies within a narrow circle. I am the sole depositary of my own secret, and it shall perish with me *.

If an honest man, and, I may truly affirm, a laborious zeal for the public service has given me any weight in your esteem, let me exhort and conjure you never to suffer an invasion of your political constitution, however minute the instance may appear, to pass by, without a determined, persevering resistance. One precedent creates another. They soon accumulate, and constitute law. What yesterday was fact, to-day is doctrine. Examples are supposed to justify the most dangerous measures, and where they do not suit exactly, the defect is supplied by analogy. Be assured that the laws, which protect us in our civil rights, grow out of the constitution, and that they must fall or flourish with it. This is not the cause of faction, or of party, or of any individual, but the common interest of every man in Britain. Although the king should continue to support his present system of government, the period is not very distant, at which you will have the means of redress in your own power. It may be nearer perhaps than any of us expect, and I would warn you to be prepared for it. The king may possibly be advised to dissolve the present Parliament a year or two before it expires of course, and precipitate a new election, in hopes of taking the nation

---

* It would appear otherwise from Private Letter, No. 8, unless it were written to mystify Woodfall, which is probable, from the great care Junius took to preserve his incognita towards the printer.—ED.

by surprise. If such a measure be in agitation, this very caution may defeat or prevent it*.

I cannot doubt that you will unanimously assert the freedom of election, and vindicate your exclusive right to choose your representatives. But other questions have been started, on which your determination should be equally clear and unanimous. Let it be impressed upon your minds, let it be instilled into your children, that the liberty of the press is the *palladium* of all the civil, political, and religious rights of an Englishman, and that the right of juries to return a general verdict, in all cases whatsoever, is an essential part of our constitution, not to be controlled or limited by the judges, nor in any shape questionable by the legislature. The power of King, Lords, and Commons is not an arbitrary power. They are the trustees, not the owners of the estate. The fee-simple is in US. They cannot alienate, they cannot waste. When we say that the legislature is *supreme*, we mean that it is the highest power known to the constitution:—that it is the highest in comparison with the other subordinate powers established by the laws. In this sense, the word *supreme* is relative, not absolute. The power of the legislature is limited, not only by the general rules of natural justice, and the welfare of the community, but by the forms and principles of our particular constitution. If this doctrine be not true, we must admit, that King, Lords, and Commons have no rule to direct their resolutions, but merely their own will and pleasure. They might unite the legislative and executive power in the same hands, and dissolve the constitution by an Act of Parliament. But I am persuaded you will not leave it to the choice of seven hundred persons, notoriously corrupted by the crown, whether seven millions of their equals shall be freemen or slaves. The certainty of forfeiting their own rights, when they sacrifice those of the nation, is no check to a brutal, degenerate mind. Without insisting upon the extravagant concession made to Harry the Eighth, there are instances, in

---

* The object to have been accomplished by obtaining a new Parliament does not appear to have been of sufficient force to have precipitated such a measure; and was, in consequence, relinquished: on which account the parliament in question was not dissolved till September 30, 1774, after having existed upwards of six years.—ED.

the history of other countries, of a formal, deliberate surrender of the public liberty into the hands of the sovereign. If England does not share the same fate, it is because we have better resources, than in the virtue of either House of Parliament.

I said that the liberty of the press is the *palladium* of all your rights, and that the right of juries to return a general verdict is part of your constitution. To preserve the whole system, you must correct your legislature. With regard to any influence of the constituents over the conduct of the representative, there is little difference between a seat in Parliament for seven years and a seat for life. The prospect of your resentment is too remote; and although the last session of a septennial Parliament be usually employed in courting the favour of the people, consider that, at this rate, your representatives have six years for offence, and but one for atonement. A death-bed repentance seldom reaches to restitution. If you reflect that in the changes of administration, which have marked and disgraced the present reign, although your warmest patriots have, in their turn, been invested with the lawful and unlawful authority of the crown, and though other reliefs or improvements have been held forth to the people, yet that no one man in office has ever promoted or encouraged a bill for shortening the duration of Parliaments, but that (whoever was minister) the opposition to this measure, ever since the septennial act passed, has been constant and uniform on the part of Government—you cannot but conclude, without a possibility of a doubt, that long parliaments are the foundation of the undue influence of the crown. This influence answers every purpose of arbitrary power to the crown, with an expense and oppression to the people, which would be unnecessary in an arbitrary Government. The best of our ministers find it the easiest and most compendious mode of conducting the King's affairs; and all ministers have a general interest in adhering to a system, which of itself is sufficient to support them in office, without any assistance from personal virtue, popularity, labour, abilities, or experience. It promises every gratification to avarice and ambition, and secures impunity.—These are truths unquestionable.— If they make no impression, it is because they are too vulgar and notorious. But the inattention or indifference of the nation has continued too long. You are roused at last to a sense of your danger.—The remedy will soon be in your power. If Junius lives, you shall often be reminded of it If, when the opportunity presents itself, you neglect to do your duty to youselves and to your posterity—to God and to your country, I shall have one consolation left, in common with the meanest and basest of mankind.—Civil liberty may still last the life of

JUNIUS.

PREFACE BY JUNIUS*.

THE encouragement given to a multitude of spurious, mangled publications of the Letters of Junius, persuades me, that a complete edition, corrected and improved by the author, will be favourably received. The printer will readily acquit me of any view to my own profit†. I undertake this troublesome task merely to serve a man who has deserved well of me, and of the public; and who, on my account, has been exposed to an expensive, tyrannical prosecution. For these reasons, I give to Mr. Henry Sampson Woodfall, and to him alone, my right, interest, and property in these letters, as fully and completely, to all intents and purposes, as an author can possibly convey his property in his own works to another.

This edition contains all the letters of Junius, Philo Junius, and of Sir William Draper and Mr. Horne to Junius, with their respective dates, and according to the order in which they appeared in the *Public Advertiser*. The auxiliary part of Philo Junius was indispensably necessary to defend or explain particular passages in Junius, in answer to plausible objections; but the subordinate character is never guilty of the indecorum of praising his principal. The fraud was innocent, and I always intended to explain it. The notes will be found not only useful, but necessary. References to facts not generally known, or allusions to the current report or opinion of the day, are in a little time unintelligible. Yet the reader will not find himself overloaded with explanations.

---

* As a literary composition, the Preface excels the Dedication. It contains more profound remarks, more cogent reasoning, more fervid eloquence. It must have been written with more elaborate care, and with a more studied unity of design. But it bears this mark of the hand of an English, rather than of a French or a Scottish author—that it is finished with felicity, pains, and skill, in particular passages, much rather than well-digested, with due congruity and combination of parts, as a whole.—ED.

† Private Letter, No. 59.

I was not born to be a commentator, even upon my own works.

It remains to say a few words upon the liberty of the press The daring spirit, by which these letters are supposed to be distinguished, seems to require that something serious should be said in their defence. I am no lawyer by profession, nor do I pretend to be more deeply read, than every English gentleman should be in the laws of his country. If therefore the principles I maintain are truly constitutional, I shall not think myself answered, though I should be convicted of a mistake in terms, or of misapplying the language of the law. I speak to the plain understanding of the people, and appeal to their honest, liberal construction of me.

Good men, to whom alone I address myself, appear to me to consult their piety as little as their judgment and experience, when they admit the great and essential advantages accruing to society from the freedom of the press, yet indulge themselves in peevish or passionate exclamations against the abuses of it. Betraying an unreasonable expectation of benefits, pure and entire, from any human institution, they in effect arraign the goodness of Providence, and confess that they are dissatisfied with the common lot of humanity. In the present instance they really create to their own minds, or greatly exaggerate the evil they complain of. The laws of England provide, as effectually as any human laws can do, for the protection of the subject, in his reputation, as well as in his person and property. If the characters of private men are insulted or injured, a double remedy is open to them, by *action* and *indictment*. If, through indolence, false shame, or indifference, they will not appeal to the laws of their country, they fail in their duty to society, and are unjust to themselves. If, from an unwarrantable distrust of the integrity of juries, they would wish to obtain justice by any mode of proceeding, more summary than a trial by their peers, I do not scruple to affirm, that they are in effect greater enemies to themselves, than to the libeller they prosecute.

With regard to strictures upon the characters of men in office and the measures of Government, the case is a little different. A considerable latitude must be allowed in the discussion of public affairs, or the liberty of the press will be of no benefit to society. As the indulgence of private malice and personal slander should be checked and resisted by every legal means, so a constant examination into the characters and conduct of ministers and magistrates should be equally promoted and encouraged. They, who conceive that our newspapers are no restraint upon bad men, or impediment to the execution of bad measures, know nothing of this country. In that state of abandoned servility and prostitution, to which the undue influence of the crown has reduced the other branches of the legislature, our ministers and magistrates have in reality little punishment to fear, and few difficulties to contend with, beyond the censure of the press, and the spirit of resistance which it excites among the people. While this censorial power is maintained, to speak in the words of a most ingenious foreigner, both minister and magistrate is compelled, in almost every instance, *to choose between his duty and his reputation.* A dilemma of this kind, perpetually before him, will not indeed work a miracle upon his heart, but it will assuredly operate, in some degree, upon his conduct. At all events, these are not times to admit of any relaxation in the little discipline we have left.

But it is alleged that the licentiousness of the press is carried beyond all bounds of decency and truth;—that our excellent ministers are continually exposed to the public hatred or derision;—that, in prosecutions for libels on Government, juries are partial to the popular side; and that, in the most flagrant cases a verdict cannot be obtained for the king. If the premises were admitted, I should deny the conclusion. It is not true that the temper of the times has, in general, an undue influence over the conduct of juries. On the contrary, many signal instances may be produced of verdicts returned for the king, when the inclinations of the people led strongly to an undistinguishing opposition to Government. Witness the cases of Mr. Wilkes and Mr. Almon *. In the late pro-

* The case of Wilkes here alluded to is his prosecution, for having written an obscene parody on Pope's Essay on Man, which he called "An Essay on Woman." Almon was prosecuted merely for having sold in a magazine, entitled "The London Museum," which he did not print, a transcript of Junius's letter to the King, first published in the Public Advertiser, and thence copied into a variety of other newspapers; and the result was a verdict against him, although it did not appear to the court that he was privy to the sale, or even knew that the magazine sold at his shop contained the letter to the king.

secutious of the printers of my address to a great personage, the juries were never fairly dealt with.—Lord Chief Justice Mansfield, conscious that the paper in question contained no treasonable or libellous matter, and that the severest parts of it, however painful to the king, or offensive to his servants, were strictly true, would fain have restricted the jury to the finding of special facts, which, as to Guilty or Not Guilty, were merely indifferent. This particular motive, combined with his general purpose to contract the power of juries, will account for the charge he delivered in Woodfall's trial. He told the jury, in so many words, that they had nothing to determine, except the fact of *printing and publishing*, and whether or no the *blanks* or *innuendoes* were properly filled up in the information; but that, whether the defendant had committed a *crime* or not, was no matter of consideration to twelve men, who yet, upon their oaths, were to pronounce their peer Guilty or Not Guilty *. When we hear such nonsense delivered from the bench, and find it supported by a laboured train of sophistry, which a plain understanding is unable to follow, and which an unlearned jury, however it may shock their reason, cannot be supposed qualified to refute, can it be wondered that they should return a verdict, perplexed, absurd, or imperfect?—Lord Mansfield has not yet explained to the world, why he accepted of a verdict, which the court afterwards set aside as illegal, and which, as it took no notice of the *innuendoes*, did not even correspond with his own charge. If he had known his duty he should have sent the jury back. —I speak advisedly, and am well assured that no lawyer of character, in Westminster Hall, will contradict me. To show the falsehood of Lord Mansfield's doctrine, it is not necessary to enter into the merits of the paper which produced the trial. If every line of it were treason, his charge to the jury would still be false, absurd, illegal, and unconstitutional. If I

* The charge delivered to the jury by Lord Chief Justice Mansfield, and which Junius so bitterly arraigns, has lost much of its interest to the present generation in consequence of the statutory change in the law that Almon's trial originated. By the Libel Bill of Mr. Fox, which was passed in 1792, juries are empowered, in cases of libel, as in felony, or any other criminal indictment, to judge of the *law* as well as of the *facts* of printing and publishing, to which their jurisdiction had been heretofore restricted by the judges. Mr. Fox's bill has always been held as a great principle established in favour of the freedom of the press.—ED.

stated the merits of my letter to *the King, I should imitate* Lord Mansfield*, and TRAVEL OUT OF THE RECORD. *When law and reason* speak plainly, we do not want *authority* to direct our understandings. Yet, for the honour of the profession, I

---

* The following quotation from a speech delivered by *Lord Chatham*, on the 11th of December, 1770, is *taken with exactness*. The reader will find it curious in itself, and very fit to be inserted here. " My Lords, the verdict, given in Woodfall's trial, was guilty of *printing and publishing* only ; upon which two motions were made in court ;—one, in arrest of judgment, by the defendant's counsel, grounded upon the ambiguity of the verdict ;—the other, by the counsel for the crown, for a rule upon the defendant, to shew cause, why the verdict should not be entered up according to the *legal* import of the words. On both motions, a rule was granted, and soon after the matter was argued before the Court of King's Bench. The noble judge, when he delivered the opinion of the Court upon the verdict, went regularly through the whole of the proceedings at *Nisi Prius*, as well the evidence that had been given, as his own charge to the jury. This proceeding would have been very proper, had a motion been made of either side for a new trial, because either a verdict given contrary to evidence, or an improper charge by the judge at *Nisi Prius*, is held to be a sufficient ground for granting a new trial. But when a motion is made in arrest of judgment, or for establishing the verdict, by entering it up according to the legal import of the words, it must be on the ground of something appearing *on the face of the record ;* and the court, in considering whether the verdict shall be established or not, are so confined to the *record*, that they cannot take notice of any thing that does not appear on the face of it ; in the legal phrase, *they cannot travel out of the record.* The noble judge did travel out of the record, and I affirm that his discourse was *irregular, extrajudicial*, and *unprecedented.* His apparent motive, for doing what he knew to be wrong, was, that he might have an opportunity of telling the public, *extrajudicially*, that the other three judges concurred in the doctrine laid down in his charge."—AUTHOR.

It will subsequently appear (vol. ii. p. xliii. and pp. 323 and 324) that this note contributed largely to identify the authorship of the Letters. Junius, introducing the quotation by vouching for it being " taken with exactness," and by copying it afterwards nearly verbatim into one of his own letters, led to the inference that he himself had reported it, and was the same person as a distinguished living individual known to have reported

am content to oppose one lawyer to another, especially when it happens that the king's Attorney General has virtually disclaimed the doctrine by which the Chief Justice meant to insure success to the prosecution. The opinion of the plaintiff's counsel (however it may be otherwise insignificant) is weighty in the scale of the defendant. My Lord Chief Justice De Grey, who filed the information *ex officio*, is directly with me. If he had concurred in Lord Mansfield's doctrine, the trial must have been a very short one. The facts were either admitted by Woodfall's counsel, or easily proved to the satisfaction of the jury. But Mr. De Grey, far from thinking he should acquit himself of his duty by barely proving the facts, entered largely, and I confess not without ability, into the demerits of the paper, which he called *a seditious libel*. He dwelt but lightly upon those points, which (according to Lord Mansfield) were the only matter of consideration to the jury. The criminal intent, the libellous matter, the pernicious tendency of the paper itself, were the topics on which he principally insisted, and of which, for more than an hour, he tortured his faculties to convince the jury. If he agreed in opinion with Lord Mansfield, his discourse was impertinent, ridiculous, and unseasonable. But understanding the law as I do, what he said was, at least, consistent and to the purpose.

If any honest man should still be inclined to leave the construction of libels to the court, I would intreat him to consider what a dreadful complication of hardships he imposes upon his fellow subject. In the first place, the prosecution commences by *information* of an officer of the crown, not by the regular constitutional mode of *indictment* before a grand jury. As the fact is usually admitted, or in general can easily be proved, the office of the petty jury is nugatory. The *court* then judges of the nature and extent of the offence, and determines *ad arbitrium*, the *quantum* of the punishment, from a small fine to a heavy one, to repeated whipping, to pillory, and unlimited imprisonment. Cutting off ears and noses *might* still be inflicted by a resolute judge; but I will be candid enough to suppose that penalties, so apparently shocking

the speeches of Lord Chatham. For the charge of Chief Justice Mansfield, upon which Chatham founded his strictures, see Appendix.—ED.

to humanity, would not be hazarded in these times. In all other criminal prosecutions, the jury decides upon the fact and the crime in one word, and the court pronounces a *certain* sentence, which is the sentence of the law, not of the judge. If Lord Mansfield's doctrine be received, the jury must either find a verdict of acquittal, contrary to evidence, (which, I can conceive, might be done by very conscientious men, rather than trust a fellow-creature to Lord Mansfield's mercy,) or they must leave to the court two offices, never but in this instance united, of finding guilty, and awarding punishment.

But, says this honest Lord Chief Justice, " If the paper be not criminal, the defendant" (though found guilty by his peers) " is in no danger, for he may move the court in arrest of judgment." True, my good Lord, but who is to determine upon the motion? Is not the court still to decide, whether judgment shall be entered up or not; and is not the defendant this way as effectually deprived of judgment by his peers, as if he were tried in a court of civil law, or in the chambers of the inquisition? It is you, my Lord, who then try the crime, not the jury. As to the probable effect of a motion in arrest of judgment, I shall only observe, that no reasonable man would be so eager to possess himself of the invidious power of inflicting punishment, if he were not predetermined to make use of it.

Again :—We are told that judge and jury have a distinct office ; that the jury is to find the fact, and the judge to deliver the law. *De jure respondent judices, de facto jurati.* The *dictum* is true, though not in the sense given to it by Lord Mansfield. The jury are undoubtedly to determine the fact, that is, whether the defendant did or did not commit the crime charged against him. The judge pronounces the sentence annexed by law to that fact so found ; and if, in the course of the trial, any question of law arises, both the counsel and the jury must, of necessity, appeal to the judge, and leave it to his decision. An *exception*, or *plea in bar*, may be allowed by the court ; but, when issue is joined, and the jury have received their charge, it is not possible, in the nature of things, for them to separate the law from the fact, unless they think proper to return a *special* verdict.

It has also been alleged that, although a common jury are sufficient to determine a plain matter of fact, they are not qualified to comprehend the meaning, or to judge of the tendency, of a seditious libel. In answer to this objection, (which, if well founded, would prove nothing as to the *strict right* of returning a general verdict,) I might safely deny the truth of the assertion. Englishmen of that rank from which juries are usually taken are not so illiterate as (to serve a particular purpose) they are now represented. Or, admitting the fact, let a special jury be summoned in all cases of difficulty and importance, and the objection is removed. But the truth is, that if a paper, supposed to be a libel upon government, be so obscurely worded, that twelve common men cannot possibly see the seditious meaning and tendency of it, it is in effect no libel. It cannot inflame the minds of the people, nor alienate their affections from government; for they no more understand what it means, than if it were published in a language unknown to them.

Upon the whole matter. it appears to *my* understanding, clear beyond a doubt, that if, in any future prosecution for a seditious libel, the jury should bring in a verdict of acquittal not warranted by the evidence, it will be owing to the false and absurd doctrines laid down by Lord Mansfield. Disgusted at the odious artifices made use of by the judge to mislead and perplex them, guarded against his sophistry, and convinced of the falsehood of his assertions, they may perhaps determine to thwart his detestable purpose, and defeat him at any rate. To *him* at least, they will do *substantial justice.* Whereas, if the whole charge, laid in the information, be fairly and honestly submitted to the jury, there is no reason whatsoever to presume that twelve men, upon their oaths, will not decide impartially between the king and the defendant. The numerous instances, in our State trials, of verdicts recovered for the king, sufficiently refute the false and scandalous imputations thrown by the abettors of Lord Mansfield upon the integrity of juries. But even admitting the supposition that, in times of universal discontent, arising from the notorious maladministration of public affairs, a seditious writer should escape punishment, it makes nothing against my general argument. If juries are fallible, to what other tribunal shall we appeal? If juries cannot safely be trusted, shall we unite the offices of judge and jury, so wisely divided by the consti tution, and trust implicitly to Lord Mansfield? Are the judges of the Court of King's Bench more likely to be unbiassed and impartial, than twelve yeomen, burgesses, or gentlemen taken indifferently from the county at large? Or, in short, shall there be *no* decision, until we have instituted a tribunal, from which no possible abuse or inconvenience whatsoever can arise? If I am not grossly mistaken, these questions carry a decisive answer along with them *.

Having cleared the freedom of the press from a restraint, equally unnecessary and illegal, I return to the use which has been made of it in the present publication.

National reflections, I confess, are not to be justified in theory, nor upon any general principles. To know how well they are deserved, and how justly they have been applied, we must have the evidence of facts before us. We must be conversant with the Scots in private life, and observe their principles of acting to *us*, and to each other;—the characteristic prudence, the selfish nationality, the indefatigable smile, the persevering assiduity, the everlasting profession of a discreet and moderate resentment.—If the instance were not too important for an experiment, it might not be amiss to confide a little in their integrity.—Without any abstract reasoning upon causes and effects, we shall soon be convinced by *experience*, that the Scots, transplanted from their own country, are always a distinct and separate body from the people who receive them. In other settlements they only love themselves;—in England, they cordially love themselves, and as cordially hate their neighbours. For the remainder of their good qualities, I must appeal to the reader's observation, unless he will accept of my Lord Barrington's authority. In a letter to the late Lord Melcombe, published by Mr. Lee, he expresses himself with a truth and accuracy not very common

---

* The questions are so decisive, and the general train of reasoning here advanced so clear and convincing, that the point has been ever since settled upon the authority of common sense, in the feelings and understanding of every man, whether professional or unprofessional. And all that remained to be done, was an interference of the legislature to prevent a revival of the question by any future judge, upon any future case whatsoever; a business patriotically undertaken by a statesman, whose name will ever be connected with genuine patriotism, the late Mr. Fox, who in 1791 introduced a bill into Parliament for this purpose, and in 1792 succeeded in carrying it through both houses. See farther, on this subject, note to Junius, Letter No. 41.

in his lordship's lucubrations.—" And Cockburn, *like most of his countrymen*, is as abject to those above him, as he is insolent to those below him." *—I am far from meaning to impeach the articles of the Union. If the true spirit of those articles were religiously adhered to, we should not see such a multitude of Scotch commoners in the lower house, as representatives of English boroughs, while not a single Scotch borough is ever represented by an Englishman. We should not see English peerages given to Scotch ladies, or to the elder sons of Scotch peers, and the number of *sixteen* doubled and trebled by a scandalous evasion of the Act of Union.—If it should ever be thought advisable to dissolve an act, the violation or observance of which is invariably directed by the advantage and interest of the Scots, I shall say very sincerely with Sir Edward Coke, "When poor England stood alone, and had not the access of another kingdom, and yet had more and as potent enemies as it now hath, yet the king of England prevailed." †

Some opinion may now be expected from me, upon a point of equal delicacy to the writer, and hazard to the printer. When the character of the chief magistrate is in question, more must be understood, than may safely be expressed. If it be really a part of our constitution, and not a mere *dictum* of the law, *that the king can do no wrong*, it is not the only instance in the wisest of human institutions, where theory is at variance with practice.—That the sovereign of this country is not amenable to any form of trial known to the laws is unquestionable. But exemption from punishment is a singular privilege annexed to the royal character, and no way excludes the possibility of deserving it. How long, and to what extent a king of England may be protected by the forms, when he violates the spirit of the constitution, deserves to be considered. A mistake in this matter proved fatal to Charles and his son.— For my own part, far from thinking that the king can do no wrong, far from suffering myself to be deterred or imposed upon by the language of forms, in opposition to the substantial evidence of truth, if it were my misfortune to live under the inauspicious reign of a prince, whose whole life was employed

* See the same passage quoted in Miscellaneous Letters, No. 111.
† Parliamentary History, Vol. 7, p. 400

in one base, contemptible struggle with the free spirit of his people, or in the detestable endeavour to corrupt their moral principles, I would not scruple to declare to him,—" Sir, you alone are the author of the greatest wrong to your subjects and to yourself. Instead of reigning in the hearts of your people, instead of commanding their lives and fortunes through the medium of their affections, has not the strength of the crown, whether influence or prerogative, been uniformly exerted, for eleven years together, to support a narrow, pitiful system of government, which defeats itself, and answers no one purpose of real power, profit, or personal satisfaction to you?—With the greatest unappropriated revenue of any prince in Europe, have we not seen you reduced to such vile, and sordid distresses, as would have conducted any other man to a prison?—With a great military, and the greatest naval power in the known world, have not foreign nations repeatedly insulted you with impunity?—Is it not notorious that the vast revenues, extorted from the labour and industry of your subjects, and given you to do honour to yourself and to the nation, are dissipated in corrupting their representatives?—Are you a prince of the House of Hanover, and do you exclude all the leading Whig families from your councils?—Do you profess to govern according to law, and is it consistent with that profession, to impart your confidence and affection to those men only, who, though now perhaps detached from the desperate cause of the Pretender, are marked in this country by an hereditary attachment to high and arbitrary principles of government?—Are you so infatuated as to take the sense of your people from the representation of ministers, or from the shouts of a mob, notoriously hired to surround your coach, or stationed at a theatre?—And if you are in reality, that public man, that king, that magistrate, which these questions suppose you to be, is it any answer to your people, to say that among your domestics you are good humoured?—that to one lady you are faithful?—that to your children you are indulgent?—Sir, the man who addresses you in these terms is your best friend. He would willingly hazard his life in defence of your title to the crown; and if *power* be your object, would still show you, how possible it is for a king of England, by the noblest means, to be the most absolute prince in Europe. You have no enemies, Sir, but those who persuade you to aim at power without right, and who think it flattery to tell you, that the character of king dissolves the natural relation between guilt and punishment."

I cannot conceive that there is a heart so callous, or an understanding so depraved as to attend to a discourse of this nature, and not to feel the force of it. But where is the man, among those who have access to the closet, resolute and honest enough to deliver it. The liberty of the press is our only resource. It will command an audience when every honest man in the kingdom is excluded. This glorious privilege may be a security to the king, as well as a resource to his people. Had there been no star-chamber, there would have been no rebellion against Charles the First. The constant censure and admonition of the press would have corrected his conduct, prevented a civil war, and saved him from an ignominious death.—I am no friend to the doctrine of precedents exclusive of right, though lawyers often tell us, that whatever has been once done, may lawfully be done again.

I shall conclude this preface with a quotation, applicable to the subject, from a foreign writer *, whose essay on the English constitution I beg leave to recommend to the public, as a performance, deep, solid, and ingenious.

" In short, whoever considers what it is that constitutes the moving principle of what we call great affairs, and the invincible sensibility of man to the opinion of his fellow-creatures, will not hesitate to affirm that, if it were possible for the liberty of the press to exist in a despotic government, and (what is not less difficult) for it to exist without changing the constitution, this liberty of the press would alone form a counterpoise to the power of the prince. If, for example, in an empire of the East, a sanctuary could be found, which, rendered respectable by the ancient religion of the people, might insure safety to those who should bring thither their observations of any kind, and that, from thence, printed papers should issue, which, under a certain seal, might be equally respected, and which, in their daily appearance, should examine, and freely discuss, the conduct of the cadis, the bashaws, the vizir, the divan, and the sultan himself, that would introduce immediately some degree of liberty."

* Monsieur De Lolme.

LETTERS OF JUNIUS.

LETTER I.

SIR,   January 21, 1769.

THE submission of a free people to the executive authority
of government, is no more than a compliance with laws which
they themselves have enacted. While the national honour is
firmly maintained abroad, and while justice is impartially ad-
ministered at home, the obedience of the subject will be
voluntary, cheerful, and I might almost say, unlimited. A
generous nation is grateful even for the preservation of its
rights, and willingly extends the respect due to the office of a
good prince into an affection for his person. Loyalty, in the
heart and understanding of an Englishman, is a rational attachment to the guardian of the laws. Prejudices and passion have sometimes carried it to a criminal length; and,
whatever foreigners may imagine, we know that Englishmen
have erred as much in a mistaken zeal for particular persons
and families, as they ever did in defence of what they thought
most dear and interesting to themselves.

It naturally fills us with resentment, to see such a temper
insulted, or abused. In reading the history of a free people,
whose rights have been invaded, we are interested in their
cause. Our own feelings tell us how long they ought to have
submitted, and at what moment it would have been treachery
to themselves not to have resisted. How much warmer will
be our resentment, if experience should bring the fatal example home to ourselves!

The situation of this country is alarming enough to rouse
the attention of every man, who pretends to a concern for
the public welfare. Appearances justify suspicion, and, when

the safety of a nation is at stake, suspicion is a just ground of inquiry. Let us enter into it with candour and decency. Respect is due to the station of ministers; and, if a resolution must at last be taken, there is none so likely to be supported with firmness, as that which has been adopted with moderation.

The ruin or prosperity of a state depends so much upon the administration of its government, that to be acquainted with the merit of a ministry, we need only observe the condition of the people *. If we see them obedient to the laws, prosperous in their industry, united at home, and respected abroad, we may reasonably presume that their affairs are conducted by men of experience, abilities and virtue. If, on the contrary, we see an universal spirit of distrust and dissatisfaction, a rapid decay of trade, dissensions in all parts of the empire, and a total loss of respect in the eyes of foreign powers, we may pronounce, without hesitation, that the government of that country is weak, distracted and corrupt. The multitude, in all countries, are patient to a certain point. Ill-usage may rouse their indignation, and hurry them into excesses, but the original fault is in government. Perhaps there never was an instance of a change in the circumstances and temper of a whole nation so sudden and extraordinary as that which the misconduct of ministers has, within these very few years, produced in Great Britain. When our gracious Sovereign ascended the throne, we were a flourishing and a contented people. If the personal virtues of a king could have insured the happiness of his subjects, the scene could not have altered so entirely as it has done. The idea of uniting all parties, of trying all characters, and of distributing the

---

* The arrangement of the ministry at the period in question, was as follows:—Duke of Grafton, First Lord of the Treasury; Lord North, Chancellor of the Exchequer; Lord Camden, Lord Chancellor; Lord Viscount Townshend, Lord Lieutenant of Ireland; Earl Rochford, Minister for the Foreign Department; Viscount Weymouth, (afterwards Marquis of Bath,) for the Home Department; Earl of Hillsborough, (afterwards Marquis of Downshire,) American Minister; Earl Gower, Lord President of the Council; Earl Bristol, Lord Privy Seal; Sir Edw. Hawke, First Lord of the Admiralty; Viscount Barrington, Secretary at War; Marquis of Granby, Master-General of the Ordnance; Lord Howe, Treasurer of the Navy; Mr. De Grey and Mr. Dunning, (subsequently Lords Walsingham and Ashburton,) Attorney and Solicitor General.

officers of state by rotation, was gracious and benevolent to an extreme, though it has not yet produced the many salutary effects which were intended by it. To say nothing of the wisdom of such a plan, it undoubtedly arose from an unbounded goodness of heart, in which folly had no share. It was not a capricious partiality to new faces; it was not a natural turn for low intrigue; nor was it the treacherous amusement of double and triple negociations. No, Sir, it arose from a continued anxiety, in the purest of all possible hearts, for the general welfare. Unfortunately for us, the event has not been answerable to the design. After a rapid succession of changes, we are reduced to that state which hardly any change can mend. Yet there is no extremity of distress, which of itself ought to reduce a great nation to despair. It is not the disorder, but the physician—it is not a casual concurrence of calamitous circumstances, it is the pernicious hand of government—which alone can make a whole people desperate.

Without much political sagacity, or any extraordinary depth of observation, we need only mark how the principal departments of the state are bestowed, and look no farther for the true cause of every mischief that befalls us.

The finances of a nation, sinking under its debts and expenses, are committed to a young nobleman already ruined by play *. Introduced to act under the auspices of Lord Chatham, and left at the head of affairs by that nobleman's retreat, he became minister by accident; but, deserting the principles and professions which gave him a moment's popularity, we see him, from every honourable engagement to the public, an apostate by design. As for business, the world yet knows nothing of his talents or resolution—unless a wayward, wavering inconsistency be a mark of genius, and caprice a

---

* The Duke of Grafton took the office of Secretary of State, with an engagement to support the Marquis of Rockingham's administration. He resigned, however, in a little time, under pretence that he could not act without Lord Chatham, nor bear to see Mr. Wilkes abandoned; but that under Lord Chatham he would act in any office. This was the signal of Lord Rockingham's dismission. When Lord Chatham came in, the Duke got possession of the Treasury. Reader, mark the consequence.—JUNIUS[1].

---

[1] Notes with this signature are from the pen of Junius, and are those inserted by him in the collective edition he revised for Mr. Woodfall in 1772. —ED.

demonstration of spirit. It may be said, perhaps, that it is his grace's province, as surely it is his passion, rather to distribute than to save the public money, and that while Lord North is chancellor of the exchequer, the first lord of the treasury may be as thoughtless and as extravagant as he pleases. I hope, however, he will not rely too much on the fertility of Lord North's genius for finance. His lordship is yet to give us the first proof of his abilities. It may be candid to suppose that he has hitherto voluntarily concealed his talents; intending, perhaps, to astonish the world, when we least expect it, with a knowledge of trade, a choice of expedients, and a depth of resources equal to the necessities, and far beyond the hopes, of his country. He must now exert the whole power of his capacity, if he would wish us to forget, that, since he has been in office, no plan has been formed, no system adhered to, nor any one important measure adopted, for the relief of public credit. If his plan for the service of the current year be not irrevocably fixed on, let me warn him to think seriously of consequences before he ventures to increase the public debt.* Outraged and oppressed as we are, this nation will not bear, after a six years' peace, to see new millions borrowed, without an eventual diminution of debt, or reduction of interest. The attempt might rouse a spirit of resentment, which might reach beyond the sacrifice of a minister. As to the debt upon the civil list, the people of England expect that it will not be paid without a strict enquiry how it was incurred. If it must be paid by parliament, let me advise the chancellor of the exchequer to think of some better expedient than a lottery. To support an expensive war, or in circumstances of absolute necessity, a lottery may perhaps be allowable; but, besides that it is at all times the very worst way of raising money upon the people, I think it ill becomes the royal dignity to have the debts of a king provided for, like the repairs of a county bridge, or a decayed hospital. The management of the king's affairs in the House of Commons cannot be more disgraced than it has been. A leading minister repeatedly called down for absolute ignorance—ridiculous motions

* The Public Debt at the conclusion of the Peace in 1763, amounted to £148,377,618.

ridiculously withdrawn—deliberate plans disconcerted, and a week's preparation of graceful oratory lost in a moment,— give us some, though not an adequate idea of Lord North's parliamentary abilities and influence. Yet, before he had the misfortune to be chancellor of the exchequer, he was neither an object of derision to his enemies, nor of melancholy pity to his friends *.

A series of inconsistent measures had alienated the colonies from their duty as subjects, and from their natural affection to their common country. When Mr. Grenville was placed at the head of the Treasury, he felt the impossibility of Great Britain's supporting such an establishment as her former successes had made indispensable, and at the same time of giving any sensible relief to foreign trade, and to the weight of the public debt. He thought it equitable that those parts of the empire, which had benefited most by the expenses of the war, should contribute something to the expenses of the peace, and he had no doubt of the constitutional right vested in parliament to raise that contribution. But, unfortunately for this country, Mr. Grenville was at any rate to be distressed, because he was minister, and Mr. Pitt† and Lord Camden were to be the patrons of America, because they were in opposition. Their declarations gave spirit and argument to the colonies, and while perhaps they meant no more than the ruin of a minister, they in effect divided one half of the empire from the other.

Under one administration the Stamp Act is made; under the second it is repealed; under the third, in spite of all experience, a new mode of taxing the colonies is invented, and

* Lord North was not a man of surpassing intellectual powers, or possessed of that comprehension and accuracy of knowledge, which are necessary to the character of the great statesman. Yet, with talents and knowledge far from despicable, he united a pleasant amenity of manners and a pliancy of spirit, which are very convenient qualities in the ostensible first servant of a government, or the leader of a party. We often yield to persons, whose gifts and pretensions are too moderate for envy, that homage which we would pertinaciously deny to him who should strive only to make us shrink into nothing before the humbling superiority of his genius. Lord North was soon after to rise to greater eminence of official power; and there was, perhaps, no man fitter to accomplish the gradual combination of a party sufficiently strong and united to combat the attacks, equally of the turbulent part of the people, and factious portion of the great Whig aristocracy.—ED.

† Yet Junius has been called the partisan of Lord Chatham!—JUNIUS.

a question revived, which ought to have been buried in ob-livion.   In these circumstances a new office is established for the business of the plantations, and the Earl of Hills-borough called forth, at a most critical season, to govern America *.   The choice at least announced to us a man of su-perior capacity and knowledge.   Whether he be so or not, let his despatches, as far they have appeared, let his measures, as far as they have operated, determine for him.   In the former we have seen strong assertions without proof, decla-mation without argument, and violent censures without dignity or moderation ; but neither correctness in the composition, nor judgment in the design.   As for his measures, let it be remembered, that he was called upon to conciliate and unite ; and that, when he entered into office, the most refractory of the colonies were still disposed to proceed by the constitu-tional methods of petition and remonstrance.   Since that period they have been driven into excesses little short of rebellion. Petitions have been hindered from reaching the throne ; and the continuance of one of the principal assemblies rested upon an arbitrary condition †, which, considering the temper they were in, it was impossible they should comply with, and which would have availed nothing as to the general question if it had been complied with.   So violent, and I believe I may call it so unconstitutional, an exertion of the prerogative, to say nothing of the weak injudicious terms in which it was conveyed, gives us as humble an opinion of his lordship's capacity, as it does of his temper and moderation.   While we are at peace with other nations, our military force may perhaps be spared to support the Earl of Hillsborough's measures in America.   Whenever that force shall be necessarily withdrawn or diminished, the dismission of such a minister will neither console us for his imprudence, nor remove the settled resent-ment of a people, who, complaining of an act of the legislature, are outraged by an unwarrantable stretch of prerogative, and,

* Upon the death of Queen Anne a third secretaryship, antecedently un known to the constitution, was created, professing to be for the superintend ence of Scotland, which terminated upon the cessation of the rebellion. In 1768, for the purpose of finding a post for the Earl of Hillsborough, the office of third secretary was revived ; and Scotland having no demand for his talents, he was denominated Secretary for America.

† That they should retract one of their resolutions, and erase the entry of it.—JUNIUS.

supporting their claims by argument, are insulted with declamation.

Drawing lots would be a prudent and reasonable method of appointing the officers of state, compared to a late disposition of the secretary's office. Lord Rochford was acquainted with the affairs and temper of the southern courts—Lord Weymouth was equally qualified for either department *. By what unaccountable caprice has it happened, that the latter, who pretends to no experience whatsoever, is removed to the most important of the two departments, and the former by preference placed in an office, where his experience can be of no use to him? Lord Weymouth had distinguished himself in his first employment by a spirited, if not judicious, conduct. He had animated the civil magistrate beyond the tone of civil authority, and had directed the operations of the army to more than military execution. Recovered from the errors of his youth, from the distraction of play, and the bewitching smiles of Burgundy, behold him exerting the whole strength of his clear, unclouded faculties, in the service of the crown. It was not the heat of midnight excesses, nor ignorance of the laws, nor the furious spirit of the House of Bedford. No, Sir, when this respectable minister interposed his authority between the magistrate and the people, and signed the mandate on which, for aught he knew, the lives of thousands depended, he did it from the deliberate motion of his heart, supported by the best of his judgment.

It has lately been a fashion to pay a compliment to the bravery and generosity of the commander-in-chief, at the expense of his understanding. They who love him least make no question of his courage, while his friends dwell chiefly on the facility of his disposition. Admitting him to be as brave as a total absence of all feeling and reflection can make him, let us see what sort of merit he derives from the remainder of his character. If it be generosity to accumulate in his own person and family a number of lucrative employments—to provide, at the public expense, for every creature that bears the name of Manners—and, neglecting the merit

* It was pretended that the Earl of Rochford, while ambassador in France, had quarrelled with the Duke of Choiseuil, and that therefore he was appointed to the northern department, out of compliment to the French minister.—JUNIUS.

and services of the rest of the army, to heap promotions upon his favourites and dependents—the present commander-in-chief is the most generous man alive. Nature has been sparing of her gifts to this noble lord; but, where birth and fortune are united, we expect the noble pride and independence of a man of spirit, not the servile, humiliating complaisance of a courtier. As to the goodness of his heart, if a proof of it be taken from the facility of never refusing, what conclusions shall we draw from the indecency of never performing? And if the discipline of the army be in any degree preserved, what thanks are due to a man, whose cares, notoriously confined to filling up vacancies, have degraded the office of commander-in-chief into a broker of commissions *!

With respect to the navy, I shall only say, that this country is so highly indebted to Sir Edward Hawke, that no expense should be spared to secure to him an honourable and affluent retreat.

The pure and impartial administration of justice is perhaps the firmest bond to secure a cheerful submission of the people, and to engage their affections to government. It is not sufficient that questions of private right and wrong are justly decided, nor that judges are superior to the vileness of pecuniary corruption. Jefferies himself, when the court had no interest, was an upright judge. A court of justice may be subject to another sort of bias, more important and pernicious, as it reaches beyond the interest of individuals, and affects the whole community. A judge under the influence of government, may be honest enough in the decision of private causes, yet a traitor to the public. When a victim is marked out by the ministry, this judge will offer himself to perform the sacrifice. He will not scruple to prostitute his dignity, and betray the sanctity of his office, whenever an arbitrary point is to be carried for government, or the resentments of a court are to be gratified.

These principles and proceedings, odious and contemptible

* Notwithstanding the depreciatory estimate of Junius, the Marquis of Granby possessed noble qualities; he was humane, brave, generous, and the most popular of all the members of the administration. But as it was the object of Junius to overthrow the Grafton ministry, he, doubtless, thought it requisite to use extra pains to damage the reputation of those of whom public opinion was inclined to think most indulgently.—ED.

as they are, in effect are no less injudicious. A wise and generous people are roused by every appearance of oppressive, unconstitutional measures, whether those measures are supported openly by the power of government, or masked under the forms of a court of justice. Prudence and self-preservation will oblige the most moderate dispositions to make common cause, even with a man whose conduct they censure, if they see him persecuted in a way which the real spirit of the laws will not justify *. The facts, on which these remarks are founded, are too notorious to require an application.

This, Sir, is the detail. In one view, behold a nation overwhelmed with debt; her revenues wasted; her trade declining; the affections of her colonies alienated; the duty of the magistrate transferred to the soldiery; a gallant army, which never fought unwillingly but against their fellow subjects, mouldering away for want of the direction of a man of common abilities and spirit: and, in the last instance, the administration of justice become odious and suspected to the whole body of the people. This deplorable scene admits but of one addition—that we are governed by councils, from which a reasonable man can expect no remedy but poison, no relief but death †.

If, by the immediate interposition of Providence, it were possible for us to escape a crisis so full of terror and despair, posterity will not believe the history of the present times. They will either conclude that our distresses were imaginary, or that we had the good fortune to be governed by men of acknowledged integrity and wisdom: they will not believe it possible that their ancestors could have survived, or recovered from so desperate a condition, while a duke of Grafton was

---

* Mr. Wilkes.

† At a first reading, we might regard this and some other similar figures, as merely useless and extravagant. But more careful consideration will induce us to forego this opinion. It is the master-art of these LETTERS OF JUNIUS, that they are addressed equally, on the one hand, to the taste, reason, and spirit of intrigue, of the *great;* and, on the other, to the prejudices, and the fierce abusive spirit of the *vulgar.* For the sake of the latter, some slight occasional sacrifices were to be made by taste. Of these the present extravagant figure is one. It seems just a sally of genius and dignity of mind, descending as far as it is possible for them to descend, to the coarseness of vulgar abuse. Never was coarseness better reconciled with dignity than in these Letters.—HERON.

prime minister, a Lord North chancellor of the exchequer,
a Weymouth and a Hillsborough secretaries of state, a Granby
commander-in-chief, and a Mansfield chief criminal judge of
the kingdom.

JUNIUS

LETTER II.

TO THE PRINTER OF THE PUBLIC ADVERTISER.

SIR,   January 26, 1769.
THE kingdom swarms with such numbers of felonious rob
bers of private character and virtue, that no honest or good
man is safe; especially as these cowardly, base assassins, stab
in the dark, without having the courage to sign their real
names to their malevolent and wicked productions. A writer,
who signs himself Junius, in the Public Advertiser of the 21st
instant, opens the deplorable situation of this country in a
very affecting manner; with a pompous parade of his candour
and decency, he tells us, that we see dissensions in all parts
of the empire, an universal spirit of distrust and disatisfaction,
and a total loss of respect towards us in the eyes of foreign
powers.   But this writer, with all his boasted candour, has
not told us the real cause of the evils he so pathetically enu-
merates.   I shall take the liberty to explain the cause for him.
Junius, and such writers as himself, occasion all the mischiefs
complained of, by falsely and maliciously traducing the best
characters in the kingdom.   For when our deluded people at
home, and foreigners abroad, read the poisonous and inflammatory libels that are daily published with impunity, to vilify
those who are in any way distinguished by their good qualities
and eminent virtues; when they find no notice taken of, or
reply given to these slanderous tongues and pens, their conclusion is, that both the ministers and the nation have been
fairly described, and they act accordingly.   I think it therefore the duty of every good citizen to stand forth, and endeavour to undeceive the public, when the vilest arts are
made use of to defame and blacken the brightest characters
among us.   An eminent author affirms it to be almost as

criminal to hear a worthy man traduced, without attempting
his justification, as to be the author of the calumny against
him.   For my own part I think it a sort of misprision of
treason against society.   No man, therefore, who knows Lord
Granby, can possibly hear so good and great a character most
vilely abused, without a warm and just indignation against
this Junius, this high priest of envy, malice, and all un-
charitableness, who has endeavoured to sacrifice our beloved
commander-in-chief at the altars of his horrid deities.   Nor
is the injury done to his lordship alone, but to the whole
nation, which may too soon feel the contempt, and consequently the attacks of our late enemies, if they can be induced to believe that the person on whom the safety of these
kingdoms so much depends, is unequal to his high station,
and destitute of those qualities which form a good general.
One would have thought that his lordship's services in the
cause of his country, from the battle of Culloden to his most
glorious conclusion of the late war, might have entitled him
to common respect and decency at least; but this uncandid,
indecent writer, has gone so far as to turn one of the most
amiable men of the age, into a stupid, unfeeling, and senseless being; possessed indeed of a personal courage, but void
of those essential qualities which distinguish the commander
from the common soldier.

A very long, uninterrupted, impartial, and I will add, a
most disinterested friendship with Lord Granby, gives me the
right to affirm, that all Junius's assertions are false and scandalous.   Lord Granby's courage, though of the brightest and
most ardent kind, is among the lowest of his numerous good
qualities; he was formed to excel in war by nature's liberality
to his mind as well as person.   Educated and instructed by
his most noble father. and a most spirited as well as excellent
scholar, the present Bishop of Bangor *, he was trained to the
nicest sense of honour, and to the truest and noblest sort of
pride, that of never doing or suffering a mean action.   A
sincere love and attachment to his king and country, and to
their glory, first impelled him to the field, where he never
gained aught but honour.   He impaired, through his bounty,
his own fortune; for his bounty, which this writer would in

vain depreciate, is founded upon the noblest of the human affections, it flows from a heart melting to goodness from the most refined humanity.   Can a man, who is described as unfeeling, and void of reflection, be constantly employed in seeking proper objects on whom to exercise those glorious virtues of compassion and generosity?   The distressed officer, the soldier, the widow, the orphan, and a long list besides, know that vanity has no share in his frequent donations ; he gives, because he feels their distresses.   Nor has he ever been rapacious with one hand to be bountiful with the other ; yet this uncandid Junius would insinuate, that the dignity of the commander-in-chief is depraved into the base office of a commission broker ; that is, Lord Granby bargains for the sale of commissions : for it must have this meaning, if it has any at all.   But where is the man living who can justly charge his lordship with such mean practices ?   Why does not Junius produce him ?   Junius knows that he has no other means of wounding this hero, than from some missile weapon, shot from an obscure corner : he seeks, as all such defamatory writers do,

—— spargere voces
In vulgum ambiguas ——

to raise suspicion in the minds of the people.   But I hope that my countrymen will be no longer imposed upon by artful and designing men, or by wretches, who, bankrupts in business, in fame, and in fortune, mean nothing more than to involve this country in the same common ruin with themselves.   Hence it is that they are constantly aiming their dark, and too often fatal, weapons against those who stand forth as the bulwark of our national safety.   Lord Granby was too conspicuous a mark not to be their object.   He is next attacked for being unfaithful to his promises and engagements. Where are Junius's proofs ?   Although I could give some instances, where a breach of promise would be a virtue, especially in the case of those who would pervert the open, unsuspecting moments of convivial mirth, into sly, insidious applications for preferment, or party systems, and would endeavour to surprise a good man, who cannot bear to see any one leave him dissatisfied, into unguarded promises. Lord Granby's attention to his own family and relations is called selfish.   Had he not attended to them, when fair and just opportunities presented themselves, I should have thought him unfeeling, and void of reflection indeed. How are any man's friends or relations to be provided for, but from the influence and protection of the patron? It is unfair to suppose that Lord Granby's friends have not as much merit as the friends of any other great man If he is generous at the public expense, as Junius invidiously calls it, the public is at no more expense for his lordship's friends than it would be if any other set of men possessed those offices. The charge is ridiculous!

The last charge against Lord Granby is of a most serious and alarming nature indeed. Junius asserts that the army is mouldering away for want of the direction of a man of common abilities and spirit. The present condition of the army gives the directest lie to his assertions. It was never upon a more respectable footing with regard to discipline, and all the essentials that can form good soldiers. Lord Ligonier delivered a firm and noble palladium of our safeties into Lord Granby's hands, who has kept it in the same good order in which he received it. The strictest care has been taken to fill up the vacant commissions with such gentlemen as have the glory of their ancestors to support, as well as their own, and are doubly bound to the cause of their king and country, from motives of private property as well as public spirit. The adjutant-general*, who has the immediate care of the troops after Lord Granby, is an officer who would do great honour to any service in Europe, for his correct arrangements, good sense, and discernment upon all occasions, and for a punctuality and precision which give the most entire satisfaction to all who are obliged to consult him. The reviewing generals, who inspect the army twice a year, have been selected with the greatest care, and have answered the important trust reposed in them in the most laudable manner. Their reports of the condition of the army are much more to be credited than those of Junius, whom I do advise to atone for his shameful aspersions, by asking pardon of Lord Granby, and the whole kingdom, whom he has offended by his abominable scandals. In short, to turn Junius's own battery against him,

* Harvey.

I 2

I must assert, in his own words, "that he has given strong
assertions without proof, declamation without argument, and
violent censures without dignity or moderation."

                                        WILLIAM DRAPER*.

————

LETTER III.

SIR,   February 7, 1769.
THE defence of Lord Granby does honour to the goodness of
your heart. You feel, as you ought to do, for the reputation
of your friend, and you express yourself in the warmest language of the passions. In any other cause, I doubt not, you
would have cautiously weighed the consequences of committing
your name to the licentious discourses and malignant opinions

* As a correspondent of Junius in this and several other letters, the following short notice of Sir William Draper cannot be unacceptable to the
reader. It is taken from Mr. Chalmers's Appendix to the Supplemental
Apology for the Believers in the supposititious Shakespeare Papers, p. 80.

"Sir William, as a scholar, had been bred at Eton, and King' College,
Cambridge; but he chose the sword for his profession. In India he ranked
with those famous warriors, Clive and Laurence. In 1761 he acted at Bell-
isle, as a Brigadier. In 1763 he commanded the troops who conquered
Manilla, which place was saved from plunder, by the promise of a ransom
that was never paid. His first appearance, as an able writer, was in his
clear refutation of the objections of the Spanish court. His services were
rewarded with the command of the sixteenth regiment of foot, which he resigned to Colonel Gisborne, for his half-pay of £200 Irish. This common
transaction furnished Junius with many a sarcasm. Sir William had scarcely
closed his contest with that formidable opponent, when he had the misfortune to lose his wife, who died on the 1st of September, 1769. As he was
foiled, he was, no doubt, mortified; and he set out, in October of that year,
to make the tour of the Northern Colonies, which had now become objects of
notice, and scenes of travel. He arrived at Charlestown, South Carolina, in
January, 1770; and travelling northward he arrived, during the summer of
that year, in Maryland; where he was received with that hospitality which
she always paid to strangers, and with the attentions that were due to the
merit of such a visitor.

"From Maryland, Sir William passed on to New York, where he married
Miss De Lancy, a lady of great connections there, and agreeable endowments,
who died in 1778, leaving him a daughter. In 1779 he was appointed
Lieutenant-Governor of Minorca: a trust which, however discharged, ended
unhappily He died at Bath, on the 8th of January, 1787."

of the world. But here, I presume, you thought it would be a breach of friendship to lose one moment in consulting your understanding; as if an appeal to the public were no more than a military *coup de main*, where a brave man has no rules to follow but the dictates of his courage. Touched with your generosity, I freely forgive the excesses into which it has led you; and, far from resenting those terms of reproach, which, considering that you are an advocate for decorum, you have heaped upon me rather too liberally, I place them to the account of an honest, unreflecting indignation, in which your cooler judgment and natural politeness had no concern. I approve of the spirit with which you have given your name to the public; and, if it were a proof of anything but spirit, I should have thought myself bound to follow your example. I should have hoped that even *my* name might carry some authority with it*, if I had not seen how very little weight or consideration a printed paper receives even from the respectable signature of Sir William Draper.

You begin with a general assertion, that writers, such as I am, are the real cause of all the public evils we complain of. And do you really think, Sir William, that the licentious pen of a political writer is able to produce such important effects? A little calm reflection might have shown you, that national calamities do not arise from the description, but from the real character and conduct of ministers. To have supported your assertion, you should have proved that the present ministry are unquestionably the *best and brightest* characters of the kingdom: and that, if the affections of the colonies have been alienated, if Corsica† has been shamefully abandoned, if commerce languishes, if public credit is threatened with a new

---

* This expression will receive some farther light from a feature of himself incidentally introduced by Junius in a letter omitted in his own edition, but inserted in the present, Miscellaneous Letter, No. 54, as also from other views of his sentiments and conduct as casually evinced in the Private Letters.

† Corsica, in modern times, was first subjugated by the Genoese, who made use of so much insolence and oppression, as to induce the natives to throw off the yoke, and endeavour to recover their independence. The contest was long and severe, and the Corsicans were reduced to beggary in the generous struggle. Nieuhoff and Paoli chiefly figured as leaders of the Corsicans, the first of whom was actually elected king, but could not maintain his throne against the invaders. The Corsicans applied to many foreign

debt, and your own Manilla ransom most dishonourably given
up*, it has all been owing to the malice of political writers,
who will not suffer the best and brightest of characters
(meaning still the present ministry) to take a single right
step for the honour or interest of the nation. But it seems
you were a little tender of coming to particulars. Your conscience insinuated to you that it would be prudent to leave
the characters of Grafton, North, Hillsborough, Weymouth,
and Mansfield to shift for themselves; and truly, Sir William,
the part you *have* undertaken is at least as much as you are
equal to.

Without disputing Lord Granby's courage, we are yet to
learn in what articles of military knowledge nature has been
so very liberal to his mind. If you have served with him, you
ought to have pointed out some instances of able disposition
and well-concerted enterprise, which might fairly be attributed
to his capacity as a general. It is you, Sir William, who
make your friend appear awkward and ridiculous, by giving
him a laced suit of tawdry qualifications, which nature never
intended him to wear.

courts for assistance, among the rest to Great Britain; and Lord Shelburne was one of the warmest supporters of their cause, and most desirous when in administration to engage in it. But his colleagues opposed
him, and the cause of Corsica was abandoned, though the citizens of London
contributed largely to its support. Yet the Genoese could not totally subdue
it; and in consequence they sold it to France to be subdued by the French
arms; and the tyranny which was at first exercised over it by the Genoese,
it was now doomed to suffer from the French. Poland, Norway, Cracow,
and Hungary afford subsequent and ready historical parallels to this brief
advertence to the past history of Corsica.—ED.

* In the preceding war with Spain, Sir William (then Col. Draper) had
commanded an expedition against the Spanish settlements in the Philippine
Isles. It succeeded completely; and the capital of Manilla was taken by
assault. Yet the generous conquerors, instead of plundering the city, consented
to accept for the value of the spoil bills drawn upon the Spanish Government
adequate to its supposed amount. These bills the Spanish Government undertook to pay, but dishonourably forfeited its word on their becoming due. Sir
William Draper, on his return from India, repeatedly pressed the English
minister to interpose upon the subject, on behalf of himself and his fellow-
soldiers. The English minister, however, did not interpose. Draper was
personally rewarded by an election into the order of the Bath, in conjunction
with certain pecuniary emoluments referred to in this correspondence; while
his colleague, Admiral Cornish, together with the soldiers and sailors under
their commands, were suffered to live and die without redress.

You say, he has acquired nothing but honour in the field. Is the Ordnance nothing? Are the Blues nothing? Is the command of the army, with all the patronage annexed to it, nothing? Where he got these *nothings* I know not; but you at least ought to have told us where he deserved them.

As to his bounty, compassion, &c., it would have been but little to the purpose, though you had proved all that you have asserted. I meddle with nothing but his character as commander-in-chief; and though I acquit him of the baseness of selling commissions, I still assert that his military cares have never extended beyond the disposal of vacancies; and I am justified by the complaints of the whole army, when I say that, in this distribution, he consults nothing but parliamentary interests, or the gratification of his immediate dependants. As to his servile submission to the reigning ministry, let me ask whether he did not desert the cause of the whole army when he suffered Sir Jeffrey Amherst to be sacrificed, and what share he had in recalling that officer to the service? Did he not betray the just interests of the army, in permitting Lord Percy to have a regiment? And does he not at this moment give up all character and dignity as a gentleman, in receding from his own repeated declarations in favour of Mr. Wilkes?

In the two next articles I think we are agreed. You candidly admit, that he often makes such promises as it is a virtue in him to violate, and that no man is more assiduous to provide for his relations at the public expense. I did not urge the last as an absolute vice in his disposition, but to prove that a *careless disinterested spirit* is no part of his character; and as to the other, I desire it may be remembered, that *I* never descended to the indecency of inquiring into his *convivial hours*. It is you, Sir William Draper, who have taken pains to represent your friend in the character of a drunken landlord, who deals out his promises as liberally as his liquor, and will suffer no man to leave his table either sorrowful or sober. None but an intimate friend, who must frequently have seen him in these unhappy, disgraceful moments, could have described him so well.

The last charge, of the neglect of the army, is indeed the most material of all. I am sorry to tell you, Sir William, that, in this article, your first fact is false; and as there is nothing more painful to me than to give a direct contradiction to a gentleman of your appearance, I could wish that, in your future publications, you would pay a greater attention to the truth of your premises, before you suffer your genius to hurry you to a conclusion. Lord Ligonier *did not* deliver the army (which you, in classical language, are pleased to call a palladium) into Lord Granby's hands. It was taken from him much against his inclination, some two or three years before Lord Granby was commander-in-chief. As to the state of the army, I should be glad to know where you have received your intelligence. Was it in the rooms at Bath, or at your retreat at Clifton? The reports of reviewing generals comprehend only a few regiments in England, which, as they are immediately under the royal inspection, are perhaps in some tolerable order. But do you know anything of the troops in the West Indies, the Mediterranean, and North America, to say nothing of a whole army absolutely ruined in Ireland? Inquire a little into facts, Sir William, before you publish your next panegyric upon Lord Granby, and, believe me, you will find there is a fault at head-quarters, which even the acknowledged care and abilities of the adjutant-general cannot correct *.

Permit me now, Sir William, to address myself personally to you, by way of thanks for the honour of your correspondence. You are by no means undeserving of notice; and it may be of consequence, even to Lord Granby, to have it determined, whether or no the man who has praised him so lavishly, be himself deserving of praise. When you returned to Europe, you zealously undertook the cause of that gallant army by whose bravery at Manilla your own fortune had been established. You complained, you threatened, you even appealed to the public in print. By what accident did it happen, that in the midst of all this bustle, and all these clamours for justice to your injured troops, the name of the Manilla ransom was suddenly buried in a profound, and, since that time, an uninterrupted, silence? Did the ministry suggest any motives to you strong enough to tempt a man of honour to desert and betray the cause of his fellow-soldiers? Was it that blushing ribband, which is now the perpetual ornament of your person? Or was it that regiment, which you afterwards (a thing unprecedented among soldiers) sold to Colonel Gisborne? Or was it that government, the full pay of which you are contented to hold, with the half-pay of an Irish colonel? And do you

* Adjutant-General Harvey.

now, after a retreat not very like that of Scipio, presume to intrude yourself, unthought of, uncalled for, upon the patience of the public?   Are your flatteries of the commander-in-chief directed to another regiment, which you may again dispose of on the same honourable terms?   We know your prudeuce, Sir William, and I should be sorry to stop your preferment.

JUNIUS.

LETTER IV

TO THE PRINTER OF THE PUBLIC ADVERTISER.

Sir William Draper severely felt the force of the argument and invective in the preceding letter, and was excited to make a second attempt to vindicate as well his own honour as that of the Marquis of Granby, and to evince, if possible, that his literary talents were not utterly contemptible in comparison with those of Junius.   His reply is of considerable merit, as a piece of exculpatory eloquence.   It is written more carefully than his former letter, and with somewhat more of oratorical art.   Yet, even here, he deals with too much of artless candour; he affects too much the use of such ornaments as are fittest to adorn the theme of a school-boy, or the laboured essay of a college pedant; he descends into detail and confession, too much in the manner of a man that felt himself humbled, awed, subdued, before his adversary.

Sir William begins with remarking what advantages Junius derives from the concealment of his person; how dishonest are the motives by which he must be prompted; how bitter his malignity; how ungenerous his misrepresentations; how powerfully his literary talents have seconded the badness of his heart.   The author next renews his defence of Lord Granby, and maintains it with a degree of skill, that seems to have been sufficient to deter Junius from returning upon that nobleman's character as a fit subject of political satire.   Of the state of the army, too, Sir William here writes with a knowledge of military fitness, and of the certain principles of human action, by which the force of the animadversions of Junius is in a great degree destroyed.   But, when he comes to speak of himself, he at once discovers the whole extent of his humiliation.   He makes confession, as if he were on the rack, and, in the fulness of his heart, brings his adversary acquainted with facts against him, which but for this too frank discovery might not have become publicly known.   Had he not thus furnished his opponent with a key to secrets, of which the notoriety was to make him odious, perhaps he might have retired from the contention without bitterness or disgrace.

February 17, 1769.

Sir,

I RECEIVED Junius's favour last night; he is determined to keep his advantage by the help of his mask: it is an excellent

protection, it has saved many a man from an untimely end
But whenever he will be honest enough to lay it aside, avow
himself, and produce the face which has so long lurked behind
it, the world will be able to judge of his motives for writing
such infamous invectives. His real name will discover his
freedom and independency, or his servility to a faction. Disappointed ambition, resentment for defeated hopes, and desire
of revenge, assume but too often the appearance of public
spirit; but be his designs wicked or charitable, Junius should
learn that it is possible to condemn measures, without a barbarous and criminal outrage against men. Junius delights to
mangle carcases with a hatchet; his language and instrument
have a great connection with Clare-market, and, to do him
justice, he handles his weapon most admirably. One would
imagine he had been taught to throw it by the savages of
America. It is therefore high time for me to step in once
more to shield my friend from this merciless weapon, although
I may be wounded in the attempt. But I must first ask
Junius, by what forced analogy and construction the moments
of convivial mirth are made to signify indecency, a violation
of engagements, a drunken landlord, and a desire that every
one in company should be drunk likewise? He must have
culled all the flowers of St. Giles's and Billingsgate to have
produced such a piece of oratory. Here the hatchet descends
with tenfold vengeance; but, alas! it hurts no one but its
master! For Junius must not think to put words into my
mouth, that seem too foul even for his own.

My friend's political engagements I know not, so cannot
pretend to explain them, or assert their consistency. I know
not whether Junius be considerable enough to belong to any
party; if he should be so, can he affirm that he has always
adhered to one set of men and measures? Is he sure that he
has never sided with those whom he was first hired to abuse?
Has he never abused those he was hired to praise? To say
the truth, most men's politics sit much too loosely about
them. But as my friend's military character was the chief
object that engaged me in this controversy, to that I shall
return.

Junius asks what instances my friend has given of his
military skill and capacity as a general? When and where
he gained his honour? When he deserved his emoluments?

The united voice of the army which served under him, the glorious testimony of Prince Ferdinand, and of vanquished enemies, all Germany will tell him. Junius repeats the complaints of the army against parliamentary influence. I love the army too well, not to wish that such influence were less. Let Junius point out the time when it has not prevailed. It was of the least force in the time of that great man, the late Duke of Cumberland, who, as a prince of the blood, was able as well as willing to stem a torrent which would have overborne any private subject. In time of war this influence is small. In peace, when discontent and faction have the surest means to operate, especially in this country, and when from a scarcity of public spirit, the wheels of government are rarely moved, but by the power and force of obligations, its weight is always too great. Yet if this influence at present has done no greater harm than the placing Earl Percy at the head of a regiment, I do not think that either the rights or best interests of the army are sacrificed and betrayed, or the nation undone. Let me ask Junius, if he knows any one nobleman in the army, who has had a regiment by seniority? I feel myself happy in seeing young noblemen of illustrious name and great property come among us. They are an additional security to the kingdom from foreign or domestic slavery. Junius needs not be told, that should the time ever come when this nation is to be defended only by those who have nothing more to lose than their arms and their pay its danger will be great indeed. A happy mixture of men of quality with soldiers of fortune is always to be wished for. But the main point is still to be contended for—I mean the discipline and condition of the army; and I still must maintain, though contradicted by Junius, that it was never upon a more respectable footing, as to all the essentials that can form good soldiers, than it is at present. Junius is forced to allow that our army at home may be in some tolerable order; yet how kindly does he invite our late enemies to the invasion of Ireland, by assuring them that the army in that kingdom is totally ruined! (The colonels of that army are much obliged to him.) I have too great an opinion of the military talents of the lord lieutenant, and of their diligence and capacity, to believe it. If from some strange, unaccountable fatality, the people of that kingdom cannot be induced to consult their own security

by such an effectual augmentation as may enable the troops
there to act with power and energy, is the commander-in
chief here to blame? Or is he to blame, because the troops
in the Mediterranean, in the West Indies, in America, labour
under great difficulties from the scarcity of men, which is but
too visible all over these kingdoms! Many of our forces are
in climates unfavourable to British constitutions: their loss
is in proportion. Britain must recruit all these regiments
from her own emaciated bosom, or, more precariously, by
Catholics from Ireland. We are likewise subject to the
fatal drains to the East Indies, to Senegal, and the alarming
emigrations of our people to other countries. Such depopula-
tion can only be repaired by a long peace, or by some sensible
bill of naturalization.

I must now take the liberty to talk to Junius on my own
account. He is pleased to tell me that he addresses himself
to me *personally*. I shall be glad to see him. It is his *im-
personality* that I complain of, and his invisible attacks; for
his dagger in the air is only to be regarded, because one cannot see the hand which holds it; but had he not wounded
other people more deeply than myself, I should not have ob-
truded myself at all on the patience of the public.

Mark how a plain tale shall put him down, and transfuse
the blush of my ribband into his own cheeks! Junius tells
me, that, at my return, I zealously undertook the cause of the
gallant army by whose bravery at Manilla my own fortunes
were established; that I complained, that I even appealed, to
the public. I did so; I glory in having done so, as I had an
undoubted right to vindicate my own character, attacked by a
Spanish memorial, and to assert the rights of my brave companions. I glory likewise that I have never taken up my
pen but to vindicate the injured. Junius asks by what accident did it happen, that in the midst of all this bustle, and
all these clamours for justice to the injured troops, the Manilla
ransom was suddenly buried in a profound, and, since that
time, an uninterrupted silence? I will explain the cause to
the public. The several ministers who have been employed
since that time have been very desirous to do us justice from
two most laudable motives, a strong inclination to assist injured bravery, and to acquire a well-deserved popularity to
themselves. Their efforts have been in vain. Some were

ingenuous enough to own, that they could not think of involving this distressed nation in another war for our private concerns.   In short, our rights for the present are sacrificed to national convenience; and I must confess that, although I may lose five-and-twenty thousand pounds by their acquiescence to this breach of faith in the Spaniards, I think they are in the right to temporize, considering the critical situation of this country, convulsed in every part by poison infused by anonymous, wicked, and incendiary writers.   Lord Shelburne will do me the justice to own that, in September last, I waited upon him with a joint memorial from the admiral Sir S. Cornish and myself, in behalf of our injured companions. His lordship was as frank upon the occasion as other secretaries had been before him.   He did not deceive us by giving any immediate hopes of relief.

Junius would basely insinuate, that my silence may have been purchased by my government, by my *blushing* ribband, by my regiment, by the sale of that regiment, and by my half-pay as an Irish colonel.

His Majesty was pleased to give me my government [Yarmouth], for my services at Madras.   I had my first regiment in 1757.   Upon my return from Manilla, his Majesty, by Lord Egremont, informed me that I should have the first vacant red ribband, as a reward for my services in an enterprise which I had planned as well as executed.   The Duke of Bedford and Mr. Grenville confirmed those assurances many months before the Spaniards had protested the ransom bills.   To accommodate Lord Clive, then going upon a most important service to Bengal, I waived my claim to the vacancy which then happened.   As there was no other vacancy until the Duke of Grafton and Lord Rockingham were joint ministers, I was then honoured with the order; and it is surely no small honour to me, that in such a succession of ministers, they were all pleased to think that I had deserved it: in my favour they were all united.   Upon the reduction of the 79th regiment, which had served so gloriously in the East Indies, his Majesty, unsolicited by me, gave me the 16th of foot as an equivalent.   My motives for retiring afterwards are foreign to the purpose; let it suffice, that his Majesty was pleased to approve of them; they are such as no man can think indecent, who knows the shocks that repeated vicissitudes of heat and cold, of dangerous and sickly climates, will give to the best constitutions in a pretty long course of service. I resigned my regiment to Colonel Gisborne, a very good officer, for his half-pay, and 200*l.* Irish annuity*; so that, according to Junius, I have been bribed to say nothing more of the Manilla ransom, and sacrifice those brave men by the strange avarice of accepting three hundred and eighty pounds per annum, and giving up eight hundred! If this be bribery, it is not the bribery of these times. As to my flattery, those who know me will judge of it. By the asperity of Junius's style, I cannot indeed call him a flatterer, unless it be as a cynic or a mastiff; if he wags his tail, he will still growl, and long to bite. The public will now judge of the credit that ought to be given to Junius's writings, from the falsities that he has insinuated with respect to myself.

WILLIAM DRAPER.

LETTER V

TO SIR WILLIAM DRAPER, KNIGHT OF THE BATH.

SIR,   February 21, 1769.
I SHOULD justly be suspected of acting upon motives of more than common enmity to Lord Granby, if I continued to give you fresh materials or occasion for writing in his defence.

---

* The letter, as it appeared in the Public Advertiser, stated, by mistake, "*twelve* hundred pounds Irish annuity !" and the error continued to be propagated through every edition of Junius's Letters, without a single exception. In a note addressed to the printer, however, and published in the same newspaper, Feb. 22, 1769, the mistake is noticed and corrected as follows :—
'Sir,   Feb. 19.
'I beg the favour of you to correct the following error in my answer to Junius. Instead of 1200*l.* please to put, 'and 200*l.* Irish annuity.'
'I am, Sir,
'Yours', &c.,
'W. DRAPER.'
But it would seem that Junius preferred the error to the correction, for in the edition of his letters revised by himself, the error in the amount of Sir William Draper's Irish annuity is retained, and thence, doubtless, continued in subsequent impressions. But it may have been an oversight, as in the next letter Junius mentions correctly the amount of Draper's Irish annuity.—ED.

Individuals who hate, and the public who despise, him have read your letters, Sir William, with infinitely more satisfaction than mine. Unfortunately for him, his reputation, like that unhappy country to which you refer me for his last military achievements, has suffered more by his friends than his enemies. In mercy to him, let us drop the subject *. For my own part, I willingly leave it to the public to determine whether your vindication of your friend has been as able and judicious, as it was certainly well intended; and you, I think, may be satisfied with the warm acknowledgments he already owes you, for making him the principal figure in a piece, in which, but for your amicable assistance, he might have passed without particular notice or distinction.

In justice to your friends, let your future labours be confined to the care of your own reputation. Your declaration, that you are happy in seeing young noblemen *come among us*, is liable to two objections. With respect to Lord Percy, it means nothing, for he was already in the army. He was aidde-camp to the king, and had the rank of colonel. A regiment, therefore, could not make him a more military man, though it made him richer, and probably at the expense of some brave, deserving, friendless officer. The other concerns yourself. After selling the companions of your victory in one instance, and after selling your profession in the other, by what authority do you presume to call yourself a soldier? The plain evidence of facts is superior to all declarations. Before you were appointed to the 16th regiment, your complaints were a distress to government; from that moment you were silent. The conclusion is inevitable. You insinuate to us that your ill state of health obliged you to quit the service. The retirement necessary to repair a broken constitution would have been as good a reason for not accepting as for resigning the command of a regiment. There is certainly an error of the press, or an affected obscurity, in that paragraph where you speak of your bargain with Colonel Gisborne. Instead of attempting to answer what I really do not understand, permit me to explain to the public what I really

* This is certainly leaving a kind-hearted man, and popular idol, in very humble plight: that Lord Granby enjoyed popularity in his day, as well as the late Duke of York, and of the same kind, may be inferred from the fact that his effigy may still be occasionally descried on the sign-boards of old country inns.—ED.

know. In exchange for your regiment you accepted of a colonel's half-pay (at least 220*l.* a year) and an annuity of 200*l.* for your own and Lady Draper's life jointly. And is this the losing bargain which you would represent to us, as if you had given up an income of 800*l.* a year for 380*l.*? Was it decent, was it honourable, in a man who pretends to love the army, and calls himself a soldier, to make a traffic of the royal favour, and turn the highest honour of an active profession into a sordid provision for himself and his family? It were unworthy of me to press you farther. The contempt with which the whole army heard of the manner of your retreat, assures me that as your conduct was not justified by precedent it will never be thought an example for imitation.

The last and most important question remains. When you receive your half-pay, do you, or do you not, take a solemn oath, or sign a declaration upon honour, to the following effect? *That you do not actually hold any place of profit, civil or military, under his Majesty.* The charge which this question plainly conveys against you, is of so shocking a complexion, that I sincerely wish you may be able to answer it well, not merely for the colour of your reputation, but for your own inward peace of mind.

JUNIUS.*

P.S. I had determined to leave the commander-in-chief in the quiet enjoyment of his friends and the bottle; but Titus deserves an answer, and *shall have* a complete one

This postscript, though accompanying the letter which appeared in the Public Advertiser, was omitted by Junius in his own collected edition.—ED.

* Heron is in raptures on the felicities of Junius in this brief rejoinder. "Not splendour of imagination," says he, "but keen energy of sentiment, forcible cogency of logic, strong propriety of application, business-like plainness, secretly combined with all the labour of eloquence, an art concealing all art, constitute the excellence of this letter of Junius. There is nothing more masterly, hardly aught equally so, in the invectives of Cicero against Antony, Catiline, or Verres. Compare the style of this letter with that of Johnson, in his pamphlet on the subject of Falkland's Islands; that of Gibbon, in his answer to Davis; or that of James Macpherson, in his famous pamphlet, intituled "A Short History of the Opposition;" and you shall perceive how much Junius here excels these great writers, by combining with happier skill than they the natural tone and manner of real business, with the ornaments of eloquence, and the artifices of rhetoric." The writhings of Sir William will be seen, if not felt, in the subjoined reply: he has obviously become more cautious in his dealings with his unknown tormentor, but the last sentence shows how bitterly he feels the scarification he has undergone.—ED.

LETTER VI.

TO THE PRINTER OF THE PUBLIC ADVERTISER.

SIR,   February 27, 1769.

I HAVE a very short answer for Junius's important question : I do not either take an oath, or declare upon honour, that I have no *place* of profit, *civil* or military, when I receive the half-pay as an Irish colonel. My most gracious sovereign gives it me as a pension ; he was pleased to think I deserved it. The annuity of 200*l.* Irish, and the equivalent for the half-pay, together produce no more than 380*l.* per annum, clear of fees and perquisites of office. I receive 167*l.* from my government of Yarmouth. Total 547*l.* per annum. My conscience is much at ease in these particulars ; my friends need not blush for me.

Junius makes much and frequent use of interrogations : they are arms that may be easily turned against himself. I could, by malicious interrogations, disturb the peace of the most virtuous man in the kingdom ; I could take the decalogue, and say to one man, Did you never steal ? To the next, Did you never commit murder ? And to Junius himself, who is putting my life and conduct to the rack, Did you never bear false witness against thy neighbour ? Junius must easily see that, unless he affirms the contrary in his real name, some people who may be as ignorant of him as I am, will be apt to suspect him of having deviated a little from the truth : therefore let Junius ask no more questions. You bite against a file : cease, viper.

W. D.

LETTER VII.

TO SIR WILLIAM DRAPER, KNIGHT OF THE BATH *.

SIR,   March 3, 1769.

AN academical education has given you an unlimited command over the most beautiful figures of speech. Masks, hatchets,

---

* Mr. Heron esteems this letter the Io Triumphe of Junius, in regard to the general result of his newspaper correspondence with Sir William

racks, and vipers dance through your letters in all the mazes
of metaphorical confusion.   These are the gloomy companions
of a disturbed imagination; the melancholy madness of poetry,
without the inspiration.   I will not contend with you in point
of composition.   You are a scholar, Sir William, and, if I am
truly informed, you write Latin with almost as much purity
as English.   Suffer me then, for I am a plain unlettered
man, to continue that style of interrogation, which suits my
capacity, and to which, considering the readiness of your
answers, you ought to have no objection.   Even Mr. Bingley*
promises to answer, if put to the torture.

Do you then really think that, if I were to ask a *most
virtuous man* whether he ever committed theft, or murder, it
would disturb his peace of mind?   Such a question might
perhaps discompose the gravity of his muscles, but I believe
it would little affect the tranquillity of his conscience.   Examine your own breast, Sir William, and you will discover
that reproaches and inquiries have no power to afflict either
the man of unblemished integrity, or the abandoned profligate.   It is the middle compound character which alone is

Draper.   The concluding paragraph bids adieu in a mitigated tone, but still
in the style of a man who looked down from an infinite distance upon his
antagonist prostrate at his feet, and assumed the authority of a conqueror, in
insulting at once the courage, the honour, and the prudence, of him whom
he had brought thus low.   It must be owned that, as Sir William Draper's
open interposition in the controversy with Junius was spontaneous, with a
knowledge of the conditions under which he was to contend, Junius cannot
be, in candour blamed, as having dealt unfairly by him.   Yet one would
rather recommend these letters to Sir William Draper as a model of controversial address, of argumentative closeness, of skill to confound the understanding by harassing the passions, than as examples of noble liberality and
candour.—ED.

* This man, being committed by the Court of King's Bench for a contempt, voluntarily made oath, that he would never answer interrogatories,
unless he should be put to the torture.—JUNIUS.

Bingley was by trade a printer, and in the character here referred to, a
witness for the crown in a cause between government and Wilkes.   It is difficult to say for what purpose this man was subpoenaed on either side, for his
obstinacy was so extreme, that he could not be induced to answer the interrogatories addressed to him on the part either of the plaintiff or defendant.
It was on this account he was committed to the King's Bench Prison, where
he continued as refractory as in the King's Bench Court: he was at length
discharged, on the motion of the Attorney-General, without any submission
on his own part, from the mere idea that he had suffered severely enough for
his contumacy.

vulnerable: the man, who, without firmness enough to avoid a dishonourable action, has feeling enough to be ashamed of it.

I thank you for your hint of the decalogue, and shall take an opportunity of applying it to some of your *most virtuous* friends in both Houses of Parliament.

You seem to have dropped the affair of your regiment; so let it rest. When you are appointed to another, I dare say you will not sell it either for a gross sum, or for an annuity upon lives.

I am truly glad (for really, Sir William, I am not your enemy, nor did I begin this contest with you,) that you have been able to clear yourself of a crime, though at the expense of the highest indiscretion. You say that your half-pay was given you by way of pension. I will not dwell upon the singularity of uniting in your own person two sorts of provision, which in their own nature, and in all military and parliamentary views, are incompatible; but I call upon you to justify that declaration wherein you charge your sovereign with having done an act in your favour, notoriously against law. The half-pay, both in Ireland and England, is appropriated by Parliament; and if it be given to persons who, like you, are legally incapable of holding it, it is a breach of law. It would have been more decent in you to have called this dishonourable transaction by its true name—a job to accommodate two persons, by particular interest and management at the Castle. What sense must Government have had of your services, when the rewards they have given you are only a disgrace to you!

And now, Sir William, I shall take my leave of you for ever. Motives very different from any apprehension of your resentment, make it impossible you should ever know me. In truth, you have some reason to hold yourself indebted to me. From the lessons I have given you, you may collect a profitable instruction for your future life. They will either teach you so to regulate your conduct as to be able to set the most malicious inquiries at defiance; or, if that be a lost hope, they will teach you prudence enough not to attract the public attention to a character which will only pass without censure when it passes without observation.

JUNIUS.

K 2

It has been said, and I believe truly, that it was signified to Sir William Draper, as the request of Lord Granby, that he should desist from writing in his Lordship's defence. Sir William Draper certainly drew Junius forward to say more of Lord Granby's character than he originally intended. He was reduced to the dilemma of either being totally silenced, or of supporting his first letter. Whether Sir William had a right to reduce him to this dilemma, or to call upon him for his name, after a voluntary attack on *his* side, are questions submitted to the candour of the public. The death of Lord Granby was lamented by Junius. He undoubtedly owed some compensations to the public, and seemed determined to acquit himself of them. In private life, he was unquestionably that good man who, for the interest of his country, ought to have been a great one. *Bonum virum facilè dixeris;—magnum libenter.* I speak of him now without partiality;—I never spoke of him with resentment. His mistakes in public conduct did not arise either from want of sentiment, or want of judgment, but in general from the difficulty of saying NO to the bad people who surrounded him.

As for the rest, the friends of Lord Granby should remember, that he himself thought proper to condemn, retract, and disavow, by a most solemn declaration in the House of Commons, that very system of political conduct which Junius had held forth to the disapprobation of the public.—JUNIUS.

The politics of Sir William Draper were certainly not violent, and he appears to have been rather a private friend of the Marquis's than a partisan on either side of the question. The following letter, published by him in the Public Advertiser, in the very midst of his dispute with Junius, is highly creditable to his liberality, and sufficiently proves the truth of the assertion of Junius, that he could not be, at least upon political principles, Sir William's enemy.

TO THE PRINTER.

SIR,   *Clifton, February* 6, 1769.
IF the voice of a well-meaning individual could be heard amidst the clamour, fury, and madness of the times, would it appear too rash and presumptuous to propose to the public, that an act of indemnity and oblivion may be made for all past transactions and offences, as well with respect to Mr. Wilkes as to our colonies? Such salutary expedients have been embraced by the wisest of nations; such expedients have been made use of by our own, when the public confusion had arrived to some very dangerous and alarming crisis; and I believe it needs not the gift of prophecy to foretell that some such crisis is now approaching. Perhaps it will be more wise and praiseworthy to make such an act immediately, in order to prevent the possibility (not to say the probability) of an insurrection at home and in our dependencies abroad, than it will be to be obliged to have recourse to one after the mischief has been done, and the kingdom has groaned under all the miseries that avarice, ambition, hypocrisy, and madness, could inflict upon it. An act of grace, indemnity, and oblivion, was passed at the restoration of King Charles the Second; but I will venture to say that had such an act been seasonably passed in the reign of his unhappy father, the civil war had been prevented, and no restoration had been necessary. Is it too late to recall all the messengers and edicts of wrath? Cannot the money that is now wasted in endless and mutual prosecutions, and in stopping the mouth of one person, and

opening that of another, be better employed in erecting a temple to Concord? Let Mr. Wilkes lay the first stone, and such a stone as I hope the builders will not refuse. May this parliament, to use Lord Clarendon's expression, be called "The healing parliament!" May our foul wounds be cleansed and then closed! The English have been as famous for good-nature as for valour—let it be not said that such qualities are degenerated into savage ferocity. If any of my friends in either house of legislature shall condescend to listen to and improve these hints, I shall think that I have not lived in vain.

WILLIAM DRAPER.

Sir William, in return, if he ever had any personal enmity against Junius, appears to have relinquished it completely a short time after the contest, if we may judge from the following anecdote given by Mr. Campbell in his Life of Hugh Boyd, p. 185.

"Some months after the Letters of Junius were published collectively, Boyd met Sir William Draper at the tennis court, where their acquaintance was originally formed in the year 1769, and where (being both great tennis players) they used often to meet; the conversation turning upon Junius, Sir William observed, "That though Junius had treated him with extreme severity, he now looked upon him as a very honest fellow; that he freely forgave him for the bitterness of his censures, and that there was no man with whom he would more gladly drink a bottle of old Burgundy."

Sir W. Draper, as far as Lord Granby was implicated, dropped the subject, though he subsequently wrote the following letter in defence of his own conduct, in which he again calls upon Junius to avow himself.

TO THE PRINTER OF THE PUBLIC ADVERTISER.

SIR,   *Clifton, April 24,* 1769.

A GENTLEMAN who signed himself *An Half-pay Subaltern,* has called upon me to stand forth in the behalf of the much distressed officers now upon half-pay. He was pleased to say, that I have an effectual method of being *really* serviceable to the officers of my reduced regiment. I should have been happy in receiving, by a private letter, that gentleman's idea of relief for them; could have wished he had made use of a more agreeable mode of application than a public newspaper, as, unluckily, these *ill-seasoned provocatives* are more apt to *disgust* than *quicken* the desire of doing good, especially when they are accompanied by invidious reflections, both rash and ill-founded; at present I am quite at a loss to find out by what means a person out of parliament, who has long retired from the *great world,* and who, of course, has but very little influence or interest, can be of much use to those gallant and distressed gentlemen, to many of whom I have the greatest obligations, of which I have, upon all occasions, made the most public and grateful acknowledgments; nor was there the smallest necessity to *wake* me in this loud manner to a remembrance of their important services, although the writer has been pleased to charge me with *forgetfulness*—a most *heavy* imputation, as it implies ingratitude towards those by whom I have been so essentially assisted, and to whom I am so much indebted for my *good fortune,* which, however, is not so *great* as the gentleman imagines: he himself forgets that the Spaniards have also *forgot* to pay the ransom. If he could quicken their memory, instead of mine, the officers would be more obliged to him.

Their bravery has given me a competency, a *golden mediocrity*, but not much affluence or luxury, which is a stranger to my house as well as to my thoughts; and I here most solemnly declare (notwithstanding the *false assertions* of a Junius, who has told the world that I had *sold the partners* of my victory, and then *gravely* asked me if I were not guilty of perjury) that my income is now less than when I first went to Manilla. It is true that its being so is by my own choice: I am voluntarily upon an equivalent for half-pay; and although I would most willingly stand forth in the service of my king and country, should the necessity of the times demand my poor assistance, yet I would not again accept of any regiment whatsoever, or interfere with the pretensions of those officers whose good fortune has been less than their merits; and I here most solemnly declare, that I never received either from the East India Company, or from the Spaniards, directly or indirectly, any *present* or *gratification* or any circumstance of emolument whatsoever, to the amount of five shillings, during the whole course of the expedition, or afterwards, my legal prize-money excepted. The Spaniards know that I refused the sum of fifty thousand pounds offered me by the Archbishop, to mitigate the terms of the ransom, and to reduce it to half a million, instead of a *whole* one, so that had I been disposed to have *basely sold* the partners of my victory, avarice herself could not have wished for a richer opportunity.

The many base insinuations that have been of late thrown out to my disadvantage in the public papers, oblige me to have recourse to the same channel for my vindication, and flatter myself that the public will be candid enough not to impute it to arrogance, vanity, or the impertinence of egotism; and hope that as much credit will be given to the assertions of a man who is ready to seal his testimony with his blood, as to a writer, who, when repeatedly called upon to avow himself, and personally maintain his accusation, still skulks in the dark, or in the *mean* subterfuge of a mask.

W. D.

LETTER VIII.

TO HIS GRACE THE DUKE OF GRAFTON.

WHEN Junius closed his correspondence with Sir William Draper, he was impatient to aim at a nobler quarry. The Duke of Grafton was now principal minister, or First Lord of the Treasury. He stood at the head of those whom this writer wished to frighten from the helm of affairs. But for the interposition of Sir William Draper, and the discussion of the character of Lord Granby, the duke would probably have been singled out the first for a particular attack. Although writing these letters, evidently, upon a preconceived and regular plan, yet Junius had so settled this plan with himself, that he could seize, towards its accomplishment in any part, whatever new events should rise upon the public notice while he was proceeding in the series of his epistolary invectives. He, in this letter, took occasion to open his attack on the Duke of Grafton, by joining in the outcry of popular re-sentiment, on account of a pardon granted to a chairman who had been condemned for murder, and whom the populace of London wished rather to have seen hanged.   The circumstances of the case are worthy of being here mentioned somewhat in detail.

The resignation of Mr. Pitt and Lord Temple, upon the rejection of the former's advice to declare war against Spain, was, perhaps, fully justified by the information and the views on which that advice was founded.   But the resignation of those ministers was made the signal for raising the outrageous clamour of unpopularity against the government of the sovereign, whose councils they had forsaken.   When the Duke of Newcastle, and his dependants, at length reluctantly followed their example, a new agency was added to increase the bluster of the storm.   The populace of London and Westminster would not, of themselves, have easily become prompt to seditious tumults, against the sway of a young monarch of an interesting person, and the fairest private character.   But the discontented great openly encouraged, to a certain length, the murmurs and tumults of the people; and what they themselves would not openly do to provoke those tumults and murmurs, that they contrived to have done more secretly by busy agitators, and anonymous writings.   The *North Briton*, the work of John Wilkes, assisted by Charles Churchill and Lord Temple, was admirably addressed to every popular prejudice and passion, and contributed, therefore, in an extraordinary degree, to inflame both high and low, especially about the metropolis, with mingled rage and contempt against the government.   When the famous Forty-fifth number of that paper appeared, the ministry thought they saw the occasion which they desired to have arrived.   They began their proceedings against its author by a measure which, though its use had been exemplified by the Whigs at the height of their power, was a violation of the fundamental laws of the constitution. This measure was the issuing of a general warrant, in the trial of the validity of which the courts of law gave the triumph to Wilkes.   Nothing animates vulgar ferocity and turbulence more than success.   The government became, therefore, doubly unpopular, after the courts of law had, in one instance, declared against it.   The Whigs in opposition saw with joy the unpopularity of the ministry, for they naturally believed that a young king, desirous of the love of his people, and personally deserving it, would not fail to dismiss his present ministers and favourites, if he should be once convinced that they, and they alone, made him odious to his subjects.   Wilkes's imprudence soon reversed his triumph.   He was expelled the House of Commons, and prosecuted to outlawry before a court of justice.   Yet the popular ferment did not subside, nor could the tumultuous spirit of the people be easily reduced under the proper restraints.   There had been irregularities in the renewed proceedings against the author of the *North Briton*, which, arising from nothing but imprudence and want of address in the ministers, were by the art of opposition represented to the people as indications of a settled design to overthrow the national liberties.   By various acts, almost all the Whigs in the opposition, directly or indirectly, engaged never to take a part in the administration, without procuring a reversal of what had been done against Wilkes, and without compensating him for his sufferings in what was esteemed to be a public cause.   On the other hand, for a while, no party would be admitted into administration, without embracing the priuciples and the consequences of the prosecution of Wilkes. The Marquis of Rockingham's administration of 1765 were reduced to the humiliation of pensioning Wilkes abroad, that they might not lose, by his return upon them, either the king or people. When the Duke of Grafton rose into greater authority, under the ministry of Lord Chatham, he taught his friend Wilkes to expect, from his good offices, all that either Wilkes himself or the public could demand in his favour. Wilkes returned, submitted himself to the laws of his country, had his outlawry annulled, and was condemned to suffer punishment under the effect of his former prosecution. The Duke of Grafton could not fulfil what he had promised, yet the vigilance and the energies of government were somehow unaccountably relaxed in favour of the daring agitator. The people were glad to see him brave the government and the parliament to the teeth. They espoused his cause with eagerness infinitely greater than they had before discovered towards him. It seemed as if the populace of London and Middlesex were the *plebs* of ancient Rome, and Wilkes a tribune. Even while he was an outlaw they would choose him at the general election, to represent the county of Middlesex in parliament. The rival candidates, whom government favoured, had a hired mob to contend with the mob of Wilkes's partisans. In a fray a man of the name of Clarke was killed by persons belonging to that which was called the *hired mob of the court*. Those persons were brought to trial. In the exasperation of the people against the court, M'Quirk was found guilty by the jury. The crown might have freely pardoned him, without publicly assigning any reason for this act of mercy. But administration was, at this time, so timid and feeble, in consequence of its former irregularities in the exercise of power, that even pardon to a condemned criminal might not be granted without rendering an account to the people. By the advice of Lord Camden, at that time Lord Chancellor, witnesses were again examined concerning the immediate cause of Clarke's death. It was rendered probable that the jury who found M'Quirk guilty might have been hastily mistaken. M'Quirk was pardoned. The reasons for the pardon were made public, perhaps not more to justify the sovereign, than to throw out an insinuation of partiality in the jury. The clamour of the public was raised high against this act of mercy. Junius marked their humour, and would not miss so fair an occasion of becoming the apologist of their prejudices, and of inflaming their passions, in order the more effectually to promote his own primary views. The contest between the ministry and the people of the metropolis was on this occasion the fiercer, because while the people complained, on the one hand, that the government was disposed to support and strengthen itself by infractions of the law, and an irregular exercise of the prerogative, the friends of government, on the other hand, alleged that juries were eager to acquit every person tried before them, however strong the evidence against him, if it were a public crime of which he was accused, and that crime some attempt to thwart and embarrass the executive power.

In this letter Junius introduces his animadversions on the pardon to M'Quirk, with accusing the Duke of Grafton of making his sovereign odious to the English nation, by exhibiting him, contrary to the design of the English constitution, as the author rather of acts of unpopular severity than of such as could be alone adopted to conciliate the favour of the people, and by making he exercise even of the royal prerogative of mercy to individuals, appear to be sullen cruelty to the public at large. These insinuations were intended both to reach the sovereign himself, in the estimation of the public, and to excite, if the letter should fall into their hands, mutual suspicions in the minds of the king and of his minister.

Junius next enters directly upon the subject which his letter was meant to discuss. He suggests that government had employed every possible exertion of undue influence to save M'Quirk at his trial. He affirms that, when his guilt had appeared too flagrant and too notorious to be by any arts saved from the justice of an English jury, then, with singular wickedness and folly, had the minister advised his sovereign to insult that jury, and encourage seditious riots, by pardoning, upon frivolous pretexts, a criminal whose profligacy mercy could not be expected to reclaim, and whose punishment would have been a highly salutary example, to command due respect for the king's peace, and due reverence for the laws.

He insinuates, as was then very industriously alleged by the demagogues and agitators of the opposition, that the ministers were not unwilling to encourage riots, and every species of tumultuous licence, in order to procure a pretence for superseding the legal functions of the civil magistracy, by the ordinary employment of a military force to keep the peace. He next examines the reasons alleged for the pardon of M'Quirk, and pronounces them absurdly frivolous. In the close of his letter he makes an eloquent transition to the case of Mr. Wilkes, by which the minds of the public had been deeply interested, and violently agitated. He strives to make the unpopular pardon to M'Quirk still more odious, by contrasting it with the obstinacy with which Government denied the only pardon which the people were greatly solicitous to obtain, and concludes with a fierce accusation of the Duke's private morals and public conduct.—HERON.

———

MY LORD,   March 18, 1769.

BEFORE you were placed at the head of affairs, it had been a maxim of the English Government, not unwillingly admitted by the people, that every ungracious or severe exertion of the prerogative should be placed to the account of the minister; but that whenever an act of grace or benevolence was to be performed, the whole merit of it should be attributed to the Sovereign himself*. It was a wise doctrine, my lord, and equally advantageous to the king and to his subjects; for while it preserved that suspicious attention with which the people ought always to examine the conduct of ministers, it tended at the same time rather to increase than to diminish their attachment to the person of their Sovereign. If there be not a fatality attending every measure you are concerned in, by what treachery or by what excess of folly has it happened,

* Les rois ne se sont réservé que les graces. Ils renvoient les condamnations vers leur officiers. *Montesquieu.*—JUNIUS.

that those ungracious acts which have distinguished your administration, and which I doubt not were entirely your own, should carry with them a strong appearance of personal interest, and even of personal enmity, in a quarter where no such interest or enmity can be supposed to exist without the highest injustice and the highest dishonour? On the other hand, by what judicious management have you contrived it that the only act of mercy to which you ever advised your Sovereign, far from adding to the lustre of a character truly gracious and benevolent, should be received with universal disapprobation and disgust? I shall consider it as a ministerial measure, because it is an odious one, and as your measure, my Lord Duke, because you are the minister.

As long as the trial of this chairman was depending, it was natural enough that Government should give him every possible encouragement and support. The honourable service for which he was hired, and the spirit with which he performed it, made common cause between your Grace and him. The minister who by secret corruption invades the freedom of elections, and the ruffian who by open violence destroys that freedom, are embarked in the same bottom. They have the same interests, and mutually feel for each other. To do justice to your Grace's humanity, you felt for M'Quirk as you ought to do, and if you had been contented to assist him indirectly, without a notorious denial of justice, or openly insulting the sense of the nation, you might have satisfied every duty of political friendship, without committing the honour of your Sovereign, or hazarding the reputation of his government. But when this unhappy man had been solemnly tried, convicted and condemned;—when it appeared that he had been frequently employed in the same services, and that no excuse for him could be drawn either from the innocence of his former life, or the simplicity of his character, was it not hazarding too much to interpose the strength of the prerogative between this felon and the justice of his country*? You ought to

---

* *Whitehall, March* 11, 1769. His Majesty has been graciously pleased to extend his royal mercy to Edward M'Quirk, found guilty of the murder of George Clarke, as appears by his royal warrant, to the tenor following:—
    GEORGE R.
WHEREAS a doubt had arisen in Our Royal breast concerning the evidence of the Death of George Clarke, from the representations of William Bromfield,

have known that an example of this sort was never so neces
sary as at present; and certainly you must have known that
the lot could not have fallen upon a more guilty object
What system of government is this? You are perpetually
complaining of the riotous disposition of the lower class of
people, yet, when the laws have given you the means of making
an example, in every sense unexceptionable, and by far the
most likely to awe the multitude, you pardon the offence, and
are not ashamed to give the sanction of Government to the
riots you complain of, and even to future murders. You are

Esq., surgeon, and Solomon Starling, apothecary; both of whom, as has been
represented to Us, attended the deceased before his death, and expressed
their opinions that he did not die of the blow he received at Brentford:
And whereas it appears to Us, that neither of the said persons were produced
as witnesses upon the trial. though the said Solomon Starling had been examined before the coroner, and the only person called to prove that the death
of the said George Clarke was occasioned by the said blow was John Foot,
surgeon, who never saw the deceased till after his death: We thought fit,
thereupon, to refer the said representations, together with the report of the
Recorder of Our City of London, of the evidence given by Richard and
William Beale, and the said John Foot, on the trial of Edward Quirk, otherwise called Edward Kirk, otherwise called Edward M'Quirk, for the murder
of the said Clarke, to the masters, wardens, and the rest of the court of examiners of the Surgeons' Company, commanding them likewise to take such
further examination of the said persons so representing, and of the said John
Foot, as they might think necessary, together with the premises above-
mentioned, to form and report to Us their opinion, "Whether it did or
did not appear to them that the said George Clarke died in consequence of
the blow he received in the riot at Brentford on the 8th of December last."
And the said court of examiners of the Surgeons' Company having thereupon
reported to us their opinion, "That it did not appear to them that he did;"
We have thought proper to extend Our royal mercy to him the said Edward
Quirk, otherwise Edward Kirk, otherwise called Edward M'Quirk, and to
grant him Our free pardon for the murder of the said George Clarke, of which
he has been found guilty: Our will and pleasure therefore is, That he, the
said Edward Quirk, otherwise called Edward Kirk, otherwise called Edward
M'Quirk, be inserted, for the said murder, in our first and next general
pardon that shall come out for the poor convicts of Newgate, without any
condition whatsoever; and that in the mean time you take bail for his
appearance in order to plead Our said pardon. And for so doing this shall
be your warrant.
    Given at Our court of St. James's, the 10th day of March, 1769, in the
    ninth year of our reign.—By his Majesty's command,
                                      ROCHFORD
To Our trusty and well-beloved James Eyre, Esq., Recorder
    of Our city of London, the Sheriffs of Our said city and
    county of Middlesex. and all others whom it may concern.

partial, perhaps, to the military mode of execution, and had rather see a score of these wretches butchered by the guards, than one of them suffer death by regular course of law *. How does it happen, my Lord, that, in *your* hands, even the mercy of the prerogative is cruelty and oppression to the subject?

The measure, it seems, was so extraordinary that you thought it necessary to give some reasons for it to the public. Let them be fairly examined.

1. You say *that Messrs. Bromfield and Starling were not examined at M'Quirk's trial.* I will tell your Grace why they were not. They must have been examined upon oath ; and it was foreseen, that their evidence would either not benefit, or might be prejudicial to the prisoner. Otherwise, is it conceivable that his counsel should neglect to call in such material evidence?

2. You say that *Mr. Foot did not see the deceased until after his death.* A surgeon, my Lord, must know very little of his profession, if, upon examining a wound or a contusion, he cannot determine whether it was mortal or not. While the party is alive, a surgeon will be cautious of pronouncing : whereas, by the death of the patient, he is enabled to consider both cause and effect in one view, and to speak with a certainty confirmed by experience.

Yet we are to thank your Grace for the establishment of a new tribunal. Your *inquisitio post mortem* is unknown to the laws of England, and does honour to your invention †. The

---

* This subject is farther touched upon in Miscellaneous Letters, No. 24.

† This sentence, in a note to one of the editions of the Letters of Junius, is said to have no correct meaning. "Junius," says the commentator, "thought that he had hit upon a forcible and quaintly allusive expression, hastily used it, and blundered into nonsense in the use." The reader, however, shall now determine whether it is the author or the commentator who has *blundered into nonsense.*

The expression is, in fact, perfectly correct, though liable to be misunderstood without some attention. Every coroner's inquest, indeed, except in the cases of shipwreck and treasure-trove, is, when exercised judicially, an *inquisitio post mortem;* but it can only *legally* take place, *super visum corporis,* "on the sight of the corpse or dead body," on the spot where the death was produced, and by a jury summoned from the neighbourhood. In the instance before us none of these constitutional requisites were attended to ; and Junius might hence remark, with the strictest accuracy, as well as with the keenest irony, " *Your inquisitio post mortem* is unknown to the laws of England."

only material objection to it is, that if Mr. Foot's evidence was insufficient because he did not examine the wound till after the death of the party, much less can a negative opinion, given by gentlemen who never saw the body of Mr. Clarke, either before or after his decease, authorize you to supersede the verdict of a jury, and the sentence of the law.

Now, my Lord, let me ask you, has it never occurred to your Grace, while you were withdrawing this desperate wretch from that justice which the laws had awarded, and which the whole people of England demanded, against him, that there is another man, who is the favourite of his country, whose pardon would have been accepted with gratitude, whose pardon would have healed all our divisions? Have you quite forgotten that this man was once your Grace's friend? Or is it to murderers only that you will extend the mercy of the crown?

These are questions you will not answer. Nor is it necessary. The character of your private life, and the uniform tenor of your public conduct, is an answer to them all.

JUNIUS.

LETTER IX.

TO HIS GRACE THE DUKE OF GRAFTON.

It is easy to see that this letter, like the former, was written chiefly on account of Wilkes. The Duke of Grafton had even lately invited Mr. Wilkes from France, and encouraged him with the hopes of pardon, preferment, and emolument. But Wilkes's demands were so high, and so fixed was still the resentment of the court against him, that the Duke could not fulfil his promise, nor gratify his own wishes. Wilkes believed that he had the public on his side, and would not be made a dupe. He chose rather to encounter the Duke's resentment, than to risk the loss of the public favour. That favour made him representative in parliament for the county of Middlesex. The Ministry procured him to be again expelled from the House of Commons. Again and again he was re-elected. Government had not, when this letter was written, taken the last steps against Wilkes in regard to the Middlesex election. Junius might perhaps hope that his threats and invectives would deter the Duke of Grafton from the contest, and give the victory to "the minion of the multitude."—HERON.

My LORD, April 10, 1769.

I HAVE so good an opinion of your Grace's discernment, that when the author of the vindication of your conduct assures us that he writes from his own mere motion, without the least authority from your Grace*, I should be ready enough to believe him, but for one fatal mark, which seems to be fixed upon every measure, in which either your personal or your political character is concerned. Your first attempt to support Sir William Proctor ended in the election of Mr. Wilkes; the second ensured success to Mr. Glynn. The extraordinary step you took to make Sir James Lowther lord paramount of Cumberland has ruined his interest in that county for ever†. The House List of Directors was cursed with the concurrence of government‡; and even the miserable Dingley could not escape the misfortune of your Grace's protection §. With this uniform experience before us, we are authorized to suspect that when a pretended vindication of your principles and conduct in reality contains the bitterest reflections upon both, it could not have been written without your immediate direction and assistance. The author, indeed, calls God to witness for him, with all the sincerity, and in the very terms of an Irish evidence, *to the best of his knowledge and belief.* My Lord, you should not encourage these appeals to heaven. The pious prince, from whom you are supposed to descend. made such frequent use of them in his public declarations, that at last the people also found it necessary to appeal to heaven in their turn. Your administration has driven us into circumstances of equal distress; —— beware at least how you remind us of the remedy.

You have already much to answer for. You have provoked this unhappy gentleman to play the fool once more in public life, in spite of his years and infirmities, and to show us that,

---

* He alludes to a pamphlet containing a long and laboured vindication of the Duke of Grafton, attributed to the pen of Mr. Edward Weston, writer of the Gazette.

† See note upon the *Nullum Tempus* bill, Junius, No. 5, in which the contest between Sir James Lowther and the Duke of Portland is detailed at large.

‡ At this period the whole four and twenty directors were annually chosen, and ten gentlemen, whose names were not inserted in the house list, were elected, notwithstanding the influence of government was exerted in its support.

§ This unfortunate person had been persuaded by the Duke of Grafton to set up for Middlesex, his Grace being determined to seat him in the House of Commons if he had but a single vote. It happened unluckily that he could not prevail upon any one freeholder to put him in nomination, and it was with difficulty he escaped out of the hands of the populace.—JUNIUS.

as you yourself are a singular instance of youth without spirit, the man who defends you is a no less remarkable example of age without the benefit of experience. To follow such a writer minutely would, like his own periods, be a labour without end. The subject too has been already discussed, and is sufficiently understood. I cannot help observing, however, that, when the pardon of Mac Quirk was the principal charge against you, it would have been but a decent compliment to your Grace's understanding to have defended you upon your own principles. What credit does a man deserve, who tells us plainly that the facts set forth in the king's proclamation were not the true motives on which the pardon was granted, and that he wishes that those chirurgical reports, which first gave occasion to certain doubts in the royal breast, had not been laid before his majesty? You see, my Lord, that even your friends cannot defend your actions without changing your principles, nor justify a deliberate measure of government without contradicting the main assertion on which it was founded.

The conviction of Mac Quirk had reduced you to a dilemma in which it was hardly possible for you to reconcile your political interest with your duty. You were obliged either to abandon an active useful partisan, or to protect a felon from public justice. With your usual spirit, you preferred your interest to every other consideration; and, with your usual judgment, you founded your determination upon the only motives which should not have been given to the public.

I have frequently censured Mr. Wilkes's conduct, yet your advocate reproaches me with having devoted myself to the service of sedition. Your Grace can best inform us for which of Mr. Wilkes's good qualities you first honoured him with your friendship, or how long it was before you discovered those bad ones in him at which, it seems, your delicacy was offended. Remember, my Lord, that you continued your connection with Mr. Wilkes long after he had been convicted of those crimes which you have since taken pains to represent in the blackest colours of blasphemy and treason. How unlucky is it that the first instance you have given us of a scrupulous regard to decorum is united with the breach of a moral obligation! For my own part, my Lord, I am proud to affirm that, if I had been weak enough to form such a friendship, I would never have been base enough to betray it. But, let Mr. Wilkes's character be what it may, this at least is certain, that, circumstanced as he is with regard to the public, even his vices plead for him. The people of England have too much discernment to suffer your Grace to take advantage of the failings of a private character, to establish a precedent by which the public liberty is affected, and which you may hereafter, with equal ease and satisfaction, employ to the ruin of the best of men in the kingdom. Content yourself, my Lord, with the many advantages which the unsullied purity of your own character has given you over your unhappy, deserted friend. Avail yourself of all the unforgiving piety of the court you live in, and bless God that "you are not as other men are; extortioners, unjust, adulterers, or even as this publican."* In a heart void of feeling, the laws of honour and good faith may be violated with impunity, and there you may safely indulge your genius. But the laws of England shall not be violated, even by your *holy zeal to oppress a sinner*, and though you have succeeded in making him the tool, you shall not make him the victim, of your ambition

JUNIUS.

LETTER X.

TO MR. EDWARD WESTON

SIR,   April 21, 1769.

I SAID you were an old man without the benefit of experience. It seems you are also a volunteer with a stipend of twenty commissions†; and at a period when all prospects are at an

---

* This is one of those frequent occasions on which Junius discovers his intimate acquaintance with the Bible, and his want of reverence for the Holy Scriptures.—ED.

† Under the presumption that the pamphlet alluded to in the preceding letter, entitled a " Vindication of the Duke of Grafton," was written by Mr. Weston, and which was avowedly defended by the author, whoever he was, in the *Public Advertiser* under the signature of a " Volunteer in the Government's Service," the following short letter, addressed to that gentleman, *obviously from the pen of Junius*, appeared in the same paper.

TO THE RIGHT HON. EDWARD WESTON.

SIR,   *April* 20, 1769.

YOUR age, though oppressed with bodily and mental infirmities, which, for the world's edification, you have published to it, demands some respect, or the cause you have embarked in would entitle you to none. The last glim-merings of your expiring taper, however, do your hero no honour; and *I*

end, you are still looking forward to rewards which you cannot enjoy. No man is better acquainted with the bounty of
government than you are

> —— " ton impudence,
> Téméraire vieillard, aura sa récompense."*

fear the principle that has kindled it obtains you no credit. You are a privy
counsellor in Ireland, writer of the Gazette, comptroller of the salt-office, a
clerk of the signet, and a pensioner on the Irish establishment: such is the
Volunteer! And you may remember, when you were under secretary of
state, the division of 500*l.* among ten people, left to your discretion, of which
you *modestly* claimed 400*l.* for yourself. So honest, so upright, and so disinterested, is the *man!* Let Junius be the *dirty rascal* you call him, I
know, you know, and all the world knows, *what* you *are.*—CRITO.

This letter produced a short reply from the *Volunteer*, in which he denies
that Mr. Weston is the author of the pamphlet, or of the letter under that
signature; and one from *Poetikastos*, who attacks Junius in the following
words:—

" You conclude your despicable vindication of an honour which you do not
possess, by asserting 'that you are a master in the art of representing the
treachery of the minister, and the abused simplicity of a ———.' Villain!
of whom? You, who write under the name of Junius, are a base scoundrel.
You lie; and you may find out who gives you the lie."

These letters occasioned the under-written answer:—

TO THE RIGHT HON. EDWARD WESTON.

April 27, 1769.

THE old fox has been unkennelled, but is ashamed of his stinking tail. Either
several people of intelligence and consideration have been grossly deceived,
or our doughty *Volunteer* declares upon *his honour* an untruth. I cannot
believe a misinformation, unless the world should have thought that no
impertinent, expectant old fellow could have been found to despatch so lame
an errand but you.

You seem ashamed of your generous distribution: I applaud your modesty!
but it shall not be at the expense of truth. You did claim 400*l.* out of 500*l.*
for your own self; and there are, I suppose, at least half a dozen people who
can attest it. And you shall find that I dare say something else to your
mortification, if you suppose the world is not heartily tired of you, your petulance, and your crudities.

I don't believe the governors of Bedlam indulge their patients with newspapers, or I should have supposed that *Poetikastos* had obtained his genteel
residence there. The poor raving creature bawls aloud for swords and
pistols, and requires the *last* argument instead of the *best*. The public has
pronounced upon his reason the judgment of *Felo de se*, from his own pen;—
I am so impressed with humanity as to wish the coroner may not have the
trouble of passing the same sentence upon his person from his sword. I
should, however, pity the elegant Junius, who well deserves the thanks of
the independent public, if he was obliged to take notice of every fool,
sycophant, and bully.—CRITO.

* A quotation from Corneille. aptly introduced.—ED.

L

But I will not descend to an altercation either with the impotence of your age, or the peevishness of your diseases. Your pamphlet†, ingenious as it is, has been so little read, that the public cannot know how far you have a right to give me the lie, without the following citation of your own words.

Page 6—' 1. That he is persuaded that the motives which he (Mr. Weston) has alleged must appear fully sufficient, with or without the opinions of the surgeons.

' 2. That those very motives MUST HAVE BEEN the foundation on which the Earl of Rochford thought proper, &c.

' 3. That he CANNOT BUT REGRET that the Earl of Rochford seems to have thought proper to lay the chirurgical reports before the king in preference to all the other sufficient motives,' &c.

Let the public determine whether this be defending government on their principles or your own.

The style and language you have adopted are, I confess, not ill suited to the elegance of your own manners, or to the dignity of the cause you have undertaken. Every common dauber writes rascal and villain under his pictures, because the pictures themselves have neither character nor resemblance. But the works of a master require no index. His features and colouring are taken from nature. The impression they make is immediate and uniform; nor is it possible to mistake his characters, whether they represent the treachery of a minister, or the abused simplicity of a king.

-JUNIUS.

† It is possible Junius, though his information was generally accurate, was incorrect in attributing this pamphlet to Mr. Weston. For, in a letter inserted by Mr. Weston in the *Public Advertiser*, a few months afterwards, October 14, he solemnly denies his having written this and a variety of pamphlets and letters attributed to him[1].

---

[1] The letter of Junius to Mr. Weston, and the letters of *Crito*, which the editor of Woodfall's edition, on not very conclusive testimony, has ascribed to him, with their rejoinders, are curious specimens of the unlicensed range of virulence and insinuation then allowed in political controversy. In the "Works of Peter Porcupine" effusions may be met with, equalling in abuse, bitterness, and unwarranted assumptions, those of the time of Junius; but such communications, with rare exceptions, would be promptly rejected by the present newspaper press.—ED.

LETTER XI.

TO HIS GRACE THE DUKE OF GRAFTON *.

MY LORD,   April 24, 1769.

THE system you seemed to have adopted when Lord Chatham unexpectedly left you at the head of affairs gave us no pro-mise of that uncommon exertion of vigour, which has since illustrated your character, and distinguished your administra-tion.   Far from discovering a spirit bold enough to invade the first rights of the people, and the first principles of the con-stitution, you were scrupulous of exercising even those powers, with which the executive branch of the legislature is legally invested.   We have not yet forgotten how long Mr. Wilkes was suffered to appear at large, nor how long he was at liberty to canvass for the city † and county, with all the terrors of an outlawry hanging over him ‡.   Our gracious sovereign has not yet forgotten the extraordinary care you took of his dignity and of the safety of his person, when at a crisis which courtiers affected to call alarming, you left the metropolis exposed for two nights together to every species of riot and dis-order.   The security of the royal residence from insult was then

* Upon the whole, this letter is a skilful and eloquent composition.   Its main object is to alarm and confound the minister, to rouse the indignation of the people, and to open the batteries of argument against the decision of the House of Commons in favour of Luttrell's election for Middlesex.—ED.

† Prior to his offering himself for the county of Middlesex, Wilkes had become a candidate for the metropolis, and it was in consequence of his failure in the city that he pressed forward to the county.   The populace, in both cases, were so numerously and so violently attached to him that many serious riots were the consequence ; and so outrageous were they in two or three instances, that the court party strenuously asserted that the city, and even the palace itself, were not free from danger.   Of these riots, the two most serious that occurred were—on the meeting of parliament, when the populace surrounded the King's Bench prison from an expectation of seeing Wilkes, who had then been elected member for Middlesex, liberated in order to take his seat in the senate, in the course of which several persons were killed by the firing of the military ; and on the counter-address to that of the city being carried to St. James's by those who were deputed for this purpose ; on which last occasion the riot act was read at the palace gate, and Lord Talbot, the lord-steward, had his staff of office broken in his hand.

‡ See APPENDIX, p. 478, for Lord Mansfield's admirable address on the reversal of the outlawry of Wilkes.—ED.

L 2

sufficiently provided for in Mr. Conway's firmness * and Lord
Weymouth's discretion; while the prime minister of Great
Britain, in a rural retirement, and in the arms of *faded beauty*†,
had lost all memory of his sovereign, his country and himself.
In these instances you might have acted with vigour, for you
would have had the sanction of the laws to support you.   The
friends of government might have defended you without
shame, and moderate men, who wish well to the peace and
good order of society, might have had a pretence for applaud-
ing your conduct.   But these, it seems, were not occasions
worthy of your Grace's interposition.   You reserved the proofs
of your intrepid spirit for trials of greater hazard and importance; and now, as if the most disgraceful relaxation of the
executive authority had given you a claim of credit to indulge
in excesses still more dangerous, you seem determined to
compensate amply for your former negligence, and to balance
the non-execution of the laws with a breach of the constitution.   From one extreme you suddenly start to the other,
without leaving, between the weakness and the fury of the
passions, one moment's interval for the firmness of the understanding.

These observations, general as they are, might easily be
extended into a faithful history of your Grace's administration,
and perhaps may be the employment of a future hour.   But

---

* The Hon. Henry Seymour Conway was brother to Lord Hertford, and
father of the late Mrs. Damer, who constituted, indeed, his only issue.   He
had enjoyed several places of high rank and confidence at court during the
beginning of his Majesty's reign.   After the prorogation of parliament, in the
year 1764, G. Grenville, then first lord of the treasury and chancellor of the
exchequer, in conjunction with the Duke of Bedford, lord president, took
from him his regiment, and dismissed him from his office as groom of the
bed-chamber to the King, in consequence of having voted, in the lower house,
in opposition to government, upon the question of *general warrants*.   Mr.
Conway was made a secretary of state in the Rockingham administration of
1765, and retained that post till Lord Chatham, who succeeded Lord Rockingham, quitted office in October 1768.   Mr. Conway was a man of an
independent mind, but often wavering in opinions, and, like his favourite
cousin, Horace Walpole, much attached to literature and the fine arts.

† The celebrated Nancy Parsons, afterwards Lady Maynard.   Unfortunate
in his first marriage, the Duke was now living in celibacy, and kept a
mistress, who, it appears, had been lovelier in the eyes of Junius when
younger; but this could be no heinous political crime in his Grace, rather his
private misfortune.—ED.

the business of the present moment will not suffer me to look back to a series of events, which cease to be interesting or important, because they are succeeded by a measure so singu larly daring that it excites all our attention, and engrosses all our resentment.

Your patronage of Mr Luttrell has been crowned with success *. With this precedent before you, with the principles on which it was established, and with a future House of

* In the contest for the county of Middlesex, the House of Commons, on the 3rd of February, 1769, had proceeded to the severe step of expelling Mr. Wilkes for, among other offences, republishing in the St. James's Chronicle Lord Weymouth's letter to Mr. Justice Ponton, one of the magistrates for Surrey, with the ensuing prefatory remarks: "I send you the following authentic state paper, the date of which, prior by more than three weeks to the fatal 10th of May, 1768, shows how long the horrid massacre in St. George's Fields had been planned and determined upon before it was carried into execution, and how long a hellish project can be brooded over by some infernal spirits without one moment's remorse." Mr. Wilkes having admitted the publication, the house resolved "That John Wilkes, Esq., a member of this house, who hath, at the bar of this house, confessed himself to be the author and publisher of what this house has resolved to be an insolent, scandalous, and seditious libel; and who has been convicted in the Court of King's Bench of having printed and published a seditious libel, and three obscene and impious libels; and, by the judgment of the said court, has been sentenced to undergo twenty-two months' imprisonment, and is now in execution under the said judgment, be expelled this house;" which was carried in the affirmative by 219 against 137. On the 16th of February, 1769, he was a second time returned for Middlesex without opposition. On the day following the election was vacated, and he was declared by a majority of the house incapable of being elected into that parliament. Notwithstanding this resolution of the house he was a third time, March 10, elected without opposition; for Dingley, as before observed, had not been able to obtain even a nomination. This election, however, was also declared void the next day. The great mass of Middlesex freeholders were, in consequence, thrown into a more violent commotion than ever, and insisted upon their right to return whomsoever they pleased, let parliament expel him as often as it pleased. Wilkes was a third time expelled; and, to oppose him with a certainty of success, another device was now contrived; and, under the promise that he should certainly be seated for the county in opposition to Wilkes, Colonel Luttrell was prevailed upon to relinquish the seat he then held, and to oppose him with all the force that could be mustered up on the occasion. With every possible effort exerted in his favour, however, Luttrell was incapable of obtaining more than two hundred and ninety-six votes, and Wilkes was again returned *almost* unanimously. The ministry were intimidated; but still resolved to carry their new device into effect. Wilkes was not now, therefore, to be openly re-expelled; but, which amounted to the same thing, to be declared incapable of sitting in parliament in consequence of his previous expulsion, and Luttrell was of course declared

Commons, perhaps less virtuous than the present, every county in England, under the auspices of the treasury, may be represented as completely as the county of Middlesex. Posterity will be indebted to your Grace for not contenting yourself with a temporary expedient, but entailing upon them the immediate blessings of your administration. Boroughs were already too much at the mercy of government. Counties could neither be purchased nor intimidated. But their solemn determined election may be rejected, and the man they detest may be appointed, by another choice, to represent them in parliament. Yet it is admitted, that the sheriffs obeyed the laws and performed their duty *. The return they made must have been legal and valid, or undoubtedly they would have been censured for making it. With every good-natured allowance for your Grace's youth and inexperience, there are some things which you cannot but know. You cannot but know that the right of the freeholders to adhere to their choice (even supposing it improperly exerted) was as clear and indisputable as that of the House of Commons to exclude one of their own members:—nor is it possible for you not to see the wide distance there is between the negative power of rejecting one man, and the positive power of appointing another. The right of expulsion, in the most favourable sense, is no more than the custom of parliament. The right of election is the very essence of the constitution. To violate that right, and much more to transfer it to any other set of men, is a step leading immediately to the dissolution of all government. So far forth as it operates, it constitutes a House of Commons which *does not* represent the people. A House of Commons

the sitting member. Yet, with an incongruity not often to be paralleled, the sheriffs, instead of being punished, were admitted to have done their duty in allowing Wilkes to have become a candidate, and in returning him as fairly elected.

The nation at large now joined in the cause of the Middlesex freeholders; the parliament from exercising the unconstitutional act of rejecting one person who was a real member of its body, without an adequate cause, and in admitting another person to be a member who had never been returned by a majority of votes, was declared to have passed into a state of political incapacity, every vote and act of which must necessarily be incompetent and illegislative and the throne was thronged with petitions and remonstrances from every part of the kingdom, beseeching his Majesty to dissolve it.

* Sir Fletcher Norton, when it was proposed to punish the sheriffs, declared in the House of Commons. that they, in returning Mr. Wilkes, had done no more than their duty.- JUNIUS.

so formed would involve a contradiction and the grossest confusion of ideas; but there are some ministers, my Lord, whose
views can only be answered by reconciling absurdities, and
making the same proposition which is false and absurd in
argument, true in fact.

This measure, my Lord, is, however attended with one consequence favourable to the people which I am persuaded you
did not foresee *. While the contest lay between the ministry
and Mr. Wilkes, his situation and private character gave you
advantages over him, which common candour, if not the
memory of your former friendship, should have forbidden you
to make use of. To religious men you had an opportunity
of exaggerating the irregularities of his past life;—to moderate men you held forth the pernicious consequences of
faction. Men who, with this character, looked no farther
than to the object before them, were not dissatisfied at seeing
Mr. Wilkes excluded from parliament. You have now taken
care to shift the question; or, rather, you have created a new
one, in which Mr. Wilkes is no more concerned than any
other English gentleman. You have united this country
against you on one grand constitutional point, on the decision
of which our existence as a free people absolutely depends.
You have asserted, not in words but in fact, that representation
in parliament does not depend upon the choice of the freeholders. If such a case can possibly happen once, it may
happen frequently;—it may happen always;—and if three
hundred votes, by any mode of reasoning whatsoever, can
prevail against twelve hundred, the same reasoning would
equally have given Mr. Luttrell his seat with ten votes, or
even with one. The consequences of this attack upon the
constitution are too plain and palpable not to alarm the dullest
apprehension. I trust you will find that the people of England are neither deficient in spirit nor understanding, though
you have treated them as if they had neither sense to feel, nor
spirit to resent. We have reason to thank God and our ancestors, that there never yet was a minister in this country
who could stand the issue of such a conflict; and, with every
prejudice in favour of your intentions, I see no such abilities
in your Grace as should entitle you to succeed in an enterprise, in which the ablest and basest of your predecessors have
found their destruction. You may continue to deceive your

* The reader is desired to mark this prophecy.—JUNIUS.

gracious master with false representations of the temper and
condition of his subjects—you may command a venal vote,
because it is the common established appendage of your office
—but never hope that the freeholders will make a tame sur
render of their rights, or that an English army will join with
you in overturning the liberties of their country. They know
that their first duty as citizens is paramount to all subsequent engagements, nor will they prefer the discipline, not
even the honours, of their profession to those sacred original
rights which belonged to them before they were soldiers,
and which they claim and possess as the birthright of Englishmen.

Return, my Lord, before it be too late, to that easy insipid
system which you first set out with. Take back your mistress *;
—the name of friend may be fatal to her, for it leads to

---

* The Duke, about this time, had separated himself from Ann Parsons,
but proposed to continue united with her on some Platonic terms of friendship,
which she rejected with contempt. His baseness to this woman is beyond
description or belief.—JUNIUS [1].

---

[1] It was the avowed principle of the writer of these letters never to spare
the man whose measures were to be condemned; but ever to mingle the
abuse of private character with the vehement disapprobation of public conduct. When a minister or adversary of any sort was to be *written down,*
Junius thought that no sort of opprobrium against him ought to be spared
that could contribute to this effect. While the *morality* of this principle is
to be condemned, its policy, in the present state of society, may be approved.
An opposition that affects too much candour towards 'its adversaries must
always be feeble and inefficient. But the use of *opprobria* against a political
opponent may be carried to excess; if harsh epithets or malicious hints
be repeated till they lose their first lively effect on the mind, the intended
result is then directly counteracted, and the abuse is not less injudicious than
unjust. Junius, vehement in spirit, and proud of his talents for obloquy and
invective, appears to have occasionally run into this error; and, perhaps, in
no instance more strikingly than in his frequent allusions, both in this and
his next address, to the liaison between the minister and Miss Parsons. We
have before us in MS. some verses on the subject, which show that the elegant
Junius could even descend to gross ribaldry, in the pursuit of his object.
The verses are headed " *Harry and Nan, an Elegy in the manner of
Tibullus.*" Excepting the first verse, which we subjoin, they are unfit for pub
lication.
> " Can Apollo resist, or a Poet refuse,
> When Harry and Nancy solicit the Muse;
> A statesman who makes the whole nation his care,
> And a nymph who is almost as chaste as she's fair."

The hand-writing is undoubtedly that of Junius.—ED.

treachery and persecution. Indulge the people Attend New-market. Mr. Luttrell may again vacate his seat; and Mr. Wilkes, if not persecuted, will soon be forgotten. To be weak and inactive is safer than to be daring and criminal; and wide is the distance between a riot of the populace and a convulsion of the whole kingdom. You may live to make the experiment, but no honest man can wish you should survive it.

JUNIUS.

LETTER XII.

TO HIS GRACE THE DUKE OF GRAFTON.

The former letters from Junius to the Duke of Grafton, whatever pain they might have given his Grace, had produced no alteration in his public conduct. Mr. Luttrell still sat in the House of Commons, as one of the re-presentatives for the county of Middlesex. Mr. Wilkes was not freed from the effects of the prosecution against him; those vigorous measures were not relaxed which government had, at length, resolutely adopted for the suppres-sion of the riots which had long triumphed in the metropolis. Neither did it appear that the duke had either lost the confidence of his sovereign, or himself wavered as to his intention of remaining in office. He was even strengthened in power by an alliance of marriage which might seem to unite him with the family and the party of the Duke of Bedford. Yet the power of Junius over public opinion was, in the mean time, greatly increased, and he was already regarded as the most formidable of the foes of the Ministry, the ablest of the allies of the opposition. He determined, therefore, to try what might be done by one general letter of satire upon the whole conduct and character of the first minister, both in public and in private life. To command new admiration of his inculpatory eloquence, to render the Duke of Grafton, if possible, odious and contemptible in the judgment of all parties, and make him shrink from the responsibility of ministerial office, were evidently the objects at which Junius, in this letter, aimed. The boldness of his address, the art with which the intermixture of truth in it is made to lend new credibility to falsehood, its wit, its elegance, its vehemence, the secret anecdotes which it brought into light, and the able discernment of political expediencies which it exhibits, gave it an influence inconceivably great on the minds of those to whom it was addressed. Political letters in newspapers, it is essential to observe, were far more attentively read when Junius wrote than at present, because the proceedings of Parliament had not yet begun to be regularly pub-lished; nor had the public journals so generally a regular and paid body of contributors, to whom is exclusively entrusted their leading commentaries on public men and measures.

MY LORD, May 30, 1769.

IF the measures in which you have been most successful had been supported by any tolerable appearance of argument, I should have thought my time not ill employed in continuing to examine your conduct as a minister, and stating it fairly to the public. But when I see questions, of the highest national importance, carried as they have been, and the first principles of the constitution openly violated without argument or decency, I confess I give up the cause in despair. The meanest of your predecessors had abilities sufficient to give a colour to their measures. If they invaded the rights of the people, they did not dare to offer a direct insult to their understanding; and, in former times, the most venal parliaments made it a condition, in their bargain with the minister, that he should furnish them with some plausible pretences for selling their country and themselves. You have had the merit of introducing a more compendious system of government and logic. You neither address yourself to the passions nor to the understanding, but simply to the touch. You apply yourself immediately to the feelings of your friends who, contrary to the forms of parliament, never enter heartily into a debate until they have divided.

Relinquishing, therefore, all idle views of amendment to your Grace, or of benefit to the public, let me be permitted to consider your character and conduct merely as a subject of curious speculation. There is something in both, which distinguishes you not only from all other ministers, but all other men. It is not that you do wrong by design, but that you should never do right by mistake. It is not that your indolence and your activity have been equally misapplied, but that the first uniform principle, or, if I may so call it, the genius of your life, should have carried you through every possible change and contradiction of conduct without the momentary imputation or colour of a virtue, and that the wildest spirit of inconsistency should never once have betrayed you into a wise or honourable action. This, I own, gives an air of singularity to your fortune, as well as to your disposition. Let us look back together to a scene in which a mind like yours will find nothing to repent of. Let us try, my Lord, how well you have supported the various relations in which you stood, to your sovereign, your country, your friends, and yourself. Give us, if it be possible, some excuse to posterity, and to ourselves, for submitting to your administration. If not the abilities of a great minister, if not the integrity of a patriot, or the fidelity of a friend, show us, at least, the firmness of a man. For the sake of your mistress, the lover shall be spared. I will not lead her into public as you have done, nor will I insult the memory of departed beauty. Her sex, which alone made her amiable in your eyes, makes her respectable in mine.

The character of the reputed ancestors of some men has made it possible for their descendants to be vicious in the extreme without being degenerate. Those of your Grace, for instance, left no distressing examples of virtue even to their legitimate posterity, and you may look back with pleasure to an illustrious pedigree in which heraldry has not left a single good quality upon record to insult or upbraid you *. You have better proofs of your descent, my Lord, than the register of a marriage, or any troublesome inheritance of reputation. There are some hereditary strokes of character by which a family may be as clearly distinguished as by the blackest features of the human face. Charles the First lived and died a hypocrite. Charles the Second was a hypocrite of another sort, and should have died upon the same scaffold. At the distance of a century we see their different characters happily revived and blended in your Grace. Sullen and severe without religion, profligate without gaiety, you live like Charles II. without being an amiable companion, and, for aught I know, may die as his father did without the reputation of a martyr.

You had already taken your degrees with credit in those schools in which the English nobility are formed to virtue when you were introduced to Lord Chatham's protection †.

* The first Duke of Grafton, as most persons know, was a natural son of Charles II. During the progress of the revolution he abandoned the Stuarts for King William, and his descendants had hitherto generally ranked themselves among the party of the Whigs.

† To understand these passages, Junius, in a note, refers the reader to a *Defence of the late Minority*. This pamphlet was written by Charles Townsend, a grandson of Lord Townsend, and brother-in-law of Sir Robert Walpole, the famous minister. Mr. Hume, in a letter to Adam Smith, speaks of Townsend as "the cleverest fellow in England." He was so charmed with the perusal of Smith's *Theory of Moral Sentiments* that he immediately resolved to honour himself by the patronage of the author. Having married the Countess Dowager of Dalkeith, mother to a former Duke of Buccleugh, he had, by consequence, considerable authority in the direction of that young nobleman's education. He invited Mr. Smith from the University of Glas-

From Newmarket, White's, and the Opposition, he gave you
to the world with an air of popularity which young men
usually set out with and seldom preserve—grave and plausible enough to be thought fit for business, too young for
treachery, and, in short, a patriot of no unpromising expecta
tions.   Lord Chatham was the earliest object of your political
wonder and attachment *.   Yet you deserted him upon the
first hopes that offered of an equal share of power with Lord
Rockingham.   When the Duke of Cumberland's first negotiation failed, and when the favourite was pushed to the last
extremity, you saved him, by joining with an administration
in which Lord Chatham had refused to engage.   Still, however, he was your friend, and you are yet to explain to the
world, why you consented to act without him, or why, after
uniting with Lord Rockingham, you deserted and betrayed
him.   You complained that no measures were taken to satisfy
your patron, and that your friend, Mr. Wilkes, who had suffered so much for the party, had been abandoned to his fate.
They have since contributed not a little to your present
plenitude of power; yet I think Lord Chatham has less

gow to accompany the Duke on his travels, upon conditions which assured
to the author of the *Wealth of Nations* an ample independence for his future
life.   Townsend was honoured with a noble encomium by Burke, and his
premature death appears to have been as much regretted as that of the late
lamented Charles Butler, whom he seems to have resembled.—ED.

   * The Duke of Grafton was first introduced into the political world at an
early period of life, under the auspices and protection of Mr. Pitt, as a determined Whig.   To the administration of Lord Bute succeeded that of G.
Grenville and the Duke of Bedford, who soon became obnoxious to Lord Bute,
the guardian of his Majesty's non-age, and confidential adviser.   The Duke
of Cumberland, uncle to the king, was deputed to propose another administration conjointly to Mr. Pitt, Lord Temple, and Lord Lyttleton.   They, however, objected to the undue influence of the noble favourite, and the proposal
was declined. Lord Rockingham was now applied to, and prevailed upon to take
the lead, and form an administration of his own; Mr. Pitt refused to unite
in it, but the Duke of Grafton deserted him, and accepted the office of secretary of state.   With this administration, however, he soon became chagrined,
and resigned his office.   Lord Chatham again received him into communion,
and in the ministry, shortly after planned and carried into effect by himself,
in which he held the privy seal, he nominated the Duke of Grafton First
Lord of the Treasury.   At the head of this new system, however, Lord
Chatham did not long continue— he withdrew in disgust; but the noble duke,
instead of following him, took the lead upon himself, and commenced an administration of his own.

reason than ever to ue satisfied ; and as for Mr. Wilkes, it is, perhaps, the greatest misfortune of his life, that you should have so many compensations to make in the closet for your former friendship with him. Your gracious master understands your character, and makes you a persecutor, because you have been a friend.

Lord Chatham formed his last administration upon principles which you certainly concurred in, or you could never have been placed at the head of the treasury. By deserting those principles, and by acting in direct contradiction to them, in which he found you were secretly supported in the closet, you soon forced him to leave you to yourself, and to withdraw his name from an administration which had been formed on the credit of it. You had then a prospect of friendships better suited to your genius and more likely to fix your disposition. Marriage is the point on which every rake is stationary at last ; and truly, my Lord, you may well be weary of the circuit you have taken, for you have now fairly travelled through every sign in the political zodiac, from the Scorpion, in which you stung Lord Chatham, to the hopes of a Virgin * in the house of Bloomsbury. One would think that you had had sufficient experience of the frailty of nuptial engagements, or, at least, that such a friendship as the Duke of Bedford's might have been secured to you by the auspicious marriage of your late Duchess with † his nephew. But ties of this tender nature cannot be drawn too close ; and it may, possibly, be a part of the Duke of Bedford's ambition, after making *her* an honest woman, to work a miracle of the same sort upon your Grace. This worthy nobleman has long dealt in virtue. There has been a large consumption of it in his own family; and, in the way of traffic, I dare say he has bought and sold more than half the representative integrity of the nation.

In a political view this union is not imprudent. The favour of princes is a perishable commodity. You have now a strength sufficient to command the closet ; and, if it be necessary to betray one friendship more, you may set even Lord Bute at defiance   Mr. Stuart Mackenzie may possibly

* His Grace had lately married Miss Wrottesley, niece of the Good Gertrude, Duchess of Bedford.—JUNIUS.

† Miss Liddel, after her divorce from the Duke, married Lord Upper Ossory.—JUNIUS.

remember what use the Duke of Bedford usually makes of
his power *; and our gracious sovereign, I doubt not, rejoices
at this first appearance of union among his servants. His
late majesty, under the happy influence of a family connection between his ministers, was relieved from the cares of
government. A more active prince may perhaps observe
with suspicion by what degrees an artful servant grows upon
his master, from the first unlimited professions of duty and
attachment to the painful representation of the necessity of the
royal service, and soon, in regular progression, to the humble
insolence of dictating in all the obsequious forms of peremptory submission. The interval is carefully employed in forming connections, creating interests, collecting a party, and
laying the foundation of double marriages †; until the deluded prince who thought he had found a creature prostituted
to his service, and insignificant enough to be always dependent upon his pleasure, finds him at last too strong to be commanded and too formidable to be removed.

Your Grace's public conduct as a minister is but the
counterpart of your private history;—the same inconsistency,
the same contradictions. In America we trace you from the
first opposition to the Stamp Act ‡ on principles of convenience, to Mr. Pitt's surrender of the right; then forward to

* Mr. Stuart Mackenzie was brother to the Earl of Bute. The Duke of
Bedford's abuse of power here referred to is again noticed in Junius, Letter
No. 36, and consisted in compelling the king to displace Mr. Mackenzie from
the office of lord privy seal of Scotland, shortly after his appointment, in
favour of Lord Frederick Campbell. In this act of coercion Mr. Grenville
bore an equal part with the noble duke. Upon the resignation of these
ministers, Mr. Stuart Mackenzie was reinstated in his former post.

† These double marriages, which Junius gloats over with remorseless
satire, have been partly explained already; they were the marriages of
the Duke of Grafton with the niece of the Duchess of Bedford, and of the
lady whom he had divorced for infidelity, with her paramour, the nephew
of the Duke. The last has not been without imitations in high circles in
more recent times, and, if not adequate compensation in such unfortunate con-
nexions, is the best proof that can be afforded by the transgressors of the sincerity of their preferences.—ED.

‡ At the period here referred to, the American colonies had acquired such
a population and proportion of public wealth, as to render it necessary to inquire more critically than had hitherto been done into the peculiar mode of
its political connection with the mother country, and to bind it to the latter
in a more definite bond. It was found that most of the provincial departments were chartered by the crown and expressly exempted from legislative
taxation, but that others were not chartered in any way, and of course pos-

Lord Rockingham's surrender of the fact; then back again to
Lord Rockingham's declaration of the right; then forward to
taxation with Mr. Townshend; and, in the last instance, from
the gentle Conway's undetermined discretion to blood and
compulsion with the Duke of Bedford *. Yet, if we may
believe the simplicity of Lord North's eloquence, at the open
ing of next session you are once more to be the patron of
America. Is this the wisdom of a great minister? or is it
the ominous vibration of a pendulum? Had you no opinion
of your own, my Lord? or was it the gratification of betraying every party with which you have been united, and of
deserting every political principle in which you had concurred?
   Your enemies may turn their eyes without regret from this
admirable system of provincial government. They will find

sessed no such privilege. From the capacity of their being now able to contribute to the exigencies of the state, from a desire to equalize the entire
colonisation, and from a professed belief that charters granted by the crown
with such an exemption as above, displayed an undue stretch of the prerogative, it was determined upon, by Mr. Grenville's administration, to bring the
matter boldly to an issue, and for the legislature to claim an authority over
the colonies by passing an act which should immediately affect them. The
statute enacted for this purpose was the *Stamp Act*, which imposed a duty
upon many of the articles most current through the colonies. The colonies
were thrown into a general commotion by this measure, the duty could not
be collected, and almost every province became ripe for rebellion.
   At home the members of opposition doubted, or affected to doubt, both the
propriety and legality of the conduct of administration. Mr. Pitt denied
the *right*, the Marquis of Rockingham admitted the right, but denied the
expediency, while many politicians, perplexed by the sophistry advanced by
the pleaders on all sides, vacillated in their opinion, and sometimes united
with one party and sometimes with another. Of this last description was the
Duke of Grafton, who occasionally favoured Mr. Pitt's opinion, occasionally the
Marquis of Rockingham's, and at last sided with Mr. Charles Townshend in a
determined resolution to carry the sytsem of taxation into effect at all hazards.
   * Mr. Knox, in his "Extra Official State Papers," narrates the following
anecdote as having happened to himself on the repeal of the Stamp Act:—
"The morning after the resolution passed in the House of Commons to repeal the Stamp Act and to bring in the declaratory bill, I was sent for to a
meeting of the Opposition at Mr. Rigby's in Parliament Street; when I came
there Mr. Grenville and Mr. Rigby came out to me, and told me the Duke
of Bedford and several others desired to know my opinion of the effects which
those resolutions would produce in America. My answer was in a few words
—*addresses of thanks and measures of rebellion.* Mr. Grenville smiled and
shook his head, and Mr. Rigby swore by G— he thought so, and both
wished me a good morning."

gratification enough in the survey of your domestic and foreign policy.

If, instead of disowning Lord Shelburne, the British court had interposed with dignity and firmness, you know, my Lord, that Corsica would never have been invaded *. The French saw the weakness of a distracted ministry, and were justified in treating you with contempt. They would probably have yielded in the first instance, rather than hazard a rupture with this country; but, being once engaged, they cannot retreat without dishonour. Common sense foresees consequences which have escaped your Grace's penetration. Either we suffer the French to make an acquisition, the importance of which you have probably no conception of, or we oppose them by an underhand management, which only disgraces us in the eyes of Europe, without answering any purpose of policy or prudence. From secret, indirect assistance, a transition to some more open decisive measures becomes unavoidable; till at last we find ourselves principals in the war, and are obliged to hazard everything for an object which might have originally been obtained without expense or danger. I am not versed in the politics of the north; but this, I believe, is certain, that half the money you have distributed to carry the expulsion of Mr. Wilkes, or even your secretary's share in the last subscription, would have kept the Turks at your devotion †. Was it economy, my Lord? or did the coy resistance you have constantly met with in the British senate, make you despair of corrupting the Divan? Your friends, indeed, have the first claim upon your

---

* Lord Shelburne, father to the present Marquis of Lansdowne, while Secretary of State, instructed our Ambassador at the Court of Versailles to remonstrate in very spirited terms on the intended invasion of Corsica by the French. His Lordship's conduct, however, was disavowed by his colleagues, and he resigned his situation, Oct. 21, 1768.

† The Ottoman Porte was at this time in the hands of French influence; the Court of Tuilleries supplying it with French officers, and instructing it, through their means, in modern tactics, so as to enable it to support more successfully the war in which it was engaged with Russia. The growing extent of French influence over the continent might, in this instance perhaps, have easily been curtailed by a little address, and even transferred to the court of St. James's. The parallel between Corsica and Hungary has been adverted to in a previous note, the chief discrepancies being that, in the first instance, Genoa and France were the aggressive powers; in the latter, Austria and Russia.—ED.

bounty, but if five hundred pounds a year can be spared in pension to Sir John Moore*, it would not have disgraced you to have allowed something to the secret service of the public.

You will say perhaps that the situation of affairs at home demanded and engrossed the whole of your attention. Here, I confess, you have been active. An amiable, accomplished prince ascends the throne under the happiest of all auspices— the acclamations and united affections of his subjects. The first measures of his reign, and even the odium of a favourite, were not able to shake their attachment. Your services, my Lord, have been more successful. Since you were permitted to take the lead we have seen the natural effects of a system of government at once both odious and contemptible. We have seen the laws sometimes scandalously relaxed, some- times violently stretched beyond their tone. We have seen the sacred person of the sovereign insulted; and, in profound peace, and with an undisputed title, the fidelity of his sub- jects brought by his own servants into public question†. Without abilities, resolution, or interest, you have done more than Lord Bute could accomplish with all Scotland at his heels.

Your Grace, little anxious perhaps either for present or future reputation, will not desire to be handed down in these colours to posterity. You have reason to flatter yourself that the memory of your administration will survive even the forms of a constitution which our ancestors vainly hoped would be immortal; and as for your personal character I will not, for the honour of human nature, suppose that you can wish to have it remembered. The condition of the present times is desperate indeed; but there is a debt due to those who come after us, and it is the historian's office to punish though he cannot correct. I do not give you to posterity as a pattern to imitate, but as an example to deter; and, as your conduct

* Sir John Moore was an old Newmarket acquaintance of his Grace's, where he succeeded in completely squandering away his private fortune. The Duke of Grafton, out of compassion, obtained for him the pension in question.

† The wise Duke, about this time, exerted all the influence of government to procure addresses to satisfy the King of the fidelity of his subjects. They came in very thick from *Scotland;* but, after the appearance of this letter, we heard no more of them.- -JUNIUS.

comprehends every thing that a wise or honest minister should avoid, I mean to make you a negative instruction to your successors for ever.

JUNIUS.

LETTER XIII.

TO THE PRINTER OF THE PUBLIC ADVERTISER.

SIR,　　　　　　　　　　　　　　　　　　　　June 12, 1769.

THE Duke of Grafton's friends, not finding it convenient to enter into a contest with Junius, are now reduced to the last melancholy resource of defeated argument, the flat general charge of scurrility and falsehood. As for his style, I shall leave it to the critics. The truth of his facts is of more importance to the public. They are of such a nature that I think a bare contradiction will have no weight with any man who judges for himself. Let us take them in the order in which they appear in his last letter.

1. Have not the first rights of the people, and the first principles of the constitution been openly invaded, and the very name of an election made ridiculous, by the arbitrary appointment of Mr. Luttrell?

2. Did not the Duke of Grafton frequently lead his mistress into public, and even place her at the head of his table, as if he had pulled down an ancient temple of Venus, and could bury all decency and shame under the ruins? Is this the man who dares to talk of Mr. Wilkes's morals?

3. Is not the character of his presumptive ancestors as strongly marked in him as if he had descended from them in a direct legitimate line? The idea of his death is only prophetic; and what is prophecy but a narrative preceding the fact?

4. Was not Lord Chatham the first who raised him to the rank and post of a minister, and the first whom he abandoned?

5. Did he not join with Lord Rockingham and betray him?

6. Was he not the bosom friend of Mr. Wilkes, whom he now pursues to destruction?

7 Did he not take his degrees with credit at Newmarket, White's, and the Opposition?

8. After deserting Lord Chatham's principles and sacrificing his friendship, is he not now closely united with a set of men, who, though they have occasionally joined with all parties, have, in every different situation, and at all times, been equally and constantly detested by this country?

9. Has not Sir John Moore a pension of five hundred pounds a year? This may probably be an acquittance of favours upon the turf; but is it possible for a minister to offer a grosser outrage to a nation which has so very lately cleared away the beggary of the civil list at the expense of more than half a million?

10. Is there any one mode of thinking or acting with respect to America, which the Duke of Grafton has not successively adopted and abandoned?

11. Is there not a singular mark of shame set upon this man, who has so little delicacy and feeling as to submit to the opprobrium of marrying a near relation of one who had debauched his wife? In the name of decency how are these amiable cousins to meet at their uncle's table? It will be a scene in Œdipus, without the distress. Is it wealth, or wit, or beauty? or is the amorous youth in love?

The rest is notorious. That Corsica has been sacrificed to the French; that in some instances the laws have been scandalously relaxed, and in others daringly violated; and that the king's subjects have been called upon to assure him of their fidelity in spite of the measures of his servants.

A writer, who builds his arguments upon facts such as these, is not easily to be confuted. He is not to be answered by general assertions or general reproaches. He may want eloquence to amuse or persuade, but, speaking truth, he must always convince.

PHILO-JUNIUS *.

* This is the first letter of Philo-Junius. In his Preface Junius admits the authorship of letters under this signature, and that it was a subordinate part he started as needful to explain and support the principal; not, he says, to "praise him," but to appear ingenuously convinced by his facts and reasoning—a puff oblique, if not direct, from the author himself.—ED.

LETTER XIV.

TO THE PRINTER OF THE PUBLIC ADVERTISER

Sir,   June 22, 1769.

THE name of *Old Noll* is destined to be the ruin of the house
of Stuart. There is an ominous fatality in it which even the
spurious descendants of the family cannot escape. Oliver
Cromwell had the merit of conducting Charles the First
to the block. Your correspondent *Old Noll* * appears
to have the same design upon the Duke of Grafton. His
arguments consist better with the title he has assumed, than
with the principles he professes; for though he pretends to
be an advocate for the Duke, he takes care to give us the best
reasons why his patron should regularly follow the fate of his
presumptive ancestor. Through the whole course of the
Duke of Grafton's life I see a strange endeavour to unite contradictions which cannot be reconciled. He marries to be
divorced, he keeps a mistress to remind him of conjugal en-
dearments, and he chooses such friends as it is a virtue in
him to desert. If it were possible for the genius of that accomplished president who pronounced sentence upon Charles
the First to be revived in some modern sycophant†, his

* A correspondent under this signature replied to the preceding letter of
Philo-Junius, in the *Public Advertiser*, dated June 19, introducing his
observations with the following paragraph :—" Though *Philo-Junius* is, in
every sense, unworthy of an answer as a writer, yet, as he has compressed
into small compass what he calls the facts advanced by Junius, I will answer
them briefly one by one, and for ever drop a subject that could only acquire
consequence by discussing it in a serious manner."—ED.

† It is hardly necessary to remind the reader of ‘the name of *Bradshaw*.—JUNIUS. And as little so that *Old Noll* was the nickname of Oliver
Cromwell. There is a peculiar severity in the comparison of the two periods
and the two families. The Duke of Grafton was a Stuart, and Bradshaw,
the president of the regicide court, was the name of the Duke's private secretary; and Junius here insinuates that he was also the author of the letter
signed *Old Noll*, which had a chance of proving as fatal to his Grace's cause
as ever the name of *Bradshaw* or *Old Noll* had proved fatal to his Grace's
ancestor. Before his present appointment, Bradshaw had been an under-
clerk in the war-office, and was raised to the rank of private secretary for his
despatch in business. In 1772 he was appointed a lord of the admiralty,
and on the Duke retiring from the premiership he was rewarded with a
pension of 1500*l.* Considering this provision unequal to his deserts or his
wants, he committed suicide.—ED.

Grace, I doubt not, would, by sympathy, discover him among the dregs of mankind, and take him for a guide in those paths, which naturally conduct a minister to the scaffold.

The assertion that two thirds of the nation approve of the *acceptance* of Mr. Luttrell (for even *Old Noll* is too modest to call it an election), can neither be maintained nor confuted by argument.   It is a point of fact on which every English gentleman will determine for himself.   As to lawyers, their profession is supported by the indiscriminate defence of right and wrong, and I confess I have not that opinion of their knowledge or integrity, to think it necessary that they should decide for me upon a plain constitutional question.   With respect to the appointment of Mr. Luttrell, the Chancellor * has never yet given any authentic opinion.   Sir Fletcher Norton † is indeed an honest, a very honest, man ; and the Attorney General ‡ is *ex officio* the guardian of liberty, to take care, I presume, that it shall never break out into a criminal excess. Doctor Blackstone is solicitor to the queen.   The Doctor recollected that he had a place to preserve, though he forgot that he had a reputation to lose.   We have now the good fortune to understand the Doctor's principles as well as his writings.   For the defence of truth, of law, and reason, the Doctor's book may be safely consulted ; but whoever wishes to cheat a neighbour of his estate §, or to rob a country of its rights ||, need make no scruple of consulting the Doctor himself.

The example of the English nobility may, for aught I know, sufficiently justify the Duke of Grafton, when he indulges his genius in all the fashionable excesses of the age; yet, considering his rank and station, I think it would do him more honour to be able to deny the fact than to defend it by such authority.   But if vice itself could be excused, there is

---

* Lord Camden.

† At this time Chief Justice in Eyre, with a salary of 3000*l.*, and just appointed a privy counsellor.

‡ Mr. De Grey, afterwards Lord Walsingham.

§ Doctor, better known as Sir William, Blackstone, and a distinguished name : he had been, unfortunately for himself, an adviser of Sir James Lowther against the Duke of Portland, in the dispute concerning the Cumberland crown lands, upon the obsolete law of *nullum tempus.*—ED.

‖ Blackstone had also supported government in its rejection of Mr. Wilkes as member for the county of Middlesex.

yet a certain display of it, a certain outrage to decency, and violation of public decorum which, for the benefit of society, should never be forgiven. It is not that he kept a mistress at home, but that he constantly attended her abroad. It is not the private indulgence but the public insult of which I complain. The name of Miss Parsons would hardly have been known, if the First Lord of the Treasury had not led her in triumph through the Opera House, even in the presence of the queen. When we see a man act in this manner we may admit the shameless depravity of his heart, but what are we to think of his understanding?

His Grace, it seems, is now to be a regular domestic man, and, as an omen of the future delicacy and correctness of his conduct, he marries a first cousin of the man who had fixed that mark and title of infamy upon him which, at the same moment, makes a husband unhappy and ridiculous. The ties of consanguinity may possibly preserve him from the same fate a second time, and as to the distress of meeting, I take for granted the venerable uncle of these common cousins has settled the etiquette in such a manner that, if a mistake should happen, it may reach no farther than from *Madame ma femme* to *Madame ma cousine.*

The Duke of Grafton has always some excellent reasons for deserting his friends. The age and incapacity of Lord Chatham*; the debility of Lord Rockingham; or the infamy of Mr. Wilkes. There was a time indeed when he did not appear to be quite so well acquainted or so violently offended with the infirmities of his friends. But now I confess they are not ill exchanged for the youthful, vigorous virtue of the Duke of Bedford, the firmness of General Conway, the blunt, or if I may call it, the aukward integrity of Mr. Rigby †, and the spotless morality of Lord Sandwich ‡.

---

* Lord Chatham, it is well known, laboured under a premature decrepitude of body, from frequent and violent attacks of the gout.

† Mr. Rigby was introduced into political life by the Duke of Bedford, to whom he had chiefly recommended himself by his convivial talents. He at length attained the lucrative post of paymaster of the British forces. His pretensions to *integrity* are well known, even to the present moment, to have been rather equivocal.

‡ It was Lord Sandwich who, in conjunction with Dr. Warburton, complained to the House of Lords, of Wilkes's *Essay on Woman,* and induced their lordships' interference, in consequence of which the writer was prose-

If a large pension to a broken gambler * be an act worthy of commendation, the Duke of Grafton's connections will furnish him with many opportunities of doing praiseworthy actions; and, as he himself bears no part of the expense, the generosity of distributing the public money for the support of virtuous families in distress will be an unquestionable proof of his Grace's humanity.

As to public affairs, *Old Noll* is a little tender of descending to particulars. He does not deny that Corsica has been sacrificed to France, and he confesses that, with regard to America, his patron's measures have been subject to some variation; but then he promises wonders of stability and firmness for the future. These are mysteries of which we must not pretend to judge by experience; and truly, I fear we shall perish in the Desert before we arrive at the Land of Promise. In the regular course of things, the period of the Duke of Grafton's ministerial manhood should now be approaching. The imbecility of his infant state was committed to Lord Chatham. Charles Townshend took some care of his education at that ambiguous age which lies between the follies of political childhood and the vices of puberty. The empire of the passions soon succeeded. His earliest principles and connections were of course forgotten or despised. The company he has lately kept has been of no service to his morals; and, in the conduct of public affairs, we see the character of his time of life strongly distinguished. An obstinate ungovernable self-sufficiency plainly points out to us that state of imperfect maturity at which the graceful levity of youth is lost, and the solidity of experience not yet acquired. It is possible the young man may in time grow wiser and reform; but, if I understand his disposition, it is not of such corrigible stuff that we should hope for any amendment in him before he has accomplished the destruction of this country. Like other rakes, he may perhaps live to see his error, but not until he has ruined his estate.

PHILO-JUNIUS.

cuted by the crown. The irony of the expression here adopted proceeds from the well-known fact that Lord Sandwich was at this very time the most profligate of all the Bedford party.

* Sir John Moore.

LETTER XV *.

TO HIS GRACE THE DUKE OF GRAFTON.

MY LORD,   July 8, 1769.

IF nature had given you an understanding qualified to keep
pace with the wishes and principles of your heart, she would
have made you, perhaps, the most formidable minister that

* In this Letter Junius with unabated severity, but less of personal crimina-
tion, renews in closer array of fact and argument his general attack on the
Duke of Grafton. His eloquence, however, and political sagacity, did not succeed any more than the petition of the livery of London, in obliging the
king to alter his plan of government, or the ministry to retire. That the
reader may better understand the position of the belligerents—of the sovereign and his ministry on one side, and the opposition on the other, consisting of the now united Whig phalanx, Junius, Wilkes and the populace, with
the agitators of the City—and that he may be the better instructed by the
truths in these Letters, without being misled by their prejudices and errors,
it is essential in the perusal of them to hold the following facts steadily in
his mind :—
    1. The plan of the breaking down of the great Whig aristocracy, by
selecting ability and loyalty from among both Whigs and Tories, did not
begin with Lord Bute, but was conceived and arranged by Bolingbroke ;
was imperfectly carried into effect in the opposition guided by Mr. Pulteney,
Sir William Wyndham, and Lord Carteret ; occasioned, in the struggle
between its supporters and opposers, all that uncertainty and weakness of
government which prevailed from the resignation of Sir Robert Walpole till
the Pelhams were fully established in ministerial power ; and was renewed
by Mr. Pitt in 1758, after the Whig aristocracy had made themselves odious
by corruption, tyranny, and failures.
    2. The Earl of Bute, in his attempt to carry this plan into effect, erred in
nothing so much as in not gaining Mr. Pitt for his confidential ally. Pitt hated
the great Whig aristocracy which had scowled on his talents, and thwarted,
by every artifice, his attempts to rise by ability and patriotism above the
native humility of his fortune. He courted the Tories of Leicester House ;
and desired nothing better than to set himself at the head of a body of
mingled Whigs and Tories, by which the aristocracy that had oppressed
him might be overthrown. Having gained the entire confidence of George
II., who had previously regarded him with aversion, Pitt learned to value
himself on cultivating the personal favour of his sovereign, not less than on
commanding the admiration of the multitude. Had the king and Lord Bute
treated him with free unbounded confidence, he would, without doubt, have
entered cordially into their new plan of combining and balancing parties, and
it might have been accomplished without occasioning that long prostration
of government which ensued in the prosecution of it without Pitt's aid. It
was the conceit of ability which he possessed not, it was a jealousy incom-

ever was employed under a limited monarch to accomplish the ruin of a free people. When neither the feelings of shame, the reproaches of conscience, nor the dread of punish-

patible with true greatness of soul, it was a servitude to sordid interests and petty prejudices, that made Bute irritate Pitt to resignation, instead of courting, in happy hour, his confidential friendship. This was the capital error of the king's elect. He meant well; when too late, he strove to regain for his sovereign the cordial service of Pitt. Even then, however, there were in his advances a hesitation and duplicity which Pitt's penetration could not fail to detect, and which his generous nature must of necessity abhor.

3. In the first dissociation of the Whigs from the Tories, in the counter-poise of those two parties in the reign of William, in their alternate success under Anne, in the triumph of the Whigs, during the two first reigns of the House of Hanover, in the efforts of St. John, of Pitt, of Bute, to displace them, and in the consummation of Tory ascendancy under the ministry of the son of Chatham, the operation of general and permanent causes is conspicuously remarkable—causes originating in the first principles of human nature, and, in the fundamental composition of society, predominating over all those secondary causes to which narrow-minded courtiers, patriots, politicians, party-writers, and historians, have attributed all the fluctuation and changes in the government and policy of Britain.

4. During the long supremacy of the Whigs, both the *Executive* and the *Legislative Powers* had made encroachments upon the rights of the people, and the first principles of the constitution. These had, indeed, been in part counterbalanced by the growing ascendancy of public opinion, the voice of which had begun to be generally listened to, and obeyed, by both the crown and the parliament. It was time, however, both for the safety of the crown and the constitution, that such encroachments should be checked. They could not have been effectually checked if it had not been for that opposition, both in parliament and among the people, in support of which the Letters of Junius were written.

5. It does not appear, that any one of the parties in the opposition, from the year 1760 to the year 1770, had thoroughly studied anything but their private and party interests and caprices of all that was in dispute. *They had no principles thoroughly understood; and, because thoroughly understood, therefore not to be abandoned.* The great utilities of government and society impelled them along in a course in which Whigs and Tories might cordially move on together. But here they were, in some sort unconscious agents; as to all else, what they called their principles continually yielded to their interests and passions. The peace of 1763, hastily concluded, was at first almost unanimously approved by all but Mr. Pitt. Even of the persecution of Wilkes, almost all, in their turn, approved, at least so far as not to make his acquittal a condition without which they would not act with government. In regard to the taxation of the Americans, it is evident from the whole conduct of all parties, that there was, *in truth*, no real dispute, except as to the possibility of carrying it into easy execution. Wilkes had his merits and his uses, but patriotism with him was merely a game of calculation. His spirit delighted in bold contention, and he desired to make his fortune. This was the sum of his impulses: and yet he happened to ex-

ment, form any bar to the designs of a minister, the people would have too much reason to lament their condition, if they did not find some resource in the weakness of his understanding. We owe it to the bounty of Providence, that the completest depravity of the heart is sometimes strangely united with a confusion of the mind which counteracts the most favourite principles, and makes the same man treacherous without art, and a hypocrite without deceiving. The measures, for instance, in which your Grace's activity has been chiefly exerted, as they were adopted without skill, should have been conducted with more than common dexterity. But truly, my Lord, the execution has been as gross as the design.

hibit more remarkable steadiness, and to be the instrument of greater good to the constitution, than was effected by all the cabals, and all the parliamentary eloquence, of the higher members of the opposition. The patriot citizens of London, had as little of virtue and intelligence in their opposition as the parliamentary leaders. The agitators who stirred them into action were mostly men actuated by base or absurd motives. The mob were inspired by prejudice, ignorance, and low insolence.

6. There was much of weakness, of narrowness, of mean artifice, and of blundering rashness, in the system of the court itself. In principle, and in its first leading views, it was considerably in the right : in almost all else, it was in the wrong. The virtue and ability of the sovereign himself, together with the insuperable necessities of government, seem to have contributed, much more than the skill or honesty of any of his secret counsellors, to avert that ruin which the weakness of the government, and the strength of the opposition, too long threatened.

7. What the Whigs, who complained of a *secret influence* at court, which, after the public retirement of Lord Bute, had no existence, continually demanded, was, in fact, that the king should never presume to think or speak of any one concern of his government, except in their presence, and in implicit submission to their control. These were the conditions to which they strove to reduce their sovereign, and which were chiefly thwarted by their own mutual treachery.

8. At the time when these Letters were written, Lord Chatham, Lord Temple, the Marquis of Rockingham, and Mr. George Grenville, acted in union. They believed it impossible that their strength should not prevail, and they were using every possible effort to take by storm the strong-holds of the administration. They had mutually vowed never more to suffer themselves to be disunited by the practices of their adversaries. But their engagements and resolutions were, *happily*, not of a nature to resist the first splendid temptations of avarice or ambition.

9. From all this it follows, that the Duke of Grafton was not, in politics and patriotism, a worse man than the other conspicuous leaders, whether of the ministry or of the opposition, despite of the revolting exhibition of him by Junius.—HERON.

By one decisive step you have defeated all the arts of writing. You have fairly confounded the intrigues of opposition, and silenced the clamours of faction. A dark, ambiguous system might require and furnish the materials of ingenious illustration ; and, in doubtful measures, the virulent exaggeration of party must be employed to rouse and engage the passions of the people. You have now brought the merits of your ad ministration to an issue on which every Englishman of the narrowest capacity may determine for himself. It is not an alarm to the passions, but a calm appeal to the judgment of the people upon their own most essential interests. A more experienced minister would not have hazarded a direct invasion of the first principles of the constitution before he had made some progress in subduing the spirit of the people. With such a cause as yours, my Lord, it is not sufficient that you have the court at your devotion unless you can find means to corrupt or intimidate the jury. The collective body of the people form that jury, and from *their* decision there is is but one appeal.

Whether you have talents to support you at a crisis of such difficulty and danger should long since have been considered. Judging truly of your disposition, you have, perhaps, mistaken the extent of your capacity. Good faith and folly have so long been received for synonymous terms, that the reverse of the proposition has grown into credit, and every villain fancies himself a man of abilities. It is the apprehension of your friends, my Lord, that you have drawn some hasty conclusion of this sort, and that a partial reliance upon your moral character has betrayed you beyond the depth of your understanding. You have now carried things too far to retreat. You have plainly declared to the people what they are to expect from the continuance of your administration. It is time for your Grace to consider what you also may expect in return from *their* spirit and *their* resentment.

Since the accession of our most gracious sovereign to the throne we have seen a system of government which may well be called a reign of experiments. Parties of all denominations have been employed and dismissed. The advice of the ablest men in this country has been repeatedly called for and rejected ; and when the royal displeasure has been signified to a minister, the marks of it have usually been proportioned to his abilities and integrity. The spirit of the FAVOURITE had some apparent influence upon every administration; and every set of ministers preserved an appearance of duration, as long as they submitted to that influence. But there were certain services to be performed for the favourite's security, or to gratify his resentments, which your predecessors in office had the wisdom or the virtue not to undertake. The moment this refractory spirit was discovered their disgrace was determined. Lord Chatham, Mr. Grenville, and Lord Rockingham have successively had the honour to be dismissed for preferring their duty as servants of the public to those compliances which were expected from their station. A submissive administration was at last gradually collected from the deserters of all parties, interests, and connections; and nothing remained but to find a leader for these gallant well-disciplined troops. Stand forth, my Lord, for thou art the man. Lord Bute found no resource of dependence or security in the proud, imposing superiority of Lord Chatham's abilities, the shrewd, inflexible judgment of Mr. Grenville *, nor in the mild but determined integrity of Lord Rockingham. His views and situation required a creature void of all these properties; and he was forced to go through every division, resolution, composition, and refinement of political chemistry, before he happily arrived at the *caput mortuum* of vitriol in your Grace. Flat and insipid in your retired state, but, brought into action, you become vitriol again. Such are the extremes of alternate indolence or fury which have governed your whole administration. Your circumstances with regard to the people soon becoming desperate, like other honest servants you determined to involve the best of masters in the same difficulties with yourself. We owe it to your Grace's well-directed labours,

* Mr. G. Grenville, younger brother of Lord Temple, and brother-in-law to Lord Chatham, was a political élève of his maternal uncle, Lord Cobham. He first attached himself to the Tory party in consequence of marrying the daughter of Sir W. Wyndham, the confidential friend of Bolingbroke, and father of Lord Egremont; and was made one of the secretaries of state when Lord Bute, in 1762, was appointed first lord of the treasury. He planned the American Stamp Act, and commenced the opposition to Wilkes. He afterwards, however, became disgusted with Lord Bute, and, upon hi' resignation, firmly attached himself to the party of Lord Rockingham, the most pure and unmixed Whig leader of his day, with whom also Lord Temple and the Earl of Chatham had now united themselves.

that your sovereign has been persuaded to doubt of the affections of his subjects, and the people to suspect the virtues of their sovereign, at a time when both were unquestionable. You have degraded the royal dignity into a base, dishonourable competition with Mr. Wilkes, nor had you abilities to carry even this last contemptible triumph over a private man, without the grossest violation of the fundamental laws of the constitution and rights of the people. But these are rights, my Lord, which you can no more annihilate than you can the soil to which they are annexed. The question no longer turns upon points of national honour and security abroad, or on the degrees of expedience and propriety of measures at home It was not inconsistent that you should abandon the cause of liberty in another country *, which you had persecuted in your own; and in the common arts of domestic corruption, we miss no part of Sir Robert Walpole's system except his abilities. In this humble imitative line you might long have proceeded, safe and contemptible. You might, probably, never have risen to the dignity of being hated, and even have been despised with moderation. But it seems you meant to be distinguished, and, to a mind like yours, there was no other road to fame but by the destruction of a noble fabric, which you thought had been too long the admiration of mankind. The use you have made of the military force introduced an alarming change in the mode of executing the laws. The arbitrary appointment of Mr. Luttrell invades the foundation of the laws themselves, as it manifestly transfers the right of legislation from those whom the people have chosen to those whom they have rejected. With a succession of such appointments we may soon see a House of Commons collected, in the choice of which the other towns and counties of England will have as little share as the devoted county of Middlesex

Yet, I trust, your Grace will find that the people of this country are neither to be intimidated by violent measures, nor deceived by refinements. When they see Mr Luttrell seated in the House of Commons by mere dint of power, and in direct opposition to the choice of a whole county, they will not listen to those subtleties by which every arbitrary exertion of authority is explained into the law and privilege of parliament.

* Corsica.

It requires no persuasion of argument, but simply the evidence of the senses, to convince them that to transfer the right of election from the collective to the representative body of the people contradicts all those ideas of a House of Commons which they have received from their forefathers, and which they have already, though vainly perhaps, delivered to their children. The principles on which this violent measure has been defended, have added scorn to injury, and forced us to feel that we are not only oppressed but insulted.

With what force, my Lord, with what protection, are you prepared to meet the united detestation of the people of England? The city of London has given a generous example to the kingdom in what manner a king of this country ought to be addressed *; and I fancy, my Lord, it is not yet in your courage to stand between your sovereign and the addresses of his subjects. The injuries you have done this country are such as demand not only redress but vengeance. In vain shall you look for protection to that venal vote which you have already paid for—another must be purchased; and to save a minister, the House of Commons must declare themselves not only independent of their constituents, but the determined enemies of the constitution. Consider, my Lord, whether this be an extremity to which their fears will permit them to advance, or, if *their* protection should fail you, how far you are authorized to rely upon the sincerity of those smiles which a pious court lavishes without reluctance upon a libertine by profession. It is not, indeed, the least of the thousand contradictions which attend you, that a man, marked to the world by the grossest violation of all ceremony and decorum, should be the first servant of a court in which prayers are morality and kneeling is religion. Trust not too far to appearances by which your predecessors have been deceived, though they have not been injured. Even the best of princes may at last discover that this is a contention in which every-thing may be lost but nothing can be gained; and, as you became minister by accident, were adopted without choice, trusted without confidence, and continued without favour, be assured that, whenever an occasion presses, you will be discarded without even the forms of regret. You will then

---

* See this subject farther noticed in Junius's Letter xxxvii.

have reason to be thankful if you are permitted to retire to that seat of learning which, in contemplation of the system of your life, the comparative purity of your manners with those of their high steward, and a thousand other recommending circumstances, has chosen you to encourage the growing virtue of their youth, and to preside over their education *. Whenever the spirit of distributing prebends and bishopricks shall have departed from you, you will find that learned seminary perfectly recovered from the delirium of an installation, and, what in truth it ought to be, once more a peaceful scene of slumber and thoughtless meditation. The venerable tutors of the university will no longer distress your modesty by proposing you for a pattern to their pupils. The learned dulness of declamation will be silent†; and even the venal muse‡, though happiest in fiction, will forget your virtues. Yet, for the benefit of the succeeding age, I could wish that your retreat might be deferred until your morals shall happily be ripened to that maturity of corruption at which the worst examples cease to be contagious.

JUNIUS.

LETTER XVI.

TO THE PRINTER OF THE PUBLIC ADVERTISER§.

SIR, July 19, 1769.

A GREAT deal of useless argument might have been saved in the political contest which has arisen upon the expulsion of

* The Duke of Grafton was chancellor, and Lord Sandwich high steward, of the University of Cambridge.

† Dr. Hinchliffe, afterwards Bishop of Peterborough, in his official situation as vice-chancellor of Cambridge, made an oration in praise of the Duke of Grafton on introducing him to the senate-house on the morning of his installation to the chancellorship of that university.

‡ Alluding to Gray's celebrated Ode to Music, composed and performed on the installation of his Grace as chancellor of the university, beginning—
Hence! avaunt! 'tis holy ground—
Comus and his midnight crew, &c.

§ This letter is perhaps the best specimen the whole collection affords of clear and cogent reasoning. It cannot be too often read by those who would learn to reason with precision, yet without elaborate refinement, who would join force and brevity with lucid clearness, whether in writing or in debate, in the ardour of real business, or in the coolness of speculation.—ED.

Mr. Wilkes, and the subsequent appointment of Mr. Luttrell, if the question had been once stated with precision, to the satisfaction of each party, and clearly understood by them both. But in this. as in almost every other dispute, it usually happens that much time is lost in referring to a multitude of cases and precedents which prove nothing to the purpose, or in maintaining propositions which are either not disputed, or, whether they be admitted or denied, are entirely indifferent as to the matter in debate, until, at last, the mind, perplexed and confounded with the endless subtleties of controversy, loses sight of the main question, and never arrives at truth. Both parties in the dispute are apt enough to practise these dishonest artifices. The man who is conscious of the weakness of his cause is interested in concealing it; and, on the other side, it is not uncommon to see a good cause mangled by advocates who do not know the real strength of it.

I should be glad to know, for instance, to what purpose, in the present case, so many precedents have been produced to prove that the House of Commons have a right to expel one of their own members; that it belongs to them to judge of the validity of elections; or that the law of parliament is part of the law of the land*? After all these propositions are admitted, Mr. Luttrell's right to his seat will continue to be just as disputable as it was before. Not one of them is at present in agitation. Let it be admitted that the House of Commons were authorized to expel Mr. Wilkes; that they are the proper court to judge of elections, and that the law of parliament is binding upon the people; still it remains to be inquired whether the House, by their resolution in favour of Mr. Luttrell, have, or have not, truly declared that law. To facilitate this inquiry, I would have the question cleared of all foreign or indifferent matter. The following state of it will probably be thought a fair one by both parties; and then, I imagine, there is no gentleman in this country who will not be capable of forming a judicious and true opinion upon it. I take the question to be strictly this: "Whether or no it be the known established law of parliament, that the expulsion of a member of the House of Commons of

* The reader will observe that these admissions are made, not as of truths unquestionable, but for the sake of argument, and in order to bring the real question to issue.—JUNIUS.

itself creates in him such an incapacity to be re-elected, that. at a subsequent election, any votes given to him are null and void, and that any other candidate, who, except the person expelled, has the greatest number of votes, ought to be the sitting member."

To prove that the affirmative is the law of parliament, I apprehend it is not sufficient for the present House of Commons to declare it to be so. We may shut our eyes indeed to the dangerous consequences of suffering one branch of the legislature to declare new laws, without argument or example, and it may perhaps be prudent enough to submit to authority; but a mere assertion will never convince, much less will it be thought reasonable to prove the right by the fact itself. The ministry have not yet pretended to such a tyranny over our minds. To support the affirmative fairly, it will either be necessary to produce some statute in which that positive provision shall have been made, that specific disability clearly created, and the consequence of it declared, or, if there be no such statute, the custom of parliament must then be referred to, and some case or cases * strictly in point must be produced, with the decision of the court upon them; for I readily admit that the custom of parliament, once clearly proved, is equally binding with the common and statute law,

The consideration of what may be reasonable or unreasonable makes no part of this question. We are inquiring what the law is, not what it ought to be. Reason may be applied to show the impropriety or expedience of a law, but we must have either statute or precedent to prove the existence of it. At the same time I do not mean to admit that the late resolution of the House of Commons is defensible on general principles of reason, any more than in law. This is not the hinge on which the debate turns.

Supposing, therefore, that I have laid down an accurate state of the question, I will venture to affirm, 1st, That there is no statute existing by which that specific disability which we speak of is created. If there be, let it be produced. The argument will then be at an end.

2ndly, That there is no precedent in all the proceedings of

---

* Precedents, in opposition to principles, have little weight with Junius; but he thought it necessary to meet the ministry upon their own ground.— Junius.

the House of Commons which comes entirely home to the
present case, viz., "where an expelled member has been
returned again, and another candidate, with an inferior number of votes, has been declared the sitting member." If
there be such a precedent, let it be given to us plainly, and I
am sure it will have more weight than all the cunning arguments which have been drawn from inferences and proba-
bilities.

The ministry, in that laborious pamphlet which, I presume, contains the whole strength of the party, have declared *, " That Mr. Walpole's † was the first and only instance, in which the electors of any county or borough had
returned a person expelled to serve in the same parliament."
It is not possible to conceive a case more exactly in point.
Mr. Walpole was expelled and, having a majority of votes at
the next election, was returned again. The friends of Mr.
Taylor, a candidate set up by the ministry, petitioned the
house that he might be the sitting member ‡.   Thus far the

* *Case of the Middlesex Election Considered*, page 38.—JUNIUS.

† This fact occurred while Mr. Walpole was in an inferior capacity to
that in which he afterwards appeared so conspicuously as prime minister of
George I. and George II.   At the period in question, the Tories having obtained a majority in parliament, expelled him for the crime of having accepted
profits upon a military contract, while secretary at war, and at the same
time possessed influence enough to have him committed to the Tower.   He
was member for Lynn Regis, the burgesses of which borough were warmly
attached to him.   It was for this borough he had been returned at an early
period of his life, by which he was enabled, while a young politician, to
head the Whig party against St. John, afterwards Lord Bolingbroke, who
took a leading part in the Tory administration of Harley.

From the disgrace into which he was hereby for a long time plunged, he
was at length relieved by the failure of the minister's favourite expedient of
the South Sea incorporation, and the extreme unpopularity in which he was
consequently involved.   Walpole now triumphed upon the ruin of his rival,
became prime minister, retained the post through the whole of the existing
and part of the next reign, and for his services was created Earl of Orford.

‡ The following are the particulars of this case as extracted from the
journals of the House of Commons :—

" On the 23rd of February, 1711, a petition of the freemen and free-
burghers of the borough of King's Lynn, in the county of Norfolk, was
presented to the house, and read ; setting forth, that Monday the eleventh
of February last, being appointed for choosing a member to serve in parliament for this borough, in the room of Robert Walpole, Esq., expelled this
house, Samuel Taylor, Esq., *was elected their* burgess ; but John Bagg,
present mayor of the said borough, *refused to return the said Samuel Taylor,*

circumstances tally exactly, except that our House of Com
mons saved Mr. Luttrell the·trouble of petitioning. The
point of law, however, was the same. It came regularly
before the house, and it was their business to determine upon
it. They did determine it, for they declared Mr. Taylor *not
duly elected*. If it be said that they meant this resolution as
matter of favour and indulgence to the borough which had
retorted Mr. Walpole upon them, in order that the burgesses,
knowing what the law was, might correct their error, I
answer,

I. That it is a strange way of arguing, to oppose a supposition, which no man can prove, to a fact which proves
itself.

II. That if this were the intention of the House of Commons, it must have defeated itself. The burgesses of Lynn
could never have known their error, much less could they
have corrected it, by any instruction they received from the
proceedings of the House of Commons. They might perhaps have foreseen that, if they returned Mr. Walpole again,
he would again be rejected; but they never could infer from
a resolution by which the candidate with the fewest votes was
declared *not duly elected* that, at a future election, and in
similar circumstances, the House of Commons would reverse

though required so to do; and returned the said Robert Walpole, though
expelled this house, and then a prisoner in the Tower, and praying the consideration of the house.

" March 6th. The order of the day being read of taking into consideration the merits of the petition of the freemen and free-burghers of the
borough of King's Lynn, in the county of Norfolk, and a motion being made
that counsel be called in, upon a division, it was resolved in the negative.
Tellers for the yeas, Sir Charles Turner, Mr. Pulteney, 127. Tellers for the
noes, Sir Simeon Stuart, Mr. Foster, 212.—A motion being made, and the
question put, that Robert Walpole, Esq., having been this session of parliament committed a prisoner to the Tower of London, and expelled this house
for an high breach of trust in the execution of his office, and notorious corruption, when secretary at war, was, and is, incapable of being elected a
member to serve in this present parliament, it was resolved, upon a division,
in the affirmative. Then a motion being made, and the question put, that
Samuel Taylor, Esq., is duly elected a burgess to serve in the present parliament for the borough of King's Lynn in the county of Norfolk, it passed in
the negative. Resolved, that the late election of a burgess to serve in the
present parliament for the said borough of King's Lynn, in the county of
Norfolk, is a void election.'

N 2

their resolution, and receive the same candidate as duly elected whom they had before rejected.

This indeed would have been a most extraordinary way of declaring the law of parliament, and what I presume no man, whose understanding is not at cross-purposes with itself, could possibly understand.

If, in a case of this importance, I thought myself at liberty to argue from suppositions rather than from facts, I think the probability in this instance is directly the reverse of what the ministry affirm ; and that it is much more likely that the House of Commons at that time would rather have strained a point in favour of Mr. Taylor than that they would have violated the law of parliament, and robbed Mr. Taylor of a right legally vested in him, to gratify a refractory borough which, in defiance of them, had returned a person branded with the strongest mark of the displeasure of the House.

But really, Sir, this way of talking, for I cannot call it argument, is a mockery of the common understanding of the nation too gross to be endured.   Our dearest interests are at stake.   An attempt has been made, not merely to rob a single county of its rights, but, by inevitable consequence, to alter the constitution of the House of Commons.   This fatal attempt has succeeded, and stands as a precedent recorded for ever.   If the ministry are unable to defend their cause by fair argument founded on facts, let them spare us at least the mortification of being amused and deluded like children.   I believe there is yet a spirit of resistance in this country, which will not submit to be oppressed; but I am sure there is a fund of good sense in this country, which cannot be deceived.

JUNIUS.

LETTER XVII.

TO THE PRINTER OF THE PUBLIC ADVERTISER.

Sir,   August 1, 1769.
It will not be necessary for Junius to take the trouble of answering your correspondent G. A. or the quotation from

a speech without doors, published in your paper of the 28th of last month *. The speech appeared before JUNIUS's letter,

* The " speech without doors" was from the pen of Sir William Blackstone, and, from the legal eminence of the writer, may not be unacceptable to the reader.

A speech without doors upon the subject of a vote given on the 9th day of May, 1769.

" Your question I will answer, having first premised that if you are satisfied we did right in setting aside Mr. Wilkes's election, I cannot believe it will be a very difficult task to convince you that the admitting of Mr. Luttrell was the unavoidable consequence. ' No (say you) : for surely you might have declared it a void election. Why go greater lengths than in former times, even the most heated and violent, it was ever thought proper to go? Or upon what ground, either of reason or authority, can you justify the vote you gave, that Mr. Luttrell, who certainly had not the majority, was duly elected?' The question you have a right to put to me, and I mean to give it a direct answer.

" Now the principle upon which I voted was this, that in all cases of election by a majority of votes, wherever the candidate for whom the most votes are given, appears to have been, at the time of the election, under a *known legal incapacity*, the person who had the next greatest number of votes ought to be considered as the person duly elected. And this, as a general principle, I take to be altogether uncontrovertible. We may differ in our ways of expressing the principle, or of explaining the grounds of it : some choosing to state it, that the electors voting for such incapable person, do for that time forfeit their right of voting; others, that their votes are thrown away; and others, that votes for a person not legally capable, are not legal votes. But in whatever way we assign the ground of the rule, the result and conclusion is still the same, that, in every such case, the election of the capable person by the inferior number of votes, is a good and valid election.

" Nor is this rule, founded as it is in sound sense and public necessity, to be put out of countenance by a little ingenious sophistry, playing upon the ambiguity of certain undefined terms, taunting us with the reproach of elections by a minority, of inverting the rules of arithmetic, and the like. Not even the sacredness of the rights of the electors can stand against its authority; for sacred as those rights ought ever to be held, the exercise of them, as well as of all the other rights of individuals, must ever be confined within such bounds, and governed by such rules, as are consistent with the attainment of the great public ends for which they were established. But could any thing be more preposterous than if, while you are securing to individuals the right they have to take part in determining who shall be appointed to discharge the several public offices and trusts, no care should be taken that the public, in all events, may be secure of having any persons appointed at all? Yet to this inconvenience the public must be perpetually exposed, if the rule were to be strictly and invariably followed, that nothing but a majority of the electors could ever make a good election. That a majority of the whole number entitled to have voice in the election is not necessary,

and, as the author seems to consider the great proposition on which all his argument depends, namely, *that Mr. Wilkes was under that known legal incapacity of which* JUNIUS *speaks,* as

will be readily admitted ; for, at that rate, the absence of one-half of the electors might defeat the possibility of any election at all.   Neither is it necessary, in order to a candidate's being duly elected, that he should have the votes of more than one-half of the electors present ; since, if it were, diversity of inclinations among the electors, and the putting up of three candidates, might as completely frustrate all possibility of supplying the vacancy, as the absence of one-half of the electors would in the former case.   Accordingly, therefore, we constantly see, that wherever there are more than two candidates for one vacancy, the election is determined, not so properly by a majority, as by a plurality of voices ; and the candidate who has more voices than any one of his competitors, although fewer than one-half of the electors present, is always determined to be well and duly elected ; there being, indeed, no other method allowed by the constitution of voting against one candidate, but by voting for another; nor any liberty of declaring whom I would prefer in the second place, in case my first vote should prove ineffectual ; either of which allowances might prevent any election being made.

" Thus far then we are guarded against the public service being disappointed, either by the remissness of the electors in absenting themselves from the election, or by such a diversity of opinions among the electors present as, though innocent in itself, would yet be of fatal consequence to the public should it be suffered to operate so far as to prevent any effectual election from taking place.   But much in vain have these rules been established, if it is still to be in the power of the same number of electors, by a little management, to effect the same purpose, and put an effectual bar to all possibility of a valid election.   Had they, by staying away, declared that they would take no part in supplying the vacancy, their fellow electors who chose to exercise their franchise, and upon whom, in that case, the complete right would have devolved, might have exercised their right accordingly, and the public service would have been provided for.   But shall they be allowed to come, and by declaring that they will vote against one candidate, but for no other, or by voting for a person whom they know to be incapable of holding the office, as truly, to all intents and purposes, deprive their fellows of their right, and the public of its due, as if, instead of coming, they had only sent a prohibition of proceeding to any election till it should be their good pleasure to suffer one ?   Against such a mockery of the public authority common sense reclaims ; and has, therefore, provided against this abuse by pointing out this farther qualification of the rule by which elections are to be decided. That as the electors who give no vote at all have no power of excluding any candidate for whom other electors do vote, so those who give their votes for a person whom they know to be by law incapable, are to be considered exactly on the same footing as if they gave no votes at all.   Not to give any vote, to declare I vote for nobody, or to vote for the Great Mogul, must undoubtedly have the same effect.

" Thus then it appeared to me, that the general rule, that in case of a *known legal incapacity* in the person having the majority of voices, the

a point granted, his speech is, in no shape, an answer to Junius, for this is the very question in debate.

As to G. A. I observe first, that if he did not admit of Junius's state of the question, he should have shown the fallacy of it, or given us a more exact one :—secondly, that considering the many hours and days which the ministry and their advocates have wasted in public debate, in compiling large quartos, and collecting innumerable precedents, expressly to prove that the late proceedings of the House of Commons are warranted by the law, custom, and practice of parliament, it is rather an extraordinary supposition to be made by one of their own party, even for the sake of argument, *that no such statute, no such custom of parliament, no such case in point can be produced.* G. A. may, however, make the supposition with safety. It contains nothing but literally the fact, except that there is a case exactly in point, with a decision of the house, diametrically opposite to that which the present House of Commons came to in favour of Mr. Luttrell.

The ministry now begin to be ashamed of the weakness of their cause, and, as it usually happens with falsehood, are driven to the necessity of shifting their ground, and changing their whole defence. At first we were told that nothing could be clearer than that the proceedings of the House of

capable person next upon the poll, although chosen by a minority, is duly elected, is consonant to reason, is the dictate of common sense.

" That it had also the sanction of authority, I was as clearly convinced. The practice of the courts of law in such cases seems not to be disputed ; they have, by repeated decisions, established the principle.

" Upon these grounds, therefore, both of reason and authority, I not only thought myself fully justified in giving my vote, that Mr. Luttrell was duly elected, but in truth I could not think myself at liberty to vote otherwise, being convinced, that as, on the one hand, by so voting I should do no wrong to the 1143 freeholders of Middlesex, who, for the chance of being able to overbear the authority of the House of Commons, which had adjudged Mr. Wilkes to be incapable, had chosen to forego their right of taking part in the nomination of a capable person in his room ; so, by a contrary decision, I should have done a most manifest injustice to Mr. Luttrell, and to the 296 freeholders who voted for him; and who, in failure of a nomination by an equal number of freeholders of any other capable candidate, had, upon every principle of reason, and every rule of law, as well as according to the uniform usage of parliament, conferred upon him a clear title to sit as one of the representatives for the county of Middlesex."

Commons were justified by the known law and uniform custom of parliament. But now it seems, if there be no law, the House of Commons have a right to make one, and if there be no precedent, they have a right to create the first; —for this, I presume, is the amount of the questions proposed to JUNIUS. If your correspondent had been at all versed in the law of parliament, or generally in the laws of this country, he would have seen that this defence is as weak and false as the former.

The privileges of either House of Parliament, it is true, are indefinite; that is, they have not been described or laid down in any one code or declaration whatsoever; but whenever a question of privilege has arisen, it has invariably been disputed or maintained upon the footing of precedents alone * In the course of the proceedings upon the Aylesbury election the House of Lords resolved, "That neither House of Parliament had any power, by any vote or declaration, to create to themselves any new privilege that was not warranted by the known laws and customs of parliament." And to this rule the House of Commons, though otherwise they had acted in a very arbitrary manner, gave their assent, for they affirmed that they had guided themselves by it in asserting their privileges. Now, Sir, if this be true with respect to matters of privilege in which the House of Commons, individually and as a body, are principally concerned, how much more strongly will it hold against any pretended power in that House to create or declare a new law by which not only the rights of the House over their own member, and those of the member himself are concluded, but also those of a third and separate party—I mean the freeholders of the kingdom. To do justice to the ministry, they have not yet pretended that any one or any two of the three estates have power to make a new law without the concurrence of the third. They know that a man who maintains such a doctrine is liable, by statute, to the heaviest penalties. They do not acknowledge that the House of Commons have assumed a *new* privilege, or declared a *new* law. On the contrary, they affirm that their proceedings have been strictly conformable to and founded

* This is still meeting the ministry upon their own ground; for, in truth, no precedents will support either natural injustice, or violation of positive right.—JUNIUS.

upon the ancient law and custom of parliament. Thus, therefore, the question returns to the point, at which Junius had fixed it, namely, *Whether or no this be the law of parlia ment.* If it be not, the House of Commons had no legal authority to establish a precedent, and the precedent itself is a mere fact, without any proof of right whatsoever.

Your correspondent concludes with a question of the simplest nature; *Must a thing be wrong, because it has never been done before?* No. But admitting it were proper to be done, that alone does not convey an authority to do it. As to the present case, I hope I shall never see the time when not only a single person, but a whole county, and, in effect, the entire collective body of the people, may again be robbed of their birthright by a vote of the House of Commons. But if, for reasons which I am unable to comprehend, it be necessary to trust that House with a power so exorbitant and so unconstitutional, at least let it be given to them by an act of the legislature.

PHILO-JUNIUS.

LETTER XVIII.

TO DR. WILLIAM BLACKSTONE, SOLICITOR GENERAL TO HER MAJESTY.

SIR,   July 29, 1769.

I SHALL make you no apology for considering a certain pamphlet, in which your late conduct is defended, as written by yourself *. The personal interest, the personal resent-

---

* This was at last admitted by the friends of the Solicitor-General. Th. pamphlet was entitled, "An Answer to the Question stated;" and was a reply to a pamphlet from Sir William Meredith, one of the most active members of parliament of the Whig party, entitled, "The Question stated," in reference to the adjudication of Wilkes's incapacity to sit in parliament after his last election; in the course of which also, the inconsistency of opinion between that delivered by the Solicitor-General in his Commentaries, and that on the point in question, was severely animadverted upon.

The press was overwhelmed with tracts on this dispute from both sides. Of these, the chief, independently of Sir William Meredith's, and the reply to it by Sir William Blackstone, were "The Case of the last Election for the County of Middlesex considered," attributed to Mr. Dyson, who was nicknamed, by his opponents, Mungo: "Serious considerations;" "Mungo on

ments, and above all, that wounded spirit, unaccustomed to reproach, and I hope not frequently conscious of deserving it, are signals which betray the author to us as plainly as if your name were in the title-page. You appeal to the public in defence of your reputation. We hold it, Sir, that an injury offered to an individual is interesting to society. On this principle the people of England made common cause with Mr. Wilkes. On this principle, if *you* are injured, they will join in your resentment. I shall not follow you through the insipid form of a third person, but address myself to you directly.

You seem to think the channel of a pamphlet more respectable and better suited to the dignity of your cause than that of a newspaper. Be it so. Yet if newspapers are scurrilous, you must confess they are impartial. They give us, without any apparent preference, the wit and argument of the ministry, as well as the abusive dulness of the opposition. The scales are equally poised. It is not the printer's fault if the greater weight inclines the balance.

Your pamphlet, then, is divided into an attack upon Mr. Grenville's character, and a defence of your own. It would would have been more consistent, perhaps, with your professed intentions, to have confined yourself to the last. But anger has some claim to indulgence, and railing is usually a relief to the mind. I hope you have found benefit from the experiment. It is not my design to enter into a formal vindication of Mr. Grenville upon his own principles. I have neither the honour of being personally known to him *, nor do I pretend to be completely master of all the facts. I need not run the risk of doing an injustice to his opinions, or to his conduct, when your pamphlet alone carries, upon the face of it, a full vindication of both.

the use of Quotations;" " Mungo's case considered;" " Letter to Junius:" " Postscript to Junius," published in a subsequent edition to Sir William Blackstone's reply, and "The False Alarm," written by Doctor Johnson. Of all these some incidental notice is taken in the course of the volumes before us.

* This, as already observed in the Preliminary Essay, is a truly singular assertion when taken in connection with the fact, that Mr. Grenville, of all the political characters of the day, appears to have been our author's favourite. He voluntarily omits every opportunity of censuring him, and readily embraces every occasion of defending and extolling his conduct and principles.

Your first reflection is, that Mr. Grenville * was, of all men, the person who should not have complained of inconsistence with regard to Mr. Wilkes †.   This, Sir, is either an unmeaning sneer, a peevish expression of resentment, or, if it means anything, you plainly beg the question ; for whether his parliamentary conduct with regard to Mr. Wilkes has or has not been inconsistent, remains yet to be proved.   But it seems he received upon the spot a sufficient chastisement for exercising *so unfairly* ‡ his talent of misrepresentation.   You are a lawyer, Sir, and know better than I do upon what particular occasions a talent for misrepresentation may be *fairly* exerted ; but to punish a man a second time, when he has been once sufficiently chastised, is rather too severe.   It is not in the laws of England, it is not in your own Commentaries, nor is it yet, I believe, in the new law you have revealed to the House of Commons.   I hope this doctrine has no existence but in your own heart.   After all, Sir, if you had consulted that sober discretion which you seem to oppose with triumph to the honest jollity of a tavern, it might have occurred to you that, although you could have succeeded in fixing a charge of inconsistence upon Mr. Grenville, it would not have tended in any shape to exculpate yourself.

Your next insinuation, that Sir William Meredith had hastily adopted the false glosses of his new ally, is of the

---

* Mr. Grenville had quoted a passage from the Doctor's excellent Commentaries, which directly contradicted the principles maintained by the Doctor in the House of Commons.—JUNIUS.

† It has been already observed that the opposition to Wilkes commenced with Mr. George Grenville, who advised the issue of the General Warrant. It is observed also in the same note, that Grenville afterwards deserted the ministry, and attached himself strenuously to the Whig party.   See note, *ante*, p. 172.   Upon this apparent inconsistency Junius shrewdly remarks, that whatever propriety or impropriety there might have been in Mr. Grenville's opposing Wilkes *personally*—the present question has nothing to do with it—as he now supports him not on account of his personal character, but as the instrument *of the people* at large, whose rights and privileges the ministry have grossly violated by their conduct towards him.—ED.

‡ An inaccurate expression in the pamphlet alluded to.   The chastisement that ensued is related, *post*, p. 191.   Blackstone was thunderstruck at the contradiction pointed out by Grenville, and was incapable of uttering a word in his defence—a pause ensued, and Mr. Grenville insultingly shook his head.   For the rest see the page just referred to.—ED.

same s rt with the first. It conveys a sneer as little worthy of the gravity of your character as it is useless to your defence. It is of little moment to the public to inquire by whom the charge was conceived, or by whom it was adopted. The only question we ask is, whether or no it be true. The remainder of your reflections upon Mr. Grenville's conduct destroy themselves. He could not possibly come prepared to traduce your integrity to the House. He could not foresee that you would even speak upon the question, much less could he foresee that you would maintain a direct contradiction of that doctrine which you had solemnly, disinterestedly, and upon soberest reflection delivered to the public. He came armed indeed with what he thought a respectable authority, to support what he was convinced was the cause of truth, and I doubt not he intended to give you, in the course of the debate, an honourable and public testimony of his esteem. Thinking highly of his abilities, I cannot however allow him the gift of divination. As to what you are pleased to call a plan coolly formed to impose upon the House of Commons, and his producing it without provocation at midnight, I consider it as the language of pique and invective, therefore unworthy of regard. But, Sir, I am sensible I have followed your example too long, and wandered from the point.

The quotation from your Commentaries is matter of record. It can neither be *altered* by your friends, nor misrepresented by your enemies ; and I am willing to take your own word for what you have said in the House of Commons. If there be a real difference between what you have written and what you have spoken you confess that your book ought to be the standard. Now, Sir, if words mean anything, I apprehend that when a long enumeration of disqualifications (whether by statute or the custom of parliament) concludes with these general comprehensive words, " but subject to these restrictions and disqualifications, *every* subject of the realm is eligible of common right," a reader of plain understanding must of course rest satisfied that no species of disqualification whatsoever had been omitted. The known character of the author, and the apparent accuracy with which the whole work is compiled, would confirm him in his opinion ; nor could he possibly form any other judgment without looking upon your

Commentaries in the same light in which you consider those penal laws which, though not repealed, are fallen into disuse, and are now in effect A SNARE TO THE UNWARY *.

You tell us indeed, that it was not part of your plan to specify any temporary incapacity, and that you could not, without a spirit of prophecy, have specified the disability of a private individual subsequent to the period at which you wrote. What your plan was I know not; but what it should have been, in order to complete the work you have given us, is by no means difficult to determine. The incapacity, which you call temporary, may continue seven years; and though you might not have foreseen the particular case of Mr. Wilkes, you might and should have foreseen the possibility of *such* a case, and told us how far the House of Commons were authorised to proceed in it by the law and custom of parliament. The freeholders of Middlesex would then have known what they had to trust to, and would never have returned Mr. Wilkes, when Colonel Luttrell was a candidate against him. They would have chosen some indifferent person, rather than submit to be represented by the object of their contempt and detestation.

Your attempt to distinguish between disabilities which affect whole classes of men, and those which affect individuals only, is really unworthy of your understanding. Your Commentaries had taught me that, although the instance in which a a penal law is exerted be particular, the laws themselves are general. They are made for the benefit and instruction of the public, though the penalty falls only upon an individual. You cannot but know, Sir, that what was Mr. Wilkes's case yesterday, may be yours or mine to-morrow, and that consequently the common right of every subject of the realm is invaded by it. Professing therefore to treat of the constitution of the House of Commons, and of the laws and customs relative to that constitution, you certainly were guilty of a most unpardonable omission in taking no notice of a right and privilege of the House, more extraordinary and more arbitrary than all

* If, in stating the law upon any point, a judge deliberately affirms that he has included *every* case, and it should appear that he has purposely omitted a material case, he does in effect lay *a snare for the unwary.*—JUNIUS. This last part of the sentence is a quotation artfully selected from Blackstone's own works, and turned against himself.—ED.

the others they possess put together. If the expulsion of a member, not under any other legal disability, of itself creates in him an incapacity to be re-elected, I see a ready way marked out, by which the majority may at any time remove the honestest and ablest men who happen to be in opposition to them. To say that they *will not* make this extravagant use of their power, would be a language unfit for a man so learned in the laws as you are. By your doctrine, Sir, they *have* the power, and laws you know are intended to guard against what men *may* do, not to trust what they *will* do.

Upon the whole, Sir, the charge against you is of a plain, simple nature—it appears even upon the face of your own pamphlet. On the contrary, your justification of yourself is full of subtlety and refinement, and in some places not very intelligible. If I were personally your enemy, I should dwell with a malignant pleasure upon those great and useful qualifications which you certainly possess, and by which you once acquired, though they could not preserve to you, the respect and esteem of your country—I should enumerate the honours you have lost, and the virtues you have dis graced ; but having no private resentments to gratify, I think it sufficient to have given my opinion of your public conduct, leaving the punishment it deserves to your closet and to yourself.

JUNIUS.

LETTER XIX

TO THE PRINTER OF THE PUBLIC ADVERTISER.

SIR,   August 14, 1769.
A CORRESPONDENT of the St. James's Chronicle first wilfully misunderstands JUNIUS, then censures him for a bad reasoner. JUNIUS does not say that it was incumbent upon Doctor Blackstone to foresee and state the crimes for which Mr. Wilkes was expelled. If, by a spirit of prophecy, he had even done so, it would have been nothing to the purpose. The question is, not for what particular offences a person may be expelled, but generally, whether by the law of

parliament expulsion alone creates a disqualification? If the affirmative be the law of parliament, Doctor Blackstone might and should have told us so. The question is not con·fined to this or that particular person, but forms one great general branch of disqualification, too important in itself, and too extensive in its consequences, to be omitted in an accurate work expressly treating of the law of parliament.

The truth of the matter is evidently this. Doctor Blackstone, while he was speaking in the House of Commons, never once thought of his Commentaries until the contradiction was unexpectedly urged and stared him in the face. Instead of defending himself upon the spot he sunk under the charge in an agony of confusion and despair. It is well known that there was a pause of some minutes in the House, from a general expectation that the Doctor would say something in his own defence; but, it seems, his faculties were too much overpowered to think of those subtleties and refinements which have since occurred to him. It was then Mr. Grenville received that severe chastisement which the Doctor mentions with so much triumph—*I wish the honourable gentleman, instead of shaking his head, would shake a good argument out of it.* If to the elegance, novelty, and bitterness of this ingenious sarcasm, we add the natural melody of the amiable Sir Fletcher Norton's pipe, we shall not be surprised that Mr. Grenville was unable to make him any reply.

As to the Doctor, I would recommend it to him to be quiet. If not, he may perhaps hear again from Junius himself.

PHILO-JUNIUS.

POSTSCRIPT* TO A PAMPHLET

INTITLED,

" AN ANSWER TO THE QUESTION STATED."

Supposed to be written by Dr. Blackstone, Solicitor to the Queen, in answer to Junius's Letter.

SINCE these papers were sent to the press, a writer in the public papers, who subscribes himself JUNIUS, has made a

* This is the Postscript, added in a subsequent edition, to Sir William Blackstone's reply to Sir William Meredith's pamphlet, as noticed, *ante,* p. 185, note. See also a further extract on this subject from a "Speech without doors," by Sir W. B., *ante,* p. 181.

feint of bringing this question to a short issue. Though the
foregoing observations contain, in my opinion at least, a full
refutation of all that this writer has offered, I shall, however,
bestow a very few words upon him. It will cost me very
little trouble to unravel and expose the sophistry of his argument.

" I take the question," says he, " to be strictly this :
Whether or no it be the known established law of Parliament,
that the expulsion of a member of the House of Commons, of
itself, creates in him such an incapacity to be re-elected, that,
at a subsequent election, any votes given to him are null and
void, and that any other candidate who, except the person
expelled, has the greatest number of votes, ought to be the
sitting member."

Waiving for the present any objection I may have to this
state of the question, I shall venture to meet our champion
upon his own ground ; and attempt to support the affirmative
of it in one of the two ways by which he says it can be alone
fairly supported. " If there be no statute," says he, " in
which the specific disability is clearly created, &c. (and we
acknowledge there is none), the custom of parliament must
then be referred to, and some case or cases strictly in point
must be produced, with the decision of the court upon them."
Now I assert, that this has been done. Mr. Walpole's case
is strictly in point, to prove that expulsion creates absolute
incapacity of being re-elected. This was the clear decision of
the House upon it, and was a full declaration that incapacity
was the necessary consequence of expulsion. The law was as
clearly and firmly fixed by this resolution, and is as binding
in every subsequent case of expulsion, as if it had been declared by an express statute, " That a member expelled by a
resolution of the House of Commons shall be deemed incapable of being re-elected." Whatever doubt, then, there might
have been of the law before Mr. Walpole's case, with respect
to the full operation of a vote of expulsion, there can be none
now. The decision of the House upon this case is strictly in
point to prove that expulsion creates absolute incapacity in
law of being re-elected.

But incapacity in law in this instance must have the same
operation and effect with incapacity in law in every other instance. Now, incapacity of being re-elected implies in its

very terms, that any votes given to the incapable person, at a subsequent election, are null and void. This is its necessary operation, or it has no operation at all. It is *vox et præterea nihil.* We can no more be called upon to prove this proposition than we can to prove that a dead man is not alive, or that twice two are four. When the terms are understood the proposition is self-evident.

Lastly, it is in all cases of election the known and established law of the land, grounded upon the clearest principles of reason and common sense, that if the votes given to one candidate are null and void, they cannot be opposed to the votes given to another candidate. They cannot affect the votes of such candidate at all. As they have, on the one hand, no positive quality to add or establish, so have they, on the other hand, no negative one to subtract or destroy. They are, in a word, a mere nonentity. Such was the determination of the House of Commons in the Malden and Bedford elections—cases strictly in point to the present question as far as they are meant to be in point. And to say that they are not in point in all circumstances, in those particularly which are independent of the proposition which they are quoted to prove, is to say no more than that Malden is not Middlesex, nor Serjeant Comyns Mr. Wilkes.

Let us see then how our proof stands. Expulsion creates incapacity ; incapacity annihilates any votes given to the incapable person. The votes given to the qualified candidate stand upon their own bottom, firm and untouched, and can alone have effect. This, one would think, would be sufficient : but we are stopped short and told that none of our precedents come home to the present case, and are challenged to produce "a precedent in all the proceedings of the House of Commons that does come home to it, viz., *where an expelled member has been returned again, and another candidate, with an inferior number of votes, has been declared the sitting member.*"

Instead of a precedent, I will beg leave to put a case which, I fancy, will be quite as decisive to the present point. Suppose another Sacheverel (and every party must have its Sacheverel) should, at some future election, take it into his head to offer himself a candidate for the county of Middlesex. He is opposed by a candidate whose coat is of a different colour; but, however, of a very good colour. The divine has an indisputable majority; nay, the poor layman is absolutely distanced. The sheriff, after having had his conscience well informed by the reverend casuist, returns him, as he supposes, duly elected. The whole House is in an uproar, at the apprehension of so strange an appearance amongst them. A motion, however, is at length made, that the person was incapable of being elected, that his election therefore is null and void, and that his competitor ought to have been returned. No, says a great orator; first show me your law for this proceeding " Either produce me a statute, in which the specific disability of a clergyman is created; or produce me a precedent *where a clergyman has been returned, and another candidate, with an inferior number of votes, has been declared the sitting member*." No such statute, no such precedent is to be found. What answer then is to be given to this demand? The very same answer which I will give to that of Junius: That there is more than one precedent in the proceedings of the House ——" where an incapable person has been returned, and another candidate, with an inferior number of votes, has been declared the sitting member; and that this is the known and established law, in all cases of incapacity, from whatever cause it may arise."

I shall now therefore beg leave to make a slight amendment to Junius's state of the question, the affirmative of which will then stand thus:—

" It is the known and established law of Parliament, that the expulsion of any member of the House of Commons creates in him an incapacity of being re-elected; that any votes given to him at a subsequent election are, in consequence of such incapacity, null and void; and that any other candidate, who, except the person rendered incapable, has the greatest number of votes, ought to be the sitting member."

But our business is not yet quite finished. Mr. Walpole's case must have a re-hearing. " It is not possible," says this writer, " to conceive a case more exactly in point. Mr. Walpole was expelled, and having a majority of votes at the next election, was returned again. The friends of Mr. Taylor, a candidate set up by the ministry, petitioned the House that he might be the sitting member. Thus far the circumstances tally exactly, except that our House of Commons saved Mr.

Luttrell the trouble of petitioning. The point of law, how ever, was the same. It came regularly before the House and it was their business to determine upon it. They did determine it; for they declared Mr. Taylor *not duly elected*."

Instead of examining the justness of this representation, I shall beg leave to oppose against it my own view of this case, in as plain a manner and as few words as I am able.

It was the known and established law of Parliament, when the charge against Mr. Walpole came before the House of Commons, that they had power to expel, to disable, and to render incapable for offences. In virtue of this power they expelled him.

Had they, in the very vote of expulsion, adjudged him, in terms, to be incapable of being re-elected, there must have been at once an end with him. But though the right of the House, both to expel and adjudge incapable, was clear and indubitable, it does not appear to me, that the full operation and effect of a vote of expulsion singly was so. The law in this case had never been expressly declared. There had been no event to call up such a declaration. I trouble not myself with the grammatical meaning of the word expulsion. I regard only its legal meaning. This was not, as I think, precisely fixed. The House thought proper to fix it, and explicitly to declare the full consequences of their former vote, before they suffered these consequences to take effect. And in this proceeding they acted upon the most liberal and solid principles of equity, justice, and law. What then did the burgesses of Lynn collect from the second vote? Their subsequent conduct will tell us; it will with certainty tell us, that they considered it as decisive against Mr. Walpole; it will also, with equal certainty, tell us, that, upon supposition that the law of election stood then as it does now, and that they knew it to stand thus, they inferred, " that, at a future election, and in case of a similar return, the House would receive the same candidate, as duly elected, whom they had before rejected." They could infer nothing but this.

It is needless to repeat the circumstance of dissimilarity in the present case. It will be sufficient to observe, that as the law of Parliament, upon which the House of Commons grounded every step of their proceedings, was clear beyond the reach of doubt, so neither could the freeholders of Mid

dlesex be at a loss to foresee what must be the inevitable consequence of their proceedings in opposition to it.   For, upon
every return of Mr. Wilkes, the House made inquiry whether
any votes were given to any other candidate?

But I could venture, for the experiment's sake, even to give
this writer the utmost he asks; to allow the most perfect
similarity throughout in these two cases; to allow, that the
law of expulsion was quite as clear to the burgesses of Lynn,
as to the freeholders of Middlesex.   It will, I am confident,
avail his cause but little.   It will only prove that the law of
election at that time was different from the present law.   It
will prove, that, in all cases of an incapable candidate returned, the law then was, that the whole election should be
void.   But now we know that this is not law.   The cases of
Malden and Bedford were, as has been seen, determined upon
other and more just principles.   And these determinations
are, I imagine, admitted on all sides to be law.

I would willingly draw a veil over the remaining part of
this paper.   It is astonishing, it is painful, to see men of
parts and ability giving into the most unworthy artifices, and
descending so much below their true line of character.   But
if they are not the dupes of their sophistry (which is hardly
to be conceived), let them consider that they are something
much worse.

The dearest interests of this country are its laws and its
constitution.   Against every attack upon these, there will, I
hope, be always found amongst us the firmest *spirit of resistance;* superior to the united efforts of faction and ambition;
for ambition, though it does not always take the lead of faction, will be sure in the end to make the most fatal advantage
of it, and draw it to its own purposes.   But, I trust, our day
of trial is yet far off; and there is *a fund of good sense in this
country which cannot long be deceived* by the arts either of
false reasoning, or false patriotism.

LETTER XX*.

SIR,   August 8, 1769.

THE gentleman who has published an answer to Sir William Meredith's pamphlet, having honoured me with a postscript of six quarto pages, which he moderately calls bestowing a *very* few words upon me, I cannot, in common politeness, refuse him a reply. The form and magnitude of a quarto imposes upon the mind; and men who are unequal to the labour of discussing an intricate argument, or wish to avoid it, are willing enough to suppose, that much has been proved, because much has been said. Mine, I confess, are humble labours. I do not presume to instruct the learned, but simply to inform the body of the people; and I prefer that channel of conveyance which is likely to spread farthest among them. The advocates of the ministry seem to me to write for fame, and to flatter themselves that the size of their works will make them immortal. They pile up reluctant quarto upon solid folio, as if their labours, because they are gigantic, could contend with truth and heaven.

The writer of the volume in question meets me upon my own ground. He acknowledges there is no statute by which the specific disability we speak of is created, but he affirms, that the custom of parliament has been referred to, and that a case strictly in point has been produced, with the decision of the court upon it. I thank him for coming so fairly to the point. He asserts that the case of Mr. Walpole is strictly in point to prove that expulsion creates an absolute incapacity of being re-elected; and for this purpose he refers generally to the first vote of the House upon that occasion, without venturing to recite the vote itself. The unfair, disingenuous artifice of adopting that part of a precedent which seems to suit his purpose and omitting the remainder, deserves some pity, but cannot excite my resentment. He takes advantage eagerly of the first resolution, by which Mr. Walpole's in-

---

* "I wish the inclosed to be announced to-morrow *conspicuously*. I am not capable of writing anything more finished."—Private Letter, No. 6, vol. ii.

capacity is declared; but as to the following, by which the candidate with the fewest votes was declared "not duly elected," and the election itself vacated, I dare say he would be well satisfied, if they were for ever blotted out of the journals of the House of Commons. In fair argument, no part of a precedent should be admitted unless the whole of it be given to us together. The author has divided his precedent, for he knew that, taken together, it produced a consequence directly the reverse of that which he endeavours to draw from a vote of expulsion. But what will this honest person say if I take him at his word, and demonstrate to him that the House of Commons never meant to found Mr. Walpole's incapacity upon his expulsion only? What subterfuge will then remain?

Let it be remembered that we are speaking of the intention of men, who lived more than half a century ago, and that such intention can only be collected from their words and actions, as they are delivered to us upon record. To prove their designs by a supposition of what they would have done, opposed to what they actually did, is mere trifling and impertinence. The vote, by which Mr. Walpole's incapacity was declared, is thus expressed: "That Robert Walpole, Esq., having been this session of parliament committed a prisoner to the Tower, and expelled this House for a high breach of trust in the execution of his office, and notorious corruption when secretary at war, was, and is, incapable of being elected a member to serve in this present parliament."[*]   Now, Sir, to my understanding, no proposition of this kind can be more evident than that the House of Commons, by this very vote, themselves understood, and meant to declare, that Mr. Walpole's incapacity arose from the crimes he had committed, not from

---

[*] It is well worth remarking, that the compiler of a certain quarto, called *The Case of the Election for the County of Middlesex considered,* has the impudence to recite this very vote, in the following terms, vide page 11 : " Resolved, that Robert Walpole, Esq., having been that session of parliament expelled the House, was and is incapable of being elected a member to serve in that present parliament." There cannot be a stronger positive proof of the treachery of the compiler, nor a stronger presumptive proof that he was convinced that the vote, if truly recited, would overturn his whole argument.— JUNIUS.

It has been already remarked that the pamphlet alluded to in the above note of the author, was from the pen of Mr. Dyson. (See *ante,* p. 185.)

the punishment of the House annexed to them. The high breach of trust, the notorious corruption, are stated in the strongest terms. They do not tell us he was incapable because he was expelled, but because he had been guilty of such offences as justly rendered him unworthy of a seat in parliament. If they had intended to fix the disability upon his expulsion alone, the mention of his crimes in the same vote would have been highly improper. It could only perplex the minds of the electers, who, if they collected anything from so confused a declaration of the law of parliament, must have concluded that their representative had been declared incapable because he was highly guilty, not because he had been punished. But even admitting them to have understood it in the other sense, they must then, from the very terms of the vote, have united the idea of his being sent to the Tower with that of his expulsion, and considered his incapacity as the joint effect of both.

I do not mean to give an opinion upon the justice of the proceedings of the House of Commons with regard to Mr. Walpole; but certainly, if I admitted their censure to be well founded, I could no way avoid agreeing with them in the consequence they drew from it. I could never have a doubt, in law or reason, that a man, convicted of a high breach of trust, and of a notorious corruption in the execution of a public office was and ought to be incapable of sitting in the same parliament. Far from attempting to invalidate that vote, I should have wished that the incapacity declared by it could legally have been continued for ever.

Now, Sir, observe how forcibly the argument returns. The House of Commons, upon the face of their proceedings, had the strongest motives to declare Mr. Walpole incapable of being re-elected. They thought such a man unworthy to sit among them. To that point they proceeded no farther; for they respected the rights of the people, while they asserted their own. They did not infer from Mr. Walpole's incapacity that his opponent was duly elected; on the contrary, they declared Mr. Taylor "not duly elected," and the election itself void.

Such, however, is the precedent which my honest friend assures us is strictly in point to prove, that expulsion of itself creates an incapacity of being elected. If it had been so, the present House of Commons should at least have followed strictly the example before them, and should have stated to us, in the same vote, the crimes for which they expelled Mr. Wilkes; whereas they resolve simply that, "having been expelled, he was and is incapable." In this proceeding I am authorized to affirm they have neither statute, nor custom, nor reason, nor one single precedent to support them. On the other side, there is indeed a precedent so strongly in point that all the enchanted castles of ministerial magic fall before it. In the year 1698 (a period which the rankest Tory dare not except against) Mr. Wollaston was expelled, re-elected, and admitted to take his seat in the same parliament. The ministry have precluded themselves from all objections drawn from the cause of his expulsion, for they affirm absolutely, that expulsion of itself creates the disability. Now, Sir, let sophistry evade, let falsehood assert, and impudence deny—here stands the precedent, a landmark to direct us through a troubled sea of controversy, conspicuous and unremoved.

I have dwelt the longer upon the discussion of this point, because, in *my* opinion, it comprehends the whole question. The rest is unworthy of notice. We are enquiring whether incapacity be or be not created by expulsion. In the cases of Bedford and Malden the incapacity of the persons returned was matter of public notoriety, for it was created by act of parliament. But really, Sir, my honest friend's suppositions are as unfavourable to him as his facts. He well knows that the clergy, besides that they are represented in common with their fellow-subjects, have also a separate parliament of their own; —that their incapacity to sit in the House of Commons has been confirmed by repeated decisions of the House, and that the law of parliament declared by those decisions, has been, for above two centuries, notorious and undisputed. The author is certainly at liberty to fancy cases, and make whatever comparisons he thinks proper; his suppositions still continue as distant from fact as his wild discourses are from solid argument.

The conclusion of his book is candid to an extreme. He offers to grant me all I desire. He thinks he may safely admit that the case of Mr. Walpole makes directly against him, for it seems he has one grand solution *in petto* for all difficulties. *If*, says he, *I were to allow all this, it will only prove that the law of election was different in Queen Anne's time from what it is at present.*

This, indeed, is more than I expected. The principle, I

know, has been maintained in fact, but I never expected to see it so formally declared. What can he mean? Does he assume this language to satisfy the doubts of the people, or does he mean to rouse their indignation? Are the ministry daring enough to affirm, that the House of Commons have a right to make and unmake the law of parliament at their pleasure? Does the law of parliament—which we are so often told is the law of the land—does the common right of every subject of the realm depend upon an arbitrary, capricious vote of one branch of the legislature? The voice of truth and reason must be silent.

The ministry tell us plainly that this is no longer a question of right, but of power and force alone. What was law yesterday is not law to-day; and now, it seems, we have no better rule to live by than the temporary discretion and fluctuating integrity of the House of Commons.

Professions of patriotism are become stale and ridiculous. For my own part, I claim no merit from endeavouring to do a service to my fellow-subjects. I have done it to the best of my understanding; and, without looking for the approbation of other men, my conscience is satisfied. What remains to be done concerns the collective body of the people. They are now to determine for themselves, whether they will firmly and constitutionally assert their rights, or make an humble, slavish surrender of them at the feet of the ministry. To a generous mind there cannot be a doubt. We owe it to our ancestors to preserve entire those rights which they have delivered to our care—we owe it to our posterity not to suffer their dearest inheritance to be destroyed. But if it were possible for us to be insensible of these sacred claims, there is yet an obligation binding upon ourselves, from which nothing can acquit us,—a personal interest, which we cannot surrender. To alienate even our own rights would be a crime as much more enormous than suicide as a life of civil security and freedom is superior to a bare existence; and, if life be the bounty of heaven, we scornfully reject the noblest part of the gift if we consent to surrender that certain rule of living without which the condition of human nature is not only miserable, but contemptible.

JUNIUS.

LETTER OF PHILO-JUNIUS

(In reference to the preceding.)

TO THE PRINTER OF THE PUBLIC ADVERTISER*.

SIR,   May 22, 1771.

VERY early in the debate upon the decision of the Middlesex
election, it was observed by Junius that the House of Commons
had not only exceeded their boasted precedent of the expulsion
and subsequent incapacitation of Mr. Walpole, but that they
had not even adhered to it strictly as far as it went.   After
convicting Mr. Dyson of giving a false quotation from the
Journals, and having explained the purpose which that contemptible fraud was intended to answer, he proceeds to state
the vote itself by which Mr. Walpole's supposed incapacity
was declared, viz.,—" Resolved, that Robert Walpole, Esq.,
having been this session of parliament committed a prisoner
to the Tower, and expelled this House for a high breach of
trust in the execution of his office, and notorious corruption
when secretary at war, was and is incapable of being elected a
member to serve in this present parliament:"—and then observes that, from the terms of the vote, we have no right to
annex the incapacitation to the *expulsion* only, for that, as
the proposition stands, it must arise equally from the expulsion and the commitment to the Tower.   I believe, Sir, no
man who knows anything of dialectics, or who understands
English, will dispute the truth and fairness of this construction.   But Junius has a great authority to support him, which,
to speak with the Duke of Grafton, I accidentally met with
this morning in the course of my reading.   It contains an
admonition which cannot be repeated too often.   Lord Somers,
in his excellent tract upon the rights of the people, after re-

---

* This letter, published long subsequent to that which here immediately
precedes it, was intended chiefly to adduce, in defence of Junius's explanation of the Commons resolution, which declared Mr. Walpole incapable of
immediate re-election, no less authority than that of Lord Somers, as clearly
expressed in his interpretation of the famous convention at the revolution, by
which King James was declared to have abdicated the throne.   The letter is
inserted here, because Junius, from the place he has given it in his own
edition, appears to have intended that it should accompany that of August 8,
1769, to which it especially refers.—ED.

citing the vote of the convention of the 28th of January, 1689, viz.,—" That King James the Second, having endeavoured to subvert the constitution of this kingdom by breaking the original contract between king and people, and by the advice of Jesuits and other wicked persons having violated the fundamental laws, and having withdrawn himself out of this kingdom, hath abdicated the government, &c."—makes this observation upon it:—" The word *abdicated* relates to *all* the clauses aforegoing, as well as to his deserting the kingdom, or else they would have been wholly in vain." And that there might be no pretence for confining the *abdication* merely to the *withdrawing*, Lord Somers farther observes, *that King James, by refusing to govern us according to that law by which he held the crown, implicitly renounced his title to it.*

If Junius's construction of the vote against Mr. Walpole be now admitted (and indeed I cannot comprehend how it can honestly be disputed), the advocates of the House of Commons must either give up their precedent entirely, or be reduced to the necessity of maintaining one of the grossest absurdities imaginable, viz.,—" That a commitment to the Tower is a constituent part of, and contributes half at least to, the incapacitation of the person who suffers it."

I need not make you any excuse for endeavouring to keep alive the attention of the public to the decision of the Middlesex election. The more I consider it, the more I am convinced that, as a *fact*, it is indeed highly injurious to the rights of the people; but that, as a *precedent*, it is one of the most dangerous that ever was established against those who are to come after us. Yet I am so far a moderate man that I verily believe the majority of the House of Commons, when they passed this dangerous vote, neither understood the question, nor knew the consequence of what they were doing. Their motives were rather despicable, than criminal, in the extreme. One effect they certainly did not foresee. They are now reduced to such a situation that, if a member of the present House of Commons were to conduct himself ever so improperly, and in reality deserve to be sent back to his constituents with a mark of disgrace, they would not dare to expel him, because they know that the people, in order to try again the great question of right, or to thwart an odious House of Commons, would probably overlook his immediate unworthiness, and return the same person to parliament. But, in time, the precedent will gain strength. A future House of Commons will have no such apprehensions, consequently will not scruple to follow a precedent which they did not establish. The miser himself seldom lives to enjoy the fruit of his extortion; but his heir succeeds to him of course, and takes possession without censure. No man expects him to make restitution, and, no matter for his title, he lives quietly upon the estate.

PHILO-JUNIUS.

LETTER XXI.

TO THE PRINTER OF THE PUBLIC ADVERTISER.

SIR,　　　　　　　　　　　　　　　　　August 22, 1769.

I MUST beg of you to print a few lines, in explanation of some passages in my last letter, which I see have been misunderstood.

1. When I said that the House of Commons never meant to found Mr. Walpole's incapacity on his expulsion *only*, I meant no more than to deny the general proposition that expulsion *alone* creates the incapacity. If there be anything ambiguous in the expression, I beg leave to explain it by saying that, in my opinion, expulsion neither creates, nor in any part contributes to create, the incapacity in question.

2. I carefully avoided entering into the merits of Mr. Walpole's case. I did not inquire whether the House of Commons acted justly, or whether they truly declared the law of parliament. My remarks went only to their apparent meaning and intention, as it stands declared in their own resolution.

3. I never meant to affirm that a commitment to the Tower created a disqualification. On the contrary, I considered that idea as an absurdity into which the ministry must inevitably fall if they reasoned right upon their own principles.

The case of Mr. Wollaston speaks for itself. The ministry assert that *expulsion alone* creates an absolute, complete incapacity to be re-elected to sit in the same parliament. This proposition they have uniformly maintained, without any con dition or modification whatsoever. Mr. Wollaston was ex- pelled, re-elected, and admitted to take his seat in the same parliament. I leave it to the public to determine whether this be a plain matter of fact, or mere nonsense and declama- tion.

JUNIUS.

LETTER XXII.

TO THE PRINTER OF THE PUBLIC ADVERTISER.

SIR,   September 4, 1769.

ARGUMENT AGAINST FACT; or, A new System of political Logic, by which the ministry have demonstrated, to the satisfaction of their friends, that expulsion alone creates a complete incapacity to be re-elected; *alias*, that a subject of this realm may be robbed of his common right by a vote of the House of Commons.

FIRST FACT.

Mr. Wollaston, in 1698, *was expelled, re-elected, and ad- mitted to take his seat.*

ARGUMENT.

As this cannot conveniently be reconciled with our general proposition, it may be necessary to shift our ground and look back to the *cause* of Mr. Wollaston's expulsion. From thence it will appear clearly that, "although he was expelled, he had not rendered himself a culprit too ignominious to sit in parliament, and that, having resigned his employment, he was no longer incapacitated by law." *Vide Serious Consider- ations*, page 23. Or thus, "The House, somewhat *inaccu- rately*, used the word EXPELLED; they should have called it A MOTION." *Vide Mungo's Case considered*, page 11. Or, in short, if these arguments should be thought insufficient, we may fairly deny the fact. For example; " I affirm that he was not re-elected. The same Mr. Wollaston who was ex- pelled was not again elected. The same individual, if you please, walked into the House, and took his seat there; but the same person in law was not admitted a member of that parliament, from which he had been discarded.' *Vide Letter to Junius*, page 12.

SECOND FACT.

Mr. Walpole having been committed to the Tower, and expelled for a high breach of trust, and notorious corruption in a public office, was declared incapable, &c.

ARGUMENT.

From the terms of this vote, nothing can be more evident than that the House of Commons meant to fix the incapacity upon the punishment, and not upon the crime; but lest it should appear in a different light to weak, uninformed persons, it may be advisable to put the resolution, and give it to the public, with all possible solemnity, in the following terms, namely, " Resolved, that Robert Walpole, Esq., having been that session of parliament expelled the House, was and is incapable of being elected a member to serve in that present parliament." *Vide Mungo, on the Use of Quotations*, page 11.

N.B.—The author of the answer to Sir William Meredith[*] seems to have made use of Mungo's quotation, for in page 18 he assures us, " That the declaratory vote of the 17th of February, 1769, was indeed a literal copy of the resolution of the House in Mr. Walpole's case."

THIRD FACT.

His opponent, Mr. Taylor, having the smallest number of votes at the next election, was declared NOT DULY ELECTED.

ARGUMENT.

This fact we consider as directly in point to prove that Mr. Luttrell ought to be the sitting member, for the following reasons, " The burgesses of Lynn could draw no other inference from this resolution, but this, that, at a future election, and in case of a similar return, the House would receive the same candidate as duly elected whom they had before rejected." *Vide Postscript to Junius*, p. 37. Or thus: "This their resolution leaves no room to doubt what part they *would*

---

[*] Sir W. Blackstone.

have taken if, upon a subsequent re-election of Mr. Walpole there had been any other candidate in competition with him. For, by their vote, they could have no other intention than to admit such other candidate." *Vide Mungo's Case considered* p. 39. Or take it in this light: the burgesses of Lynn, having, in defiance of the House, retorted upon them a person whom they had branded with the most ignominious marks of their displeasure, were thereby so well entitled to favour and indulgence, that the House could do no less than rob Mr. Taylor of a right legally vested in him, in order that the burgesses might be apprized of the law of parliament, which law the House took a very direct way of explaining to them by resolving that 'the candidate with the fewest votes was not duly elected:—" And was not this much more equitable, more in the spirit of that equal and substantial justice, which is the end of all law, than if they had violently adhered to the strict maxims of law?" *Vide Serious Considerations*, pp. 33 and 34. "And if the present House of Commons had chosen to follow the spirit of this resolution, they would have received and established the candidate with the fewest votes." *Vide Answer to Sir W. M.*, p. 18.

Permit me now, Sir, to show you that the worthy Dr. Blackstone sometimes contradicts the ministry as well as himself. The speech without doors asserts *, p. 9, "That the legal effect of an incapacity founded on a judicial determination of a competent court is precisely the same as that of an incapacity created by act of parliament." Now for the Doctor.—*The law and the opinion of the judge are not always convertible terms, or one and the same thing; since it sometimes may happen that the judge may mistake the law.* Commentaries, vol. i. p. 71.

The answer to Sir W. M. asserts, page 23, "That the returning officer is not a judicial, but a purely ministerial officer. His return is no judicial act." At 'em again, Doctor.—*The Sheriff, in his judicial capacity, is to hear and determine causes of forty shillings value and under in his county court. He has also a judicial power in divers other civil cases. He is likewise to decide the elections of knights of the shire (subject to the control of the House of Commons), to*

* Letter 17.

judge of the qualification of voters, and to return such as he shall DETERMINE *to be duly elected.* Vide Commentaries, page 332, vol. i.

What conclusion shall we draw from such facts, such arguments, and such contradictions? I cannot express my opinion of the present ministry more exactly than in the words of Sir R. Steele, "that we are governed by a set of drivellers, whose folly takes away all dignity from distress, and makes even calamity ridiculous."*

PHILO-JUNIUS.

* In a pamphlet written by Steele upon the issue of the South-Sea Company, at the period when Walpole was beginning to take a higher and more decided part in the management of public affairs. It was supposed to have been written by Walpole and Steele conjointly. But Steele seems to have been as much superior to Walpole in the knowledge of matters of trade and national revenue as in the art of elegant writing.

Before entering with Junius on a new theme, it may not be amiss to contrast the whole strength of the ministerial arguments in favour of the decision of the House of Commons, in the case of the Middlesex election, with those which have been urged by Junius to prove the illegality of that decision. The ministerial cause was argued by Dr. Johnson, in his pamphlet of *The False Alarm,* much better than by any one else who undertook to plead it. The following is a summary of Johnson's arguments.

1. Wilkes was so very worthless a fellow, that the electors disgraced themselves, and offered an insult to the electors in all the burghs and counties of Great Britain, to the House of Commons, and even to the other two branches of the Legislature, by sending him to be their representative in parliament.

2. By natural expediency, and by custom expressed in a long series of precedents, the House of Commons have collectively an unlimited authority over their own members, in the exercise of which they cannot be controlled, as even for its abuse they cannot be called to account.

3. A man attainted of felony cannot sit in parliament. The House of Commons must have considered the crimes of Wilkes as little less heinous than felony. They, justly, therefore, assumed the liberty of treating him as a felon.

4. From the time of his expulsion, Wilkes could not be a legal candidate for the representation of any county or burgh. Votes given for one incapable of being legally a candidate, could have no legal effect. Having no legal effect, were they not, of course, null?

5. Selden has maintained that the House of Commons have even power to impose perpetual disability upon any one of their members.

6. Only that power which cannot be exercised without the agency of others terminates to the Commons at the end of a Session. But that of which the exercise is in themselves alone, and only while they sit, endures from one general election to another.

7. It appears to have always been the law, that no Member of the House

of Commons, once expelled, for whatever cause, could again obtain a seat in the same parliament, if there were not some statutory exception in his favour.

8. If a county or burgh were left free to return, by continually repeated election, any obnoxious member, as often as the House should think fit to expel him, the business of Parliament might be entirely interrupted by a mischievous concert between that member and his electors; and the whole attention of the Commons might be confined, even at any crisis, however important, to this ridiculous contest ; therefore, to protect the order of its proceedings, the House of Commons *must* necessarily possess authority to prevent the re-election of any member whom they have expelled.

9. Were it even true that the decision in favour of Mr. Luttrell, and in opposition to the claims of Mr. Wilkes and the majority of the Middlesex electors, were unjust and unconstitutional, yet how happy, in comparison, that nation which suffers from its government no wrongs heavier than this!

These are the arguments of Johnson. Let us oppose to them a summary of those of Junius.

1. It was not his immorality that recommended Wilkes to the choice of the electors of Middlesex; but his zeal and firmness in opposing wicked ministers and irregular acts of power; his sufferings in the cause he had espoused, sufferings by which he was certainly recommended to the esteem and favour of his country ; and the consideration that the man, *whoever he might be,* in respect to whom any great principle of the constitution had been violated, ought to be firmly supported by all who thought that constitution worthy of defence, till his wrongs should be redressed, and the laws, in the violation of which he was injured, should be effectually vindicated.

2. Unless there be statute or precedent to the contrary, the House of Commons can possess no other authority over either their own members or any one else, save what, in addition to the effect of the common and statute law, and to the care of the King to maintain the peace in favour of his Commons, may be necessary to support the freedom and order of their proceedings. Having it so much in their power to discover and promote whatever new laws may be wanted, they can easily procure an act of the legislature whenever new and more effectual protection to their legislative agency may become necessary. And it cannot be supposed that *they* should choose to retain aught in uncertainty which they may procure to be decisively settled, if that were requisite, by a law of unquestionable validity.

3. But the power of excluding an expelled member is not indispensably necessary to maintain the order and dignity of the proceedings of the House of Commons. Or, if it be necessary, it is at least of such a nature that it might be defined by law without inconvenience either to the public in general or to the House of Commons. Or it may be at least rendered effectual by the Commons alone, without depriving those electors of the right of voting who may incline to send back the expelled member into the bosom of the House.

4. The power of excluding an expelled member *on account simply of his expulsion,* has not been bestowed on the House of Commons by any statute, and does not appear in any precedent, to have been ever exercised by them. Neither do they appear to have ever on any former occasion supposed that

LETTER XXIII*

TO HIS GRACE THE DUKE OF BEDFORD.

MY LORD,   September 19, 1769.

You are so little accustomed to receive any marks of respect
or esteem from the public †, that if in the following lines a

they had power to annul the votes which were given in favour of candidates
who had been previously disqualified by expulsion from the House.

5. All the precedents which have been quoted in defence of the decision
of the House upon the Middlesex election have been found to be in this
case inaccurately applied, and of course to contradict the very position which
they have been quoted to maintain.

6. Consequences the most fatal to the British Constitution would ensue if the
House of Commons were suffered to annul at pleasure, by their sole authority,
the votes of their electors. Every burgh, every county, might be forced to
forego its first choice in order to escape the danger of being deprived of the
liberty to make a second.

These are the chief arguments on both sides. It is easy to see that those
of Junius exceedingly preponderate. And happily, at the time when, at the
close of the American War, the Whigs of the school of Charles Fox—Charles
Fox, the true political representative of Temple and of Chatham—came for a
short time into power, the precedent of the decision in the case of the Middlesex election was erased from the records of the House of Commons.

* In requesting the announcement of this letter, Junius says, "I mean to
make it worth printing." Private Letter, No. 9, vol. ii.

† The unpopular peace of 1763 was negotiated by the Duke of Bedford,
and gave rise to a variety of public commotions, which at length broke out
into acts of open insurrection among the Spitalfield weavers, who exclaimed
that their trade was ruined by its commercial stipulations. The rumour
became current that the French Court had purchased this peace by bribes to
the Princess Dowager of Wales, Lord Bute, the Duke of Bedford, and Mr.
Henry Fox, afterwards Lord Holland; and such was its general belief that
the House of Commons thought proper to appoint a committee to examine
into its truth; who traced it chiefly to a Dr. Musgrave, who, nevertheless,
does not appear to have suffered from this libellous report, which, as he
affirmed, he had brought home with him from Paris. The public disfavour
with which the terms of the peace were received, produced a fresh disagreement between Lord Bute and the Duke of Bedford on his return home, and
he resigned the office of lord privy seal. Upon the death of Lord Egremont,
however, Lord Bute found himself compelled once more to apply to the Duke
of Bedford for his interest, who, conscious of his importance, exacted not only
from Lord Bute but from the King himself a submission to whatever terms
he chose to impose. After the Regency Bill, which had been recommended
in a speech from the throne in April, 1765, had passed both Houses, an
attempt was made to change the administration, from a belief that this bill

compliment or expression of applause should escape me, I fear you would consider it as a mockery of your established character, and perhaps an insult to your understanding. You have nice feelings, my Lord, if we may judge from your resentments. Cautious, therefore, of giving offence where you have so little deserved it, I shall leave the illustration of your virtues to other hands. Your friends have a privilege to play upon the easiness of your temper, or possibly they are better acquainted with your good qualities than I am. You have done good by stealth. The rest is upon record. You have still left ample room for speculation when panegyric is exhausted.

You are indeed a very considerable man. The highest rank, a splendid fortune, and a name, glorious till it was yours, were sufficient to have supported you with meaner abilities than I think you possess. From the first, you derived a constitutional claim to respect; from the second, a natural extensive authority; the last created a partial expectation of hereditary virtues. The use you have made of these uncommon advantages might have been more honourable to yourself, but could not be more instructive to mankind. We may trace it in the veneration of your country, the choice of your friends, and in the accomplishment of every sanguine hope which the public might have conceived from the illustrious name of Russell.

had not received their cordial support during its progress through Parliament, but without success. It was upon this occasion that the Duke of Bedford insisted upon the dismissal of Lord Bute's brother, Mr. Stuart Mackenzie, from his office, although Mackenzie had received his Majesty's solemn promise that he should preserve it for life; that he recalled Lord Northumberland from the lord-lieutenancy of Ireland, and removed Lord Holland from the pay office.

Incapable of submitting to such severe treatment, his Majesty soon afterwards entreated the Duke of Newcastle and Lord Rockingham to rescue him from the Bedford party. They consented, and the duke was again dismissed with contumely. When his Majesty became disgusted, as he soon did, with this ministry also, Lord Bute applied in the King's name to George Grenville for support, and the Duke of Bedford, who was on terms of the closest friendship with him, once more strove to enter into the cabinet; but on this occasion Lord Bute had spirit enough to treat his offer with the utmost contempt. Lord Chatham was next applied to, who consented to take the lead, and on his resignation the Duke of Grafton was made prime minister, who, to strengthen his own hands, re-introduced the Duke of Bedford into the cabinet, without, however, appointing him to any particular office.

P 2

The eminence of your station gave you a commanding pro
spect of your duty.   The road which led to honour was open
to your view.   You could not lose it by mistake, and you had
no temptation to depart from it by design.   Compare the
natural dignity and importance of the richest peer of England—the noble independence which he might have maintained in parliament, and the real interest and respect which
he might have acquired, not only in parliament, but through
the whole kingdom—compare these glorious distinctions with
the ambition of holding a share in government, the emoluments of a place, the sale of a borough, or the purchase of a
corporation, and though you may not regret the virtues which
create respect, you may see with anguish how much real importance and authority you have lost.   Consider the character
of an independent, virtuous Duke of Bedford; imagine what
he might be in this country, then reflect one moment upon
what you are.   If it be possible for me to withdraw my attention from the fact, I will tell you in theory what such a
man might be.

Conscious of his own weight and importance, his conduct
in parliament would be directed by nothing but the constitutional duty of a peer.   He would consider himself as a guardian of the laws.   Willing to support the just measures of
government, but determined to observe the conduct of the
minister with suspicion, he would oppose the violence of fac
tion with as much firmness as the encroachments of prerogative.   He would be as little capable of bargaining with the
minister for places for himself or his dependents as of descending to mix himself in the intrigues of opposition.
Whenever an important question called for his opinion in
parliament, he would be heard by the most profligate minister
with deference and respect.   His authority would either
sanctify or disgrace the measures of government.   The people would look up to him as their protector, and a virtuous
prince would have one honest man in his dominions in whose
integrity and judgment he might safely confide.   If it should
be the will of Providence to afflict him with a domestic misfortune *, he would submit to the stroke with feeling, but not

---

* The duke had lately lost his only son, by a fall from his horse. —
JUNIUS.

without dignity. He would consider the people as his children, and receive a generous heart-felt consolation in the sympathising tears and blessings of his country.

Your Grace may probably discover something more intelligible in the negative part of this illustrious character. The man I have described would never prostitute his dignity in parliament by an indecent violence either in opposing or defending a minister. He would not at one moment rancorously persecute, at another basely cringe to, the favourite of his sovereign. After outraging the royal dignity with peremptory conditions little short of menace and hostility, he would never descend to the humility of soliciting an interview * with the favourite, and of offering to recover, at any price, the honour of his friendship. Though deceived, perhaps, in his youth, he would not, through the course of a long life, have invariably chosen his friends from among the most profligate of mankind. His own honour would have forbidden him from mixing his private pleasures or conversation with jockeys, gamesters, blasphemers, gladiators, or buffoons. He would then have never felt, much less would he have submitted to, the humiliating, dishonest necessity of engaging in the interest and intrigues of his dependents, of supplying their vices, or relieving their beggary, at the expense of his country. He would not have betrayed such ignorance or such contempt of the constitution as openly to avow, in a court of justice, the purchase and sale † of a borough. He would not have thought it consistent with his rank in the state, or even with his personal importance, to be the little tyrant of a little corporation ‡. He would never have been insulted with virtues which he had laboured to extinguish, nor suffered the disgrace

---

* At this interview, which passed at the house of the late Lord Eglintoun, Lord Bute told the duke that he was determined never to have any connection with a man who had so basely betrayed him.—JUNIUS.

† In an answer in Chancery, in a suit against him to recover a large sum paid him by a person whom he had undertaken to return to Parliament for one of his Grace's boroughs. He was compelled to repay the money.—JUNIUS.

‡ Of Bedford, where the tyrant was held in such contempt and detestation, that, in order to deliver themselves from him, they admitted a great number of strangers to the freedom. To make his defeat truly ridiculous. he tried his whole strength against Mr. *Horne,* and was beaten upon his own ground.—JUNIUS.

of a mortifying defeat which has made him ridiculous and contemptible even to the few by whom he was not detested. I reverence the afflictions of a good man—his sorrows are sacred. But how can we take part in the distresses of a man whom we can neither love nor esteem; or feel for a calamity of which he himself is insensible? Where was the father's heart when he could look for, or find an immediate consolation for the loss of an only son, in consultations and bargains for a place at court, and even in the misery of balloting at the India House!

Admitting, then, that you have mistaken or deserted those honourable principles which ought to have directed your conduct, admitting that you have as little claim to private affection as to public esteem, let us see with what abilities, with what degree of judgment, you have carried your own system into execution. A great man in the success, and even in the magnitude, of his crimes finds a rescue from contempt. Your Grace is every way unfortunate. Yet I will not look back to those ridiculous scenes by which, in your earlier days, you thought it an honour to be distinguished—the recorded stripes *, the public infamy, your own sufferings, or Mr. Rigby's fortitude. These events undoubtedly left an impression, though not upon your mind. To *such* a mind it may, perhaps, be a pleasure to reflect that there is hardly a corner of any of His Majesty's kingdoms, except France, in which, at one time or other, your valuable life has not been in danger. Amiable man! we see and acknowledge the protection of Providence, by which you have so often escaped the personal detestation of your fellow-subjects, and are still reserved for the public justice of your country.

Your history begins to be important at that auspicious period at which you were deputed to represent the Earl of Bute at the court of Versailles. It was an honourable office,

---

* Mr. Heston Homphrey, a country attorney, horsewhipped the duke with equal justice, severity, and perseverance, on the course at Litchfield. *Rigby* and *Lord Trentham* were also cudgelled in a most exemplary manner. This gave rise to the following story: "When the late king heard that Sir Edward Hawke had given the French a *drubbing*, his Majesty, who had never received that kind of chastisement, was pleased to ask Lord Chesterfield the meaning of the word. "Sir," says Lord Chesterfield "the meaning of the word—but here comes the Duke of Bedford, who is better able to explai 1 it to your Majesty than I am."—JUNIUS.

and executed with the same spirit with which it was accepted. Your patrons wanted an ambassador who would submit to make concessions without daring to insist upon any honourable condition for his sovereign. Their business required a man who had as little feeling for his own dignity as for the welfare of his country; and they found him in the first rank of the nobility. Belleisle, Goree, Guadaloupe, St. Louis, Martinique, the Fishery, and the Havanna, are glorious monuments of your Grace's talents for negotiation*. My Lord, we are too well acquainted with your pecuniary character to think it possible that so many public sacrifices should be made without some private compensations. Your conduct carries with it an internal evidence beyond all the legal proofs of a court of justice. Even the callous pride of Lord Egremont was alarmed †. He saw and felt his own dishonour in corresponding with you; and there certainly was a moment at which he meant to have resisted, had not a fatal lethargy prevailed over his faculties, and carried all sense and memory away with it.

I will not pretend to specify the secret terms on which you were invited to support an administration ‡ which Lord Bute pretended to leave in full possession of their ministerial authority, and perfectly masters of themselves. He was not of a temper to relinquish power, though he retired from employment. Stipulations were certainly made between your Grace and him, and certainly violated. After two years submission, you thought you had collected a strength sufficient to controul his influence, and that it was your turn to be a tyrant, because you had been a slave. When you found yourself mistaken in your opinion of your gracious master's firmness, disappointment got the better of all your humble discretion, and carried you to an excess of outrage to his person, as distant from

---

* The peace of 1763, negotiated by the duke; the conquests specified were relinquished by its conditions, and the rumour, as already observed, was in general circulation that the duke and his friends had been bribed into so prodigal a surrender.

† This man, notwithstanding his pride and Tory principles, had some English stuff in him. Upon an official letter he wrote to the Duke of Bedford, the duke desired to be recalled, and it was with the utmost difficulty that Lord Bute could appease him.—JUNIUS.

‡ Mr. Grenville, Lord Halifax, and Lord Egremont.—JUNIUS.

true spirit, as from all decency and respect*. After robbing him of the rights of a king, you would not permit him to preserve the honour of a gentleman. It was then Lord Weymouth was nominated to Ireland, and dispatched (we well remember with what indecent hurry) to plunder the treasury of the first fruits of an employment which you well knew he was never to execute†.

This sudden declaration of war against the favourite might have given you a momentary merit with the public, if it had either been adopted upon principle, or maintained with resolution. Without looking back to all your former servility, we need only observe your subsequent conduct to see upon what motives you acted. Apparently united with Mr. Grenville, you waited until Lord Rockingham's feeble administration should dissolve in its own weakness. The moment their dismission was suspected, the moment you perceived that another system was adopted in the closet, you thought it no disgrace to return to your former dependence, and solicit once more the friendship of Lord Bute. You begged an interview, at which he had spirit enough to treat you with contempt.

It would now be of little use to point out by what a train of weak, injudicious measures, it became necessary, or was thought so, to call you back to a share in the administration‡. The friends, whom you did not in the last instance desert, were not of a character to add strength or credit to government, and at that time your alliance with the Duke of Grafton was, I presume, hardly foreseen. We must look for other stipulations to account for that sudden resolution of the closet, by which three of your dependants§ (whose characters, I think, cannot be less respected than they are) were advanced

---

* The ministry having endeavoured to exclude the Dowager out of the regency bill, the Earl of Bute determined to dismiss them. Upon this the Duke of Bedford demanded an audience of the King, reproached him in plain terms with his duplicity, baseness, falsehood, treachery, and hypocrisy—repeatedly gave him the lie, and left him in convulsions.—JUNIUS.

† He received three thousand pounds for plate and equipage money.—JUNIUS.

‡ When Earl Gower was appointed president of the council, the King, with his usual sincerity, assured him that he had not had one happy moment since the Duke of Bedford left him.—JUNIUS.

§ Lords Gower, Weymouth, and Sandwich.—JUNIUS.

to offices through which you might again controul the minister, and probably engross the whole direction of affairs.

The possession of absolute power is now once more within your reach. The measures you have taken to obtain and confirm it, are too gross to escape the eyes of a discerning, judicious prince. His palace is besieged; the lines of circumvallation are drawing round him; and, unless he finds a resource in his own activity, or in the attachment of the real friends of his family, the best of princes must submit to the confinement of a state prisoner until your Grace's death or some less fortunate event shall raise the siege. For the present, you may safely resume that style of insult and menace which even a private gentleman cannot submit to hear without being contemptible. Mr. Mackenzie's history is not yet forgotten, and you may find precedents euough of the mode in which au imperious subject may signify his pleasure to his sovereign. Where will this gracious monarch look for assistance, when the wretched Grafton could forget his obligations to his master, and desert him for a hollow alliance with *such* a man as the Duke of Bedford!

Let us consider you, then, as arrived at the summit of worldly greatness; let us suppose that all your plans of avarice and ambition are accomplished, and your most sanguine wishes gratified in the fear as well as the hatred of the people. Can age itself forget that you are now in the last act of life? Can grey hairs make folly venerable? and is there no period to be reserved for meditation and retirement? For shame! my Lord: let it not be recorded of you, that the latest moments of your life were dedicated to the same unworthy pursuits, the same busy agitations, in which your youth and manhood were exhausted. Consider that, although you cannot disgrace your former life, you are violating the character of age, and exposing the impotent imbecility, after you have lost the vigour, of the passions.

Your friends will ask, perhaps, Whither shall this unhappy old man retire? Can he remain in the metropolis, where his life has been so often threatened, and his palace so often attacked? If he returns to Woburn, scorn and mockery await him. He must create a solitude round his estate, if he would avoid the face of reproach and derision. At Plymouth, his destruction would be more than probable: at Exeter, inevita-

ble.   No honest Englishman will ever forget his attachment,
nor any honest Scotchman forgive his treachery, to Lord
Bute.   At every town he enters he must change his liveries
and his name.   Which ever way he flies, the *Hue and Cry* of
the country pursues him.

In another kingdom, indeed, the blessings of his administration have been more sensibly felt ; his virtues better understood ; or at worst, they will not, for him alone, forget
their hospitality.   As well might Verres have returned to
Sicily.   You have twice escaped, my Lord ; beware of a third
experiment.   The indignation of a whole people, plundered,
insulted, and oppressed as they have been, will not always be
disappointed.

It is in vain therefore to shift the scene.   You can no more
fly from your enemies than from yourself.   Persecuted abroad,
you look into your own heart for consolation, and find nothing
but reproaches and despair.   But, my Lord, you may quit the
field of business, though not the field of danger ; and though
you cannot be safe, you may cease to be ridiculous.   I fear
you have listened too long to the advice of those pernicious
friends with whose interests you have sordidly united your
own, and for whom you have sacrificed everything that ought
to be dear to a man of honour.   They are still base enough to
encourage the follies of your age, as they once did the vices
of your youth.   As little acquainted with the rules of decorum
as with the laws of morality, they will not suffer you to profit
by experience, nor even to consult the propriety of a bad character.   Even now they tell you, that life is no more than a
dramatic scene, in which the hero should preserve his consistency to the last, and that, as you lived without virtue, you
should die without repentance *.

JUNIUS.

* As some apprehension was entertained by the printer, that he might be
brought before the House of Lords for inserting this letter in his paper,
Junius wrote to him in Private Letter, No. 10, as follows :—"As to you, it
is clearly my opinion that you have nothing to fear from the Duke of Bedford.   I reserve some things expressly to awe him, in case he should think of
bringing you before the House of Lords.   I am sure I can threaten him privately with such a storm as would make him tremble even in his grave."

This letter, viewed as an effort of personal satire, is one of the ablest
specimens of the peculiar eloquence of Junius.   The contrast of a fancied
good character with the assumed bad one of the Duke of Bedford ; the artful

LETTER XXIV.

SIR WILLIAM DRAPER TO JUNIUS

SIR,   September 14, 1769.

HAVING accidentally seen a *republication* * of your letters, wherein you have been pleased to *assert*, that I had *sold* the companions of my success; I am again obliged to declare the said assertion to be a most *infamous* and *malicious false-hood;* and I *again* call upon you to stand forth, avow yourself, and *prove* the charge. If you can make it out to the satisfaction of any one man in the kingdom, I will be content to be thought the worst man in it; if you do not, what must the nation think of you? *Party* has nothing to do in this affair: you have made a personal attack upon my honour, defamed me by a most vile calumny, which might possibly have sunk into oblivion, had not such uncommon pains been taken to renew and perpetuate this scandal, chiefly because it has been told in good language; for I give you full credit for your elegant diction, well-turned periods, and Attic wit †; but wit

imputation of treachery won by bribes in the negotiating of the peace; the hinted coarseness and vulgarity of the object of his disparagement in his private pleasures; the recalling of that outrage to recollection with which the duke had, on a former occasion, treated his sovereign; the suggestion that the duke might now fancy all his plans of ambition consummated, and himself indisputable master of the cabinet; above all, the alarming earnestness with which, in the concluding paragraphs, the duke is taught to believe the whole empire to be, as it were, in arms against him;—compose, together, an assemblage of splendid parts, forming one of the most powerful and elaborate compositions of the author. The general excellence of the letter, however, is in some measure impaired by a *quaintness* inconsistent with that chaste delicacy of writing which can alone deserve the approbation of true taste. By *quaintness* is meant the use of that cast of thought, and that mould of style, which in propriety belong only to true wit, upon occasions when there is no genuine wit produced, and when indeed the use of such wit would be unseasonable.—ED.

* The *italics* are in the Junius edition of 1772, and are in consequence retained both in this and the other letters of the work.—ED.

† This is a palpable misnomer. No two things of the same species can be more unlike than the wit of Junius and that which both the ancients and well-informed moderns have distinguished by the appellation of *Attic wit.* A delicate propriety that pollutes itself with no grossness, hazards none of those experiments in which the distinctions between *true* and *false* wit seem to become uncertain, an ease that seems to aim at nothing striking, a simplicity that wears the air of expressing the first thoughts that can arise to an

is oftentimes false, though it may appear brilliant; which is
exactly the case of your *whole performance*. But, Sir, I am
obliged in the most *serious* manner to accuse you of being
guilty of *falsities*. You have said the thing that is *not*. To
support your story, you have recourse to the following *irresistible* argument: " You *sold* the companions of your victory,
because, when the 16th regiment was given to *you*, you was
silent. The conclusion is inevitable." I believe that such
deep and *acute reasoning* could only come from such an extraordinary writer as Junius. But, unfortunately for you, the
premises as well as the *conclusion* are absolutely *false*. Many
applications have been made to the ministry on the subject of
the Manilla ransom, *since* the time of my being colonel of that
regiment. As I have for some years quitted London, I was
obliged to have recourse to the honourable Colonel Monson
and Sir Samuel Cornish *, to *negotiate* for me; in the last
autumn, I personally delivered a memorial to the Earl of
Shelburne at his seat in Wiltshire. As you have told us of
your importance, that you are a person of *rank* and *fortune*,
and above a *common* bribe †, you may in all probability be not
unknown to his lordship, who can satisfy you of the truth of
what I say. But I shall now take the liberty, Sir, to seize
your battery, and turn it against yourself. If your puerile and
tinsel logic could carry the least weight or conviction with it,
how must you stand affected by the *inevitable conclusion*, as
you are pleased to term it? According to Junius, *silence* is
guilt. In many of the public papers, you have been called in
the most direct and offensive terms a *liar* and a *coward*.
When did you reply to these foul accusations? you have been
quite *silent*—quite chopfallen—therefore, *because* you was
silent, the nation has a right to pronounce you to be both a
liar and a coward from your own argument; but, Sir, I will
give you fairer play—will afford you an opportunity to wipe off

inartificial mind, in the most natural, unstudied language, an archness that,
under all this disguise, misses no occasion of presenting the happiest combina-
tions of ideas which, though never before associated, yet refuse not to meet
together, faultless purity of phrase, correctness of syntax, and an absence of
everything, whether in style or in thought, that might strike the ear as
affected or unfamiliar, are the characteristic qualities of Attic wit.—HERON.

* These gentlemen accompanied Sir William as brother officers in his expedition against the Philippines.

† See Miscellaneous Letter of the author, No. 54, vol. ii.

the first appellation by desiring the proofs of your charge against me. Produce them! To wipe off the last, produce *yourself*. People cannot bear any longer your *lion's skin*, and the despicable *imposture* of the *old Roman name* which you have *affected*. For the future assume the name of some *modern** bravo and dark assassin: let your appellation have some affinity to your practice. But if I must *perish*, Junius, let me *perish* in the face of day; be for *once* a generous and open enemy. I allow that Gothic *appeals* to cold iron are no better proofs of a man's honesty and veracity, than hot iron and burning ploughshares are of *female chastity*; but a soldier's honour is as delicate as a woman's; it must not be suspected; you have dared to throw more than a suspicion upon mine—you cannot but know the consequences, which even the meekness of Christianity would pardon me for, after the injury you have done me.

WILLIAM DRAPER.

LETTER XXV

Hæret lateri lethalis arundo.

JUNIUS TO SIR WILLIAM DRAPER, K.B.

SIR,   September 25, 1769.

AFTER so long an interval, I did not expect to see the debate revived between us. My answer to your last letter shall be short; for I write to you with reluctance, and I hope we shall now conclude our correspondence for ever.

---

* Was *Brutus* an *ancient* bravo and dark assassin? or does Sir W. D. think it criminal to stab a tyrant to the heart?—JUNIUS.

Sir William was certainly unfortunate in throwing out a contemptuous phrase against the character of the illustrious Roman. He beside commits an egregious error, unpardonable in an ostentatious pretender to classical learning, by confounding *Lucius Junius* Brutus, the expeller of the Tarquins and founder of the Roman republic, with *Marcus Junius* Brutus, who conspired against Julius Cæsar to restore the Commonwealth after its subversion. 'T was from the former, doubtless, that JUNIUS assumed his name, and he was unquestionably no " bravo and dark assassin," as Sir William insinuates, but the open and courageous foe of tyrants.—ED.

Had you been originally and without provocation attacked by an anonymous writer, you would have some right to demand his name. But in this cause you are a volunteer. You engaged in it with the unpremeditated gallantry of a soldier. You were content to set your name in opposition to a man who would probably continue in concealment. You understood the terms upon which we were to correspond, and gave at least a tacit assent to them. After voluntarily attacking me under the character of Junius, what possible right have you to know me under any other? Will you forgive me if I insinuate to you, that you foresaw some honour in the apparent spirit of coming forward in person, and that you were not quite indifferent to the display of your literary qualifications?

You cannot but know that the republication of my letters was no more than a catchpenny contrivance of a printer, in which it was impossible I should be concerned, and for which I am no way answerable. At the same time I wish you to understand that, if I do not take the trouble of reprinting these papers, it is not from any fear of giving offence to Sir William Draper.

Your remarks upon a signature* adopted merely for distinction, are unworthy of notice; but when you tell me I have submitted to be called a liar and a coward, I must ask you in my turn, whether you seriously think it any way incumbent upon me to take notice of the silly invectives of every simpleton who writes in a newspaper? and what opinion would you have conceived of my discretion, if I had suffered myself to be the dupe of so shallow an artifice?

Your appeal to the sword, though consistent enough with your late profession, will neither prove your innocence nor clear you from suspicion. Your complaints with regard to the Manilla ransom were, for a considerable time, a distress to government. You were appointed (greatly out of your turn) to the command of a regiment, and *during that administration* we heard no more of Sir William Draper. The facts, of which I speak, may indeed be variously accounted for, but they are

* Despite of his vigilance, Junius does not appear to have detected Sir William's error, remarked on in a previous note, in regard to the two Brutii, and the true derivation of his own *nom de guerre*. His reasoning in regard to the propriety of concealing his name, in spite of provocation, is however sufficiently conclusive.—ED.

too notorious to be denied; and I think you might have learnt at the university that a false conclusion is an error in argument, not a breach of veracity. Your solicitations, I doubt not, were renewed under *another* administration. Admitting the fact, I fear an indifferent person would only infer from it, that experience had made you acquainted with the benefits of complaining. Remember, Sir, that you have yourself confessed that, *considering the critical situation of this country, the ministry are in the right to temporize with Spain.* This confession reduces you to an unfortunate dilemma. By renewing your solicitations, you must either mean to force your country into a war at a most unseasonable juncture; or, having no view or expectation of that kind, that you look for nothing but a private compensation to yourself.

As to me, it is by no means necessary that I should be exposed to the resentment of the worst and the most powerful men in this country, though I may be indifferent about yours. Though *you* would fight, there are others who would assassinate.

But after all, Sir, where is the injury? You assure me that my logic is puerile and tinsel; that it carries not the least weight or conviction; that my premises are false and my conclusions absurd. If this be a just description of me, how is it possible for such a writer to disturb your peace of mind, or to injure a character so well established as yours? Take care, Sir William, how you indulge this unruly temper, lest the world should suspect that conscience has some share in your resentments. You have more to fear from the treachery of your own passions than from any malevolence of mine.

I believe, Sir, you will never know me. A considerable time must certainly elapse before we are personally acquainted. You need not, however, regret the delay, or suffer an apprehension that any length of time can restore you to the Christian meekness of your temper and disappoint your present indignation. If I understand your character, there is in your own breast a repository in which your resentments may be safely laid up for future occasions, and preserved without the hazard of diminution. The *Odia in longum jaciens, quæ reconderet, auctaque promeret* *, I thought, had only be-

---

* Written of Tiberius by Tacitus, a favourite author, it would seem, and is likely, of Junius.—ED.

longed to the worst character of antiquity. The text is in
Tacitus;—you know best where to look for the commentary

JUNIUS.

LETTER XXVI.

A WORD AT PARTING TO JUNIUS.

This is, on the whole, a well-written letter. The tone of sentiment in
which Sir William Draper bids adieu to the hope of direct personal explanation from Junius, is that of a man who feels himself humbled, yet takes comfort from the thought that he has been harshly dealt with, and that scarcely
any other man would have stood the same trial better than himself. His interposition in favour of the Duke of Bedford, is artfully contrived to excite
the public indignation against the barbarous cruelty of Junius's attacks. His
account of the dissensions, the mutual treacheries, and the unsettling changes
of the ministers, and other great political leaders, is in all respects happy, save
that it produces ludicrous ideas where it was meant to give serious ones.—ED.

SIR *,   October 7, 1769.

As you have not favoured me with either of the *explanations*
demanded of you, I can have nothing more to say to you upon
my *own* account. Your mercy to me, or tenderness for yourself, has been very great. The public will judge of your
motives. If your excess of modesty forbids you to produce
either the proofs or yourself, I will excuse it. Take courage;
I have not the temper of Tiberius any more than the rank or

---

* *Measures and not men*, is the common cant of affected moderation; a base,
counterfeit language, fabricated by knaves, and made current among fools. Such
gentle censure is not fitted to the present degenerate state of society. What
does it avail to expose the absurd contrivance or pernicious tendency of measures, if the man who advises or executes shall be suffered not only to escape
with impunity, but even to preserve his power, and insult us with the favour
of his sovereign? I would recommend to the reader the whole of Mr. Pope's
letter to Doctor Arbuthnot, dated 26th July, 1734, from which the following is
an extract:—" To reform and not to chastise, I am afraid is impossible; and that
the best precepts, as well as the best laws, would prove of small use if there
were no examples to enforce them. To attack vices in the abstract, without
touching persons, may be safe fighting indeed, but it is fighting with shadows.
My greatest comfort and encouragement to proceed has been to see that those
who have no shame, and no fear of anything else, have appeared touched by
my satires."—JUNIUS.

power. You, indeed, are a tyrant of another sort, and upon your political bed of torture can excruciate any subject, from a first minister down to such a grub or butterfly as myself; like another detested tyrant of antiquity, can make the wretched sufferer fit the bed if the bed will not fit the sufferer, by disjointing or tearing the trembling limbs until they are stretched to its extremity. But courage, constancy, and patience, under torments, have sometimes caused the most hardened monsters to relent, and forgive the object of their cruelty. You, Sir, are determined to try all that human nature can endure until she expires; else, was it possible that you could be the author of that most inhuman letter to the Duke of Bedford? I have read it with astonishment and horror. Where, Sir, where were the feelings of your own heart when you could upbraid a most affectionate father with the loss of his only and most amiable son? Read over again those cruel lines of yours, and let them wring your very soul! Cannot political questions be discussed without descending to the most odious personalities? Must you go wantonly out of your way to torment declining age, because the Duke of Bedford may have quarrelled with those whose cause and politics you espouse? For shame! for shame! As you have *spoke daggers* to him you may justly dread the *use* of them against your own breast, did a want of courage or of noble sentiments stimulate him to such mean revenge. He is above it; he is brave. Do you fancy that your own base arts have infected our whole island? But your own reflections, your own conscience must and will, if you have any spark of humanity remaining, give him most ample vengeance. Not all the power of words with which you are so graced will ever wash out, or even palliate, this foul blot in your character. I have not time at present to dissect your letter so minutely as I could wish, but I will be bold enough to say, that it is (as to reason and argument) the most extraordinary piece of *florid impotence* * that was ever imposed upon the eyes and ears of the too credulous and deluded mob. It accuses the Duke of Bedford of high treason. Upon what foundation? You tell us "that the duke's *pecuniary character* makes it

---

* Sir William errs as much in imputing *florid impotence* to the writing of Junius, as in praising it for *Attic wit.*—HERON.

more than *probable* that he could not have made such sacrifices at the peace without *some private compensations;* that his conduct carried with it an interior evidence beyond all the legal proofs of a court of justice."

My academical education, Sir, bids me tell you that it is necessary to establish the truth of your first proposition before you presume to draw inferences from it. First prove the avarice before you make the rash, hasty, and most wicked conclusion. This father, Junius, whom you call avaricious, allowed that son eight thousand pounds a year. Upon his most unfortunate death, which your usual good nature took care to remind him of, he greatly increased the jointure of the afflicted lady, his widow. Is this avarice? Is this doing good by *stealth?* It is upon record.

If exact order, method, and true economy as a master of a family, if splendour and just magnificence, without wild waste and thoughtless extravagance, may constitute the character of an avaricious man, the duke is guilty. But for a moment let us admit that an ambassador may love money too much; what proof do you give that he has taken any to betray his country? Is it hearsay; or the evidence of letters, or ocular; or the evidence of those concerned in this black affair? Produce your authorities to the public. It is a most impudent kind of sorcery to attempt to blind us with the smoke without convincing us that the fire has existed. You first brand him with a vice that he is free from to render him odious and suspected. Suspicion is the foul weapon with which you make all your chief attacks—with that you stab, But shall one of the first subjects of the realm be ruined in his fame; shall even his life be in constant danger from a charge built upon such sandy foundations? Must his house be besieged by lawless ruffians, his journeys impeded, and even the asylum of an altar be insecure from assertions so base and false? Potent as he is, the duke is amenable to justice; if guilty, punishable. The parliament is the high and solemn tribunal for matters of such great moment. To that be they submitted. But I hope, also, that some notice will be taken of, and some punishment inflicted upon, false accusers, especially upon such, Junius, who are *wilfully false*. In any truth I will agree even with Junius; will agree with him that it is highly unbecoming the dignity of Peers to tamper

with boroughs. Aristocracy is as fatal as democracy. Our
constitution admits of neither. It loves a King, Lords, and
Commons really chosen by the unbought suffrages of a free
people. But if corruption only shifts hands, if the wealthy
commoner gives the bribe instead of the potent peer, is the
state better served by this exchange? Is the real emancipa-
tion of the borough effected because new parchment bonds
may possibly supersede the old? To say the truth, wherever
such practices prevail, they are equally criminal to and destructive of our freedom.

The rest of your declamation is scarce worth considering,
excepting for the elegance of the language. Like Hamlet in
the play, you produce two pictures. You tell us that one is
not like the Duke of Bedford; then you bring a most hideous
caricatura, and tell us of the resemblance; but *multum ablu-
dit imago.*

All your long tedious accounts of the ministerial quarrels
and the intrigues of the cabinet are reducible to a few short
lines; and to convince you, Sir, that I do not mean to flatter
any minister, either past or present, these are my thoughts:
they seem to have acted like lovers or children; have pouted,
quarrelled, cried, kissed, and been friends again *; as the
objects of desire, the ministerial rattles have been put into
their hands. But such proceedings are very unworthy of the
gravity and dignity of a great nation. We do not want men
of abilities—but we have wanted steadiness—we want unani-
mity; your letters, Junius, will not contribute thereto. You
may one day expire by a flame of your own kindling. But it
is my humble opinion that lenity and moderation, pardon and
oblivion, will disappoint the efforts of all the seditious in the
land, and extinguish their wide-spreading fires. I have lived
with this sentiment; with this I shall die.

WILLIAM DRAPER †.

---

* Sir William gives us a pleasant account of men who, in *his* opinion at
least, are the best-qualified to govern an empire.—JUNIUS.

† Sir William Draper appears to have been a generous and accomplished
man, with too great a susceptibility to newspaper strictures. He married a
daughter of the second son of the Duke of St. Albans; her ladyship died in
1778, leaving him no issue. Sir William died in January, 1787. In the
year 1768 he erected a magnificent cenotaph in his garden, at Clifton, near
Bristol, in honour of the 79th regiment, of which he had been colonel in the

LETTER XXVII.

SIR,   October 13, 1769.

IF Sir William Draper's bed be a bed of torture, he has
made it for himself. I shall never interrupt his repose.
Having changed the subject, there are parts of his last letter
not undeserving of a reply. Leaving his private character
and conduct out of the question, I shall consider him merely
in the capacity of an author, whose labours certainly do no
discredit to a newspaper.

We say, in common discourse, that a man may be his own
enemy, and the frequency of the fact makes the expression
intelligible. But that a man should be the bitterest enemy
of his friends, implies a contradiction of a peculiar nature!
There is something in it which cannot be conceived without a
confusion of ideas, nor expressed without a solecism in language. Sir William Draper is still that fatal friend Lord
Granby found him. Yet I am ready to do justice to his
generosity; if, indeed, it be not something more than generous to be the voluntary advocate of men who think themselves injured by his assistance, and to consider nothing in
the cause he adopts but the difficulty of defending it. I
thought, however, he had been better read in the history of
the human heart than to compare or confound the tortures of
the body with those of the mind. He ought to have known,
though perhaps it might not be his interest to confess that
no outward tyranny can reach the mind. If conscience plays
the tyrant, it would be greatly for the benefit of the world
that she were more arbitrary, and far less placable than some
men find her.

But it seems I have outraged the feelings of a father's
heart. Am I indeed so injudicious? Does Sir William
Draper think I would have hazarded my credit with a generous nation by so gross a violation of the laws of humanity?

preceding war, and whose bravery had been conspicuous against the French,
and in laying the foundation of our Indian empire. Three field-officers, ten
captains, thirteen lieutenants, five ensigns, three surgeons, and one thousand
private men, belonging to that regiment, fell in the course of the war.—ED.

Does he think I am so little acquainted with the first and noblest characteristic of Englishmen? Or how will he reconcile such folly with an understanding so full of artifice as mine? Had *he* been a father he would have been but little offended with the severity of the reproach, for his mind would have been filled with the justice of it. He would have seen that I did not insult the feelings of a father, but the father who felt nothing. He would have trusted to the evidence of his own paternal heart, and boldly denied the possibility of the fact, instead of defending it. Against whom, then, will this honest indignation be directed, when I assure him, that this whole town beheld the Duke of Bedford's conduct, upon the death of his son, with horror and astonishment. Sir William Draper does himself but little honour in opposing the general sense of his country. The people are seldom wrong in their opinions;—in their sentiments they are never mistaken. There may be a vanity, perhaps, in a singular way of thinking; but when a man professes a want of those feelings which do honour to the multitude, he hazards something infinitely more important than the character of his understanding. After all, as Sir William may possibly be in earnest in his anxiety for the Duke of Bedford, I should be glad to relieve him from it. He may rest assured that this worthy nobleman laughs, with equal indifference, at *my* reproaches, and Sir William's distress about him. But here let it stop. Even the Duke of Bedford, insensible as he is, will consult the tranquillity of his life, in not provoking the moderation of my temper. If from the profoundest contempt I should ever rise into anger, he should soon find that all I have already said of him was lenity and compassion *.

Out of a long catalogue Sir William Draper has confined himself to the refutation of two charges only. The rest he had not time to discuss; and, indeed, it would have been a laborious undertaking. To draw up a defence of such a series of enormities would have required a life at least as long as that which has been uniformly employed in the practice of them. The public opinion of the Duke of Bedford's extreme economy is, it seems, entirely without foundation. Though not very prodigal abroad, in his own family, at least,

* Private Letter, No. 10.

he is regular and magnificent. He pays his debts, abhors a beggar, and makes a handsome provision for his son. His charity has improved upon the proverb, and ended where it began. Admitting the whole force of this single instance of his domestic generosity (wonderful, indeed, considering the narrowness of his fortune and the little merit of his only son) the public may still, perhaps, be dissatisfied, and demand some other less equivocal proofs of his munificence. Sir William Draper should have entered boldly into the detail— of indigence relieved—of arts encouraged—of science patronized—men of learning protected—and works of genius rewarded; in short, had there been a single instance, besides Mr. Rigby *, of blushing merit brought forward by the duke, for the service of the public, it should not have been omitted †.

I wish it were possible to establish my inference with the same certainty on which I believe the principle is founded. My conclusion, however, was not drawn from the principle alone. I am not so unjust as to reason from one crime to another, though I think, that of all the vices, avarice is most apt to taint and corrupt the heart. I combined the known temper of the man with the extravagant concessions made by the ambassador; and, though I doubt not sufficient care was taken to leave no document of any treasonable negotiation, I still maintain that the conduct ‡ of this minister carries with it an internal and a convincing evidence

* This gentleman is supposed to have the same idea of *blushing* that a man blind from his birth has of scarlet or skyblue.—JUNIUS.

† In answer to this heavy charge, two instances of the noble duke's benevolence were brought forward in two separate letters in the Public Advertiser. The one dated Oct. 17, and signed Frances, which states that his Grace had relieved with a *patent employment*, the husband of the writer of a series of sentimental letters of "Henry and Frances," in which the author, a Mrs. Griffiths, fictitiously depicted their own real distress. The other dated Oct. 20, and signed Jere. Mears, lieut. of the 29th regiment, relates the duke's generous and unsolicited bestowal upon him of a pair of colours, upon being informed, when lord-lieutenant of Ireland, of the writer's destitute situation.

‡ If Sir W. D. will take the trouble of looking into Torcy's Memoirs, he will see with what little ceremony a bribe may be offered to a duke, and with what little ceremony it was *only not accepted.*—JUNIUS.

The first Duke of Marlborough is the nobleman referred to; but the bribe was not refused, according to Philo-Janius, *post*, Letter 2S.—ED.

against him. Sir William Draper seems not to know the value or force of such a proof. He will not permit us to judge of the motives of men by the manifest tendency of their actions, nor by the notorious character of their minds. He calls for papers and witnesses with a sort of triumphant security, as if nothing could be true but what could be proved in a court of justice. Yet a religious man might have re membered upon what foundation some truths, most interesting to mankind, have been received and established. If it were not for the internal evidence, which the purest of religions carries with it, what would have become of his once well-quoted decalogue, and of the meekness of his Christianity?

The generous warmth of his resentment makes him confound the order of events. He forgets that the insults and distresses which the Duke of Bedford has suffered, and which Sir William has lamented with many delicate touches of the true pathetic, were only recorded in my letter to his Grace, not occasioned by it. It was a simple candid narrative of facts; though, for aught I know, it may carry with it something prophetic. His Grace undoubtedly has received several ominous hints; and I think, in certain circumstances, a wise man would do well to prepare himself for the event.

But I have a charge of a heavier nature against Sir William Draper. He tells us that the Duke of Bedford is amenable to justice; that parliament is a high and solemn tribunal; and that, if guilty, he may be punished by due course of law; and all this he says with as much gravity as if he believed every word of the matter. I hope indeed, the day of impeachments will arrive, before this nobleman escapes out of life; but to refer us to that mode of proceeding now, with such a ministry and such a House of Commons as the present, what is it, but an indecent mockery of the common sense of the nation? I think he might have contented himself with defending the greatest enemy, without insulting the distresses, of his country.

His concluding declaration of his opinion, with respect to the present condition of affairs, is too loose and undetermined to be of any service to the public. How strange it is that this gentleman should dedicate so much time and argument to the defence of worthless or indifferent characters, while he gives

but seven solitary lines to the only subject which can deserve
his attention, or do credit to his abilities.

JUNIUS.

The Duke of Bedford, so mercilessly arraigned by Junius, had, as is
usually the fortune of public men, his defenders as well as assailants, and
it seems to have been the practice of the *Public Advertiser* fairly to open
its columns to both sides.   Examples of this impartiality have been referred
to in the preceding note, and the subjoined is an extract from an able reply
to the several attacks of Junius on his Grace, subscribed *M. Tullius*, dated
Dec. 8.

" In these strictures I have principally in view the treatment which
Junius, in two publications, has thought proper to offer to the Duke of Bedford.   His animadversions on this illustrious nobleman are intended to reflect both on his public and private character.   With regard to the first of
these, nothing of consequence is urged besides his Grace's conduct as ambassador at the court of Versailles in the making of the late peace.   I mean
not to enter here into the merits or demerits of that important transaction.
Thus much is known to all : the riches of the nation were at that time well
nigh exhausted, public credit was on the brink of ruin, the national debt increased to such an enormous height as to threaten us with a sudden and universal crash; and whatever be said of the concessions that were made to
bring that memorable event to bear, Canada, among other instances, will
ever remain a glorious monument; the interests of this kingdom were not
forgotten in that negociation.   But Junius, hackneyed in the tricks of controversy, where a man's open and avowed actions are innocent, has the art to
hint at secret terms and private compensations; and though he is compelled
by the force of truth to own ' no document of any treasonable practice is to
be found,' we are given plainly to understand, so many public sacrifices were
not made at that period without a valuable consideration, and that in practice
there is very little difference in the ceremony of offering a bribe, and of that
duke's accepting it.   To a charge that is alleged, not only without proof, but
even with a confession that no proof is to be expected, no answer is to be returned but that of a contemptuous silence.   When a writer takes upon him
to attack the character of a nobleman of the highest rank, and in a matter of
so capital a nature as that of selling his country for a bribe, common policy,
as well as prudence, require that an accusation of such importance be supported with at least some show of evidence, and that even this be not done
but with the utmost moderation of temper and expression; but so sober a
conduct would have been beside the purpose of Junius, whose business it
was not to reason, but rail.   The Roman rhetorician, among the other arts
of oratory, mentions one which he dignifies under the title of a ' Canine
eloquence,' that of filling up the empty places of an argument with railings,
convitiis implere vacua causarum.   In the knowledge of this rule Junius is
without a rival, and the present instance, among a thousand others, is a convincing testimony of his dexterity in the application of it.

" But here it will be said, it is not from circumstance and conjecture alone
that this charge against the Duke of Bedford is founded; the general character

of every one takes its colour and complexion from that quality in him which predominates, and the allowed avarice of the man affords an evidence not to be resisted of the rapacity of the ambassador; and is it then so incontestable a point that the duke is indeed the sordid man which Junius has delineated? are there no instances to be produced that denote a contrary disposition? one would think if a vicious thirst of gain had borne so large a share as is pretended, in his Grace's composition, this would have discovered itself in the pecuniary emoluments he had secured for himself when he engaged in a share of Government. But what advantages of this kind has he obtained, or to what bargains with the minister does Junius allude, when he knows that his Grace, though willing to assist the friends of administration with his interest and weight, has not accepted any department either of power or profit? Had Junius and *candour* not shaken hands, this circumstance alone would have afforded him an evidence beyond all the legal proofs of a court of justice, of the iniquity of his own insinuations. But we are not at a loss for other instances, and those no ordinary ones, of the duke's munificence. To what principle shall we attribute the payment of the elder brother's debts to the amount of not much less than one hundred thousand pounds? the splendid provision he made for his unfortunate son, and afterwards for that son's more unfortunate widow? what shall we say to his known attachments to the interests of his friends, his kindness to his domestics, and annual bounty to those who have served him faithfully? his indulgence to his dependants? or what are, if these be not, unequivocal proofs of genuine liberality and benevolence?

"When to these symptoms of an enlarged and generous mind we add what are equally constituent parts of his Grace's character, the decency and decorum of his conduct in private life, his regularity in his family, and what is now so rare a virtue among the great, his constant attendance on all the public offices of Divine worship, we shall hardly find, in the whole circle of the nobility, a man that has a juster and much more a constitutional claim to respect, or one that less deserved the censures of a satirist such as Junius, than his Grace of Bedford. But in the reflections of Junius there is a more surprising piece of profligacy yet behind. As if all the former instances of his malignity had been too little, he has filled up the measure of his crimes by calling back to our remembrance the loss, which not the father alone, but the kingdom, sustained in the death of his only son, and to reproach him for the insensibility he supposes him to have discovered on that affecting occasion. The cruelty of this accusation is only to be paralleled by the falsehood of it, and, in a better age than the present, would have been deemed a prodigy. To one who possessed the proper sentiments of a man, the dwelling at all on a calamity which is still so recent, which in all its circumstances was so truly pitiable, would have appeared in the highest degree ungenerous and mean; but to represent the principal sufferer in this scene of woe as the only one not sensible of his misfortune, to paint a father destitute of a father's love, and even professing a want of those feelings which do honour to the multitude, is an instance of barbarity of which a savage would have been ashamed, and which no prettiness of style, no powers of language, no literary merit, can ever excuse or expiate: and indeed, corrupt as the times are said to be, I have the satisfaction to observe Junius, for once, has reckoned without his host, and mistaken the taste and temper of his countrymen: we can allow for the petulance which want and hunger extort

from an opposition; we can pity the wretch who is obliged to draw his venal
quill, and say and unsay as is dictated to him by his superiors; but we are
not yet so far gone in the road to ruin, or dead to all the movements of compassion, as to behold without abhorrence the man who can so totally resign
all pretences to humanity, or regard him in any other light than as the object
of general detestation.

"Junius, in his letter to the Duke of Bedford, amuses himself with describing, in theory, the dignity and importance of an independent nobleman;
by way of conclusion to these remarks, I shall delineate for him, in return,
what I conceive should be character of one who sets up for a political writer,
and this in imitation of his own method, both by the positive and negative
marks which may be given of it. A writer, then, of this class, though he
will ever be suspicious of the conduct of those in power, will be sure to
watch with equal jealousy over himself, lest, in his zeal for exciting a reasonable love of liberty, he encourage a dangerous spirit of licentiousness; he
will be as cautious of weakening the constitutional powers of the prince, as
he will be careful of supporting the undoubted rights of the people; and
will expose with the same freedom, in their turns, the excesses of prerogative and the lawless efforts of a faction. In the negative parts of his
character he will not give occasion to the most distant suspicion that his
opposition to government proceeds not so much from a dislike to measures
as to men; in times of real security he will not inflame the minds of the
populace with affected apprehensions; before he complains of grievances he
will be sure they exist; in his freest writings he will never violate, knowingly, the laws of truth and justice; he will not causelessly expose the follies
of youth, the infirmities of age, or the irregularities of private life, in which
the public interests are not concerned; he will be restrained by a sense of
honour from calumniating the innocent or satirizing the unhappy: in a word,
he will not take advantage of his own security to stab in the dark, or with
Solomon's fool, divert himself with holding out the most respectable characters
as objects of contempt and ridicule, and say, am not I in sport."—M. TULLIUS.

LETTER XXVIII.

TO THE PRINTER OF THE PUBLIC ADVERTISER.

SIR,   October 20, 1769.

I VERY sincerely applaud the spirit with which a lady has
paid the debt of gratitude to her benefactor *. Though I
think she has mistaken the point, she shows a virtue which
makes her respectable The question turned upon the per

---

* The letter of Mrs. Griffiths, signed Frances, already referred to (p. 230.)
Junius had demanded to hear of but a *single instance* of indigence relieved,
and works of genius rewarded, by the Duke of Bedford. Mrs. Griffiths produced that instance; and no small impression was made by it on the mind
of the public in favour of the duke.—HERON.

sonal generosity or avarice of a man whose private fortune is immense. The proofs of his munificence must be drawn from the uses to which he has applied that fortune. I was not speaking of a lord-lieutenant of Ireland, but of a rich English duke, whose wealth gave him the means of doing as much good in this country, as he derived from his power in another. I am far from wishing to lessen the merit of this single benevolent action; perhaps it is the more conspicuous from standing alone. All I mean to say is, that it proves nothing in the present argument.

JUNIUS*.

LETTER XXIX.

TO THE PRINTER OF THE PUBLIC ADVERTISER.

SIR, October 19, 1769.

I AM well assured that Junius will never descend to a dispute with such a writer as Modestus (whose letter appeared in the Gazetteer of Monday †), especially as the dispute must be chiefly about words. Notwithstanding the partiality of the public, it does not appear that Junius values himself upon any superior skill in composition, and I hope his time will always be more usefully employed than in the trifling refinements of verbal criticism. Modestus, however, shall have no reason to triumph in the silence and moderation of Junius. If he knew as much of the propriety of language as I believe he does of the facts in question, he would have been as cautious of attacking Junius upon his composition as he seems to be of entering

* This letter, to a lady who had distinguished herself by some clever writings, is smart and polite, but not satisfactory. It is an after-thought of Junius to distinguish between what the duke did as lord lieutenant of Ireland, and what he should have done as Duke of Bedford. This is a distinction which he had not thought of making when he boldly asserted that no one instance of discriminating generosity by the duke could be mentioned. But it is the interest of a disputant, and Junius was a well-trained one, to grant nothing to his adversary unless he can gain more than he loses by the concession.—ED.

† The gentleman who wrote several letters under this signature in the Gazetteer, and subsequently in the Public Advertiser, was a Mr. Dalrymple, a Scotch advocate. For a specimen of his style, see Miscellaneous Letters, No. 67, vol. ii.—ED.

into the subject of it; yet, after all, the last is the only article of any importance to the public.

I do not wonder at the unremitted rancour with which the Duke of Bedford and his adherents invariably speak of a nation which we well know has been too much injured to be easily forgiven. But why must Junius be an Irishman? *The absurdity of his writings betrays him.* Waiving all consideration of the insult offered by Modestus to the declared judgment of the people (they may well bear this among the rest), let us follow the several instances, and try whether the charge be fairly supported.

First then—the leaving a man to enjoy such repose as he can find upon a bed of torture, is severe indeed; perhaps too much so, when applied to such a trifler as Sir William Draper; but there is nothing absurd either in the idea or expression. Modestus cannot distinguish between a sarcasm and a contradiction.

2. I affirm with Junius, that it is the *frequency* of the fact which alone can make us comprehend how a man can be his own enemy. We should never arrive at the complex idea conveyed by those words if we had only seen one or two instances of a man acting to his own prejudice. Offer the proposition to a child, or a man unused to compound his ideas, and you will soon see how little either of them understand you. It is not a simple idea arising from a single fact, but a very complex idea arising from many facts well observed and accurately compared.

3. Modestus could not, without great affectation, mistake the meaning of Junius when he speaks of a man who is the bitterest enemy of his friends. He could not but know, that Junius spoke, not of a false or hollow friendship, but of a real intention to serve, and that intention producing the worst effects of enmity. Whether the description be strictly applicable to Sir William Draper, is another question. Junius does not say that it is more *criminal* for a man to be the enemy of his friends than his own, though he might have affirmed it with truth. In a moral light a man may certainly take greater liberties with himself than with another. To sacrifice ourselves merely, is a weakness we may indulge in if we think proper, for we do it at our own hazard and expense; but, under the pretence of friendship, to sport

with the reputation, or sacrifice the honour, of another, is something worse than weakness; and if, in favour of the foolish intention, we do not call it a crime, we must allow at least that it arises from an overweening, busy, meddling impudence. Junius says only, and he says truly, that it is more extraordinary, that it involves a greater contradiction, than the other; and is it not a maxim received in life, that in general we can determine more wisely for others than for ourselves? The reason of it is so clear in argument that it hardly wants the confirmation of experience. Sir William Draper, I confess, is an exception to the general rule, though not much to his credit.

4. If this gentleman will go back to his ethics, he may perhaps discover the truth of what Junius says, *that no outward tyranny can reach the mind.* The tortures of the body may be introduced by way of ornament or illustration to represent those of the mind, but strictly there is no similitude between them. They are totally different both in their cause and operation. The wretch who suffers upon the rack is merely passive; but when the mind is tortured, it is not at the command of any outward power. It is the sense of guilt which constitutes the punishment, and creates that torture with which the guilty mind acts upon itself.

5. He misquotes what Junius says of conscience, and makes the sentence ridiculous by making it his own.

So much for composition. Now for fact. Junius it seems has mistaken the Duke of Bedford. His Grace had all the proper feelings of a father, though he took care to suppress the appearance of them. Yet it was an occasion, one would think, on which he need not have been ashamed of his grief; on which less fortitude would have done him more honour. I can conceive indeed a benevolent motive for his endeavouring to assume an air of tranquillity in his own family, and I wish I could discover anything in the rest of his character to justify my assigning that motive to his behaviour. But is there no medium? Was it necessary to appear abroad, to ballot at the India House, and make a public display, though it were only of an apparent insensibility? I know we are treading on tender ground, and Junius, I am convinced, does not wish to urge this question farther. Let the friends of the Duke of Bedford observe that humble silence which becomes their situation. They should recollect that there are some facts in store at which human nature would shudder. I shall be understood by those whom it concerns when I say that these facts go farther than to the duke *.

It is not inconsistent to suppose that a man may be quite indifferent about one part of a charge, yet severely stung with another, and though he feels no remorse that he may wish to be revenged. The charge of insensibility carries a reproach indeed, but no danger with it. Junius had said, *there are others who would assassinate.* Modestus, knowing his man, will not suffer the insinuation to be divided, but fixes it all upon the Duke of Bedford.

Without determining upon what evidence Junius would *choose to be condemned*, I will venture to maintain, in opposition to Modestus, or to Mr. Rigby (who is certainly not Modestus), or any other of the Bloomsbury gang, that the evidence against the Duke of Bedford is as strong as any presumptive evidence can be. It depends upon a combination of facts and reasoning which require no confirmation from the anecdote of the Duke of Marlborough. This anecdote was referred to merely to show how ready a great man may be to receive a great bribe; and if Modestus could read the original, he would see that the expression, *only not accepted*, was probably the only one in our language that exactly fitted the case. The bribe offered to the Duke of Marlborough was not refused.

I cannot conclude without taking notice of this honest gentleman's learning, and wishing he had given us a little more of it. When he accidentally found himself so near speaking truth, it was rather unfair of him to leave out the

---

* Within a fortnight after Lord Tavistock's death, the venerable Gertrude had a rout at Bedford House. The good duke (who had only sixty thousand pounds a year) ordered an inventory to be taken of his son's wearing apparel, down to his slippers, sold them all, and put the money in his pocket. The amiable marchioness, shocked at such brutal, unfeeling avarice, gave the value of the clothes to the Marquis's servant out of her own purse. That incomparable woman did not long survive her husband. When she died, the Duchess of Bedford treated her as the duke had treated his only son. She ordered every gown and trinket to be sold, and pocketed the money. These are the monsters whom Sir William Draper comes forward to defend. May God protect *me* from doing anything that may require such defence or deserve such friendship.—JUNIUS.

non potuisse refelli. As it stands, the *pudct hæc opprobria* may be divided equally between Mr. Rigby and the Duke of Bedford. Mr. Rigby, I take for granted, will assert his natural right to the modesty of the quotation, and leave all the opprobrium to his Grace.

PHILO-JUNIUS*.

LETTER XXX.

TO THE PRINTER OF THE PUBLIC ADVERTISER.

SIR, October 17, 1769.

IT is not wonderful that the great cause in which this country is engaged should have roused and engrossed the whole attention of the people. I rather admire the generous spirit with which they feel and assert their interest in this important question than blame them for their indifference about any other. When the constitution is openly invaded, when the first original right of the people, from which all laws derive their authority, is directly attacked, inferior grievances naturally lose their force, and are suffered to pass by without punishment or observation. The present ministry are as singularly marked by their fortune as by their crimes. Instead of atoning for their former conduct by any wise or popular measure, they have found, in the enormity of one fact, a cover and defence for a series of measures which must have been fatal to any other administration. I fear we are too remiss in observing the whole of their proceedings. Struck with the principal figure, we do not sufficiently mark in what

* In the preceding letter, Junius employs his wonted artifice and force of argumentation. He begins with disclaiming all pretensions to eloquence and fine writing; then, in every instance in which he had seemed to be successfully harassed by the strictures of Modestus, either brings forward a satisfactory refutation, or turns his adversary so effectually into ridicule, that the reader entirely loses sight of the truth of the criticism. Nor is even his Grace of Bedford suffered to escape without having the severity of the former invective against him increased, on account of the officious interposition of his defender. According to Heron, this letter is a "model for any man to study who may, in like manner, wish to vindicate himself against the attack of bold, malignant criticism."—ED.

manner the canvass is filled up. Yet surely it is not a less
crime, nor less fatal in its consequences, to encourage a
flagrant breach of the law by a military force, than to make
use of the forms of parliament to destroy the constitution.
The ministry seem determined to give us a choice of difficulties, and, if possible, to perplex us with the multitude of
their offences. The expedient is well worthy of the Duke
of Grafton. But though he has preserved a gradation and
variety in his measures, we should remember that the principle is uniform. Dictated by the same spirit, they deserve
the same attention. The following fact, though of the most
alarming nature, has not yet been clearly stated to the public,
nor have the consequences of it been sufficiently understood.
Had I taken it up at an earlier period I should have been
accused of an uncandid, malignant precipitation, as if I
watched for an unfair advantage against the ministry, and
would not allow them a reasonable time to do their duty.
They now stand without excuse. Instead of employing the
leisure they have had in a strict examination of the offence
and punishing the offenders, they seem to have considered
that indulgence as a security to them, that, with a little time
and management, the whole affair might be buried in silence
and utterly forgotten.

A major-general of the army is arrested by the sheriffs'
officers for a considerable debt*. He persuades them to

* Major-General Gansel, who forms the subject of this letter, was arrested
September 21, 1769, in Piccadilly, for two thousand pounds. He told the
bailiff if he would go down with him to the Tilt Yard he should there find a
friend, and would, on his not giving bail, go with him to a spunging-house.
When they came to the Horse Guards, the officer sent for a serjeant and file
of musqueteers to secure the bailiff, on a pretence that he had been insulted
by him, which they did, while the prisoner escaped. Adjutant-General
Harvey having heard of the affair, ordered the serjeant and his men close
prisoners to the Savoy, and sent Captain Cox to notify to the Sheriffs the
steps he had taken in consequence of the proceedings of General Gansel, who
had, in the meanwhile, surrendered himself into custody. In consequence
of the above circumstance, on the 21st of April following, was issued to the
brigade of guards the Order as under:—
"Parole Hounslow,
"B. O. His Majesty has signified to the field officer in waiting, that he
has been acquainted that Serjeant Bacon of the first regiment, and Serjeant Parke of the Coldstream regiment, William Powell, William Hart,
James Porter, and Joseph Collins, private soldiers in the first regiment of

conduct him to the Tilt-yard in St. James's Park, under some pretence of business, which it imported him to settle before he was confined.   He applies to a serjeant, not immediately on duty, to assist with some of his companions in favouring his escape.   He attempts it.   A bustle ensues.   The bailiffs claim their prisoner.   An officer of the guards not then on duty takes part in the affair, applies to the lieutenant commanding the Tilt-yard guard, and urges him to turn out his guard to relieve a general officer.   The lieutenant declines interfering in person, but stands at a distance and suffers the business to be done.   The other officer takes upon himself to order out the guard.   In a moment they are in arms, quit their guard, march, rescue the general, and drive away the sheriffs' officers, who in vain represent their right to the prisoner, and the nature of the arrest.   The soldiers first conduct the general into their guard-room, then escort him to a place of safety with bayonets fixed, and in all the forms of military triumph.   I will not enlarge upon the various circumstances which attended this atrocious proceeding.   The

foot-guards, were more or less concerned in the rescue of Major-General Gansel in September last; the King hopes, and is willing to believe, they did not know the major-general was arrested, and only thought they were delivering an officer in distress: however his Majesty commands, that they should be severely reprimanded for acting in this business as they have done; and strictly orders for the future, that no commissioned officer or soldier do presume to interfere with bailiffs, or arrests, on any account or pretence whatsoever, the crime being of a very atrocious nature; and if any are found guilty of disobeying this order, they will be most severely punished.   This order to be read immediately at the head of every company in the brigade of guards, that no man may plead ignorance for the future."

It would appear from this brigade order that the ministry were not indifferent but partial in their cognizance of the military outrages, and it evinces considerable alacrity of inculpation to impute as a crime to them the unauthorized act of a few individuals of the guards.   But their approbation of the conduct of the soldiers upon occasions when riots had been suppressed with bloodshed, was supposed to have encouraged the soldiers to dare almost any act of wanton audacity against the civil power.   Hence, though not directly and immediately guilty of the rescue of General Gansel, the ministers were regarded as being primarily the authors of that, and of whatever other like irregularity the soldiery might proceed to commit.—HERON.

The General appears to have been of a violent temper.   Almon mentions that, on a subsequent arrest for debt, in 1773, he fired at the bailiffs, and was tried for it; and, though the fact was clearly proved, yet, under the direction of Judge Nares, he was acquitted.   But he was detained upon the arrest, and committed to the Fleet, where he died suddenly in July 1774.—ED.

personal injury received by the officers of the law in the execution of their duty may, perhaps, be atoned for by some private compensation. I consider nothing but the wound which has been given to the law itself, to which no remedy has been applied, no satisfaction made. Neither is it my design to dwell upon the misconduct of the parties concerned any farther than is necessary to show the behaviour of the ministry in its true light. I would make every compassionate allowance for the infatuation of the prisoner, the false and criminal discretion of one officer, and the madness of another I would leave the ignorant soldiers entirely out of the question. They are certainly the least guilty, though they are the only persons who have yet suffered, even in the appearance of punishment. The fact itself, however atrocious, is not the principal point to be considered. It might have happened under a more regular government, and with guards better disciplined than ours. The main question is, in what manner have the ministry acted on this extraordinary occasion. A general officer calls upon the king's own guard, then actually on duty, to rescue him from the laws of his country; yet, at this moment, he is in a situation no worse than if he had not committed an offence equally enormous in a civil and military view. A lieutenant upon duty designedly quits his guard, and suffers it to be drawn out by another officer, for a purpose which he well knew (as we may collect from an appearance of caution which only makes his behaviour the more criminal) to be in the highest degree illegal. Has this gentleman been called to a court-martial to answer his conduct? No. Has it been censured? No. Has it been in any shape inquired into? No. Another lieutenant, not upon duty, nor even in his regimentals, is daring enough to order out the king's guard, over which he had properly no command, and engages them in a violation of the laws of his country, perhaps the most singular and extravagant that ever was attempted. What punishment has *he* suffered? Literally none. Supposing he should be prosecuted at common law for the rescue, will that circumstance from which the ministry can derive no merit, excuse or justify their suffering so flagrant a breach of military discipline to pass by unpunished and unnoticed? Are they aware of the outrage offered to their sovereign when his own proper guard is ordered out to stop, by main force, the execution of his laws? What are we to conclude from so scandalous a neglect of their duty, but that they have other views which can only be answered by securing the attachment of the guards? The minister would hardly be so cautious of offending them if he did not mean, in due time, to call for their assistance.

With respect to the parties themselves, let it be observed, that these gentlemen are neither young officers nor very young men. Had they belonged to the unfledged race of ensigns who infest our streets and dishonour our public places, it might, perhaps, be sufficient to send them back to that discipline from which their parents, judging lightly from the maturity of their vices, had removed them too soon. In this case, I am sorry to see not so much the folly of youth as the spirit of the corps and the connivance of government. I do not question that there are many brave and worthy officers in the regiment of guards. But, considering them as a corps, I fear it will be found that they are neither good soldiers nor good subjects. Far be it from me to insinuate the most distant reflection upon the army. On the contrary, I honour and esteem the profession; and if these gentlemen were better soldiers, I am sure they would be better subjects. It is not that there is any internal vice or defect in the profession itself, as regulated in this country, but that it is the spirit of this particular corps to despise their profession, and that, while they vainly assume the lead of the army, they make it a matter of impertinent comparison and triumph over the bravest troops in the world (I mean our marching regiments) that *they* indeed stand upon higher ground, and are privileged to neglect the laborious forms of military discipline and duty. Without dwelling longer upon a most invidious subject, I shall leave it to military men who have seen a service more active than the parade to determine whether or no I speak truth.

How far this dangerous spirit has been encouraged by government, and to what pernicious purposes it may be applied hereafter, well deserves our most serious consideration. I know, indeed, that when this affair happened, an affectation of alarm ran through the ministry. Something must be done to save appearances. The case was too flagrant to be passed by absolutely without notice. But how have they acted?

R 2

Instead of ordering the officers concerned (and who, strictly speaking, are alone guilty) to be put under arrest and brought to trial, they would have it understood that they did their duty completely in confining a serjeant and four private soldiers until they should be demanded by the civil power; so that, while the officers who ordered or permitted the thing to be done escape without censure, the poor men who obeyed those orders, who in a military view are in no way responsible for what they did, and who for that reason have been discharged by the civil magistrates, are the only objects whom the ministry have thought proper to expose to punishment. They did not venture to bring even these men to a court-martial, because they knew their evidence would be fatal to some persons whom *they* were determined to protect. Otherwise, I doubt not, the lives of these unhappy, friendless soldiers would long since have been sacrificed, without scruple, to the security of their guilty officers.

I have been accused of endeavouring to inflame the passions of the people. Let me now appeal to their understanding. If there be any tool of administration daring enough to deny these facts, or shameless enough to defend the conduct of the ministry, let him come forward. I care not under what title he appears. He shall find me ready to maintain the truth of my narrative and the justice of my observations upon it at the hazard of my utmost credit with the public.

Under the most arbitrary governments the common administration of justice is suffered to take its course. The subject, though robbed of his share in the legislature, is still protected by the laws. The political freedom of the English constitution was once the pride and honour of an Englishman. The civil equality of the laws preserved the property and defended the safety of the subject. Are these glorious privileges the birthright of the people, or are we only tenants at the will of the ministry? But that I know there is a spirit of resistance in the hearts of my countrymen, that they value life, not by its conveniences, but by the independence and dignity of their condition, I should, at this moment, appeal only to their discretion. I should persuade them to banish from their minds all memory of what we were; I should tell them this is not a time to remember that we were

Englishmen; and give it as my last advice, to make some early agreement with the minister that, since it has pleased him to rob us of those political rights which once distinguished the inhabitants of a country where honour was happiness, he would leave us at least the humble, obedient security of citizens, and graciously condescend to protect us in our submission.

JUNIUS.

LETTER XXXI.

TO THE PRINTER OF THE PUBLIC ADVERTISER.

SIR, November 14, 1769.

THE variety of remarks which have been made upon the last letter of Junius, and my own opinion of the writer, who, whatever may be his faults, is certainly not a weak man, have induced me to examine with some attention the subject of that letter. I could not persuade myself that, while he had plenty of important materials, he would have taken up a light or trifling occasion to attack the ministry; much less could I conceive that it was his intention to ruin the officers concerned in the rescue of General Gansel, or to injure the general himself. These are little objects, and can no way contribute to the great purposes he seems to have in view by addressing himself to the public. Without considering the ornamented style he has adopted, I determined to look farther into the matter before I decided upon the merits of his letter. The first step I took was to inquire into the truth of the facts; for if these were either false or misrepresented, the most artful exertion of his understanding in reasoning upon them would only be a disgrace to him. Now, Sir, I have found every circumstance stated by Junius to be literally true. General Gansel persuaded the bailiffs to conduct him to the parade, and certainly solicited a corporal and other soldiers to assist him in making his escape. Captain Dodd did certainly apply to Captain Garth for the assistance of his guard. Captain Garth declined appearing himself, but stood aloof, while the other took upon him to order out the king's guard, and by main force rescued the general. It is also strictly true, that

the general was escorted by a file of musqueteers to a place of
security.   These are facts. Mr. Woodfall, which I promise you
no gentleman in the guards will deny.   If all or any of them
are false, why are they not contradicted by the parties themselves?   However secure against military censure, they have
yet a character to lose, and surely, if they are innocent, it is
not beneath them to pay some attention to the opinion of the
public.

   The force of Junius's observations upon these facts cannot
be better marked than by stating and refuting the objections
which have been made to them.   One writer says, " Admitting
the officers have offended, they are punishable at common law,
and will you have a British subject punished twice for the
same offence?"   I answer that they have committed two
offences, both very enormous, and violated two laws.   The
rescue is one offence, the flagrant breach of discipline another,
and hitherto it does not appear that they have been punished,
or even censured for either.   Another gentleman lays much
stress upon the calamity of the case, and, instead of disproving
facts, appeals at once to the compassion of the public.   This
idea, as well as the insinuation *that depriving the parties of
their commissions would be an injury to their creditors*, can
only refer to General Gansel.   The other officers are in no
distress, therefore have no claim to compassion, nor does it
appear that their creditors, if they have any, are more likely
to be satisfied by their continuing in the guards.   But this
sort of plea will not hold in any shape.   Compassion to an
offender who has grossly violated the laws, is in effect a
cruelty to the peaceable subject who has observed them ; and,
even admitting the force of any alleviating circumstances, it
is nevertheless true that, in this instance, the royal compassion has interposed too soon.   The legal and proper mercy of
a king of England may remit the punishment, but ought not
to stop the trial.

   Besides these particular objections, there has been a cry
raised against Junius for his malice and injustice in attacking
the ministry upon an event which they could neither hinder
nor foresee.   This, I must affirm, is a false representation of
his argument.   He lays no stress upon the event itself as a
ground of accusation against the ministry, but dwells entirely
upon their subsequent conduct.   He does not say that they

are answerable for the offence, but for the scandalous neglect of their duty in suffering an offence so flagrant to pass by without notice or inquiry. Supposing them ever so regardless of what they owe to the public, and as indifferent about the opinion as they are about the interests of their country, what answer, as officers of the crown, will they give to Junius. when he asks them, *Are they aware of the outrage offered to their sovereign, when his own proper guard is ordered out to stop, by main force, the execution of his laws?* And when we see a ministry giving such a strange unaccountable protection to the officers of the guards, is it unfair to suspect that they have some secret and unwarrantable motives for their conduct? If they feel themselves injured by such a suspicion, why do they not immediately clear themselves from it by doing their duty? For the honour of the guards I cannot help express ing another suspicion, that if the commanding officer had not received a secret injunction to the contrary, he would, in the ordinary course of his business, have applied for a court-martial to try the two subalterns; the one for quitting his guard, the other for taking upon him the command of the guard, and employing it in the manner he did. I do not mean to enter into or defend the severity with which Junius treats the guards. On the contrary I will suppose for a mo ment that they deserve a very different character. If this be true, in what light will they consider the conduct of the two subalterns, but as a general reproach and disgrace to the whole corps? And will they not wish to see them censured in a military way, if it were only for the credit and discipline of the regiment?

Upon the whole, Sir, the ministry seem to me to have taken a very improper advantage of the good-nature of the public, whose humanity they found considered nothing in this affair but the distress of General Gansel. They would persuade us that it was only a common rescue by a few dis orderly soldiers, and not the formal deliberate act of the king's guard, headed by an officer, and the public has fallen into the deception. I think, therefore, we are obliged to Junius for the care he has taken to inquire into the facts. and for the just commentary with which he has given them to the world. For my own part, I am as unwilling as any man to load the unfortunate; but really, Sir, the prece dent, with respect to the guards, is of a most important nature, and alarming enough (considering the consequences with which it may be attended) to deserve a parliamentary inquiry: when the guards are daring enough, not only to violate their own discipline, but publicly and with the most atrocious violence to stop the execution of the laws, and when such extraordinary offences pass with impunity, believe me, Sir, the precedent strikes deep.

PHILO-JUNIUS*.

LETTER XXXII.

TO THE PRINTER OF THE PUBLIC ADVERTISER.

SIR,   November 15, 1769.

I ADMIT the claim of a gentleman, who publishes in the Gazetteer under the name of *Modestus* †. He has some right to expect an answer from me; though I think not so much from the merit or importance of his objections as from my own voluntary engagement. I had a reason for not taking notice of him sooner, which, as he is a candid person, I believe he will think sufficient. In my first letter, I took for granted, from the time which had elapsed, that there was no intention to censure, nor even to try the persons concerned in the rescue of General Gansel; but *Modestus* having since either affirmed, or strongly insinuated, that the offenders might still be brought to a legal trial, any attempt to prejudge the cause, or to prejudice the minds of a jury, or a court-martial, would be highly improper.

A man more hostile to the ministry than I am would not so often remind them of their duty. If the Duke of Grafton will not perform the duty of his station, why is he minister? I will not descend to a scurrilous altercation with any man:

---

* This letter was originally printed in the *Public Advertiser*, with the signature of *Moderatus*. It shows that Junius himself was pleased with this composition, or he would not have raised it in his own edition to the rank of those letters which were published under the signature of his *chief* auxiliary, Philo-Junius.

† In the copy corrected by the author, and from which the original edition of these letters was printed, Junius gives directions to omit the letters under this signature in the following words:—"*Modestus* is too stupid, and must not be inserted."

b**t this is a subject too important to be passed over with silent indifference. If the gentlemen whose conduct is in question are not brought to a trial, the Duke of Grafton shall hear from me again.

The motives on which I am supposed to have taken up this cause are of little importance compared with the facts themselves, and the observations I have made upon them. Without a vain profession of integrity, which, in these times, might justly be suspected, I shall show myself in effect a friend to . the interests of my countrymen, and leave it to them to determine whether I am moved by a personal malevolence to three private gentlemen, or merely by a hope of perplexing the ministry, or whether I am animated by a just and honourable purpose of obtaining a satisfaction to the laws of this country, equal, if possible, to the violation they have suffered

JUNIUS.

LETTER XXXIII.

TO HIS GRACE THE DUKE OF GRAFTON.

My Lord,   November 29, 1769.

THOUGH my opinion of your Grace's integrity was but little affected by the coyness with which you received Mr. Vaughan's proposals *, I confess I gave you some credit for your discretion. You had a fair opportunity of displaying a certain delicacy of which you had not been suspected; and you were in the right to make use of it. By laying in a moderate stock of reputation, you undoubtedly meant to provide for the future

---

* The facts are detailed by Junius in a note, and in Letter 36. Mr. Samuel Vaughan was a merchant in the City, of hitherto unblemished character, and strongly attached to the popular cause. The office he attempted to procure had at times been previously disposed of for a pecuniary consideration, and had on one particular occasion been sold by an order of the Court of Chancery, and consisted in the reversion of the clerkship to the Supreme Court in the Island of Jamaica. A Mr. Howell was, in fact, at this very time in treaty with the patentee for the purchase of his resignation, which clearly disproved any criminal intention in Mr. V. He was however prosecuted, obviously from political motives, but which was dropped, as subsequently stated by Junius, after the affair of Hine's patent was brought before the public.

necessities of your character, that, with an honourable resistance upon record, you might safely indulge your genius, and yield to a favourite inclination with security. But you have discovered your purposes too soon ; and, instead of the modest reserve of virtue, have shown us the termagant chastity of a prude who gratifies her passions with distinction, and prosecutes one lover for a rape, while she solicits the lewd embraces of another.

Your cheek turns pale ; for a guilty conscience tells you you are undone Come forward, thou virtuous minister, and tell the world by what interest Mr. Hine has been recommended to so extraordinary a mark of his Majesty's favour ; what was the price of the patent he has bought, and to what honourable purpose the purchase-money has been applied. Nothing less than many thousands could pay Colonel Burgoyne's expenses at Preston*. Do you dare to prosecute such a creature as Vaughan while you are basely setting up the royal patronage to auction? Do you dare to complain of an attack upon your own honour, while you are selling the favours of the crown to raise a fund for corrupting the morals of the people? And do you think it possible such enormities should escape without impeachment? It is indeed highly your interest to maintain the present House of Commons. Having sold the nation to you in gross, they will undoubtedly protect you in the detail ; for while they patronize *your* crimes they feel for their own.

JUNIUS.

LETTER XXXIV.

TO HIS GRACE THE DUKE OF GRAFTON

My Lord,   December 12, 1769.
I FIND with some surprise that you are not supported as you deserve. Your most determined advocates have scruples about them which *you* are unacquainted with ; and, though there be nothing too hazardous for your Grace to engage in, there are some things too infamous for the vilest prostitute of

---

* See the ensuing letter, as also Private Letter, No. 15, vol. ii.

a newspaper to defend *. In what other manner shall we account for the profound, submissive silence which you and your friends have observed upon a charge which called immediately for the clearest refutation, and would have justified the severest measures of resentment? I did not attempt to blast your character by an indirect, ambiguous insinuation, but candidly stated to you a plain fact, which struck directly at the integrity of a privy counsellor, of a first commissioner of the treasury, and of a leading minister who is supposed to enjoy the first share in his Majesty's confidence†. In every one of these capacities I employed the most moderate terms to charge you with treachery to your sovereign and breach of trust in your office. I accused you of having *sold*, or permitted to be *so'd*, a patent place in the collection of the customs at Exeter, to one Mr. Hine, who, unable or unwilling to deposit the whole purchase-money himself, raised part of it by contribution, and has now a certain Doctor Brooke quartered upon the salary for one hundred pounds a year. No sale by the candle was ever conducted with greater formality. I affirm that the price at which the place was knocked down (and which, I have good reason to think, was not less than three thousand five hundred pounds) was, with your connivance and consent ‡, paid to Colonel Burgoyne, to reward

* From the publication of the preceding to this date, not one word was said in defence of the infamous Duke of Grafton. But vice and impudence soon recovered themselves, and the sale of the royal favour was openly avowed and defended. We acknowledge the piety of St. James's; but what is become of *his* morality?—JUNIUS.

† And by the same means preserves it to this hour.—JUNIUS.

‡ The following is the answer to the charge of Junius:—

TO THE PRINTER OF THE PUBLIC ADVERTISER.

SIR,   *Dec.* 14, 1769.
THE infamous traduction of that libeller Junius, his daring falsehoods and gross misrepresentations, excite in me the utmost abhorrence and contempt, and I hope all his deadly poisons will be sheathed in the natural antidote every good mind has to malevolent and bitter invective. What act of delinquency has the Duke of Grafton committed by Colonel Burgoyne disposing of a patent obtained of his Grace? Will Junius dare to assert it was with the duke's privity, or for his emolument? Let us state the fact, and disarm the assassin at once. A place in the Custom House at Exeter becomes vacant—Colonel Burgoyne asks it of the Duke of Grafton—he gives it. The

him. I presume, for the decency of his deportment at **Pres-**
ton * ; or to reimburse him, perhaps, for the fine of one thousand pounds which, for that very deportment, the Court of
King's Bench thought proper to set upon him. It is not
often that the Chief Justice and the Prime Minister are so
strangely at variance in their opinions of men and things.

I thank God there is not in human nature a degree of impudence daring enough to deny the charge I have fixed upon
you. Your courteous secretary †, your confidential architect ‡,
are silent as the grave. Even Mr. Rigby's countenance fails
him. He violates his second nature, and blushes whenever
he speaks of you §. Perhaps the noble colonel himself will
relieve you. No man is more tender of his reputation. He
is not only nice, but perfectly sore in everything that touches
his honour. If any man, for example, were to accuse him of
taking his stand at a gaming-table, and watching with the

colonel says, I cannot hold it myself; will you give it my friend?—The
duke consents—the colonel nominates—the duke appoints; but, says
Junius, the colonel set it up to sale, and actually received a sum of money
for it. Be it so—he took a gross sum for what was given him as an annual
income; and who is injured by this? If the Duke of Grafton sold it, he is
impeachable; if he gave it to be sold, he is blameable; but if his Grace did
neither, which is the fact, he is basely belied, and most impudently and
wickedly vilified.   JUSTICE.

* Colonel, afterwards General, Burgoyne, was a candidate, together with
Sir Harry Houghton, for Preston, at the general election in 1768, on the interest of the Earl of Derby, who had a house in the town in which he occasionally resided, who was accustomed to return one, if not both the members,
and whose daughter the colonel had run away with. The corporation supported Sir Frank Standish and Sir Peter Leicester, who were returned.
Burgoyne and Houghton petitioned the House of Commons, and set up the
right of the inhabitants at large to vote, which was so decided by the house.
The corporation endeavoured to controvert this decision in 1784, and supported Mr. M. A. Taylor and Mr. Clayton; a double return ensued. Mr.
Fox was nominee of Burgoyne and his colleague, when the committee, after
a very long hearing, confirmed the decision of 1768. It was during the
former contest that Colonel Burgoyne suffered his partisans to commit the
most disgraceful excesses, and for which he was, upon the close of the election, prosecuted and fined, as stated in the text.

† Tommy Bradshaw.

‡ Mr. Taylor. He and George Ross (the Scotch agent and worthy con-
fidant of Lord Mansfield) managed the business.—JUNIUS.

§ Mr. Rigby was proverbially remarked for a countenance not easily
abashed by any occurrence.

soberest attention for a fair opportunity of engaging a drunken young nobleman at piquet, he would undoubtedly consider it as an infamous aspersion upon his character, and resent it like a man of honour. Acquitting him therefore of drawing a regular and splendid subsistence from any unworthy practices, either in his own house or elsewhere, let me ask your Grace for what military merits you have been pleased to reward him with a military government*? He had a regiment of dragoons, which one would imagine was at least an equivalent for any services *he* ever performed. Besides he is but a young officer, considering his preferment, and, except in his activity at Preston, not very conspicuous in his profession. But it seems the sale of a civil employment was not sufficient, and military governments which were intended for the support of worn out veterans must be thrown into the scale to defray the extensive bribery of a contested election. Are these the steps you take to secure to your sovereign the attachment of his army? With what countenance dare you appear in the royal presence branded as you are with the infamy of a notorious breach of trust? With what countenance can you take your seat at the treasury-board or in council when you *feel* that every circulating whisper is at *your* expense alone, and stabs you to the heart? Have you a single friend in parliament so shameless, so thoroughly abandoned, as to undertake your defence? You know, my Lord, that there is not a man in either house whose character, however flagitious, would not be ruined by mixing his reputation with yours; and does not your heart inform you that you are degraded below the condition of a man when you are obliged to hear these insults with submission, and even to thank me for my moderation?

We are told by the highest judicial authority, that Mr. Vaughan's offer† to purchase the reversion of a patent in

---

* Col. Burgoyne, only a few days before the date of this letter, had been promoted to the government of Fort William.

† A little before the publication of this and the preceding letter the chaste Duke of Grafton had commenced a prosecution against Mr. Samuel Vaughan, for endeavouring to corrupt his integrity, by an offer of five thousand pounds for a patent place in Jamaica. A rule to show cause why an information should not be exhibited against Vaughan for certain misdemeanours, being granted by the Court of King's Bench, the matter was solemnly argued on the 27th of November, 1769, and, by the unanimous opinion of the four judges, the rule was made absolute. The pleadings and speeches were accu-

Jamaica (which he was otherwise sufficiently entitled to)
amounted to a high misdemeanour. Be it so ; and, if he deserves it, let him be punished. But the learned judge might
have had a fairer opportunity of displaying the powers of his
eloquence. Having delivered· himself with so much energy
upon the criminal nature and dangerous consequences of any
attempt to corrupt a man in your Grace's station, what would
he have said to the minister himself, to that very privy counsellor, to that first commissioner of the treasury who does not
wait for, but impatiently solicits, the touch of corruption, who
employs the meanest of his creatures in these honourable
services, and, forgetting the genius and fidelity of his secretary, descends to apply to his house-builder for assistance ?

This affair, my Lord, will do infinite credit to government,
if to clear your character, you should think proper to bring it
into the House of Lords, or into the Court of King's Bench.
But, my Lord, you dare not do either.

                                                    JUNIUS.

rately taken in short-hand and published. The whole of Lord Mansfield's
speech, and particularly the following extracts from it, des rve the reader's
attention. "A practice of the kind complained of here is certainly dishonourable and scandalous. If a man, standing under the relation of an officer
under the king, or of a person in whom the king puts confidence, or of a
minister, takes money for the use of that confidence the king puts in him, he
basely betrays the king—he basely betrays his trust. If the king sold the
office, it would be acting contrary to the trust the constitution hath reposed
in him. The constitution does not intend the crown should sell those offices
to raise the revenue out of them. Is it possible to hesitate whether this would
not be criminal in the Duke of Grafton—contrary to his duty as a privy
counsellor—contrary to his duty as a minister—contrary to his duty as a subject. His advice should be free according to his judgment—it is the duty of
his office ;—he has sworn to it." Notwithstanding all this, the chaste Duke
of Grafton certainly sold a patent place to Mr. Hine for three thousand
five hundred pounds, and, for so doing, is now lord privy seal to the chaste
George, with whose piety we are perpetually deafened. If the House of Commons had done their duty, and impeached the black duke for this most infamous breach of trust, how woefully must poor honest Mansfield have been
puzzled ! His embarrassment would have afforded the most ridiculous scene
that ever was exhibited. To save the worthy judge from this perplexity, and
the no less worthy duke from impeachment, the prosecution against *Vaughan*
was immediately dropped upon my discovery and publication of the duke's
treachery. The suffering this charge to pass without any inquiry, fixes
shameless prostitution upon the face of the House of Commons, more strongly
than even the Middlesex election.—Yet the licentiousness of the press is
complained of !—JUNIUS.

Of the Colonel Burgoyne of the above letter, a few additional particulars may not be out of place; he was a conspicuous figure in his time, and acquired many distinctions as soldier, man of fashion, dramatist, and member of parliament. Respectable by descent, he entered the army at an early age, and displayed superior abilities in the Portuguese war of 1756. After the peace his services were rewarded as Junius has related. In London his military fame, added to taste, wit, intelligence, and proficiency in fashionable amusements, made him a leader in the gay world. He was an adept in gaming, and is understood to have used his proficiency in the way Junius insinuates. He possessed parliamentary talents, and it was requisite to his advancement in the army that he should have a seat in parliament. Hence the struggle and the corruption, in which he unsuccessfully expended not less than ten thousand pounds to obtain the representation of Preston in the Parliament which met in 1768. He possessed talents for elegant literature, and successfully distinguished these in that happy and fantastic trifle, the *Maid of the Oaks*, which Horace Walpole has peevishly branded with the charge of dulness, and in the *Heiress*, one of the standard comedies of the stage. When the American war broke out, General Burgoyne was appointed to a command in it under Sir William Howe. His service was able, but finally unfortunate, terminating in the surrender of himself and army to the Americans. He returned home a prisoner upon parole; was ungraciously received by the ministers; was refused admission to his sovereign's presence; threw himself into the arms of Opposition; aided their efforts by his complaints and information; took up his pen to vindicate his military character; and succeeded in showing, at least, that for what had happened he was not solely to blame. He died some years afterwards, not indeed dishonoured, but without that splendour of fortune, or of military character, which his earlier services in Portugal had seemed to promise.—ED.

LETTER XXXV*.

FOR THE PUBLIC ADVERTISER.

December 19, 1769.

WHEN the complaints of a brave and powerful people are observed to increase in proportion to the wrongs they have

---

* The address to the king through the medium of this letter, made a very great impression upon the public mind at the moment of its appearance, and though 1750 copies of the P. A. were printed in addition to the usual number circulated, not a single copy was to be procured a few hours after its publication. The author himself, indeed, seemed to entertain a very favourable opinion of it, as in Private Letter, No. 15, speaking of this letter, he says, "I am now meditating a capital and, I hope, a final piece." It was for this production that the printer was prosecuted, and obtained the celebrated verdict of "guilty of printing and publishing only," the consequence of which,

suffered; when, instead of sinking into submission, they are roused to resistance, the time will soon arrive at which every inferior consideration must yield to the security of the sovereign, and to the general safety of the state. There is a moment of difficulty and danger at which flattery and false hood can no longer deceive, and simplicity itself can no longer be misled. Let us suppose it arrived. Let us suppose a gracious, well-intentioned prince, made sensible at last of the great duty he owes to his people, and of his own disgraceful situation—that he looks round him for assistance, and asks for no advice but how to gratify the wishes and secure the happiness of his subjects. In these circumstances, it may be matter of curious SPECULATION to consider if an honest man were permitted to approach a king, in what terms he would address himself to his sovereign. Let it be imagined, no matter how improbable, that the first prejudice against his character is removed, that the ceremonious difficulties of an audience are surmounted, that he feels himself animated by the purest and most honourable affections to his king and country, and that the great person whom he addresses has spirit enough to bid him speak freely, and understanding enough to listen to him with attention. Unacquainted with the vain impertinence of forms, he would deliver his sentiments with dignity and firmness, but not without respect.

as appears from Woodfall's trial (see APPENDIX), was that two distinct motions were made in court; one by the counsel for the defendant in arrest of judgment, grounded on its ambiguity, and another by the counsel for the crown, to compel the defendant to show cause why the verdict should not be entered up according to the legal import. The case being argued, the Court of King's Bench ultimately decided that a new trial should be granted. This accordingly commenced, when the Attorney-General observing to the Chief Justice that he had not the original newspaper by which he could prove the publication, his lordship laconically replied, "that's not my fault, Mr. Attorney," and in this manner terminated the second trial. The fact is, that the foreman of the jury upon the first trial had pocketed the paper upon its being handed to the jury box for inspection, and had afterwards destroyed it. The expense the defendant was put to in this prosecution, as stated in Private Letter, No. 19, amounted to about 120*l*. Mr. Almon, with others, were also prosecuted for selling a reprint of this letter; and in a note to his edition of *Junius* (vol. i. 327) the former states, that the Attorney-General (Mr. De Grey, afterwards Lord Walsingham) copied the whole of the address into the information, which he filed *ex officio*, thereby extending the instrument to above 140 sheets, and considerably increasing the law expenses, which he asserts amounted in his case to between five and six hundred pounds!—ED.

"SIR,—It is the misfortune of your life, and originally the cause of every reproach and distress which has attended your government, that you should never have been acquainted with the language of truth until you heard it in the complaints of your people. It is not, however, too late to correct the error of your education. We are still inclined to make an indulgent allowance for the pernicious lessons you received in your youth, and to form the most sanguine hopes from the natural benevolence of your disposition*. We are far from thinking you capable of a direct, deliberate purpose to invade those original rights of your subjects on which all their civil and political liberties depend. Had it been possible for us to entertain a suspicion so dishonourable to your character, we should long since have adopted a style of remonstrance very distant from the humility of complaint. The doctrine inculcated by our laws, *That the king can do no wrong*, is admitted without reluctance. We separate the amiable, good-natured prince from the folly and treachery of his servants, and the private virtues of the man from the vices of his government. Were it not for this just distinction, I know not whether your Majesty's condition or that of the English nation would deserve most to be lamented. I would prepare your mind for a favourable reception of truth by removing every painful, offensive idea of personal reproach. Your subjects, Sir, wish

* The plan of tutelage and future dominion over the heir apparent, laid many years ago at Carlton House, between the Princess Dowager and her favourite the Earl of Bute, was as gross and palpable as that which was concerted between Anne of Austria and Cardinal Mazarin, to govern Lewis the Fourteenth, and in effect to prolong his minority until the end of their lives. That prince had strong natural parts, and used frequently to blush for his own ignorance and want of education which had been wilfully neglected by her mother and her minion. A little experience, however, soon showed him how shamefully he had been treated, and for what infamous purposes he had been kept in ignorance. Our great Edward too, at an early period, had sense enough to understand the nature of the connection between his abandoned mother and the detested Mortimer. But since that time human nature, we may observe, is greatly altered for the better. Dowagers may be chaste, and minions may be honest. When it was proposed to settle the present king's household as Prince of Wales, it is well known that the Earl of Bute was forced into it in direct contradiction to the late king's inclination. *That* was the salient point from which all the mischiefs and disgraces of the present reign took life and motion. From that moment Lord Bute never suffered the Prince of Wales to be an instant out of his sight. We need not look farther.—JUNIUS.

for nothing but that, as *they* are reasonable and affectionate enough to separate your person from your government, so *you,* in your turn, should distinguish between the conduct which becomes the permanent dignity of a king and that which serves only to promote the temporary interest and miserable ambition of a minister.

"You ascended the throne with a declared and, I doubt not, a sincere resolution of giving universal satisfaction to your subjects *. You found them pleased with the novelty of a young prince whose countenance promised even more than his words, and loyal to you not only from principle but passion. It was not a cold profession of allegiance to the first magistrate, but a partial, animated attachment to a favourite prince, the native of their country. They did not wait to examine your conduct, nor to be determined by experience, but gave you a generous credit for the future blessings of your reign, and paid you in advance the dearest tribute of their affections. Such, Sir, was once the disposition of a people who now surround your throne with reproaches and complaints. Do justice to yourself. Banish from your mind those unworthy opinions with which some interested persons have laboured to possess you. Distrust the men who tell you that the English are naturally light and inconstant—that they complain without a cause. Withdraw your confidence equally from all parties— from ministers, favourites, and relations; and let there be one moment in your life in which you have consulted your own understanding.

"When you affectedly renounced the name of Englishman†, believe me, Sir, you were persuaded to pay a very ill-judged compliment to one part of your subjects at the expense of another. While the natives of Scotland are not in actual rebellion, they are undoubtedly entitled to protection, nor do I mean to condemn the policy of giving some encouragement to the novelty of their affections for the house of Hanover. I am ready to hope for everything from their new-born zeal,

* " Born and educated in this country, I glory in the name of Briton, and the peculiar happiness of my life will ever consist in promoting the welfare of a people whose loyalty and warm affection to me I consider as the greatest and most permanent security of my throne."—*Speech of the King, Nov.* 18, 1760.

† Alluding to the king's substitution of the word Briton.

and from the future steadiness of their allegiance. But hitherto
they have no claim to your favour. To honour them with a
determined predilection and confidence, in exclusion of your
English subjects who placed your family, and in spite of
treachery and rebellion have supported it, upon the throne, is
a mistake too gross even for the unsuspecting generosity of
youth. In this error we see a capital violation of the most
obvious rules of policy and prudence. We trace it, however, to
an original bias in your education, and are ready to allow for
your inexperience.

" To the same early influence we attribute it that you have
descended to take a share not only in the narrow views and
interests of particular persons, but in the fatal malignity of
their passions. At your accession to the throne the whole
system of government was altered, not from wisdom or deliberation, but because it had been adopted by your predecessor. A little personal motive of pique and resentment was
sufficient to remove the ablest servants of the crown *; but it
is not in this country, Sir, that such men can be dishonoured
by the frowns of a king. They were dismissed, but could not
be disgraced. Without entering into a minuter discussion of
the merits of the peace, we may observe, in the imprudent
hurry with which the first overtures from France were accepted, in the conduct of the negociation, and terms of the
treaty, the strongest marks of that precipitate spirit of con
cession with which a certain part of your subjects have been
at all times ready to purchase a peace with the *natural ene
mies* of this country. On *your* part we are satisfied that
everything was honourable and sincere, and if England was
sold to France, we doubt not that your Majesty was equally
betrayed. The conditions of the peace were matter of grief
and surprise to your subjects, but not the immediate cause of
their present discontent.

" Hitherto, Sir, you had been sacrificed to the prejudices
and passions of others. With what firmness will you bear the
mention of your own?

---

* One of the first acts of the present reign was to dismiss Mr. Legge,
because he had some years before refused to yield his interest in Hampshire
to a Scotchman recommended by Lord Bute. This was the reason publicly
assigned by his lordship.—JUNIUS.
The Scotchman alluded to was Sir Simeon Stuart.

" A man, not very honourably distinguished in the world, commences a formal attack upon your favourite, considering nothing but how he might best expose his person and principles to detestation, and the national character of his countrymen to contempt. The natives of that country, Sir, are as much distinguished by a peculiar character as by your Majesty's favour. Like another chosen people, they have been conducted into the land of plenty, where they find themselves effectually marked, and divided from mankind. There is hardly a period at which the most irregular character may not be redeemed. The mistakes of one sex find a retreat in patriotism; those of the other in devotion. Mr. Wilkes brought with him into politics the same liberal sentiments by which his private conduct had been directed, and seemed to think, that as there are few excesses in which an English gentlemen may not be permitted to indulge, the same latitude was allowed him in the choice of his political principles, and in the spirit of maintaining them. I mean to state, not entirely to defend, his conduct. In the earnestness of his zeal he suffered some unwarrantable insinuations to escape him. He said more than moderate men would justify, but not enough to entitle him to the honour of your Majesty's personal resentment. The rays of royal indignation collected upon him served only to illuminate, and could not consume. Animated by the favour of the people on one side, and heated by persecution on the other, his views and sentiments changed with his situation. Hardly serious at first, he is now an enthusiast. The coldest bodies warm with opposition, the hardest sparkle in collision. There is a holy mistaken zeal in politics as well as in religion. By persuading others, we convince ourselves. The passions are engaged, and create a maternal affection in the mind, which forces us to love the cause for which we suffer. Is this a contention worthy of a king? Are you not sensible how much the meanness of the cause gives an air of ridicule to the serious difficulties into which you have been betrayed? the destruction of one man has been now for many years the sole object of your government; and if there can be anything still more disgraceful, we have seen for such an object the utmost influence of the executive power and every ministerial artifice exerted, without success. Nor can you ever succeed, unless *he* should be imprudent enough to forfeit the protection of those laws to which you owe your crown, or unless your ministers should persuade you to make it a question of force alone, and try the whole strength of government in opposition to the people. The lessons *he* has received from experience, will probably guard him from such excess of folly, and in your Majesty's virtues we find an unquestionable assurance that no illegal violence will be attempted.

" Far from suspecting you of so horrible a design, we would attribute the continued violation of the laws, and even this last enormous attack upon the vital principles of the constitution, to an ill-advised, unworthy personal resentment. From one false step you have been betrayed into another, and as the cause was unworthy of you, your ministers were determined that the prudence of the execution should correspond with the wisdom and dignity of the design. They have reduced you to the necessity of choosing out of a variety of difficulties—to a situation so unhappy, that you can neither do wrong without ruin, nor right without affliction. These worthy servants have undoubtedly given you many singular proofs of their abilities. Not contented with making Mr. Wilkes a man of importance, they have judiciously transferred the question from the rights and interests of one man to the most important rights and interests of the people, and forced your subjects from wishing well to the cause of an individual, to unite with him in their own. Let them proceed as they have begun, and your Majesty need not doubt that the catastrophe will do no dishonour to the conduct of the piece.

" The circumstances to which you are reduced will not admit of a compromise with the English nation. Undecisive, qualifying measures will disgrace your government still more than open violence, and without satisfying the people will excite their contempt. They have too much understanding and spirit to accept of an indirect satisfaction for a direct injury. Nothing less than a repeal, as formal as the resolution itself, can heal the wound which has been given to the constitution, nor will anything less be accepted. I can readily believe that there is an influence sufficient to recall that pernicious vote. The House of Commons undoubtedly consider their duty to the crown as paramount to all other obligations. To *us* they are only indebted for an accidental existence, and have justly transferred their gratitude from their parents to their benefactors—from those who gave them birth to the minister from whose benevolence they derive the comforts and pleasures of their political life, who has taken the tenderest care of their infancy, and relieves their necessities without offending their delicacy. But, if it were possible for their integrity to be degraded to a condition so vile and abject that, compared with it, the present estimation they stand in is a state of honour and respect, consider, Sir, in what manner you will afterwards proceed. Can you conceive that the people of this country will long submit to be governed by so flexible a House of Commons? It is not in the nature of human society that any form of government, in such circumstances, can long be preserved? In ours, the general contempt of the people is as fatal as their detestation. Such, I am persuaded, would be the necessary effect of any base concession made by the present House of Commons, and, as a qualifying measure would not be accepted, it remains for you to decide whether you will, at any hazard, support a set of men who have reduced you to this unhappy dilemma, or whether you will gratify the united wishes of the whole people of England by dissolving the parliament.

"Taking it for granted, as I do very sincerely, that you have personally no design against the constitution, nor any views inconsistent with the good of your subjects, I think you cannot hesitate long upon the choice, which it equally concerns your interest and your honour to adopt. On one side you hazard the affections of all your English subjects—you relinquish every hope of repose to yourself, and you endanger the establishment of your family for ever. All this you venture for no object whatsoever, or for such an object as it would be an affront to you to name. Men of sense will examine your conduct with suspicion, while those who are incapable of comprehending to what degree they are injured, afflict you with clamours equally insolent and unmeaning. Supposing it possible that no fatal struggle should ensue, you determine at once to be unhappy, without the hope of a compensation either from interest or ambition. If an English king be hated or despised, he *must* be unhappy; and this, perhaps, is the only political truth which he ought to be convinced of without experiment. But if the English people should no longer confine their resentment to a submissive representation of their wrongs—if, following the glorious example of their ancestors, they should no longer appeal to the creature of the constitution, but to that high Being who gave them the rights of humanity, whose gifts it were sacrilege to surrender—let me ask you, Sir, upon what part of your subjects would you rely for assistance?

" The people of Ireland have been uniformly plundered and oppressed. In return, they give you every day fresh marks of their resentment. They despise the miserable governor you have sent them *, because he is the creature of Lord Bute ; nor is it from any natural confusion in their ideas that they are so ready to confound the original of a king with the disgraceful representation of him.

" The distance of the colonies would make it impossible for them to take an active concern in your affairs if they were as well affected to your government as they once pretended to be to your person. They were ready enough to distinguish between *you* and your ministers. They complained of an act of the legislature, but traced the origin of it no higher than to the servants of the crown ; they pleased themselves with the hope that their sovereign, if not favourable to their cause, at least was impartial. The decisive, personal part you took against them has effectually banished that first distinction from their minds †. They consider you as united with your servants against America, and know how to distinguish the sovereign and a venal parliament on one side from the real sentiments of the English people on the the other. Looking forward to independence, they might possibly receive you for their king ; but, if ever you retire to America, be assured they will give you such a covenant to

---

* Viscount Townshend, sent over on the plan of being resident governor. The history of his ridiculous administrations shall not be lost to the public.—JUNIUS.

This promise Junius did not fulfil ; but see his Miscellaneous Letter, No. 4, on the appointment of this nobleman to the lord-lieutenarcy.

† In the King's speech of November 8, 1768, it was declared " That the spirit of faction had broken out afresh in some of the colonies, and, in one of them, proceeded to acts of violence and resistance to the execution of the laws ; —that Boston was in a state of disobedience to all law and government, and had proceeded to measures subversive of the constitution, and attended with circumstances that manifested a disposition to throw off their dependence on Great Britain."—JUNIUS.

digest as the presbytery of Scotland would have been ashamed
to offer to Charles the Second. They left their native land in
search of freedom, and found it in a desert. Divided as they
are into a thousand forms of policy and religion, there is one
point in which they all agree—they equally detest the
pageantry of a king and the supercilious hypocrisy of a
bishop.

" It is not then from the alienated affections of Ireland or
America that you can reasonably look for assistance; still
less from the people of England, who are actually contending
for their rights, and in this great question are parties against
you. You are not, however, destitute of every appearance of
support — you have all the Jacobites, Nonjurors, Roman
Catholics, and Tories of this country, and all Scotland without exception. Considering from what family you are descended, the choice of your friends has been singularly directed; and truly, Sir, if you had not lost the Whig interest
of England, I should admire your dexterity in turning the
hearts of your enemies. Is it possible for you to place any
confidence in men who, before they are faithful to you, must
renounce every opinion and betray every principle, both in
church and state, which they inherit from their ancestors,
and are confirmed in by their education? whose numbers are
so inconsiderable that they have long since been obliged to give
up the principles and language which distinguish them as a
party, and to fight under the banners of their enemies?
Their zeal begins with hypocrisy, and must conclude in
treachery. At first they deceive—at last they betray.

"As to the Scotch, I must suppose your heart and understanding so biassed from your earliest infancy in their favour,
that nothing less than *your own* misfortunes can undeceive
you. You will not accept of the uniform experience of your
ancestors; and when once a man is determined 'to believe,
the very absurdity of the doctrine confirms him in his faith
A bigoted understanding can draw a proof of attachment to
the house of Hanover from a notorious zeal for the house of
Stuart, and find an earnest of future loyalty in former rebel-
lions. Appearances are, however, in their favour; so strongly,
indeed, that one would think they had forgotten that you are
their lawful king, and had mistaken you for a pretender to
the crown. Let it be admitted, then, that the Scotch are as

sincere in their present professions as if you were in reality not an Englishman, but a Briton of the North. You would not be the first prince of their native country against whom they have rebelled, nor the first whom they have basely betrayed. Have you forgotten, Sir, or has your favourite concealed from you that part of our history when the unhappy Charles (and he too had private virtues) fled from the open, avowed indignation of his English subjects, and surrendered himself at discretion to the good faith of his own countrymen? Without looking for support in their affections as subjects, he applied only to their honour as gentlemen for protection. They received him as they would your Majesty, with bows, and smiles, and falsehood, and kept him until they had settled their bargain with the English parliament; then basely sold their native king to the vengeance of his enemies. This, Sir, was not the act of a few traitors, but the deliberate treachery of a Scotch parliament representing the nation. A wise prince might draw from it two lessons of equal utility to himself. On one side he might learn to dread the undisguised resentment of a generous people, who dare openly assert their rights, and who, in a just cause, are ready to meet their sovereign in the field. On the other side, he would be taught to apprehend something far more formidable —a fawning treachery against which no prudence can guard, no courage can defend. The insidious smile upon the cheek would warn him of the canker in the heart.

" From the uses to which one part of the army has been too frequently applied *, you have some reason to expect that there are no services they would refuse. Here, too, we trace the partiality of your understanding. You take the sense of the army from the conduct of the guards, with the same justice with which you collect the sense of the people from the representations of the ministry. Your marching regiments, Sir, will not make the guards their example either as soldiers or subjects. They feel and resent, as they ought to do, that invariable, undistinguishing favour with which the guards are treated †; while those gallant troops by whom every

* Miscellaneous Letter, No. 24, vol. ii., in which the author discusses this subject more at large.

† The number of commissioned officers in the guards are to the marching regiments as one to eleven ; the number of regiments given to the guards,

hazardous, every laborious service is performed, are left to perish in garrisons abroad, or pine in quarters at home, neglected and forgotten. If they had no sense of the great original duty they owe their country, their resentment would operate like patriotism, and leave your cause to be defended by those to whom you have lavished the rewards and honours of their profession. The prætorian bands, enervated and debauched as they were, had still strength enough to awe the Roman populace; but when the distant legions took the alarm, they marched to Rome and gave away the empire.

"On this side, then, whichever way you turn your eyes you see nothing but perplexity and distress. You may determine to support the very ministry who have reduced your affairs to this deplorable situation—you may shelter yourself under the forms of a parliament, and set your people at defiance. But be assured, Sir, that such a resolution would be as imprudent as it would be odious. If it did not immediately shake your establishment, it would rob you of your peace of mind for ever.

"On the other, how different is the prospect! How easy, how safe and honourable is the path before you! The English nation declare they are grossly injured by their representatives, and solicit your Majesty to exert your lawful prerogative, and give them an opportunity of recalling a trust which, they find, has been scandalously abused. You are not to be told that the power of the House of Commons is not original, but delegated to them for the welfare of the people from whom they received it. A question of right arises between the constituent and the representative body. By what authority shall it be decided? Will your Majesty interfere in a question in which you have properly no immediate concern? It would be a step equally odious and unnecessary.

compared with those given to the line, is about three to one at a moderate computation; consequently the partiality in favour of the guards is as thirty-three to one. So much for the officers. The private men have fourpence a day to subsist on, and five hundred lashes if they desert. Under this punishment they frequently expire. With these encouragements it is supposed they may be depended upon whenever a certain person thinks it necessary to butcher his *fellow-subjects.*—JUNIUS.

The impolicy here pointed out has been since acknowledged and acted upon; and the soldier of the present day has no reason to complain either of poverty of income or severity of discipline.

Shall the Lords be called upon to determine the rights and privileges of the Commons? They cannot do it without a flagrant breach of the constitution. Or will you refer it to the judges? They have often told your ancestors that the law of parliament is above them. What party then remains but to leave it to the people to determine for themselves? They alone are injured; and, since there is no superior power to which the cause can be referred, they alone ought to determine.

" I do not mean to perplex you with a tedious argument upon a subject already so discussed that inspiration could hardly throw a new light upon it. There are, however, two points of view in which it particularly imports your Majesty to consider the late proceedings of the House of Commons. By depriving a subject of his birthright, they have attributed to their own vote an authority equal to an act of the whole legislature; and, though perhaps not with the same motives, have strictly followed the example of the Long Parliament, which first declared the regal office useless, and soon after, with as little ceremony, dissolved the House of Lords. The same pretended power which robs an English subject of his birthright may rob an English king of his crown. In another view, the resolution of the House of Commons, apparently not so dangerous to your Majesty, is still more alarming to your people. Not contented with divesting one man of his right, they have arbitrarily conveyed that right to another. They have set aside a return as illegal, without daring to censure those officers who were particularly apprized of Mr. Wilkes's incapacity, not only by the declaration of the House, but expressly by the writ directed to them, and who, nevertheless, returned him as duly elected. They have rejected the majority of votes, the only criterion by which our laws judge of the sense of the people; they have transferred the right of election from the collective to the representative body; and, by these acts, taken separately or together, they have essentially altered the original constitution of the House of Commons. Versed as your Majesty undoubtedly is in the English history, it cannot easily escape you how much it is your interest, as well as your duty, to prevent one of the three estates from encroaching upon the province of the other two, or assuming the authority of them all. When once they have departed from the great constitutional line by which all their proceedings should be directed, who will answer for their future moderation? Or what assurance will they give you that when they have trampled upon your equals they will submit to a superior? Your Majesty may learn hereafter how nearly the slave and tyrant are allied.

"Some of your council, more candid than the rest, admit the abandoned profligacy of the present House of Commons, but oppose their dissolution upon an opinion, I confess not very unwarrantable, that their successors would be equally at the disposal of the treasury. I cannot persuade myself that the nation will have profited so little by experience. But if that opinion were well founded, you might then gratify our wishes at an easy rate, and appease the present clamour against your government, without offering any material injury to the favourite cause of corruption.

"You have still an honourable part to act. The affections of your subjects may still be recovered. But before you sub-due *their* hearts you must gain a noble victory over your own. Discard those little personal resentments which have too long directed your public conduct. Pardon this man the remain-der of his punishment; and, if resentment still prevails, make it what it should have been long since—an act, not of mercy, but contempt. He will soon fall back into his na-tural station—a silent senator, and hardly supporting the weekly eloquence of a newspaper. The gentle breath of peace would leave him on the surface neglected and unre-moved. It is only the tempest that lifts him from his place *.

"Without consulting your minister, call together your whole council. Let it appear to the public that you can determine and act for yourself. Come forward to your people.

---

* It is evident from other passages, as well as the present, that Junius was not, strictly speaking, a partisan of Mr. Wilkes, though he was a deter-mined enemy to the decision of the House of Commons with respect to the Middlesex election. Wilkes, at this time, was confined in the King's Bench prison, under sentence of a fine of 1000*l.* and twenty-two months' imprison-ment, for the publication of the *North Briton*, No. 45, and the *Essay on Woman.*—ED.

Lay aside the wretched formalities of a king, and speak to your subjects with the spirit of a man, and in the language of a gentleman. Tell them you have been fatally deceived. The acknowledgment will be no disgrace, but rather an honour to your understanding. Tell them you are determined to remove every cause of complaint against your government, that you will give your confidence to no man who does not possess the confidence of your subjects; and leave it to themselves to determine, by their conduct at a future election, whether or no it be in reality the general sense of the nation that their rights have been arbitrarily invaded by the present House of Commons, and the constitution betrayed. They will then do justice to their representatives and to themselves.

"These sentiments, Sir, and the style they are conveyed in, may be offensive, perhaps, because they are new to you. Accustomed to the language of courtiers, you measure their affections by the vehemence of their expressions; and, when they only praise you indirectly, you admire their sincerity But this is not a time to trifle with your fortune. They deceive you, Sir, who tell you that you have many friends whose affections are founded upon a principle of personal attachment. The first foundation of friendship is not the power of conferring benefits, but the equality with which they are received and *may* be returned. The fortune which made you a king forbad you to have a friend. It is a law of nature which cannot be violated with impunity. The mistaken prince who looks for friendship will find a favourite, and in that favourite the ruin of his affairs.

"The people of England are loyal to the house of Hanover, not from a vain preference of one family to another, but from a conviction that the establishment of that family was necessary to the support of their civil and religious liberties. This, Sir, is a principle of allegiance equally solid and rational; fit for Englishmen to adopt, and well worthy of your majesty's encouragement. We cannot long be deluded by nominal distinctions, The name of Stuart, of itself, is only contemptible; armed with the sovereign authority, their principles are formidable. The prince who imitates their conduct should be warned by their example; and, while he plumes himself upon the security of his title to the crown.

should remember that, as it was acquired by one revolution. it may be lost by another."

JUNIUS.

———

The above celebrated address appeared when the Whigs hoped at last to force themselves in a body into administration on their own terms. The Grenvilles, the Earl of Chatham, the Marquis of Rockingham, with their respective adherents, were now united, and professed to believe that their purposes, whether of patriotism, avarice, or ambition, could be accomplished only by unswerving fidelity to their union. The opening of the session of parliament was near. They supposed that the business of government could not be performed in that session unless the king should implicitly resign the whole ministerial powers into their hands. They were preparing, by every means, to secure, beyond the possibility of disappointment, the grand object of their expectations. Not unconscious of the strength of public opinion, they used every artifice to make it raise a voice continually louder and more furious in their favour. Junius, privy to *their* secrets, though *they* were not privy to *his*, was willing to promote, by an attempt bolder and of greater effort than any he had hitherto made, that success of his party in which he expected probably to share. He, with this view, raised the level of his invective higher than either the Duke of Grafton or the Duke of Bedford, and dared to try whether he might not make Majesty itself quail before his attacks.

The address exhibits dignity in its tone; and preserves, even in the bitterness of invective, somewhat of that language of respect which is becoming in a subject who proffers counsel to his sovereign. It is comprehensive in its survey of characters, events, political measures, and party interests. It manages the leading points of the appeal with great skill, as being addressed to a good prince who loved his people, and sincerely desired to obtain, by good government, their love. It blends sublimity and vehemence with brevity and pathos. Yet by some it has been judged inferior to what, after the former letters, so great an occasion might have been expected to call forth from so consummate a master as Junius.—HERON.

———

LETTER XXXVI.

TO HIS GRACE THE DUKE OF GRAFTON.

MY LORD, February 14, 1770

IF I were personally your enemy, I might pity and forgive you. You have every claim to compassion that can arise from misery and distress. The condition you are reduced to would disarm a private enemy of his resentment, and leave no consolation to the most vindictive spirit, but that such an object as you are would disgrace the dignity of revenge*. But in the relation you have borne to this country, you have no title to indulgence ; and if I had followed the dictates of my own opinion, I never should have allowed you the respite of a moment.   In your public character you have injured every subject of the empire ; and though an individual is not authorized to forgive the injuries done to society, he is called upon to assert his separate share in the public resentment. I submitted, however, to the judgment of men more moderate, perhaps more candid, than myself.   For my own part, I do not pretend to understand those prudent forms of decorum, those gentle rules of discretion which some men endeavour to unite with the conduct of the greatest and most hazardous affairs.   Engaged in the defence of an honourable cause, I would take a decisive part, I should scorn to provide for a future retreat, or to keep terms with a man who preserves no measures with the public.   Neither the abject submission of deserting his post in the hour of danger, nor even the sacred shield of cowardice should protect him †.   I would pursue him through life, and try the last exertion of my abilities to preserve the perishable infamy of his name and make it immortal.

What then, my Lord, is this the event of all the sacrifices you have made to Lord Bute's patronage and to your own unfortunate ambition ?   Was it for this you abandoned your earliest friendships —the warmest connections of your youth, and all those honourable engagements by which you once solicited, and might have acquired, the esteem of your country ? Have you secured no recompense for such a waste of honour ? Unhappy man ! What party will receive the common deserter of all parties ?   Without a client to flatter, without a friend to console you, and with only one companion from the honest

---

* The duke had now resigned the office of first lord of the treasury, worn out by the attacks of Lord Chatham and the combined Whig phalanx in parliament, of Junius, and the petitioners and remonstrators from all parts of the country out of parliament.   His Grace resigned abruptly, and left the cabinet in some confusion, Lord Camden having not long before been compelled to leave the office of lord chancellor, and Mr. Charles Yorke, who had been called to succeed him, having killed himself through political vexation or some other cause. The Duke of Grafton was succeeded by Lord North.—ED.

† ——— *Sacro tremuere timore.* Every coward pretends to be planet struck.—JUNIUS.

house of Bloomsbury, you must now retire into a dreadful
solitude.   At the most active period of life you must quit
the busy scene and conceal yourself from the world if you
would hope to save the wretched remains of a ruined reputation.   The vices operate like age—bring on disease before its
time, and in the prime of youth leave the character broken
and exhausted.

Yet your conduct has been mysterious as well as contemptible.   Where is now that firmness or obstinacy so long
boasted of by your friends and acknowledged by your enemies?
We were taught to expect that you would not leave the ruin
of this country to be completed by other hands, but were determined either to gain a decisive victory over the constitu
tion, or to perish bravely at least behind the last dyke of the
prerogative.   You knew the danger and might have been provided for it.   You took sufficient time to prepare for a meeting
with your parliament, to confirm the mercenary fidelity of
your dependants, and to suggest to your sovereign a language
suited to his dignity, at least, if not to his benevolence and
wisdom.   Yet, while the whole kingdom was agitated with
anxious expectation upon one great point, you meanly evaded
the question, and instead of the explicit firmness and decision
of a king, gave us nothing but the misery of a ruined grazier*,
and the whining piety of a Methodist.   We had reason to
expect that notice would have been taken of the petitions
which the king has received from the English nation ; and
although I can conceive some personal motives for not yield-
ing to them, I can find none, in common prudence or decency,
for treating them with contempt.   Be assured, my Lord, the
English people will not tamely submit to this unworthy
treatment ; they had a right to be heard, and their petitions,
if not granted, deserved to be considered.   Whatever be the

---

* There was something wonderfully pathetic in the mention of the *horned
cattle.*—JUNIUS.

The royal speech with which parliament was opened, Jan. 9, 1770, treated
with silent contempt the petitions from the City, Westminster, York, and
Surrey, but was pathetic on the cattle distemper. Contemporary with the
murrain this year, there happening to be a great many divorces, it gave rise
to numberless witticisms. Among the nuptial dissolutions were those of the
Duke of Grafton and Lord Grosvenor ; and Almon relates that these two
noble lords bowed to each other while the king was reading this part of his
speech.—ED.

real views and doctrine of a court, the sovereign should be taught to preserve some forms of attention to his subjects, and if he will not redress their grievances, not to make them a topic of jest and mockery among lords and ladies of the bed-chamber. Injuries may be atoned for and forgiven; but insults admit of no compensation. They degrade the mind in its own esteem, and force it to recover its level by revenge. This neglect of the petitions was, however, a part of your original plan of government, nor will any consequences it has produced account for your deserting your sovereign in the midst of that distress in which you and your new friends * had involved him. One would think, my Lord, you might have taken this spirited resolution before you had dissolved the last of those early connections which once, even in your own opinion, did honour to your youth; before you had obliged Lord Granby to quit a service he was attached to†; before you had discarded one chancellor and killed another‡. To what an abject condition have you laboured to reduce the best of princes, when the unhappy man who yields at last to such personal instance and solicitation as never can be fairly employed against a subject feels himself degraded by his compliance. and is unable to survive the disgraceful honours which his gracious sovereign had compelled him to accept! He was a man of spirit, for he had a quick sense of shame, and death has redeemed his character. I know your Grace too well to appeal to your feelings upon this event; but there is another heart, not yet, I hope, quite callous to the touch of humanity, to which it ought to be a dreadful lesson for ever§.

Now, my Lord, let us consider the situation to which you have conducted, and in which you have thought it advisable

* The Bedford party.

† As well as the Marquis of Granby, the Dukes of Beaufort and Manchester, Lord Coventry, and Mr. Dunning, the solicitor-general, resigned; they expected, by early resignation, to be included in the new ministry of the Earl of Chatham and Lord Rockingham; but the appointment of Lord North to be premier disappointed all the expectants—Junius among them.—ED.

‡ Mr. Yorke, brother of Lord Hardwicke, on being induced to accept the chancellorship by the powerful solicitation above alluded to, found himself estranged from all his friends, who would not listen to his explanations, in consequence of which Almon says he destroyed himself the same day.—ED.

§ The most secret particulars of this detestable transaction shall, in due time, be given to the public. The people shall know what kind of man they have to deal with.—JUNIUS.

to abandon, your royal master. Whenever the people have complained and nothing better could be said in defence of the measures of government, it has been the fashion to answer us. though not very fairly, with an appeal to the private virtues of our sovereign. "Has he not, to relieve the people, surrendered a considerable part of his revenue? Has he not made the judges independent by fixing them in their places for life?" My Lord, we acknowledge the gracious principle which gave birth to these concessions, and have nothing to regret but that it has never been adhered to. At the end of seven years, we are loaded with a debt of above five hundred thousand pounds upon the civil list, and we now see the chancellor of Great Britain tyrannically forced out of his office, not for want of abilities, not for want of integrity, or of attention to his duty, but for delivering his honest opinion in parliament upon the greatest constitutional question that has arisen since the revolution *. We care not to whose private virtues you appeal; the theory of such a government is falsehood and mockery; the practice is oppression. You have laboured then (though I confess to no purpose) to rob your master of the only plausible answer that ever was given in defence of his government—of the opinion which the people had conceived of his personal honour and integrity. The Duke of Bedford was more moderate than your Grace. He

---

* The question here alluded to was the legality of the vote of the House of Commons, which seated Mr. Luttrell for the county of Middlesex. A great debate arose upon this subject in the House of Lords on the opening of the session, January 9, 1770, in which Lord Camden expressed his decided disapprobation of the conduct pursued by the Lower House, in the following energetic terms :—" I consider the decision upon that affair as a direct attack upon the first principles of the constitution ; and if, in the judicial exercise of my office I were to pay any regard to that or to any other such vote passed in opposition to the known and established laws of the land, I should look upon myself as a traitor to my trust and an enemy to my country."

This public avowal of an opinion so contrary to the proceedings if not the views of administration, was considered by them as a total defection ; and on the 17th of the same month, Lord Camden received a message from the Secretary of State, desiring, in his Majesty's name, that he would deliver up the seals that evening at seven o'clock ; which he did accordingly into his Majesty's own hands.

Besides his speech, Lord Camden was suspected by the court of betraying the secrets of the Cabinet to Lord Chatham.—ED.

only forced his master to violate a solemn promise made to an individual *. But you, my Lord, have successfully extended your advice to every political, every moral engagement, that could bind either the magistrate or the man. The condition of a king is often miserable, but it required your Grace's abilities to make it contemptible.

You will say perhaps that the faithful servants in whose hands you have left him are able to retrieve his honour, and to support his government. You have publicly declared, even since your resignation, that you approved of their measures and admired their character, particularly that of the Earl of Sandwich †. What a pity it is, that with all this approbation, you should think it necessary to separate yourself from such amiable companions! You forget, my Lord, that while you are lavish in the praise of men whom you desert, you are publicly opposing your conduct to your opinions, and depriving yourself of the only plausible pretence you had for leaving your sovereign overwhelmed with distress; I call it plausible, for, in truth, there is no reason whatsoever less than the frowns of your master that could justify a man of spirit for abandoning his post at a moment so critical and important. It is in vain to evade the question. If you will not speak out, the public have a right to judge from appearances. We are au thorized to conclude that you either differed from your col leagues whose measures you still affect to defend, or that you thought the administration of the king's affairs no longer tenable. You are at liberty to choose between the hypocrite and the coward. Your best friends are in doubt which way they shall incline. Your country unites the characters, and gives you credit for them both. For my own part I see nothing inconsistent in your conduct. You began with betraying the people—you conclude with betraying the king.

In your treatment of particular persons you have preserved the uniformity of your character. Even Mr. Bradshaw declares that no man was ever so ill used as himself. As to the provision ‡ you have made for his family, he was intitled to it

---

* Mr. Stuart Mackenzie, note, *ante*, p. 211.

† Lord Sandwich had been First Lord of the Admiralty, and was again nominated to this post in 1771.

‡ A pension of £1500 per annum, insured upon the four-and-a-half per cents (he was too cunning to trust to Irish security), for the lives of himself and

by the house he lives in. The successor of one Chancellor
might well pretend to be the rival of another. It is the
breach of private friendship which touches Mr. Bradshaw ;
and to say the truth, when a man of his rank and abilities
had taken so active a part in your affairs, he ought not to have
been let down at last with a miserable pension of fifteen hundred pounds a year. Colonel Luttrell, Mr. Onslow, and
Governor Burgoyne, were equally engaged with you, and have
rather more reason to complain than Mr. Bradshaw. These
are men, my lord, whose friendship you should have adhered
to, on the same principle on which you deserted Lord Rockingham, Lord Chatham, Lord Camden, and the Duke of
Portland. We can easily account for your violating your engagements with men of honour, but why should you betray
your *natural* connections ? Why separate yourself from
Lord Sandwich, Lord Gower, and Mr. Rigby, or leave the
three worthy gentlemen above-mentioned to shift for themselves ? With all the fashionable indulgence of the times, this
country does not abound in characters like theirs ; and you
may find it a difficult matter to recruit the black catalogue of
your friends.

The recollection of the royal patent you sold to Mr. Hine
obliges me to say a word in defence of a man whom you have
taken the most dishonourable means to injure. I do not refer
to the sham prosecution which you affected to carry on against
him. On that ground I doubt not he is prepared to meet you
with tenfold recrimination, and set you at defiance. The
injury you have done him affects his moral character. You
knew that the offer to purchase the reversion of a place which
has heretofore been sold under a decree of the Court of
Chancery, however imprudent in his situation, would no way

---

all his sons. This gentleman, who a few years ago was clerk to a contractor
for forage, and afterwards exalted to a petty post in the war-office, thought
it necessary (as soon as he was appointed secretary to the Treasury) to take
that great house in Lincoln's-Inn Fields in which the Earl of Northington
had resided while he was Lord High Chancellor of Great Britain. As to
the pension, Lord North very solemnly assured the House of Commons that
no pension was ever so well deserved as Mr. Bradshaw's.—N.B. Lord Camden and Sir Jeffery Amherst are not near so well provided for ; and Sir
Edward Hawke, who saved the state, retires with two thousand pounds a
year, on the Irish establishment, from which he in fact receives less than
Mr. Bradshaw's pension.—JUNIUS

tend to cover him with that sort of guilt which you wished to fix upon him in the eyes of the world. You laboured, then, by every species of false suggestion, and even by publishing counterfeit letters, to have it understood that he had proposed terms of accommodation to you, and had offered to abandon his principles, his party, and his friends. You consulted your own breast for a character of consummate treachery, and gave it to the public for that of Mr. Vaughan. I think myself obliged to do this justice to an injured man, because I was deceived by the appearances thrown out by your Grace, and have frequently spoken of his conduct with indignation. If he really be what I think him, honest, though mistaken, he will be happy in recovering his reputation, though at the expense of his understanding. Here, I see, the matter is likely to rest. Your Grace is afraid to carry on the prosecution. Mr. Hine keeps quiet possession of his purchase; and Governor Burgoyne, relieved from the apprehension of refunding the money, sits down for the remainder of his life *infamous and contented.*

I believe, my Lord, I may now take my leave of you for ever. You are no longer that resolute minister who had spirit to support the most violent measures—who compensated for the want of great and good qualities by a brave determination (which some people admired and relied on) to maintain himself without them. The reputation of obstinacy and perseverance might have supplied the place of all the absent virtues. You have now added the last negative to your character, and meanly confessed that you are destitute of the common spirit of a man. Retire then, my Lord, and hide your blushes from the world; for, with such a load of shame, even BLACK may change its colour. A mind such as yours, in the solitary hours of domestic enjoyment, may still find topics of consolation. You may find it in the memory of violated friendship; in the afflictions of an accomplished prince whom you have disgraced and deserted, and in the agitations of a great country driven by *your* counsels to the brink of destruction.

The palm of ministerial firmness is now transferred to Lord North. He tells us so himself with the plenitude of the *ore rotundo* *; and I am ready enough to believe that,

---

* This eloquent person has got as far as the *discipline* of Demosthenes. He constantly speaks with pebbles in his mouth to improve his articulation.—JUNIUS.

while he can keep his place. he will not easily be persuaded to resign it. Your Grace was the firm minister of yesterday: Lord North is the firm minister of to-day. To-morrow, perhaps, his Majesty in his wisdom may give us a rival for you both. You are too well acquainted with the temper of your late allies to think it possible that Lord North should be permitted to govern this country. If we may believe common fame, they have shown him their superiority already. His Majesty is indeed too gracious to insult his subjects, by choosing his first minister from among the domestics of the Duke of Bedford. That would have been too gross an outrage to the three kingdoms. Their purpose, however, is equally answered by pushing forward this unhappy figure *, and forcing it to bear the odium of measures which they in reality direct. Without immediately appearing to govern, they possess the power and distribute the emoluments of government as they think proper. They still adhere to the spirit of that calculation which made Mr. Luttrell representative of Middlesex. Far from regretting your retreat, they assure us very gravely that it increases the real strength of the ministry. According to this way of reasoning they will probably grow stronger and more flourishing every hour they exist; for I think there is hardly a day passes in which some one or other of his Majesty's servants does not leave them to improve by the loss of his assistance. But, alas! their countenances speak a different language. When the members drop off, the main body cannot be insensible of its approaching dissolution. Even the violence of their proceedings is a signal of despair. Like broken tenants, who have had warning to quit the premises, they curse their landlord, destroy the fixtures, throw everything into confusion, and care not what mischief they do to the estate.

JUNIUS.

* Junius describes the " unhappy figure " of the new minister in a note of Letter No. 88.—Ed.

LETTER XXXVII.

TO THE PRINTER OF THE PUBLIC ADVERTISER.

SIR,   March 19, 1770.

I BELIEVE there is no man, however indifferent about the interests of this country, who will not readily confess that the
situation to which we are now reduced, whether it has arisen
from the violence of faction, or from an arbitrary system of
government, justifies the most melancholy apprehensions, and
calls for the exertion of whatever wisdom or vigour is left
among us.   The king's answer to the remonstrance of the city
of London *, and the measures since adopted by the ministry

---

* The city of London, the city and liberty of Westminster, the counties
of Middlesex, Surrey, &c., had presented petitions to his Majesty to dissolve
the parliament, in consequence of the illegal rejection of Wilkes by the Lower
House, after he had been returned for the fourth time as a knight of the shire
for the county of Middlesex.   These petitions not having been graciously received, the petitioners assumed a bolder tone, and approached the throne with
remonstrances upon the answers they had received.   To the remonstrance
of the city on the 14th of March, the king returned the following answer :—
   " I shall always be ready to receive the requests, and to listen to the complaints of my subjects ; but it gives me great concern to find that any of
them should have been so far misled as to offer me an address and remonstrance, the contents of which I cannot but consider as disrespectful to me,
injurious to my parliament, and irreconcilable to the principles of the constitution.
   " I have ever made the law of the land the rule of my conduct, esteeming
it my chief glory to reign over a free people ; with this view I have always
been careful, as well to execute faithfully the trust reposed in me, as to avoid
even the appearance of invading any of those powers which the constitution has
placed in other hands.   It is only by persevering in such a conduct that I
can either discharge my own duty, or secure to my subjects the free enjoyment of those rights which my family were called to defend, and, while I act
upon these principles, I shall have a right to expect, and I am confident I
shall continue to receive, the steady and affectionate support of my people."
   There was at the same time a declaration against the remonstrance, drawn
up and subscribed by the aldermen on the ministerial side ; and an address was
jointly presented by both Houses of Parliament in support of the crown and
the propriety of the king's answer.   This and his Majesty's reply gave rise
to a second remonstrance from the city, of which the following is the most
remarkable portion :—
   " Perplexed and astonished as we are, by the awful sentence of censure
lately passed upon the citizens of London, in your Majesty's answer from the
throne, we cannot, without surrendering all that is dear to Englishmen, for

amount to a declaration that the principle on which Mr. Lut
trell was seated in the House of Commons is to be supported
in all its consequences, and carried to its utmost extent. The
same spirit which violated the freedom of election now invades
the declaration and bill of rights, and threatens to punish the
subject for exercising a privilege hitherto undisputed, of petitioning the crown. The grievances of the people are aggra
vated by insults; their complaints not merely disregarded.
but checked by authority; and every one of those acts against
which they remonstrated, confirmed by the king's decisive approbation. At such a moment no honest man will remain
silent or inactive. However distinguished by rank or property,
in the rights of freedom we are all equal. As we are Englishmen, the least considerable man among us has an interest
equal to the proudest nobleman, in the laws and constitution

bear most humbly to supplicate that your Majesty will deign to grant a more
favourable interpretation to this dutiful, though persevering, claim to our invaded birthrights, nothing doubting that the benignity of your Majesty's nature will, to our unspeakable comfort, at length break through all the secret
and visible machinations to which the city of London owes its late severe re-
pulse, and that your kingly justice, and fatherly tenderness, will disclaim the
malignant and pernicious advice which suggested the answer we deplore, an
advice of most dangerous tendency, inasmuch as thereby the exercise of the
clearest rights of the subject, namely, to petition the king for redress of grievances, to complain of the violation of the freedom of election, and to pray
dissolution of parliament, to point out malpractices in administration, and to
urge the removal of evil ministers, hath, by the generality of one compendious word, been indiscriminately checked with reprimand; and your Majesty's afflicted citizens of London have heard from the throne itself, that the
contents of their humble address, remonstrance, and petition, laying their
complaints and injuries at the feet of their sovereign cannot but be con
sidered by your Majesty as disrespectful to yourself, injurious to your parlia
ment, and irreconcilable to the principles of the constitution."

His Majesty's Answer, delivered the 23rd May, 1770:—

"I should have been wanting to the public, as well as to myself, if I had
not expressed my dissatisfaction at the late address. My sentiments on that
subject continue the same, and I should ill deserve to be considered as the
Father of my People, if I should suffer myself to be prevailed upon to make
such an use of my prerogative as I cannot but think inconsistent with the
interest and dangerous to the constitution of the kingdom."

The lord mayor, Mr. Beckford, then adopted the unusual course of re-
plying to the king, and addressed his Majesty in the following words:—

"Most gracious Sovereign,

"Will your Majesty be pleased so far to condescend as to permit the

of his country, and is equally called upon to make a generous contribution in support of them;—whether it be the heart to conceive, the understanding to direct, or the hand to execute. It is a common cause in which we are all interested, in which we should all be engaged. The man who deserts it at this alarming crisis is an enemy to his country, and, what I think of infinitely less importance, a traitor to his sovereign. The subject who is truly loyal to the chief magistrate will neither advise nor submit to arbitrary measures. The city of London have given an example which, I doubt not, will be followed by the whole kingdom. The noble spirit of the metropolis is the life-blood of the state collected at the heart: from that point it circulates with health and vigour through every artery of the constitution. The time is come when the body of the English people must assert their own cause: conscious of their strength, and animated by a sense of their duty, they will not surrender their birthright to ministers, parliaments, or kings.

The city of London have expressed their sentiments with freedom and firmness; they have spoken truth boldly; and,

mayor of your loyal city of London to declare in your royal presence, on behalf of his fellow citizens, how much the bare apprehension of your Majesty's displeasure would at all times affect their minds. The declaration of that displeasure has already filled them with inexpressible anxiety, and with the deepest affliction. Permit me, Sire, to assure your Majesty, that your Majesty has not in all your dominions any subjects more faithful, more dutiful, or more affectionate to your Majesty's person and family, or more ready to sacrifice their lives and fortunes in the maintenance of the true honour and dignity of your crown.

"We do, therefore, with the greatest humility and submission, most earnestly supplicate your Majesty that you will not dismiss us from your presence without expressing a more favourable opinion of your faithful citizens, and without some comfort, without some prospect at least of redress.

"Permit me, Sire, farther to observe, that whoever has already dared, or shall hereafter endeavour, by false insinuations and suggestions, to alienate your Majesty's affections from your loyal subjects in general, and from the city of London in particular, and to withdraw your confidence in, and regard for, your people, is an enemy to your Majesty's person and family, a violator of the public peace, and a betrayer of our happy constitution, as it was established at the glorious revolution."

This is the famous reply which the corporation has had engraven beneath the statue erected to the memory of Mr. Beckford, at the north side of Guildhall. Mr. Beckford, it may be added, was an enthusiastic admirer of Lord Chatham, and the main stay of the popularity of that haughty and ambitious leader in the city.—Ed.

in whatever light their remonstrance may be represented by courtiers, I defy the most subtle lawyer in this country to point out a single instance in which they have exceeded the truth. Even that assertion which we are told is most offensive to parliament in the theory of the English constitution, is strictly true. If any part of the representative body be not chosen by the people, that part vitiates and corrupts the whole. If there be a defect in the representation of the people, that power which alone is equal to the making of laws in this country is not complete, and the acts of parliament, under that circumstance, are not the acts of a pure and entire legislature. I speak of the theory of our constitution; and, whatever difficulties or inconveniences may attend the practice. I am ready to maintain that, as far as the fact deviates from the principle, so far the practice is vicious and corrupt. I have not heard a question raised upon any other part of the remonstrance. That the principle on which the Middlesex election was determined is more pernicious in its effects than either the levying of ship-money, by Charles the First, or the suspending power assumed by his son, will hardly be disputed by any man who understands or wishes well to the English con stitution. It is not an act of open violence done by the king, or any direct and palpable breach of the laws attempted by his minister, that can ever endanger the liberties of this country. Against such a king or minister the people would immediately take the alarm, and all parties unite to oppose him. The laws may be grossly violated in particular instances without any direct attack upon the whole system. Facts of that kind stand alone; they are attributed to necessity, not defended upon principle. We can never be really in danger until the forms of parliament are made use of to destroy the substance of our civil and political liberties;—until parliament itself betrays its trust by contributing to establish new principles of government, and employing the very weapons committed to it by the collective body, to stab the constitution.

As for the terms of the remonstrance, I presume it will not be affirmed by any person less polished than a gentleman usher that this is a season for compliments. Our gracious king indeed is abundantly civil to himself. Instead of an answer to a petition, his Majesty very gracefully pronounces his

own panegyric; and I confess that as far as his personal
behaviour, or the royal purity of his intentions is concerned, the truth of those declarations which the minister has
drawn up for his master cannot decently be disputed.   In
every other respect I affirm that they are absolutely unsup-
ported either in argument or fact.   I must add, too, that supposing the speech were otherwise unexceptionable, it is not a
direct answer to the petition of the city.   His Majesty is
pleased to say that he is always ready to receive the requests
of his subjects; yet the sheriffs were twice sent back with an
excuse, and it was certainly debated in council whether or no
the magistrates of the city of London should be admitted to
an audience.   Whether the remonstrance be or be not injurious to parliament, is the very question between the parliament and the people, and such a question as cannot be decided
by the assertion of a third party, however respectable.   That
the petitioning for a dissolution of parliament is irreconcilable with the principles of the constitution, is a new doctrine.
His Majesty perhaps has not been informed that the House of
Commons themselves have, by a formal resolution, admitted
it to be the right of the subject.   His Majesty proceeds to
assure us that he has made the laws the rule of his conduct.
Was it in ordering or permitting his ministers to apprehend Mr. Wilkes by a general warrant?   Was it in suffering
his ministers to revive the obsolete maxim of *nullum tempus*
to rob the Duke of Portland of his property, and thereby give
a decisive turn to a county election *?   Was it in erecting a
chamber consultation of surgeons, with authority to examine
into and supersede the legal verdict of a jury †?   Or did his
Majesty consult the laws of this country, when he permitted
his secretary of state to declare that whenever the civil magistrate is trifled with, a military force must be sent for, *without
the delay of a moment*, and effectually employed ?   Or was it
in the barbarous exactness with which this illegal, inhuman
doctrine was carried into execution?   If his Majesty had recollected these facts, I think he would never have said, at
least with any reference to the measures of his government,
that he had made the laws the rule of his conduct.   To talk
of preserving the affections, or relying on the support of his

---

* Letters 59 and 67, and notes.   † Ante, p. 133.

subjects while he continues to act upon these principles, is in deed paying a compliment to their loyalty, which I hope they have too much spirit and understanding to deserve.

His Majesty, we are told, is not only punctual in the performance of his own duty, but careful not to assume any of those powers which the constitution has placed in other hands. Admitting this last assertion to be strictly true, it is no way to the purpose. The city of London have not desired the king to assume a power placed in other hands. If they had, I should hope to see the person who dared to present such a petition immediately impeached *.   They solicit their sovereign to exert that constitutional authority which the laws have vested in him, for the benefit of his subjects. They call upon him to make use of his lawful prerogative in a case which our laws evidently supposed might happen, since they have provided for it by trusting the sovereign with a discretionary power to dissolve the parliament. This request will, I am confident, be supported by remonstrances from all parts of the kingdom. His Majesty will find at last that this is the sense of his people, and that it is not his interest to support either ministry or parliament, at the hazard of a breach with the collective body of his subjects. That he is the king of a free people, is indeed his greatest glory. That he may long continue the king of a free people, is the second wish that animates my heart. The first is, THAT THE PEOPLE MAY BE FREE.

                                        JUNIUS.

The resignation of the Duke of Grafton and his replacement by Lord North are notable events in the progress of these Letters. A ministerial change had ensued, but not that change which the Whig chieftains, the livery of London, or the ardour of Junius, had sought to force upon the crown. In consequence, the war against the king and his ministry continued

---

* " When his Majesty had done reading his speech [ante, p. 279] the lord mayor, &c. had the honour of kissing his Majesty's hand ; after which, as they were withdrawing, his Majesty instantly turned round to his courtiers and burst out a laughing.

" Nero fiddled whilst Rome was burning."—JUNIUS.

Mr. Horne, having furnished the printer of the Public Advertiser with a detail of the proceedings which took place on presenting the address on the 14th of March, concluded it with the above words quoted by JUNIUS; for which a prosecution was commenced against the printer, but was not persevered in.

with unabated vehemence; the bold harangues of Chatham breathed a more democratic spirit, the city continued to besiege the court with alternate petition and remonstrance, and Junius thundered forth his terrible philippics in the columns of the *Advertiser*. Despite of these onslaughts, the nation became gradually alienated from the assailants, and the great penman laboured to inflame an ardour that was continually dying away. Lord North held on his course—disastrously enough sometimes—for twelve years; and, with the exception of the Pelham ministry, it was the first stable government the country had had since the overthrow of Sir Robert Walpole, twenty-eight years before. The event has been briefly commemorated in a previous publication of the editor, and as throwing light on the political aspects of the time, the subjoined extract may not be misplaced:— •

" The establishment of Lord North's ministry in 1770 forms an epoch in the history of party. By it the Whigs lost their monopoly of power which they did not recover till sixty years after. The aristocratic pressure that the king had vainly tried to remove at the commencement of his reign was quietly removed by the course of events. Popular excitement subsided, and an entire change came over the public mind. The reasons for this issue are not difficult to assign. By the appointment of a *new man* to the head of the treasury, the apple of discord was abstracted, and Grenville, Rockingham, Chatham, and Bedford, it is probable, were less mortified at the award of this prize to a stranger to their divisions than if the selection had been made from one of themselves. The second reason was the new tone assumed at the royal court. Attempts were made to keep up national discontents, by procuring addresses and remonstrances to the throne, especially from the city of London; these were received either with dignified silence, or met with gentle rebuke, by which happy union of temper, firmness and moderation, the public mind was tranquillized and even conciliated."— *British History*. Fifth edition, p. 465.

LETTER XXXVIII.

TO THE PRINTER OF THE PUBLIC ADVERTISER.

SIR,   April 3, 1770.

In my last letter I offered you my opinion of the truth and propriety of his Majesty's answer to the city of London, considering it merely as the speech of a minister, drawn up in his own defence, and delivered, as usual, by the chief magistrate. I would separate, as much as possible, the king's personal character and behaviour from the acts of the present government. I wish it to be understood that his Majesty had in effect no more concern in the substance of what he said,

than Sir James Hodges * had in the remonstrance, and that
as Sir James, in virtue of his office, was obliged to speak the
sentiments of the people, his Majesty might think himself
bound, by the same official obligation, to give a graceful utter-
ance to the sentiments of his minister. The cold formality
of a well-repeated lesson is widely distant from the animated
expression of the heart.

This distinction, however, is only true with respect to the
measure itself. The consequences of it reach beyond the
minister, and materially affect his Majesty's honour. In their
own nature they are formidable enough to alarm a man of
prudence, and disgraceful enough to afflict a man of spirit.
A subject whose sincere attachment to his Majesty's person
and family is founded upon rational principles, will not, in
the present conjuncture, be scrupulous of alarming, or even of
afflicting his sovereign. I know there is another sort of
loyalty, of which his Majesty has had plentiful experience.
When the loyalty of Tories, Jacobites, and Scotchmen, has
once taken possession of an unhappy prince, it seldom leaves
him without accomplishing his destruction. When the poison
of their doctrines has tainted the natural benevolence of his
disposition, when their insidious counsels have corrupted the
stamina of his government, what antidote can restore him to
his political health and honour but the firm sincerity of his
English subjects?

It has not been usual in this country, at least since the
days of Charles the First, to see the sovereign personally at
variance, or engaged in a direct altercation with his subjects.
Acts of grace and indulgence are wisely appropriated to him,
and should constantly be performed by himself. He never
should appear but in an amiable light to his subjects. Even
in France, as long as any ideas of a limited monarchy were
thought worth preserving, it was a maxim, that no man should
leave the royal presence discontented. They have lost or
renounced the moderate principles of their government, and
now, when parliaments venture to remonstrate, the tyrant
comes forward, and answers absolutely for himself. The

* Town-clerk to the city of London, who signed for the corporation the
city petition and remonstrance.

spirit of their present constitution requires that the king should be feared, and the principle I believe is tolerably supported by the fact. But, in *our* political system, the theory is at variance with the practice, for the king should be beloved. Measures of greater severity may, indeed, in some circumstances, be necessary; but the minister who advises, should take the execution and odium of them entirely upon himself. He not only betrays his master, but violates the spirit of the English constitution, when he exposes the chief magistrate to the personal hatred or contèmpt of his subjects. When we speak of the firmness of government, we mean an uniform system of measures, deliberately adopted, and resolutely maintained by the servants of the crown, not a peevish asperity in the language or behaviour of the sovereign. The government of a weak, irresolute monarch may be wise, moderate, and firm ;—that of an obstinate, capricious prince, on the contrary, may be feeble, undetermined, and relaxed. The reputation of public measures depends upon the minister. who is responsible, not upon the king, whose private opinions are not supposed to have any weight against the advice of his counsel, whose personal authority should therefore never be interposed in public affairs. This, I believe, is true constitutional doctrine. But, for a moment, let us suppose it false. Let it be taken for granted, that an occasion may arise, in which a king of England shall be compelled to take upon himself the ungrateful office of rejecting the petitions, and censuring the conduct of his subjects; and let the city remonstrance be supposed to have created so extraordinary an occasion. On this principle, which I presume no friend of administration will dispute, let the wisdom and spirit of the ministry be examined. They advise the king to hazard his dignity, by a positive declaration of his own sentiments; they suggest to him a language full of severity and reproach. What follows? When his Majesty had taken so decisive a part in support of his ministry and parliament, he had a right to expect from *them* a reciprocal demonstration of firmness in their own cause, and of zeal for *his* honour. He had reason to expect (and such, I doubt not, were the blustering promises of Lord North) that the persons, whom he had been advised to charge with having failed in their respect to him, with having injured parliament. and violated the principles of the constitution, should not have been permitted to escape without some severe marks of the displeasure and vengeance of parliament. As the matter stands, the minister, after placing his sovereign in the most unfavourable light to his subjects, and after attempting to fix the ridicule and odium of his own precipitate measures upon the royal character, leaves him a solitary figure upon the scene, to recall if he can, or to compensate by future compliances for one unhappy demonstration of ill-supported firmness and ineffectual resentment. As a man of spirit his Majesty cannot but be sensible that the lofty terms in which he was persuaded to reprimand the city, when united with the silly conclusion of the business, resemble the pomp of a mock tragedy, where the most pathetic sentiments, and even the sufferings of the hero, are calculated for derision.

Such has been the boasted firmness and consistency of a minister*, whose appearance in the House of Commons was thought essential to the king's service; —whose presence was to influence every divison :—who had a voice to persuade, an eye to penetrate, a gesture to command. The reputation of these great qualities has been fatal to his friends. The little dignity of Mr. Ellis has been committed. The mine was sunk ;—combustibles provided, and Welbore Ellis, the Guy Faux of the fable, waited only for the signal of command. All of a sudden the country gentlemen discover how grossly they have been deceived;—the minister's heart fails him, the grand plot is defeated in a moment, and poor Mr. Ellis and his motion taken into custody. From the event of Friday last one would imagine that some fatality hung over this gentleman. Whether he makes or suppresses a motion, he is equally sure of his disgrace. But the complexion of the times will suffer no man to be vice-treasurer of Ireland with impunity †

* Lord North. This graceful minister is oddly constructed. His tongue is a little too big for his mouth, and his eyes a great deal too big for their sockets. Every part of his person sets natural proportion at defiance. At this present writing, his head is supposed to be much too heavy for his shoulders.—JUNIUS.

† About this time the courtiers talked of nothing but a bill of pains and penalties against the lord mayor and sheriffs, or impeachment at the least. Little *mannikin Ellis* told the king that, if the business were left to his management, he would engage to do wonders. It was thought very odd that a

I do not mean to express the smallest anxiety for the minister's reputation. He acts separately for himself, and the most shameful inconsistency may perhaps be no disgrace to him. But when the sovereign, who represents the majesty of the state, appears in person, his dignity should be supported. The occasion should be important;—the plan well considered;—the execution steady and consistent. My zeal for his Majesty's real honour compels me to assert that it has been too much the system of the present reign, to introduce him personally, either to act for, or to defend his servants. They persuade him to do what is properly *their* business, and desert him in the midst of it *. Yet this is an inconvenience to which he must for ever be exposed, while he adheres to a ministry divided among themselves, or unequal in credit and ability to the great task they have undertaken. Instead of reserving the interposition of the royal personage, as the last resource of government, their weakness obliges them to apply it to every ordinary occasion, and to render it cheap and common in the opinion of the people. Instead of supporting their master they look to *him* for support; and for the emolument of remaining one day more in office, care not how much his sacred character is prostituted and dishonoured.

If I thought it possible for this paper to reach the closet, I would venture to appeal at once to his Majesty's judgment. I would ask him, but in the most respectful terms, " As you are a young man, Sir, who ought to have a life of happiness in prospect,—as you are a husband,—as you are father (your filial duties I own have been religiously performed), is it *bonâ fide* for your interest or your honour to sacrifice your

---

motion of so much importance should be entrusted to the most contemptible little piece of machinery in the whole kingdom. His honest zeal, however, was disappointed. The minister took fright, and at the very instant that little Ellis was going to open, sent him an order to sit down. All their magnanimous threats ended in a ridiculous vote of censure, and a still more ridiculous address to the king. This shameful desertion so afflicted the generous mind of George the Third, that he was obliged to live upon potatoes for three weeks, to keep off a malignant fever.—Poor man !—*quis talia fando temperet a lacrymis !*—JUNIUS.

* After a certain person had succeeded in cajoling Mr. Yorke, he told the Duke of Grafton, with a witty smile, " My Lord, you may kill the next Percy yourself."—N. B. He had but that instant wiped the tears away which overcame Mr. Yorke.—JUNIUS.

domestic tranquillity, and to live in a perpetual disagreement
with your people, merely to preserve such a chain of beings
as North, Barrington, Weymouth, Gower, Ellis, Onslow,
Rigby, Jerry Dyson, and Sandwich? Their very names are
a satire upon all government, and I defy the gravest of your
chaplains to read the catalogue without laughing."

For my own part, Sir, I have always considered addresses
from parliament as a fashionable unmeaning formality. Usurp-
ers, idiots, and tyrants have been successively complimented
with almost the same professions of duty and affection. But
let us suppose them to mean exactly what they profess.
The consequences deserve to be considered. Either the
sovereign is a man of high spirit and dangerous ambition,
ready to take advantage of the treachery of his parliament,
ready to accept of the surrender they make him of the public
liberty;—or he is a mild undesigning prince, who, provided
they indulge him with a little state and pageantry, would of
himself intend no mischief. On the first supposition, it must
soon be decided by the sword, whether the constitution should
be lost or preserved. On the second, a prince no way qualified for the execution of a great and hazardous enterprise, and
without any determined object in view, may nevertheless be
driven into such desperate measures as may lead directly to
his ruin, or disgrace himself by a shameful fluctuation between
the extremes of violence at one moment, and timidity at another. The minister perhaps may have reason to be satisfied
with the success of the present hour, and with the profits of
his employment. He is the tenant of the day, and has no
interest in the inheritance   The sovereign himself is bound
by other obligations, and ought to look forward to a superior,
a permanent interest. His paternal tenderness should remind
him how many hostages he has given to society. The ties of
nature come powerfully in aid of oaths and protestations.
The father who considers his own precarious state of health,
and the possible hazard of a long minority, will wish to see
the family estate free and unincumbered *. What is the
dignity of the crown, though it were really maintained;—
what is the honour of parliament, supposing it could exist

* Every true friend of the house of Brunswick sees with affliction how
rapidly some of the principal branches of the family have dropped off.—
JUNIUS.

without any foundation of integrity and justice;—or what is the vain reputation of firmness, even if the scheme of government were uniform and consistent, compared with the heartfelt affections of the people, with the happiness and security of the royal family, or even with the grateful acclamations of the populace? Whatever style of contempt may be adopted by ministers or parliaments, no man sincerely despises the voice of the English nation. The House of Commons are only interpreters, whose duty it is to convey the sense of the people faithfully to the crown. If the interpretation be false or imperfect, the constituent powers are called upon to deliver their own sentiments. Their speech is rude, but intelligible; —their gestures fierce, but full of explanation. Perplexed by sophistries, their honest eloquence rises into action. The first appeal was to the integrity of their representatives;— the second to the king's justice;—the last argument of the people, whenever they have recourse to it, will carry more perhaps than persuasion to parliament, or supplication to the throne.

JUNIUS.

LETTER XXXIX *.

TO THE PRINTER OF THE PUBLIC ADVERTISER.

SIR, May 28, 1770.

WHILE parliament was sitting, it would neither have been safe nor perhaps quite regular to offer any opinion to the public upon the justice or wisdom of their proceedings. To pronounce fairly upon their conduct, it was necessary to wait until we could consider, in one view, the beginning, progress,

* In parliament, in the city, in the newspapers, the contest with the court was continued by the Whigs. The society for the support of the Bill of Rights had discharged or compromised all Mr. Wilkes's debts, to the amount of seventeen thousand pounds. The term of Wilkes's confinement had expired; and he had been elected alderman for the ward of Farringdon Without.

In this state of things Junius wrote the following letter. His object in it was, to prevent the people from adopting the persuasion either that Government was not greatly in the wrong, or that redress was hopeless, and that no part remained for the complainers but tame acquiescence. He re-

and conclusion of their deliberations. The cause of the public
was undertaken and supported by men whose abilities and
united authority, to say nothing of the advantageous ground
they stood on, might well be thought sufficient to determine a
popular question in favour of the people. Neither was the
House of Commons so absolutely engaged in defence of the
ministry, or even of their own resolutions, but that *they* might
have paid some decent regard to the known disposition of
their constituents, and, without any dishonour to their firmness, might have retracted an opinion, too hastily adopted,
when they saw the alarm it had created, and how strongly it
was opposed by the general sense of the nation. The ministry,
too, would have consulted their own immediate interest in
making some concession satisfactory to the moderate part of
the people. Without touching the fact, they might have consented to guard against, or give up the dangerous principle on
which it was established. In this state of things, I think it was
highly improbable at the beginning of the session, that the
complaints of the people upon a matter, which, in *their* apprehension at least, immediately affected the life of the consti
tution, would be treated with as much contempt by their own
representatives, and by the House of Lords, as they had been
by the other branch of the legislature. Despairing of their
integrity, we had a right to expect something from their prudence, and something from their fears. The Duke of Grafton
certainly did not foresee to what an extent the corruption of a
parliament might be carried. He thought, perhaps, that
there was still some portion of shame or virtue left in the
majority of the House of Commons, or that there was a line
in public prostitution beyond which they would scruple to proceed. Had the young man been a little more practised in the
world, or had he ventured to measure the characters of other
men by his own, he would not have been so easily discouraged.

views the proceedings of parliament during the session, which had ended on
the 19th of May; blames both the Lords and Commons equally for what
they had done, and for what they had neglected; arraigns the unskilfulness
of the financial measures which the new minister had adopted; and introduces a disadvantageous comparison of the character of the present sovereign,
with those of some of the worst and most unfortunate of his predecessors.
In this way he dexterously afforded ready topics of abuse for those who desired to keep up the popular flame.—ED.

The prorogation of parliament naturally calls upon us to review their proceedings, and to consider the condition in which they have left the kingdom. I do not question but they have done what is usually called the king's business much to his Majesty's satisfaction *. We have only to lament that, in consequence of a system introduced or revived in the present reign, this kind of merit should be very consistent with the neglect of every duty they owe to the nation. The interval between the opening of the last and the close of the former session was longer than usual †. Whatever were the views of the minister in deferring the meeting of parliament, sufficient time was certainly given to every member of the House of Commons, to look back upon the steps he had taken, and the consequences they had produced. The zeal of party, the violence of personal animosities, and the heat of contention had leisure to subside. From that period, whatever resolution they took was deliberate and prepense. In the preceding session the dependants of the ministry had affected to believe that the final determination of the question would have satisfied the nation, or at least put a stop to their complaints; as if the certainty of an evil could diminish the sense of it, or the nature of injustice could be altered by decision. But they found the people of England were in a temper very distant from submission; and although it was contended that the House of Commons could not themselves reverse a resolution which had the force and effect of a judicial sentence, there were other constitutional expedients which would have given a security against any similar attempts for the future. The general proposition, in which the whole country had an interest, might have been reduced to a particular fact, in which Mr. Wilkes and Mr. Luttrell would alone have been concerned   The House of Lords might interpose—the king might dissolve the parliament—or, if every other resource failed, there still lay a grand constitutional writ of error, in behalf of the people, from the decision of one court to the wisdom of the whole legislature. Every one of these remedies

* The temper with which you have conducted all your proceedings has given me great satisfaction."—*King's Speech on closing the Session of Parliament, May* 19, 1770.
† There was no autumnal session this year. Parliament did not meet till January 9, 1769-70.

has been successively attempted. The people performed *their*
part with dignity, spirit, and perseverance. For many months
his Majesty heard nothing from his subjects but the language
of complaint and resentment; unhappily for this country, it
was the daily triumph of his courtiers that he heard it with an
indifference approaching to contempt.

The House of Commons having assumed a power unknown
to the constitution, were determined not merely to support it
in the single instance in question, but to maintain the doctrine
in its utmost extent, and to establish the fact as a precedent
in law, to be applied in whatever manner his Majesty's servants should hereafter think fit. Their proceedings upon
this occasion are a strong proof that a decision, in the first
instance illegal and unjust, can only be supported by a continuation of falsehood and injustice. To support their former
resolutions they were obliged to violate some of the best
known and established rules of the House. In one instance
they went so far as to declare, in open defiance of truth and
common sense, that it was not the rule of the House to
divide a complicated question, at the request of a member *.
But after trampling upon the laws of the land, it was not
wonderful that they should treat the private regulations of
their own assembly with equal disregard. The speaker,
being young in office, began with pretending ignorance, and

* This extravagant resolution appears in the votes of the House, but, in
the minutes of the committees, the instances of resolutions contrary to law
and truth, and of refusals to acknowledge law and truth when proposed to
them, are innumerable.—JUNIUS.

The following is a more particular explanation of the fact alluded to by
Junius :—

The House having, on the 30th of January, 1770, resolved itself into a
committee on the state of the nation, the ensuing declaration was proposed:
"That, in the exercise of its jurisdiction, the House ought to judge of elections by the law of the land, and by the custom of parliament, which is part
of that law." This being the first of a string of resolutions that were to lead
to a condemnation of the principles on which the determination of the Middlesex election had taken place, it was contended on the part of the ministry
that, according to the usage of the House, the entire series could not be divided, to which the speaker having assented, the ministry next moved, that
the whole of the intended resolutions, except the first, should be omitted, and
that the following amendment should be added to it :—" And that the judgment of this House in the case of John Wilkes was agreeable to the law of
the land, and fully authorized by the practice of parliament." This was
carried by 224 to 180.

ended with deciding for the ministry. We were not surprised at the decision; but he hesitated and blushed at his own baseness *, and every man was astonished †.

The interest of the public was vigorously supported in the House of Lords. Their right to defend the constitution against any encroachment of the other estates, and the necessity of exerting it at this period, was urged to them with every argument that could be supposed to influence the heart or the understanding. But it soon appeared that they had already taken their part, and were determined to support the House of Commons, not only at the expense of truth and decency, but even by a surrender of their own most important rights. Instead of performing that duty which the constitution expects from them in return for the dignity and independence of their station—in return for the hereditary share it has given them in the legislature—the majority of them made common cause with the other House in oppressing the people, and established another doctrine as false in itself, and, if possible, more pernicious to the constitution, than that on which the Middlesex election was determined. By resolving " that they had no right to impeach a judgment of the House of Commons, in any case whatsoever, where that House has a competent jurisdiction," ‡ they in effect gave up that con-

* Sir Fletcher Norton was now speaker of the House of Commons. He had commenced his political career as a violent Whig; but for some time past had exhibited the most complete tergiversation, and had been as warm in the cause of Toryism as the warmest of its oldest espousers. He was elected to the chair, January 22, 1770, on the resignation of Sir John Cust, through ill health, and who died on the same day that Sir Fletcher succeeded him.

† When the king first made it a measure of his government to destroy Mr. Wilkes, and when for this purpose it was necessary to run down privilege, Sir Fletcher Norton, with his usual prostituted effrontery, assured the House of Commons that he should regard one of their votes no more than a resolution of so many drunken porters. This is the very lawyer whom Ben Jonson describes in the following lines :—

> " Gives forked counsel ; takes provoking gold,
> *On either hand,* and puts it up.
> So wise, so grave, of so perplex'd a tongue,
> And *loud* withal, that would not wag, nor scarce
> Lie still without *a fee.*"—JUNIUS.

‡ A motion similar to that recited in the note to p. 294 was made by the Marquis of Rockingham, in the House of Lords, declaring, " That the law of the land and the established customs of parliament were the sole rule of

stitutional check and reciprocal control of one branch of the
legislature over the other, which is perhaps the greatest and
most important object provided for by the division of the
whole legislative power into three estates ; and now, let the
judicial decisions of the House of Commons be ever so extravagant, let their declarations of the law be ever so flagrantly
false, arbitrary, and oppressive to the subject, the House of
Lords have imposed a slavish silence upon themselves; they
cannot interpose—they cannot protect the subject—they
cannot defend the laws of their country. A concession so
extraordinary in itself, so contradictory to the principles of
their own institution, cannot but alarm the most unsuspecting
mind. We may well conclude, that the Lords would hardly
have yielded so much to the other House, without the certainty
of a compensation, which can only be made to them at the
expense of the people. The arbitrary power they have
assumed of imposing fines, and committing, during pleasure,
will now be exercised in its full extent *. The House of
Commons are too much in their debt to question or interrupt
their proceedings. The crown too, we may be well assured,
will lose nothing in this new distribution of power. After
declaring that to petition for a dissolution of Parliament is
irreconcilable with the principles of the constitution † his
Majesty has reason to expect that some extraordinary compliment will be returned to the royal prerogative. The three
branches of the legislature seem to treat their separate rights
and interests as the Roman Triumvirs did their friends—

determination in all cases of election," which having been lost, was met by
one to the purport of that before quoted, which was carried by a large
majority ; in consequence of which, two most strong and able protests were
entered upon the journals of the House, which were signed by no less than
forty-two peers. In the last of these the protesting lords pledged themselves to the public that they would avail themselves, as far as in them lay,
of every right and every power with which the constitution had armed them
for the good of the whole, in order to obtain full relief in behalf of the
injured electors of Great Britain.

* The man who resists and overcomes this iniquitous power assumed by
the lords must be supported by the whole people. We have the laws of
our side, and want nothing but an intrepid leader. When such a man stands
forth let the nation look to it. It is not *his* cause, but our own.—JUNIUS.

See Private Letters, Nos. 80, 81, and 82, in which Wilkes gives an
intimation of an intended attack upon the House of Lords.

† Note to Letter 37, *ante*, p. 279.

they reciprocally sacrifice them to the animosities of each other, and establish a detestable union among themselves, upon the ruin of the laws and liberty of the commonwealth.

Through the whole proceedings of the House of Commons in this session, there is an apparent, a palpable consciousness of guilt, which has prevented their daring to assert their own dignity, where it has been immediately and grossly attacked. In the course of Doctor Musgrave's examination, he said everything that can be conceived mortifying to individuals, or offensive to the House. They voted his information frivolous, but they were awed by his firmness and integrity, and sunk under it *. The terms in which the sale of a patent to Mr. Hine were communicated to the public †, naturally called for a parliamentary inquiry. The integrity of the House of Commons was directly impeached ; but they had not courage to move in their own vindication, because the inquiry would have been fatal to Colonel Burgoyne and the Duke of Grafton. When Sir George Saville branded them with the name of traitors to their constituents—when the lord mayor,the sheriffs, and Mr. Trecothick expressly avowed and maintained every part of the city remonstrance—why did they tamely submit to be insulted ? Why did they not immediately expel those refractory members? Conscious of the motives on which they had acted, they prudently preferred infamy to danger, and were better prepared to meet the contempt than to rouse the indignation of the whole people. Had they expelled those five members ‡, the consequences of the new doctrine of incapacitation would have come immediately home to every man. The truth of it would then have been fairly tried, without any reference to Mr. Wilkes's private character, or the dignity of the House, or the obstinacy of one particular county. These topics, I know, have had their weight with men who, affecting a character of moderation, in reality consult nothing but their own immediate ease—who are weak enough to acquiesce under a

---

* The examination of this firm, honest man is printed for Almon. The reader will find it a most curious and a most interesting tract. Doctor Musgrave, with no other support but truth, and his own firmness, resisted and overcame the whole House of Commons.—JUNIUS.

† Junius, Letter 33, ante, p. 249.

‡ The five members alluded to are Sir George Saville, Mr. Beckford, Mr. Townshend, Mr. Sawbridge, and Mr. Trecothick.

flagrant violation of the laws, when it does not directly touch themselves, and care not what injustice is practised upon a man whose moral character they piously think themselves obliged to condemn.   In any other circumstances, the House of Commons must have forfeited all their credit and dignity, if, after such gross provocation, they had permitted those five gentlemen to sit any longer among them.   We should then have seen and felt the operation of a precedent which is represented to be perfectly barren and harmless.   But there is a set of men in this country whose understandings measure the violation of law by the magnitude of the instance, not by the important consequences which flow directly from the principle; and the minister, I presume, did not think it safe to quicken their apprehension too soon.   Had Mr. Hampden reasoned and acted like the moderate men of these days, instead of hazarding his whole fortune in a law-suit with the crown, he would have quietly paid the twenty shillings demanded of him; the Stuart family would probably have continued upon the throne ; and, at this moment, the imposition of ship-money would have been an acknowledged prerogative of the crown.

What, then, has been the business of the session, after voting the supplies, and confirming the determination of the Middlesex election?   The extraordinary prorogation of the Irish parliament*, and the just discontents of that kingdom, have been passed by without notice.   Neither the general situation of our colonies, nor that particular distress which forced the inhabitants of Boston to take up arms in their defence, have been thought worthy of a moment's consideration†.   In the

---

* A law had lately passed in the Irish legislature, rendering the Irish parliaments octennial.   Prior to this period they had been of longer duration, and it was against the will of the court that the law was enacted. The parliament that passed it was prorogued immediately afterwards, and then dissolved, under the hope of a more tractable parliament in future. The minister, however, was deceived; for the new parliament objected, shortly after its meeting, to passing the proposed money bill, in consequence of its having originated in the privy council instead of in the House of Commons.   Lord Townshend, the lord-lieutenant, on December 2, entered a protest on the journals of the Upper House against the rejection of this bill; and intended to have done the same on the journals of the House of Commons, but the latter would not suffer him.

† After the repeal of the stamp act, it was tried whether the Americans would submit to certain custom-house duties, as upon glass, red-lead, tea,

repeal of those acts, which were most offensive to America, the parliament have done everything but remove the offence. They have relinquished the revenue, but judiciously taken care to preserve the contention. It is not pretended that the continuance of the tea duty is to produce any direct benefit whatsoever to the mother country. What is it, then, but an odious, unprofitable exertion of a speculative right, and fixing a badge of slavery upon the Americans, without service to their masters? But it has pleased God to give us a ministry and a parliament who are neither to be persuaded by argu ment nor instructed by experience.

Lord North, I presume, will not claim an extraordinary merit from anything he has done this year in the improvement or application of the revenue. A great operation, directed to an important object, though it should fail of success, marks the genius and elevates the character of a minister. A poor contracted understanding deals in little schemes, which dishonour him if they fail, and do him no credit when they succeed. Lord North had fortunately the means in his possession of reducing all the four per cents at once *. The failure of his first enterprise in finance is not

&c. But it was the *principle* itself that was obnoxious to the Americans; and hence this attempt was as strenuously resisted as the former. These latter duties were in consequence all relinquished, excepting that on *tea*. The Americans, however, would not submit to this mortification, which as much infringed upon their principle as if no part whatever had been relinquished. Government nevertheless insisted upon retaining this impost, and the result is well known. Yet hostilities may be said to have commenced in the first instance at Boston, from a private dispute between two or three soldiers quartered there and a party of ropemakers. The soldiers in this quarrel were joined by their comrades, and even by their officers, and the ropemakers by the inhabitants of the town; in the scuffle that ensued, the officers were struck, the soldiers fired, and several persons in the mob were killed or wounded. Captain Preston, the commanding officer, was after wards tried but acquitted.

* The stock denominated three per cents had arisen from a loan of two millions raised by government in the 29th of Geo. II., for which a lottery and redeemable annuities at three pounds ten shillings per cent. had been granted and secured. Of the annuities, one quarter had been paid off, and the sinking fund, which was charged with the remainder, was at this time so fully capable of liquidating it, that a notice to this effect had been given by an order of the House of Commons, dated April 26, 1770.

In consequence of this flourishing state of the three per cents, into which almost every one was buying, the four per cents had been much for

half so disgraceful to his reputation as a minister as the enterprise itself is injurious to the public. Instead of striking one decisive blow, which would have cleared the market at once, upon terms proportioned to the price of the four per cents six weeks ago, he has tampered with a pitiful portion of a commodity which ought never to have been touched but in gross—he has given notice to the holders of that stock, of a design formed by government to prevail upon them to surrender it by degrees, consequently has warned them to hold up and enhance the price; so that the plan of reducing the four per cents must either be dropped entirely, or continued with an increasing disadvantage to the public. The minister's sagacity has served to raise the value of the thing he means to purchase, and to sink that of the three per cents, which it is his purpose to sell. In effect, he has contrived to make it the interest of the proprietor of four per cents to sell out and buy three per cents in the market, rather than subscribe his stock upon any terms that can possibly be offered by government.

The state of the nation leads us naturally to consider the situation of the king. The prorogation of parliament has the effect of a temporary dissolution. The odium of measures adopted by the collective body sits lightly upon the separate members who composed it. They retire into summer quarters, and rest from the disgraceful labours of the campaign. But as for the sovereign, *it is not so with him*. HE has a permanent existence in this country. HE cannot withdraw himself from the complaints, the discontents, the

---

taken, and had sunk below their level. Lord North, by a small bonus, might have induced all the holders of this stock to have transferred it into three per cents instead of receiving four, which would have been a great relief to the public debt ; but, though the minister was open to this conviction, he went to work with a timid hand, and took so much time to complete what he did intend, as to forfeit every advantage he might at first have derived. Instead of making a proposal of this kind to embrace the *whole* of the four per cents, he proposed to convert only two millions and a quarter of them into three per cents, and that the bonus should be a lottery for five hundred thousand pounds, divided into fifty thousand tickets, of which every holder of a hundred pounds capital should be entitled, for this supposed difference of fourteen pounds sterling, to two of such lottery tickets. In the prospect of this scheme the four per cents began to rise at the expense of the three per cents, and the object, so far as regarded pecuniary advantage, was completely frustrated.

reproaches of his subjects   They pursue him to his retirement, and invade his domestic happiness, when no address
can be obtained from an obsequious parliament to encourage
or console him.   In other times, the interest of the king
and people of England was, as it ought to be, entirely the same.
A new system has not only been adopted in fact, but professed upon principle.   Ministers are no longer the public
servants of the state, but the private domestics of the
sovereign.   One particular class of men are permitted to
call themselves the king's friends*, as if the body of the
people were the king's enemies; or as if his Majesty looked
for a resource or consolation in the attachment of a few
favourites against the general contempt and detestation of
his subjects.   Edward and Richard the Second made the
same distinction between the collective body of the people,
and a contemptible party who surrounded the throne.   The
event of their mistaken conduct might have been a warning
to their successors.   Yet the errors of those princes were not
without excuse.   They had as many false friends as our
present gracious sovereign, and infinitely greater temptations
to seduce them.   They were neither sober, religious, nor
demure.   Intoxicated with pleasure, they wasted their inheritance in pursuit of it.   Their lives were like a rapid
torrent, brilliant in prospect, though useless or dangerous in
its course.   In the dull, unanimated existence of other
princes, we see nothing but a sickly, stagnant water, which
taints the atmosphere without fertilizing the soil.   The
morality of a king is not to be measured by vulgar rules.
His situation is singular.   There are faults which do him
honour, and virtues that disgrace him.   A faultless, insipid
equality in his character, is neither capable of vice nor virtue
in the extreme; but it secures his submission to those
persons whom he has been accustomed to respect, and makes
him a dangerous instrument of *their* ambition.   Secluded
from the world, attached from his infancy to one set of
persons, and one set of ideas, he can neither open his heart
to new connections, nor his mind to better information.   A

---

* "An ignorant, mercenary, and servile crew; unanimous in evil, diligent in mischief, variable in principles, constant to flattery, talkers for
liberty, but slaves to power—styling themselves the court party and the
prince's only friends."—*Davenant, quoted by* JUNIUS.

character of this sort is the soil fittest to produce that ob
stinate bigotry in politics and religion which begins with a
meritorious sacrifice of the understanding, and finally con-
ducts the monarch and the martyr to the block.

At any other period, I doubt not, the scandalous disorders
which have been introduced into the government of all the
dependencies of the empire would have roused and engaged
the attention of the public.   The odious abuse and prostitution of the prerogative at home, the unconstitutional employment of the military, the arbitrary fines and commitments
by the House of Lords, and Court of King's Bench, the
mercy of a chaste and pious prince extended cheerfully to a
wilful murderer, because that murderer is the brother of a
common prostitute, would, I think, at any other time, have
excited universal indignation*.   But the daring attack upon
the constitution in the Middlesex election, makes us callous
and indifferent to inferior grievances.   No man regards an
eruption upon the surface when the noble parts are invaded,
and he feels a mortification approaching to his heart.   The
free election of our representatives in parliament comprehends, because it is the source and security of, every right
and privilege of the English nation.   The ministry have
realized the compendious ideas of Caligula.   They know that
the liberty, the laws, and property of an Englishman have in
truth but one neck, and that, to violate the freedom of election,
strikes deeply at them all.

JUNIUS.

* Matthew and Patrick Kennedy had been condemned to suffer death for
the murder of John Bigby, a watchman.   Their sister, Miss Kennedy, was
a prostitute well known to many of the courtiers of the day, and her intercession availed to obtain for them, first a respite, and afterwards a pardon.
The widow of Bigby, nevertheless, laid an appeal against the murderers,
and a new trial was appointed.   The friends of Miss Kennedy, however,
bought them off, by a present to the widow of three hundred and fifty
pounds, and, in consequence, she desisted from appearing against the
prisoners when they were arraigned.

LETTER XL*.

TO LORD NORTH.

My Lord,   August 22, 1770.

Mr Luttrell's services were the chief support and ornament of the Duke of Grafton's administration. The honour of rewarding them was reserved for your lordship. The duke, it seems, had contracted an obligation he was ashamed to acknowledge, and unable to acquit. You, my Lord, had no scruples. You accepted of the succession with all its incumbrances, and have paid Mr. Luttrell his legacy, at the hazard of ruining the estate.

When this accomplished youth declared himself the champion of government, the world was busy in inquiring what honours or emoluments could be a sufficient recompense, to a young man of his rank and fortune for submitting to mark his entrance into life with the universal contempt and detestation of his country. His noble father had not been so precipitate. To vacate his seat in parliament—to intrude upon a county in which he had no interest or connection—to possess himself of another man's right, and to maintain it in defiance of public shame as well as justice, bespoke a degree of zeal or of depravity which all the favour of a pious prince could hardly requite. I protest, my Lord, there is in this young man's conduct a strain of prostitution, which, for its singularity, I cannot but admire. He has discovered a

* In the perusal of the strictures of Junius, it should be borne in mind, that, in regard to the great constitutional grounds on which the two adverse parties of the Crown and the Opposition had taken each its separate stand, both were in the right. The executive power did well to maintain its dignity with firmness, in spite of factious importunity, or popular outrage. It did well to preserve the sovereign from the humiliation of being treated merely as a lunatic in the hands of the Whigs. The Opposition, on the other hand, acted a part which, however intended, had substantially the effect of true patriotism when they resisted the execution of general warrants, branded with reprobation what they esteemed an ignominious peace, supported Wilkes, notwithstanding his private errors, against ministerial oppression, asserted the violated rights of the electors of Middlesex, and eagerly watched against any undue interposition of the military force in the ordinary exercise of the civil authority. Such were the good and evil of the struggle. Junius belonged to the constitutional or resisting party, and for his purpose the present letter is written with admirable force, liveliness, and propriety.— Ed

new line in the human character—he has degraded even the
name of Luttrell, and gratified his father's most sanguine
expectations

The Duke of Grafton, with every possible disposition to
patronise this kind of merit, was contented with pronouncing
Colonel Luttrell's panegyric*. The gallant spirit, the disinterested zeal of the young adventurer, were echoed through
the House of Lords. His Grace repeatedly pledged himself
to the House, as an evidence of the purity of his friend
Mr. Luttrell's intentions, that he had engaged without any
prospect of personal benefit, and that the idea of compensation would mortally offend him†. The noble Duke could
hardly be in earnest; but he had lately quitted his employment, and began to think it necessary to take some care of
his reputation. At that very moment the Irish negotiation
was probably begun. Come forward, thou worthy representative of Lord Bute, and tell this insulted country, who
advised the king to appoint Mr. Luttrell ADJUTANT-GENERAL
to the army in Ireland. By what management was Colonel
Cuninghame prevailed on to resign his employment, and the
obsequious Gisborne to accept of a pension for the government
of Kinsale‡? Was it an original stipulation with the Princess
of Wales, or does he owe his preferment to your Lordship's partiality, or to the Duke of Bedford's friendship?
My Lord, though it may not be possible to trace this measure to its source, we can follow the stream, and warn the
country of its approaching destruction. The English nation
must be roused, and put upon its guard. Mr. Luttrell has
already shown us how far he may be trusted whenever an
open attack is to be made upon the liberties of this country

---

* At this time he was only lieutenant-colonel.

† He now says that his great object is the rank of colonel, and that he
will have it.—JUNIUS.

‡ This infamous transaction ought to be explained to the public. Colonel
Gisborne was quarter-master-general in Ireland. Lord Townshend persuades
him to resign to a Scotch officer, one Fraser, and gives him the government
of Kinsale. Colonel Cuninghame was adjutant-general in Ireland. Lord
Townshend offers him a pension to induce him to resign to Luttrell. Cuninghame treats the offer with contempt. What's to be done? Poor Gisborne must move once more. He accepts of a pension of 500l. a year until
a government of greater value shall become vacant. Colonel Cuninghame
is made governor of Kinsale; and Luttrell, at last, for whom the whole
machinery is put in motion, becomes adjutant-general, and in effect takes
the command of the army in Ireland.—JUNIUS.

I do not doubt that there is a deliberate plan formed. Your Lordship best knows by whom ; the corruption of the legis lative body on this side, a military force on the other, and then *farewell to England!* It is impossible that any minister shall dare to advise the king to place such a man as Luttrell in the confidential post of adjutant-general, if there were not some secret purpose in view which only such a man as Lut- trell is fit to promote. The insult offered to the army in general is as gross as the outrage intended to the people of England. What! Lieutenant-colonel Luttrell to be adjutant- general of an army of sixteen thousand men! One would think his Majesty's campaigns at Blackheath and Wimble- don might have taught him better. I cannot help wish- ing General Harvey joy of a colleague who does so much honour to the employment. But, my Lord, this measure is too daring to pass unnoticed, too dangerous to be received with indifference or submission. You shall not have time to remodel the Irish army. They will not submit to be garbled by Colonel Luttrell. As a mischief to the English constitution (for he is not worth the name of enemy), they already detest him. As a boy, impudently thrust over their heads, they will receive him with indignation and contempt. As for you, my Lord, who perhaps are no more than the blind unhappy instrument of Lord Bute and her Royal Highness the Princess of Wales, be assured that you shall be called upon to answer for the advice which has been given, and either discover your accomplices, or fall a sacrifice to their security.

JUNIUS.

LETTER XLI.

TO THE RIGHT HONOURABLE LORD MANSFIELD *.

MY LORD, November 14, 1770.

THE appearance of this letter will attract the curiosity of the public, and command even your Lordship's attention.

* In the *envelope* to this address, Junius makes the following observation :— " The inclosed, though begun within these few days, has been greatly laboured." Private Letter, No. 24.

Warned by their adventures with Wilkes, the ministers, though sorely

I am considerably in your debt, and shall endeavour, once for all, to balance the account. Accept of this address, my Lord, as a prologue to more important scenes, in which you will probably be called upon to act or suffer.

You will not question my veracity when I assure you, that it has not been owing to any particular respect for your person that I have abstained from you so long. Besides the distress and danger with which the press is threatened, when your Lordship is party, and the party is to be judge, I confess I have been deterred by the difficulty of the task. Our language has no term of reproach, the mind has no idea of detestation, which has not already been happily applied to you, and exhausted. Ample justice has been done by abler pens than mine to the separate merits of your life and character. Let it

galled by Junius, did not think it politic to combat him by the shield and spear of legal prosecution till his *Letter to the King* appeared to them to have proceeded to an audacity of seditious invective which could not fail to provoke the indignation of every Englishman in whose breast false patriotism had not utterly extinguished all sentiments of loyalty. Mr. Woodfall, therefore, the original publisher of that and the other letters of Junius, Mr. Almon, who had sold it in a publication called the *London Museum*, Mr. Miller, the publisher of the *London Evening Post*, and others who had also reprinted the same letter to the king, were brought, at different times, to trial. Almon's trial came on first; he was found guilty of selling the letter by the jury. The sentence pronounced upon him was, to pay a fine of ten marks, and to find sureties for his good behaviour for two years; himself to be bound in four hundred pounds, his sureties in two hundred pounds each. Woodfall was found guilty by the jury, of *printing and publishing* only. Miller and Baldwin were acquitted. At the trial of Robinson, one of the jurymen, starting up while the judge was giving his charge, cried, *You need not say any more, for I am determined to acquit him.* And, in consequence of this irregularity, the trial was put off till the next term. On these trials the court wished to confine the juries to find simply the fact of printing or publishing, without giving any opinion of its guilt or innocence.

It was after the issue of these trials had shown what the publishers of the letters of Junius had to dread, that the author addressed the present long and eloquent one to Lord Mansfield. In this letter Junius professes to write an invective of revenge: relates, in opprobrium against Lord Mansfield, some particulars of his lordship's early life; condemns the general tenor of his conduct as a judge; accuses him of endeavouring continually to sophisticate the spirit of the law of England, by debasing additions out of the civil law of Rome; blames him for giving evil political advice to his sovereign; and concludes with threatening fiercer invective if the printers of this letter should be harassed by prosecution.—ED.

be *my* humble office to collect the scattered sweets, till their united virtue tortures the sense.

Permit me to begin with paying a just tribute to Scotch sincerity wherever I find it. I own I am not apt to confide in the professions of gentlemen of that country; and when they smile, I feel an involuntary emotion to guard myself against mischief. With this general opinion of an ancient nation, I always thought it much to your Lordship's honour, that in your earlier days, you were but little infected with the prudence of your country. You had some original attachments, which you took every proper opportunity to acknowledge. The liberal spirit of youth prevailed over your native discretion. Your zeal in the cause of an unhappy prince was expressed with the sincerity of wine, and some of the solemnities of religion *. This, I conceive, is the most amiable point of view in which your character has appeared. Like an honest man, you took that part in politics which might have been expected from your birth, education, country, and connections†. There was something generous in your attach-

---

* This man was always a rank jacobite. Lord Ravensworth produced the most satisfactory evidence of his having frequently drunk the Pretender's health upon his knees.— JUNIUS.

† This statement of Lord Mansfield's immediate connection with the Pretender's secretary has been disputed ; and the charge advanced by Lord Ravensworth of his having drunk the Pretender's health upon his knees, was made the subject of investigation before the Privy Council and the House of Lords, in the year 1753, which terminated in Mr. Murray's acquittal, both tribunals declaring the charge to be a foul calumny. That Lord Mansfield, however, lay under the public imputation of being a relative of the Pretender's secretary is certain ; as, in a memorial in Dodington's Diary, p. 441, edit. 1809, anonymously addressed to General Hawley, and written for the avowed purpose of procuring the Solicitor-General's dismission, he is thus spoken of :—" To have a Scotsman, of a most disaffected family, and allied to the Pretender's *first minister*, consulted in the education of the Prince of Wales, must tend to alarm and disgust the friends of the present royal family. Dodington, who was intimate with Lord Mansfield, then Mr. Murray, nowhere contradicts the supposed connection ; who, nevertheless, it is presumed, would have done so if the assertion had not been true. Mr. Murray, when a student in the Temple, was an intimate acquaintance of Mr. Vernon, a rich jacobite mercer on Ludgate Hill, and the toast referred to is said to have been frequently drunk in the house of this gentleman. Mr. Vernon on his death bequeathed to Mr. Murray an estate in the counties of Chester and Derby.

x 2

ment to the banished house of Stuart. We lament the mistakes of a good man, and do not begin to detest him until he
affects to renounce his principles. Why did you not adhere
to that loyalty you once professed? Why did you not follow
the example of your worthy brother *? With him you might
have shared in the honour of the Pretender's confidence—
with him you might have preserved the integrity of your
character, and England, I think, might have spared you
without regret. Your friends will say, perhaps, that, although
you deserted the fortune of your liege lord, you have adhered
firmly to the principles which drove his father from the
throne; that without openly supporting the person, you have
done essential service to the cause, and consoled yourself for
the loss of a favourite family, by reviving and establishing
the maxims of their government. This is the way in which
a Scotchman's understanding corrects the error of his heart.
My Lord, I acknowledge the truth of the defence, and can
trace it through all your conduct. I see through your whole
life one uniform plan to enlarge the power of the crown at
the expense of the liberty of the subject. To this object
your thoughts, words, and actions have been constantly
directed. In contempt or ignorance of the common law of
England, you have made it your study to introduce into the
court where you preside maxims of jurisprudence unknown
to Englishmen. The Roman code, the law of nations, and
the opinion of foreign civilians are your perpetual theme;
but who ever heard you mention Magna Charta or the Bill
of Rights with approbation or respect? By such treacherous
arts the noble simplicity and free spirit of our Saxon laws
were first corrupted. The Norman conquest was not complete until Norman lawyers had introduced their laws, and
reduced slavery to a system. This one leading principle
directs your interpretation of the laws, and accounts for your
treatment of juries. It is not in political questions only
(for there the courtier might be forgiven), but let the cause
be what it may, your understanding is equally on the rack,
either to contract the power of the jury, or to mislead their

---

* Confidential secretary to the late Pretender. This circumstance confirmed the friendship between the brothers.—JUNIUS.

judgment. For the truth of this assertion, I appeal to the doctrine you delivered in Lord Grosvenor's cause. An action for criminal conversation being brought by a peer against a prince of the blood *, you were daring enough to tell the jury that, in fixing the damages, they were to pay no regard to the quality or fortune of the parties; that it was a trial between A. and B.; that they were to consider the offence in a moral light only, and give no greater damages to a peer of the realm than to the meanest mechanic. I shall not attempt to refute a doctrine which, if it was meant for law, carries falsehood and absurdity upon the face of it; but, if it was meant for a declaration of your political creed, is clear and consistent. Under an arbitrary government all ranks and distinctions are confounded. The honour of a nobleman is no more considered than the reputation of a peasant, for, with different liveries, they are equally slaves.

Even in matters of private property we see the same bias and inclination to depart from the decisions of your predecessors, which you certainly ought to receive as evidence of the common law. Instead of those certain positive rules by which the judgment of a court of law should invariably be determined, you have fondly introduced your own unsettled notions of equity and substantial justice. Decisions given upon such principles do not alarm the public so much as they ought, because the consequence and tendency of each particular instance is not observed or regarded. In the meantime the practice gains ground; the Court of King's Bench becomes a court of equity, and the judge, instead of consulting strictly the law of the land, refers only to the wisdom of the court, and to the purity of his own conscience. The name of Mr. Justice Yates will naturally revive in your mind some of those emotions of fear and detestation with

---

* The action was brought by Lord Grosvenor against the Duke of Cumberland for criminal conversation with Lady Grosvenor; and the cause in which Lord Mansfield delivered the opinion here charged to him, was tried before his Lordship in the Court of King's Bench, July 5, 1770. The damages were laid at 100,000l. : the verdict was for 10,000l. The doctrine here objected against by Junius has since been relinquished in courts of justice, and his own substituted.

which you always beheld him*. That great lawyer, that
honest man, saw your whole conduct in the light that I do.
After years of ineffectual resistance to the pernicious principles introduced by your Lordship, and uniformly supported
by your *humble friends* upon the bench, he determined to
quit a court whose proceedings and decisions he could neither
assent to with honour nor oppose with success.

The injustice done to an individual is sometimes of service
to the public†. Facts are apt to alarm us more than the
most dangerous principles. The sufferings and firmness of
a printer have roused the public attention. You knew and
felt that your conduct would not bear a parliamentary inquiry,
and you hoped to escape it by the meanest, the basest sacrifice of dignity and consistency that ever was made by a great
magistrate. Where was your firmness, where was that vindictive spirit, of which we have seen so many examples, when
a man, so inconsiderable as Bingley, could force you to confess, in the face of this country that, for two years together,
you had illegally deprived an English subject of his liberty
and that he had triumphed over you at last? Yet I own, my
Lord, that yours is not an uncommon character. Women, and
men like women, are timid, vindictive, and irresolute. Their
passions counteract each other, and make the same creature
at one moment hateful, at another contemptible. I fancy, my
Lord, some time will elapse before you venture to commit
another Englishman for refusing to answer interrogatories‡.

* Sir Joseph Yates was lately dead. The facts which Junius relates are
true. Yates was an able and upright judge, but incapable of improving the
spirit of the law in his interpretation of it. There was opposition of juridical principles and of personal views between him and Lord Mansfield.
He passed to the Court of Common Pleas on the 4th of May; his death
happened on the 7th of June, 1770.—ED.

† The oppression of an obscure individual gave birth to the famous
Habeas Corpus Act of 31 Car. II. which is frequently considered as another
Magna Charta of the kingdom.—*Blackstone,* iii. 135.—JUNIUS.

‡ " Bingley was committed for contempt in not submitting to be examined.
He lay in prison two years, until the Crown thought the matter might
occasion some serious complaint, and therefore he was let out, in the same
contumacious state he had been put in, with all his sins about him, un-
anointed and unannealed. There was much coquetry between the Court
and the Attorney-General about who should undergo the ridicule of letting
him escape."—*Vide another Letter to* ALMON, p. 189.—JUNIUS.

The doctrine you have constantly delivered in cases of libel, is another powerful evidence of a settled plan to contract the legal power of juries, and to draw questions inseparable from facts within the *arbitrium* of the court.   Here, my Lord, you have fortune of your side.   When you invade the province of the jury in matter of libel, you, in effect, attack the liberty of the press, and, with a single stroke, wound two of your greatest enemies.   In some instances you have succeeded, because jurymen are too often ignorant of their own rights, and too apt to be awed by the authority of a chief justice.   In other criminal prosecutions the malice of the design is confessedly as much the subject of consideration to a jury as the certainty of the fact.   If a different doctrine prevails in the case of libels, why should it not extend to *all* criminal cases?   Why not to capital offences?   I see no reason (and I dare say you will agree with me that there is no good one) why the life of the subject should be better protected against you than his liberty or property.   Why should you enjoy the full power of pillory, fine, and imprisonment, and not be indulged with hanging or transportation?   With your Lordship's fertile genius and merciful disposition, I can conceive such an exercise of the power you have, as could hardly be aggravated by that which you have not *.

But, my Lord, since you have laboured (and not unsuccessfully) to destroy the substance *of the trial*, why should you suffer the form of the *verdict* to remain?   Why force twelve honest men, in palpable violation of their oaths, to pronounce their fellow-subject a *guilty* man, when, almost at the same moment, you forbid their inquiring into the only circumstance which, in the eye of law and reason, constitutes guilt—the malignity or innocence of his intentions?   But I understand your Lordship.   If you could succeed in making the trial by jury useless and ridiculous, you might then with greater safety introduce a bill into parliament for enlarging the jurisdiction of the court, and extending your favourite

* An act of parliament already mentioned, declaratory of the rights of juries in cases of libel, which Mr. Fox, with the assistance of Mr. Erskine, introduced, established the principle, " that the jury is, in regard to libels, to judge of law as well as of fact, of intention as well as of the extent of act."—ED.

trial by interrogatories to every question in which the life of liberty of an Englishman is concerned*.

Your charge to the jury, in the prosecution against Almon and Woodfall, contradicts the highest legal authorities as well as the plainest dictates of reason. In Miller's cause, and still more expressly in that of Baldwin, you have proceeded a step further, and grossly contradicted yourself. You may know, perhaps, though I do not mean to insult you by an appeal to your experience, that the language of truth is uniform and consistent. To depart from it safely requires memory and discretion. In the two last trials your charge to the jury began, as usual, with assuring them that they had nothing to do with the law, that they were to find the bare fact, and not concern themselves about the legal inferences drawn from it, or the degree of the defendant's guilt. Thus far you were consistent with your former practice. But how will you account for the conclusion? You told the jury that, " if, after all, they would take upon themselves to determine the law, *they might do it*, but they must be very sure that they determined according to law, for it touched their consciences, and they acted at their peril." If I understand your first proposition, you meant to affirm, that the jury were not competent judges of the law in the criminal case of a libel—that it did not fall within *their* jurisdiction; and that, with respect to *them*, the malice or innocence of the defendant's intentions would be a question *coram non judice*. But the second proposition clears away your own difficulties, and restores the jury to all their judicial capacities. You make the competence of the court to depend upon the legality of the decision†. In the first instance you deny

---

* "The philosophical poet doth notably describe the damnable and damned proceedings of the Judge of Hell:

" Gnossius hic Rhadamanthus habet durissima regna,

" Castigatque, auditque dolos, *subigitque fateri.*

First he punisheth and *then* he heareth; and, lastly, compelleth to confess, and makes and mars laws at his pleasure; like as the Centurion in the holy history did to St. Paul, for the text saith, *Centurio apprehendi Paulum jussit, et se catenis ligari, et* tunc INTERROGABAT, *quis fuisset, et quid fecisset:* but good judges and justices abhor these courses."—*Coke* 2, *Inst.* 55.— JUNIUS.

† Directly the reverse of the doctrine he constantly maintained in the House of Lords and elsewhere upon the decision of the Middlesex election.

the power absolutely. In the second, you admit the power, provided it be legally exercised. Now, my Lord, without pretending to reconcile the distinctions of Westminster Hall with the simple information of common sense or the integrity of fair argument, I shall be understood by your Lordship when I assert that, if a jury or any other court of judicature (for jurors are judges) have no right to entertain a cause or question at law, it signifies nothing whether their decision be or be not according to law. Their decision is in itself a mere nullity; the parties are not bound to submit to it; and, if the jury run any risk of punishment, it is not for pronouncing a corrupt or illegal verdict, but for the illegality of meddling with a point on which they have no legal authority to decide *.

I cannot quit this subject without reminding your Lordship of the name of Mr. Benson. Without offering any legal objection, you ordered a special juryman to be set aside in a cause where the king was prosecutor. The novelty of the fact required explanation. Will you condescend to tell the world by what law or custom you were authorized to make a peremptory challenge of a juryman? The parties, indeed, have this power, and perhaps your Lordship, having accustomed yourself to unite the characters of judge and party, may claim it in virtue of the new capacity you have assumed, and profit by your own wrong. The time within which you might have been punished for this daring attempt to pack a jury is, I fear, elapsed; but no length of time shall erase the record of it.

The mischiefs you have done this country are not confined to your interpretation of the laws. You are a minister, my Lord, and, as such, have long been consulted; let us candidly examine what use you have made of your ministerial influence; I will not descend to little matters, but come at once to those

He invariably asserted that the decision must be *legal*, because the court was *competent;* and never could be prevailed on to enter further into the question.—JUNIUS.

* These iniquitous prosecutions cost the best of princes six thousand pounds, and ended in the total defeat and disgrace of the prosecutors. In the course of one of them, Judge Aston had the unparalleled impudence to tell Mr. Morris (a gentleman of unquestionable honour and integrity, and who was then giving his evidence on oath), that *he should pay very little regard to any affidavit he should make.*—JUNIUS.

important points on which your resolution was waited for, on which the expectation of your opinion kept a great part of the nation in suspense. A constitutional question arises upon a declaration of the law of parliament, by which the freedom of election and the birthright of the subject were supposed to have been invaded; the king's servants are accused of violating the constitution; the nation is in a ferment; the ablest men of all parties engage in the question, and exert their utmost abilities in the discussion of it—what part has the honest Lord Mansfield acted? As an eminent judge of the law, his opinion would have been respected; as a peer, he had a right to demand an audience of his sovereign, and inform him that his ministers were pursuing unconstitutional measures; upon other occasions, my Lord, you have no difficulty in finding your way into the closet. The pretended neutrality of belonging to no party will not save your reputation; in questions merely political an honest man may stand neuter, but the laws and constitution are the general property of the subject—not to defend is to relinquish; and who is there so senseless as to renounce his share in a common benefit, unless he hopes to profit by a new division of the spoil? As a lord of parliament you were repeatedly called upon to condemn or defend the new law declared by the House of Commons; you affected to have scruples, and every expedient was attempted to remove them; the question was proposed and urged to you in a thousand different shapes; your prudence still supplied you with evasion, your resolution was invincible; for my own part I am not anxious to penetrate this solemn secret. I care not to whose wisdom it is entrusted, nor how soon you carry it with you to your grave*. You have betrayed your opinion by the very care you have taken to conceal it. It is not from Lord Mansfield that we expect any reserve in declaring his real sentiments in favour of Government, or in opposition to the people; nor is it difficult to account for the motions of a timid, dishonest heart, which neither has virtue enough to acknowledge truth, nor courage to contradict it. Yet you continue to support an administration which you know is univer-

* He said in the House of Lords that he believed he should carry his opinion with him to the grave. It was afterwards reported that he had entrusted it, in special confidence, to the ingenious Duke of Cumberland.—JUNIUS.

sally odious, and which, on some occasions, you yourself speak of with contempt. You would fain be thought to take no share in government, while, in reality, you are the main spring of the machine. Here, too, we trace the *little*, prudential policy of a Scotchman. Instead of acting that open, generous part which becomes your rank and station, you meanly skulk into the closet, and give your sovereign such advice as you have not spirit to avow or defend. You secretly engross the power, while you decline the title of minister ; and though you dare not be chancellor, you know how to secure the emoluments of the office. Are the seals to be for ever in commission, that you may enjoy five thousand pounds a year? I beg pardon, my Lord*, your fears have interposed at last, and forced you to resign ; the odium of continuing speaker of the House of Lords upon such terms was too formidable to be resisted. What a multitude of bad passions are forced to submit to a constitutional infirmity! But though you have relinquished the salary, you still assume the rights of a minister ; your conduct it seems must be defended in parliament. For what other purpose is your wretched friend, that miserable serjeant, posted to the House of Commons? Is it in the abilities of Mr. Leigh to defend the great Lord Mansfield? or is he only the Punch of the puppet-show, to speak as he is prompted by the chief juggler behind the curtain†?

In public affairs, my Lord, cunning, let it be ever so well wrought, will not conduct a man honourably through life; like bad money, it may be current for a time, but it will soon be cried down ; it cannot consist with a liberal spirit, though it be sometimes united with extraordinary qualifications. When I acknowledge your abilities you may believe I am sincere. I feel for human nature, when I see a man so gifted

---

* Upon the death of Charles Yorke, whose suicide has been already mentioned (p. 271,) on his appointment to the Chancellorship, the great seal was held in commission by Sir Sydney Stafford Smythe, the hon. Henry Bathurst, and Sir Richard Aston; while Lord Mansfield was appointed Speaker of the Upper House, and received the fees attached to that important situation. Lord Apsley, about the date of this letter, succeeded to both offices.

† This paragraph gagged poor *Leigh*. I really am concerned for the man, and wish it were possible to open his mouth. He is a very pretty orator.—— JUNIUS.

as you are descend to such vile practice ; yet do not suffer your vanity to console you too soon. Believe me, my good Lord, you are not admired in the same degree in which you are detested. It is only the partiality of your friends that balances the defects of your heart with the superiority of your understanding; no learned man, even among your own tribe, thinks you qualified to preside in a court of common law ; yet it is confessed that, under *Justinian*, you might have made an incomparable *Prætor*. It is remarkable enough, but I hope not ominous, that the laws you understand best, and the judges you affect to admire most, flourished in the decline of a great empire, and are supposed to have contributed to its fall.

Here, my Lord, it may be proper for us to pause together. It is not for my own sake that I wish you to consider the delicacy of your situation. Beware how you indulge the first emotions of your resentment. This paper is delivered to the world, and cannot be recalled. The persecution of an innocent printer cannot alter facts nor refute arguments. Do not furnish me with farther materials against yourself. An honest man, like the true religion, appeals to the understanding, or modestly confides in the internal evidence of his conscience ; the impostor employs force instead of argument, imposes silence where he cannot convince. and propagates his character by the sword.

JUNIUS.

LETTER XLII*.

TO THE PRINTER OF THE PUBLIC ADVERTISER.

SIR,   January 30, 1771.

IF we recollect in what manner the *king's friends* have been constantly employed, we shall have no reason to be surprised

---

* Falkland Islands, adjacent to the continent of South America, were discovered by the early navigators more than two centuries and a half since. The Spaniards considered them as included in the grant to their sove-

at any condition of disgrace to which the once respected name of Englishmen may be degraded. His Majesty has no cares but such as concern the laws and constitution of this country In his royal breast there is no room left for resentment, no place for hostile sentiments against the natural enemies of his crown. The system of government is uniform: violence and oppression at home can only be supported by treachery and submission abroad. When the civil rights of the people are daringly invaded on one side, what have we to expect but that their political rights should be deserted and betrayed, in the same proportion, on the other? The plan of domestic policy which has been invariably pursued from the moment of his present Majesty's accession engrosses all the attention of his servants; they know that the security of their places depends upon their maintaining, at any hazard, the secret system of the closet. A foreign war might embarrass, an unfavourable event might ruin the minister, and defeat the deep-laid scheme of policy to which he and his associates owe their employments. Rather than suffer the execution of that scheme to be delayed or interrupted, the king has been advised to make a public surrender, a solemn sacrifice, in the

reigns from the Roman Pontiff. The English claimed them by the right supposed to be conferred by priority of discovery. They remained desolate and neglected till late in the eighteenth century. It was at last judged by the English, that, as a station from which the Spaniards of South America might be annoyed in war, or visited for commercial purposes during peace, these isles might be seized and colonised with advantage. They were accordingly occupied by an English force, and some slight fortifications erected. Aware of the danger to their empire in South America if a flourishing English colony should be established so near, the Spaniards sent an armament from an American port, which dispossessed the English, and sent them ignominiously home. An act of such hostility was to be resented. Complaints were made to the Court of Madrid; and preparations were at the same time commenced for going to war if the Spaniards should refuse to restore the islands without a contest. Negotiations were protracted, but the Spaniards at length agreed to make the required restitution, but without relinquishing their right; while it was secretly stipulated that England, soon after the surrender, should evacuate the disputed possession. On the 22nd of January, 1771, the king was enabled to inform his parliament of the settlement of the dispute with Spain. Opposition arraigned the dishonour of the implied conditions. Junius undertook to rouse public opinion on their side in the present letter, which is more ably written than those on the subject of the London petitions.—ED.

face of all Europe, not only of the interests of his subjects. but of his own personal reputation, and of the dignity of that crown which his predecessors have worn with honour. These are strong terms, Sir, but they are supported by fact and argument.

The king of Great Britain has been for some years in possession of an island, to which, as the ministry themselves have repeatedly asserted, the Spaniards had no claim of right. The importance of the place is not in question; if it were, a better judgment might be formed of it from the opinions of Lord Anson and Lord Egmont, and from the anxiety of the Spaniards, than from any fallacious insinuations thrown out by men whose interest it is to undervalue that property which they are determined to relinquish. The pretensions of Spain were a subject of negotiation between the two courts; they had been discussed but not admitted; the king of Spain, in these circumstances, bids adieu to amicable negotiation, and appeals directly to the sword. The expedition against Port Egmont does not appear to have been a sudden, ill-concerted enterprise; it seems to have been conducted not only with the usual military precautions, but in all the forms and ceremonies of war. A frigate was first employed to examine the strength of the place; a message was then sent, demanding immediate possession, in the catholic king's name, and ordering our people to depart; at last, a military force appears, and compels the garrison to surrender. A formal capitulation ensues, and his Majesty's ship, which might at least have been permitted to bring home his troops immediately, is detained in port twenty days, and her rudder forcibly taken away. This train of facts carries no appearance of the rashness or violence of a Spanish governor; on the contrary, the whole plan seems to have been formed and executed in consequence of deliberate orders, and a regular instruction from the Spanish court. Mr. Bucarelli is not a pirate, nor has he been treated as such by those who employed him *. I feel for the honour of a gentleman, when I affirm that our king owes him a signal reparation. Where will the humiliation of this country end! A king of Great Britain, not contented with placing himself

---

* The governor of Buenos Ayres, under whose direction the expedition sent to take possession of Port Egmont was forwarded; and who, it was well known, did not act without authority.

upon a level with a Spanish governor, descends so low as to do a notorious injustice to that governor. As a salvo for his own reputation, he has been advised to traduce the character of a brave officer, and to treat him as a common robber, when he knew with certainty that Mr. Bucarelli had acted in obedience to his orders, and had done no more than his duty. Thus it happens in private life, with a man who has no spirit nor sense of honour: one of his equals orders a servant to strike him; instead of returning the blow to his master, his courage is contented with throwing an aspersion, equally false and public, upon the character of the servant.

This short recapitulation was necessary to introduce the consideration of his Majesty's speech of 13th November, 1770, and the subsequent measures of government. The excessive caution with which the speech was drawn up had impressed upon me an early conviction that no serious resentment was thought of, and that the conclusion of the business, whenever it happened, must, in some degree, be dishonourable to England. There appears through the whole speech a guard and reserve in the choice of expression, which shows how careful the ministry were not to embarrass their future prospects by any firm or spirited declaration from the throne. When all hopes of peace are lost, his Majesty tells his parliament that he is preparing, not for barbarous war, but (with all his mother's softness *) *for a different situation.* An open act of hostility, authorised by the catholic king, is called *an act of a governor.* This act, to avoid the mention of a regular siege and surrender, passes under the piratical description of *seizing by force;* and the thing taken is described, not as a part of the king's territory or proper dominion, but merely as a *possession*—a word expressly chosen in contradistinction to, and exclusion of, the idea of *right,* and to prepare us for a future surrender both of the right and of the possession. Yet this speech, Sir, cautious and equivocal as it is, cannot, by any sophistry, be accommodated to the measures which have since been adopted; it seemed to promise that whatever might be given up by secret stipulation, some care would be taken to save appearances to the public. The event shows us that

* Alluding to the vulgar report of the day, that the Princess Dowager of Wales had interfered in the Spanish negotiation.

to depart, in the minutest article, from the nicety and strict ness of punctilio, is as dangerous to national honour as to female virtue. The woman who admits of one familiarity seldom knows where to stop, or what to refuse; and when the counsels of a great country give way in a single instance, when once they are inclined to submission, every step accelerates the rapidity of the descent. The ministry themselves, when they framed the speech, did not foresee that they should ever accede to such an accommodation as they have since advised their master to accept of.

The king says, *the honour of my crown and the rights of my people are deeply affected.* The Spaniard, in his reply, says, *I give you back possession, but I adhere to my claim of prior right, reserving the assertion of it for a more favourable opportunity.*

The speech says, *I made an immediate demand of satisfaction, and, if that fails, I am prepared to do myself justice* This immediate demand must have been sent to Madrid on the 12th of September, or in a few days after. It was certainly refused, or evaded, and the king *has not* done himself justice; when the first magistrate speaks to the nation, some care should be taken of his apparent veracity.

The speech proceeds to say, *I shall not discontinue my preparations until I have received proper reparation for the injury.* If this assurance may be relied on, what an enormous expense is entailed, *sine die*, upon this unhappy country! Restitution of a possession, and reparation of an injury, are as different in substance as they are in language; the very act of restitution may contain, as in this instance it palpably does, a shameful aggravation of the injury. A man of spirit does not measure the degree of an injury by the mere positive damage he has sustained; he considers the principle on which it is founded, he resents the superiority asserted over him, and rejects with indignation the claim of right which his adversary endeavours to establish and would force him to acknowledge

The motives on which the catholic king makes restitution are, if possible, more insolent and disgraceful to our sovereign than even the declaratory condition annexed to it. After taking four months to consider whether the expedition was undertaken by his own orders or not, he condescends to dis avow the enterprise and to restore the island, not from any regard to justice, not from any regard he bears to his Britannic Majesty, but merely *from the persuasion in which he is of the pacific sentiments of the king of Great Britain;* at this rate, if our king had discovered the spirit of a man, if he had made a peremptory demand of satisfaction, the king of Spain would have given him a peremptory refusal.   But why this unseasonable, this ridiculous mention of the king of Great Britain's pacific intentions?   Have they ever been in question?   Was *he* the aggressor?   Does he attack foreign powers without provocation?   Does he even resist when he is insulted?   No, Sir, if any ideas of strife or hostility have entered his royal mind, they have a very different direction.   The enemies of England have nothing to fear from them.

After all, Sir, to what kind of disavowal has the king of Spain at last consented?   Supposing it made in proper time, it should have been accompanied with instant restitution, and if Mr. Bucarelli acted without orders, he deserved death.   Now, Sir, instead of immediate restitution we have a four months' negotiation; and the officer, whose act is disavowed, returns to court and is loaded with honours.

If the actual situation of Europe be considered, the treachery of the king's servants, particularly of Lord North, who takes the whole upon himself, will appear in the strongest colours of aggravation.   Our allies were masters of the Mediterranean   The king of France's present aversion from war and the distraction of his affairs are notorious; he is now in a state of war with his people; in vain did the catholic king solicit him to take part in the quarrel against us; his finances were in the last disorder, and it was probable that his troops might find sufficient employment at home.   In these circumstances we might have dictated the law to Spain.   There are no terms to which she might not have been compelled to submit; at the worst, a war with Spain alone carries the fairest promise of advantage.   One good effect at least would have been immediately produced by it—the desertion of France would have irritated her ally, and, in all probability, have dissolved the family compact.   The scene is now fatally changed; the advantage is thrown away, the most favourable opportunity is lost; hereafter we shall know the value of it.   When the

French king is reconciled to his subjects, when Spain has completed her preparations, when the collected strength of the house of Bourbon attacks us at once, the king himself will be able to determine upon the wisdom or imprudence of his present conduct. As far as the probability of argument extends, we may safely pronounce that a conjuncture, which threatens the very being of this country, has been wilfully prepared and forwarded by our own ministry. How far the people may be animated to resistance under the present administration I know not; but this I know with certainty, that, under the present administration, or if anything like it should continue, it is of very little moment whether we are a conquered nation or not.*

Having travelled thus far in the high road of matter of fact, I may now be permitted to wander a little into the field of imagination. Let us banish from our minds the persuasion that these events have really happened in the reign of the best of princes; let us consider them as nothing more than the materials of a fable, in which we may conceive the sovereign of some other country to be concerned. I mean to violate all the laws of probability, when I suppose that this imaginary king, after having voluntarily disgraced himself in the eyes of his subjects, might return to a sense of his dishonour!—that he might perceive the snare laid for him by his ministers, and feel a spark of shame kindling in his breast The part he must then be obliged to act would overwhelm him with confusion. To his parliament he must say, *I called you together to receive your advice, and have never asked your*

* The king's acceptance of the Spanish Ambassador's declaration is drawn up in barbarous French, and signed by the Earl of Rochford. This diplomatic lord has spent his life in the study and practice of *etiquettes*, and is supposed to be a profound master of the ceremonies. I will not insult him by any reference to grammar or common sense. If he were even acquainted with the common forms of his office, I should think him as well qualified for it as any man in his Majesty's service. The reader is requested to observe Lord Rochford's method of authenticating a public instrument. "En foi de quoi, *moi* soussigné un des principaux secretaires d'eta. de S. M. B. *ai* signé la presente de ma signature ordinaire, et à icelle fait apposer le cachet de *nos* armes." In three lines there are no less than seven false concords. But the man does not even know the style of his office;—if he had known it, he would have said, " *nous* soussigné, secretaire d'etat de S. M. B. *avons* signé," &c.—JUNIUS.

opinion; to the merchant, *I have distressed your commerce, I have dragged your seamen out of your ships, I have loaded you with a grievous weight of insurances;* to the landholder, *I told you war was too probable when I was determined to submit to any terms of accommodation, I extorted new taxes from you before it was possible they could be wanted, and am now unable to account for the application of them;* to the public creditor, *I have delivered up your fortunes a prey to foreigners, and to the vilest of your fellow-subjects.* Perhaps this repenting prince might conclude with one general acknowledgment to them all, *I have involved every rank of my subjects in anxiety and distress, and have nothing to offer you in return but the certainty of national dishonour, an armed truce, and peace without security.*

If these accounts were settled there would still remain an apology to be made to his navy and to his army. To the first he would say, *you were once the terror of the world, but go back to your harbours; a man dishonoured, as I am, has no use for your service.* It is not probable that he would appear again before his soldiers, even in the pacific ceremony of a review*. But, wherever he appeared, the humiliating confession would be extorted from him. *I have received a blow, and had not spirit to resent it; I demanded satisfaction, and have accepted a declaration in which the right to strike me again is asserted and confirmed.* His countenance at least would speak this language, and even his guards would blush for him.

But to return to our argument. The ministry, it seems, are labouring to draw a line of distinction between the honour of the crown and the rights of the people. This new idea has yet been only started in discourse, for, in effect, both objects have been equally sacrificed. I neither understand the distinction, nor what use the ministry propose to make of it. The king's honour is that of his people. *Their* real honour and real interest are the same; I am not contending for a vain punctilio. A clear, unblemished character comprehends not only the integrity that will not offer, but the spirit that will not submit to an injury; and whether it belongs to an individual or to a community it is the foundation of peace, of independence,

---

* A mistake. He appears before them every day with the mark of a blow upon his face.—*Proh pudor!—*JUNIUS.

and of safety Private credit is wealth, public honour is
security ; the feather that adorns the royal bird, supports its
flight ; strip him of his plumage, and you fix him to the earth

                                                    JUNIUS.

_____

It was against the preceding letter that Dr. Johnson was engaged by the
ministry to muster his argumentative powers. His answer, published in 1771,
is entitled, "Thoughts on the late Transactions respecting Falkland's Islands;"
from which the following is worth transcribing :—

"Of Junius it cannot be said, as of Ulysses, that he scatters ambiguous expressions among the vulgar ; for he cries *havoc* without reserve, and endeavours to let slip the dogs of foreign and of civil war, ignorant whither they
are going, and careless what may be their prey. Junius has sometimes made
his satire felt, but let not injudicious admiration mistake the venom of the
shaft for the vigour of the bow. He has sometimes sported with lucky
malice ; but to him that knows his company, it is not hard to be sarcastic in
a mask. While he walks like Jack the Giant Killer in a coat of darkness,
he may do much mischief with little strength. Novelty captivates the super-
ficial and thoughtless ; vehemence delights the discontented and turbulent.
He that contradicts acknowledged truth will always have an audience ; he
that vilifies established authority will always find abettors.

"Junius burst into notice with a blaze of impudence which has rarely
glared upon the world before, and drew the rabble after him as a monster
makes a show. When he had once provided for his safety by impenetrable
secrecy, he had nothing to combat but truth and justice, enemies whom he
knows to be feeble in the dark. Being then at liberty to indulge himself in
all the immunities of invisibility ; out of the reach of danger, he has been
bold ; out of the reach of shame—he has been confident. As a rhetorician,
he has the art of persuading when he seconded desire ; as a reasoner, he has
convinced those who had no doubt before ; as a moralist, he has taught that
virtue may disgrace ; and as a patriot, he has gratified the mean by insults
on the high. Finding sedition ascendant, he has been able to advance it ;
finding the nation combustible, he has been able to inflame it. Let us
abstract from his wit the vivacity of insolence, and withdraw from his efficacy
the sympathetic favour of plebeian malignity ; I do not say that we shall
leave him nothing ; the cause that I defend scorns the help of falsehood ;
but if we leave him only his merit, what will be his praise?

"It is not by his liveliness of imagery, his pungency of periods, or his
fertility of allusion, that he detains the cits of London and the boors of
Middlesex. Of style and sentiment they take no cognizance. They admire
him for virtues like their own, for contempt of order and violence of outrage, for rage of defamation and audacity of falsehood. The supporters of
the Bill of Rights feel no niceties of composition, nor dexterities of sophistry;
their faculties are better proportioned to the bawl of Bellas or barbarity of
Beckford ; but they are told that Junius is on their side, and they are therefore sure that Junius is infallible. Those who know not whither he would
lead them, resolve to follow him ; and those who cannot find his meaning,
hope he means rebellion.

" Junius is an unusual phenomenon on which some have gazed with wonder, and some with terror, but wonder and terror are transitory passions. He will soon be more closely viewed, or more attentively examined, and what folly has taken for a comet that, from its flaming hair, shook pestilence and war, inquiry will find to be only a meteor formed by the vapours of putrefying democracy, and kindled into flame by the effervescence of interest struggling with conviction, which after having plunged its followers in a bog, will leave us inquiring why we regarded it.

" Yet though I cannot think the style of Junius secure from criticism, though his expressions are often trite, and his periods feeble, I should never have stationed him where he has placed himself, had I not rated him by his morals rather than his faculties. ' What,' says Pope, ' must be the priest, where the monkey is a god ?' What must be the drudge of a party of which the heads are Wilkes and Crosby, Sawbridge and Townshend ?

" Junius knows his own meaning, and can therefore tell it. He is an enemy to the ministry, he sees them hourly growing stronger. He knows that a war at once unjust and unsuccessful would have certainly displaced them, and is therefore, in his zeal for his country, angry that war was not unjustly made, and unsuccessfully conducted; but there are others whose thoughts are less clearly expressed, and whose schemes, perhaps, are less consequentially digested, who declare that they do not wish for a rupture, yet condemn the ministry for not doing that from which a rupture would naturally have followed."

Of this pamphlet the ministry were not a little proud; and especially as they made no doubt that Junius would hereby be drawn into a paper contest with Dr. Johnson, and that hence they would possess a greater facility of detecting him. Junius seems to have been aware of the trap laid for him, and made no direct reply whatever.

LETTER XLIII

TO THE PRINTER OF THE PUBLIC ADVERTISER.

SIR,   February 6, 1771.

I HOPE your correspondent Junius is better employed than in answering or reading the criticisms of a newspaper. This is a task from which, if he were inclined to submit to it, his friends ought to relieve him*. Upon this principle I shall undertake to answer *Anti-Junius*, more, I believe, to his conviction than to his satisfaction. Not daring to attack the main body of Junius's last letter, he triumphs in having, as

---

* In his Preface (p. 91), Junius says his " subordinate character is never guilty of the indecorum of praising his principal;" but does not this commencement savour strongly of laudation ?—ED.

he thinks, surprised an outpost, and cut off a detached argument, a mere straggling proposition. But even in this petty warfare, he shall find himself defeated.

Junius does not speak of the Spanish *nation* as the *natural enemies* of England. He applies that description, with the strictest truth and justice, to the Spanish *Court*. From the moment when a prince of the House of Bourbon ascended that throne, their whole system of government was inverted and became hostile to this country. Unity of possession introduced a unity of politics, and Lewis the Fourteenth had reason when he said to his grandson, "*The Pyrenees are removed.*" The history of the present century is one continued confirmation of the prophecy.

The assertion "*That violence and oppression at home can only be supported by treachery and submission abroad,*" is applied to a free people whose rights are invaded, not to the government of a country where despotic or absolute power is confessedly vested in the prince; and with this application, the assertion is true. An absolute monarch having no points to carry at home will naturally maintain the honour of his crown in all his transactions with foreign powers. But if we could suppose the sovereign of a free nation possessed with a design to make himself absolute, he would be inconsistent with himself if he suffered his projects to be interrupted or embarrassed by a foreign war, unless that war tended, as in some cases it might, to promote his principal design. Of the three exceptions to this general rule of conduct (quoted by *Anti-Junius*) that of Oliver Cromwell is the only one in point. Harry the Eighth, by the submission of his parliament, was as absolute a prince as Lewis the Fourteenth. Queen Elizabeth's government was not oppressive to the people; and as to her foreign wars, it ought to be considered that they were *unavoidable*. The national honour was not in question. She was compelled to fight in defence of her own person and of her title to the crown. In the common course of selfish policy, Oliver Cromwell should have cultivated the friendship of foreign powers, or at least have avoided disputes with them the better to establish his tyranny at home. Had he been only a bad man, he would have sacrificed the honour of the nation to the success of his domestic policy. But, with all his crimes, he had the spirit of an Englishman. The conduct of such a man must always be an exception to vulgar rules. He had abilities sufficient to reconcile contradictions, and to make a great nation at the same moment unhappy and formidable. If it were not for the respect I bear the minister, I could name a man who, without one grain of understanding, can do half as much as Oliver Cromwell.

Whether or no there be a *secret system* in the closet, and what may be the object of it, are questions which can only be determined by appearances, and on which every man must decide for himself.

The whole plan of Junius's letter proves that he himself makes no distinction between the real honour of the crown and the real interest of the people. In the climax, to which your correspondent objects, Junius adopts the language of the court, and by that conformity, gives strength to his argument. He says that, "*the king has not only sacrificed the interests of his people, but* (what was likely to touch him more nearly) *his personal reputation, and the dignity of his crown.*"

The queries put by *Anti-Junius* can only be answered by the ministry*. Abandoned as they are, I fancy they will not confess that they have, for so many years, maintained possession of another man's property. After admitting the assertion of the ministry, viz., *that the Spaniards had no rightful claim*, and after justifying them for saying so, it is *his* business, not *mine*, to give us some good reason for their *suffering the pretensions of Spain to be a subject of negotiation.* He admits the facts;—let him reconcile them if he can.

The last paragraph brings us back to the original question, whether the Spanish declaration contains such a satisfaction as the king of Great Britain ought to have accepted. This was the field upon which he ought to have encountered Junius openly and fairly. But here he leaves the argument as no longer defensible. I shall therefore conclude with one general admonition to my fellow-subjects;—that, when they hear these matters debated, they should not suffer themselves to be misled by general declamations upon the conveniences of peace, or the miseries of war. Between peace and war,

* A writer, subscribing himself *Anti-Junius*, attacked the preceding letter of Junius in three successive numbers of the Public Advertiser, in February, 1771; but, after the extracts inserted from Dr. Johnson, his letters are hardly entitled to further notice.

nbstractedly, there is not, there cannot be, a question in the
mind of a rational being. The real questions are, *Have we
any security that the peace we have so dearly purchased will
last 'a twelvemonth?* and if not,—*have we, or have we not,
sacrificed the fairest opportunity of making war with advantage?*

PHILO-JUNIUS.

LETTER XLIV *.

TO THE PRINTER OF THE PUBLIC ADVERTISER.

SIR,   April 22, 1771.

To write for profit without taxing the press, to write for
fame and to be unknown, to support the intrigues of faction

---

* The debates in parliament had never yet been regularly and avowedly
published in the newspapers. But various artifices had been used in order to
make them known, under some affectation of disguise, by which the general
curiosity might be gratified without provoking parliamentary censure.
Even this disguise began to be laid aside under the freedom of the press,
which had begun to be exercised since the commencement of the present
reign. This freedom was, however, frequently checked by both Houses of
Parliament. The printers of any publication in which either House was
mentioned were liable to be summoned before that House, confined,
reprimanded, severely fined, and only dismissed after they had made the
most humiliating submissions, and paid large sums of money in fines and
fees. A Lord Marchmont, especially, used to watch with suspicious vigilance
over the newspapers, and to make motions against their printers in the
House of Peers, whenever any of the proceedings of that House were, however
slightly, mentioned in the papers. The public endured this severe use of the
privilege of parliament with great impatience. The printers of the newspapers were from time to time encouraged to set it at defiance. At length,
in the beginning of March, 1771, the matter was brought to trial between
the people and the House of Commons.
    Accounts of the proceedings in parliament had been printed in the different
newspapers. Colonel Onslow made a motion in the House of Commons
against the printers, as guilty of a violation of the privileges of parliament.
The printers were summoned to attend the House. Those who obeyed the
summons, obtained, on easy terms, their pardon. Robert Thompson, and
John Wheble, printers of the *Gazetteer*, and the *Middlesex Journal*, slighted
the order; and a proclamation was therefore issued, offering a reward of fifty
pounds to apprehend them. On the 13th of March, the printers of the
Morning Chronicle, the *St. James's Chronicle*, the *London*, the *Whitehall*,
and the *General Evening*, *Posts*, and the *London Packet*, were also ordered
to attend the House of Commons. J. Miller, printer of the *London Evening*

and to be disowned, as a dangerous auxiliary, by every party
in the kingdom, are contradictions which the minister must

Post, slighting this order, a messenger from the Commons was, on the 14th,
sent to take him into custody.

While these proceedings went on in the House of Commons against the
printers, the city was in a commotion against their vexatious measures. Mr.
Wilkes, now alderman of the Ward of Farringdon Without, concerted a
plan to baffle all the wrath of the Commons. Wheble was apprehended, in
consequence of the proclamation, on the 15th, and was brought before him,
then the sitting alderman at Guildhall. In contempt of the authority of the
House of Commons, and the proclamation, Wilkes discharged Wheble; bound
him over to prosecute the person by whom he had been apprehended;
obliged that person to give bail for his future appearance in trial; and sent
notice of these proceedings to Lord Halifax, then one of the secretaries of
state. A messenger from the Serjeant-at-Arms attending on the House of
Commons was sent to take into custody Miller, the refractory printer of the
London Evening Post. Miller was instructed to charge that messenger as
guilty of an assault, if he should attempt to seize him, to call in a constable
to take him into custody, and to carry him before the city magistrates. All
this was done. Whittam, the messenger from the Serjeant-at-Arms, attempting to seize Miller, was, by him, carried before the Lord Mayor; who, with
Aldermen Wilkes and Oliver, committed Whittam to Wood Street-compter,
and afterwards held him to bail for his future appearance.

At the news of this invasion of their privileges, the Commons were highly
enraged. They summoned Crosby, the Lord Mayor, to attend in his place, and
give an account of his conduct in committing a messenger from the House of
Commons into custody. Mr. Wilkes was ordered to attend the House, but
refused, unless he might attend in his place as Member for Middlesex. On
the 19th, Crosby and Oliver obeyed the order of the Commons. They justified, or attempted to justify, their conduct, by pleading their obligation to
maintain inviolate the rights of the city. The ministers and their friends
earnestly proposed that the Lord Mayor, and Mr. Oliver, should be at least
committed to the Tower during the pleasure of the House. The minority
contended with every argument which zeal could suggest in their favour.
Oliver was sent to the Tower immediately after the close of the debate. The
recognizance of Whittam the messenger was erased out of the minute book
of recognizances belonging to the Lord Mayor's court. The determination
in respect to Crosby, the Mayor, was delayed, only because illness made him
unable to continue in the House till the close of the proceedings of the day.
On the 27th, the Lord Mayor again attended in his place, refused all concessions, and was also sent to the Tower. Wilkes had received a second
order to attend the House, which he slighted equally as the first. He was
a third time summoned to attend on the 8th of April. But the leaders of the
majority, aware that he would still slight their summons, contrived to waive
the contention which he courted by adjourning over the day on which he was
last ordered to attend, and then ceasing from any farther repetition of their
summons.

In the mean time Crosby, Wilkes, and Oliver were extolled as the firm

reconcile, before I forfeit my credit with the public. I may
quit the service, but it would be absurd to suspect me of
desertion. The reputation of these papers is an honourable
pledge for my attachment to the people. To sacrifice a
respected character, and to renounce the esteem of society,
requires more than Mr. Wedderburne's resolution *; and
though, in him, it was rather a profession than a desertion of
his principles (I speak tenderly of this gentleman, for when

friends of the freedom of discussion. The thanks of the Common Council were
eagerly voted to them. A committee of the Common Council was appointed
to assist them in their defence. To defray the necessary expense, a sum of
money was zealously granted. In their passage through the streets, between
the Mansion House, the House of Commons, and the Tower, they were
followed by an immense crowd, consisting not merely of the populace, but of
the livery, who were zealous in whatever could thwart the House of Commons
or the views of the administration. In the Tower, the Mayor and Alderman
Oliver were visited by the leaders of the minority in parliament; and had a
table kept for them at the expense of the city. Application was made to the
Chief Justices of the Courts of King's Bench and Common Pleas, to admit
them to bail. Both these judges, however, acknowledged the authority of
the House of Commons, and refused to interpose between that House and
the prisoners. They remained, therefore, in confinement till the prorogation
of that session of parliament. They were then, of course, set at liberty; as
the authority of the House of Commons had ceased. They were received,
when they left the Tower, with many expressions of congratulation by their
fellow-citizens. The printers were presented with a gratification in money
from the supporters of the Bill of Rights. Whittam, the messenger, was
saved by a *noli prosequi* from the prosecution which was in the printer's
name urged against him. The city, after Crosby and Oliver were at liberty,
again petitioned the king against the House of Commons. From the period
of this spirited resistance, the printers of newspapers have been tacitly suffered to publish such accounts as they could procure of the debates in the
two Houses of parliament without punishment, unless when those accounts
have misrepresented or vilified the proceedings of either House.

    On the 22nd of April, while the Lord Mayor and Alderman Oliver were
still in the Tower, Junius wrote the present letter (No. 44). Its design is to
prove that the House of Commons had no right to imprison for any contempt of
their authority. It may not be one of his most powerful or constitutional
productions, yet it contains much force of reasoning, authority, and eloquence.
In a private note to Alderman Wilkes (Private Letters, No. 70, vol. ii.) he
says, " the pains I took with that paper are greater than I can express to
you."—ED.

    * Mr. Wedderburne, progressively Baron Loughborough and Earl of Ross-
lyn, had, on the 12th of January preceding the date of this letter, been promoted to the offices of Solicitor-General, and cofferer to the queen. His politics
may, therefore, be ascertained without trouble; yet he had been inducted
into public life under the auspices of George Grenville after the latter had

treachery is in question, I think we should make allowances for a Scotchman), yet we have seen him in the House of Commons overwhelmed with confusion, and almost bereft of his faculties. But in truth, Sir, I have left no room for an accommodation with the piety of Saint James's. My offences are not to be redeemed by recantation or repentance. On one side, our warmest patriots would disclaim me as a burthen to their honest ambition. On the other, the vilest prostitution, if Junius could descend to it, would lose its natural merit and influence in the cabinet, and treachery be no longer a recommendation to the royal favour.

The persons who till within these few years, have been most distinguished by their zeal for high church and prerogative, are now, it seems, the great assertors of the privileges of the House of Commons. This sudden alteration of their sentiments or language carries with it a suspicious appearance. When I hear the undefined privileges of the popular branch of the legislature exalted by Tories and Jacobites, at the expense of those strict rights which are known to the subject, and limited by the laws, I cannot but suspect that some mischievous scheme is in agitation to destroy both law and privilege by opposing them to each other. They who have uniformly denied the power of the whole legislature to alter the descent of the crown, and whose ancestors, in rebellion against his Majesty's family, have defended that doctrine at the hazard of their lives, now tell us that privilege of parliament is the only rule of right, and the chief security of the public freedom. I fear, Sir, that while forms remain, there has been some material change in the substance of our constitution. The opinions of these men were too absurd to be so easily renounced. Liberal minds are open to conviction—liberal doctrines are capable of improvement. There are proselytes from atheism, but none from superstition. If their present professions were sincere, I think they could not but be highly offended at seeing a question concerning parliamentary privilege unnecessarily started at a season so unfavourable to the House of Commons, and by so very mean

professed the principles of Whiggism, and while he was a partisan of Lord Rockingham ; and it is to this defection from the tenets Mr. Wedderburne avowed till this period, that our author here alludes.

and insignificant a person as the minor *Onslow**. They knew that the present House of Commons, having commenced hostilities with the people, and degraded the authority of the laws by their own example, were likely enough to be resisted, *per fas et nefas*. If they were really friends to privilege, they would have thought the question of right too dangerous to be hazarded at this season, and, without the formality of a convention, would have left it undecided.

I have been silent hitherto, though not from that shameful indifference about the interests of society which too many of us profess, and call moderation. I confess, Sir, that I felt the prejudices of my education, in favour of a House of Commons, still hanging about me. I thought that a question between law and privilege † could never be brought to a formal decision without inconvenience to the public service, or a manifest diminution of legal liberty;—that it ought, therefore, to be carefully avoided: and when I saw that the violence of the House of Commons had carried them too far to retreat, I determined not to deliver a hasty opinion upon a matter of so much delicacy and importance.

The state of things is much altered in this country since it was necessary to protect our representatives against the direct power of the crown. We have nothing to apprehend from prerogative, but everything from undue influence. Formerly it was the interest of the people that the privileges of parlia- should be left unlimited and undefined. At present it is not only their interest, but I hold it to be essentially necessary to the preservation of the constitution, that the privileges of par liament should be strictly ascertained and confined within the narrowest bounds the nature of their institution will admit of. Upon the same principle on which I would have resisted prerogative in the last century, I now resist privilege. It is indifferent to me whether the crown, by its own immediate

---

* It was this gentleman, afterwards Lord Onslow, who moved the resolution against the printers already noticed; and who commenced a prosecution for defamation against Horne, in which he was not successful.

† The transaction referred to is the resistance of the authority of a mere royal proclamation, and a mere order of the House of Commons by the magistrates of the city; the arrests and counter-arrests that followed; and the commitment of the Lord Mayor and Aldermen to the Tower. See pre- vious note, p. 328, and Miscellaneous Letter, No. 92.—Ed.

act, imposes new, and dispenses with old laws, or whether the same arbitrary power produces the same effects through the medium of the House of Commons. We trusted our representatives with privileges for their own defence and ours. We cannot hinder their desertion, but we can prevent their carrying over their arms to the service of the enemy. It will be said that I begin with endeavouring to reduce the argument concerning privilege to a mere question of convenience—that I deny at one moment what I would allow at another—and that to resist the power of a prostituted House of Commons, may establish a precedent injurious to all future parliaments. To this I answer generally, that human affairs are in no instance governed by strict positive right. If change of circumstances were to have no weight in directing our conduct and opinions, the mutual intercourse of mankind would be nothing more than a contention between positive and equitable right. Society would be a state of war, and law itself would be injustice. On this general ground it is highly reasonable that the degree of our submission to privileges, which have never been defined by any positive law, should be considered as a question of convenience, and proportioned to the confidence we repose in the integrity of our representatives. As to the injury we may do to any future and more respectable House of Commons, I own I am not now sanguine enough to expect a more plentiful harvest of parliamentary virtue in one year than another. Our political climate is severely altered; and, without dwelling upon the depravity of modern times, I think no reasonable man will expect that, as human nature is constituted, the enormous influence of the crown should cease to prevail over the virtue of individuals. The mischief lies too deep to be cured by any remedy less than some great convulsion which may either carry back the constitution to its original principles or utterly destroy it. I do not doubt that, in the first session after the next election, some popular measures may be adopted. The present House of Commons have injured themselves by a too early and public profession of their principles; and if a strain of prostitution, which had no example, were within the reach of emulation, it might be imprudent to hazard the experiment too soon. But after all, Sir, it is very immaterial whether a House of Commons shall preserve their virtue for a week. a

month, or a year. The influence which makes a septennial
parliament dependent upon the pleasure of the crown has a
permanent operation and cannot fail of success. My premises,
I know, will be denied in argument, but every man's conscience
tells him they are true.   It remains, then, to be considered
whether it be for the interests of the people that privilege of
parliament (which *, in respect to the purposes for which it
has hitherto been acquiesced under, is merely nominal) should
be contracted within some certain limits, or whether the subject shall be left at the mercy of a power arbitrary upon the
face of it, and notoriously under the direction of the crown.

I do not mean to decline the question of *right*. On the contrary, Sir, I join issue with the advocates for privilege, and affirm
that, "excepting the cases wherein the House of Commons are
a court of judicature (to which, from the nature of their office,
a coercive power must belong), and excepting such contempts
as immediately interrupt their proceedings, they have no legal
authority to imprison any man for any supposed violation of
privilege whatsoever."—It is not pretended that privilege, as
now claimed, has ever been defined or confirmed by statute ;
neither can it be said, with any colour of truth, to be a part of
the common law of England which had grown into prescription long before we knew anything of the existence of a House of
Commons.   As for the law of parliament, it is only another
name for the privilege in question; and since the power of creating new privileges has been formally renounced by both
Houses—since there is no code, in which we can study the law
of parliament, we have but one way left to make ourselves
acquainted with it, that is, to compare the nature of the in
stitution of a House of Commons with the facts upon record.
To establish a claim of privilege in either House, and to dis-

---

    * The necessity of securing the House of Commons against the king's
power, so that no interruption might be given either to the attendance of the
members in parliament, or to the freedom of debate, was the foundation of
parliamentary privilege; and we may observe, in all the addresses of new
appointed speakers to the sovereign, the utmost privilege they demand is
liberty of speech and freedom from arrests.   The very word privilege, means
no more than immunity or a safe-guard to the party who possesses it, and
can never be construed into an active power of invading the rights of others."
—JUNIUS.

    This and some of the following notes form part of a letter signed a Whig,
and will be found in the Miscellaneous Collection, No. 95.

tinguish original right from usurpation, it must appear that it is indispensably necessary for the performance of the duty they are employed in, and also that it has been uniformly allowed. From the first part of this description it follows clearly, that whatever privilege does of right belong to the present House of Commons did equally belong to the first assembly of their predecessors, was as completely vested in them, and might have been exercised in the same extent. From the second, we must infer that privileges which, for several centuries, were not only never allowed, but never even claimed by the House of Commons, must be founded upon usurpation. The constitutional duties of a House of Commons are not very complicated nor mysterious. They are to propose or assent to wholesome laws for the benefit of the nation. They are to grant the necessary aids to the king; petition for the redress of grievances, and prosecute treason or high crimes against the state. If unlimited privilege be necessary to the performance of these duties, we have reason to conclude that, for many centuries after the institution of the House of Commons, they were never performed. I am not bound to prove a negative, but I appeal to the English history when I affirm that, with the exceptions already stated (which yet I might safely relinquish), there is no precedent, from the year 1265 to the death of Queen Elizabeth, of the House of Commons having imprisoned any man (not a member of their House) for contempt or breach of privilege In the most flagrant cases, and when their acknowledged privileges were most grossly violated, the *poor Commons*, as they then styled themselves, never took the power of punishment into their own hands. They either sought redress by petition to the king, or, what is more remarkable, applied for justice to the House of Lords; and when satisfaction was denied them or delayed, their only remedy was to refuse proceeding upon the king's business. So little conception had our ancestors of the monstrous doctrines now maintained concerning privilege, that, in the reign of Elizabeth, even liberty of speech, the vital principle of a deliberative assembly, was restrained, by the queen's authority, to a simple *aye* or *no*, and this restriction, though imposed upon three successive parliaments*, was never once disputed by the House of Commons

* In the years 1593 1597, and 1601.

I know there are many precedents of arbitrary commitments for contempt. But, besides that they are of too modern a date to warrant a presumption that such a power was originally vested in the House of Commons—*Fact* alone does not constitute *Right*. If it does, general warrants were lawful. An ordinance of the two houses has a force equal to law; and the criminal jurisdiction assumed by the Commons in 1621, in the case of Edward Lloyd *, is a good precedent, to warrant the like proceedings against any man who shall unadvisedly mention the folly of a king or the ambition of a princess. The truth is, Sir, that the greatest and most exceptionable part of the privileges now contended for, were introduced and asserted by a House of Commons which abolished both monarchy and peerage, and whose proceedings, although they ended in one glorious act of substantial justice, could no way be reconciled to the forms of the constitution. Their successors profited by the example, and confirmed their power by a moderate or a popular use of it. Thus it grew by degrees from a notorious innovation at one period, to be tacitly admitted as the privilege of parliament at another.

If, however, it could be proved, from considerations of necessity or convenience, that an unlimited power of commitment ought to be intrusted to the House of Commons, and that, *in fact*, they have exercised it without opposition, still, in contemplation of law, the presumption is strongly against them. It is a leading maxim of the laws of England (and without it all laws are nugatory), that there is no right without a remedy, nor any legal power without a legal course to carry it into effect. Let the power now in question be tried by this rule. The speaker issues his warrant of attachment. The party attached either resists force with force, or appeals to a magistrate, who declares the warrant illegal, and discharges the prisoner. Does the law provide no legal means

* Lloyd, while a prisoner in the Fleet, had ridiculed the daughter of James the First and her consort, for which complaint was made to the House of Commons, who, on investigation, chose to think the words sufficiently proved, and sentenced him to be " set on the pillory at Westminster for two hours, to ride backward upon a horse without a saddle with the horse's tail in his hand, to have labels affixed on his head, indicating that he had been found guilty of using ' false, malicious, and despiteful speeches against the king's daughter and her husband,' to be again pilloried in Cheapside, and to be fined 1000*l*.

for enforcing a legal warrant? Is there no regular proceeding pointed out in our law books to assert and vindicate
the authority of so high a court as the House of Commons?
The question is answered directly by the fact. Their unlawful commands are resisted, and they have no remedy.
The imprisonment of their own members is revenge indeed,
but it is no assertion of the privilege they contend for *.
Their whole proceeding stops, and there they stand,
ashamed to retreat, and unable to advance. Sir, these
ignorant men should be informed that the execution of the
laws of England is not left in this uncertain, defenceless condition. If the process of the courts of Westminster Hall be
resisted, they have a direct course sufficient to enforce submission. The Court of King's Bench commands the sheriff
to raise the *posse comitatûs*. The Courts of Chancery and
Exchequer issue a *writ of rebellion* which must also be supported, if necessary, by the power of the county. To whom
will our honest representatives direct *their* writ of rebellion?
The guards, I doubt not, are willing enough to be employed,
but they know nothing of the doctrine of writs, and may
think it necessary to wait for a letter from Lord Barrington†.

It may now be objected to me that my arguments prove too
much; for that certainly there may be instances of contempt
and insult to the House of Commons which do not fall within
my own exceptions, yet, in regard to the dignity of the House,
ought not to pass unpunished. Be it so. The courts of
criminal jurisdiction are open to prosecutions which the
Attorney-General may commence by information or indictment. A libel, tending to asperse or vilify the House of
Commons or any of their members, may be as severely
punished in the Court of King's Bench as a libel upon the
king. Mr. De Grey thought so, when he drew up the
information upon my letter to his Majesty, or he had no
meaning in charging it to be a scandalous libel upon the

* Upon their own principles they should have committed Mr. Wilkes,
who had been guilty of a greater offence than even the Lord Mayor or
Alderman Oliver. But after repeatedly ordering him to attend, they at last
adjourned beyond the day appointed for his attendance, and by this mean,
pitiful evasion, gave up the point. Such is the force of conscious guilt!—
JUNIUS.

† In allusion to his letter of thanks to the guards for their conduct in St.
George's Fields.

House of Commons. In *my* opinion, they would consult their real dignity much better by appealing to the laws when they are offended than by violating the first principle of natural justice, which forbids us to be judges when we are parties to the cause *.

I do not mean to pursue them through the remainder of their proceedings. In their first resolutions it is possible they might have been deceived by ill-considered precedents. For the rest there is no colour of palliation or excuse. They have advised the king to resume a power of dispensing with the laws by royal proclamation†; and kings, we see, are ready enough to follow such advice. By mere violence, and without the shadow of right, they have expunged the record of a judicial proceeding‡. Nothing remained but to attribute to their own vote a power of stopping the whole distribution of criminal and civil justice.

The public virtues of the chief magistrate have long since ceased to be in question. But it is said that he has private good qualities, and I myself have been ready to acknowledge them. They are now brought to the test. If he loves his people, he will dissolve a parliament which they can never confide in or respect. If he has any regard for his own honour, he will disdain to be any longer connected with such abandoned prostitution. But if it were conceivable that a

---

* " If it be demanded in case a subject should be committed by either House for a matter manifestly out of their jurisdiction, what remedy can he have ? I answer, that it cannot well be imagined that the law, which favours nothing more than the liberty of the subject should give us a remedy against commitments by the king himself, appearing to be illegal, and yet give us no manner of redress against a commitment by our fellow-subjects, equally appearing to be unwarranted. But as this is a case which I am persuaded will never happen, it seems needless over nicely to examine it." *Hawkins* 2, 110.—*N.B. He was a good lawyer, but no prophet.*—JUNIUS.

† That their practice might be every way conformable to their principles, the House proceed to advise the crown to publish a proclamation universally acknowledged to be illegal. Mr. Moreton publicly protested against it before it was issued ; and Lord Mansfield, though not scrupulous to an extreme, speaks of it with horror. It is remarkable enough that the very men who advised the proclamation, and who hear it arraigned every day both within doors and without, are not daring enough to utter one word in its defence, nor have they ventured to take the least notice of Mr. Wilkes for discharging the persons apprehended under it.—JUNIUS.

‡ Lord Chatham very properly called this the act of a mob not of a senate —JUNIUS.

king of this country had lost all sense of personal honour, and all concern for the welfare of his subjects, I confess, Sir, I should be contented to renounce the forms of the constitution once more, if there were no other way to obtain substantial justice for the people*.

JUNIUS.

LETTER XLV.

TO THE PRINTER OF THE PUBLIC ADVERTISER.

SIR,   May 1, 1771.

THEY who object to detached parts of Junius's last letter, either do not mean him fairly, or have not considered the general scope and course of his argument. There are degrees in all the private vices. Why not in public prostitution? The influence of the crown naturally makes a septennial parliament dependent. Does it follow that every House of Commons will plunge at once into the *lowest depths* of prostitution? Junius supposes that the present House of Commons, in going such enormous lengths, have been *imprudent to themselves*, as well as wicked to the public; that their

---

* When Mr. Wilkes was to be punished they made no scruple about the privileges of parliament; and, although it was as well known as any matter of public record and uninterrupted custom could be, *that the members of either house are privileged, except in case of treason, felony, or breach of peace,* they declared without hesitation *that privilege of parliament did not extend to the case of a seditious libel;* and undoubtedly they would have done the same if Mr. Wilkes had been prosecuted for any other misdemeanor whatsoever. The ministry are of a sudden grown wonderfully careful of privileges which their predecessors were as ready to invade. The known laws of the land, the rights of the subject, the sanctity of charters, and the reverence due to our magistrates, must all give way, without question or resistance, to a privilege of which no man knows either the origin or the extent. The House of Commons judge of their own privileges without appeal :—they may take offence at the most innocent action, and imprison the person who offends them during their arbitrary will and pleasure. The party has no remedy;—he cannot appeal from their jurisdiction; and if he questions the privilege which he is supposed to have violated, it becomes an aggravation of his offence. Surely this doctrine is not to be found in Magna Charta. If it be admitted without limitation, I affirm that there is neither law nor liberty in this kingdom. We are the slaves of the House of Commons, and through them, we are the slaves of the king and his ministers.— ANONYMOUS.

z 2

example is *not within the reach of emulation;* and that, in the first session after the next election, *some* popular measures may probably be adopted. He does not expect that a dissolution of parliament will destroy corruption, but that at least it will be a check and terror to their successors, who will have seen that, *in flagrant cases*, their constituents *can* and *will* interpose with effect. After all, Sir, will you not endeavour to remove or alleviate the most dangerous symptoms because you cannot eradicate the disease? Will you not punish *treason* or *parricide*, because the sight of a gibbet does not prevent highway robberies? When the main argument of Junius is admitted to be unanswerable, I think it would become the minor critic who hunts for blemishes, to be a little more distrustful of his own sagacity. The other objection is hardly worth an answer. When Junius observes that kings are ready enough to follow *such* advice, he does not mean to insinuate that, if the advice of parliament were good, the king would be so ready to follow it.

PHILO-JUNIUS.

LETTER XLVI.

TO THE PRINTER OF THE PUBLIC ADVERTISER.

SIR,   May 22, 1771.

VERY early in the debate upon the decision of the Middlesex election, it was well observed by Junius, that the House of Commons had not only exceeded their boasted precedent of the expulsion and subsequent incapacitation of Mr. Walpole, but that they had not even adhered to it strictly as far as it went. After convicting Mr. Dyson of giving a false quotation from the journals*, and having explained the purpose which that contemptible fraud was intended to answer, he proceeds to state the vote itself by which Mr. Walpole's supposed incapacity was declared, viz., "Resolved, that Robert Walpole, Esq., having been this session of parliament committed a prisoner to the Tower, and expelled this House for a high breach of trust in the execution of his office, and notorious corruption when secretary at war, was, and is, incapable of

* Letter 20, note, ante, p. 198.

being elected a member to serve in this present parliament:
and then observes, that, from the terms of the vote, we have
no right to annex the incapacitation to the *expulsion* only, for
that, as the proposition stands, it must arise equally from the
expulsion and the commitment to the Tower.   I believe, Sir,
no man, who knows anything of dialectics, or who understands English, will dispute the truth and fairness of this
construction.   But Junius has a great authority to support
him which, to speak with the Duke of Grafton, I accidentally
met with this morning in the course of my reading.   It contains an admonition which cannot be repeated too often.
Lord Somers, in his excellent tract upon the rights of the
people, after reciting the vote of the convention of the 28th
of January, 1689, viz., "That King James the Second,
having endeavoured to subvert the constitution of this kingdom by breaking the original contract between king and
people, and by the advice of Jesuits and other wicked persons having violated the fundamental laws, and having
withdrawn himself out of this kingdom, hath abdicated the
government," &c., makes this observation upon it:—"The
word *abdicated* relates to *all* the clauses aforegoing, as well
as to his deserting the kingdom, or else they would have
been wholly in vain."   And, that there might be no pretence
for confining the *abdication* merely to the *withdrawing*, Lord
Somers farther observes, *that King James, by refusing to
govern us according to that law by which he held the crown,
did implicitly renounce his title to it.*

If Junius's construction of the vote against Mr. Walpole
be now admitted (and indeed I cannot comprehend how it
can honestly be disputed), the advocates of the House of
Commons must either give up their precedent entirely, or be
reduced to the necessity of maintaining one of the grossest
absurdities imaginable, viz., "That a commitment to the
Tower is a constituent part of, and contributes half at least,
to the incapacitation of the person who suffers it."

I need not make you any excuse for endeavouring to keep
alive the attention of the public to the decision of the Middlesex election.   The more I consider it, the more I am
convinced that, as a *fact*, it is indeed highly injurious to the
rights of the people ; but that, as a *precedent*, it is one of
the most dangerous that ever was established against those
who are to come after us.   Yet I am so far a moderate man

that I verily believe the majority of the House of Commons, when they passed this dangerous vote, neither understood the question, nor knew the consequence of what they were doing. Their motives were rather despicable than criminal in the extreme. One effect they certainly did not foresee. They are now reduced to such a situation, that if a member of the present House of Commons were to conduct himself ever so improperly, and in reality deserve to be sent back to his constituents with a mark of disgrace, they would not dare to expel him ; because they know that the people, in order to try again the great question of right, or to thwart an odious House of Commons, would probably overlook his immediate unworthiness, and return the same person to parliament. But in time the precedent will gain strength. A future House of Commons will have no such apprehensions, consequently will not scruple to follow a precedent which they did not establish. The miser himself seldom lives to enjoy the fruit of his extortion ; but his heir succeeds to him of course, and takes possession without censure. No man expects him to make restitution, and no matter for his title, he lives quietly upon the estate.

PHILO-JUNIUS.

Mr. Wilkes having been again returned as one of the members for the county of Middlesex, in the parliaments of 1774 and 1780, made various fruitless efforts to get the decision of the House of Commons on this interesting controversy erased from their journals, which he at length effected on the dissolution of the administration of which Lord North had been at the head, from the time of the resignation of the Duke of Grafton in the year 1770. This occurred May 3, 1782. His address on this occasion, as a specimen of the oratory of the great popular leader of his time, and as his statement of his case, is subjoined. The expulsion of Mr. Wilkes from the House of Commons, and its resolution declaring his ineligibility to sit in the House after such expulsion, though returned by a majority of parliamentary electors, form such prominent events, that it may be convenient to state the final issue of the struggle.

Mr. Wilkes prefaced his motion in the following address to the House :—
" MR. SPEAKER,

" I think myself peculiarly happy at the present moment, that I have the honour of submitting to the House an important national question respecting the rights of election, when the friends and favourites of the people enjoy, with the smiles of our sovereign, the offices of trust and power in the state, accompanied with that fair influence which is necessarily created by great ability, perfect integrity, the purest political virtue, and the remembrance of their former upright conduct in the cause of the people. If the people of

England, Sir, have at any period explicitly and fully declared an opinion on a momentous constitutional question, it has been in regard to the Middlesex election in 1768, and the subsequent most profligate proceedings of an administration, hostile by system to the rights of this country, and every part of the British Empire. An instance cannot be found in our history of a more general concurrence of sentiment among the freeholders of England, and they were joined by almost every borough and corporation in the southern part of the island. I am satisfied, therefore, that I now shall find the real friends of the people determined and zealous in the support of their just claims and undoubted privileges.

" Hitherto, Sir, every attempt for the recovery of this invaluable franchise has been rendered fruitless by the arts and machinations of power in the hands of wicked men ; and I may with truth assert, that the body of the people long addressed, petitioned, and remonstrated with manly firmness and perseverance, without the least effect or even impression. The full redress demanded by this injured nation seems reserved to distinguish the present propitious era of public liberty, among the early and blooming honours of an administration which possesses the confidence, and daily conciliates the affections, of a brave and sensible people. Their voice was never heard in a more clear and distinct manner than on this point of the first magnitude for all the electors of this kingdom; and I trust will now be heard favourably. The general resentment and indignation ran so high against the House of Commons which committed the outrage, that their immediate dissolution became the prayer of numberless petitions to the throne. No man scrupled to declare them unworthy to exist in their political capacity. The public pronounced them *guilty* of sacrificing and betraying the rights which they were called upon, by every tie of justice and duty, to defend. The noble spirit of the freeholders of Middlesex, persevering in the best of causes, undaunted by all the menaces of power, was the subject of the most general applause and admiration. The voice of the people was then in the harsh and sharp tone of passion and anger against ministers. It will, I am persuaded, soon be in the soft and pleasing accents of joy and thankfulness to our deliverers.

" It is scarcely possible, Sir, to state a question in which the people of this free country are more materially interested than in the right of election for it is the share which they have reserved to themselves in the legislature When it was wrested from them by violence, the constitution was torn up by the roots.

" I have now the happiness of seeing the treasury bench filled with the friends of the constitution, the guardians and lovers of liberty, who have been unwearied and uniform in the defence of all our rights, and in particular of this invaluable franchise. I hail the present auspicious moment, and with impatience expect the completion of what I have long and fervently desired for my friends and country, for the present age, and a free posterity. The former conduct of those now in power affords me the most sanguine hopes of this day seeing justice done to a people to whom they have so frequently appealed, who now look up to them with ardent expectation, with pleasure and esteem. Consistency, Sir, has drawn the right line of their political conduct to this period. It will now point out the same path of public virtue and honour. May I be indulged in a hint, which I mean to extend much

beyond the business of the day, when I say that consistency will be attended
with that stability and perfect security which are the objects of every good
man's wishes for them? They have given us a fair earnest of their reverence for the constitution by their support of two bills essentially necessary
to restore the purity and independency of parliament; *I mean the bill for
preventing contractors from sitting in the House of Commons, and the bill for
disabling officers of the revenue from voting at elections.*" Mr. Wilkes was
here interrupted with a message by Sir Francis Molyneaux, gentleman usher
of the *black rod*, desiring the immediate attendance of the House of Commons
in the House of Lords. The Speaker then went up to the House of Peers;
and after his return and report of what had passed,

    Mr. Wilkes said :—

    " MR. SPEAKER,

    " I return my thanks to the *black* rod for so luckily interposing in favour
of this House, when I might possibly have again tired them with the important, however stale, case of the *Middlesex election,* which their patient
ear has for several years with much good nature suffered. I will now make
some return to their indulgence in profiting by the circumstance of this happy
interruption, and not saying a single word about *Walpole* or *Wollaston,
Coke* or *Blackstone.* I will not detain the House longer than by observing
the parliamentary form of desiring the clerk to read the resolution of the
17th of February, 1769." Which having been complied with, he then
moved " That the entry of the resolution of the 17th of February, 1769,
' That John Wilkes, Esq., having been in this session of parliament expelled
this House, was, and is, incapable of being elected a member to serve in this
present parliament,' might be expunged from their journals, it being subversive of the rights of the whole body of the electors of this kingdom." This
motion was (after some opposition from the late Mr. Fox, then Secretary of
State, and from the late Lord Melville, then Lord Advocate for Scotland, the
former of whom had strenuously supported the whole of the resolutions
passed by the House of Commons in respect of the Middlesex election)
carried on a division, by 185 to 47. Mr. Wilkes, as soon as this question was
disposed of, moved " That all the declarations, orders and resolutions of the
House respecting his election for the county of Middlesex as a void election,
the due and legal election of Mr. Luttrell into parliament for the said county,
and his own incapacity to be elected a member to serve in the said parliament, be expunged;" which motion was, for the reasons before given, carried
without a division.

    Thus terminated one of the most severe, and on the part of the servants of
the crown, unconstitutional and impolitic contests, that ever agitated the people
of this country; not leaving *a rack behind* to constitute, as our author empha-
tically terms it, " A precedent the most dangerous that ever was established
against those who are to come after us." As the merit of the erasure of
these obnoxious resolutions from the journals of the House of Commons is
solely due to the talents and perseverance of Mr. Wilkes, it will not be unfair
to defend his motives and pretensions as a patriot, from the detraction of
contemporary adversaries as well as from his more modern opponents. The
first political offence of which he appears to have been guilty, was the severity
with which he attacked the administration of Lord Bute, and which was
characterized as being deficient in ability, as it was odiously unconstitutional.

For this attack a general warrant was issued, his papers were seized, and himself committed a close prisoner to the Tower. He was afterwards prosecuted for the republication of the *North Briton*, No. 45, the vehicle of his political lucubrations, and for the " Essay on Woman," which had been surreptitiously stolen from him by a man of the name of Curry, employed in printing it at his private press, at the instigation of, and under the promise of ample reward and protection from, Philip Carteret Webb, the solicitor to the treasury. Previous to the trial, Wilkes fled to France, where he remained for some years; in the mean time he had been found guilty in the King's Bench of printing and publishing both libels; and not appearing in due time to receive the judgment of the court, he was outlawed. A short time previous to the dissolution of parliament in the year 1768, he returned to this country, and was elected member for the county of Middlesex. In the meanwhile, he surrendered himself to the King's Bench, and having claimed the benefit of certain errors in the writ of outlawry, the same were, after solemn argument, admitted by the court, and the outlawry was reversed. A few days subsequent to this determination, the judgment of the court was pronounced on him for publishing the libels; for the former he was sentenced to pay a fine of 500*l.* to the king, and to be imprisoned ten months ; and for the latter, he was fined in the like sum, and sentenced to twelve months' imprisonment ; and was further ordered to find security for his good behaviour for seven years, himself in 1000*l.* and two sureties in 500*l.* each. His expulsion from the House of Commons, and the consequences of it, are the subject of several of the letters of these volumes, as well as of the notes which have been added to them. Not long previous to his release from prison, he was elected alderman of Farringdon Without; shortly afterwards one of the sheriffs of London, and in due course Lord Mayor; and on the death of Mr. Hopkins, chamberlain. At a subsequent period of Mr. Wilkes's life, when the violence of the politics which had raised him to these several respectable situations had altogether subsided, he was attacked more than once, on the annual election of chamberlain, and other city offices, with a demand of the previous resignation of his gown as an alderman of London, which he always most resolutely refused, declaring that no consideration on earth should induce him to forego the honour which he felt had been conferred upon him by his election to the magistracy of the City of London, and by which determination he ran considerable risk of losing his election to the former lucrative situation ; an instance of disinterestedness not often to be met with in those who most confidently lay claim to patriotism, which certainly places his character in a higher point of view than many have been willing to allow to it : and in so far as the motives which actuated his political conduct can be called in question, adds to the value of the obligations conferred upon the public by his able and successful opposition to general warrants ; by the aid and assistance afforded the printers in resisting the violence of their representatives on the subject of reporting the debates in parliament; and by his perseverance in vindicating the rights of the electors of Great Britain in procuring the erasure from the journals of the House of Commons of their most unconstitutional determination, on the much-agitated question of the Middlesex election. With respect to the private character of Mr. Wilkes in early life, the writer of this note will not venture to make any defence, though he trusts to be excused if he quotes the apology which was made for

him by a friend in the year 1769. " As to his private foibles, I shall only
add that he may apply what a very eccentric genius of this age has said of
himself : my own passions, and the passions and interests of other people
still more, have led me aside. I launched into the deep before I had loaded
ballast enough. If the ship did not sink, the cargo was thrown overboard.
The storm itself threw me into port." Mr. Wilkes, after he lost his election
for the county of Middlesex in the year 1790, lived in considerable retirement, and much respected. His literary attainments were of the higher
order, and, as a political controversialist, few men were equal to him. Not
many years before his death, he was applied to by the late Mr. H. S. Woodfall
to write some explanatory notes for a new edition of these letters, which by
some have been erroneously attributed to his pen, but declined it on the
ground, as he stated, of not wishing to pay a second visit to the prison of the
King's Bench. Mr. Wilkes died December 26, 1797, in the 71st year of
his age.

LETTER XLVII.

TO THE PRINTER OF THE PUBLIC ADVERTISER.

SIR,   May 25, 1771.

I CONFESS my partiality to Junius, and feel a considerable
pleasure in being able to communicate anything to the public
in support of his opinions. The doctrine laid down in his
last letter concerning the power of the House of Commons
to commit for contempt is not so new as it appeared to many
people who, dazzled with the name of *privilege*, had never
suffered themselves to examine the question fairly. *In the course
of my reading this morning* I met with the following passage in
the journals of the House of Commons (vol. i., p. 603). Upon
occasion of a jurisdiction unlawfully assumed by the House, in
the year 1621, Mr. Attorney-General *Noye* gave his opinion
as follows:—" No doubt but, in some cases, this House may
give judgment, in matters of returns, and concerning members
of our House, or falling out in our view in parliament ; but,
for foreign matters, knoweth not how we can judge it ; knoweth
not that we have been used to give judgment in any case but
those before mentioned."

Sir Edward Coke, upon the same subject, says (page 604),
" No question but this is a house of record, and that it hath
power of judicature in some cases—have power to judge of
returns and members of our House ; one, no member offending

out of the parliament, *when he came hither and justified it,* was censured for it."

Now, Sir, if you will compare the opinion of these great sages of the law with Junius's doctrine, you will find they tally exactly. He allows the power of the House to commit their own members (which, however, they may grossly abuse); he allows their power in cases where they are acting as a court of judicature, viz., elections, returns, &c.; and he allows it in such contempts as immediately interrupt their proceedings, or, as Mr. Noye expresses it, *falling out in their view in parliament.*

They who would carry the privileges of parliament farther than Junius, either do not mean well to the public, or know not what they are doing. The government of England is a government of law. We betray ourselves, we contradict the spirit of our laws, and we shake the whole system of English jurisprudence, whenever we intrust a discretionary power over the life, liberty, or fortune of the subject, to any man or set of men whatsoever, upon a presumption that it will not be abused.

PHILO-JUNIUS.

LETTER XLVIII *.

SIR,   May 28, 1771.

ANY man who takes the trouble of perusing the journals of the House of Commons will soon be convinced that very little if any regard at all ought to be paid to the resolutions of one branch of the legislature declaratory of the law of the land, or even what they call the law of parliament. It will appear that these resolutions have no one of the properties by which, in this country particularly, *law* is distinguished from

* Junius, since his last letter, had discovered, by more diligent search, in the records of the House of Commons, an instance in which that House carried its claim of privileges considerably beyond what the present parliament regarded as just. The parliament in which such extravagance of privilege was arrogated, had, by the violence of their proceedings, obliged Queen Anne to prorogue, and then dissolve them. He hastened to lay before the public these facts, from which his own inference was, that the law of parliament was

mere *will* and *pleasure*; but that, on the contrary, they bear
every mark of a power arbitrarily assumed and capriciously
applied; that they are usually made in times of contest, and
to serve some unworthy purpose of passion or party; that the
law is seldom declared until *after* the fact by which it is supposed to be violated; that legislation and jurisdiction are
united in the same persons, and exercised at the same moment; and that a court from which there is no appeal assumes
an *original* jurisdiction in a criminal case; in short, Sir, to
collect a thousand absurdities into one mass, " we have a law
which cannot be known because it is *ex post facto*, the party
is both legislator and judge, and the jurisdiction is without
appeal." Well might the judges say, *the law of parliament is
above us*.

You will not wonder, Sir, that with these qualifications the
declaratory resolutions of the House of Commons should
appear to be in perpetual contradiction, not only to common
sense and to the laws we are acquainted with (and which alone
we can obey), but even to one another. I was led to trouble
you with these observations by a passage which, to speak in
lutestring, *I met with this morning in the course of my reading*,
and upon which I mean to put a question to the advocates for
privilege: on the 8th of March, 1704 (*vide* Journals, vol. xiv.,
p. 565), the House thought proper to come to the following
resolutions:—1, " That no commoner of England committed
by the House of Commons for breach of privilege, or contempt
of that House, ought to be, by any writ of *Habeas Corpus*,
made to appear in any other place, or before any other judicature, during that session of parliament wherein such person
was so committed."

altogether unsettled, and it may be added, so continues; but that it was
usual for the sovereign to dissolve his parliament when their own refractory
conduct, or the general wishes of the people, strongly recommended such a
measure.

In the first paragraph of this letter, Junius skilfully discriminates between
a resolution of the House of Commons, and an act of the whole legislature. He
then states from the journals for the year 1704 the great fact for the purpose of proclaiming which this letter was written. An application of this
fact to the support of his own former doctrine concerning the law of parliament, fills the next paragraph. In the closing sentences, he employs, with
triumph, the inference which he had deduced to expose to still stronger ridicule and more abhorrent odium, that act of authority by which the House of
Commons had sent Crosby and Oliver to the Tower.—ED.

2. " That the serjeant-at-arms attending this House do make no return of, or yield any obedience to, the said writs of *Habeas Corpus*, and for such his refusal, that he have the protection of the House of Commons."*

Welbore Ellis, what say you? Is this the law of parliament, or is it not? I am a plain man, Sir, and cannot follow you through the phlegmatic forms of an oration. Speak out, Grildrig †,—say yes or no! If you say *yes*, I shall then enquire by what authority Mr. De Grey, the honest Lord Mansfield, and the barons of the exchequer, dared to grant a writ of *Habeas Corpus* for bringing the bodies of the lord mayor and Mr. Oliver before them, and why the lieutenant of the Tower made any return to a writ which the House of Commons had, in a similar instance, declared to be unlawful. If you say *no*, take care you do not at once give up the cause in support of which you have so long and so laboriously tortured your understanding. Take care you do not confess that there is no test by which we can distinguish, no evidence by which we can determine, what is and what is not the law of parliament. The resolutions I have quoted stand upon your journals uncontroverted and unrepealed; they contain a declaration of the law of parliament, by a court competent to the question, and whose decision, as you and Lord Mansfield say, must be law, because there is no appeal from it; and they were made not hastily, but after long deliberation upon a constitutional question. What farther sanction or solemnity will you annex to any resolution of the present House of Commons beyond what appears upon the face of those tow resolutions, the legality of which you now deny? If you say that parliaments

* If there be in reality any such law in England as the *law of parliament*, which (under the exceptions stated in my letter on privilege), I confess, after long deliberation, I very much doubt, it certainly is not constituted by, nor can it be collected from, the resolutions of either House, whether *enacting* or *declaratory*. I desire the reader will compare the above resolution of the year 1704, with the following of the 3rd of April, 1628.—"*Resolved*, That the writ of *Habeas Corpus* cannot be denied, but ought to be granted to every man that is committed or detained in prison, or otherwise restrained by the command of the king, the privy council, or any other, he praying the same."—JUNIUS.

† The diminutive stature of Mr. Welbore Ellis, afterwards Lord Mendip, hence in another place called, by our author, little *mannikin* Ellis, has been already noticed. The term Grildrig preserves the same idea, this being the name bestowed on Gulliver by the gigantic inhabitants of Brobdignag.

are not infallible, and that Queen Anne, in consequence of the violent proceedings of that House of Commons, was obliged to prorogue and dissolve them, I shall agree with you very heartily, and think that the precedent ought to be followed immediately. But you, Mr. Ellis, who hold this language, are inconsistent with your own principles. You have hitherto maintained that the House of Commons are the sole judges of their own privileges, and that their declaration does, *ipso facto*, constitute the law of parliament; yet now you confess that parliaments are fallible, and that their resolutions may be illegal, consequently that their resolutions *do not* constitute the law of parliament. When the king was urged to dissolve the present parliament, you advised him to tell his subjects that *he was careful not to assume any of those powers which the constitution had placed in other hands*, &c. Yet Queen Anne, it seems, was justified in exerting her prerogative to stop a House of Commons whose proceedings, compared with those of the assembly of which you are a most worthy member, were the perfection of justice and reason.

In what a labyrinth of nonsense does a man involve himself who labours to maintain falsehood by argument! How much better would it become the dignity of the House of Commons to speak plainly to the people, and tell us at once *that their will must be obeyed, not because it is lawful and reasonable, but because it is their will!* Their constituents would have a better opinion of their candour, and, I promise you, not a worse opinion of their integrity.

PHILO-JUNIUS.

LETTER XLIX*.

TO HIS GRACE THE DUKE OF GRAFTON.

MY LORD,   June 22, 1771.
THE profound respect I bear to the gracious prince who governs this country with no less honour to himself than satisfaction

* The death of George Grenville, the indiscreet violence of the livery of London, with the mingled firmness and moderation of the government, had, since the commencement of the session of parliament for 1770-71, given new stability to the administration which Junius opposed. Persons who, a few

to his subjects, and who restores you to your rank under his
standard, will save you from a multitude of reproaches. The
attention I should have paid to your failings is involuntarily
attracted to the hand that rewards them; and though I am
not so partial to the royal judgment as to affirm that the favour
of a king can remove mountains of infamy, it serves to lessen
at least, for undoubtedly it divides, the burden. While I
remember how much is due to *his* sacred character, I cannot,
with any decent appearance of propriety, call you the meanest
and the basest fellow in the kingdom. I protest, my Lord, I
do not think you so. You will have a dangerous rival in that

months before, had shown an inclination to abandon the ministry, now
returned to proffer their aid, and to court its alliance. Nor were their
offers hastily slighted. The opposition were still numerous, powerful, and
active; and no means were to be neglected likely to fortify the government
against their attacks.

In this state of things, the Duke of Grafton, who had almost withdrawn
from the administration, renewed his connection with it, and obtained new
proofs of royal favour. He was appointed, on the 12th of June, 1771, lord
keeper of the privy seal, instead of Lord Suffolk, who succeeded the Earl of
Halifax, as secretary of state for the northern department. On the 14th day
of the same month, he was appointed in succession to the Earl of Halifax,
ranger and warden of Salcey Park, in Northamptonshire. Thus gratified
with honours and emoluments, yet not placed in a situation of dangerous
responsibility, he was more closely than ever attached to the king and his
ministry. Junius appeared to have menaced and inveighed in vain. He felt
himself insulted by this new hardihood of the duke. He was enraged
equally, that the duke should dare to accept ministerial appointment, and
that the king should presume to employ and reward him. He determined to
resume his strain of invective against the faithless friend of Wilkes, the
deserter of Chatham, and not to spare even Majesty itself; since it was
probable that, however outrageous, he might still find protection for his
printers in the favour of a London jury.

At the outset he aims his invective more against the king himself than
against his minister. He then ingenuously hints that the loudest outcry of
some of the patriots had been but hollow pretence. He indignantly enume-
rates those acts of imputed perfidy, by which alone, as he would insinuate,
the Duke of Grafton had gained his sovereign's cordial favour. He involves,
in the current of his outpouring, various other names; exhausts his present
stores of satirical eloquence, and menaces new terrors, in a tone somewhat
between the bullying of weakness, and the haughty threat of conscious
power.

This letter, according to his own estimate, and with reason, appears to
have been considered one of his greatest efforts. In a private note (No.
35) he says, "I am strangely partial to the inclosed. It is finished with
the utmost care. If I find myself mistaken in my judgment of this paper,
I positively will never write again."—ED.

kind of fame to which you have hitherto so happily directed your ambition, as long as there is one man living who thinks you worthy of his confidence, and fit to be trusted with any share in his government. I confess you have great intrinsic merit, but take care you do not value it too highly; consider how much of it would have been lost to the world, if the king had not graciously affixed his stamp, and given it currency among his subjects. If it be true that a virtuous man, struggling with adversity, be a scene worthy of the gods, the glorious contention between you and the best of princes deserves a circle equally attentive and respectable; I think I already see other gods rising from the earth to behold it.

But this language is too mild for the occasion. The king is determined that our abilities shall not be lost to society. The perpetration and description of new crimes will find employment for us both. My Lord, if the persons who have been loudest in their professions of patriotism had done their duty to the public with the same zeal and perseverance that I did, I will not assert that government would have recovered its dignity, but at least our gracious sovereign must have spared his subjects this last insult *, which, if there be any feeling left among us, they will resent more than even the real injuries they received from every measure of your Grace's administration. In vain would he have looked round him for another character so consummate as yours. Lord Mansfield shrinks from his principles †, his ideas of government perhaps go farther than your own, but his heart disgraces the theory of his understanding. Charles Fox ‡ is yet in blossom; and as for Mr. Wedderburne, there is something about him which

* The duke was lately appointed lord privy seal.—JUNIUS. He succeeded Lord Suffolk, who had just taken possession of the post of the northern department upon the death of the Earl of Halifax.—ED.

† Alluding to Lord Mansfield's call of the House upon the subject of the opinion of the judges, in consequence of the verdict of the jury upon Woodfall's trial, which embraced the question whether juries were judges of the fact alone, or of both the fact and law. An important motion was expected, but his Lordship, as Junius states it, *shrunk* from the principles he had advanced, and merely informed the House that he had left a paper with their clerk, containing the unanimous judgment of the Court of King's Bench upon the verdict in question, and the doctrine it necessarily embraced, and that their Lordships were welcome to copies of it if they chose.

‡ Afterwards the celebrated leader of the Whigs, though then a member of a Tory administration, as a lord of the admiralty.—ED.

even treachery cannot trust; for the present, therefore, the best of princes must have contented himself with Lord Sandwich. You would long since have received your final dismission and reward; and I, my Lord, who do not esteem you the more for the high office you possess, would willingly have followed you to your retirement. There is surely something singularly benevolent in the character of our sovereign. From the moment he ascended the throne there is no crime of which human nature is capable (and I call upon the recorder * to witness it), that has not appeared venial in his sight†. With any other prince, the shameful desertion of him in the midst of that distress, which you alone had created, in the very crisis of danger, when he fancied he saw the throne already surrounded by men of virtue and abilities, would have outweighed the memory of your former services. But his Majesty is full of justice, and understands the doctrine of compensations; he remembers with gratitude how soon you had accommodated your morals to the necessities of his service; how cheerfully you had abandoned the engagements of private friendship, and renounced the most solemn professions to the public. The sacrifice of Lord Chatham was not lost upon him. Even the cowardice and perfidy of deserting him may have done you no disservice in his esteem The instance was painful, but the principle might please.

You did not neglect the magistrate while you flattered the *man.* The expulsion of Mr. Wilkes, predetermined in the cabinet; the power of depriving the subject of his birthright, attributed to a resolution of one branch of the legislature; the constitution impudently invaded by the House of Commons; the right of defending it treacherously renounced by the House of Lords: these are the strokes, my Lord, which, in the present reign, recommend to office and constitute a minister. They would have determined your sovereign's judgment if they had made no impression upon his heart. We need not look for any other species of merit to account for his taking the earliest opportunity to recall you to his councils; yet you have other merit in abundance. Mr. Hine, the Duke of Portland, and

---

* The late Chief Justice Eyre was, at this time, recorder of London.—Ed.
† The author here more particularly alludes to the pardon of M‘Quirk and the Kennedys. See Letter 8.

A A

Mr. Yorke,—breach of trust, robbery, and murder *. You would think it a compliment to your gallantry if I added rape to the catalogue, but the style of your amours secures you from resistance. I know how well these several charges have been defended. In the first instance, the breach of trust is supposed to have been its own reward. Mr. Bradshaw affirms upon his honour (and so may the gift of smiling never depart from him!) that you reserved no part of Mr. Hine's purchase-money for your own use, but that every shilling of it was scrupulously paid to Governor Burgoyne. Make haste, my Lord, another patent, applied in time, may keep the Oaks † in the family; if not, Birnham Wood, I fear, must come to the *macaroni* ‡.

The Duke of Portland was in life your earliest friend. In defence of his property he had nothing to plead but equity against Sir James Lowther, and prescription against the crown §. You felt for your friend, *but the law must take its course*. Posterity will scarce believe that Lord Bute's son-in-law had barely interest enough at the Treasury to get his grant completed before the general election ‖.

Enough has been said of that detestable transaction, which ended in the death of Mr. Yorke. I cannot speak of it without horror and compassion. To excuse yourself, you publicly impeach your accomplice, and to *his* mind, perhaps, the accusation may be flattery; but in murder you are both principals. It was once a question of emulation, and if the event had not disappointed the immediate schemes of the closet, it might

---

* These points have all been elucidated; they relate to Hine's patent place; Inglewood Forest, &c., in Cumberland, granted to Sir James Lowther by the crown, although it had been in possession of the Duke of Portland's family for seventy years; and the suicide of Charles Yorke, the lord chancellor, who cut his throat from political chagrin, immediately after his appointment.

† A superb villa of Colonel Burgoyne, about this time advertised for sale.

‡ The person alluded to is the father of the late Mr. Christie, who was the auctioneer employed to sell the estate.

§ Sir James Lowther was son-in-law to Lord Bute by the marriage of one of his daughters.

‖ It will appear by a subsequent letter, that the duke's precipitation proved fatal to the grant. It looks like the hurry and confusion of a young highwayman, who takes a few shillings, but leaves the purse and watch behind him. And yet the duke was an old offender.—JUNIUS.

still have been a hopeful subject of jest and merriment between you

This letter, my Lord, is only a preface to my future correspondence; the remainder of the summer shall be dedicated to your amusement. I mean now and then to relieve the severity of your morning studies, and to prepare you for the business of the day. Without pretending to more than Mr. Bradshaw's sincerity, you may rely upon my attachment as long as you are in office.

Will your Grace forgive me if I venture to express some anxiety for a man whom I know you do not love? My Lord Weymouth has cowardice to plead, and a desertion of a later date than your own. You know the privy seal was intended for him; and if you consider the dignity of the post he deserted, you will hardly think it decent to quarter him on Mr. Rigby. Yet he must have bread, my Lord; or rather he must have wine *. If you deny him the cup, there will be no keeping him within the pale of the ministry.

JUNIUS.

LETTER L.

TO HIS GRACE THE DUKE OF GRAFTON

City business is the burthen of this letter. Junius connects it with the Duke of Grafton's name, solely for the sake of holding out his Grace, as much as possible, to public odium and obloquy. It relates that the secretary to the treasury under Lord North was as busy in dishonourable practices as Mr. Bradshaw, the secretary under the Duke of Grafton, had been. It insults

* Lord Weymouth, upon deserting the ministry, was succeeded in the foreign department by the Earl of Rochford. The former nobleman resigned Dec. 10, 1770, and the Duke of Grafton on the preceding 28th of January. Lord Weymouth's attachment to the bottle furnishes the ground for the imagery with which the letter concludes. White's, in St. James's Street, was his favourite house, and his boon companions were the Duke of Bridgewater, Lord Gower, Lord Thurlow, Mr. Rigby, and Mr. Garnier. He loved play but not deep. Although a bon vivant, he kept faithfully the secrets of the closet, which gained him the esteem of the king, who honoured him with the garter, and made him a marquis without the recommendation of any minister.—ED.

A A 2

over the death of Mr. Dingley, and brings into quaint comparison with his fate and his relations to the duke, the name and character of the sovereign; lastly Mr. Horne is assailed, and accused of wavering, if not the desertion of his former friends and principles. It is not one of Junius's best letters, yet it is not without some admirable strokes of genius and indignation.—ED.

MY LORD,   July 9, 1771.

THE influence of your Grace's fortune still seems to preside over the treasury; the genius of Mr. Bradshaw inspires Mr. Robinson *. How remarkable it is (and I speak it not as a matter of reproach, but as something peculiar to your character), that you have never yet formed a friendship which has not been fatal to the object of it. nor adopted a cause to which, one way or other, you have not done mischief. Your attachment is infamy while it lasts, and whichever way it turns, leaves ruin and disgrace behind it. The deluded girl who yields to such a profligate, even while he is constant, forfeits her reputation as well as her innocence, and finds herself abandoned at last to misery and shame. Thus it happened with the best of princes. Poor Dingley, too †! I protest I hardly know which of them we ought most to lament, the unhappy man who sinks under the sense of his dishonour, or him who survives it; characters so finished are placed beyond the reach of panegyric. Death has fixed his seal upon Dingley; and you, my Lord, have set your mark upon the other.

The only letter I ever addressed to the king was so unkindly received that I believe I shall never presume to trouble his Majesty in that way again; but my zeal for his service is superior to neglect, and, like Mr. Wilkes's patriotism, thrives by persecution. Yet his Majesty is much addicted to useful reading. and, if I am not ill informed, has honoured the *Public Adver-*

* By an intercepted letter from the secretary of the treasury, it appeared, *that the friends of government were to be very active* in supporting the ministerial nomination of sheriffs.—JUNIUS.

Robinson was now secretary of the treasury, and filled the same post of confidential agent to Lord North that Bradshaw had before filled to the Duke of Grafton.

† Dingley was now just dead: and our author insinuates that he died of a broken heart in consequence of having been so contemptuously treated at the preceding election for Middlesex, in which he had offered himself a candidate at the request of the Duke of Grafton, but could not obtain a nomination from any one freeholder, and was afraid even to nominate himself.

tiser with particular attention. I have endeavoured, therefore, and not without success (as perhaps you may remember), to furnish it with such interesting and edifying intelligence as probably would not reach him through any other channel The services you have done the nation, your integrity in office, and signal fidelity to your approved good master, have been faithfully recorded. Nor have his own virtues been entirely neglected. These letters, my Lord, are read in other countries and in other languages; and I think I may affirm, without vanity, that the gracious character of the best of princes is by this time not only perfectly known to his subjects, but tolerably well understood by the rest of Europe. In this respect, alone, I have the advantage of Mr. Whitehead*. His plan, I think, is too narrow. He seems to manufacture his verses for the sole use of the hero who is supposed to be the subject of them; and, that his meaning may not be exported in foreign bottoms, sets all translation at defiance.

Your Grace's re-appointment to a seat in the cabinet was announced to the public by the ominous return of Lord Bute to this counntry†. When that noxious planet approaches England, he never fails to bring plague and pestilence along with him. The king already feels the malignant effect of your influence over his councils; your former administration made Mr. Wilkes an alderman of London and representative of Middlesex; your next appearance in office is marked with his election to the shrievalty; in whatever measure you are concerned, you are not only disappointed of success, but always contrive to make the government of the best of princes contemptible in his own eyes and ridiculous to the whole world. Making all due allowance for the effect of the minister's declared interposition, Mr. Robinson's activity‡, and Mr

* Poet-laureate of the day.

† From the continent, over a part of which he had been for some time travelling.

‡ Junius was charged by the writers of the day, as well as by a more recent opponent, with having "debased his pretensions to greatness by engaging unsuccessfully *in city politics*." He, however, does not appear to have been the only unsuccessful politician who had plunged into the mire of London politics, as the following letter from that celebrated character, Jack Robinson, written during the election of sheriffs of London, will evince:—

" Mr. Robinson presents his compliments to Mr. Smith. Mr. Harley

Horne's new zeal in support of administration*, we still want the genius of the Duke of Grafton to account for committing the whole interest of government in the city to the conduct of Mr. Harley.   I will not bear hard upon your faithful friend and emissary, Mr. Touchet, for I know the difficulties of his situation, and that a few lottery tickets are of use to his economy.   There is a proverb concerning persons in the predicament of this gentleman, which, however, cannot be strictly applied to him : *they commence dupes and finish knaves.*

meets his ward publicly to day, to support Aldermen Plumbe and Kirkman. The friends of government will be very active, and it is earnestly desired that you will exert yourself to the utmost of your power to support those aldermen.   It is thought it will be very advantageous to push the poll to day with as many friends as possible, therefore it is desired that you will pursue that conduct.   Mr. Harley will be early in the city today, and to be heard of at his counting-house in Bridge Yard, Bucklersbury, and if you, or such person as you intrust in this matter, could see him to consult thereon, it might be beneficial to the cause.

" Tuesday Morning, 25th of June, 1771, six o'clock.

J. Robinson."

" To Benj. Smith, Esq."

This letter, intended for Mr. Benjamin Smith, the partner of Mr. Alderman Nash, of Cannon Street, was, through the mistake of the messenger, delivered to Mr. Smith of Budge Row, who published it, together with an affidavit as to its verity, which had such an effect on the election, that Mr. Bull, who at the time was fourth on the poll, was ultimately returned as one of the sheriffs of London, in conjunction with Mr. Wilkes, another of the candidates for that important office.

* Mr. Horne (the celebrated Horne Tooke of a later period), had long zealously fought on the side of the staunchest Whigs, and was an active member of the society for the support of the Bill of Rights which had just discharged Wilkes's debts.   Alderman Oliver, who had also been as zealous an advocate on the same side, and had suffered himself to be committed with the lord mayor to the Tower, in support of his principles, for some reason or other became at this time jealous of the popularity of Wilkes, affected to rival him, and refused to serve in the office of sheriff if Wilkes were allowed to be his colleague.   Horne joined with Townshend, and the society for the support of the Bill of Rights became divided into two grand parties.

Wilkes united with Alderman Bull in proposing himself for the shrievalty, and in the contest that ensued between them with Oliver Kirkman, and Plumbe, obtained a large majority both for himself and his colleague, leaving Oliver, though supported by all the efforts of Horne, the lowest on the poll.

It was in consequence of the conduct thus pursued by Horne, and which was fatal to the popular cause, that Junius chose to represent him as bribed by the ministry.

Now, Mr. Touchet's character is uniform I am convinced that his sentiments never depended upon his circumstances, and that, in the most prosperous state of his fortune, he was always the very man he is at present; but was there no other person of rank and consequence in the city whom government could confide in but a notorious Jacobite? Did you imagine that the whole body of the dissenters *, that the whole Whig interest of London would attend at a levee, and submit to the directions of a notorious Jacobite? Was there no Whig magistrate in the city to whom the servants of George the Third could intrust the management of a business so very interesting to their master as the election of sheriffs? Is there no room at St. James's but for Scotchmen and Jacobites? My Lord, I do not mean to question the sincerity of Mr. Harley's attachment to his Majesty's government. Since the commencement of the present reign I have seen still greater contradictions reconciled. The principles of these worthy Jacobites are not so absurd as they have been represented; their ideas of divine right are not so much annexed to the person or family as to the political character of the sovereign. Had there ever been an honest man among the *Stuarts*, his Majesty's present friends would have been Whigs upon principle. But the conversion of the best of princes has removed their scruples. They have forgiven him the sins of his Hanoverian ancestors, and acknowledge the hand of Providence in the descent of the crown upon the head of a true *Stuart*. In you, my Lord, they also behold, with a kind of predilection which borders upon loyalty, the natural representative of that illustrious family. The mode of your descent from Charles the Second is only a bar to your pretensions to the crown, and no way interrupts the regularity of your succession to all the virtues of the *Stuarts*.

The unfortunate success of the Rev. Mr. Horne's endeavours in support of the ministerial nomination of sheriffs, will, I fear, obstruct his preferment. Permit me to recommend him to your Grace's protection; you will find him copiously gifted with those qualities of the heart which usually direct you in the choice of your friendships. He, too, was

---

* The family of the Harleys were originally dissenters, and the allusion is to this fact.

Mr Wilkes's friend, and as incapable as you are of the liberal
resentment of a gentleman. No, my Lord, it was the solitary,
vindictive malice of a monk, brooding over the infirmities of
his friend, until he thought they quickened into public life,
and feasting with a rancorous rapture upon the sordid catalogue of his distresses*. Now let him go back to his cloister,
—the church is a proper retreat for him; in his principles
he is already a bishop.

The mention of this man has moved me from my natural
moderation. Let me return to your Grace. You are the
pillow upon which I am determined to rest all my resentments.
What idea can the best of sovereigns form to himself of his
own government? In what repute can he conceive that he
stands with his people, when he sees, beyond the possibility
of a doubt, that, whatever be the office, the suspicion of his
favour is fatal to the candidate, and that when the party he
wishes well to has the fairest prospect of success, if his royal
inclination should unfortunately be discovered, it drops like
an acid, and turns the election. This event, among others,
may perhaps contribute to open his Majesty's eyes to his real
honour and interest. In spite of all your Grace's ingenuity,
he may at last perceive the inconvenience of selecting, with
such a curious felicity, every villain in the nation to fill the
various departments of his government. Yet I should be
sorry to confine him in the choice either of his footmen or his
friends.

JUNIUS.

LETTER LI.

FROM THE REVEREND MR. HORNE TO JUNIUS.

SIR, July 13, 1771.
Farce, Comedy, and *Tragedy*—*Wilkes, Foote,* and *Junius*†—
united at the same time against one poor parson, are fearful

* See note to Letter 52, *post,* p. 365.
† In consequence of his defection from the Whigs, Mr. Horne had lost
his popularity; upon which reverse Foote, the great mimic and farce writer,
ventured to caricature Horne's negligence of dress on the stage. While Mr.
Horne pretends to tremble beneath the *comic* efforts of Foote and the *tragic*
efforts of Junius, he still wishes the world to regard Wilkes's opposition to him
is a mere *farce.*

cdds; the two former are ouly labouring in their vocation, and may equally plead, in excuse, that their aim is a livelihood. I admit the plea for the *second*—his is an honest calling, and my clothes were lawful game; but I cannot so readily approve Mr. Wilkes, or commend him for making patriotism a trade, and a fraudulent trade.   But what shall I say to Junius ? the grave, the solemn, the didactic !   Ridicule, indeed, has been ridiculously called the test of truth; but surely to confess that you lose your *natural moderation* when mention is made of the man, does not promise much truth or justice when you speak of him yourself.

You charge me with " a new zeal in support of administration," and with " endeavours in support of the ministerial nomination of sheriffs."   The reputation which your talents have deservedly gained to the signature of Junius, draws from me a reply which I disdained to give to the anonymous lies of Mr. Wilkes.   You make frequent use of the word *gentleman*, I only call myself a *man*, and desire no other distinction; if you are either, you are bound to make good your charges, or to confess that you have done me a hasty injustice upon no authority.

I put the matter fairly to issue.   I say, that so far from any new " zeal in support of administration," I am possessed with the utmost abhorrence of their measures; and that I have ever shown myself, and am still ready, in any rational manner, to lay down all I have—my life—in opposition to those measures.   I say, that I have not, and never have had, any communication or connection of any kind, directly or indirectly, with any courtier or ministerial man, or any of their adherents; that I never have received, or solicited, or expected, or desired, or do now hope for, any reward of any sort, from any party or set of men in administration or opposition; I say, that I never used any " endeavours in support of the ministerial nomination of sheriffs."   That I did not solicit any one liveryman for his vote for any one of the candidates, nor employ any other person to solicit; and that I did not write one single line or word in favour of Messrs. Plumbe and Kirkman*, whom I understand to have been supported by the ministry.

* Plumbe and Kirkman were the real government candidates for the shrievalty.   Oliver stood alone.   Yet Junius, availing himself of this last

You are bound to refute what I here advance, or to lose your credit for veracity : you must produce facts; surmise and general abuse, in however elegant language, ought not to pass for proofs; you have every advantage, and I have every disadvantage; you are unknown, I give my name; all parties both in and out of administration have their reasons (which I shall relate hereafter) for uniting in their wishes against me; and the popular prejudice is as strongly in your favour as it is violent against the parson *.

gentleman's opposition to Wilkes, was shrewdly desirous of impressing on the world an idea that they had all been supported by government with a view of throwing out Wilkes and his avowed colleague Bull.

* This paragraph Mr. Horne was accused of borrowing from Mr. Hugh Kelly, author of *False Delicacy*, and several other dramatic pieces, as will appear from the following letter addressed to that gentleman :—

For the Public Advertiser.

TO THE REV. MR. HORNE.

SIR,   *July 20th*, 1771.

Happening to be at a distance from London, your letter to Junius did not fall into my hands till yesterday, when I confess I read it with equal astonishment and indignation; and, though it may be inconsistent with the generosity of an Englishman to strike the *fallen*, there is something so peculiarly unmanly in your conduct, that it is impossible to let you escape without some *memorandums* of your judgment when the case *is*, and when the case *is not* your own.

Do you remember, Sir, Friday, April 30, 1771, when you harangued the freeholders for Middlesex for three tedious hours, at the assembly room at Mile End; when you urged random accusations yourself against others, for their supposed connection with government; when you particularly attacked Mr. Kelly as the immediate champion of administration, and affirmed with great pathos that he was employed at the soldier's trial at Guildford to vindicate the wanton effusion of innocent blood ?

I have no connection with Mr. Kelly, Sir, nor do I by any means profess myself of his political faith; but if fame says true, he has been no apostate to his principles; has betrayed no friendship; and I introduce him solely here, that the world may see how conformable the tenor of Mr. Horne's conduct is to the candour of his professions. The following, Sir, is your speech relative to the Guildford affair :

" It is necessary to give you an account of Maclean's trial, because the judge forbad it being taken down by any one, *except it was government*. It has never been published. A very false account of this trial has indeed been published by Mr. Kelly, who was *paid* and *brought* down to Guildford for that *purpose*, and who had lodgings taken for him there, and who was familiarly conversant with a gentleman, whose name I shall not mention now, lest it should seem to proceed from resentment in me for an account I have to settle with him next week. However, one circumstance I ought to tell you, this gentleman was foreman of the grand jury."

Singular as my present situation is, it is neither painful, nor was it unforeseen. He is not fit for public business who does not, even at his entrance, prepare his mind for such an event. Health, fortune, tranquillity, and private connections I have sacrificed upon the altar of the public; and the only return I receive, because I will not concur to dupe and mislead a senseless multitude, is barely that they have not yet torn me in pieces ; that this has been the only return is my pride, and a source of more real satisfaction than honours or prosperity I can practise before I am old the lessons I learned in my youth, nor shall I ever forget the words of my ancient monitor *,

> " ' Tis the last key-stone
> That makes the arch : the rest that there were put,
> Are nothing till that comes to bind and shut.
> Then stands it a triumphal mark ! then men
> Observe the strength, the height, the why and when
> It was erected ; and still walking under,
> Meet some new matter to look up at and wonder !"

JOHN HORNE.

" Mr. Kelly, in the address prefixed to his play, which you and other advocates for the *freedom* of the press so basely drove from the theatre, after saying some civil things relative to the character which he had heard of your disposition, and which your perfidy to that true friend of the constitution, Mr. Wilkes, has clearly proved you never merited, thus expresses himself:

" ' But though Mr. Kelly readily makes this concession in favour of Mr. Horne's private character, he must observe that the constitution of this country, for the purity of which Mr. Horne is so strenuous an advocate, does not allow the mere *belief* of any man to be *positive* evidence; nor compliment his simple *conjecture* with the force of a *fact.* For this reason Mr. Horne should be extremely cautious how he asserts anything to the prejudice of another's reputation. *Hearsay* authority is not enough for this purpose; he should know of his own *knowledge* what he asserts upon his own *word ;* and be certain in his *proof* where he is peremptory in his *accusation.*'

" Honestly, now, Mr. Horne, had you not this paragraph either in your head, or your heart, at the time you were writing the following passage to Junius ?

' You are bound to *refute,*' &c. "WHIPCORD."

To this letter Mr. Horne did not return any answer.

* B. Jonson, of whose writings Mr. Horne Tooke was remarkably fond. The *Sad Shepherd* of that author is called his favourite poem in the " Diversions of Purley." The present quotation is from his Underwoods : *vide* an epistle to Sir Edward Sackville, now Earl of Dorset. Folio, 1692, p. 553.

LETTER LII.

TO THE REVEREND MR. HORNE.

SIR,   July 24, 1771.

I CANNOT descend to an altercation with you in the newspapers. But since I have attacked your character, and you
complain of injustice, I think you have some right to an
explanation. You defy me to prove that you ever solicited a
vote, or wrote a word in support of the ministerial aldermen.
Sir, I did never suspect you of such gross folly. It would
have been impossible for Mr. Horne to have solicited votes,
and very difficult to have written for the newspapers in
defence of that cause, without being detected and brought to
shame.   Neither do I pretend to any intelligence concerning
you, or to know more of your conduct than you yourself have
thought proper to communicate to the public. It is from
your own letters I conclude that you have sold yourself to
the ministry*; or, if that charge is too severe, and supposing
it possible to be deceived by appearances so very strongly
against you, what are your friends to say in your defence?
Must they not confess that, to gratify your personal hatred of
Mr. Wilkes, you sacrificed, as far as depended upon *your*
interest and abilities, the cause of the country?   I can make
allowance for the violence of the passions, and, if ever I
should be convinced that you had no motive but to destroy
Wilkes, I shall then be ready to do justice to your character,
and to declare to the world, that I despise you somewhat less
than I do at present. But, as a public man, I must for ever
condemn you. You cannot but know, nay, you dare not pretend to be ignorant, that the highest gratification of which
the most detestable ——— in this nation is capable would
have been the defeat of Wilkes. I know *that man* much
better than any of you. Nature intended him only for a
good-humoured fool. A systematical education, with long
practice, has made him a consummate hypocrite. Yet this
man, to say nothing of his worthy ministers, you have most
assiduously laboured to gratify. To exclude Wilkes, it was

---

* The letters written by Mr. Horne in the dispute with Mr. Wilkes. See
the subsequent note as well as one appended to Private Letter, No. 35.

not necessary you should solicit votes for his opponents. We incline the balance as effectually by lessening the weight in one scale as by increasing it in the other.

The mode of your attack upon Wilkes (though I am far from thinking meanly of your abilities) convinces me, that you either want judgment extremely, or that you are blinded by your resentment. You ought to have foreseen that the charges you urged against Wilkes could never do him any mischief. After all, when we expected discoveries highly interesting to the community, what a pitiful detail did it end in! Some old clothes—a Welch pony—a French footman, and a hamper of claret*. Indeed, Mr. Horne, the

---

* The facts here alluded to were as follow :—The late Mr. Tooke, then Mr. Horne, while travelling on the continent was introduced to Mr. Wilkes, at that time resident in Paris, which led to a subsequent intimacy, and apparently warm friendship. Mr. Horne, on leaving that gay metropolis, left behind him, in the care of Mr. Wilkes, several suits of clothes of the most fashionable Parisian manufacture, being ill adapted to the clerical profession, as well as ill calculated to please the taste or suit the manners of the people of this country. In a political quarrel which occurred between these gentlemen, shortly previous to the date of this letter, and which was the subject of a long and acrimonious altercation in the *Public Advertiser*, Mr. Horne accused Mr. Wilkes with having, in the midst of his distress, pawned the clothes intrusted to his custody ; with commissioning Mr. Horne's brother-in-law to purchase a pony which he never paid for ; with drinking claret while detained in the King's Bench prison ; with endeavouring to make his brother chamberlain of London ; and with retaining in his service six domestics, three of whom were French. As these, with several other charges, were detailed to the public by Mr. Horne in thirteen or fourteen very long letters, the editor will not here transcribe them, but content himself with inserting several detached parts of Mr. Wilkes's defence against these accusations, as they contain some curious facts, and are illustrative of the subject more particularly adverted to in the text by the author.

For the Public Advertiser.

TO THE REV. MR. HORNE.

SIR, *Prince's Court, Saturday, May 18.*

Your *first* letter of May 14, told me that you " blamed my public conduct," and " would not open any account with me on the score of private character." A *third* letter is this day addressed to me. Not a word hitherto " of my public conduct," but many false and malignant attacks about Mr. Wildman, your brother-in-law, who formerly kept the Bedford Head, in Southampton Street, Covent Garden, and your *old clothes*. The public will impute the impertinence of such a dispute to its author, and pardon my calling their attention for a few moments to scenes of so trifling a nature, because it is in justification of an innocent man.

When you left Paris in May 1767, you desired me to take care of

public should, and *will*, forgive him his claret and his footmen, and even the ambition of making his brother chamberlain of London, as long as he stands forth against a ministry

your *old clothes*, for you meant to return in a few months, and they could be
of no use to you in England.   The morning of your departure you sent me
the following letter :
    " Dear Sir,
    " According to your permission I leave with you
            1 suit of scarlet and gold ⎱ cloth.
            1 suit of white and silver ⎰ cloth.
            1 suit of blue and silver——camblet.
            1 suit of flowered silk.
            1 suit of black silk.
    And 1 black velvet surtout.
    " If you have any fellow-feeling you cannot but be kind to them ; since they
too, as well as yourself, are outlawed in England ; and on the same account
—their superior worth.
                        " I am, Dear Sir,
                            " Your very Affectionate,
                                " Humble Servant,
    " Paris, *May* 25, 1767."   " JOHN HORNE."

    This letter I returned to you at the King's Bench, and at the bottom of it
the following memorandum in my own hand-writing : " Nov. 21, 1767, sent
to Mr. Panchaud's in the Rue St. Sauveur."   I left Paris Nov. 22, 1767,
and therefore thought it proper the day before to send your clothes *where* I
was sure they would be perfectly safe, to Mr. Panchaud's, the great English banker's.   They remained in my house, Rue des Saint Peres, only from
May till the November following, nor was any demand, or request, made to
me about them by Mr. Wildman, or any one else.   You are forced to own " I
have received a letter within the last three months from Mr. Panchaud, in-
forming me that they (*the clothes*) have *long* been in his possession."   Examine
the banker's books.   You will find the date is Nov. 21, 1767.   You say,
" for my own part I never made the least inquiry after my clothes."   I suppose for the plainest reason in the world.   You knew where they were,
and that they could be no part of a clergyman's dress in England, but
that you were sure of so *rich a wardrobe* on your next tour to France or
Italy, as Paris would probably be your route.   This is all I know of the
vestimenta pretiosa of *Eutrapelus*.   I hope, Sir, the putting them on
will not have the same effect on you as they formerly had on his acquaintance.

            Cum *pulchris tunicis* sumet nova consilia et spes ;
            Dormiet in lucem ; *scorto* postponet honestum
            Officium ; *nummos alienos* pascet.

    Your charge about your brother-in-law, Mr. Wildman, is equally unjust.
When I was in England, in October, 1766, I lodged at Mr. Wildman's house
in Argyle Buildings, on his own most pressing invitation.   I had long known
him, and for several years belonged to a club which met once a week at the

and parliament who are doing everything they can to enslave the country. and as long as he is a thorn in the king's side. You will not suspect me of setting up *Wilkes* for a perfect cha-

Bedford Head. Mr. Wildman desired to be considered at this time as the warm partisan of Mr. Wilkes. He begged that he might be useful as far as he could to me and my friends. I asked him to buy a little Welch horse for a lady in France, to whom I was desirous of paying a compliment. I fixed the price, and insisted on paying him at that very time, which I did. About a year afterwards Mr. Wildman fulfilled my commission, purchased me a Welch pony, and sent it to Calais. This was the single transaction of my own with your brother-in-law at that time. I gave him two or three trifling commissions from Monsieur *Saint Foy* for arrack, &c., which were to be forwarded to Paris. I believe they were sent, but they never passed through my hands, nor do I know whether Mr. Wildman has yet been paid for those trifles, the whole of which amounted only, as he told me, to about thirty pounds.

Your endeavours to create a coolness between Mr. Cotes and me are clearly seen through, and will prove ineffectual. You made the same attempt on the late Mr. Sterne and me with the same success. In your letter to me at Paris, dated Jan. 3, 1766, you say, "I passed a week with Sterne at Lyons, and am to meet him again at Sienna in the summer. Forgive my question, and do not answer it if it is impertinent. Is there any cause of coldness between you and Sterne; he speaks very handsomely of you, when it is absolutely necessary to speak at all; but not with that *warmth and enthusiasm* that I expect from every one that knows you. Do not let me cause a coldness between you if there is none. I am sensible my question is at least imprudent, and my jealousy blameable."

In your second letter you say, "the nature of our *intercourse*, for it cannot be called a *connection*," and afterwards, "in my return from Italy to England in the year 1767, I saw reasons sufficient *never more to trust you with a single line;*" and in your third letter you pretend that you had even in 1767, "infinite contempt for the very name of Mr. Wilkes." However, on the 17th of last May, you write me another letter on my going to Fulham, while my house here was repairing, to recommend *six* tradesmen to me, to tell me how *most sincerely* you were mine, &c. You add, "I could not forbear showing my *friendship* to you by letting you know your friends." You will find, Sir, that it requires more memory as well as wit than falls to one man's share, to support a long chain of falsehoods. You are lost and bewildered in the intricacies of error. The path of truth you would find more easy and honourable.

You assert "I found that all the private letters of your friends were regularly pasted in a book, and read over indiscriminately, not only to your friends and acquaintance, but to every visitor." I glory, Sir, in having four large volumes of manuscript letters, many of them written by the first men of this age. I esteem them my most valuable possession. Why is the pleasure of an elegant and instructive epistle to perish with the hour it is received? To the care and attention of Cicero's friends in preserving that great Roman's letters we owe the best history of Rome for a most interesting

racter. The question to the public is, where shall we find a
man who, with purer principles, will go the lengths and run

period of about forty years. You mistake when you talk of *all the private
letters of your friends.* My care has extended only to letters of particular
friends on particular occasions, or to letters of business, taste, or literature.
The originals of such I have preserved; never any copies of my own letters,
unless when I wrote to a secretary of state, to a Talbot, a Martin, or a Horne.
When you add, "that they are read over indiscriminately, not only to your
friends and acquaintance, but to every visitor," you knowingly advance a
falsehood. So much of your time has passed with me that you are sensible very few of my friends have ever heard of the volumes I mentioned.
The preservation of a letter is surely a compliment to the writer. But,
although I approve the preservation in general, I highly disapprove the publication of any private letters. However, there are cases which justly call
them forth to light. Mr. Onslow's first letter was after great importunity
from you printed by me, to justify what you had said at Epsom. The
second you printed, without my consent, from a copy I suffered you
to take.

The *pamphlet* you mention has *not yet been published.* I have now before
me the copy, corrected with your own hand, which you gave me at Paris.
The following passage I am sure you will read at this time with particular
satisfaction, and I reserve it for you, *pour la bonne bouche.*

"We have seen, by *Mr. Wilkes's* treatment, that no man who is not, and
who has not always been, absolutely perfect himself, must dare to arraign the
measures of a minister.

"It is not sufficient that he pay an inviolable regard to the laws;
that he be a man of the strictest and most unimpeached honour; that he be
endowed with superior abilities and qualifications; that he be blessed with a
benevolent, generous, noble, free soul; that he be inflexible, incorruptible,
and brave; that he prefer infinitely the public welfare to his own interest,
peace, and safety; that his life be ever in his hand, ready to be laid down
cheerfully for the liberty of his country; and that he be dauntless and unwearied in her service. All this avails him nothing.

"If it can be proved (though by the base means of *treachery* and *theft*)
that in some unguarded, wanton hour, he has uttered an indecent word or
penned a loose expression—away with such a fellow from the earth—it is not
fit that he should live."

* * * * *

After a variety of accusations of *private* crimes, you effect to cover the
whole with the veil of *hypocrisy.* You say, "I have mentioned these circumstances not as any charges against you, though no doubt they will
operate as such." Had your turn, Sir, been to divinity, in the subtleties of
the schools you would have outshone Thomas Aquinas or Duns Scotus, in
treachery even the priest *Malagrida.*

You have in your late letters to me accused me of almost *every crime,*
of which the most diabolical heart is capable. When you wrote the letters
to Sir William Beauchamp Proctor, I had only *one crime,* of which I own I
have not repented. "Mr. Wilkes's crime is well known to have been his
opposing and exposing the measures of *Lord Bute.*

the hazards that he has done? the season calls for such a
man, and he ought to be supported. What would have been

"The two Humes, Johnson, Murphy, Ralph, Smollett, Shebbeare, &c.,
&c., all authors pensioned, or promised, had been let loose on him in vain.
The lord steward of his Majesty's household (who has *therefore* continued
in that post through every revolution of ministry), and the treasurer to
the Princess Dowager of Wales (who together with that office has a pension
for himself and a reversion for his son), had separately endeavoured to commit a murder on his body, with as little success as *others had attempted his
reputation ;* for they found him *tam Marte quam Mercurio.*

"The intended assassination of him by *Forbes* and *Dun* had miscarried.

"The secretaries of state had seized his papers, and confined his person to close imprisonment. They had trifled with and eluded the Habeas
Corpus. But still *he rose superior to them all, and baffled alone the insati-
able malice of all his persecutors ;* for though they had in a manner ruined
his private fortunes, *his public character remained entire.* They had spilt
his blood indeed ; but they had not taken his life, and with it still were left

'The unconquerable mind, and freedom's holy flame.'

It remained then to make one general attack upon him at once of every
power of the state, each in its separate capacity. The reverend name of
Majesty itself was misapplied to this business. The House of Lords, the
House of Commons, and the Court of King's Bench, through the little agency
of Carrington, Kidgell, Curry, Webb, Faden, Sandwich, make one general
assault."

* * * * * *

As you mentioned a promise you had obtained of being one of the *chaplains to his Majesty,* I shall conclude my present extracts with the following
passage which will show how peculiarly fitted you are to be a *domestic
chaplain* to our *present sovereign.*

"Sheridan is at Blois *by order of his Majesty,* and with a pension, invent-
ing a method to give the proper pronunciation of the English language to
strangers, by means of sounds borrowed from their own. And he begins
with the French.

"I remember a few years ago when an attempt was made to prove Lord
Harborough an *idiot.* The counsel on both sides produced the same instance ;
one of his wit, the other of his folly. His servants were puzzled once to un-
pack a large box, and his lordship advised them to do with it as they did
with oysters—put it in the fire, and it would gape.

"This commission of Sheridan appears to me equally equivocal. And
should *a similar statute be at any time attempted against his Majesty,* they
who do not know him may be apt to suspect that he employed Sheridan in
this manner, not so much for the sake of foreigners as of his own subjects,
and had permitted him to amuse himself abroad, to prevent his spoiling our
pronunciation at home."

* * * * * *

Am I to answer your impertinence about claret and French servants? It
shall be in one word. I have not purchased a bottle of claret since I
left the King's Bench. Only two French servants are in my family. As

the triumph of that odious hypocrite and his minions, if
Wilkes had been defeated! It was not *your* fault, reverend
Sir, that he did not enjoy it completely. But now, I promise

old woman who has many years attended my daughter, and a footman, whom
I esteem, as I have often told you, not as a Frenchman, but for his *singular
fidelity* to an Englishman during a course of several years when I had the
honour of being exiled. I have reason to believe that from hence originated
your hatred to him.

* * * * * *

You assert " though I knew not the person of any one man in opposition,
I quitted all my friends and connections when I joined the public cause ;
and with my eyes open, exchanged ease and fair fame for labour and reproach." I desire to know what one friend, and what single connection you
have quitted for the public cause. Your *fair fame* at Eaton and Cambridge survived a very short time your abode at either of these places. Will
you call an Italian gentleman now in town, your confident during your
whole residence at *Genoa*, to testify the morality of your conduct in Italy ?
But I will not write the life of Jonathan Wild, nor of Orator Henley.

You declare " *ministerial and court favour* I know I can never have, and
for *public favour* I will never be a candidate. I chose to tell them that, as
far as it affects myself, *I laugh at the displeasure of both.*" You well
know that no minister will ever dare *openly* to give you any mark of *court
favour*, at least in the *church ;* many *secret favours* you may, you do expect,
and some I believe actually receive. The *public* you have abandoned in
despair, after an assiduous courtship of near four years, but remember,
Sir, when you say, that *you laugh at their displeasure*, the force of truth
has extorted even from Lord Mansfield the following declaration : " The people
are almost always in the right. The great may sometimes be in the wrong,
but the body of the people are always in the right."

* * * * *

In your *first* letter you declare " it is necessary to give a short history of
the *commencement*, progress, and conclusion of the intercourse between us."
In your *second* you say " The nature of our intercourse (for it cannot be called
a connection), will best appear from the *situation* of each of us at its *commencement.*" Your *situation* shall be explained by yourself from the words
of the first letter you ever wrote to me.

" You are entering into a correspondence with a *parson*, and I am a little
apprehensive lest that title should disgust you ; but give me leave to assure
you I am not ordained a hypocrite.

" It is true I have suffered the infectious hand of a bishop to be waved
over me, whose imposition, like the sop given to Judas, is only a signal for
the devil to enter. It is true that usually at that touch——fugiunt pudor,
verumque, fidesque. ' In quorum sobeunt locum fraudes, dolique, insidiæque,
&c., &c., but I hope I have escaped the contagion : and if I have not, if you
should at any time discover the BLACK spot under the tongue, assist me
kindly to conquer the prejudices of education and profession."

                                            I am, Sir, &c.,
                                                JOHN WILKES.

you, you have so little power to do mischief, that I much question whether the ministry will adhere to the promises they have made you. It will be in vain to say that *I* am a partisan of Mr. Wilkes, or personally *your* enemy. You will convince no man, for you do not believe it yourself. Yet, I confess, I am a little offended at the low rate at which you seem to value my understanding. I beg, Mr. Horne, you will hereafter believe that I measure the integrity of men by their conduct, not by their professions. Such tales may entertain Mr. Oliver or your grandmother, but, trust me, they are thrown away upon Junius.

You say you are a *man*. Was it generous, was it manly, repeatedly to introduce into a newspaper the name of a young lady*, with whom you must heretofore have lived on terms of politeness and good humour? But I have done with you. In *my* opinion your credit is irrecoverably ruined. Mr. Townshend, I think, is nearly in the same predicament. Poor Oliver has been shamefully duped by you. You have made him sacrifice all the honour he got by his imprisonment. As for Mr. Sawbridge†, whose character I really respect, I am astonished he does not see through your duplicity. Never was so base a design so poorly conducted. This letter, you see, is not intended for the public; but if you think it will do you any service, you are at liberty to publish it.

JUNIUS‡.

---

* Horne had taken liberties with the name of Miss Wilkes in his public letters in some of the newspapers—and liberties which no misconduct of hers had entitled him to take.

† Townshend and Sawbridge had been persuaded by Horne to unite in supporting Oliver against Wilkes; and both, in consequence hereof, forfeited much of their popularity from this moment, and were accused of gross want of understanding, and by some of tergiversation.

‡ This letter was transmitted privately by the printer to Mr. Horne, by Junius's request. Mr. Horne returned it to the printer with directions to publish it.—JUNIUS.

The reason for such private transmission was, that it was not Junius's wish to increase those divisions which Horne and Oliver had so unwisely provoked in the Bill of Rights Society by an open contest between himself and any one of its members.

B B 2

LETTER LIII.

FROM THE REVEREND MR. HORNE TO JUNIUS.

SIR,   July 31, 1771.

You have disappointed me. When I told you that surmise
and general abuse, in however elegant language, ought not
to pass for proofs, I evidently hinted at the reply which I
expected; but you have dropped your usual elegance, and
seem willing to try what will be the effect of surmise and
general abuse in very coarse language. Your answer to my
letter (which, I hope, was cool and temperate and modest),
has convinced me that my idea of a *man* is superior to yours
of a *gentleman*. Of your former letters I have always said
materiem superabat opus: I do not think so of the present;
the principles are more detestable than the expressions are
mean and illiberal. I am contented that all those who adopt
the one should for ever load me with the other.

I appeal to the common sense of the public, to which I
have ever directed myself. I believe they have it; though
I am sometimes half inclined to suspect that Mr. Wilkes
has formed a truer judgment of mankind than I have.
However, of this I am sure, that there is nothing else upon
which to place a steady reliance. Trick and low cunning,
and addressing their prejudices and passions, may be the
fittest means to carry a particular point; but if they have
not common sense, there is no prospect of gaining for them
any real permanent good. The same passions which have
been artfully used by an honest man for their advantage,
may be more artfully employed by a dishonest man for their
destruction. I desire them to apply their common sense to
this letter of Junius, not for my sake, but their own; it
concerns them most nearly, for the principles it contains lead
to disgrace and ruin, and are inconsistent with every notion of
civil society.

The charges which Junius has brought against me are
made ridiculous by his own inconsistency and self-contradic-
tion. He charges me positively with "a new zeal in support
of administration;" and with "endeavours in support of the
ministerial nomination of sheriffs." And he assigns two

inconsistent motives for my conduct; either that I have
"*sold* myself to the ministry," or am instigated "by the
solitary vindictive *malice* of a monk;" either that I am influenced by a sordid desire of *gain*, or am hurried on by "personal *hatred* and blinded by *resentment*." In his letter to
the Duke of Grafton he supposes me actuated by both; in
his letter to me he at first doubts which of the two, whether
interest or revenge is my motive; however, at last he determines for the former, and again positively asserts that "the
ministry have made me promises;" yet he produces no instance of corruption, nor pretends to have any intelligence
of a ministerial connection: he mentions no *cause* of personal hatred to Mr. Wilkes, nor any *reason* for my resentment
or revenge; nor has Mr. Wilkes himself ever hinted any,
though repeatedly pressed*.   When Junius is called upon to

---

* In one of the letters addressed to Mr. Wilkes by Mr. Horne, during the
altercation spoken of in the preceding notes, the latter thus explains himself
with respect to his support of the former, as well as to the motives which induced him to withdraw it.   In this extract Mr. Horne also gives a general
and able outline of his political opinions, from which he does not appear to
have materially varied to the day of his death.   "I was your friend only for
the sake of the public cause; that reason does in certain matters remain; as
far as it remains, so far I am still your friend, and therefore, I said in my
first letter, 'the public should know how far they *ought*, and how far they
ought not to support you.'   To bring to punishment the great delinquents
who have corrupted the parliament and the seats of justice; who have encouraged, pardoned, and rewarded murder; to heal the breaches made in the
constitution, and by salutary provisions to prevent them for the future; to
replace once more, not the *administration* and *execution*, for which they are
very unfit, but the *checks* of government *really* in the hands of the governed.
   "For these purposes, if it were possible to suppose that the great enemy
of mankind could be rendered instrumental to their happiness, so far the
devil himself should be supported by the people; for a human instrument they should go farther, he should not only be supported but thanked
and rewarded for the good which, perhaps, he did not intend, as an encouragement to others to follow his example.   But if the foul fiend, having
gained their support, should endeavour to delude the weaker part, and entice
them to an idolatrous worship of himself, by persuading them that what he
suggested was their voice, and their voice the voice of God; if he should
attempt to obstruct everything that leads to their security and happiness,
and to promote every wickedness that tends only to his own emolument; if
when the cause—the cause—reverberates on their ears, he should divert
them from the original sound, and direct them towards the opposite unfaithful echo; if confusion should be all his aim, and mischief his sole enjoyment,
would not he act the part of a faithful monitor to the people who should
save them from their snares by reminding them of the true object of their

justify his accusation, he answers " he cannot descend to an
altercation with me in the newspapers." Junius, who *exists*
only in the newspapers, who acknowledges " he has attacked
my character" *there*, and "thinks I have some right to an
explanation ;" yet this Junius "cannot descend to an altercation in the newspapers !" and because he cannot descend to
an altercation with me in the newspapers, he sends a letter of
abuse by the printer, which he finishes by telling me " I am
at liberty to *publish* it." This, to be sure, is a most excellent
method to avoid an altercation in the newspapers !

The *proofs* of his positive charges are as extraordinary.
" He does not pretend to any intelligence concerning me, or

constitutional worship, expressed in those words of holy writ (for to me it is
so) *Rex, Lex loquens ; Lex, Rex mutus.* This is—the cause—the cause. To
make this union indissoluble is the only cause I acknowledge. As far as the
support of Mr. Wilkes tends to this point I am as warm as the warmest.
But all the lines of your projects are drawn towards a different centre—yourself ; and if with a good intention I have been diligent to gain you powers
which may be perverted to mischief, I am bound to be doubly diligent to
prevent their being so employed.

" The diligence I have used for two years past, and the success I have had
in defeating all your shameful schemes, is the true cause of the dissension between us. I have never had any private pique or quarrel with you. It was
your policy in paragraphs and anonymous letters to pretend it, but you cannot
mention any private cause of pique or quarrel.

" To prevent the mischief of division to a popular opposition, those who
saw both your bad intentions and your actions were silent ; and whilst they
defeated all your projects, they were cautious to conceal your defects. They
studied so much the more to satisfy your voracious prodigality, and thought,
as I should have done if a minister, that if feeding it would keep you from
mischief, a few thousands would be well employed by the public for that
purpose. But I can never, merely for the sake of strengthening opposition, join in those actions which would prevent all the good effects to be
hoped for from opposition, and for the sake of which alone any opposition to government can be justifiable. Such a practice would very well
suit those who wish a change of ministers. For my part I wish no such
thing ; bad as the present are, I am afraid the next will not be better, though
I am sure they cannot be worse, I care not under whose administration good
comes. But the people must owe it to themselves, nor ought they to receive
the restoration of their rights as a favour from any set of men, minister, or
king. The moment they accept it as a grant, a favour, an act of grace, the
people have not the prospect of a right left. They will from that time become like the mere possessors of an estate without a title, and of which they
may be dispossessed at pleasure. If the people are not powerful enough to make
a bad administration or a bad king do them justice, they will not often have
a good one. Would to God the time were come, which I am afraid is very
distant beyond the period of my life, when an honest man could not be in

to know more of my conduct than I myself have thought proper to communicate to the public." He does not suspect me of such gross folly as to have solicited votes, or to have written anonymously in the newspapers; because it is impossible to do either of these without being detected and brought to shame. Junius says this! Who yet imagines that he has himself written two years under that signature (and more under *others*) without being detected!—his warmest admirers will not hereafter add, without being brought to shame. But though he did never suspect me of such gross folly as to run the *hazard* of being detected and brought to shame by *anonymous* writing, he insists that I have been

---

opposition! I declare I should rejoice to find the patronage of a minister in the smallest degree my honour and interest. I never have pretended to any more than to prefer the former to the latter. But it is not upon me alone that you have poured forth your abuse, but upon every man of honour who has deserved well of the public. And if you were permitted to proceed without interruption, there would shortly not be found one honest man who would not shudder to deserve well of the people.

"The true reason of our dissension being made public is, that you could not get on a step without it; and you trust that the popularity of your name, and your diligence in paragraphing the papers, will outweigh with the people the most essential services of others; and that you shall get rid of all control by taking away from those who mean well the confidence of the people. If you can once get them affronted by the public whom they have faithfully served, you flatter yourself that disgust will make them retire from a scene where such a man as you are, covered with infamy like yours, has the disposal of honour and disgrace, and the characters of honest men at his mercy.

"JOHN HORNE."

To the second paragraph of this extract Mr. Wilkes makes the following attempt at a reply:—

"I thank you for the entertainment of your sixth letter. The idea of an unfaithful echo, although not quite new and original, is perfectly amusing; but, like Bayes, you love to elevate and surprise. I wish you would give the list of echoes of this kind, which you have heard in your travels through France and Italy. I have read of only one such in a neighbouring kingdom. If you ask, *How do you?* it answers, *Pretty well I thank you.* The sound of your unfaithful echo can only be paralleled by Jack Home's silence with a stilly sound, in the tragedy of Douglas.

'The torrent rushing o'er its pebbly banks,
Infuses silence with a stilly sound.'

"I have heard of the babbling, the mimic, the shrill echo. The discovery of an unfaithful echo was reserved for Mr. Horne. Really, Sir, I should have thought, notwithstanding all your rage, you might have suffered an echo to be faithful. I did not expect novelty or variety, much less infidelity from an echo."

guilty of a much grosser folly—of incurring the certainty of shame and detection by writings *signed* with my name! But this is a small flight for the towering Junius. "He is FAR from thinking meanly of my abilities," though he is 'convinced that I want judgment extremely," and can, "really respect Mr. Sawbridge's character," though he de-clares* him to be so poor a creature as not to be able to "see through the basest design conducted in the poorest manner!" And this most base design is conducted in the poorest manner by a man whom he does not suspect of gross folly, and of whose abilities he is FAR from thinking meanly!

Should we ask Junius to reconcile these contradictions and explain this nonsense, the answer is ready; "he cannot descend to an altercation in the newspapers." He feels no reluctance to attack the character of any man—the throne is not too high nor the cottage too low—his mighty malice can grasp both extremes—he hints not his accusations as *opinion*, *conjecture*, or *inference*, but delivers them as *positive asser-tions*. Do the accused complain of injustice? He acknow-ledges they have some sort of right to an *explanation*; but if they ask for *proofs* and *facts*, he begs to be excused; and though he is nowhere else to be encountered, "he can-not descend to an altercation in the newspapers."

And this, perhaps, Junius may think "the *liberal resent ment of a gentleman*"—this skulking assassination he may call courage. In all things, as in this, I hope we differ.

> " I thought that fortitude had been a mean
> 'Twixt fear and rashness; not a lust obscene,
> Or appetite of offending; but a skill
> And nice discernment between good and ill.

* I beg leave to introduce Mr. Horne to the character of the *Double Dealer*. I thought they had been better acquainted.—" Another very wrong objec-tion has been made by some, who have not taken leisure to distinguish the characters. The hero of the play (meaning *Mellefont*) is a gull, and made a fool, and cheated. Is every man a gull and a fool that is deceived? At that rate I am afraid the two classes of men will be reduced to one, and the knaves themselves be at a loss to justify their title. But if an open, honest-hearted man, who has an entire confidence in one whom he takes to be his friend, and who (to confirm him in his opinion) in all appearance and upon several trials has been so; if this man be deceived by the treachery of the other, must he of necessity commence fool immediately, only because the other has proved a villain?"—YES, says parson *Horne*. No, says *Congreve*, and he, I think, is allowed to have known something of human nature.—JUNIUS.

Her ends are honesty and public good,
And without these she is not understood." *

Of two things, however, he has condescended to give proof.
He very properly produces a *young lady*, to prove that I am
not a man ; and a good *old woman*, my grandmother, to
prove Mr. Oliver a fool. Poor old soul ! she read her Bible
far otherwise than Junius ! she often found there that the
sins of the fathers had been visited on the children ; and
therefore was cautious that herself and her immediate descendants should leave no reproach on her posterity ; and
they left none. How little could she foresee this reverse of
Junius, who visits my political sins upon my *grandmother !*
I do not charge this to the score of malice in him,—it proceeded entirely from his propensity to blunder,—that whilst
he was reproaching me for introducing in the most harmless
manner the name of *one* female, he might himself, at the
same instant, introduce *two*.

I am represented alternately, as it suits Junius's purpose,
under the opposite characters of a *gloomy monk*, and a man
of *politeness and good humour*. I am called " *a solitary
monk*," in order to confirm the notion given of me in
Mr. Wilkes's anonymous paragraphs, that I *never laugh ;*
and the terms of *politeness* and *good humour*, on which I am
said to have lived heretofore with the *young lady*, are intended to confirm other paragraphs of Mr. Wilkes, in which
he is supposed to have offended me by *refusing his daughter*.
Ridiculous ! Yet I cannot deny but that Junius has proved
me *unmanly* and *ungenerous* as clearly as he has shown me
corrupt and *vindictive :* and I will tell him more ; I have paid
the present ministry as many *visits* and *compliments* as ever
I paid to the *young lady*, and shall all my life treat them with
the *same politeness and good humour*.

* This quotation is also from the epistle to Sackvile. Mr. Horne here made
some slight alterations : perhaps he quoted from memory. For B. Jonson's
" Or science of a discerning good and ill,"
he prints,
And nice discernment between, &c.
For
" And where they want she is not understood,"
And without these, &c.
One of his alterations disturbs, however astonishing, the grammatical con-
struction : a *skill* between *good* and *ill* is not English.

But Junius "begs me to believe that he measures the integrity of men by their *conduct*, not by their *professions.*" Surely this Junius must imagine his readers as void of understanding as he is of modesty! Where shall we find the standard of HIS integrity? By what are we to measure the *conduct* of this lurking assassin? And he says this to me, whose conduct, wherever I could personally appear, has been as direct and open and public as my words; I have not, like him, concealed myself in my chamber to shoot my arrows out the window; nor contented myself to view the battle from afar, but publicly mixed in the engagement and shared the danger. To whom have I, like him, refused my name upon complaint of injury? what printer have I desired to conceal me? in the infinite variety of business in which I have been concerned, where it is not so easy to be faultless, which of my actions can he arraign? to what danger has any man been exposed to which I have not faced? *information, action, imprisonment,* or *death!* what labour have I refused? what expense have I declined? what pleasure have I not renounced? But Junius, *to whom no conduct belongs,* "measures the integrity of men by their *conduct,* not by their professions;" himself all the while being nothing but *professions,* and those too *anonymous!* the political ignorance or wilful falsehood of this *declaimer* is extreme: his own *former* letters justify both my conduct and those whom his *last* letter abuses; for the public measures, which Junius has been all along defending, were ours, whom he attacks; and the uniform opposer of those measures has been Mr. Wilkes, whose bad actions and intentions he endeavours to screen.

Let Junius now, if he pleases, change his abuse; and, quitting his loose hold of *interest* and *revenge,* accuse me of *vanity,* and call this defence *boasting.* I own I have a pride to see statues decreed, and the highest honours conferred for measures and actions which all men have approved; whilst those who counselled and caused them are execrated and insulted. The darkness in which Junius thinks himself shrouded has not concealed him; nor the artifice of only *attacking under that signature* those he would pull down (whilst he *recommends by other ways* those he would have promoted), disguised from me whose partisan he is. When Lord Chatham can forgive the awkward situation in which

for the sake of the public he was designedly placed by the
thanks to him from the city*; and when *Wilkes's name*
ceases to be necessary to Lord Rockingham to keep up a
clamour against the *persons* of the ministry, without obliging
the different factions now in opposition to bind themselves
beforehand to some certain points, and to stipulate some precise advantages to the public, then, and not till then, may
those whom he now abuses expect the approbation of Junius.
The approbation of the public for our faithful attention to
their interest by endeavours for those stipulations which
have made us as obnoxious to the factions in opposition as to
those in administration, is not perhaps to be expected till
some years hence, when the public will look back and see
how shamefully they have been deluded, and by what arts
they were made to lose the golden opportunity of preventing
what they will surely experience, a change of ministers,
without a *material* change of measures, and without any
security for a tottering constitution.

But what cares Junius for the security of the constitution? He has now unfolded to us his diabolical principles.
As a public man he must ever condemn any measure which
may tend even accidentally to *gratify* the sovereign; and
Mr. Wilkes is to be supported and assisted in all his attempts
(no matter how ridiculous or mischievous his projects) *as long
as he continues to be a thorn in the king's side!* The cause
of the country, it seems, in the opinion of Junius, is merely
to vex the king; and any rascal is to be supported in any
roguery, provided he can only thereby plant *a thorn in the
king's side.* This is the very extremity of faction, and the
last degree of political wickedness. Because Lord Chatham
has been ill-treated by the king, and treacherously betrayed
by the Duke of Grafton, the latter is to be " the pillow on
which Junius will rest his resentment!" and the public are
to oppose the measures of government from mere motives of
personal enmity to the sovereign! These are the avowed
principles of the man who in the same letter says, " if ever
he should be convinced that I had no motive but to destroy
Wilkes, he shall then be ready to do justice to my character,
and to declare to the world that he despises me somewhat

* See note, *post*, p. 384.

less than he does at present!" Had I ever acted from personal affection or enmity to Mr. Wilkes, I should justly be despised; but what does he deserve whose avowed motive is personal enmity to the sovereign? The contempt which I should otherwise feel for the absurdity and glaring inconsistency of Junius is here swallowed up in my abhorrence of his principle. The *right divine* and *sacredness* of kings is to me a senseless jargon. It was thought a daring expression of Oliver Cromwell in the time of Charles the First, that if he found himself placed opposite the king in battle, he would discharge his piece into his bosom as soon as into any other man's. I go farther: had I lived in those days, I would not have waited for chance to give me an opportunity of doing my duty; I would have sought him through the ranks, and, without the least personal enmity, have discharged my piece into his bosom *rather* than into any other man's*. The king

* Mr. Horne was charged with having stolen this idea from a note of Mr. Wilkes, annexed to that passage in Clarendon to which the writer here more particularly alludes. The letter is short, and as it also explains a subsequent fact, it ought not to be omitted.

For the Public Advertiser.

TO THE REV. MR. HORNE.

SIR,   *Aug.* 6, 1771.

You declare in your letter to Junius, that Mr. Wilkes told the Rockingham administration, "it cost me a year and a half to write down the last administration." Unluckily for Mr. Horne the administration said to be wrote down by Mr. Wilkes did not last *one year*, and Mr. Wilkes is certainly too well informed to have made so gross a mistake. Lord Bute was made first commissioner of the treasury, May 29, 1762, and resigned April 8, 1763. The *North Briton* made its first appearance June 5, 1762. The paper war, therefore, did not last quite one year before the enemy abandoned the capital post he had seized. Mr. Horne when he invents, should be careful not to give absurd fictions. I am acquainted both with Mr. Wilkes and Mr. Horne. It is amusing to observe how the parson has, on a variety of occasions, purloined from the alderman. Many of their former common friends have been amused with the instances. The late passage about Cromwell is curious. Mr. Horne says, "it was thought a daring expression of Oliver Cromwell, &c." Mr. Wilkes has probably forgot the little anecdote; but I breakfasted with him at the King's Bench with Mr. Horne, who copied in my presence the following note from Mr. Wilkes's Clarendon, which I likewise preserved :—" Cromwell ought to have declared, that he would rather choose to single out the king, and discharge his pistol upon him, as the first author of the guilt of a civil war, and whose death then might probably extinguish it." The whole passage of Clarendon is so curious, your readers will not be displeased to find it in your paper. " Cromwell, though the greatest dis-

whose actions justify rebellion to his government deserves death from the hand of every subject. And should such a time arrive I shall be as free to act as to say. But till then my attachment to the person and family of the sovereign shall ever be found more zealous and sincere than that of his flatterers. I would offend the sovereign with as much reluctance as the parent; but, if the happiness and security of the whole family made it necessary, so far and no farther I would offend him without remorse.

But let us consider a little whither these principles of Junius would lead us. Should Mr. Wilkes once more commission Mr. Thomas Walpole to procure for him a pension of *one thousand pounds* upon the Irish establishment for thirty years, he must be supported in the demand by the public, because it would mortify the king!

Should he wish to see Lord Rockingham and his friends once more in administration, *unclogged by any stipulations for the people*, that he might again enjoy a *pension of one thousand and forty pounds* a year, viz., from the *first lord of the*

sembler living, always made his hypocrisy of singular use and benefit to him, and never did anything, how ungracious or imprudent soever it seemed to be, but what was necessary to the design; even his roughness and unpolishedness, which, in the beginning of the parliament, he affected contrary to the smoothness and complacency which his cousin, and bosom friend, Mr. Hampden, practised towards all men, was necessary; and his first public declaration, in the beginning of the war, to his troop when it was first mustered, that he would not deceive or cozen them by the perplexed and involved expressions in his commission, to fight for king and parliament, and therefore told them, that if the king chanced to be in the body of the enemy that he was to charge, he would as soon discharge his pistol upon him as any other private person; and if their conscience would not permit them to do the like he advised them not to list themselves in his troop, or under his command, which was generally looked upon as imprudent and malicious, and might, by the professions the parliament then made, have proved dangerous to him, yet served his turn, and severed from others, and united among themselves, all the furious and incensed men against the government, whether ecclesiastical or civil, to look upon him as a man for their turn, upon whom they might depend, as one who would go through the work that he undertook."

The passage I have quoted from Mr. Horne's letter appears to me in flat contradiction to what he says at the end of the same letter, "whoever or whatever is sovereign demands the respect and support of the people." Is it possible that the last paragraph could be written by the same person who printed in all the papers that the king's smiling when the city remonstrance was presented reminded him that "Nero fiddled while Rome was burning!"

W. R.

treasury 300*l.*; from the *lords of the treasury* 60*l.* each; from the *lords of trade* 40*l.* each *, &c. The public must give up their attention to points of national benefit, and assist Mr. Wilkes in his attempt—because it would mortify the king!

Should he demand the government of *Canada*, or of *Jamaica*, or the embassy to *Constantinople*, and, in case of refusal, to write them down, as he had before served another administration, in a year and an half, he must be supported in his pretensions, and upheld in his insolence—because it would mortify the king!

Junius may choose to suppose that these things cannot happen! But that they have happened, notwithstanding Mr. Wilkes's denial, I do aver. I maintain that Mr. Wilkes did commission Mr. Thomas Walpole to solicit for him a pension of *one thousand pounds* on the *Irish* establishment for *thirty years*, with which, and a pardon, he declared he would be satisfied, and that, notwithstanding his letter to Mr. Onslow, he did accept a *clandestine*, *precarious* and *eleemosynary* pension from the Rockingham administration, which they paid in proportion to and out of their salaries; and so entirely was it ministerial, that as any of them went out of the ministry, their names were scratched out of the list, and they contributed no longer. I say, he did solicit the governments and the embassy. and threatened their refusal nearly in these words—" It cost me a year and an half to write down the last administration; should I employ as much time upon you, very few of you would be in at the death." When these threats did not prevail, he came over to England to embarrass them by his presence; and when he found that Lord Rockingham was something firmer and more manly than he expected, and refused to be bullied into what he could not perform, Mr. Wilkes declared that he could not leave England without money; and the Duke of Portland and Lord Rockingham purchased his absence with *one hundred pounds a-piece;* with which he returned to Paris. And for the truth of what I here advance, I appeal to the Duke of Portland, to Lord Rocking-

---

* The Rockingham party had consented to unite with the Bedford administration on the express stipulation of a reversal of the proceedings against Wilkes. They were not, however, able to obtain this stipulation at last; and, as some indemnification to Wilkes for the promise they had made to him in this respect, they granted him a pension *out of their own salaries,* upon the proportions stated above, with which, at their entreaty, he again returned to the continent.

nam, to Lord John Cavendish, to Mr. Walpole, &c.—I appeal to the hand-writing of Mr. Wilkes, which is still extant.

Should Mr. Wilkes afterwards (failing in this wholesale trade) choose to dole out his popularity by the pound, and expose the city offices to sale to his brother, his attorney, &c. Junius will tell us it is only an *ambition* that he has to make them *chamberlain, town clerk*, &c., and he must not be opposed in thus robbing the ancient citizens of their birth-right—because any defeat of Mr. Wilkes would gratify the king!

Should he, after consuming the whole of his own fortune and that of his wife, and incurring a debt of *twenty thousand pounds* merely by his own private extravagance, without a single service or exertion all this time for the public whilst his estate remained—should he, at length being undone, commence patriot, have the good fortune to be illegally persecuted, and in consideration of that illegality be espoused by a few gentlemen of the purest public principles—should his debts (though none of them were contracted for the public) and all his other incumbrances be discharged—should he be offered 600*l.* or 1000*l.* a year to make him independent for the future—and should he, after all, instead of gratitude for these services, insolently forbid his benefactors to bestow their own money upon any other object but himself *, and revile them for setting any bounds to their supplies—Junius (who, any more than Lord Chatham, never contributed one farthing to these enormous expenses) will tell them, that if they think of converting the supplies of Mr. Wilkes's private extravagance to the support of public measures they are as great fools as my *grandmother ;* and that Mr. Wilkes ought to hold the strings of their purses—*as long as he continues to be a thorn in the king's side!*

Upon these principles I never have acted, and I never will act. In my opinion, it is less dishonourable to be the creature of a court than the tool of a faction. I will not be either. I understand the two great leaders of opposition to be Lord Rockingham and Lord Chatham; under one of whose banners all the opposing members of both Houses, who desire to get

---

* The quarrel between Mr. Wilkes and Mr. Horne is said to have originated in the mode of appropriating the contributions to the Bill of Rights Society, the funds of which were professedly subscribed for the purpose of paying the debts of the former.

places, enlist.   I can place no confidence in either of them,
or in any others, unless they will now engage, whilst they
are OUT, to grant certain essential advantages for the security
of the public when they shall be IN administration.   These
points they refuse to stipulate, because they are fearful lest
they should prevent any future overtures from the court.   To
force them to these stipulations has been the uniform endeavour of Mr Sawbridge, Mr. Townshend, Mr. Oliver, &c., and,
THEREFORE, they are abused by Junius. I know no reason but
my zeal and industry in the same cause that should entitle
me to the honour of being ranked by his abuse with persons
of their fortune and station. It is a duty I owe to the memory
of the late Mr. Beckford to say, that he had no other aim
than this when he provided that sumptuous entertainment at
the Mansion House for the members of both Houses in opposition *.   At that time he drew up the heads of an engagement which he gave to me with a request that I would couch
it in terms so cautious and precise as to leave no room for
future quibble and evasion, but to oblige them either to fulfil
the intent of the obligation, or to sign their own infamy, and
leave it on record ; and this engagement he was determined
to propose to them at the Mansion House, that either by their
refusal they might forfeit the confidence of the public, or by
the engagement lay a foundation for confidence.   When they
were informed of the intention, Lord Rockingham and his
friends flatly refused any engagement; and Mr. Beckford as
flatly swore, they should then " eat none of his broth ;" and
he was determined to put off the entertainment ; but Mr.
Beckford was prevailed upon by ———— to indulge them in
the ridiculous parade of a popular procession through the
city, and to give them the foolish pleasure of an imaginary
consequence for the real benefit only of the cooks and pur-
veyors.

It was the same motive which dictated the thanks of the
city to Lord Chatham, which were expressed to be given for his
declaration in favour of *short parliaments†*; in order thereby

---

* On the 22nd of March, 1770, at which forty-five noblemen, besides a
great number of members of parliament, and other persons of distinction, were
present.

† The vote of thanks and answer were as follow :—

At a Common Council holden on the 14th of May, 1770, it was resolved to fix Lord Chatham at least to that one constitutional remedy without which all others can afford no security. The embarrassment no doubt was cruel. He had his choice either

"That the grateful thanks of this court be presented to the Right Hon. William Earl of Chatham, for the zeal he has shown in support of those most valuable and sacred privileges, the right of election, and the right of petition; and for his wishes and declaration, that his endeavours shall hereafter be used that parliaments may be restored to their original purity, by shortening their duration, and introducing a more full and equal representation, an act which will render his name more honoured by posterity than the memorable successes of the glorious war he conducted."

To this vote of thanks the Earl of Chatham made the following reply to the committee deputed to present it to his Lordship:

"GENTLEMEN,

"It is not easy for me to give expression to all I feel on the extraordinary honour done to my public conduct by the city of London; a body so highly respectable on every account, but above all, for their constant assertion of the birthrights of Englishmen in every great crisis of the constitution.

"In our present unhappy situation my duty shall be, on all proper occasions, to add the zealous endeavours of an individual to those legal exertions of constitutional rights, which, to their everlasting honour, the city of London has made in defence of freedom of election and freedom of petition, and for obtaining effectual reparation to the electors of Great Britain.

"As to the point among the declarations which I am understood to have made, of my wishes for the public, permit me to say there has been some misapprehension, for with all my deference to the sentiments of the city, I am bound to declare, that I cannot recommend triennial parliaments as a remedy against that canker of the constitution, venality in elections; but I am ready to submit my opinion to better judgment if the wish for that measure shall become prevalent in the kingdom. Purity of parliament is the corner stone in the commonwealth; and as one obvious means towards this necessary end is to strengthen and extend the natural relation between the constituents and the elected, I have, in this view, publicly expressed my earnest wishes for a more full and equal representation by the addition of one knight of the shire in a county, as a further balance to the mercenary boroughs.

"I have thrown out this idea with the just diffidence of a private man when he presumes to suggest anything new on a high matter. Animated by your approbation, I shall with better hope continue humbly to submit it to the public wisdom, as an object most deliberately to be weighed, accurately examined, and maturely digested.

"Having many times, when in the service of the crown, and when retired from it, experienced, with gratitude, the favour of my fellow-citizens, I am now particularly fortunate, that, with their good liking, I can offer anything towards upholding this wisely-combined frame of mixed government against the decays of time, and the deviations incident to all human institutions; and I shall esteem my life honoured indeed, if the city of London can vouchsafe to think that my endeavours have not been wanting to maintain the national honour, to defend the colonies, and extend the commercial greatness of my

to offend the Rockingham party who declared *formally* against short parliaments, and with the assistance of whose numbers in both Houses he must expect again to be minister, or to give up the confidence of the public, from whom finally all real consequence must proceed. Lord Chatham chose the latter, and I will venture to say that, by his *answer* to those thanks, he has given up the people without gaining the friendship or cordial assistance of the Rockingham faction, whose little politics are confined to the making of matches, and extending their family connections, and who think they gain more by procuring one additional vote to their party in the House of Commons, than by adding to their languid property and feeble character, the abilities of a *Chatham*, or the confidence of the public.

Whatever may be the event of the present wretched state of politics in this country the principles of Junius will suit no form of government. They are not to be tolerated under any constitution. Personal enmity is a motive fit only for the devil. Whoever or whatever is sovereign demands the respect and support of the people. The union is formed for their happiness, which cannot be had without mutual respect; and he counsels maliciously who would persuade either to a wanton breach of it. When it is banished by either party, and when every method has been tried in vain to restore it, there is no remedy but a divorce; but even then he must have a hard and a wicked heart indeed who punishes the greatest criminal merely for the sake of the punishment; and who does not let fall a tear for every drop of blood that is shed in a public struggle, however just the quarrel.

JOHN HORNE.

country, as well as to preserve from violation the law of the land, and the essential rights of the constitution."

On the subject of triennial parliaments, Lord Chatham appears subsequently to have changed his opinion, as will be seen by reference to his speech in the Lords, April 30, 1771, in which he declares himself "a convert to triennial parliaments."—ED.

LETTER LIV*.

TO THE PRINTER OF THE PUBLIC ADVERTISER.

SIR,   August 13, 1771.

I OUGHT to make an apology to the Duke of Grafton for suffering any part of my attention to be diverted from his Grace to Mr. Horne.   I am not justified by the similarity of their dispositions.   Private vices, however detestable, have not dignity sufficient to attract the censure of the press unless they are united with the power of doing some signal mischief to the community.   Mr. Horne's situation does not correspond with his intentions.   In my own opinion (which I know, will be attributed to my usual vanity and presumption) his letter to me does not deserve an answer.   But I understand that the public are not satisfied with my silence; that an answer is expected from me, and that if I persist in refusing to plead, it will be taken for conviction.   I should be inconsistent with the principles I profess if I declined an appeal to the good sense of the people, or did not willingly submit myself to the judgment of my peers.

If any coarse expressions have escaped me I am ready to agree that they are unfit for Junius to make use of, but I see no reason to admit that they have been improperly applied.

Mr. Horne, it seems, is unable to comprehend how an extreme want of conduct and discretion can consist with the abilities I have allowed him ; nor can he conceive that a very honest man, with a very good understanding, may be deceived by a knave.   His knowledge of human nature must be limited indeed.   Had he never mixed with the world one would think that even his books might have taught him better.   Did he hear Lord Mansfield when he defended his doctrine concerning libels? Or when he stated the law in prosecutions for criminal conversation? Or when he delivered his reasons for calling the House of Lords together to receive a copy of his charge to the jury in Woodfall's trial? Had he been present

---

* Junius, in Private Letter, No. 37, makes the following observation : " If Mr. Horne answers this letter handsomely, and in point, he shall be my great Apollo."

c c 2

upon any of these occasions he would have seen how possible it is for a man of the first talents to confound himself in ab surdities which would disgrace the lips of an idiot. Perhaps the example might have taught him not to value his own understanding so highly. Lord Littleton's integrity and judgment are unquestionable; yet he is known to admire that cunning Scotchman, and verily believes him an honest man. I speak to facts with which all of us are conversant. I speak to men and to their experience, and will not descend to answer the little sneering sophistries of a collegian. Distinguished talents are not necessarily connected with discretion. If there be anything remarkable in the character of Mr. Horne, it is that extreme want of judgment should be united with his very moderate capacity. Yet I have not forgotten the acknowledgment I made him. He owes it to my bounty; and though his letter has lowered him in my opinion, I scorn to retract the charitable donation.

I said it would be *very difficult* for Mr. Horne to write directly in defence of a ministerial measure and not be detected; and even that difficulty I confined to *his* particular situation. He changes the terms of the proposition, and supposes me to assert that it would be *impossible* for *any* man to write for the newspapers and not be discovered.

He repeatedly affirms, or intimates at least, that he knows the author of these letters. With what colour of truth then can he pretend *that I am nowhere to be encountered but in a newspaper?* I shall leave him to his suspicions. It is not necessary that I should confide in the honour or discretion of a man who already seems to hate me with as much rancour as if I had formerly been his friend. But he asserts that he has traced me through a variety of signatures. To make the discovery of any importance to his purpose, he should have proved either that the fictitious character of Junius has not been consistently supported, or that the author has maintained different principles under different signatures. I can not recall to my memory the numberless trifles I have written; but I rely upon the consciousness of my own integrity, and defy him to fix any colourable charge of inconsistency against me.

I am not bound to assign the secret motives of his apparent hatred of Mr. Wilkes; nor does it follow that I may not judge fairly of *his* conduct. though it were true *that I had no conduct of my own.* Mr. Horne enlarges, with rapture, upon the importance of his services ; the dreadful battles which he might have been engaged in, and the dangers he has escaped. In support of the formidable description, he quotes verses without mercy. The gentleman deals in fiction and naturally appeals to the evidence of the poets. Taking him at his word, he cannot but admit the superiority of Mr. Wilkes in this line of service. On one side we see nothing but imaginary distresses.   On the other we see real prosecutions—real penalties—real imprisonment—life repeatedly hazarded— and, at one moment, almost the certainty of death.   Thanks are undoubtedly due to every man who does his duty in the engagement ; but it is the wounded soldier who deserves the reward.

I did not mean to deny that Mr. Horne had been an active partisan.   It would defeat my own purpose not to allow him a degree of merit which aggravates his guilt.   The very charge *of contributing his utmost efforts to support a ministerial measure* implies an acknowledgment of his former services. If he had not once been distinguished by his apparent zeal in defence of the common cause he could not now be distinguished by deserting it.   As for myself, it is no longer a question *whether I shall mix with the throng, and take a single share in the danger.* Whenever Junius appears, he must encounter a host of enemies.   But is there no honourable way to serve the public without engaging in personal quarrels with insignificant individuals, or submitting to the drudgery of canvassing votes for an election ?   Is there no merit in dedicating my life to the information of my fellow-subjects ? What public question have I declined? what villain have I spared? Is there no labour in the composition of these let-ters ? Mr. Horne, I fear, is partial to me, and measures the facility of *my* writings by the fluency of his own.

He talks to us, in high terms, of the gallant feats he would have performed if he had lived in the last century.   The unhappy Charles could hardly have escaped him.   But living princes have a claim to his attachment and respect.   Upon these terms there is no danger in being a patriot.   If he means anything more than a pompous rhapsody, let us try how well his argument holds together.   I presume he is not yet so much a courtier as to affirm that the constitution has not been grossly and daringly violated under the present reign. He will not say that the laws have not been shamefully broken or perverted; that the rights of the subject have not been invaded, or that redress has not been repeatedly solicited and refused. Grievances like these were the foundation of the rebellion in the last century, and, if I understand Mr. Horne, they would, at that period, have justified him, to his own mind, in deliberately attacking the life of his sovereign. I shall not ask him to what political constitution this doctrine can be reconciled. But, at least, it is incumbent upon him to show, that the present king has better excuses than Charles the First for the errors of his government. He ought to demonstrate to us that the constitution was better understood a hundred years ago than it is at present; that the legal rights of the subject, and the limits of the prerogative were more accurately defined and more clearly comprehended. If propositions like these cannot be fairly maintained, I do not see how he can reconcile it to his conscience, not to act immediately with the same freedom with which he speaks. I reverence the character of Charles the First as little as Mr. Horne; but I will not insult his misfortunes by a comparison that would degrade him.

It is worth observing by what gentle degrees the furious persecuting zeal of Mr. Horne has softened into moderation. Men and measures were yesterday his object. What pains did he once take to bring that great state criminal *Mac Quirk* to execution! To-day he confines himself to measures only. No penal example is to be left to the successors of the Duke of Grafton. To-morrow I presume both men and measures will be forgiven. The flaming patriot who so lately scorched us in the meridian sinks temperately to the west, and is hardly felt as he descends.

I comprehend the policy of endeavouring to communicate to Mr. Oliver and Mr. Sawbridge a share in the reproaches with which he supposes me to have loaded him. My memory fails me if I have mentioned their names with disrespect;—unless it be reproachful to acknowledge a sincere respect for the character of Mr. Sawbridge, and not to have questioned the innocence of Mr. Oliver's intentions.

It seems I am a partisan of the great leader of the opposition. If the charge had been a reproach, it should have been better supported. I did not intend to make a public declaration of the respect I bear Lord Chatham. I well knew what unworthy conclusions would be drawn from it. But I am called upon to deliver my opinion; and surely it is not in the little censure of Mr. Horne to deter me from doing signal justice to a man who, I confess, has grown upon my esteem. As for the common, sordid views of avarice, or any purpose of vulgar ambition, I question whether the applause of Junius would be of service to Lord Chatham. My vote will hardly recommend him to an increase of his pension, or to a seat in the cabinet. But if his ambition be upon a level with his understanding — if he judges of what is truly honourable for himself, with the same superior genius which animates and directs him to eloquence in debate, to wisdom in decision, even the pen of Junius shall contribute to reward him. Recorded honours shall gather round his monument and thicken over him. It is a solid fabric, and will support the laurels that adorn it. I am not conversant in the language of panegyric. These praises are extorted from me; but they will wear well, for they have been dearly earned.

My detestation of the Duke of Grafton is not founded upon his treachery to any individual; though I am willing enough to suppose that, in public affairs, it would be impossible to desert or betray Lord Chatham without doing an essential injury to this country. My abhorrence of the Duke arises from an intimate knowledge of his character, and from a thorough conviction that his baseness has been the cause of greater mischief to England than even the unfortunate ambition of Lord Bute.

The shortening the duration of parliaments is a subject on which Mr. Horne cannot enlarge too warmly; nor will I question his sincerity. If I did not profess the same sentiments I should be shamefully inconsistent with myself. It is unnecessary to bind Lord Chatham by the written formality of an engagement. He has publicly declared himself a convert to triennial parliaments; and though I have long been convinced that this is the only possible resource we have left to preserve the substantial freedom of the constitution, I do not think we have a right to determine against the integrity of Lord Rockingham or his friends. Other measures may undoubtedly be supported in argument, as better adapted to the disorder, or more likely to be obtained.

Mr. Horne is well assured that I never was the champion of Mr. Wilkes. But, though I am not obliged to answer for the firmness of his future adherence to the principles he professes, I have no reason to presume that he will hereafter disgrace them. As for all those imaginary cases which Mr. Horne so petulantly urges against me, I have one plain, honest answer to make to him. Whenever Mr. Wilkes shall be convicted of soliciting a pension, an embassy, or a government, he must depart from that situation, and renounce that character, which he assumes at present, and which, in *my* opinion, entitle him to the support of the public. By the same act, and at the same moment, he will forfeit his power of mortifying the king; and, though he can never be a favourite at St. James's, his baseness may administer a solid satisfaction to the royal mind. The man I speak of has not a heart to feel for the frailties of his fellow-creatures. It is their virtues that afflict, it is their vices that console him.

I give every possible advantage to Mr. Horne when I take the facts he refers to for granted. That they are the produce of his invention, seems highly probable; that they are exaggerated, I have no doubt. At the worst, what do they amount to but that Mr. Wilkes, who never was thought of as a perfect pattern of morality, has not been at all times proof against the extremity of distress! How shameful is it in a man who has lived in friendship with him, to reproach him with failings too naturally connected with despair! Is no allowance to be made for banishment and ruin? Does a two years' imprisonment make no atonement for his crimes? The resentment of a priest is implacable. No sufferings can soften, no penitence can appease him. Yet he himself, I think, upon his own system, has a multitude of political offences to atone for. I will not insist upon the nauseous detail with which he so long disgusted the public. He seems to be ashamed of it. But what excuse will he make to the friends of the constitution for labouring to promote *this consummately bad man* to a station of the highest national trust and importance? Upon what honourable motives did he recommend him to the livery of London for their representative;—to the ward of Farringdon for their alderman;—to the county of Middlesex for their knight? Will he affirm that, at that time, he was ignorant of Mr. Wilkes's solicita tions to the ministry? That he should say so is indeed very necessary for his own justification, but where will he find cre· dulity to believe him?

In what school this gentleman learned his ethics I know not. His *logic* seems to have been studied under Mr. Dyson. That miserable pamphleteer, by dividing the only precedent in point, and taking as much of it as suited his purpose, had reduced his argument upon the Middlesex election to something like the shape of a syllogism. Mr. Horne has conducted himself with the same ingenuity and candour. I had affirmed that Mr. Wilkes would preserve the public favour, " as long as he stood forth against a ministry and parliament, who were doing everything they could to enslave the country, *and* as long as he was a thorn in the king's side." Yet, from the exulting triumph of Mr. Horne's reply, one would think that I had rested my expectation that Mr. Wilkes would be supported by the public, upon the single condition of his mortifying the king. This may be logic at Cambridge or at the treasury, but among men of sense and honour it is folly or villany in the extreme.

I see the pitiful advantage he has taken of a single unguarded expression in a letter not intended for the public. Yet it is only the *expression* that is unguarded. I adhere to the true meaning of that member of the sentence, taken separately as *he* takes it; and now, upon the coolest deliberation, re-assert that, for the purposes I referred to, it may be highly meritorious to the public to wound the personal feelings of the sovereign. It is not a general proposition, nor is it generally applied to the chief magistrate of this, or any other constitution. Mr. Horne knows, as well as I do, that the best of princes is not displeased with the abuse which he sees thrown upon his ostensible ministers. It makes them, I presume, more properly the objects of his royal compassion. Neither does it escape his sagacity, that the lower they are degraded in the public esteem the more submissively they must depend upon his favour for protection. This, I affirm, upon the most solemn conviction, and the most cer tain knowledge, is a leading maxim in the policy of the closet. It is unnecessary to pursue the argument any farther.

Mr. Horne is now a very loyal subject. He laments the wretched state of politics in this country, and sees in a new light the weakness and folly of the opposition. *Whoever or whatever is sovereign demands the respect and support of the people**; it was not so, *when Nero fiddled while Rome was burning*†. Our gracious sovereign has had wonderful success i. creating new attachments *to his person and family.* He owes it, I presume, to the regular system he has pursued in the mystery of conversion. He began with an experiment upon the Scotch, and concludes with converting Mr. Horne. What a pity it is that the *Jews* should be condemned by Providence to wait for a Messiah of their own.!

The priesthood are accused of misinterpreting the scriptures. Mr. Horne has improved upon his profession. He alters the text, and creates a refutable doctrine of his own. Such artifices cannot long delude the understanding of the people; and, without meaning an indecent comparison. I may venture to foretel, that the Bible and Junius will be read when the commentaries of the Jesuits are forgotten.

JUNIUS.

LETTER LV.

TO THE PRINTER OF THE PUBLIC ADVERTISER.

SIR,   August 26, 1771.

THE enemies of the people, having now nothing better to object to my friend Junius, are at last obliged to quit his politics, and to rail at him for crimes he is not guilty of. His vanity and impiety are now the perpetual topics of their abuse. I do not mean to lessen the force of such charges (supposing they were true), but to show that they are not founded. If I admitted the premises, I should readily agree in all the consequences drawn from them. Vanity, indeed, is a venial error, for it usually carries its own punishment with it ; but if I thought Junius capable of uttering a disrespectful word of the religion of his country, I should be the first

---

* The very soliloquy of Lord Suffolk before he passed the Rubicon.

† This forms a sentence of Mr. Horne's own writing. and was one of his bitterest sarcasms against the king.

to renounce and give him up to the public contempt and indignation. As a man, I am satisfied that he is a Christian upon the most sincere conviction. As a writer, he would be grossly inconsistent with his political principles if he dared to attack a religion established by those laws which it seems to be the purpose of his life to defend. Now for the proofs. Junius is accused of an impious allusion to the holy sacrament, where he says that, *if Lord Weymouth be denied the cup, there will be no keeping him within the pale of the ministry* Now, Sir, I affirm that this passage refers entirely to a ceremonial in the Roman Catholic Church which denies the cup to the laity. It has no manner of relation to the Protestant creed, and is, in this country, as fair an object of ridicule as *transubstantiation*, or any other part of Lord *Peter's* history in the Tale of the Tub.

But Junius is charged with equal vanity and impiety in comparing his writings to the holy scripture. The formal protest he makes against any such comparison avails him nothing. It becomes necessary, then, to show that the charge destroys itself. If he be *vain* he cannot be *impious*. A vain man does not usually compare himself to an object which it is his design to undervalue. On the other hand, if he be *impious* he cannot be *vain*. For his impiety, if any, must consist in his endeavouring to degrade the holy scriptures by a comparison with his own contemptible writings. This would be folly indeed of the grossest nature; but where lies the vanity? I shall now be told, " Sir, what you say is plausible enough, but still you must allow that it is shamefully impudent in Junius to tell us that his works will live as long as the Bible." My answer is, *Agreed; but first prove that he has said so.* Look at his words, and you will find that the utmost he expects is that the Bible and Junius will survive the commentaries of the Jesuits, which may prove true in a fortnight. The most malignant sagacity cannot show that his works are, *in his opinion*, to live as long as the Bible. Suppose I were to foretel that *Jack* and *Tom* would survive *Harry*;—does it follow that *Jack* must live as long as *Tom?* I would only illustrate my meaning, and protest against the least idea of profaneness.

Yet this is the way in which Junius is usually answered, arraigned, and convicted. These candid critics never remem-

ber anything he says in honour of our holy religion; though
it is true that one of his leading arguments is made to rest
*upon the internal evidence which the purest of all religions
carries with it.* I quote his words, and conclude from them
that he is a true and hearty Christian, in substance, not in
ceremony; though possibly he may not agree with my reverend Lords the Bishops, or with the Head of the Church, *that
prayers are morality, or that kneeling is religion.*

PHILO-JUNIUS.

LETTER LVI.

FROM THE REV. MR. HORNE TO JUNIUS.

August 16, 1771.

I CONGRATULATE you, Sir, on the recovery of your wonted
style, though it has cost you a fortnight. I compassionate
your labour in the composition of your letters, and will com
municate to you the secret of my fluency. Truth needs no
ornament, and, in my opinion, what she borrows of the pencil
is deformity.

You brought a positive charge against me of corruption. I
denied the charge, and called for your proofs. You replied
with abuse and reasserted your charge. I called again for
proofs. You reply again with abuse only and drop your accusation. In your fortnight's letter there is not one word
upon the subject of my corruption.

I have no more to say but to return thanks to you for your
condescension, and to a *grateful* public and *honest* ministry for
all the favours they have conferred upon me. The two latter,
I am sure, will never refuse me any grace I shall solicit; and
since you have been pleased to acknowledge that you told a
deliberate lie in my favour out of bounty, and as a charitable
donation, why may I not expect that you will hereafter (if
you do not forget you ever mentioned my name with disrespect) make the same acknowledgment for what you have
said to my prejudice? This second recantation will perhaps
be more abhorrent from your disposition; but should you decline it, you will only afford one more instance how much
easier it is to be generous than just, and that men are sometimes bountiful who are not honest

At all events, I am as well satisfied with your panegyric as Lord Chatham can be.   Monument I shall have none; but over my grave it will be said, in your own words, "*Horne's situation did not correspond with his intentions.*"*

JOHN HORNE.

LETTER LVII†.

TO HIS GRACE THE DUKE OF GRAFTON.

MY LORD,   September 28, 1771.

THE people of England are not apprized of the full extent of their obligations to you.   They have yet no adequate idea of the endless variety of your character.   They have seen you distinguished and successful in the continued violation of those moral and political duties by which the little, as well as the great, societies of life are collected and held together. Every colour, every character, became you.   With a rate of abilities which Lord Weymouth very justly looks down upon with contempt, you have done as much mischief to the community as *Cromwell* would have done if *Cromwell* had been a coward, and as much as *Machiavel* if *Machiavel* had not known that an appearance of morals and religion are useful in society.

To a thinking man, the influence of the crown will, in no view, appear so formidable as when he observes to what enormous excesses it has safely conducted your Grace, without a ray of real understanding, without even the pretension to common decency or principle of any kind, or a single spark of

---

* The epitaph would not be ill-suited to the character.   At the best it is but equivocal.—JUNIUS.

† "The inclosed is of such importance, so very material, that it must be given to the public immediately."—*Private Letter, No.* 38.

Junius's rage against the quondam friend of Lord Chatham and Mr. Wilkes, was not to be appeased.   He had been unwillingly entangled in the controversy with Mr. Horne, and he, therefore, made this escape from it with as much haste as was possible.   But he delighted to hurl all his invectives against the Duke of Grafton ; and on this subject he was, therefore, earnestly disposed to dwell as long the public were not unwilling to listen.   Nothing is more remarkable than the wonderful power to diversify invective, which the writer displays in this letter; and the most damaging portion of it, as will be discovered in a note at the conclusion, is founded upon false facts.—ED.

personal resolution. What must be the operation of that pernicious influence (for which our kings have wisely exchanged the nugatory name of prerogative) that, in the highest stations, can so abundantly supply the absence of virtue, courage, and abilities, and qualify a man to be the minister of a great nation whom a private gentleman would be ashamed and afraid to admit into his family! Like the universal passport of an ambassador, it supersedes the prohibition of the laws, banishes the staple virtues of the country, and introduces vice and folly triumphantly into all the departments of the state. Other princes, besides his Majesty, have had the means of corruption within their reach, but they have used it with moderation. In former times corruption was considered as a foreign auxiliary to government, and only called in upon extraordinary emergencies. The unfeigned piety, the sanctified religion, of George the Third, have taught him to new model the civil forces of the state. The natural resources of the crown are no longer confided in. Corruption glitters in the van, collects and maintains a standing army of mercenaries, and, at the same moment, impoverishes and enslaves the country. His Majesty's predecessors (excepting that worthy family, from which you, my Lord, are unquestionably descended) had some generous qualities in their composition, with vices, I confess, or frailties in abundance. They were kings or gentlemen, not hypocrites or priests. They were at the head of the church, but did not know the value of their office. They said their prayers without ceremony, and had too little priestcraft in their understanding to reconcile the sanctimonious forms of religion with the utter destruction of the morality of their people. My Lord, this is fact, not declamation. With all your partiality to the house of Stuart, you must confess that even Charles II. would have blushed at that open encouragement, at those eager, meretricious caresses, with which every species of private vice and public prostitution is received at St. James's. The unfortunate House of Stuart has been treated with an asperity which, if comparison be a defence, seems to border upon injustice. Neither Charles nor his brother were qualified to support such a system of measures as would be necessary to change the government and subvert the constitution of England. One of them was too much in earnest in his pleasures—the other in his religion. But the danger to this country would cease to be problematical, if the crown should ever descend to a prince whose apparent simplicity might throw his subjects off their guard—who might be no libertine in behaviour—who should have no sense of honour to restrain him, and who, with just religion enough to impose upon the multitude, might have no scruples of conscience to interfere with his morality. With these honourable qualifications, and the decisive advantage of situation, low craft and falsehood are all the abilities that are wanting to destroy the wisdom of ages, and to deface the noblest monument that human policy has erected. I know *such* a man—my Lord, I know you both—and, with the blessing of God (for I, too, am religious), the people of England shall know you as well as I do. I am not very sure that greater abilities would not, in effect, be an impediment to a design which seems, at first sight, to require a superior capacity. A better understanding might make him sensible of the wonderful beauty of that system he was endeavouring to corrupt. The danger of the attempt might alarm him. The meanness, and intrinsic worthlessness of the object (supposing he could attain to it) would fill him with shame, repentance, and disgust. But these are sensations which find no entrance into a barbarous, contracted heart. In some men there is a malignant passion to destroy the works of genius, literature, and freedom. The Vandal and the monk find equal gratification in it.

Reflections like these, my Lord, have a general relation to your Grace, and inseparably attend you in whatever company or situation your character occurs to us ; they have no immediate connection with the following recent fact, which I lay before the public for the honour of the best of sovereigns, and for the edification of his people.

A prince (whose piety and self-denial, one would think, might secure him from such a multitude of worldly necessities,) with an annual revenue of near a million sterling, unfortunately *wants money*. The navy of England, by an equally strange concurrence of unforeseen circumstances (though not quite so unfortunately for his Majesty), is in equal want of timber. The world knows in what a hopeful condition you delivered the navy to your successor, and in what a condition we found it in the moment of distress; you were determined it should con

tinue in the situation in which you left it *; it happened, however, very luckily for the privy purse, that one of the above
wants promised fair to supply the other.   Our religious,
benevolent, generous sovereign, has no objection to selling *his
own* timber to *his own* admiralty to repair *his own* ships, nor
to putting the money into *his own* pocket.   People of a
religious turn naturally adhere to the principles of the church.
Whatever they acquire falls into *mortmain.*   Upon a representation from the admiralty of the extraordinary want of timber
for the indispensable repairs of the navy, the surveyor-general
was directed to make a survey of the timber in all the royal
chases and forests in England.   Having obeyed his orders
with accuracy and attention he reported that the finest timber
he had anywhere met with, and the properest in every respect
for the purposes of the navy, was in Whittlebury Forest, of
which your Grace, I think, is hereditary ranger.   In consequence of this report, the usual warrant was prepared at the
Treasury, and delivered to the surveyor, by which he or his
deputy were authorised to cut down any trees in Whittlebury
Forest, which should appear to be proper for the purposes
above mentioned.   The deputy being informed that the warrant was signed and. delivered to his principal in London,
crosses the country to Northamptonshire, and, with an officious
zeal for the public service, begins to do his duty in the forest.
Unfortunately for him, he had not the warrant in his pocket
The oversight was enormous, and you have punished him for
it accordingly; you have insisted that an active, useful officer
should be dismissed from his place; you have ruined an innocent man and his family.   In what language shall I address
so black, so cowardly a tyrant, thou worse than *one* of the

---

* When the armament took place, in consequence of the dispute with
Spain respecting Falkland's Islands, the navy was found to be in a most
deplorable state.   By the exertions of the late Earl of Sandwich, then and
for many years afterwards first lord of the admiralty, it was greatly reno-
vated.   It is, however, to later periods, to the superintendence of the present Earl Spencer and some of his very able successors, that we are to look
for its true pinnacle of glory — for the manifestation of that expert and
chivalrous courage which has made it indeed the envy of an individual
tyrant, but the admiration of the universe.—[This observation, it should be
remembered, was made by the former editor (Dr. Mason Good) in 1814,
or earlier. in reference to the French emperor, Napoleon I.—ED.]

Brunswicks, and all the *Stuarts!* To them who know Lord
North it is unnecessary to say that he was mean and base
enough to submit to you; this, however, is but a small part of
the fact. After ruining the surveyor's deputy for acting without the warrant, you attacked the warrant itself. You declared
it was illegal, and swore, in a fit of foaming, frantic passion,
that it never should be executed. You asserted, upon your
honour, that in the grant of the rangership of Whittlebury
Forest, made by Charles the Second (whom, with a modesty
that would do honour to Mr. Rigby, you are pleased to call
your ancestor) to one of his bastards (from whom I make no
doubt of your descent), the property of the timber is vested in
the ranger. I have examined the original grant, and now, in
the face of the public, contradict you directly upon the fact.
The very reverse of what you have asserted, upon your honour,
is the truth. The grant, *expressly, and by a particular clause*,
reserves the property of the timber for the use of the crown.
In spite of this evidence, in defiance of the representations of
the admiralty, in perfect mockery of the notorious distresses
of the English navy, and those equally pressing. and almost
equally notorious, necessities of your pious sovereign, here the
matter rests. The lords of the treasury recall their warrant,
the deputy-surveyor is ruined for doing his duty, Mr. John
Pitt (whose *name* I suppose is offensive to you) submits to be
brow-beaten and insulted, the oaks keep their ground, the king
is defrauded, and the navy of England may perish for want of
the best and finest timber in the island. And all this is submitted to, to appease the Duke of Grafton!—to gratify the
man who has involved the king and his kingdom in confusion
and distress, and who, like a treacherous coward, deserted his
sovereign in the midst of it!

There has been a strange alteration in your doctrines since
you thought it advisable to rob the Duke of Portland of his
property, in order to strengthen the interest of Lord Bute's
son-in-law before the last general election *. *Nullum tempus*

* Few persons have yet forgotten the commotion into which the nation
was thrown by this outrageous attempt of the minister to enlarge the royal
prerogative. By the common law of England no man can be disturbed in
his title who has been in quiet possession of an estate for sixty years; but
by an old obsolete law, a wretched remnant of ancient tyranny, it was
asserted that *nullum tempus occurrit regi*, and such was the commencement

occurrit regi was then your boasted motto, and the cry of all
your hungry partisans.   Now it seems a grant of Charles II.
to one of his bastards is to be held sacred and inviolable!
It must not be questioned by the king's servants, nor submitted to any interpretation but your own.   My Lord, this
was not the language you held when it suited you to insult
the memory of the glorious deliverer of England from that
detested family to which you are still more nearly allied in
principle than in blood.   In the name of decency and common
sense, what are your Grace's merits, either with king or
ministry, that should entitle you to assume this domineering
authority over both?   Is it the fortunate consanguinity you
claim with the House of Stuart?   Is it the secret correspondence you have for so many years carried on with Lord Bute,
by the assiduous assistance of your *cream-coloured parasite* *?
Could not your gallantry find sufficient employment for him
in those *gentle* offices by which he first acquired the tender
friendship of Lord Barrington?   Or is it only that wonderful sympathy of manners which subsists between your
Grace and one of your superiors, and does so much honour to
you both?   Is the union of *Blifil* and *Black George* no longer
a romance?   From whatever origin your influence in this

of the law itself, in plain English, that no term of possession, whether
sixty or a hundred and sixty years, can defend against a claim of the
crown.   This law was attempted to be revived in the reign of James I.;
but the attempt was so effectually opposed in its outset by that sound con-
stitntional lawyer, Sir Edward Coke, that a bill of a contrary tendency was
suffered to pass in its stead, which expressly secured every estate of sixty
years' possession "against all and every person having or pretending to
have any estate, right, or title, by force or colour of any letters patent, or
grants, upon suggestion of concealment, or defective titles, of or for which
said manors, lands, and tenements, no verdict, judgment, or decree, hath
been had or given."
    This extrnordinary and unconstitutional prerogative of the crown was
attempted to be revived by the Duke of Grafton in 1767, who, for the
mere purpose of carrying an election for the county of Cumberland in favour
of Sir James Lowther against the Duke of Portland, had admitted the
former to become a royal grantee of an enormous portion of what had formerly been crown lands, but which had been for upwards of seventy years
in the different families of the actual possessors.   This attempt introduced
Sir George Savile's famous bill, which was called the Quieting Bill, and
was intended to render more valid the Act of James I. in favour of the
subject against the crown.
    * Mr. Bradshaw.—ALMON.

country arises, it is a phenomenon in the history of human virtue and understanding. Good men can hardly believe the fact. Wise men are unable to account for it. Religious men find exercise for their faith, and make it the last effort of their piety not to repine against Providence.

JUNIUS.

To this Letter the following answer was returned, which, as it proves Junius to have been mistaken as to the facts relative to Whittlebury Forest, is here inserted on the score of impartiality.

FOR THE PUBLIC ADVERTISER.

The STORY of the OAKS, addressed to the Public and to JUNIUS.

The principles upon which Junius fabricates all his declamations to the public have been fairly unmasked and plainly exhibited in two former letters. They need only an exposure to nullify everything he promulgates, and render him abominable in the eyes of common sense and honesty. But to follow so gross a falsifier through the infinity of his wicked libels and virulent attacks upon the king, and many of the worthiest characters in the nation, is a task too foul for any gentleman to undertake. Suffice it, therefore, to observe, that Junius's labours all tend to sinister ends, and they are glossed over with a high varnish only to conceal the coarseness of the design. Men and not measures are his aim. He avails himself of the unhappy licentiousness of the times, and levels all his rhetoric at your passions, not at your reason.

He began his career upon the old infamous maxim in political writing, that lies are swifter of foot than truth, and, when they are roundly and boldly asserted, will find believers; but luckily for us, that left-handed wisdom called cunning always detects and frustrates itself.

The last charge which he has blazoned in such fiery colours against the Duke of Grafton relative to the Oaks may serve as a specimen of his veracity. The fact is in no one instance as he has represented it. An officer was sent down by the commissioners of the navy (as he declared) to inspect the timber in Salcey and Whittlebury Forests in Northamptonshire; and was ordered to make a return of what he found fit for the purposes of ship building. He accordingly marked upwards of four thousand trees in the latter, which are almost all that deserve the name of timber in the whole forest. In consequence of his return, an application was made to the treasury for permission to cut down thirteen hundred loads, and, to make a just parody upon Junius's own words, "to them who know Lord North it is unnecessary to say that he was very ready to give his assent;" as the advancement of every public good has ever been the invariable rule of his Lordship's conduct. But it was never intended nor suspected that it would be carried into a rash unseasonable execution, without due regard being first paid to the circumstances attendant upon such an operation; nor was the exigency so urgent as to warrant a flagrant violation of private property which the adjacent parishes must have suffered in their right of commonage, and the Duke in his hereditary right to the underwood. Had he not remon-

D D 2

strated against it. Besides, the season for felling timber was so far passed, that the bark (which is a valuable article, and will never run except in April or May, while the sap is rising,) would have been entirely lost. But there is another argument to be adduced, still more cogent than all the rest, it being a great national concern, which is to preserve the succession of young trees. This can only be done by carefully clearing away the common underwood, so as to expose them to plain view, otherwise they would be inevitably demolished, partly by the falling of the trees, and partly by the carelessness of workmen, as they grow mostly under them from the acorns which drop.

There is an established and legal rule against cutting the underwood oftener than once in twenty-one years; for nine years after it is cut, the same regulation prescribes that the respective coppices shall be fenced in to prevent the cattle and deer from destroying the young tender shoots; during which time the vicinage is deprived of the pasture; and for the remaining twelve years of that term the neighbouring villages have a positive right of common. Underwood is as necessary to draw young trees up straight and produce good timber, as a hotbed is for raising melons and mushrooms. There are many secondary considerations which ought to have their weight, though it is not requisite, after what has been advanced, to swell this narrative by enumerating them. Without deliberating upon these essential points, so ardent was the zeal of the surveyor-general for the public service (for the trifling perquisites of the lop and chips, amounting to little more than half the value of the timber, cannot be deemed a sufficient incentive for committing such a depredation), that he immediately dispatched a person unauthorized, to back and hew, without the least previous intimation being given to the hereditary ranger, deputy-ranger, or the king's wood ward. In opposition to all this strange precipitancy and irregularity, the Duke of Grafton did no more than interpose a candid representation of the case, which wisely put a stop to such unjust proceedings. He never once made use of those absurd declarations which Junius has so invidiously put in his mouth, "that the property of the timber was vested in the ranger." And to retort a few more of his own precious words, he must here be "contradicted in the face of the public directly upon the fact. The very reverse of what he has asserted is the truth;" for neither the present Duke nor his predecessor ever allowed a single stick of timber to be cut down for any purpose, without first having obtained a regular order from the treasury; on the contrary (as it has been heretofore justly remarked) it has been preserved for the use of the public, with an attention and integrity not to be paralleled in any other royal forest.

For the better convenience of supplying the industrious poor of the circumjacent country with firing, it has been always a custom to arrange the coppices in a regular progression, so as to cut two or more annually. There are, however, two coppices (which contain a great quantity of fine timber) exempt from commonage; and as none of the stated periods for the others are yet expired, though they are too young, yet rather than withhold the wood from the navy, the Duke has given orders for fencing and clearing them, which will be effected long ere the proper season arrives for felling the trees. The rest will be cut as they fall in course. "Mr. Junius, this is fact not declaration." The oaks will come down; the king will not be defrauded: nor will the navy of England perish for want of them !

How must it scandalise all our patriots, that their omniscient Junius should discover such consummate ignorance as to be reduced to the necessity of examining the original grant to inform himself of a notorious point which he might have learned from every attorney's clerk throughout the kingdom ; nay, even from Brass Crosby, who was only a menial servant to an attorney, " that the timber in royal forests is reserved for the use of the crown !"

This, I say, may serve for a damning proof of Junius's veracity, and all his slanderous productions are equally refutable and false. In the abundance of his modesty he has somewhere told us that his writings will be handed down to posterity like the Bible ! It is needless for me to censure his irreverent comparison ; nor will I altogether deny his prediction ; for while the Bible endures as a monument of truth, his writings may stand in odious contrast as a monument of lies.—PHILALETHES.

It is likely that this refutation proceeded from Mr. John Pitt, at that time surveyor-general of the royal forests, for Mr. Almon in his edition of *Junius*, vol ii. p. 200, states, that Mr. Pitt had assured him that Junius's statement of the matter was erroneous throughout, and that no blame whatever could attach to the Duke of Grafton on the subject.—ED.

LETTER LVIII*.

TO THE LIVERY OF LONDON.

GENTLEMEN,   September 30, 1771.

IF *you* alone were concerned in the event of the present election of a chief magistrate of the metropolis, it would be the highest presumption in a stranger to attempt to influence

* The period was arrived for the election of a lord mayor for the city of London for the year 1771-2. That election was regulated principally, though not exclusively, by the rule of seniority among the aldermen. If the senior alderman should be on this occasion advanced to the mayoralty, Mr. Nash, a gentleman unentangled in politics, would be the lord mayor of the ensuing year. During his authority the powers of the city would not be, as on former years, at the command of Wilkes and the opposition. For these reasons the patriots exercised all their activity and influence to disappoint the hopes of Mr. Nash. But their divisions had greatly diminished their influence, and the better part of the citizens were sick of the turbulence which they had so long kept up : the case was not thought of sufficient magnitude to justify the violation of the wonted rule ; Mr. Nash was elected, and the letter of Junius failed in its aim. Its excellence consists in the pertinency of its application to the design of the writer, in the brevity and plainness with which the arguments are stated, and in the skill with which the eloquence of bold metaphor and vehement interrogation is associated with simple language and the greatest closeness of reasoning.

your choice, or even to offer you his opinions. But the situation of public affairs has annexed an extraordinary importance to your resolutions. You cannot, in the choice of your magistrate, determine for *yourselves only;* you are going to determine upon a point in which every member of the community is interested. I will not scruple to say that the very being of that law, of that right, of that constitution, for which we have been so long contending, is now at stake. They who would ensnare your judgment tell you it is a *common, ordinary* case, and to be decided by ordinary precedent and practice. They artfully conclude from moderate peaceable times to times which *are not* moderate, and which *ought not* to be peaceable ; while they solicit, your favour, they insist upon a rule of rotation which excludes all idea of election*.

Let me be honoured with a few minutes of your attention The question to those who mean fairly to the liberty of the people (which we all profess to have in view), lies within a very narrow compass. Do you mean to desert that just and honourable system of measures which you have hitherto pursued in hopes of obtaining from Parliament or from the crown a full redress of past grievances, and a security for the future ? Do you think the cause desperate, and will you declare that you think so to the whole people of England ? If this be your meaning and opinion, you will act consistently with it in choosing Mr. Nash. I profess to be unacquainted with his private character. But he has acted as a magistrate, as a public man ; as such I speak of him. I see his name in a protest against one of your remonstrances to the crown; he has done everything in his power to destroy the freedom of popular elections in the city, by publishing the poll upon a former occasion ; and I know, in general, that he has distinguished himself by slighting and thwarting all those public measures

* The party interest likely to be served by an observance of the rule of rotation and consequent elevation of Alderman Nash to the mayoralty, has been already noticed ; and the object of the present letter, therefore, is to persuade the livery to overlook Mr. Nash, and by an extraordinary exercise of their elective franchise, to return Mr. Crosby or Mr. Sawbridge in his stead, whose politics were well known to be of the Whig school. But the divisions which had been introduced into the Bill of Rights Society, through the vanity of Oliver and Horne, had now spread to the city, and almost ruined the popular cause. Many were suspicious of the purity of its leaders, and still more were grown indifferent as to its result.

which *you* have engaged in with the greatest warmth, and hitherto thought most worthy of your approbation. From his past conduct what conclusion will you draw, but that he will act the same part as *lord mayor* which he has invariably acted as *alderman* and *sheriff?* He cannot alter his conduct without confessing that he never acted upon principle of any kind. I should be sorry to injure the character of a man, who perhaps may be honest in his intentions, by supposing it *possible* that he can ever concur with you in any political measure or opinion.

If, on the other hand, you mean to persevere in those resolutions for the public good, which, though not always successful, are always honourable, your choice will naturally incline to those men who (whatever they be in other respects) are most likely to co-operate with you in the great purposes which you are determined not to relinquish. The question is not of what metal your instruments are made, but *whether they are adapted to the work you have in hand!* The honours of the city, *in these times*, are improperly, because exclusively, called a *reward*. You mean not merely to *pay*, but to *employ*. Are Mr. Crosby and Mr. Sawbridge likely to execute the extraordinary, as well as the ordinary duties of lord mayor? Will they grant you common halls when it shall be necessary? Will they go up with remonstrances to the king? Have they firmness enough to meet the fury of a venal House of Commons? Have they fortitude enough not to shrink at imprisonment? Have they spirit enough to hazard their lives and fortunes in a contest, if it should be necessary, with a prostituted legislature? If these questions can fairly be answered in the affirmative, your choice is made. Forgive this passionate language, I am unable to correct it ; the subject comes home to us all, it is the language of my heart*.

JUNIUS.

* Private Letter, No. 56, vol. ii.

LETTER LIX*

SIR,　　　　　　　　　　　　　　　　　　October 5, 1771.

No man laments more sincerely than I do the unhappy differ
ences which have arisen among the friends of the people, and
divided them from each other.　The cause undoubtedly suffers

---

* The dissensions among the reformers were discrediting their cause and
defeating all their purposes.　The Rockingham Whigs and the followers of
Lord Chatham had each a particular creed respecting the government of
America.　The society for the support of the Bill of Rights had been
divided, and in some sort broken up, by mutual recriminations between
Wilkes and Horne.　Amid these divisions the city liberals especially forgot
their complaints and efforts against those whom they had accounted the
common enemy.　The aversion which Horne excited against Wilkes, and
the still greater aversion which was raised against Horne, hindered their
respective friends from due co-operation to defeat Nash's election.　The
ministry grew daily stronger in the weakness of the patriots.　The former
letter of Junius had not proved successful; but he was not without hopes
that, as in the affair of the shrievalty, the friends of Wilkes had succeeded,
so they might now, by a struggle, achieve their object.

The purport of this letter is to persuade the subdivided reformers that,
notwithstanding the differences existing among themselves, they ought to
act in union for a purpose so important as that of electing a mayor favourable
to their cause.　Junius produces a number of specious arguments.　As if
ashamed of the meanness of city politics, he endeavours to dignify his
theme by deriving his illustrations from subjects of grandeur and moment.
He contrives to escape to the examination of the parliamentary conduct of
the opposition; and, showing that its leaders refused no aid, and sacrificed,
in furtherance of the common cause, some of its own private sentiments,
strives to recommend, by this example, the same conduct to the city.
He pleads again the apology of Wilkes.　He hints anew at the mischievously-
perplexing spirit of Horne.　He pronounces the encomium of Sawbridge, and
soothes the grumblings of Townshend.　He artfully endeavours to rouse
anew, among the citizens, an indignation against the leaders in the government that should withdraw their minds from their own mutual discontents.
To Lord Mansfield he turns, as to a favourite subject of invective, and
strives to represent him as the worst, because he was the ablest and the
most artful, of all the associates of the ministry.　He kindles into wrath
as he proceeds, and endeavours to animate against the House of Commons
and against septennial elections that indignation which began to flag.
The reader cannot but remark, with pleasure and surprise, how artfully
the latter part of this letter is addressed to rouse a public spirit that should
stifle those private dissensions which its first part strives to soothe.—HERON

as well by the diminution of that strength which union carries
with it as by the separate loss of personal reputation, which
every man sustains when his character and conduct are fre
quently held forth in odious or contemptible colours. These
differences are only advantageous to the common enemy of the
country ; the hearty friends of the cause are provoked and dis
gusted ; the lukewarm advocate avails himself of any pretence
to relapse into that indolent indifference about everything that
ought to interest an Englishman, so unjustly dignified with
the title of moderation ; the false, insidious partisan, who
creates or foments the disorder, sees the fruit of his dishonest
industry ripen beyond his hopes, and rejoices in the promise
of a banquet, only delicious to such an appetite as his own.
It is time for those who really mean the *cause* and the *people* *,
who have no view to private advantage, and who have virtue
enough to prefer the general good of the community to the
gratification of personal animosities,—it is time for such men to
interpose ; let us try whether these fatal dissensions may not
yet be reconciled ; or, if that be impracticable, let us guard at
least against the worst effects of division, and endeavour to
persuade these furious partisans, if they will not consent to
draw together, to be separately useful to that cause which they
all pretend to be attached to. Honour and honesty must not
be renounced, although a thousand modes of right and wrong
were to occupy the degrees of morality between Zeno and
Epicurus. The fundamental principles of Christianity may
still be preserved, though every zealous sectary adheres to
his own exclusive doctrine, and pious ecclesiastics make it
part of their religion to persecute one another. The civil constitution, too, that legal liberty, that general creed, which
every Englishman professes, may still be supported, though
Wilkes and Horne, Townshend and Sawbridge, should obstinately refuse to communicate ; and even if the fathers of the
church, if Savile, Richmond, Camden, Rockingham, and
Chatham, should disagree in the ceremonies of their political
worship, and even in the interpretation of twenty texts in
Magna Charta. I speak to the people as one of the people.
Let us employ these men in whatever departments their
various abilities are best suited to, and as much to the

advantage of the common cause as their different inclinations
will permit. They cannot serve *us* without essentially serving
themselves.

If Mr. Nash be elected, he will hardly venture, after so
recent a mark of the personal esteem of his fellow-citizens, to
declare himself immediately a courtier. The spirit and activity
of the sheriffs will, I hope, be sufficient to counteract any
sinister intentions of the lord mayor; in collision with *their*
virtue, perhaps he may take fire.

It is not necessary to exact from Mr. Wilkes the virtues of
a Stoic. *They* were inconsistent with themselves who, almost
at the same moment, represented him as the basest of mankind, yet seemed to expect from him such instances of fortitude and self-denial as would do honour to an apostle; it is
not, however, flattery to say, that he is obstinate, intrepid, and
fertile in expedients; that he has no possible resource but in
the public favour, is, in my judgment, a considerable recommendation of him. I wish that every man who pretended to
popularity were in the same predicament; I wish that a
retreat to St. James's were not so easy and open as patriots
have found it. To Mr. Wilkes there is no access. However
he may be misled by passion or imprudence, I think he cannot be guilty of a deliberate treachery to the public; the favour
of his country constitutes the shield which defends him against
a thousand daggers, desertion would disarm him.

I can more readily admire the liberal spirit and integrity
than the sound judgment of any man who prefers a republican
form of government, in this or any other empire of equal
extent, to a monarchy so qualified and limited as ours. I am
convinced that neither is it in theory the wisest system of
government, nor practicable in this country. Yet, though I
hope the English constitution will for ever preserve its original
monarchical form, I would have the manners of the people
purely and strictly republican. I do not mean the licentious
spirit of anarchy and riot, I mean a general attachment to the
common weal, distinct from any partial attachment to persons
or families; an implicit submission to the laws only, and an
affection to the magistrate, proportioned to the integrity and
wisdom with which he distributes justice to his people, and
administers their affairs. The present habit of our political
body appears to me the very reverse of what it ought to be

The form of the constitution leans rather more than enough to the popular branch; while, in effect, the manners of the people (of those at least who are likely to take a lead in the country) incline too generally to a dependance upon the crown. The real friends of arbitrary power combine the facts, and are not inconsistent with their principles when they strenuously support the unwarrantable privileges assumed by the House of Commons. In these circumstances it were much to be desired that we had many such men as Mr. Sawbridge to represent us in parliament. I speak from common report and opinion only when I impute to him a speculative predilection in favour of a republic; in the personal conduct and manners of the man I cannot be mistaken; he has shown himself possessed of that republican firmness which the times require, and by which an English gentleman may be as usefully and as honourably distinguished as any citizen of ancient Rome, of Athens, or Lacedæmon.

Mr. Townshend complains that the public gratitude has not been answerable to his desert; it is not difficult to trace the artifices which have suggested to him a language so unworthy of his understanding. A great man commands the affections of the people, a prudent man does not complain when he has lost them: yet they are far from being lost to Mr. Townshend; he has treated our opinion a little too cavalierly. A young man is apt to rely too confidently upon himself, to be as attentive to his mistress as a polite and passionate lover ought to be. Perhaps he found her at first too easy a conquest; yet I fancy she will be ready to receive him whenever he thinks proper to renew his addresses. With all his youth, his spirit, and his appearance, it would be indecent in the lady to solicit his return.

I have too much respect for the abilities of Mr. Horne to flatter myself that these gentlemen will ever be cordially reunited; it is not, however, unreasonable to expect that each of them should act his separate part with honour and integrity to the public. As for differences of opinion upon speculative questions, if we wait until *they* are reconciled, the action of human affairs must be suspended for ever. But neither are we to look for perfection in any one man, nor for agreement among many. When Lord Chatham affirms that the authority of the British legislature is not supreme over the colonies in the

same sense in which it is supreme over Great Britain; when
Lord Camden supposes a necessity (which the king is to judge
of), and, founded upon that necessity, attributes to the crown
a legal power (not given by the Act itself) to suspend the
operation of an act of the legislature, I listen to them both
with diffidence and respect, but without the smallest degree of
conviction or assent; yet I doubt not they delivered their
real sentiments, nor ought they to be hastily condemned. I,
too, have a claim to the candid interpretation of my country,
when I acknowledge an involuntary compulsive assent to one
very unpopular opinion. I lament the unhappy necessity,
whenever it arises, of providing for the safety of the state by
a temporary invasion of the personal liberty of the subject*.
Would to God it were practicable to reconcile these important
objects in every possible situation of public affairs ! I regard
the legal liberty of the meanest man in Britain as much as
my own, and would defend it with the same zeal. I know we
must stand or fall together. But I never can doubt that the
community has a right to command, as well as to purchase,
the service of its members. I see that right founded originally
upon a necessity which supersedes all argument; I see it
established by usage immemorial, and admitted by more than
a tacit assent of the legislature. I conclude there is no remedy
in the nature of things for the grievance complained of; for
if there were, it must long since have been redressed. Though
numberless opportunities have presented themselves highly
favourable to public liberty, no successful attempt has ever
been made for the relief of the subject in this article. Yet it
has been felt and complained of ever since England had a
navy. The conditions which constitute this right must be
taken together; separately, they have little weight. It is not
fair to argue from any abuse in the execution to the illegality
of the power, much less is a conclusion to be drawn from the
navy to the land service. A seaman can never be employed
but against the enemies of his country †. The only case in

---

* Junius alludes to the practice of impressing men for sea-service; the
legality of which he allows, but confines it to seafaring men alone.

† At the time when the dispute between this country and Spain existed
relative to Falkland's Islands, for a brief account of which, see note to
Miscellaneous Letter, No. 88 ; under a persuasion that war was inevitable
an armament took place, and press warrants were issued. The legality of

which the king can have a right to arm his subjects in general, is that of a foreign force being actually landed upon our coast. Whenever that case happens, no true Englishman will inquire whether the king's right to compel him to defend his country be the custom of England or a grant of the legislature. With regard to the press for seamen, it does not follow that the symptoms may not be softened, although the distemper cannot be cured. Let bounties be increased as far as the public

these, in regard to the city, though backed by the lord mayor, was questioned by Mr. Wilkes and several other aldermen, who discharged all persons brought before them so impressed. In consequence of these discordant views of the subject, the three following questions were submitted by the lord mayor to the opinion of three of the most celebrated counsel of the day, which, together with their answers, it has been thought right to subjoin.

Query 1. May the Lords of the Admiralty of themselves, by virtue of their commission, or under the direction of the Privy Council, legally issue warrants for the impressing of seamen?

Query 2. If yea, is the warrant annexed, in point of form, legal?

Query 3. Is the lord mayor compellable to back such warrants? if he is, what may be the consequence of a refusal?

" The power of the crown to compel persons pursuing the employment and occupation of seamen to serve the public in times of danger and necessity, which has its foundation in that universal principle of the laws of all countries, that private interest must give way to the public safety, appears to us to be well established by ancient and long-continued usage frequently recognised ; and, in many instances, regulated by the legislature, and noticed at least without censure by courts of justice ; and we see no objection to this power being exercised by the lords of the admiralty under the authority of his Majesty's orders in council.

" The form of the warrant, as well as the manner in which such warrants have been usually executed, appear to us to be liable to many considerable objections ; but the nature of those objections leads us to think it the more expedient that the authority of a civil magistrate should interpose in the execution of them, to check and control the abuses to which they are liable ; and, therefore, although we do not think that the lord mayor is compellable to back the warrants, or liable to any punishment in case of his refusal, we think it right to submit it to his Lordship's consideration, whether it will not be more conducive to the preservation of the peace of the city, and the protection of the subject from oppression, if he conforms, in this instance, to what we understand to have been the practice of most of his predecessors upon the like occasion.

" AL. WEDDERBURN,
" J. GLYNN,
" J. DUNNING.'

" November 22nd, 1770."

purse can support them *. Still they have a limit, and when
every reasonable expense is incurred, it will be found, in fact,
that the spur of the press is wanted to give operation to the
bounty.

Upon the whole, I never had a doubt about the strict right
of pressing, until I heard that Lord Mansfield had applauded
Lord Chatham for delivering something like this doctrine in
the House of Lords. That consideration staggered me not a
little. But, upon reflection, his conduct accounts naturally
for itself. He knew the doctrine was unpopular, and was
eager to fix it upon the man who is the first object of his fear
and detestation. The cunning Scotchman never speaks truth
without a fraudulent design. In council he generally affects
to take a moderate part. Besides his natural timidity, it
makes part of his political plan never to be known to recommend violent measures. When the guards are called forth to
murder their fellow-subjects, it is not by the ostensible advice
of Lord Mansfield. That odious office, his prudence tells
him, is better left to such men as Gower and Weymouth, as
Barrington and Grafton. Lord Hillsborough wisely confines
his firmness to the distant Americans. The designs of
Mansfield are more subtle, more effectual, and secure.—Who
attacks the liberty of the press?—Lord Mansfield. Who invades the constitutional power of juries?—Lord Mansfield.
What judge ever challenged a juryman, but Lord Mansfield?
Who was that judge, who, to save the king's brother,
affirmed that a man of the first rank and quality, who obtains
a verdict in a suit for criminal conversation, is entitled to no
greater damages than the meanest mechanic?—Lord Mansfield? Who is it makes commissioners of the great seal?—
Lord Mansfield? Who is it forms a decree for those commissioners, deciding against Lord Chatham †, and afterwards
(finding himself opposed by the judges) declares in Parliament
that he never had a doubt that the law was in direct opposition to that decree?—Lord Mansfield. Who is he that has

---

* This suggestion was adopted by the cities of London, Bristol and
Edinburgh, and the towns of Montrose, Aberdeen, Cambletown, and
Lynn.

† On the Burton Pynsent estate, which was disputed by the relatives of
the deceased with the Earl of Chatham. See note, *post*, p. 428.

made it the study and practice of his life to undermine and
alter the whole system of jurisprudence in the Court of King's
Bench?—Lord Mansfield. There never existed a man but
himself who answered exactly to so complicated a description.
Compared to these enormities, his original attachment to the
Pretender (to whom his dearest brother was confidential
secretary) is a virtue of the first magnitude. But the hour
of impeachment *will* come, and neither he nor Grafton shall
escape me. Now let them make common cause against England and the House of Hanover. A Stuart and a Murray
should sympathise with each other.

When I refer to signal instances of unpopular opinions delivered and maintained by men who may well be supposed to
have no view but the public good, I do not mean to renew the
discussion of such opinions. I should be sorry to revive the
dormant questions of *Stamp Act, Corn Bill,* or *Press Warrant.*
I mean only to illustrate one useful proposition, which it is
the intention of this paper to inculcate:—*That we should not
generally reject the friendship or services of any man because
he differs from us in a particular opinion.* This will not appear a superfluous caution if we observe the ordinary conduct
of mankind. In public affairs, there is the least chance of a
perfect concurrence of sentiment or inclination. Yet every
man is able to contribute something to the common stock, and
no man's contribution should be rejected. If individuals have
no virtues, their vices may be of use to us. I care not with
what principle the new-born patriot is animated, if the measures he supports are beneficial to the community. The nation
is interested in his conduct. His motives are his own. The
properties of a patriot are perishable in the individual, but
there is a quick succession of subjects, and the breed is worth
preserving. The spirit of the Americans may be an useful
example to us. Our dogs and horses are English only upon
English ground; but patriotism, it seems, may be improved
by transplanting. I will not reject a bill which tends to
confine parliamentary privilege within reasonable bounds,
though it should be stolen from the House of Cavendish, and
introduced by Mr. Onslow. The features of the infant are a
proof of the descent, and vindicate the noble birth from the
baseness of the adoption. I willingly accept of a sarcasm
from Colonel Barré, or a simile from Mr. Burke. Even the

silent vote of Mr. Calcraft is worth reckoning in a division. What though he riots in the plunder of the army, and has only determined to be a patriot when he could not be a peer*? Let us profit by the assistance of such men while they are with us, and place them, if it be possible, in the post of danger, to prevent desertion.   The wary Wedderburne, the pompous Suffolk †, never threw away the scabbard, nor ever went upon a forlorn hope.   They always treated the king's servants as men with whom, some time or other, they might possibly be in friendship.   When a man who stands forth for the public has gone that length from which there is no practicable retreat, when he has given that kind of personal offence, which a pious monarch never pardons, I then begin to think him in earnest. and that he never will have occasion to solicit the forgiveness of his country.   But instances of a determination so entire and unreserved are rarely met with. Let us take mankind *as they are*.   Let us distribute the virtues and abilities of individuals according to the offices they affect, and, when they quit the service, let us endeavour to supply their places with better men than we have lost.   In this country there are always candidates enough for popular favour.   The temple of *fame* is the shortest passage to riches and preferment.

Above all things, let me guard my countrymen against the meanness and folly of accepting of a trifling or moderate compensation for extraordinary and essential injuries.   Our enemies treat us as the cunning trader does the unskilful Indian.   They magnify their generosity when they give us baubles, of little proportionate value, for ivory and gold.   The same House of Commons, who robbed the constituent body of their right of free election, who presumed to *make* a law

---

* Calcraft was introduced into political notice by Lord Holland, to whom he had been private secretary, and afterwards accumulated an immense private property by becoming army agent.   He subsequently deserted his patron, and strove to obtain a peerage from administration.   He died without having obtained his object.   One of his mistresses was the celebrated George Ann Bellamy.

† In allusion to his Lordship's manner.   Yet it must also be recollected that he headed the renegade Whigs who deserted to the ministry on the death of George Grenville.   See Miscellaneous Letters, Nos. 96 and 97, vol. ii., in which his Lordship's conduct is reprobated in very severe terms, particularly so in the latter.

under pretence of *declaring* it *; who paid our good king's debts, without once inquiring how they were incurred; who gave thanks for repeated murders committed at home, and for national infamy incurred abroad; who screened Lord Mansfield; who imprisoned the magistrates of the metropolis for asserting the subject's right to the protection of the laws; who erased a judicial record, and ordered all proceedings in a criminal suit to be suspended †;—this very House of Commons have graciously consented that their own members may be compelled to pay their debts, and that contested elections shall for the future be determined with some decent regard to the merits of the case. The event of the suit is of no consequence to the crown. While parliaments are septennial, the purchase of the sitting member or of the petitioner makes but the difference of a day. Concessions such as these are of little moment to the sum of things; unless it be to prove that the worst of men are sensible of the injuries they have done us, and perhaps to demonstrate to us the imminent danger of our situation. In the shipwreck of the state, trifles float and are preserved, while everything solid and valuable sinks to the bottom, and is lost for ever.

JUNIUS.

LETTER LX.

TO THE PRINTER OF THE PUBLIC ADVERTISER.

SIR, October 15, 1771.

I AM convinced that Junius is incapable of wilfully misrepresenting any man's opinion, and that his inclination leads him to treat Lord Camden with particular candour and respect. The doctrine attributed to him by Junius, as far as it goes, corresponds with that stated by your correspondent Scævola ‡, who seems to me to make a distinction without a

---

* The *Nullum Tempus* bill, which was passed in the year 1769.

† For a further explanation on this subject, see note to Miscellaneous Letter, No. 92.

‡ The letter of Scævola here referred to occurs in the *Public Advertiser* of October 12, and is as follows:—

TO JUNIUS.

SIR,

YOU have mistaken Lord Camden's opinion, and changed it into as weak

difference. Lord Camden, it is agreed, did certainly maintain
that, in the recess of parliament, the king (by which we all
mean the *king in council*, or the executive power) might suspend the operation of an act of the legislature; and he founded
his doctrine upon a supposed necessity, of which the king, *in
the first instance*, must be judge. The Lords and Commons
cannot be judges of it in the first instance, for they do not
exist: thus far Junius.

But, says Scævola, Lord Camden made *parliament*, and
not the *king*, judges of the necessity. That parliament may
review the acts of ministers, is unquestionable; but there is a
wide difference between saying that the crown has a *legal*
power, and that ministers may act *at their peril*. When we
say an act is *illegal*, we mean that it is forbidden by a joint
resolution of the three estates. How a subsequent resolution
of two of those branches can make it *legal ab initio*, will require explanation. If it could, the consequence would be
truly dreadful, especially in these times. There is no act of
arbitrary power which the king might not attribute to *neces-*

and mischievous a tenet as could have proceeded from Scroggs or Jefferies.
You have made it the counterpart of the ship-money doctrine. In this
representation you follow Lord Mansfield, who gave that colour to the
argument in the House of Lords. The great point of difference between
the *representation* and the *truth* is, that the former makes Lord Camden
pronounce the king judge of the necessity, and the latter, namely, my Lord
Camden's real speech, makes parliament the judge of it, and exposes the
head of the minister who advised the illegal act upon the plea of its necessity, to the mercy of parliament. Lord Camden's opinion, which I heard
him twice deliver in the House of Lords, was this:—That "if the king
should, in the recess of parliament, issue a proclamation, directing a step to
be taken flat against a subsisting law, and at the next meeting of parliament, the step should appear *to them* to have been necessary for the good
of the state, *their* declaration of that necessity would operate as a retrospect,
so as to make the act legal *ab initio*"—(which is an idea countenanced by
Mr. Locke).

That this was the scope and tenor of the noble Lord's argument, I appeal
to himself and all that heard him. Whether the opinion so restored be or
be not erroneous in point of law is a question foreign to this letter, which
has no other view but to convince the public that his Lordship never
delivered that pernicious and foolish opinion which Junius, by mistake, and
Lord Mansfield, by the basest misrepresentation, has imputed to him.

SCÆVOLA.

For Junius's opinion of this writer, see the note to Private Letter,
No 47

rity, and for which he would not be secure of obtaining the approbation of his prostituted Lords and Commons. If Lord Camden admits that the subsequent sanction of parliament was necessary to make the proclamation *legal*, why did he so obstinately oppose the bill, which was soon after brought in, for indemnifying all those persons who had acted under it? If that bill had not been passed, I am ready to maintain, in direct contradiction to Lord Camden's doctrine (taken as Scævola states it), that a litigious exporter of corn, who had suffered in his property in consequence of the proclamation, might have laid his action against the custom house officers, and would infallibly have recovered damages. No jury could refuse them; and if I, who am by no means litigious, had been so injured, I would assuredly have instituted a suit in Westminster Hall, on purpose to try the question of right. I would have done it upon a principle of defiance of the pretended power of either or both Houses to make declarations inconsistent with law, and I have no doubt, that, with an act of parliament on my side, I should have been too strong for them all. This is the way in which an Englishman should speak and act, and not suffer dangerous precedents to be established because the circumstances are favourable or palliating.

With regard to Lord Camden, the truth' is that he inadvertently overshot himself, as appears plainly by that unguarded mention of a *tyranny of forty days*, which I myself heard. Instead of asserting that the proclamation was *legal*, he *should* have said, " My Lords. I know the proclamation was *illegal*, but I advised it because it was indispensably necessary to save the kingdom from famine, and I submit myself to the justice and mercy of my country."

Such language as this would have been manly. rational, and consistent : not unfit for a lawyer, and every way worthy of a great man.

PHILO-JUNIUS.

P.S. If Scævola should think proper to write again upon this subject, I beg of him to give me a *direct* answer, that is, a plain affirmative or negative to the following questions :—In the interval between the publishing such a proclamation (or order in council) as that in question. and its receiving the

# #

# #

sanction of the two Houses, of what nature is it—is it *legal* or *illegal?* or is it neither one nor the other? I mean to be candid, and will point out to him the consequence of his answer either way. If it be *legal* it wants no farther sanction. If it be *illegal* the subject is not bound to obey it, consequently it is a useless, nugatory act, even as to its declared purpose. Before the meeting of parliament, the whole mischief which it means to prevent will have been completed*.

---

* The following extract of a subsequent letter from Scævola, inserted in the *Public Advertiser*, October 24, 1771, proves sufficiently that this writer at last admitted Lord Camden to have maintained an erroneous doctrine.

" My Lord Camden certainly thought the vote of the two Houses *in this case* equivalent to a parliamentary declaration ; he also thought such declaration made the act (illegal before) legal *ab initio*. Now as Lord Camden is no patron of mine, I am free to declare that I am satisfied he was wrong in both those points, on the foot of strict law ; that he was wrong upon his conviction, Junius himself has once admitted ; and that he was wrong upon fair and rational though not satisfactory grounds, will appear to every man of good understanding. The shade between his erroneous doctrine and the true one being in sense and reason hardly distinguishable ; both doctrines admit the proclamation to be illegal, and at the minister's peril till the meeting of parliament—both doctrines admit the two Houses of Parliament (in this or that mode) sole judges of the necessity—both doctrines agree in exposing the minister to impeachment if the two Houses of Parliament should decide against his plea of necessity. Whether upon the declaration of necessity the act becomes good in law *ab initio*, or not, is the only question. Locke (no Tory) holds the affirmative. The law, in my opinion, strictly taken, is in the negative ; for I conceive that nothing but an indemnity bill could justify the crown for having superseded a positive act of parliament."

To these remarks Junius, on the following day, puts the subjoined questions :—

1st. " In what part of Mr. Locke's writings is it maintained that the king may suspend an act of parliament, and that the subsequent approbation of the two Houses makes the suspension *legal ab initio*, or to that effect ?"

2nd. " Does Scævola think that an act of the whole legislature is as easily obtained and completed as a vote of the Lords or Commons ?"—The rest is a dispute about words not worth continuing.

LETTER LXI.

TO ZENO*.

SIR, October 17, 1771.

THE sophistry of your letter in defence of Lord Mansfield is adapted to the character you defend. But Lord Mansfield is a man of *form*, and seldom in his behaviour transgresses the

---

* The letter of Zeno here referred to occurs in the *Public Advertiser*, dated October 15, 1771, and is addressed "To Junius, alias Edmund the Jesuit of St Omer's." This writer, however, was not the only one of the same period who erred in attributing the letters of Junius to Mr. Burke. See Preliminary Essay, in which the reasons for disbelieving that gentleman to have been the author of them are more particularly given.

As Junius thought Zeno's letter worthy of a reply, the reader may not think it unworthy of a perusal. It is as follows:—

SIR,

YOUR letter of the 8th is a greater miracle than any you have hitherto produced. I do not mean in its argument, language, and arrangement. In these particulars you have been invested with a creative power, and whatever you are pleased to bring forth is not for us to approve, but to admire; but, Sir, your letter of the 8th is not written in the single spirit of calumny; you have now turned the efforts which formerly were exerted in creating divisions amongst the good, to cement those which never fail to arise amongst the bad. I have no objection to your success in this undertaking. Let the fathers of your church and the sons of the city unite. Let them club their arts and their powers. Let Wilkes enjoy his fertility in expedients, he will have need for it all. But neither that fertility, the republican firmness of Sawbridge, no, nor the youth, spirit, and graces of Townshend will avail to overturn the constitution, or even procure to them or to you the ultimate object of your desires—a little money.

Yet, Sir, why, in a letter professedly written to reconcile the patriots of the city, do you make a digression to abuse Lord Mansfield! Is it because of the diametrical opposition of his character to theirs? Certainly it must be so; and Junius is less a fool than I believed him. Nothing more likely to reconcile rogues who rail at each other than railing at honest men. If your dogs are of the true breed they will leave off worrying one another, and join in the cry against the common enemy.

It is on the subject of this abuse that I take the liberty to address the mighty Junius.

This phœnix of politicians and of reasoners tells the public that "he never had a doubt about the strict right of pressing, till he knew Lord Mansfield was of the same opinion. That indeed staggered him not a little;" and to be sure it was a staggering consideration: for who is to learn that Lord Mansfield is utterly ignorant of the law? and that his judgment is avowedly so weak and perverse, that a wise politician (I mean so very wise a politician as Junius) will examine no further, but at once

rules of decorum   I shall imitate his Lordship's good manners, and leave *you* in full possession of his principles.   I
will not call you *liar, jesuit,* or *villain;* but, with all the politeness imaginable, perhaps I may prove you so.

conclude that preposition in law to be false, which Lord Mansfield holds to
be true.

Sir, when you are only puerile, blundering, inconsistent, and absurd, I
treat you as you deserve, with ridicule and contempt. But when you assert
positive falsehoods, the mildest usage you can expect is to have them
crammed down the foul throat from which they issued. Of this nature are
the questions you make, and the answers you are pleased to give to yourself,
in relation to Lord Mansfield. So many infamous lies as these answers
contain were never crowded together before—not even by Junius. You
insinuate (and you dare but insinuate) that Lord Mansfield was the secret
adviser of sending out the guards when the affair of St. George's Fields
happened. That his Lordship was in any shape ostensibly or otherwise concerned in that matter, that he knew of it till days after it happened, is a lie
of the first magnitude; and I dare you to bring even the shadow of proof
of your infamous assertion.

It is also a lie that Lord Mansfield attacks the liberty of the press. He
has endeavoured, indeed, by legal and constitutional methods, to restrain
the abuse of that liberty, and in doing so he has shown himself a good
citizen. Are you a politician, and ignorant that the abuse of the best
things makes them degenerate into the worst? Are you a pretender to
reason, and ignorant that the abuse of a valuable privilege is the certain
means to lose it? Are not you a public defamer of every respectable character in the nation? Have not you carried the licence of the press beyond
the bounds not only of decency and humanity, but even of human conception? And dare you complain that its liberty is attacked? Your reliance
on the ignorance of those to whom you write must be great indeed, when
you dare affirm a fact which is contradicted and proved a lie by the very
affirmation of its truth.

Nor is it less false that Lord Mansfield invades the constitutional power
of juries. I refer all who are not willing to believe a lie upon the credit of
a common liar, to the letters of Phileleutherus Anglicanus, and those under
the signature of A Candid Enquirer, for information on this subject. The
letters are in the *Public Advertisers* of November and December last; and
from them, all who are able to form a judgment on a question of law, will
see it clearly demonstrated that Lord Mansfield's opinion with respect to
the power of juries is no less the law of the land than the advantage of
the subject.

Your question relating to Lord Mansfield's challenging a juryman, I confess I do not understand, neither do I know to what it alludes; a charge of
that nature ought to have been accompanied with circumstances of time,
place, and occasion. When, where, and on what account was this done?
Answer me these questions, and I pledge myself to the public that I shall
prove, to the conviction of every reasonable man, that if it was so done it
was legally done.

Like other fair pleaders in Lord Mansfield's school of justice, you answer Junius by misquoting his words, and misstating his propositions. If I am candid enough to admit that this is the very logic taught at St. Omer's, you will readily allow that

Your next accusation shows you no less void of judgment and consistency than of justice and truth. You accuse Lord Mansfield to the public, for saying a lord is entitled to no greater damages in a suit for the debauching of his wife than a mechanic. Lord Mansfield did say that, in an action of damages for criminal conversation, the law did not consider the rank of the person injured; and in this he uttered not only the dictates of law, but the dictates of common sense and humanity, neither of which you seem to understand. Had Lord Mansfield said that the law did not consider the rank of the injuring person, it might have been argued that he meant to screen the king's brother; but the difference between light and darkness is not greater than between this proposition and the proposition he maintained. None but an Irish understanding could possibly take the change, or suppose them convertible propositions. But can you, Junius, seriously make your court to the people by telling them there is a wide difference between the crime of debauching the wife of a lord and one of their own? Yo were bred at St. Omer's. You were destined for a church, not that indeed of which Savile, &c., are the fathers; but, however, a church which requires some reading. Reading the Scriptures, it is true, is forbid by your canons; but surely you have heard of the prophet Nathan's address to David on a subject of this nature? The prophet, worse than Lord Mansfield, thought that debauching the wife of a poor man was a greater crime than debauching the wife of a lord; for this plain and humane reason, that a poor man's wife was his all, his only comfort and consolation, whereas a rich man had many others; yet Junius, the popular Junius, tells the people plainly that debauching one of their wives is nothing in comparison of lying with a lord's, and arraigns the upright and discerning judge who says that the injury to the husband is in both cases equal. Who makes commissioners of the great seal? Lord Mansfield. Indeed, I thought that power had only resided in the king. To see how plain men may mistake! If you, Junius, by making commissioners mean advising the king to make commissioners I understand you. The expression is rather inaccurate, but that one is often obliged to pass over in Junius. In my turn give me leave to ask you a question. Who so proper to advise his Majesty in the choice of a law officer as Lord Mansfield?

But Lord Mansfield not only made the commissioners of the great seal, he also framed their decree, and then disavowed the decree of his own framing in the House of Peers. This is an absurd and an improbable lie. It is absurd and improbable to suppose Lord Mansfield framed a decree for three judges very capable to frame one themselves. It is more absurd to suppose Lord Mansfield would disavow the decree which he himself had made, in the presence of the three commissioners for whom he had made it, and who could so easily have detected his duplicity. And it is a direct and public lie that Lord Mansfield said he never had a doubt that the law was in direct opposition to that decree. He did not give an opinion in the

it is the constant practice in the Court of King's Bench
Junius *does not say* that he never had a doubt about the strict
right of pressing *till he knew Lord Mansfield was of the same
opinion.* His words are, *until he heard that Lord Mansfield
had applauded Lord Chatham for maintaining that doctrine
in the House of Lords.* It was not the accidental concurrence
of Lord Mansfield's opinion, but the suspicious applause given
by a cunning Scotchman to the man he detests, that raised
and justified a doubt in the mind of Junius. The question is
not whether Lord Mansfield be a man of learning and abilities (which Junius has never disputed), but whether or no he
abuses and misapplies his talents.

Junius did *not* say that Lord Mansfield had advised the
calling out the guards. On the contrary, his plain meaning is that he left that odious office to men less cunning than
himself. Whether Lord Mansfield's doctrine concerning libels
be or be not an attack upon the liberty of the press, is a question which the public in general are very well able to determine. I shall not enter into it at present. Nor do I think

House of Peers. He only stated the question; and the decree was reversed
on the unanimous opinion of the eight judges who attended. For the truth
of this I appeal to all who were present.

The last charge of Junius represents Lord Mansfield making it his study
to undermine and alter the whole system of jurisprudence in the King's
Bench. One would scarcely believe that there could be an understanding
so twisted, or a heart so corruptly malignant as to make that an article of
accusation, which, fairly taken, includes in it the most exalted merit and
virtue. If there be a superlatively eminent quality in Lord Mansfield's
great and deserved character, it is the unremitting and unwearied efforts he
constantly has made to rescue injured and oppressed innocence from the
harpy fangs of chicane and quibble. The nation does him justice in this
particular; and all the arts and lies that have been employed to defame
him have never been able to stagger the public confidence in his judgment
and integrity. The proof of this is in the breast of every man to whom I
write; and the crowd of suitors in the court where he presides gives the
most honourable testimony to the truth which I affirm, and the most palpable lie to the assertion of the abandoned Junius.

And now, Sir, having answered all your questions, you are worth no
further notice. I shall, in my turn, address a few queries to the public;
and I am sorry that the temper of the times should oblige me to recall to
their memory things which ought to be indelibly engraven on the heart of
every Englishman.

By whose advice was it that his Majesty, immediately on his accession to
the throne, made the judges places for life, thereby rendering them independent on king or minister? Lord Mansfield. When Lord Chatham and

it necessary to say much to a man who had the daring confidence to say to a jury, " Gentlemen, you are to bring in a verdict *guilty* or *not guilty*, but whether the defendant be guilty or innocent is not matter for *your* consideration." Clothe it in what language you will this is the sum total of Lord Mansfield's doctrine. If not, let Zeno show us the difference.

But it seems *the liberty of the press may be abused* and *the abuse of a valuable privilege is the certain means to lose it.* The *first* I admit; but let the *abuse* be submitted to a jury, a sufficient and indeed the only legal and constitutional check upon the licence of the press. The *second* I flatly deny. In direct contradiction to Lord Mansfield, I affirm, that " the abuse of a valuable privilege *is not* the *certain* means to lose it." If it were, the English nation would have few privileges left, for where is the privilege that has not, at one time or other, been abused by individuals? But it is false in reason and equity, that particular abuses should produce a general forfeiture. Shall the community be deprived of the protection of the laws, because there are robbers and murderers?

Lord Camden attempted to revive the impious and unconstitutional doctrine of a power in the crown to dispense with the laws of the land (which was precisely the point on which the glorious revolution hinged, and the doctrine for maintaining of which James II. lost his crown), who stood in the breach, and with eloquence and argument, more than human, defeated the pernicious attempt? Lord Mansfield. Who supported and carried through the House of Peers the bill called the *Nullum Tempus* bill; that law by which the minds of the people were quieted against apprehension of claims on the part of the crown? Lord Mansfield. To whom do we owe the success of the bill for restraining the privilege of parliament, of such essential service to the internal commerce of the nation, and especially to that part of it which could least afford to lie under any disadvantage, the industrious shopkeeper and tradesman? Lord Mansfield. Who carried Mr. Grenville's last legacy to the nation through the House of Peers, that bill by which questions of elections in the House of Commons are henceforth to be tried in a manner which will prevent the injustice supposed to have been done in the Middlesex election, and guard against the bad consequences which it was feared might follow from that determination? Lord Mansfield.

I might add many other constitutional questions in which Lord Mansfield has ever been on the side of public liberty. But if what I have already said be not sufficient to vindicate the first character in the nation from the false aspersions of an unprincipled scribbler, I am bold to say that the time is now arrived when it is unworthy of an honest man to labour for the public; and the character of an Englishman, once so respectable, will no longer be known but by its folly and ingratitude.—ZENO.

Shall the community be punished, because individuals have offended? Lord Mansfield says so, consistently enough with his principles, but I wonder to find him so explicit. Yet, for one concession, however extorted, I confess myself obliged to him The liberty of the press is, after all, a *valuable privilege*. I agree with him most heartily, and will defend it against him.

You ask me, What *juryman* was challenged by Lord Mansfield? I tell you his name was Benson. When his name was called Lord Mansfield ordered the clerk to pass him by. As for his reasons, you may ask himself, for he assigned none *. But I can tell you what all men thought of it. This Benson † had been refractory upon a former jury, and would not accept of the law as delivered by Lord Mansfield, but had the impudence to pretend to think for himself. But you it seems, honest Zeno, know nothing of the matter! You never read Junius's letter to your patron! You never heard of the intended instructions from the city to impeach Lord Mansfield! You never heard by what dexterity of Mr. Paterson that measure was prevented ‡! How wonderfully ill some people are informed!

Junius did *never* affirm that the crime of seducing the wife of a mechanic or a peer is not the same, taken in a moral or religious view. What he affirmed, in contradiction to the levelling principle so lately adopted by Lord Mansfield, was, *that the damages should be proportioned to the rank and for-*

---

* On a motion made in the House of Commons, Nov. 27, 1770, by the Hon. Mr. Phipps, for leave to bring in a bill to amend the act of William the Third, which empowers the attorney-general to file informations *ex officio*, the late Lord, then Mr., Thurlow, solicitor-general, thus defended Lord Mansfield from the charge here brought against him by Junius :—" Indeed, if a juryman has been rejected without a challenge from the parties, there is room for clamour. Such an act is highly criminal. No man is able, no honest man would wish, to defend it. But let us not be rash in passing sentence. Let the fact be well authenticated before we condemn. Rumour is not a sufficient ground for proceeding. As we found it a liar in other articles, we have this reason to doubt its veracity; though I frequent Westminster Hall, I know nothing of it; but I must confess that I cannot give it the least credit. The great judge who is suspected was incapable of such an action."

† See Letter 63, *post*, p. 432.

‡ Mr. Paterson was one of the common council for the ward of Farringdon Within, and took an active part in favour of government.

tune of the parties; and for this plain reason (admitted by every other judge that ever sat in Westminster Hall), because what is a compensation or penalty to one man is none to another. The sophistical distinction you attempt to draw between the person *injured* and the person *injuring* is Mansfield all over. If you can once establish the proposition that the injured party is not entitled to receive large damages, it follows pretty plainly that the party *injuring* should not be compelled to *pay* them; consequently the king's brother is effectually screened by Lord Mansfield's doctrine. Your reference to Nathan and David comes naturally in aid of your patron's professed system of jurisprudence. He is fond of introducing into the *Court of King's Bench* any law that contradicts or excludes the common law of England; whether it be *canon, civil, jus gentium,* or *Levitical.* But, Sir, the Bible is the code of our religious faith, and not of our municipal jurisprudence; and though it was the pleasure of God to inflict a particular punishment upon David's crime (taken as a breach of his divine commands), and to send his prophet to denounce it, an English jury have nothing to do either with David or the prophet. They consider the crime only as it is a breach of order, an injury to an individual, and an offence to society, and they judge of it by certain positive rules of law, or by the practice of their ancestors. Upon the whole, the man *after God's own heart* is much indebted to you for comparing him to the Duke of Cumberland. That his Royal Highness may be the man after Lord Mansfield's own heart seems much more probable, and you I think, Mr. Zeno, might succeed tolerably well in the character of Nathan. The evil deity, the prophet, and the royal sinner, would be very proper company for one another.

You say, Lord Mansfield did not *make* the commissioners of the great seal*, and that he only advised the king to appoint. I believe Junius meant no more, and the distinction is hardly worth disputing.

You say he *did not* deliver an opinion upon Lord Chatham's

---

* It has been already observed, that the great seal was put in commission, upon the sudden death of Charles Yorke through political chagrin. Lord Mansfield was upon this occasion made speaker of the House of Lords, and received the fees, which were supposed to amount to 5000*l.* per annum.

appeal. I affirm that he *did*, directly in favour of the appeal *. This is a point of fact to be determined by evidence only But you assign no reason for his supposed silence, nor for his desiring a conference with the judges the day before. Was not all Westminster Hall convinced that he did it with a view to puzzle them with some perplexing question, and in hopes of bringing some of them over to him? You say the com missioners were *very capable of framing a decree for themselves* By the fact it only appears that they were capable of framing an *illegal* one, which, I apprehend, is not much to the credit either of their learning or integrity.

We are both agreed that Lord Mansfield has incessantly laboured to introduce new modes of proceeding in the court where he presides; but *you* attribute it to an honest zeal in behalf of innocence oppressed by quibble and chicane. *I* say that he has introduced *new law* too, and removed the landmarks established by former decisions. *I* say that his view is to change a court of common law into a court of equity, and to bring everything within the *arbitrium* of a *prætorian* court. The public must determine between us. *But now for his merits. First*, then, the establishment of the judges in their places for life (which you tell us was advised by Lord Mansfield) was a concession merely to catch the people. It bore the appearance of royal bounty, but had nothing real in it. The judges were already for life, excepting in the case of a *demise*. Your boasted bill only provides that it shall not be in the power of the king's successor to remove them. At the best, therefore, it is only a legacy, not a gift, on the part of his present Majesty, since for himself he gives up nothing. That he did oppose Lord Camden and Lord Northington upon the proclamation against the exportation of corn, is most true, and with great ability With his talents, and taking the right side of so clear a question, it was impossible to speak ill. His motives are not so easily penetrated. They who are acquainted with the state of politics at that period, will judge of them somewhat

---

* Sir Wm. Pynsent had bequeathed an estate to Lord Chatham, which bequest was contested by his immediate heirs. The chancellorship, then in commission, was appealed to. Lord Chatham lost his cause by the decision of the commissioners; but gained it upon a further appeal to the House of Lords.

differently from Zeno. Of the popular bills, which you
say he supported in the House of Lords, the most material
is unquestionably that of Mr. Grenville for deciding contested elections. But I should be glad to know upon what
possible pretence any member of the Upper House could
oppose such a bill, after it had passed the *House of Commons!* I do not pretend to know what share he had in promoting the other two bills, but I am ready to give him all the
credit you desire. Still you will find that a whole life of deliberate iniquity is ill-atoned for by doing now and then a
laudable action upon a mixed or doubtful principle. If it be
unworthy of him, thus ungratefully treated, to labour any
longer for the public, in God's name let him retire. His
orother's patron (whose health he once was anxious for) is
dead, but the son of that unfortunate prince survives, and, I
dare say, will be ready to receive him.

PHILO-JUNIUS.

LETTER LXII.

TO AN ADVOCATE IN THE CAUSE OF THE PEOPLE*.

SIR,   October 18. 1771.
You do not treat Junius fairly. You would not have condemned him so hastily, if you had ever read Judge Foster's

---

* The letter thus subscribed appeared in the *Public Advertiser*, Oct. 16,
1771, and deserves a perusal, as it was deemed entitled to a reply.

TO JUNIUS.

SIR,
THERE is a bigotry in politics as well as in religion. Precepts which, on
examination, we should have found to be erroneous, are often implicitly
received by us, because we have formed an opinion of the integrity and
sound judgment of those by whom they were penned; but the majority of
the people are biassed by those principles entirely which they have imbibed
in their youth, and pay deference to those persons and things which their
parents instructed them to revere. The greater, therefore, the reputation of
a writer, the stricter guard I must keep over my belief, for the easier he
might lead my judgment astray. I even think it my duty, when such
a writer errs, to sound the alarm, lest my fellow-citizens be unwarily misled.
Junius is their favourite guide; but shall they follow him blindfold be

argument upon the legality of pressing seamen. A man who has not read that argument is not qualified to speak accurately upon the subject. In answer to strong facts and fair reasoning, you produce nothing but a vague comparison between two things which have little or no resemblance to each other. *General warrants*, it is true, had been often issued, but they had never been regularly questioned or resisted until the case of Mr. Wilkes. He brought them to trial, and the moment they were tried they were declared *illegal*. This is not the case of *press warrants*. They have been complained of, questioned, and resisted, in a thousand instances; but still the legislature have never interposed, nor has there ever been a formal decision against them in any of the superior courts On the contrary, they have been frequently recognized and ad-

cause he affirms it to be dark? No, let them walk with their eyes open, and see if there be not a ray of light. Credulity and superstitious veneration have ever held in darkness the human mind. It was not till the Pope and his priests had forfeited their character of holiness and infallibility that the Reformation took place, and mankind began to think for themselves; the Scriptures began to be understood in their original meaning, though many to this day interpret them, not as they have considered them in their own minds, but as, by their priests or their parents, they are taught to believe. It was not till the prerogative of the crown was abused by the House of Stuart, that the revolution succeeded in the government of Britain. Men then lost that fear and reverence with which they used to behold their king; and they began to imagine it would be better for the common weal that his power and prerogative were curtailed. The authority of the monarchical law-writers became also disregarded; and customs which, before that period, were peaceably received as the laws of the land, were then found to be illegal and inconsistent with the rights of a free man. Our minds are becoming still daily more enlightened; general warrants have lately been abolished as illegal; and you, Junius, have publicly arraigned the conduct of our chief magistrate with a freedom hitherto unknown. A few years ago a jury of your own countrymen would have perused your sentiments of their king with almost the same horror and detestation as they would have read blasphemy against their God. You have indeed, Sir, been the greatest reformer of our political creed, and I revere you for your enlarged mind. But, though in general I assent to the articles of your faith, I cannot entirely agree with you in the opinions delivered to us in your letter of the 8th of this month. What you have there written on the subject of press warrants does not become your pen. I wish, Sir, for your own honour you would give that matter a second consideration. You say, " I see the right (of pressing men into the sea service) founded originally upon necessity, which supersedes all argument. I see it established by usage immemorial, and admitted by more than a tacit assent of the legislature. I conclude there is no remedy in the nature of

mitted by parliament, and there are judicial opinions given in
their favour by judges of the first character. Under the
various circumstances stated by Junius, he has a right to conclude *for himself* that there is no remedy. If you have a good
one to propose, you may depend upon the assistance and applause of Junius. The magistrate who guards the liberty of
the individual deserves to be commended. But let him remember that it is also his duty to provide for, or at least not
to hazard, the safety of the community. If, in the case of a
foreign war, and the expectation of an invasion, you would
rather keep your fleet in harbour than man it by pressing
seamen who refuse the bounty, I have done.

You talk of disbanding the army, with wonderful ease and

things for the grievance complained of; for, if there were, it must long
since have been redressed."—Now really, Sir, this conclusion is more like
the argument of a bigoted priest of the church of Rome than the sound
reasoning of a Protestant divine. You might as well have told us to reverence the Pope, to believe in transubstantiation, and to kneel to all the
images of the popish saints, because, if it were not proper so to do, our
ancestors would not have done so before us. Would you not have been
laughed at if, in the debate on the legality of general warrants, you had
declared there was no remedy against them, because, if there were, they
must long since have been declared illegal? Were not general warrants as
much established, by usage immemorial, as is the arbitrary custom of pressing men? and were they not as anciently admitted by the tacit assent of
the legislature? Surely, Sir, if you had been seriously inclined to investigate the truth, you would have delivered yourself in a more rational style.

A man of your fertile imagination could easily have thought of a remedy
against the grievance complained of in the custom of pressing men. You
could have shown us that a body of seamen kept in constant pay was much
more necessary for the defence of this country than a standing army. You
could, during the peace, have found employment for those seamen in the
dock-yards, in the herring fishery, in the custom-house cutters, and in fully
manning those inactive men-of-war now most improperly called guard-ships,
though originally intended to guard our isle. In short, Sir, if those seamen
were to do nothing during the peace, they would still be more requisite
than an army in peace, only employed to add force to the prerogative of the
crown. But Junius was not in earnest. He is, perhaps, one of our discarded ministers (or rather one of their secretaries, for ministers rarely write
so well). He expects to be employed again; and as he may then have
occasion for men, suddenly to put a fleet to sea, he must not deliver his
opinion against press warrants; if it were received, he might hereafter find
a difficulty to equip his fleet; the remedy, though found by him, being
not yet applied to the grievance of which the nation would complain.

AN ADVOCATE IN THE CAUSE OF THE PEOPLE.

indifference. If a wiser man held such language, I should be apt to suspect his sincerity.

As for keeping up a *much greater* number of seamen in time of peace, it is not to be done. You will oppress the merchant, you will distress trade, and destroy the nursery of your seamen. He must be a miserable statesman who voluntarily, by the same act, increases the public expense and lessens the means of supporting it

PHILO-JUNIUS.

LETTER LXIII.

October 22, 1771.

A FRIEND of Junius desires it may be observed (in answer to *A Barrister-at-Law* *)—

1. That the fact of Lord Mansfield's having ordered a jury man to be passed by (which poor Zeno never heard of), is now

* The letter here referred to appeared in the *Public Advertiser* of Oct. 19, 1771, and is as follows :—

LORD MANSFIELD DEFENDED AGAINST JUNIUS AND HIS PARTY.

JUNIUS derives importance from every reply. His pride is flattered by the number of his opponents ; and even detection itself is a triumph to a man who has no honour, no fame to lose. In the absence of all character he enjoys the security which others owe to a reputation invulnerable on every side ; and he is singularly independent of rebuke, under the unparalleled depravity of his mind. But there are charges which require an answer, notwithstanding the discredit which is annexed to them on account of the quarter from which they come. Junius is not more wicked than some of his readers are credulous; and this consideration was the sole inducement to the following dispassionate answer to his late attack upon a great law Lord who is an ornament to the present age.

The charge *that his Lordship challenged a juror* is at once impossible and absurd. It answers itself, and bears the lie on its face. But Junius may found his accusation upon a misrepresented fact. A juryman, about fifteen years ago, for a suspicion conceived upon something which happened in court, was passed by with the acquiescence and consent of the counsel on both sides. Neither of the parties complained. A factious attorney, to gain consequence to himself, began to mutter. He met with no encouragement, and he dropped the affair. Junius ought to know that jurors are passed by with the acquiescence of both parties, without a *formal challenge.* Without the consent of *both*, it cannot be done. Such a measure would be a *mis-trial;* and, upon motion, would be set aside of course by the

formally admitted. When Mr. Benson's name was called, Lord Mansfield was observed to flush in the face (a signal of guilt not uncommon with him), and cried out, *pass him by* This I take to be something more than a peremptory chal· lenge. It is an *unlawful command*, without any reason

court. But when the parties are satisfied, nobody else has any right to complain.

His Lordship has destroyed the liberty of the press. Junius, in this charge, gives himself the lie. No writer ever used the liberty of the press with such unrestrained freedom as himself; no times were ever so much marked as the present with public scurrility and defamation. A reply to the charge is in *every* column of *every* paper. They are the most dangerous enemies who abuse the liberty of the press like Junius and his adherents.

His lordship, not content with destroying the liberty of the press, has, if we believe Junius, *restrained the power of juries.* Juries, it has never yet been doubted, have a power of doing either right or wrong, according to their will and pleasure. The only question is, by what rules should they govern themselves if they mean to do right. Till the year 1730, there was some doubt whether the construction of a libel was not a question of law; but in Franklin's trial, the rule, which has been invariably ever since followed, was admitted by Lord Hardwicke, then attorney-general, agreed to by eminent counsel on the other side, and adopted by the court. Lord Mansfield made a late opinion of the court very public, undoubtedly with a view that it should be taken up constitutionally in parliament by those who pretended to differ from him in opinion, by a *bill*, in the progress of which the matter might be discussed, with the assistance of the judges. It was in this light understood; and the most considerable part of those who differed from that opinion in the House of Commons, being clear that there was no colour for a declaratory law, moved for a bill to make a law for the future, which was rejected. The enormous crime trumped up by Junius and his party then is, that a judge tells the jury what, in his opinion, *the law is*, and leaves them afterwards to do as they please, without interposition. If he thinks his opinion right, as he most certainly does, it is not in his power to do otherwise; and he *must* repeat the same conduct whenever a similar case comes before him.

Junius next affirms, that "t, save the king's brother, Lord Mansfield declared that, in a verdict for criminal conversation, a man of the first quality is entitled to no greater damages than the meanest mechanic." I have talked with some who attended the trial, have read the spurious accounts of it in print. We know how falsely and ignorantly such notes are taken, even when the writers mean no harm. They are generally unintelligible till they are corrected by the persons concerned. But I suspect that malice joined issue with blunder in what is made Lord Mansfield's opinion. It is full of nonsense, contradictory, and manifestly imperfect. Much depends upon a word or two, a restriction or a qualification. The published opinion makes Lord Mansfield tell the jury that the measure of damages must be formed from all the circumstances of the case taken together. In another place, it makes him state many of the circumstances.

assigned.   That the counsel did not resist, is true; but this
might happen either from inadvertence or a criminal complaisance to Lord Mansfield.   You *Barristers* are too apt to
be civil to my Lord Chief Justice, at the expense of your
clients.

and say they are not at all material, without any restriction or qualification.
But the scope and occasion of the direction are very plain, in whatever
words the direction itself was expressed.

A very eminent and able counsel had, with a torrent of eloquence, applied
to the passions of the jury.   He laboured with great art and address to
carry them, it is impossible to say where, merely on account of the rank
and situation of the parties.   The Duke of York, he informed the jury,
recovered one hundred thousand pounds against a man for calling him a
papist, which was no additional damage to his character, for all England
knew him to be actually a papist.   If, therefore, continued the counsel, the
king's brother recovered so much, the rule should be reciprocal, and the
defendant ought to pay much more, as the injury was greater.   The learned
counsel judiciously passed over the many cases in England—of a Duke of
Norfolk. a Duke of Beaufort, a Duke of Grafton, and many other peers
who had recovered moderate damages from men of fortune.   But he rested
on an Irish case, of which he stated no circumstances, where the rule was
to give such damages as should ruin the defendant. He, therefore, contended
for an exorbitant verdict by way of punishment.

It was the indispensable duty of the judge to extricate the matter from
the passions of the jury, worked up and biassed by inflammatory eloquence,
that powerful instrument of deceit, and to bring it back to their cool and
sound judgments.   They were, therefore, told that damages are by way of
retribution or compensation to the plaintiff for the injury, and to be esti-
mated from all the circumstances.   The rank and situation of the parties
were not of themselves decisive.   A peer, under some circumstances, may
be entitled to less damages for this injury than a tradesman under other
circumstances.   That it might be just, in certain situations, to give small
damages for this injury against a defendant of great wealth, and in other
situations to give ten thousand pounds against a person of low degree.
Even from the spurious opinion published, the case appears to have been
left to the jury, upon all the circumstances, without a single remark on any
of them, without a word of alleviation.   No cases were mentioned where
moderate damages had been given to peers of the highest rank for this
injury against persons of great fortune.

The next charge of Junius and his party against the noble Lord is, " that
he has changed the system of jurisprudence."   The uncandid party do not
recollect that Lord Mansfield has had three assistants most eminent for
knowledge and integrity.   The only change we of Westminster Hall either
know or have heard of is, that the decisions inform and satisfy the bar .
that hitherto no one has been reversed, and, which is a main point to the
suitor, and perhaps new, there is *no delay*. Since Lord Mansfield sat there.
the business which flows into that channel, and leaves every other almost
dry, is increased beyond belief.   I have been assured that, besides all the

2. Junius did never say that Lord Mansfield had *destroyed* the liberty of the press. "That his lordship has *laboured to destroy*—that his doctrine is an *attack* upon the liberty of the press—that it is an *invasion* of the right of juries," are the propositions maintained by Junius. His opponents never answer him in point, for they never meet him fairly upon his own ground.

3. Lord Mansfield's policy, in endeavouring to screen his unconstitutional doctrines behind an act of the legislature, is easily understood. Let every Englishman stand upon his guard; the right of juries to return a general verdict, in all cases whatsoever, is a part of our constitution. It stands in no need of a bill, either *enacting* or *declaratory*, to confirm it *.

4. With regard to the *Grosvenor cause*, it is pleasant to observe that the doctrine attributed by Junius to Lord

other business, there are not fewer than *seven* or *eight hundred* causes entered every year at the sittings before his Lordship for London and Middlesex. It is at once unjust and uncandid to take from him all merit while he goes through the immense fatigue which arises from a high reputation.

As to Lord Chatham's cause, the malevolent writer has sat down to invent a lie, without giving himself the trouble to inquire into what passed in public upon that subject. I, as many more of the profession, attended that cause. Lord Mansfield moved the question, which was put to the judges, penned with a view to that point, upon which, it appeared afterwards, he thought the cause depended. Though it had been argued, both above and below, upon another point, the judges considered the point on which it had been argued. They were divided and prepared to give different opinions. Lord Mansfield, apprized of the disagreement among the judges, suggested that point upon which he thought the cause turned, be the other as it might. He proposed to the judges to consider it in that light. The House was adjourned expressly for this purpose; and when the judges came to consider the cause on the point suggested by Lord Mansfield, they were unanimous, which terminated the cause, whatever the law might be upon the other point on which it was decided below. The allegation that Lord Mansfield made the decree for the commissioners, bears on its face the marks of a palpable falsehood. It is a mere invention of Junius; never mentioned, never suspected by any other writer. I am convinced, both from the delicacy of the commissioners and that of his Lordship, that not a single word ever passed between them on the subject.

Temple, Oct. 16. A BARRISTER-AT-LAW.

* This subject was agitated in the House of Commons, in the spring of the year 1771, on the motion of Mr. Dowdeswell for leave to bring in an enacting bill; which was rejected by a majority of 218 against 72. See also note, *ante*, p. 94.—ED.

Mansfield is admitted by Zeno, and directly defended. The *Barrister* has not the assurance to deny flatly, but he evades the charge, and softens the doctrine by such poor contemptible quibbles as cannot impose upon the meanest understanding.

5. The quantity of business in the *Court of King's Bench* proves nothing but the litigious spirit of the people, arising from a great increase of wealth and commerce. These however are now upon the decline. and will soon leave nothing but *law suits* behind them. When Junius affirms that Lord Mansfield has laboured to alter the system of jurisprudence in the court where his Lordship presides, he speaks to those who are able to look a little further than the vulgar. Besides that the multitude are easily deceived by the imposing names of *equity* and *substantial justice*, it does not follow that a judge, who introduces into his court new modes of proceeding and new principles of law, intends, *in every instance*, to decide unjustly. Why should he where he has no interest? We say that Lord Mansfield is a bad *man* and a worse *judge;* but we do not say that he is a *mere devil*. Our adversaries would fain reduce us to the difficulty of proving too much. This artifice, however, shall not avail him. The truth of the matter is plainly this:—When Lord Mansfield has succeeded in his scheme of changing a court of *common law* to a court of *equity*, he will have it in his power to do justice *whenever he thinks proper*. This, though a wicked purpose, is neither absurd nor unattainable *.

* The unfavourable constructions by Junius of the judicial merits of Lord Mansfield have not been ratified by the deliberate opinions of a later generation. In the above paragraph he is charged with "making it his study to undermine and alter the whole system of jurisprudence in the King's Bench; upon which allegation the explanatory defence of Lord Mansfield's biographer may be fitly introduced. "His Lordship's ideas," says Mr. Holliday, " went to the gradual melioration of the law, by making its liberality keep pace with the demands of justice, and the actual concerns of the world; not restricting the infinitely-diversified occasions of men and the rules of national justice within artificial circumscriptions. Cases in law depend on the circumstances that give rise to them. A statute can seldom take in all cases. Therefore the common law, which *works itself pure* by rules drawn from the fountain of justice, is for this reason superior to act of parliament. From the period of Lord Mansfield to the present time the law has gone on continually working itself pure by rules (to use his Lordship's expression) drawn from the fountain of justice. ' General rules,' said he on the bench, 'are wisely established for obtaining justice with ease, certainty, and

6. The last paragraph, relative to Lord Chatham's cause, cannot be answered. It partly refers to facts of too secret a nature to be ascertained, and partly is unintelligible. " Upon *one* point the cause is decided against Lord Chatham; upon *another* point it is decided for him." Both the *law* and *language* are well suited to a *Barrister!* If I have any guess at this honest gentleman's meaning it is, that " whereas the commissioners of the great seal saw the question in a point of view unfavourable to Lord Chatham, and decreed accord ingly, Lord Mansfield, out of sheer love to Lord Chatham, took the pains to place it in a point of view more favourable to the *appellant.*"—*Credat Judæus Apella.* So curious an assertion would stagger the faith of Mr. Sylva.

LETTER LXIV.

TO THE PRINTER OF THE PUBLIC ADVERTISER.

SIR,   November 2, 1771.

WE are desired to make the following declaration in behalf of Junius, upon three material points, on which his opinion has been mistaken or misrepresented.

1. Junius considers the right of taxing the colonies, by an act of the British legislature, as a *speculative* right merely, never to be *exerted* nor ever to be *renounced.* To *his* judgment it appears plain, " that the general reasonings which were employed against that power, went directly to our whole legislative right, and that one part of it could not be yielded

despatch. But the great end of them being to do justice, the court will see that it be really obtained.' "—*Life of Lord Mansfield,* pp. 121-3.

Lord Brougham, in his great speech on the *State of the Law,* Feb. 8, 1828, makes honourable mention of the Chief Justice, with a reference to the opinion of Junius.

" Lord Mansfield, whose luminous mind was never understood except by those who were either jealous of his fame or ignorant of his value in the science of jurisprudence—whom no man ever attacked for a deficiency in his knowledge of the laws (with the exception of *one great writer,* whose style gave currency for a time to the assertion, though accompanied by an obvious want of legal knowledge in himself), that great man had noticed many of the discrepancies of the law with the eye of a philosopher, which were not to be changed by the habits of the practitioner."—ED.

to such arguments without a virtual surrender of all the rest."

2. That, with regard to press warrants, his argument should be taken in his own words and answered strictly: that comparisons may sometimes illustrate, but prove nothing; and that, in this case, an appeal to the passions is unfair and unnecessary. Junius feels and acknowledges the evil in the most express terms, and will show himself ready to concur in any rational plan that may provide for the liberty of the individual without hazarding the safety of the community. At the same time he expects that the evil, such as it is, be not exaggerated or misrepresented. In general it is *not* unjust that, when the rich man contributes his wealth, the *poor* man should serve the state in person; otherwise the latter contributes nothing to the defence of that law and constitution from which he demands safety and protection. But the question does not lie between *rich* and *poor*. The laws of England make no such distinctions. Neither is it true that the poor man is torn from the care and support of a wife and family helpless without him. The single question is, whether the *seaman**, in times of public danger, shall serve the merchant or the state in that profession to which he was bred, and by the exercise of which alone he can honestly support himself and his family. General arguments against the doctrine of *necessity*, and the dangerous use that may be made of it, are of no weight in this particular case. *Necessity* includes the idea of *inevitable*. Whenever it is so, it creates a law to which all *positive* laws and all *positive* rights must give way. In this sense the levy of *ship-money* by the king's warrant was not *necessary*, because the business might have been as well or better done by parliament. If the doctrine maintained by Junius be confined within this limitation, it will go but very little way in support of arbitrary power. That the king is to judge of the occasion is no objection, unless we are told how it can possibly be otherwise. There are other instances not less important in the exercise, nor less dangerous in the abuse, in which the constitution relies entirely upon the king's judgment. The executive power proclaims war and peace, binds the nation by treaties,

---

* I confine myself strictly to *seamen*;—if any others are pressed, it is a gross abuse, which the magistrates can and should correct.—JUNIUS.

orders general embargoes, and imposes quarantines, not to mention a multitude of prerogatives which, though liable to the greatest abuses, were never disputed.

3. It has been urged as a reproach to Junius, that he has not delivered an opinion upon the game laws, and particularly the late *Dog Act*. But Junius thinks he has much greater reason to complain that he is never assisted by those who are able to assist him*, and that almost the whole labour of the press is thrown upon a single hand, from which a discussion of *every* public question whatsoever is unreasonably expected. He is not paid for his labour, and certainly has a right to choose his employment. As to the *game laws*, he never scrupled to declare his opinion that they are a species of the *forest laws*, that they are oppressive to the subject, and that the spirit of them is incompatible with legal liberty; that the penalties imposed by these laws bear no proportion to the nature of the offence ; that the mode of trial, and the degree and kind of evidence necessary to convict, not only deprive the subject of all the benefits of a trial by jury, but are in themselves too summary, and to the last degree arbitrary and oppressive; that, in particular, the late acts to prevent dog-stealing, or killing game between sun and sun, are distinguished by their absurdity, extravagance, and pernicious tendency.   If these terms are weak or ambiguous, in what language can Junius express himself?   It is no excuse for Lord Mansfield to say that he *happened* to be absent when these bills passed the House of Lords.   It was his duty to be present.   Such bills could never have passed the House of Commons without his knowledge.   But we very well know by what rules he regulates his attendance.   When that order was made in the House of Lords in the case of Lord Pomfret* at which every Englishman shudders, my honest Lord Mansfield found himself *by mere accident* in the Court of King's Bench.   Otherwise he would have done wonders in defence of law and property !   The pitiful evasion is adapted

* In Private Letter, No. 66, addressed to Mr. Wilkes, Junius complains of his want of " support in the newspapers."

+ A case brought by Lord Pomfret before the House, from one of the inferior courts, in reference to a tract of ground claimed by the parish in which he resided as common land, but maintained by his Lordship to be a part of his own freehold.

to the character. But Junius will never justify himself by the example of this bad man. The distinction between *doing wrong* and *avoiding to do right* belongs to Lord Mansfield. Junius disclaims it.

———

LETTER LXV.

TO LORD CHIEF JUSTICE MANSFIELD.

November 2, 1771.

AT the intercession of three of your countrymen you have bailed a man, who, I presume, is also a Scotchman, and whom the lord mayor of London had refused to bail * I do not mean to enter into an examination of the partial, sinister motives of your conduct; but, confining myself strictly to the fact, I affirm, that you have done that which by law you were not warranted to do. The thief was taken in the theft, the stolen goods were found upon him, and he made no defence. In these circumstances (the truth of which you dare not deny, because it is of public notoriety), it could not stand indifferent whether he was guilty or not, much less could there be any presumption of his innocence ; and, in these circumstances, I affirm, in contradiction to YOU, LORD CHIEF JUSTICE MANSFIELD, that, by the laws of England, he was *not bailable*. If ever Mr. Eyre should be brought to

———

* In explanation of this assertion, the editor extracts the following paragraph from the *Public Advertiser*, Oct. 20, 1771 :—

" Yesterday application was made to the lord mayor by the friends of John Eyre, Esq., committed on the oaths of Thomas Fielding, William Holder, William Payne, and William Nash, for feloniously stealing eleven quires of writing paper. The circumstances were so strong against the prisoner, on whom the goods were found, and no defence whatever being set up by him before the magistrate who made the commitment, that the lord mayor refused to bail him. The alderman who committed him had before refused to bail him, as it was alleged that no instance whatever had been known of a person being bailed under such circumstances. Mr. Eyre was, however, bailed yesterday by Lord Mansfield, himself in only 300*l.* and three Scottish securities in 100*l.* each, a Kinloch, Farquar, and Innis. *Eyre has since made his escape.*"

trial*, we shall hear what you have to say for yourself ; and I pledge myself before God and my country, in proper time and place, to make good my charge against you.

JUNIUS.

LETTER LXVI.

FOR THE PUBLIC ADVERTISER.

November 9, 1771.

JUNIUS engages to make good his charge against LORD CHIEF JUSTICE MANSFIELD, some time before the meeting of parliament, in order that the House of Commons may, if they think proper, make it one article in the impeachment of the said Lord Chief Justice.

LETTER LXVII†.

TO HIS GRACE THE DUKE OF GRAFTON.

November 28, 1771.

WHAT is the reason, my Lord, that, when almost every man in the kingdom, without distinction of principles or party,

---

* The facts of the case were as follow :—On the 2nd Oct., 1771, Eyre was committed to Wood Street Compter, by Mr. Alderman Halifax, for privately stealing out of a room at Guildhall three quires of writing-paper which were found upon him ; on searching his lodgings, there were discovered in a box eight quires more of the same sort of paper, which had been marked privately for the discovery of the thief. Eyre had attended at the justice-room for a considerable time, under the pretence of learning the business of a magistrate, to which situation, he said, he shortly expected to be appointed. On the day preceding the date of this letter, he surrendered himself at the Old Bailey to take his trial for stealing the paper, to which charge he pleaded guilty, and threw himself on the mercy of the court. He was sentenced to be transported. This sordid wretch was asserted at the time of committing so miserable a theft to be worth at least thirty thousand pounds.

† The litigation which had arisen in consequence of the attempt to grant away the Duke of Portland's estate to Sir James Lowther, had ended in favour of the Duke. Inglewood Forest was found to have been not legally

exults in the ridiculous defeat of Sir James Lowther*, when
good and bad men unite in one common opinion of that
baronet, and triumph in his distress, as if the event (without
any reference to vice or virtue) were interesting to human
nature, your Grace alone should appear so miserably de-
pressed and afflicted? In such universal joy I know not
where you will look for a compliment of condolence, unless
you appeal to the tender sympathetic sorrows of Mr. Bradshaw. That cream-coloured gentleman's tears†, affecting as
they are, carry consolation along with them. He never
weeps but, like an April shower, with a lambent ray of sunshine upon his countenance. From the feelings of honest
men upon this joyful occasion I do not mean to draw any
conclusion to your Grace. *They* naturally rejoice when they
see a signal instance of tyranny resisted with success, of
treachery exposed to the derision of the world, an infamous
informer defeated, and an impudent robber dragged to the
public gibbet. But in the *other* class of mankind, I own
I expected to meet the Duke of Grafton. Men who have no

granted to Sir James, and to be not legally resumable from the Duke of
Portland. The Duke of Grafton was minister when the grant to Sir James
Lowther passed from the treasury; and Junius, therefore, eagerly seizes
this last opportunity to insult his feelings.

The letter chiefly repeats the old themes of opprobrium levelled against
the Duke, is interspersed with digressions respecting the Luttrells, with
exultations over Sir James Lowther, and with hinted abuse of the king. It
is eloquent and caustic; but contains little to demand new illustration. In
his Private Letter, No. 44, Junius declares that it was written in conse-.
quence of a communication from Garrick to Ramus, and from the latter to
the king, that Junius would write no more; and hence the questions in the
concluding paragraph. His words are, " David Garrick has literally forced
me to break my resolution of writing no more," for the subsequent letter
addressed to Lord Mansfield was completed sometime previous to the date
of this letter, as may be seen in Private Letter, No. 40, where, and in that
which follows it, will be found an explanation of the curious circumstance of
the communication to the king, the author's early knowledge of the fact,
and a copy of the very severe letter which he sent to Mr. Garrick, in consequence of the information which he had given to Mr. Ramus.—ED.

* He refers to the case of Lowther against the Duke of Portland, in the
contest concerning Inglewood Forest, &c., in Cumberland. See the detail
and determination of the dispute (which last had now just taken place) in
note, *ante*, p. 402.

† Miscellaneous Letter 71, vol. ii.

regard for justice, nor any sense of honour, seem as heartily pleased with Sir James Lowther's well-deserved punishment as if it did not constitute an example against themselves. The unhappy baronet has no friends, even among those who resemble him.   You, my Lord, are not yet reduced to so deplorable a state of dereliction.   Every villain in the kingdom is your friend, and, in compliment to such amity, I think you should suffer your dismal countenance to clear up. Besides, my Lord, I am a little anxious for the consistency of your character.   You violate your own rules of decorum when you do not insult the man whom you have betrayed.

The divine justice of retribution seems now to have begun its progress.   Deliberate treachery entails punishment upon the traitor.   There is no possibility of escaping it, even in the highest rank to which the consent of society can exalt the meanest and worst of men.   The forced, unnatural union of Luttrell and Middlesex was an omen of another unnatural union, by which indefeasible infamy is attached to the House of Brunswick.   If one of those acts was virtuous and honourable, the best of princes, I thank God, is happily rewarded for it by the other.   Your Grace, *it has been said*, had some share in recommending Colonel Luttrell to the king. Or, was it only the gentle Bradshaw who made himself answerable for the good behaviour of his friend?   An intimate connection has long subsisted between him and the worthy Lord Irnham. It arose from a fortunate similarity of principles, cemented by the constant mediation of their common friend, Miss Davis*.

* There is a certain family in this country, on which nature seems to have entailed an hereditary baseness of disposition. As far as their history has been known, the son has regularly improved upon the vices of his father, and has taken care to transmit them pure and undiminished into the bosom of his successor. In the senate, their abilities have confined them to those humble, sordid services, in which the scavengers of the ministry are usually employed. But in the memoirs of private treachery they stand first and unrivalled. The following story will serve to illustrate the character of this respectable family, and to convince the world that the present possessor has as clear a title to the infamy of his ancestors as he has to their estate. It deserves to be recorded for the curiosity of the fact, and should be given to the public as a warning to every honest member of society.

The present Lord Irnham, who is now in the decline of life, lately cultivated the acquaintance of a younger brother of a family with which he had lived in some degree of intimacy and friendship. The young man had long been the dupe of a most unhappy attachment to a common prostitute.

Yet I confess I should be sorry that the opprobrious infamy of this match should reach beyond the family. We have now a better reason than ever to pray for the long life of the best of princes, and the welfare of his royal *issue*. I will not mix anything ominous with my prayers, but let parliament look to it. A *Luttrell* shall never succeed to the crown of England*. If the hereditary virtues of the family deserve a kingdom, Scotland will be a proper retreat for them.

The next is a most remarkable instance of the goodness of Providence. The just law of retaliation has at last overtaken the little, contemptible tyrant of the north. To this son-in-law of your dearest friend, the Earl of Bute, you meant to transfer the Duke of Portland's property†; and you hastened the grant, with an expedition unknown to the treasury, that he might have it time enough to give a decisive turn to the election for the county. The immediate consequence of this flagitious robbery was that he lost the election, which you meant to ensure to him, and with such signal circumstances of scorn, reproach, and insult, (to say nothing of the general exultation of all parties,) as (excepting the king's brother-in-law, Colonel Luttrell‡, and old Simon, his father-in-law,) hardly ever fell upon a gentleman in this country. In the

His friends and relations foresaw the consequences of this connection, and did everything that depended upon them to save him from ruin. But he had a friend in Lord Irnham, whose advice rendered all their endeavours ineffectual. This hoary letcher, not contented with the enjoyment of his friend's mistress [the notorious Polly Davis, mentioned in the letter above], was base enough to take advantage of the passions and folly of a young man, and persuaded him to marry her. He descended even to perform the office of father to the prostitute. He gave her to his friend, who was on the point of leaving the kingdom, and the next night lay with her himself. Whether the depravity of the human heart can produce anything more base and detestable than this fact, must be left undetermined until the son shall arrive at his father's age and experience.—JUNIUS.

This note appeared in the *Public Advertiser*, April 7, 1769, under the signature of *Recens*; and was republished by Junius in the edition of his *Letters*, revised by himself.—ED.

* The Duke of Cumberland was now married to Mrs. Horton, Colonel Luttrell's sister. Miscellaneous Letter, No. 102, vol. ii.

† See note, p. 402.

‡ Miscellaneous Letter, No. 102. Our author thus denominates his Majesty, because, by the marriage of Luttrell's sister, Mrs. Horton, with the Duke of Cumberland, Luttrell was legally become brother-in-law to the king's brother; as was Luttrell's father, father-in-law to him.

event, he loses the very property of which he thought he had gotten possession, and after an expense which would have paid the value of the land in question twenty times over; the forms of villany, you see, are necessary to its success. Hereafter you will act with greater circumspection, and not drive so directly to your object. To *snatch a grace*, beyond the reach of common treachery, is an exception, not a rule.

And now, my good Lord, does not your conscious heart inform you that the justice of retribution begins to operate, and that it may soon approach your person? Do you think that Junius has renounced the Middlesex election? Or that the king's timber shall be refused to the royal navy with impunity *? Or that you shall hear no more of the sale of that patent to Mr. Hine, which you endeavoured to screen by suddenly dropping your prosecution of Samuel Vaughan†, when the rule against him was made absolute? I believe, indeed, there never was such an instance, in all the history of negative impudence. But it shall not save you. The very sunshine you live in is a prelude to your dissolution. When you are ripe you shall be plucked.

JUNIUS.

P.S.—I beg you will convey to our gracious master my humble congratulations upon the glorious success of peerages and pensions, so lavishly distributed as the rewards of Irish virtue

---

LETTER LXVIII‡.

TO LORD CHIEF JUSTICE MANSFELD

January 21, 1772.

I HAVE undertaken to prove that when, at the intercession of three of your countrymen, you bailed John Eyre, you did that

* Note, *ante*, p. 403.
† Letter 33, *ante*, p. 249, and Private Letter, No. 15, for the particulars of the transaction here alluded to.
‡ This is the threatened proof of the charge of illegality in the admitting of Eyre to bail. It attempts to show that the superior power of the

which by law you were not warranted to do, and that a felon,
under the circumstances *of being taken in the fact, with the
stolen goods upon him, and making no defence*, is *not bailable*
by the laws of England.   Your learned advocates have inter
preted this charge into a denial that the Court of King's Bench,
or the judges of that court during the vacation, have any
greater authority to bail for criminal offences than a justice of
peace.   With the instance before me I am supposed to question your power of doing wrong, and to deny the existence of
a power, at the same moment that I arraign the illegal exercise
of it.   But the opinions of such men, whether wilful in their
malignity or sincere in their ignorance, are unworthy of my
notice.   You, Lord Mansfield, did not understand me so, and
I promise you your cause requires an abler defence.   I am
now to make good my charge against you.   However dull my
argument, the subject of it is interesting.   I shall be honoured
with the attention of the public, and have a right to demand
the attention of the legislature ; supported, as I am, by the
whole body of the criminal law of England, I have no doubt of
establishing my charge.   If, on your part, you should have no
plain, substantial   defence, but should endeavour to shelter
yourself under the quirk and evasion of a practising lawyer, or
under the mere insulting assertion of power without right, the
reputation you pretend to is gone for ever ; you stand degraded
from the respect and authority of your office, and are no longer,
de jure, lord chief justice of England.   This letter, my Lord,
is addressed not so much to *you* as to the public,   Learned as
you are, and quick in apprehension, few arguments are necessary to satisfy you, that you have done that which by law you
were not warranted to do; your conscience already tells you that
you have sinned against knowledge, and that whatever defence
you make contradicts your own internal conviction.   But other

Court of King's Bench to bail rests not upon positive law ; that in a case
so clear as that of Eyre, there was no scope for the discretion of the judges ;
that, considering all the circumstances of that case, no juridical authority
known to the law of England could legally admit the culprit to bail.   There
are infinite ingenuity and elaborate erudition in the argument. *Valeat quantum valere potest.* The invective connected with it degenerates occasionally
into vulgar abuse, and is inconsistent with the gravity of the investigation.
   Junius, in speaking of this letter, says, " The paper itself is, in my
opinion, of the highest style of Junius, and cannot fail to sell." Private
Letter, No. 49.

men are willing enough to take the law upon trust. They rely upon authority, because they are too indolent to search for information ; or, conceiving that there is some mystery in the laws of their country which lawyers are only qualified to explain, they distrust their judgment, and voluntarily renounce the right of thinking for themselves. With all the evidence of history before them. from Tresillian to Jefferies, from Jefferies to Mansfield, they will not believe it possible that a learned judge can act in direct contradiction to those laws which he is supposed to have made the study of his life, and which he has sworn to administer faithfully Superstition is certainly not the characteristic of this age. Yet some men are bigoted in politics who are infidels in religion.—I do not despair of making them ashamed of their credulity.

The charge I brought against you is expressed in terms guarded and well considered. They do not deny the strict power of the judges of the Court of King's Bench to bail in cases not bailable by a justice of peace, nor replevisable by the common writ, or *ex officio* by the sheriff. I well knew the practice of the court, and by what legal rules it ought to be directed ; but far from meaning to soften or diminish the force of those terms I have made use of, I now go beyond them, and affirm—

I. That the superior power of bailing for felony, claimed by the Court of King's Bench. is founded upon the opinion of lawyers, and the practice of the court ; that the assent of the legislature to this power is merely negative, and that it is not supported by any positive provision in any statute whatsoever : if it be, produce the statute

II. Admitting that the judges of the Court of King's Bench are vested with a discretionary power to examine and judge of circumstances and allegations which a justice of the peace is not permitted to consider. I affirm that the judges, in the use and application of that discretionary power, are as strictly bound by the spirit, intent, and meaning. as the justice of peace is by the words of the legislature. Favourable circumstances, alleged before the judge, may justify a doubt whether the prisoner be guilty or not; and where the guilt is doubtful a presumption of innocence should in general be admitted. But when any such probable circumstances are alleged, they alter the state and condition of the prisoner.

He is no longer that *all-but-convicted* felon, whom the law
intends, and who by law is *not bailable at all.* If no circumstances whatsoever are alleged in his favour,—if no
allegation whatsoever be made to lessen the force of that
evidence which the law annexes to a positive charge of felony,
and particularly to the fact of *being taken with the maner,*
—I then say that the lord chief justice of England has no
more right to bail him than a justice of peace. The discretion of an English judge is not of mere will and pleasure—
it is not arbitrary—it is not capricious; but, as that great
lawyer (whose authority I wish you respected half as much as
I do) truly says*, " Discretion, taken as it ought to be, is
discernere per legem quid sit justum. If it be not directed
by the right line of the law, it is a crooked cord, and appeareth to be unlawful." If discretion were arbitrary in the
judge, he might introduce whatever novelties he thought
proper; but, says Lord Coke, " Novelties without warrant
of precedents are not to be allowed; some certain rules are
to be followed—*Quicquid judicis authoritati subjicitur, novi-
tati non subjicitur;*" and this sound doctrine is applied to the
Star Chamber, a court confessedly arbitrary. If you will
abide by the authority of this great man, you shall have all
the advantage of his opinion wherever it appears to favour
you. Excepting the plain, express meaning of the legislature, to which all private opinions must give way, I desire no
better judge between us than Lord Coke.

III. I affirm that, according to the obvious, indisputable
meaning of the legislature repeatedly expressed, a person
positively charged with *feloniously stealing,* and taken *in
flagrante delicto,* with the stolen goods upon him, *is not
bailable.* The law considers him as differing in nothing from
a *convict* but in the form of conviction, and (whatever a corrupt judge may do) will accept of no security but the confinement of his body within four walls. I know it has been
alleged in your favour that you have often bailed for murders,
rapes, and other manifest crimes. Without questioning the
fact, I shall not admit that you are to be justified by your
own example. If that were a protection to you, where is the
crime that, as a judge, you might not now securely commit?

* 4 *Inst.* 41, 66.

But neither shall I suffer myself to be drawn aside from my present argument, nor *you* to profit by your own wrong To prove the meaning and intent of the legislature will require a minute and tedious deduction. To investigate a question of law demands some labour and attention, though very little genius or sagacity. As a *practical profession* the study of the law requires but a moderate portion of abilities. The learning of a pleader is usually upon a level with his integrity. The indiscriminate defence of right and wrong contracts the understanding while it corrupts the heart Subtlety is soon mistaken for wisdom, and impunity for virtue. If there be any instances upon record, as some there are undoubtedly, of genius and morality united in a lawyer, they are distinguished by their singularity, and operate as exceptions.

I must solicit the patience of my readers. This is no light matter, nor is it any more susceptible of ornament than the conduct of Lord Mansfield is capable of aggravation.

As the law of bail, in charges of felony, has been exactly ascertained by acts of the legislature, it is at present of little consequence to inquire how it stood at common law before the statute of Westminster. And yet it is worth the reader's attention to observe how nearly, in the ideas of our ancestors, the circumstance of being taken *with the maner* approached to the conviction of the felon. It " fixed the authoritative stamp of verisimilitude upon the accusation, and, by the common law, when a thief was taken *with the maner* (that is, with the thing stolen upon him *in manu*,) he might, so detected, *flagrante delicto*, be brought into court, arraigned, and tried *without indictment;* as, by the Danish law, he might be taken and hanged upon the spot, without accusation or trial."* It will soon appear that our statute law in this behalf, though less summary in point of proceeding, is directed by the same spirit. In one instance the very form is adhered to. In offences relating to the forest, if a man was taken with *vert*, or venison, it was declared to be equivalent to indictment†. To enable the reader to judge for himself, I shall state, in due order, the several statutes relative to bail in criminal cases, or as much of them as may

* *Blackstone,* iv. 303.
† 1 Ed. III. cap. 8—and 7 Rich. II. cap. 4.

be material to the point in question, omitting superfluous words. If I misrepresent, or do not quote with fidelity, it will not be difficult to detect me.

The statute of Westminster the first *, in 1275, sets forth, that, " Forasmuch as sheriffs and others, who have taken and kept in prison persons detected of felony, and incontinent have let out by replevin such as were *not replevisable*, because they would gain of the one party and grieve the other; and forasmuch as before this time it was not determined which persons were replevisable and which not, it is provided, and by the king commanded, that such prisoners, &c., as be *taken with the maner*, &c., or for *manifest* offences, shall be *in no wise* replevisable by the common writ, nor without writ."† Lord Coke, in his exposition of the last part of this quota tion, accurately distinguishes between *replery* by the common writ or *ex officio*, and *bail* by the King's Bench. The words of the statute certainly do not extend to the judges of that court. But besides that the reader will soon find reason to think that the legislature, in their intention, made no dif ference between *bailable* and *replevisable*, Lord Coke himself (if he be understood to mean nothing but an exposition of the statute of Westminster, and not to state the law generally), does not adhere to his own distinction. In expounding the other offences which, by this statute, are declared *not reple visable*, he constantly uses the words *not bailable*. " That outlaws, for instance, are *not bailable at all;* that persons who have abjured the realm are attainted upon their own confession, and therefore *not bailable at all by law;* that provers are *not bailable;* that notorious felons are *not bail able*." The reason why the superior courts were not named in the statute of Westminster was plainly this, " because anciently most of the business touching bailment of prisoners for felony or misdemeanors was performed by the sheriffs, or

---

* " *Videtur que le statute de mainprise nest que rehersall del comen iey.*"—Bro. Mainp. 61.

† " There are three points to be considered in the construction of all remedial statutes—the old law, the mischief, and the remedy ;—that is, how the common law stood at the making of the act, what the mischief was for which the common law did not provide, and what remedy the parliament hath provided to cure this mischief. It is the business of the judges so to construe the act as to suppress the mischief and advance the remedy."— *Blackstone*, i. 87.

special bailiffs of liberties, either by writ or *virtute officii ;*" *
consequently the superior courts had little or no opportunity
to commit those abuses which the statute imputes to the
sheriffs.   With submission to Doctor Blackstone, I think he
has fallen into a contradiction which, in terms at least
appears irreconcilable.   After enumerating several offences
not bailable, he asserts, without any condition or limitation
whatsoever, "all which are clearly not admissible to bail."†
Yet in a few lines after he says, "*it is agreed* that the Court
of King's Bench may bail for any crime whatsoever, *according
to the circumstance of* the case."   To his first proposition he
should have added *by sheriffs* or *justices*, otherwise the two
propositions contradict each other, with this difference, however, that the first is absolute, the second limited by *a consideration of circumstances.*   I say this without the least
intended disrespect to the learned author.   His work is of
public utility, and should not hastily be condemned.

The statute of 17 Richard II. cap. 10, in 1393, sets forth,
that "Forasmuch as thieves notoriously defamed, *and others,
taken with the maner,* by their long abiding in prison were
delivered by charters, and favourable inquests procured, to the
great hinderance of the people, two men of law shall be
assigned in every commission of the peace to proceed to the
deliverance of such felons," &c.   It seems by this act that
there was a constant struggle between the legislature and the
officers of justice.   Not daring to admit felons *taken with
the maner* to bail or mainprise, they evaded the law by
keeping the party in prison a long time, and then delivering
him without due trial.

The statute of 1 Richard III., in 1483, sets forth, that
"Forasmuch as divers persons have been daily arrested and
imprisoned for *suspicion* of felony, sometime of malice, and
sometime of *a light suspicion,* and so kept in prison without
bail or mainprize, be it ordained, that every justice of peace
shall have authority by his discretion to let such prisoners
and persons so arrested to bail or mainprize."   By this act it
appears that there had been abuses in matter of imprisonment, and that the legislature meant to provide for the immediate enlargement of persons arrested on *light suspicion* of
felony.

* 2 *Hale,* P. C. 128. 136   † *Blackstone,* iv. 299.

The statute of 3 Henry VII. in 1486, declares, that "under colour of the preceding act of Richard the Third, persons, *such as were not mainpernable*, were oftentimes let to bail or mainprize, by justices of the peace, whereby many murderers and felons escaped, the king, &c., hath ordained, that the jus tices of the peace, or two of them at the least (whereof one to be of the *quorum*) have authority to let any such prisoners or persons, mainpernable by the law, to bail or mainprize."

The statute of 1st and 2nd of Philip and Mary, in 1554, sets forth, that "notwithstanding the preceding statute of Henry the Seventh, *one* justice of the peace hath oftentimes, by sinister labour and means, set at large the greatest and notablest offenders, *such as be not replevisable by the laws of this realm;* and yet, the rather to hide their affections in that behalf, have signed the cause of their apprehension to be but only for *suspicion* of felony, whereby the said offenders have escaped unpunished, and do daily, to the high displeasure of Almighty God, the great peril of the king and queen's true subjects, and encouragement of all thieves and evil-doers;— for reformation whereof be it enacted, that no justices of peace shall let to bail or mainprize any such persons, which, for any offence by them committed, be declared *not* to be *replevised* or *bailed*, or be forbidden to be *replevised* or *bailed* by the statute of Westminster the first; and, furthermore. that any persons arrested for manslaughter or felony, *being bailable by the law*, shall not be let to bail or mainprize by any justices of peace, but in the form thereinafter prescribed." In the two preceding statutes, the words *bailable, replevisable*, and *mainpernable* are used synonymously *, or promiscuously to express the same single intention of the legislature, viz., *not to accept of any security but the body of the offender;* and when the latter statute prescribes the form in which persons arrested on *suspicion* of felony (*being bailable by the law*) may be let to bail, it evidently supposes that there are some cases *not* bailable by the law. It may be thought, perhaps, that I attribute to the legislature an appearance of inaccuracy in the use of terms, merely to serve my present purpose. But, in truth, it would make more forcibly for my argument to pre- sume that the legislature were constantly aware of the strict

---

* 2 *Hale*, P. C. ii. 124.

legal distinction between *bail* and *replevy*, and that they always meant to adhere to it*; for if it be true that *replevy* is by the sheriffs, and *bail* by the higher courts at Westminster (which I think no lawyer will deny), it follows that, when the legislature expressly say that any particular offence is by law *not bailable*, the superior courts are comprehended in the prohibition, and bound by it. Otherwise, unless there was a positive exception of the superior courts (which I affirm there never was in any statute relative to bail), the legislature would grossly contradict themselves, and the manifest intention of the law be evaded. It is an established rule that, when the law is *special*, and the reason of it general, it is to be *generally* understood; and though, by custom, a latitude be allowed to the Court of King's Bench (to consider circumstances inductive of a doubt whether the prisoner be guilty or innocent), if this latitude be taken as an arbitrary power to bail, when no circumstances whatsoever are alleged in favour of the prisoner. it is a power without right, and a daring violation of the whole English law of bail.

The Act of the 31st of Charles the Second (commonly called the *Habeas Corpus* Act) particularly declares that it is not meant to extend to treason or felony plainly and specially expressed in the warrant of commitment. The prisoner is therefore left to seek his *habeas corpus* at common law; and so far was the legislature from supposing that persons (committed for treason or felony plainly and specially expressed in the warrant of commitment) could be let to bail by a single judge, or by the whole court, that this very act provides a remedy for such persons in case they are not indicted in the course of the term or session subsequent to their commitment. The law neither suffers them to be enlarged before trial, nor to be imprisoned after the time in which they ought regularly to be tried. In this case the law says, " It shall and may be lawful to and for the judges of the Court of King's Bench and justices of oyer and terminer, or general gaol delivery, and they are hereby required, upon motion to them made in open court, the last day of the term, session, or gaol delivery, either by the prisoner or any one in his behalf, to set at liberty the

---

* *Vide* 2 *Inst.* 150. 186.—" The word *replevisable* never signifies *bailable*. *Bailable* is in a court of record by the king's justices; but *replevisable* is by the sheriff."—*Selden, State Tr.,* vii. 149.

prisoner upon bail; unless it appear to the judges and justices, upon oath made, that the witnesses for the king could not be produced the same term, sessions, or gaol delivery." Upon the whole of this article I observe—

1. That the provision made in the first part of it would be in a great measure useless and nugatory if any single judge might have bailed the prisoner *ex arbitrio*, during the vacation; or if the court might have bailed him immediately after the commencement of the term or sessions. 2. When the law says, *It shall and may be lawful* to bail for felony under particular circumstances, we must presume that, before the passing of that act, it was *not* lawful to bail under those circumstances. The terms used by the legislature are *enacting*, not *declaratory*. 3. Notwithstanding the party may have been imprisoned during the greatest part of the vacation, and during the whole session, the court are expressly forbidden to bail him from that session to the next, if oath be made that the witnesses of the king could not be produced that same term or sessions.

Having faithfully stated the several acts of parliament relative to bail in criminal cases, it may be useful to the reader to take a short historical review of the law of bail, through its various gradations and improvements.

By the ancient common law, before and since the Conquest, all felonies were bailable till murder was excepted by statute; so that persons might be admitted to bail, before conviction, almost in every case. The statute of Westminster says that, before that time, it had not been determined which offences were replevisable and which were not, whether by the common writ *de homine replegiando*, or *ex officio* by the sheriff. It is very remarkable that the abuses arising from this unlimited power of replevy, dreadful as they were and destructive to the peace of society, were not corrected or taken notice of by the legislature until the Commons of the kingdom had obtained a share in it by their representatives; but the House of Commons had scarce begun to exist when these formidable abuses were corrected by the statute of Westminster. It is highly probable that the mischief had been severely felt by the people, although no remedy had been provided for it by the Norman kings or barons. "The iniquity of the times was so great, as it even forced the subjects to forego that which was in account a great liberty, to stop the course of a growing mischief."* The preamble of the statutes made by the first parliament of Edward the First assigns the reason of calling it: "because the people had been otherwise entreated than they ought to be, the peace less kept, the laws less used, and *offenders less punished* than they ought to be, by reason whereof the people feared less to offend;"† and the first attempt to reform these various abuses was by contracting the power of replevying felons.

For above two centuries following it does not appear that any alteration was made in the law of bail, except that *being taken with vert* or *venison* was declared to be equivalent to indictment. The legislature adhered firmly to the spirit of the statute of Westminster. The statute of 27th of Edward the First directs the justices of assize to inquire and punish officers bailing such as were *not bailable*. As for the judges of the superior courts, it is probable that, in those days, they thought themselves bound by the obvious intent and meaning of the legislature. They considered not so much to what particular persons the prohibition was addressed, as what the *thing* was which the legislature meant to prohibit, well knowing that in law, *quando aliquid prohibetur, prohibetur et omne, per quod devenitur ad illud*. "When anything is forbidden, all the means by which the same thing may be compassed or done are equally forbidden."

By the statute of Richard the Third the power of bailing was a little enlarged. Every justice of peace was authorized to bail for felony; but they were expressly confined to persons arrested *on light suspicion;* and even this power, so limited, was found to produce such inconveniences that, in three years after, the legislature found it necessary to repeal it. Instead of trusting any longer to a single justice of peace, the act of 3rd Henry VII. repeals the preceding act, and directs "that no prisoner (*of those who are mainpernable by the law*) shall be let to bail or mainprize by less than *two* justices, whereof one to be of the quorum." And so indispensably necessary was this provision thought for the administration of justice, and for the security and peace of society, that at this time an oath was proposed by the king, to be taken by the knights

---

* *Selden*, by *N. Bacon*, 182.   † *Parliamentary History* I. 82.

and esquires of his household, by the members of the House of Commons, and by the peers spiritual and temporal, and accepted and sworn to *quasi und voce* by them all, which, among other engagements, binds them "not to let any man to bail or mainprize, knowing and deeming him to be a felon, upon your honour and worship. So help you God and all saints."*

In about half a century, however, even these provisions were found insufficient. The act of Henry the Seventh was evaded, and the legislature once more obliged to interpose. The act of 1st and 2nd of Philip and Mary takes away entirely from the justices all power of bailing for offences declared *not bailable* by the statute of Westminster.

The illegal imprisonment of several persons who had refused to contribute to a loan exacted by Charles the First, and the delay of the *habeas corpus* and subsequent refusal to bail them, constituted one of the first and most important grievances of that reign. Yet when the House of Commons which met in the year 1628 resolved upon measures of the most firm and strenuous resistance to the power of imprisonment assumed by the king or privy council, and to the refusal to bail the party on the return of the *habeas corpus*, they did expressly, in all their resolutions, make an exception of commitments where the cause of the restraint was expressed, and did by law justify the commitment. The reason of this distinction is that, whereas when the cause of commitment is expressed, the crime is then known, and the offender must be brought to the ordinary trial; if, on the contrary, no cause of commitment be expressed, and the prisoner be thereupon remanded, it may operate to perpetual imprisonment. This contest with Charles the First produced the act of the 16th of that king, by which the Court of King's Bench are directed, within three days after the return of the *habeas corpus*, to examine and determine the legality of any commitment by the king or privy council, and to do *what to justice shall appertain* in delivering, bailing, or *remanding* the prisoner. *Now*, it seems, it is unnecessary for the judge to do what appertains to justice. The same scandalous traffic in which we have seen the privilege of parliament exerted or

* *Parliamentary History,* ii. 419.

relaxed to gratify the present humour, or to serve the immediate purpose, of the crown, is introduced into the administration of justice. The magistrate, it seems, has now no rule to follow but the dictates of personal enmity, national partiality, or perhaps the most prostituted corruption.

To complete this historical inquiry it only remains to be observed, that the *Habeas Corpus* Act of 31st of Charles the Second, so justly considered as another magna charta of the kingdom, "extends only to the case of commitments for such criminal charge as can produce no inconvenience to public justice by a temporary enlargement of the prisoner."* So careful were the legislature, at the very moment when they were providing for the liberty of the subject, not to furnish any colour or pretence for violating or evading the established law of bail in the higher criminal offences. But the exception, stated in the body of the act, puts the matter out of all doubt. After directing the judges how they are to proceed to the discharge of the prisoner upon recognizance and surety, having regard to the quality of the prisoner and nature of the offence, it is expressly added, "unless it shall appear to the said lord chancellor, &c., that the party so committed is detained for such matters or offences for the which BY THE LAW THE PRISONER IS NOT BAILABLE."

When the laws, plain of themselves, are thus illustrated by facts, and their uniform meaning established by history, we do not want the authority of opinions, however respectable, to inform our judgment or to confirm our belief. But I am determined that you shall have no escape. Authority of every sort shall be produced against you, from Jacob to Lord Coke, from the dictionary to the classic. In vain shall you appeal from those upright judges whom you disdain to imitate, to those whom you have made your example. With one voice they all condemn you.

"To be taken with the *maner*, is where a thief, having stolen anything, is taken with the same about him, as it were in his hands, which is called *flagrante delicto*. Such a criminal is *not bailable by law*."—*Jacob, under the word Maner.*

"Those who are taken with the *maner* are excluded by the statute of Westminster from the benefit of a replevin"—*Hawkins' P. C.* ii. 98.

* *Blackstone,* iv. 137.

"Of such heinous offences no one, who is notoriously guilty, seems to be *bailable* by the intent of this statute."— *Hawkins' P. C.* 99.

" The common practice and allowed general rule is, that bail is only then proper where it stands *indifferent* whether the party were guilty or innocent."—*Ibid*

" There is no doubt but the bailing of a person, *who is not bailable by law* is punishable, either at common law as a negligent escape, or as an offence against the several statutes relative to bail."—*Ibid*. 89.

" It cannot be doubted but that neither the judges of this nor of any other superior court of justice are strictly within the purview of that statute, yet they will always, in their discretion, pay a due regard to it, and not admit a person to bail who is expressly declared by it irreplevisable, *without some particular circumstance in his favour ;* and therefore it seems difficult to find an instance where persons attainted of felony, or notoriously guilty of treason or manslaughter, &c., by their own confession or *otherwise*, have been admitted to the benefit of bail without some special motive to the court to grant it."—*Ibid*. 114.

" If it appears that any man hath injury or wrong by his imprisonment, we have power to deliver and discharge him ; if otherwise, *he is to be remanded* by us to prison again."— *Lord Chief Justice Hyde—State Trials*, vii. 115.

" The statute of Westminster was especially for direction to the sheriffs and others, but to say courts of justice are excluded from this statute, I conceive it cannot be."—*Attorney-General Heath—State Trials*, 132.

" The court, upon review of the return, judgeth of the sufficiency or insufficiency of it. If they think the prisoner *in law* to be *bailable*, he is committed to the marshal and bailed ; if not, he is remanded." Through that whole debate the objection on the part of the prisoners was, that no cause of commitment was expressed in the warrant; but it was uniformly admitted by their counsel that, if the cause of commitment had been expressed for treason or felony, the court would then have done right in remanding them.

The Attorney-General having urged, before a committee of both Houses, that, in Beckwith's case and others, the lords of the council sent a letter to the Court of King's Bench to bail, it was replied by the managers for the House of Commons that this was of no moment, "for that either the prisoner was *bailable by the law* or *not bailable;* if bailable by the law, then he was to be bailed without any such letter; if not bailable by the law, then plainly the judges could not have bailed him upon the letter without breach of their oath, which is, *that they are to do justice according to the law, &c.*" —*State Trials*, vii. 176.

"So that, in bailing upon such offences of the highest nature, a kind of discretion rather than a constant law hath been exercised when it stands *wholly indifferent* in the eye of the court, whether the prisoner be guilty or not."—*Selden*— *State Trials*, vii. 230-1.

"I deny that a man is always bailable when imprisonment is imposed upon him for custody."—*Attorney-General Heath*— *State Trials*, 238. By these quotations from the State Trials, though otherwise not of authority, it appears plainly that, in regard to *bailable* or *not bailable*, all parties agreed in admitting one proposition as incontrovertible.

"In relation to capital offences, there are especially these acts of parliament, that are the common *landmarks* * touching offences bailable or not bailable."— *Hale's P. C.* ii. 127. The enumeration includes the several acts cited in this paper.

"Persons taken with the *manouvre* are not bailable, because it is *furtum manifestum.*" – *Ibid.* 133.

"The writ of *habeas corpus* is of a high nature; for, if persons be wrongfully committed, they are to be discharged upon this writ returned, or if bailable, they are to be bailed; *if not bailable, they are to be committed.*"—*Ibid.* 143. This doctrine of Lord Chief Justice Hale refers immediately to the superior courts from whence the writ issues. "After the return is filed the court is either to discharge or bail, or *commit* him, as the nature of the cause requires." — *Ibid.* 146.

"If bail be granted *otherwise than the law alloweth*, the party that alloweth the same shall be fined, imprisoned, render damages, or forfeit his place, as the case shall require."— *Selden*, by *N. Bacon*, 182.

---

* It has been the study of Lord Mansfield to remove landmarks.

" This induces an absolute necessity of expressing upon every commitment the reason for which it is made, that the court, upon a *habeas corpus*, may examine into its validity, and, *according to the circumstances of the case*, may discharge, admit to bail, or *remand* the prisoner." — *Blackstone*, iii. 133.

" Marriot was committed for forging indorsements upon bank bills, and, upon a *habeas corpus*, was bailed, because the crime was only a great misdemeanor; for, though the forging the bills be felony, yet forging the indorsement is not."— *Salkeld*, i. 104.

" Appell de mahem, &c., ideo ne fuit lesse a baille, nient plus que in appell de robbery ou murder; quod nota, et que in robry et murder le partie n'est baillable."—*Bro. Mainprise*, 67.

" The intendment of the law in bails is *quod stat indifferenter*, whether he be guilty or no; but when he is convict by verdict or confession, then he must be deemed in law to be guilty of the felony, and therefore *not bailable at all*."— *Coke* ii. *Inst.* 188—iv. 178.

" Bail is *quando stat indifferenter*, and *not* when the offence is open and manifest."—2 *Inst.* 189.

" In this case *non stat indifferenter*, whether he be guilty or no, being taken with the *maner*, that is with the thing stolen, as it were in his hand."—*Ibid.*

" If it appeareth that this imprisonment be just and lawful, he *shall be remanded* to the former gaoler; but, if it shall appear to the court that he was imprisoned against the law of the land, they ought by force of the statute to deliver him; if it be *doubtful* and under consideration, he may be bailed."—2 *Inst.* 55.

It is unnecessary to load the reader with any further quotations. If these authorities are not deemed sufficient to establish the doctrine maintained in this paper, it will be in vain to appeal to the evidence of law books or to the opinions of judges. They are not the authorities by which Lord Mansfield will abide. He assumes an arbitrary power of doing right, and, if he does wrong, it lies only between God and his conscience.

Now, my Lord, although I have great faith in the preceding argument, I will not say that every minute part of it is absolutely invulnerable. I am too well acquainted with the practice of a certain court directed by your example, as it is governed by your authority, to think there ever yet was an argument, however conformable to law and reason, in which a cunning quibbling attorney might not discover a flaw. But, taking the whole of it together, I affirm that it consti tutes a mass of demonstration than which nothing more complete or satisfactory can be offered to the human mind. How an evasive indirect reply will stand with your reputation, or how far it will answer in point of defence at the bar of the House of Lords, is worth your consideration. If, after all that has been said, it should still be maintained that the Court of King's Bench, in bailing felons, are exempted from all legal rules whatsoever, and that the judge has no direction to pursue but his private affections or mere unquestionable will and pleasure, it will follow plainly that the distinction between *bailable* and *not bailable* uniformly expressed by the legislature, current through all our law books and admitted by all our great lawyers without exception, is in one sense a nugatory, in another a pernicious distinction. It is nugatory, as it supposes a difference in the bailable quality of offences, when, in effect, the distinction refers only to the rank of the magistrate. It is pernicious, as it implies a rule of law which yet the judge is not bound to pay the least regard to, and impresses an idea upon the minds of the people that the judge is wiser and greater than the law.

It remains only to apply the law thus stated to the fact in question. By an authentic copy of the *mittimus*, it appears that John Eyre was committed for felony plainly and specially expressed in the warrant of commitment. He was charged before Alderman Halifax, by the oath of Thomas Fielding, William Holder, William Payne, and William Nash for *feloniously stealing* eleven quires of writing-paper, value six shillings, the property of Thomas Beach, &c. By the examinations upon oath of the four persons mentioned in the *mittimus*, it was proved that large quantities of paper had been missed, and that eleven quires (previously marked, from a suspicion that Eyre was the thief,) were found upon him. Many other quires of paper marked in the same manner were found at his lodgings; and, after he had been some time in Wood Street Compter, a key was found in his room there, which appeared to be a key to the closet a: Guildhall, from whence the paper was stolen. When asked what he had to say in his defence, his only answer was, " *I hope you will bail me.*" Mr. Holder, the clerk, replied, " *That is impossible. There never was an instance of it when the stolen goods were found upon the thief.*" The lord mayor was then applied to, and refused to bail him. Of all these circumstances it was your duty to have informed yourself minutely. The fact was remarkable, and the chief magistrate of the city of London was known to have refused to bail the offender. To justify your compliance with the solicitations of your three countrymen, it should be proved that such allegations were offered to you in behalf of their associate as honestly and *bonâ fide* reduced it to a matter of doubt and indifference whether the prisoner was innocent or guilty Was anything offered by the Scotch triumvirate that tended to invalidate the positive charge made against him by four credible witnesses upon oath? Was it even insinuated to you, either by himself or his bail, that no felony was committed, or that *he* was not the felon; that the stolen goods were *not* found upon him, or that he was only the receiver, not knowing them to be stolen? Or, in short, did they attempt to produce any evidence of his insanity? To all these questions I answer for you, without the least fear of contradiction, positively NO. From the moment he was arrested he never entertained any hope of acquittal; therefore thought of nothing but obtaining bail, that he might have time to settle his affairs, convey his fortune to another country, and spend the remainder of his life in comfort and affluence abroad. In this prudential scheme of future happiness the Lord Chief Justice of England most readily and heartily concurred. At sight of so much virtue in distress your natural benevolence took the alarm. Such a man as Mr. Eyre, struggling with adversity, must always be an interesting scene to Lord Mansfield. Or was it that liberal anxiety by which your whole life has been distinguished to enlarge the liberty of the subject? My Lord, we did not want this new instance of the liberality of your principles. We already knew what kind of subjects they were for whose liberty you were anxious. At all events the public are much indebted to you for fixing a price at which felony may be committed with impunity. You bound a felon, notoriously worth thirty thousand pounds, in the sum of three hundred. With your natural turn to equity, and knowing as you are in the doctrine of precedents, you undoubtedly meant to settle the proportion between the fortune of the felon and the fine by which he may compound for his felony. The ratio now upon record, and transmitted to posterity under the auspices of Lord Mansfield, is exactly one to a hundred. My Lord, without intending it, you have laid a cruel restraint upon the genius of your countrymen. In the warmest indulgence of their passions they have an eye to the expense, and, if their other virtues fail us, we have a resource in their economy.

By taking so trifling a security from John Eyre, you invited and manifestly exhorted him to escape. Although in bailable cases, it be usual to take four securities, you left him in the custody of three Scotchmen, whom he might have easily satisfied for conniving at his retreat. That he did not make use of the opportunity you industriously gave him, neither justifies your conduct, nor can it be any way accounted for, but by his excessive and monstrous avarice. Any other man, but this bosom friend of three Scotchmen, would gladly have sacrificed a few hundred pounds, rather than submit to the infamy of pleading guilty in open court. It is possible, indeed, that he might have flattered himself, and not unreasonably, with the hopes of a pardon. That he would have been pardoned seems more than probable if I had not directed the public attention to the leading step you took in favour of him. In the present gentle reign, we well know what use has been made of the lenity of the court and of the mercy of the crown. The Lord Chief Justice of England accepts of the hundredth part of the property of a felon taken in the fact, as a recognizance for his appearance. Your brother Smythe browbeats a jury, and forces them to alter their verdict, by which they had found a Scotch serjeant guilty of murder; and though the Kennedys were convicted of a most deliberate and atrocious murder, they still had a claim to the royal mercy*. They were saved by the chastity of their con-

* The case of the Kennedys is stated in note, ante, p. 302. That of John Taylor is as follows:—He was a serjeant in the first, or royal Scots regiment of foot, and was tried at the Guildford summer assizes in the year 1770, for the murder of James Smith, the master of the Wheatsheaf,

nexions.   They had a sister;—yet it was not her beauty, but the pliancy of her virtue that recommended her to the king.

near Westminster Bridge. It appeared upon the trial, that the deceased had uttered some aggravating expressions against the Scots; in consequence of which, the prisoner being suddenly thrown off his guard, drew his sword and stabbed him.   The jury, after deliberating a considerable time, brought in a verdict of *guilty*, on which Mr. Baron Smythe expressed his surprise, adding, that he had told them it was only manslaughter, and desired that a *special* verdict should be drawn up, which the *intimidated* jury signed.   On this Mr. Jasper Smith, a near relation of the deceased, addressed the court in the following words :—" My Lord, I am the nearest of kin to the unfortunate man who was murdered. I always thought, my Lord, when a verdict was once given it was unalterable, but by the present method of proceeding, there need not have been any jury at all.   It is as plain a murder as can be, and I am persuaded your Lordship thinks so."   To this speech no reply was given.   The decision of the judge, in the above case, occasioned some severe animadversions on his conduct, and several queries were addressed to him upon the subject, which were repeatedly inserted in the *Public Advertiser*, so as to become extremely conspicuous.   This account, however, extracted from that paper, does not seem to contain the whole train of the circumstances which preceded this unfortunate catastrophe, for when Taylor was brought to the bar of the King's Bench, February 8, 1771, Lord Mansfield, who read the minutes of the evidence as taken down by Baron Smythe, who presided at the trial, observed, that it appeared that the prisoner had been three times assaulted by Smith, the deceased, collared and violently thrown backward upon a bench without any provocation, turned out of the house, and called by the most opprobrious names; and further, that when out in the street, he was pursued and attacked by two men, before he offered to draw his sword; from which circumstances the court was unanimously of opinion that he had only been guilty of manslaughter, and sentenced him to be burnt in the hand, which was performed accordingly, behind the bar.   Mr. Dunning, also, a strong oppositionist, defended Mr. Baron Smythe's conduct in respect to the trial alluded to by Junius, in a speech spoken on a motion made by Mr. Serjeant Glynn, December 6, 1770, " for an inquiry into the administration of criminal justice, and the proceedings of the judges in Westminster Hall, particularly in cases relating to the liberty of the press and the constitutional power and duty of juries."   Mr. Dunning's words are as follow :—" It is not that the characters of the judges are not traduced by groundless accusations and scandalous aspersions.   These are grievances which every one sees, and every one laments.   Judge Smythe, for example, has, to my knowledge, been very injuriously treated.   His conduct in trying the Scotch serjeant at Guildford, for which he has been so much abused in print, and now arraigned in Parliament, was, in my opinion, very fair and honourable.   I was consulted on the affair as an advocate, and I must say that I perfectly coincided with him in sentiment. Had I been in his place, I must have fallen under the same odium, for my conscience would not have allowed me to use any other language but that of Baron Smythe."

The holy author of our religion was seen in the company of sinners ; but it was his gracious purpose to convert them from their sins. Another man, who in the ceremonies of our faith might give lessons to the great enemy of it, upon different principles keeps much the same company. He advertises for patients, collects all the diseases of the heart, and turns a royal palace into an hospital for incurables. A man of honour has no ticket of admission at St. James's. They receive him, like a virgin at the Magdalen:—*Go thou and do likewise.*

My charge against you is now made good. I shall, however, be ready to answer or to submit to fair objections*. If, whenever this matter shall be agitated, you suffer the doors of the House of Lords to be shut, I now protest that I shall consider you as having made no reply. From that moment, in the opinion of the world, you will stand self-convicted. Whether your reply be quibbling and evasive, or liberal and in point, will be matter for the judgment of your peers ;— but if, when every possible idea of disrespect to that noble House (in whose honour and justice the nation implicitly confides,) is here most solemnly disclaimed, you should endeavour to represent this charge as a contempt of their authority, and move their Lordships to censure the publisher of this paper, I then affirm that you support injustice by violence, that you are guilty of a heinous aggravation of your offence, and that you contribute your utmost influence to promote, on the part of the highest court of judicature, a positive denial of justice to the nation.

JUNIUS.

LETTER LXIX†.

TO THE RIGHT HONOURABLE LORD CAMDEN.

My Lord,

I TURN with pleasure from that barren waste, in which no salutary plant takes root, no verdure quickens, to a character

---

* Miscellaneous Letter, No. 106, in which Junius defends the present letter against several attacks which had been made upon it in the *Public Advertiser.*

† Lord Camden stood in rivalship to the Earl of Mansfield. He had

fertile, as I willingly believe, in every great and good qualification. I call upon you, in the name of the English nation,
to stand forth in defence of the laws of your country, and to
exert, in the cause of truth and justice, those great abilities
with which you were intrusted for the benefit of mankind.
To ascertain the facts set forth in the preceding paper, it may
be necessary to call the persons mentioned in the *mittimus* to
the bar of the House of Lords *. If a motion for that purpose should be rejected, we shall know what to think of Lord
Mansfield's innocence. The legal argument is submitted to
you Lordship's judgment. After the noble stand you made
against Lord Mansfield upon the question of libel, we did expect that you would not have suffered that matter to have remained undetermined. But it was said that Lord Chief
Justice Wilmot had been *prevailed upon* to vouch for an
opinion of the late Judge Yates, which was supposed to make
against you; and we admit of the excuse. When such detestable arts are employed to prejudge a question of right, it
might have been imprudent at that time to have brought it to
a decision. In the present instance you will have no such
opposition to contend with. If there be a judge or lawyer of
any note in Westminster Hall who shall be daring enough
to affirm that according to the true intendment of the laws of
England, a felon, taken with the *maner, in flagrante delicto*,
is bailable, or that the discretion of an English judge is
merely arbitrary, and not governed by rules of law, I should
be glad to be acquainted with him. Whoever he be, I will

threatened him in the last session of parliament. But Lord Mansfield eluded
every attempt to draw him into an open and lengthened contention relative
to his principles of decision. Hopes were entertained that another session
of parliament might see the contest renewed with Lord Mansfield. It was
with a view to this that Junius so laboriously resumed his attack against
the Chief Justice. In this letter he calls on Lord Camden, almost with
threats and with reproach,.to make the bailing of Eyre the subject of a new
motion against Lord Mansfield in the House of Peers. The call was
fruitless.

This letter ends the political series, and followed the preceding in the
Public Advertiser, appearing under the same date as that addressed to Lord
Mansfield, namely, January 21, 1772.—ED.

* In the case of Lord Mansfield's having bailed Eyre, Lord Camden had
openly expressed his opinion that the bail was illegal, and had given reason
to expect that he would make it the subject of a parliamentary inquiry on
the commencement of the ensuing session.

take care that he shall not give you much trouble. Your Lordship's character assures me that you will assume that principal part which belongs to you, in supporting the laws of England against a wicked judge, who makes it the occupation of his life to misinterpret and pervert them. If you decline this honourable office, I fear it will be said that for some months past you have kept too much company with the Duke of Grafton. When the contest turns upon the interpretation of the laws you cannot, without a formal surrender of all your reputation, yield the post of honour even to Lord Chatham. Considering the situation and abilities of Lord Mansfield, I do not scruple to affirm, with the most solemn appeal to God for my sincerity, that, in *my* judgment, he is the very worst and most dangerous man in the kingdom. Thus far I have done my duty in endeavouring to bring him to punishment. But mine is an inferior ministerial office in the temple of justice. I have bound the victim, and dragged him to the altar.

JUNIUS.

POSTSCRIPT.

The Reverend Mr. John Horne having, with his usual veracity and honest industry, circulated a report that Junius, in a letter to the supporters of the Bill of Rights, had warmly declared himself in favour of long parliaments and rotten boroughs, it is thought necessary to submit to the public the following extract from his letter to John Wilkes, Esq., dated the 7th of September, 1771, and laid before the society on the 24th of the same mouth *.

"With regard to the several articles, taken separately, I own I am concerned to see that the great condition, which ought to be the *sine quâ non* of parliamentary qualification, which ought to be the basis (as it assuredly will be the only support) of every barrier raised in defence of the constitution, I mean *a declaration upon oath to shorten the duration of*

* This letter is given entire in the private correspondence between Junius and Mr. Wilkes, No. 66, vol. ii. of the present edition. It is a remarkable production, both from the important political questions it discusses, and its bearings on the great secret of the anonymous authorship of the Letters.—ED.

parliaments, is reduced to the fourth rank in the esteem
of the society; and even in that place, far from being insisted
on with firmness and vehemence, seems to have been particularly slighted in the expression. *You shall endeavour
to restore annual parliaments!*—Are these the terms which
men, who are in earnest, make use of when the *salus rei-
publicæ* is at stake? I expected other language from Mr.
Wilkes. Besides my objection in point of form, I disapprove
highly of the meaning of the fourth article as it stands.
Whenever the question shall be seriously agitated I will endeavour (and if I live will assuredly attempt it) to convince the
English nation, by arguments to *my* understanding unanswerable, that they ought to insist upon a triennial, and banish
the idea of an annual, parliament . . . . I am
convinced that, if shortening the duration of parliaments
(which, in effect, is keeping the representative under the rod
of the constituent) be not made the basis of our new parliamentary jurisprudence, other checks or improvements signify
nothing. On the contrary, if this be made the foundation,
other measures may come in aid, and, as auxiliaries, be of considerable advantage. Lord Chatham's project, for instance,
of increasing the number of knights of shires, appears to me
admirable . . . . As to cutting away the rotten
boroughs, I am as much offended as any man at seeing so
many of them under the direct influence of the crown, or at
the disposal of private persons. Yet, I own, I have both
doubts and apprehensions in regard to the remedy you propose. I shall be charged perhaps with an unusual want of
political intrepidity, when I honestly confess to you that I am
startled at the idea of so extensive an amputation. In the
first place, I question the power, *de jure*, of the legislature to
disfranchise a number of boroughs, upon the general ground
of improving the constitution. There cannot be a doctrine
more fatal to the liberty and property we are contending for
than that which confounds the idea of a *supreme* and an *arbitrary* legislature. I need not point out to you the fatal purposes to which it has been, and may be, applied. If we are
sincere in the political creed we profess, there are many
things which we ought to affirm cannot be done by King,
Lords, and Commons. Among these I reckon the disfran-
chising of boroughs with a general view to improvement. I

consider it as equivalent to robbing the parties concerned of their freehold, of their birthright. I say, that, although this birthright may be forfeited, or the exercise of it suspended in particular cases, it cannot be taken away by a general law for any real or pretended purpose of improving the constitution. Supposing the attempt made, I am persuaded you cannot mean that either King or Lords should take an active part in it. A bill which only touches the representation of the people, must originate in the House of Commons. In the formation and mode of passing it the exclusive right of the Commons must be asserted as scrupulously as in the case of a money bill. Now, Sir, I should be glad to know by what kind of reasoning it can be proved, that there is a power vested in the representative to destroy his immediate constituent. From whence could he possibly derive it? A courtier, I know, will be ready enough to maintain the affirmative. The doctrine suits him exactly, because it gives an unlimited operation to the influence of the crown. But we, Mr. Wilkes, ought to hold a different language. It is no answer to me to say, that the bill, when it passes the House of Commons, is the act of the majority, and not of the representatives of the particular boroughs concerned. If the majority can disfranchise ten boroughs, why not twenty, why not the whole kingdom? Why should not they make their own seats in parliament for life? When the Septennial Act passed, the legislature did what, apparently and palpably, they had no power to do; but they did more than people in general were aware of: they, in effect, disfranchised the whole kingdom for four years.

" For argument's sake, I will now suppose, that the expediency of the measure, and the power of parliament are unquestionable. Still you will find an insurmountable difficulty in the execution. When all your instruments of amputation are prepared, when the unhappy patient lies bound at your feet, without the possibility of resistance, by what infallible rule will you direct the operation? When you propose to cut away the *rotten* parts, can you tell us what parts are perfectly *sound?* Are there any certain limits in fact or theory, to inform you at what point you must stop, at what point the mortification ends? To a man so capable of observation and reflection as you are, it is unnecessary to say all that might be said upon the subject. Besides that I approve highly of Lord Chatham's idea, *of infusing a portion of new health into the constitution to enable it to bear its infirmities* (a brilliant expression, and full of intrinsic wisdom), other reasons concur in persuading me to adopt it. I have no objection," &c.

The man who fairly and completely answers this argument, shall have my thanks and my applause. My heart is already with him. I am ready to be converted. I admire his morality, and would gladly subscribe to the articles of his faith. Grateful as I am to the GOOD BEING whose bounty has imparted to me this reasoning intellect, whatever it is, I hold myself proportionably indebted to him from whose enlightened understanding another ray of knowledge communicates to mine. But neither should I think the most exalted faculties of the human mind a gift worthy of the Divinity, nor any assistance in the improvement of them a subject of gratitude to my fellow-creature, if I were not satisfied that really to inform the understanding corrects and enlarges the heart.

JUNIUS.

APPENDIX.

MR. WOODFALL'S TRIAL*.

An Account of the Trial at Guildhall of the original Publisher of JUNIUS'S
Letter to the King.

YESTERDAY morning, (June 13, 1770), about nine o'clock, came on before
Lord Mansfield, in the Court of King's Bench at Guildhall, the trial of Mr.
Woodfall, the original printer of Junius's Letter in the Public Advertiser of
December 19.   Only seven of the special jury attended, viz. William Bond,
foreman ; Peter Cazalet, Alexander Peter Allen, Frederick Commerell, Her-
men Meyer, John Thomas, and Barrington Buggin.

Upon which the following five talesmen were taken out of the box, viz.
William Hannard, Paul Verges, William Sibley, William Willett, and William Davis.

The trial was opened by Mr. Wallis.

Nathaniel Crowder swore he bought the paper of Mr. Woodfall's publishing servant, whom he named.

Mr. Harris proved that the duty for the advertisements and stamps were
paid by Mr. Woodfall.   And

A clerk of Sir John Fielding proved, by a receipt from Mr. Woodfall, his
concern in and for the paper.

The publication and direction of the paper by Mr. Woodfall being thus
proved,

Lord Mansfield, in his charge, told the jury, that there were only two
points for their consideration : the first, the printing and publishing the
paper in question ; the second, the sense and meaning of it :   That as to the
charges of its being malicious, seditious, &c., they were inferences in law
about which no evidence need be given, any more than that part of an indictment need be proved by evidence, which charges a man with being moved
by the instigation of the Devil :   That therefore the printing and sense of
the paper were alone what the jury had to consider of; and that if the paper
should really contain no breach of the law, that was a matter which might
afterwards be moved in arrest of judgment: That he had no evidence to
sum up to them, as the defendant's counsel admitted the printing and publication to be well proved: That as to the sense, they had not called in doubt
the manner in which the dashes in the paper were filled up in the record, by

---

* For the remarks of Junius on this celebrated Trial, see Preface, p. 94,
† note.

giving any other sense to the passages; if they had, the jury would have
been to consider which application was the true one, that charged in the information, or suggested by the defendant : That the jury might now compare
the paper with the information : That if they did not find the application
wrong, they must find the defendant guilty ; and if they did find it wrong,
they must acquit him : That this was not the time for alleviation or aggravation, that being for future consideration : That every subject was under the
control of the law, and had a right to expect from it protection for his
person, his property, and his good name : That if any man offended the laws,
he was amenable to them, and was not to be censured or punished but in a
legal course : That any person libelled had a right either to bring a civil or a
criminal prosecution : That in the latter, which is by information or indictment, it is immaterial whether the publication be false or true : That it is no
defence to say it is true, because it is a breach of the peace, and therefore
criminal; but in a civil prosecution it is a defence to say the charges in the
publication are true, because the plaintiff there sues only for a pecuniary satisfaction to himself; and that this is the distinction as to that nature of defence.
His lordship said he was afraid it was too true that few characters in the
kingdom escaped libels : That many were very injuriously treated—and if
so, that the best way to prevent it was by an application to the law, which
is open to every man : That the liberty of the press consisted in every man
having the power to publish his sentiments without first applying for a licence
to any one ; but if any man published what was against law, he did it at his
peril, and was answerable for it in the same manner as he who suffers his
hand to commit an assault, or his tongue to utter blasphemy."

Between eleven and twelve the jury withdrew, at four the court adjourned,
and a little after nine the jury waited on Lord Mansfield at his house in
Bloomsbury Square, with their verdict, which was *Guilty of* PRINTING *and*
PUBLISHING ONLY.

This charge having been laid upon the table of the House of Lords, December 10, 1770, by the Lord Chief Justice, the following questions were put to
him in his place by Lord Camden, on the day ensuing.

1. Does the opinion mean to declare that upon the general issue of Not
Guilty, in the case of a seditious libel, the jury have no right, by law, to examine the innocence or criminality of the paper, if they think fit, and to form
their verdict upon such examination ?

2. Does the opinion mean to declare, that in the case above mentioned,
when the jury have delivered in their verdict, *Guilty*, that this verdict has
found the fact only and not the law?

3. Is it to be understood by this opinion, that if the jury come to the bar,
and say that they find the printing and publishing, but that the paper is no,
libel, that in that case the jury have found the defendant guilty generally,
and the verdict must be so entered up ?

4. Whether the opinion means to say, that if the judge, after giving his
opinion of the innocence or criminality of the paper, should leave the consideration of that matter, together with the printing and publishing, to the jury,
such a direction would be contrary to law ?

5. I beg leave to ask, whether dead, and living judges then absent, did
declare their opinions in open court, and whether the noble Lord has any
note of such opinions ?

6. Whether they declared such opinions after solid arguments, or upon any point judicially before them?

To these queries Lord Mansfield made no reply, briefly observing, that he would not answer interrogatories.

The subject was introduced into the Lower House, December 6, 1770, on a motion made by Mr. Serjeant Glynn, "That a committee should be appointed to inquire into the administration of criminal justice, and the proceedings of the judges in Westminster Hall, particularly in cases relating to the liberty of the press, and the constitutional power and duty of juries." In the course of the discussion the speakers on both sides alluded not only to the charge in Mr. Woodfall's case, but also to Mr. Baron Smythe's conduct in trying a Scotch serjeant at Guildford, which will be found more particularly detailed in the note to Junius's Letter, No. 68. Amongst the chief speakers on this occasion were, on the side of the ministry, Mr. Fox, and on that of the people, Mr. Burke.

" To the Honourable the Commons of Great Britain in Parliament assembled.

" The humble Petition of HENRY SAMPSON WOODFALL, in custody of the Serjeant-at-Arms attending this House.

"SHEWETH,

"That your Petitioner, having justly incurred the displeasure of this House by printing a letter highly reflecting on the character of the Speaker of this House, was summoned to attend on Monday the 14th of this instant, at this honourable House.

"That your Petitioner did readily obey that summons, and did attend this House accordingly.

"That your Petitioner having offended inadvertently, and through a very blameable neglect, which kind of neglect in future he will do his utmost endeavour to avoid, of examining, as he ought to have done, the contents of what he printed, and your petitioner having already incurred very heavy expenses which, if longer continued, must end in the ruin of himself and numerous and innocent family, who must be sufferers together with him.

"Your petitioner therefore humbly prays that all punishment he has already undergone by expenses, confinement, and interruption of his business may be taken into consideration, and, though the enormity of his offence is confessedly great, yet, trusting to the well-known mercy and clemency of this Honourable House, your Petitioner humbly hopes he may be discharged from the further effects of their displeasure.

" And your Petitioner,
" As in duty bound,
" shall pray.
" HENRY SAMPSON WOODFALL.

N.B.—The above is in the handwriting of H. S. W.

Mr. Woodfall's Fees.

	£	s.	d.
To the Serjeant-at-Arms, Caption Fees	3	6	8
Seventeen days in custody	17	0	0
Bringing to the bar	0	6	8
Housekeeper	0	5	0
Messenger 17 days at 6s. 8d. per day	5	13	4
Serving the Speaker's order and warrant	0	13	4
Doorkeepers	0	5	0
The Speaker's secretary	1	0	0
The clerk and clerk's assistant	1	4	0
	29	14	0

Mr. Woodfall's Bill.

		£	s.	d.
February 14.	3 Bottles of Port	0	7	6
,,	2 ditto Sherry	0	4	0
,,	Beer	0	1	4
,,	5 Suppers, beefsteaks	0	7	6
15.	3 Breakfasts	0	3	0
,,	2 Fowls, bacon, greens, leg of pork	1	1	0
,,	6 Bottles of Port	0	15	0
,,	2 Ditto Sherry	0	6	0
,,	Biscakes	0	0	3
,,	7 Suppers, duck, mince pies, and cold beef	0	14	0
,,	7 Teas and coffee	0	7	0
,,	Beer	0	3	0
16.	2 Breakfasts	0	2	0
,,	3 Bottles of Sherry	0	6	0
,,	10 Ditto Port	1	5	0
,,	6 Dinners, leg of lamb, 2 ducks, sallat, &c.	0	18	0
,,	Supper, beef and mutton, steaks, sallat, &c.	0	10	6
,,	Biscakes	0	0	3
,,	Beer	0	3	0
17.	2 Breakfasts	0	2	0
,,	5 Dinners, salt-fish, sauce, and loin of mutton	0	15	0
,,	2 Bottles of Sherry	0	4	0
,,	2 Ditto Port	0	5	0
,,	Suppers	0	2	6
,,	Beer	0	1	6
18.	2 Breakfasts	0	2	0
,,	7 Dinners, sirloin of beef, sallat, &c.	0	18	0
,,	Sherry, 1 bottle	0	2	0
,,	Port, 7 ditto	0	17	6
,,	Brandy	0	0	6
,,	Biscakes	0	0	3
,,	4 Teas	0	3	4
,,	Suppers, beef, sallat, &c.	0	5	0
	Carried forward	11	12	11

			£	s.	d.
		Brought forward	11	12	11
February 18.	Beer	0	3	0
„	19.	4 Breakfasts	0	4	0
„		7 Dinners, mutton, 2 chickens, and sallat	1	1	0
„		Sherry, 2 bottles	0	4	0
„		Port, 4 ditto	0	10	0
„		Biscakes	0	0	3
„		6 Teas and coffee	0	6	0
„		Suppers, veal collops, sallat, &c.	0	5	0
„		Beer	0	2	0
„	20.	4 Breakfasts	0	4	0
„		6 Dinners, veal, bacon, and greens	0	12	6
„		Sherry, 2 bottles	0	4	0
„		Port, 2 ditto	0	5	0
„		12 Teas	0	10	0
„		6 Suppers, cold duck, beef, and sallat	0	7	6
„		Beer	0	2	6
„		Lipsalve	0	0	3
„	21.	3 Breakfasts	0	3	0
„		4 Dinners, stewed beef, &c.	0	8	0
„		2 Bottles of Sherry	0	4	0
„		4 Ditto, Port	0	10	0
„		4 Suppers, mutton chops, cold beef, &c.	0	5	0
„		Beer	0	2	6
„	22.	2 Breakfasts	0	2	0
„		7 Dinners, leg of pork and potatoes	0	12	6
„		Port, 3 bottles	0	7	6
„		Sherry, 1 ditto	0	2	0
„		4 Teas	0	3	4
„		6 Suppers	0	3	0
„		Beer	0	3	0
„		Oranges and sugar	0	0	6
„	23.	3 Breakfasts	0	3	0
„		7 Dinners, fish, sauce, leg of mutton, &c.	1	1	0
„		Sherry, 1 bottle	0	2	0
„		Port, 3 ditto	0	7	6
„		2 Teas	0	1	8
„		6 Suppers	0	6	0
„		Beer and tobacco	0	4	10
„	24.	3 Breakfasts	0	3	0
„		7 Dinners, veal cutlets, &c.	0	17	6
„		Sherry, 2 bottles	0	4	0
„		Port, 2 ditto	0	5	0
„		5 Teas	0	4	2
„		7 Suppers, beef and mutton steaks	0	7	6
„		Beer	0	3	0
„	25.	3 Breakfasts	0	3	0
		Carried forward	24	13	5

				£	s.	d.
		Brought forward	. . . .	24	13	3
February	25.	3 Dinners, mutton, &c.	.	0	7	6
,,		Port, 4 bottles	.	0	10	0
,,		Sherry, 2 ditto	.	0	4	0
,,		4 Teas	.	0	3	4
,,		6 Suppers, fowls and mutton chops .	.	0	10	6
,,		Beer	.	0	3	0
,,	26.	3 Breakfasts	.	0	3	0
,,		8 Dinners, stewed beef and fowl .	.	1	0	0
,,		Sherry, 2 bottles	.	0	4	0
,,		Brandy	.	0	2	0
,,		7 Teas	.	0	5	10
,,		6 Suppers, fowls and chops . .	.	0	10	6
,,		Beer	.	0	4	0
,,	27.	3 Breakfasts	.	0	3	0
,.		6 Dinners, beef and tart . . .	.	0	18	0
,,		Sherry, 3 bottles	.	0	6	0
,,		Port, 4 ditto	.	0	10	0
,,		6 Teas	.	0	5	0
,,		3 Suppers	.	0	3	0
,,		Beer and tobacco	.	0	3	10
,,	28.	3 Breakfasts	.	0	3	0
,,		5 Dinners, mutton and sauce . .	.	0	10	6
,,		Port, 3 bottles	.	0	7	6
,,		Sherry, 2 ditto	.	0	4	0
,,		Beer	.	0	3	0
,,		4 Suppers, cold beef, &c. . . .	.	0	5	0
March 1.		3 Breakfasts	.	0	3	0
,,		5 Dinners, veal and brocoli . .	.	0	12	6
,,		4 Teas	.	0	3	4
,,		Port, 1 bottle	.	0	2	6
,,		4 Suppers, mutton chops and sallat .	.	0	5	0
,,		Beer	.	0	3	6
,,	2.	3 Breakfasts	.	0	3	0
,,		5 Dinners, mutton, &c. . . .	.	0	10	0
,,		Sherry, 1 bottle	.	0	2	0
,,		Beer	.	0	1	6
				35	9	3
		Deduct for fowl, overcharged		0	5	0
				35	4	3
		Use of room and linen		1	11	6
		Servants		1	1	0
				37	16	9
		Fees		29	14	0
		Carried forward		67	10	9

	£	s.	d.
Brought forward	67	10	9
The barber and messenger	2	11	6
	70	2	3
Messenger, &c.	1	17	9
Received, March 7, 1774, the above contents in full	72	0	0

(Signed)   JOHN BELLAMY.

MR. WOODFALL to THOS. BARRAT DR.

	£	s.	d.
For seven times shaving	0	3	6
To seven times shaving	0	3	6
	0	7	0
Servants	0	2	6
	0	9	6
Gave Wood, messenger	2	2	0 *

ORIGINAL LETTER OF DAVID GARRICK.

"By what dropt yesterday from our friend Beckets, I imagine that I am but a poor *caput mortuum* among my brethren of the *Publick Advertiser*, and what is worse, I have a property the very reverse of that of a boy's top, for the more I am whipped the less I spin.   I must therefore desire you to dispose of my share to any Gentleman   *   *   *   *   *   *
Paper and the Publisher, though no one wish better to both than

Dear Sir,
Your most
Humble servant

(Signed)   DAVID GARRICK.
                 Outside.
To MR. WOODFALL,
      Publisher of
         The Publick Advertiser."

N.B.—The top of the above note is torn off, which accounts for the hiatus.

---

* The celebrated Mr. Wilkes, who was nearly contemporary in duress with the printer of the *Public Advertiser*, was more fortunate in the public sympathy he excited, and received numerous largesses during his incarceration.   The subjoined extract is from ALMON:—

"When Mr. Wilkes was confined in the King's Bench prison, he received many private presents. The Duchess of Queensbery (patroness of Gay, &c.) sent him 100*l.*; and Lady Elizabeth Germain also transmitted to him a similar donation.   Wine of all sorts, game and wild fowl, fruit, turkeys, poultry, &c., were sent to him daily from most parts of England."—*Correspondence of John Wilkes with his Friends*, vol. v. p. 44.—ED.

REVERSAL OF THE OUTLAWRY OF MR. WILKES.*

As Junius was extremely severe in his censures on Lord Mansfield, it is deemed a mere act of justice to extract a part of his lordship's speech on the reversal of Mr. Wilkes's outlawry, by which it will appear, such was the temper of the times, that the Chief Justice was even privately threatened upon the occasion, should his decision of the cause be in opposition to the popular opinion of the day. The extract is well worthy the reader's perusal, as a specimen of eloquence not often equalled, and rarely excelled; it forms the conclusion of his address.

"I have now gone through the several errors assigned by the defendant, and which have been ingeniously argued, and confidently relied on by his counsel at the bar; I have given my sentiments upon them, and if upon the whole, after the closest attention to what has been said, and with the strongest inclination in favour of the defendant, no arguments which have been urged, no cases which have been cited, no reasons that occur to me, are sufficient to satisfy me in my conscience and judgment that this outlawry should be reversed, I am bound to affirm it—and here let me make a pause.

"Many arguments have been suggested, both in and out of court, upon the consequences of establishing this outlawry, either as they may affect the defendant as an individual, or the public in general. As to the first, whatever they may be, the defendant has brought them upon himself; they are inevitable consequences of law arising from his own act; if the penalty, to which he is thereby subjected, is more than a punishment adequate to the crime he has committed, he should not have brought himself into this unfortunate predicament, by flying from the justice of his country; he thought proper to do so, and he must take the fruits of his own conduct, however bitter and unpalatable they may be; and although we may be heartily sorry for any person who has brought himself into this situation, it is not in our power, God forbid it should ever be in our power, to deliver him from it; we cannot prevent the judgment of the law by creating irregularity in the proceedings; we cannot prevent the consequences of that judgment by pardoning the crime; if the defendant has any pretensions to mercy, those pretensions must be urged, and that power exercised in another place, where the constitution has wisely and necessarily vested it: the crown will judge for itself; it does not belong to us to interfere with punishment, we have only to declare the law; none of us had any concern in the prosecution of this business, nor any wishes upon the event of it; it was not our fault that the defendant was prosecuted for the libels upon which he has been convicted; I took no share in another place in the measures which were taken to prosecute him for one of them; it was not our fault that he was convicted; it was not our fault that he fled; it was not our fault that he was outlawed; it was not our fault that he rendered himself up to justice; none of us revived the prosecution against him, nor could any one of us stop that prosecution when it was revived; it is not our fault if there are not any errors upon the record, nor is it in our power to create any if there are none; we are bound by our oath and in our consciences, to give such a judgment as the law will war-

---

* The occasion of this address is referred to in Letter 11, p. 147.

rant, and as our reason can prove; such a judgment as we must stand or fall
by, in the opinion of the present times, and of posterity ; in doing it, therefore, we must have regard to our reputation as honest men, and men of skill
and knowledge competent to the stations we hold ; no considerations whatsoever should mislead us from this great object, to which we ever ought, and
I trust ever shall, direct our attention. But consequences of a public nature,
reasons of state, political ones, have been strongly urged, (private anonymous
letters sent to me, I shall pass over,) open avowed publications which have
been judicially noticed, and may therefore be mentioned, have endeavoured
to influence or intimidate the court, and so prevail upon us to trifle and pre-
varicate with God, our consciences, and the public : it has been intimated
that consequences of a frightful nature will flow from the establishment of
this outlawry ; it is said the people expect the reversal, that the temper of
the times demand it ; that the multitude will have it so ; that the continuation
of the outlawry in full force, will not be endured ; that the execution of the
law upon the defendant will be resisted : these are arguments which will not
weigh a feather with me. If insurrection and rebellion are to follow our
determination, we have not to answer for the consequences, though we should
be the innocent cause—we can only say, *Fiat justitia, ruat cœlum ;* we
shall discharge our duty, without expectations of approbation or the apprehensions of censure ; if we are subjected to the latter unjustly, we must
submit to it ; we cannot prevent it, we will take care not to deserve it. He
must be a weak man indeed who can be staggered by such a consideration.

" The misapprehension, or the misrepresentation of the ignorant or wicked,
the *Mendax Infamia*, which is the consequence of both, are equally indifferent to, unworthy the attention of, and incapable of making any impression on men of firmness and intrepidity. Those who imagine judges are
capable of being influenced by such unworthy, indirect means, most grossly
deceive themselves ; and, for my own part, I trust that my temper, and the
colour and conduct of my life, have clothed me with a suit of armour to
shield me from such arrows. If I have ever supported the king's measures ;
if I have ever afforded any assistance to government ; if I have discharged
my duty as a public or private character, by endeavouring to preserve pure
and perfect the principles of the constitution, maintaining unsullied the
honour of the courts of justice, and, by an upright administration of, to give
a due effect to, the laws,—I have hitherto done it without any other gift or
reward than that most pleasing and most honourable one, the conscientious
conviction of doing what was right. I do not affect to scorn the opinion of
mankind ; I wish earnestly for popularity ; I will seek and will have popularity ; but I will tell you how I will obtain it ; I will have that popularity
which follows, and not that which is run after. It is not the applause of a
day, it is not the huzzas of thousands, that can give a moment's satisfaction
to a rational being ; that man's mind must indeed be a weak one, and his
ambition of a most depraved sort, who can be captivated by such wretched
allurements, or satisfied with such momentary gratifications. I say with the
Roman orator, and can say it with as much truth as he did, ' *Ego hoc ani ac
semper fui, ut invidiam virtute partam, gloriam non infamiam putarem.*
But the threats have been carried further ; personal violence has been
denounced, unless public humour be complied with ; I do not fear such
threats ; I do not believe there is any reason to fear them ; it is not the

genius of the worst of men in the worst of times, to proceed to such shocking extremities: but if such an event should happen, let it be so; even such an event might be productive of wholesome effects; such a stroke might rouse the better part of the nation from their lethargic condition to a state of activity, to assert and execute the law, and punish the daring and impious hands which had violated it; and those who now supinely behold the danger which threatens all liberty, from the most abandoned licentiousness, might, by such an event, be awakened to a sense of their situation, as drunken men are oftentimes stunned into sobriety. If the security of our persons and our property, of all we hold dear and valuable, are to depend upon the caprice of a giddy multitude, or to be at the disposal of a giddy mob; if, in compliance with the humours, and to appease the clamours of those, all civil and political institutions are to be disregarded or overthrown, a life somewhat more than sixty is not worth preserving at such a price, and he can never die too soon who lays down his life in support and vindication of the policy, the government, and the constitution of his country."—ED.

END OF VOL I.

LONDON: PRINTED BY WILLIAM CLOWES AND SONS, LIMITED, STAMFORD STREET
AND CHARING CROSS.